Classic Tales
of Christmas

Classic Tales of Christmas

Introduction by Ken Mondschein, PhD

Canterbury Classics
San Diego

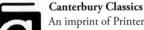

Canterbury Classics
An imprint of Printers Row Publishing Group
9717 Pacific Heights Blvd, San Diego, CA 92121
www.canterburyclassicsbooks.com • mail@canterburyclassicsbooks.com

Introduction and compilation copyright © 2023 Printers Row Publishing Group

Printers Row Publishing Group is a division of Readerlink Distribution Services, LLC. Canterbury Classics is a registered trademark of Readerlink Distribution Services, LLC.

Correspondence regarding the content of this book should be sent to Canterbury Classics, Editorial Department, at the above address.

Publisher: Peter Norton
Associate Publisher: Ana Parker
Art Director: Charles McStravick
Editorial Director: April Graham
Editor: Dan Mansfield
Production Team: Beno Chan, Julie Greene, Rusty von Dyl

Cover design: Linda Lee Mauri

Library of Congress Cataloging-in-Publication Data

Names: Mondschein, Ken, writer of introduction.
Title: Classic tales of Christmas / introduction by Ken Mondschein, PhD.
Description: San Diego : Canterbury Classics, [2022] | Summary: "A
   collection of more than twenty stories and poems celebrating Christmas,
   including works from esteemed authors such as Charles Dickens, Louisa
   May Alcott, and Hans Christian Andersen. With favorites such as O.
   Henry's "The Gift of the Magi" and L. Frank Baum's The Life and
   Adventures of Santa Claus, this elegant leather-bound volume will hold a
   special place on your bookshelf, sure to be enjoyed during the Christmas
   season, or at any time of the year"-- Provided by publisher.
Identifiers: LCCN 2021058934 | ISBN 9781645178637 (hardcover)
Subjects: LCSH: Christmas stories. | LCGFT: Christmas fiction. | Short stories.
Classification: LCC PN6120.95.C6 C56 2022 | DDC 808.83/9334--dc23/eng/20220215
LC record available at https://lccn.loc.gov/2021058934

Printed in Dongguan, China
Third printing, July 2024. RRD/07/24
28 27 26 25 24 3 4 5 6 7

MIX
Paper | Supporting
responsible forestry
FSC® C144853

Editor's Note: These works have been published in their original form to preserve the authors' intent and style.

CONTENTS

Introduction

This book contains the stories and poems that made Christmas.

That may seem a bit of an odd assertion. After all, Christmas, with its nostalgic sights, smells, and tastes, seems as old as time, not something invented. But things weren't always as they are today. For instance, the flavors that we associate with the season were popular at medieval feasts, but fell out of favor in haute cuisine in the eighteenth and nineteenth centuries. Today, they are so strongly associated with the holiday that it just seems wrong to serve "pumpkin spice" (a very Christmassy mixture of cinnamon, ginger, cloves, nutmeg, and allspice) at, for instance, a Fourth of July barbecue. Surely, we feel, Mary and Joseph must have dined on plum pudding on the road to Bethlehem. In the same way, we can't imagine that there was ever a time when we didn't have Christmas trees and mistletoe. The truth, however, is that Christmas trees were only brought to the English-speaking world in the eighteenth century when the House of Hanover came from Germany to inherit the British throne. In the same way, while the garb worn by Father Christmas formerly evoked a medieval bishop, the red and white outfit now worn by Santa Claus in countries all over the world owes much to the nineteenth-century American illustrator Thomas Nast.

So, Christmas was not always what it is now. In fact, Christmas is, in large part, a thoroughly modern invention.

Now, this doesn't mean that somebody in a corporate marketing department just came up with the idea for the holiday a few generations ago. To be sure, the celebration of Christmas goes back to at least the fourth century—but its importance, and the way we celebrate it, came about only in the nineteenth century. In years past, Epiphany (the day after Twelfth Night, celebrated on January 6) was far more important. In Western Christianity, this holiday commemorates the visitation of the Three Magi. It is still of great importance in Spanish- and French-speaking cultures.

There are other dates and practices around the season that have fallen out of favor, as well. In times past, Advent, the forty days before Christmas now most associated with chocolate "countdown calendars," was a sacred season akin to Lent. Like Lent, Advent was a solemn season, commemorated with fasts. It still has its own special liturgy in many churches, and is celebrated with wreaths and candles.

But the joyful Anglo-American Christmas, celebrated on December 25, has eclipsed all of these seasonal practices worldwide. Even in Japan, where most religious practice is a mix of Buddhism and Shintoism, Christmas has become a celebration of togetherness, love, and commerce. Christmas trees and images of Santa Claus abound, stollen cake is imported from Germany, and, thanks to a successful advertising campaign that began in the 1970s, there is a national tradition of eating Kentucky Fried Chicken on Christmas Day.

How did we get from a solemn celebration to fried chicken in Japan? Where did Christmas come from, and how and why has it changed? To discover the significance of the stories and poems in this book, we'll first need to look at the modern origins of the holiday.

The Origins of Christmas

The conventional date of December 25 for the birth of Jesus is an invention. Most likely, by biblical accounts, he would have been born in the fall, when the Jewish people would make pilgrimages to Jerusalem for Yom Kippur, the sacred holiday of atonement. However, midwinter around the time of the solstice was the time of various pagan celebrations; in particular, the Romans celebrated the joyful Saturnalia with feasts, gift-giving, and general mirth. There was a topsy-turvy aspect to the Roman holiday: masters waited on slaves, gambling was permitted, and a "king of Saturnalia" presided over the merrymaking. Meanwhile, in the snowy north of Europe, Germanic peoples would decorate sacred trees (originally, with human and animal sacrifices instead of tinsel and ornaments) and feast in fire-lit halls. It is also speculated that midwinter was the festival of the Sol Invictus (Unconquered Sun) in the Mithraic religion, which originated in Persia but was, like Christianity, a popular religion in the army of the late Roman Empire.

In the fourth century, Pope Julius I co-opted these pagan celebrations into a Christian religious festival, and December 25 was, on very scant evidence, declared the date of Christ's nativity. (Thus the Spanish *navidad*, from the Latin *dies nativitatis*, or "day of birth," whereas in English the holiday is named "Christmass," that is, a mass for Christ.) Additional political significance was added to the holiday in the early Middle Ages. For instance, Charlemagne was crowned Holy Roman Emperor on December 25, 800, and William the Conqueror was similarly crowned on Christmas Day of 1066. It also became customary for monarchs to hold lavish Christmas feasts. The fourteenth-century romance poem *Sir Gawain and the Green Knight* begins with King Arthur holding fifteen days of Christmas celebrations. There was a good reason for this: late autumn to early winter was the time to slaughter animals you didn't want to feed over the winter, and it was one of the few times fresh meat was available for many people.

By the 1500s, however, Christmas had acquired a bad reputation. The pagan-derived celebrations were deemed too drunken and rowdy, the traditions of electing a "lord of misrule" too disreputable, the kissing under the mistletoe too licentious. Young men and women would go from door to door, caroling and demanding food and drink from the better-off under threat of vandalism or violence. "Men dishonor Christ more in the 12 days of Christmas than in all the 12 months besides," wrote the sixteenth-century reformer Hugh Latimer. In fact, many claimed, on good grounds, that Christmas was nothing but a pagan festival with a thin veneer of Christianity. When Oliver Cromwell and his Puritan armies took over England in the mid-seventeenth century, they outlawed the holiday. The Pilgrim immigrants to the New World were just as strict: there was no Christmas in colonial New England—it was even illegal in Massachusetts from 1659 to 1681.

But the disorderly Christmas celebrations never really went away. In fact, in 1828, a so-called Christmas parade—more of a moving riot—began in the working-class Bowery neighborhood in New York City, attacked an African American church, smashed up the homes of the wealthy, and continued back down Broadway before facing down the city's rudimentary police force.

In response, writers began to reinvent the holiday, transforming it into the celebration of togetherness, family, light, and hope that we know today. Washington Irving, for instance, portrayed an idealized version of an English Christmas for his American readers in *The Sketchbook of Geoffrey Crayon, Gent.* (1819), one that "brought the peasant and the peer together, and blended all ranks in one warm, generous flow of joy and kindness." Clement Clarke Moore's "A Visit from St. Nicholas" (1823) is, above all, a poem about tranquility and peace, which is only broken by a benevolent (and unseen except by the narrator) St. Nicholas. Charles Dickens's *A Christmas Carol* (1843) portrays those who are against Christmas as miserly and misanthropic. Before long, Christmas in the English-speaking world began to be seen as it had been idealized on the page: a quiet family holiday, celebrated at home, when gifts were lavished on children. Scary pre-Christian figures, such as the Germanic Krampus—a horned beast that torments misbehaving children—were banished.

This was in keeping with many of the themes of the Victorian (1837–1901) and Edwardian (1901–1910) periods. The early nineteenth century was a time of rapid social change. Rural life had been disrupted by industrialization; many poor families were forced to move to cities and take factory work, where they labored and lived in squalid conditions. These tensions erupted in such events as the 1828 New York City Christmas Day riot, which was in many ways an expression of economic dissatisfaction. Even the "parade" mob's destruction of a Black church cannot be separated from the fact that poor white people competed with free African Americans for jobs.

The growing middle class, however, distinguished itself by drawing a sharp line between the public (and adult male) sphere of business and the private sphere of women, children, and home. Whereas working-class children had always had to labor outside the home, the middle class viewed childhood as an innocent time of joy, and idealized women as mothers and homemakers. These helped shape the ideals we think of when we imagine a "traditional" Christmas—a domestic time of comfort, hope, joy, plenty, and togetherness, when we rekindle the hearth fires in our hearts. So popular was this new envisioning that it quickly replaced the older, rowdier, disruptive version through all levels of society. In the United States, Christmas became a federal holiday in 1870, and not celebrating it became unthinkable.

But in the twenty-first century, a time of vast social change, new forces of darkness once again threaten Christmas. For some Americans, Christmas churchgoing has been replaced by Christmas shopping, while Advent has been replaced by a commercial season that begins on "Black Friday" after Thanksgiving and continues through the after-Christmas sales. Even those who are not Christian often feel compelled to participate in holiday festivities—for instance, the Jewish festival of Hanukkah, which falls around the same time as Christmas, was raised from a relatively minor celebration to a major festivity observed by even nonobservant Jews. In other words, for many people Christmas has become desacralized and commodified. It is a make-or-break season for movie studios, toy companies, and retailers. Altogether, Americans spend about $1 trillion per year on Christmas, including about $1,000 per person on gifts.

Perhaps even worse, some Christmas celebrations have become positively antisocial. For instance, New York City's Santa-Con bar crawl brings back the rowdiness of pre-Victorian celebrations while the anarchic and frightening figure of the Krampus has experienced something of a revival. In a sense, some have reverted to the chaos of pre-Victorian Christmas—only instead of protesting against social norms and hierarchies, they are using Christmas to crassly reinforce them. More quietly, but no less tragically, with the decline of the traditional family structure in America has come a new cynicism and ironic detachment about Christmas. More Americans live alone than ever before, and many have come to associate the holiday season with sadness, loss, and loneliness.

But these negative aspects—very similar to the ones our Victorian authors so staunchly opposed—are only one side of modern Christmas. Millions of people, both in the United States and around the world, still view the holiday as a joyous religious celebration. For many Christians, Christmas is the only time of year they do go to church to receive the message of love, hope, and forgiveness. Nor is this message exclusively Christian: Those who celebrate Christmas as a secular holiday use it as an opportunity to spend time with loved ones; enjoy festive decorating, cooking, and baking; do volunteer work and support charities; and celebrate family and cultural traditions, all in true Victorian fashion. Is it not true that the myth of Santa Claus persists to this day because he represents the magic and wonder of the holiday for both children and adults?

Perhaps, then, it's time for a revival. We hope this book will bring back something of the Victorian spirit of Christmas—a holiday of light, love, hope, and closeness. At the same time, we should pay attention to what these stories say about charity, generosity, and forgiveness. After all, family isn't necessarily something we're born with—it's something we are actively creating all the time. In that spirit, whether you spend the season with your family of birth, your family of choice, or both, we hope that this book brings you both comfort and joy in the holiday season, and inspires you to go out into the world and do good for others. Now, more than ever, we need to fight against cynicism and alienation, connect with our friends and neighbors, and come together in the true spirit of Christmas.

About the Authors and Works

Born in the city of Köningsberg (now Kaliningrad, Russia, but then part of the German state of Prussia), E. T. A. Hoffmann (1776–1822) was more than just a writer: he was also an artist, composer, music critic, government official, and legal scholar. Hoffmann's full name was actually Ernst Theodor Wilhelm, but he changed the initial "W" to "A" for "Amadeus" out of admiration for Mozart. The best known of Hoffmann's works is, of course, *The Nutcracker and the Mouse King* (1816). *The Nutcracker* is one of the first fantasy stories, mixing nineteenth-century domesticity (the Christmas setting) with magic and an epic battle between good and evil. In his emphasis on inward feeling, Hoffman is a quintessential romantic. *The Nutcracker* was championed in France by Alexandre Dumas and translated into English as early as 1853—though its best-known adaption was the 1892 Russian ballet, with music by the composer Pyotr Ilyich Tchaikovsky. Both Dumas's translation-cum-adaptation and the ballet lighten the dark tone of Hoffmann's original work.

Clement Clarke Moore (1779–1863) was a professor at the General Theological Seminary of the Episcopal Church in New York City—an institution he helped endow from his considerable inherited wealth—and also a supporter of the Federalist Party founded by Alexander Hamilton. Moore's poem "A Visit from St. Nicholas" (also known as "The Night Before Christmas" from its famous first line) was published anonymously in 1823. Moore, mindful of his reputation as an academic, did not acknowledge authorship until fourteen years later. There has been some discussion of whether he was the true author of the poem, but most scholars are convinced of Moore's authorship.

Rather than red and white, Moore's Santa wears soot-blackened furs—Haddon Sundblom did not draw his Coca-Cola illustrations, now inseparable from how we picture Santa Claus, until the 1930s. The idea of Santa's sleigh being pulled by reindeer is not Moore's invention, but can be traced to an illustrated poem for children, "Old Santeclaus with Much Delight," published anonymously in 1831—though in that version, there is only one reindeer. Moore, however, gives us the names of eight of Santa's reindeer (Rudolph wasn't invented until 1939). That the poem's roots date back to when New York was still New Amsterdam shows in Blitzen and Donner's names perhaps having been taken from the Dutch. In 1809 Washington Irving, in his satirical *A History of New York*, had presented St. Nicholas as a sort of founding saint of the city.

Besides fairy tales such as "The Little Mermaid" and "The Snow Queen" (the basis for the animated movie *Frozen*), the Danish author Hans Christian Andersen (1805–1875) was a travel writer and pan-Scandinavian nationalist. Like the Brothers Grimm, his writing was intended to show the "spirit of the people," but unlike the middle-class Grimms, Andersen was born into a working-class family, which made his rise to become Denmark's foremost writer that much more remarkable. Yet there is a deep melancholy in many of his stories. "The Fir Tree" (1844) relates the story of a little tree who wants to grow up too quickly, experiences the greatest joy and the culmination of his existence as a Christmas tree, and is then discarded. Meanwhile, "The Little Match Girl" (1845), which presents the very opposite of an innocent vision of childhood and home comforts, is tailor-made to wring feelings of pathos from the reader. Andersen seems to say that while this world will always be cruel, cold, and unjust, there will always be hope in the world to come.

Charles Dickens's *A Christmas Carol* (1843) may be the greatest, and most famous, Christmas story ever told. Dickens (1812–1870) was the quintessential Victorian writer. Having been forced into a workhouse while his father languished in debtor's prison, Dickens possessed a keen eye for the injustices of contemporary society and a longing for domestic comforts. He also possessed a flair for dramatic storytelling. These all show up in *A Christmas Carol*: Scrooge's miserliness, and his transformation through supernatural means into a kinder and more generous man, are not only what Dickens wished to have happen in contemporary society, but a character study of how individuals shape society for good or ill. In his depiction of Christmas, he captured all the qualities with which Victorians sought to imbue the holiday: making it a special time of year for family gatherings, festivities, and joy.

A Christmas Carol is far from Dickens's only holiday story. We have also included *The Chimes* (1844), *The Cricket on the Hearth* (1845), *The Battle of Life* (1846), and *The Haunted Man and the Ghost's Bargain* (1848). These were all conversion tales, similar to *A Christmas Carol*, albeit less well known. All carry Dickens's themes of social criticism and faith in people's ability to improve both their characters and their lives.

Bret Harte (1836–1902) was an American reporter, poet, satirist, and short story writer. While best known for his Westerns, as well as for his friendship—and eventual falling out—with Mark Twain, Harte wrote one notable holiday tale: "The Christmas Gift that Came to Rupert: A Story for Little Soldiers" (1873). While evoking a call to arms and patriotic duty—something thought quite laudable back in the nineteenth century—it comes off as somewhat macabre to modern readers. There is a certain irony to it, as well—though Harte had reported on the horrors of violence, particularly the massacre of up to 200 members of the Wiyot tribe in 1860, he had spent the Civil War in California. Yet, in "The Christmas Gift that Came to Rupert," he gives voice to what World War I poet Wilfred Owen would later call "The old Lie: *Dulce et decorum est / Pro patria mori.*"* He also overturns the earlier tradition of pacifist gift-giving such as that seen in "Old Santeclaus with Much Delight."

While best known for her 1852 abolitionist novel *Uncle Tom's Cabin*, Harriet Beecher Stowe (1811–1896) was also the author of two notable holiday stories, "The First Christmas of New England" and "Betty's Bright Idea," both published in 1876 alongside another story, "Deacon Pitkin's Farm." Stowe was born into a religious family that took part in the evangelical movement, which placed a high priority on women's education. "Betty's Bright Idea" militates against the commercialization of Christmas and drives home the point that "giving is better than receiving," while "The First Christmas of New England" ignores the Pilgrims' historical aversion to the holiday to present a sketch of a Christmas as pious as it is patriotic. Much as in her other writing, and that of other evangelical-tinged women writers of the era, Stowe plays on readers' emotions to try to shape their sympathies in pro-social directions.

The Russian writer Fyodor Dostoyevsky (1821–1881) is best known for his harrowing psychological novel *Crime and Punishment* (1866), as well as *The Idiot* (1869) and *The Brothers Karamazov* (1880), but it is his short story "The Beggar Boy at Christ's Christmas Tree" (1876) that we include in this collection. (The more accurate translation of the title is "The Heavenly Christmas Tree.") It was first published in Dostoyevsky's magazine, *A Writer's Diary*, in 1876, and shares its pathetic theme of a neglected child freezing to death and being reunited in

---

* "It is sweet and fitting / To die for one's country," originally from the *Odes* of the Roman poet Horace.

heaven with loved ones with Hans Christian Andersen's "The Little Match Girl." According to Dostoyevsky, the genesis was a lavish party he attended with his daughter Aimée, contrasted with his visit to a home for "juvenile delinquents" and repeated encounters with a beggar boy. Certainly nineteenth-century Russia, which was experiencing a great deal of social upheaval, had no shortage of either rural or urban poverty—circumstances that would ultimately result in the partially successful 1905 revolution, as well as the February and October Revolutions of 1917.

Dostoyevsky himself had experienced great suffering in his life. Raised in comfortable circumstances in the working-class neighborhood where his father worked, he was haunted through his life by many of the cruelties and injustices he had witnessed firsthand. He was bookish, religious, epileptic, and had always had a keen interest in social justice, all of which made the military career his parents chose for him a strange choice of vocation. He quit the army at the age of twenty-four to concentrate on his blossoming literary career, but fell into poverty. His participation in radical political and literary circles soon led to his imprisonment in Siberia for four years. While Dostoyevsky would later recover his position in society, marry twice, travel in western Europe, and publish many more literary works, his gambling and ill health led to recurrent financial troubles.

We would be remiss if we did not include "Tilly's Christmas" and "Tessa's Surprises" (both 1872), as well as "A Christmas Dream, and How It Came True" (1885) by Louisa May Alcott (1832–1888). Like Harriet Beecher Stowe, Alcott was active in abolition, feminism, and temperance, though she came to these social-justice movements from the perspective of transcendentalist philosophy, not religious evangelism. While Alcott wrote numerous anonymous pieces of commercial fiction, including disreputable Gothic thrillers, she is best known for *Little Women*, followed by *Little Men* and *Jo's Boys*. "Tilly's Christmas" and "Tessa's Surprises" are both from the first volume of *Aunt Jo's Scrap Bag*, a short-story collection. The former is a homey little story about a rescued bird, while the latter is a bit more social-realist, about a poor girl, the daughter of an Italian immigrant, who struggles to make an American Christmas for her siblings. "A Christmas Dream, and How It Came True" is a sort of meta-Christmas story, a rewriting of Dickens for children in which a spoiled little girl's feelings about Christmas are changed through supernatural means.

Besides his attempts to craft national epics such as *The Song of Hiawatha* and "Paul Revere's Ride," Henry Wadsworth Longfellow (1807–1882) also wrote "The Three Kings" (1877). Born in Portland, Maine (then part of Massachusetts), Longfellow was a writer from a young age. He attended Bowdoin College and traveled in Europe, where he learned several languages, a skill that served him later in life when he translated Dante Alighieri's *Divine Comedy*. Upon his return from Europe, his alma mater hired him as a professor; he later moved to Harvard. Longfellow's long and successful career as a teacher, writer, and public intellectual was marked by two tragedies: the death of his first wife, Mary, in 1835 after she suffered a miscarriage while the two were in Europe; and the gruesome and tragic death of his wife Frances in 1861 after her dress caught fire. Longfellow never stopped mourning her.

"The Three Kings" retells the story of the Three Wise Men in verse but mirrors the melancholy of the aging, grieving Longfellow. The poet takes a moment to linger on Mary and her knowledge of her son's future sacrifice, and the myrrh offered by Baltasar (Balthasar) is "for the body's burying." Longfellow's other notable Christmas poem, not included in this volume, is "The Bells." It was inspired by his son Charles being wounded in the Civil War. Later, set to music, it became the carol "I Heard the Bells on Christmas Day." Like "The Three Kings," it has a somewhat dark tone: it speaks of the narrator's despair for Christmas peace while the war rages on, but ends with hope of divine justice.

Continuing on the theme of the Three Magi is "The Story of the Other Wise Man" (1895) by Henry van Dyke (1852–1933). (Besides this short story, van Dyke also wrote another popular Christmas story that does not appear in this collection, "The First Christmas Tree," and the lyrics to the carol "Joyful, Joyful, We Adore Thee.") Like so many other Christmas tales, van Dyke's story, which centers around Artaban, his invented Wise Man supposedly left out of the Gospels, is one of longing, failure, disappointment, and ultimate redemption. "I do not know where this little story came from," the author remarked. "Out of the air, perhaps. One thing is certain, it is not written in any other book, nor is it to be found among the ancient lore of the East. And yet I have never felt as if it were my own. It was a gift, and it seemed to me as if I knew the Giver." But, in writing apocrypha such as this, van Dyke—as well as the other continuers of biblical stories, as well as all of the "inventors" of Santa Claus—were acting in a long tradition. Saints' lives, including "fan fiction" for biblical personages such as Mary Magdalene, were popular in the Middle Ages, the legends growing with each retelling of the tales. In this way, contemporary people are able to take part in the stories of long ago through their own creativity.

The other notable thing about "The Story of the Other Wise Man" is van Dyke's educated prose and well-researched details. He was educated at Poly Prep in Brooklyn, attended Princeton University and Princeton Theological Seminary, and then served as a professor of English at Princeton. Van Dyke was also active in the Presbyterian Church. His most notable public accomplishment, however, was that, like so many other Princeton intellectuals, he was appointed to a government post by former Princeton president Woodrow Wilson—in his case, minister to the Netherlands and Luxembourg, a post he took just as World War I broke out. The inexperienced van Dyke nonetheless carried out his role with grace and aplomb.

Though best known as the inventor of *The Wizard of Oz*, L. Frank Baum (1856–1919) also wrote "The Life and Adventures of Santa Claus" (1902) and its sequel, "A Kidnapped Santa Claus" (1904). The former is, of course, the basis for the Rankin-Bass animated special, while the second began the "Santa is missing!" trope that is perhaps most familiar from Tim Burton's 1993 film *The Nightmare Before Christmas*. In these, Baum completely throws out the history of St. Nicholas and creates a new, fantastical origin for Santa Claus, one based on a mix-up of Old World myths—a very American thing to do, but one that takes the symbols he is playing with and divorces them from their original contexts and meanings. A writer from a young age, Baum also worked as a theater impresario, newspaper publisher, and a shopkeeper in South Dakota before finding success with the Oz books.

O. Henry's "The Gift of the Magi" (1905) is well known as a classic study in irony. Born William Sydney Porter, O. Henry (1862–1910) was an acclaimed writer of short stories, and particularly stories with surprise endings. Porter was born in North Carolina, where he became a pharmacist, but moved to Texas while still a young man. In Texas he worked on a ranch, courted and married his first wife, and then, by turns, found employment at the Texas General Land Office, at a bank, and then at a newspaper. Charged with embezzling from the bank, he fled to Honduras but returned when he learned his wife was dying of tuberculosis. Porter ultimately spent three years in prison. Released in 1901, he reunited with his daughter and moved to New York City, where he remarried and began the most prolific phase of his writing career. He died in 1910 from complications from alcoholism.

"The Gift of the Magi" was first published on December 10, 1905, in *The New York Sunday World* as "Gifts of the Magi" and appeared in the short-story collection *The Four Million* the following year. Instead of seeing Della and Jim's gift-buying as a tragic farce, we would encourage the perspective that the real gift was the sacrifices they were willing to make for one another.

Lucy Maud Montgomery (1874–1942) is best known as the author of *Anne of Green Gables*. Her short stories "The Christmas Surprise at Enderly Road" (1905) and "Clorinda's Gifts" (1906) were published before the novel that made her famous, when she was still living in Cavendish on Prince Edward Island and working as a schoolteacher. They both share with *Anne of Green Gables* the rural

Canadian setting in which Montgomery found inspiration and from which she wished to escape.

Though she was a beloved, acclaimed, and wildly successful writer in her lifetime—albeit one dismissed by critics as one who wrote for girls—Montgomery was not nearly so happy in her private life. Her marriage to a moody, erratic Presbyterian minister was not a joyful one, and she herself suffered from depression and migraines. It was in her writing that she found escape and hope—and brought escape and hope to others.

The Enduring Impact of Christmas Stories

Christmas stories have evolved over the years from the serious and often tragic to the joyful and whimsical. All share, however, the desire to impart moral lessons to their audience—to inspire them with the sense of love and community that Christmas represents. Even dark stories, such as "The Little Match Girl" and "The Beggar Boy at Christ's Christmas Tree," served a purpose, endeavoring to elicit feelings of pathos from their middle-class readers and move them toward the light. Today, Christmas stories are still a vital genre, from the literary (the *New Yorker* routinely republishes stories by Vladimir Nabokov, Alice Cook, and John Updike) to the hilarious-but-cynical (David Sedaris's "Santaland Diaries") to the humorous-but-educational (Lemony Snicket's *The Latke Who Couldn't Stop Screaming: A Christmas Story*). All of these more recent contributions share one very important thing with the Christmas tales of yore: the notion that storytelling can inspire us to create a better world, one with less injustice and more light, warmth, hope, and humanity.

Ken Mondschein, PhD
Philadelphia, Pennsylvania

The Nutcracker and the Mouse King

E. T. A. Hoffman

CHRISTMAS EVE

During the long, long day of the twenty-fourth of December, the children of Doctor Stahlbaum were not permitted to enter the parlor, much less the adjoining drawing room. Frederic and Maria sat nestled together in a corner of the back chamber; dusky twilight had come on, and they felt quite gloomy and fearful, for, as was commonly the case on this day, no light was brought in to them. Fred, in great secrecy, and in a whisper, informed his little sister (she was only just seven years old), that ever since morning he had heard a rustling and a rattling, and now and then a gentle knocking, in the forbidden chambers. Not long ago also he had seen a little dark man, with a large chest under his arm, gliding softly through the entry, but he knew very well that it was nobody but Godfather Drosselmeier. Upon this Maria clapped her little hands together for joy, and exclaimed, "Ah, what beautiful things has Godfather Drosselmeier made for us this time!"

Counsellor Drosselmeier was not a very handsome man; he was small and thin, had many wrinkles in his face, over his right eye he had a large black patch, and he was without hair, for which reason he wore a very nice white wig; this was made of glass however, and was a very ingenious piece of work. The Godfather himself was very ingenious also, he understood all about clocks and watches, and could even make them. Accordingly, when any one of the beautiful clocks in Doctor Stahlbaum's house was sick, and could not sing, Godfather Drosselmeier would have to attend it. He would then take off his glass wig, pull off his brown coat, put on a blue apron, and pierce the clock with sharp-pointed instruments, which usually caused little Maria a great deal of anxiety. But it did the clock no harm; on the contrary, it became quite lively again, and began at once right merrily to rattle, and to strike, and to sing, so that it was a pleasure to all who heard it. Whenever he came, he always brought something pretty in his pocket for the children, sometimes a little man who moved his eyes and made a bow, at others, a box, from which a little bird hopped out when it was opened—sometimes one thing, sometimes another.

When Christmas Eve came, he had always a beautiful piece of work prepared for them, which had cost him a great deal of trouble, and on this account it was always carefully preserved by their parents, after he had given it to them. "Ah, what beautiful present has Godfather Drosselmeier made for us this time!" exclaimed Maria. It was Fred's opinion that this time it could be nothing else than a castle, in which all kinds of fine soldiers marched up and down and went through their exercises; then other soldiers would come, and try to break into the castle, but the soldiers within would fire off their cannon very bravely, until all roared and cracked again. "No, no," cried Maria, interrupting him, "Godfather Drosselmeier has told me of a lovely garden where there is a great lake, upon which beautiful swans swim about, with golden collars around their necks, and sing their sweetest songs. Then there comes a little girl out of the garden down along the lake, and coaxes the swans to the shore, and feeds them with sweet cake."

"Swans never eat cake," interrupted Fred, somewhat roughly, "and even Godfather Drosselmeier himself can't make a whole garden. After all, we have little good of his playthings; they are all taken right away from us again. I like what Papa and Mamma give us much better, for we can keep their presents for ourselves, and do as we please with them." The children now began once more to guess what it could be this time. Maria thought that Miss Trutchen (her great doll) was growing very old, for she fell almost every moment upon the floor, and more awkwardly than ever, which could not happen without leaving sad marks upon her face, and as to neatness in dress, this was now altogether out of the question with her. Scolding did not help the matter in the least. Frederic declared, on the other hand, that a bay horse was wanting in his stable, and his troops were very deficient in cavalry, as his Papa very well knew.

By this time it had become quite dark. Frederic and Maria sat close together, and did not venture again to speak a word. It seemed now as if soft wings rustled around them, and very distant, but sweet music was heard at intervals. At this moment a shrill sound broke upon their ears—kling, ling, kling, ling—the doors flew wide open, and such a dazzling light broke out from the great chamber, that with the loud exclamation, "Ah! ah!" the children stood fixed at the threshold. But Papa and Mamma stepped to the door, took them by the hand, and said, "Come, come, dear children, and see what Christmas has brought you this year."

THE GIFTS

Kind reader, or listener, whatever may be your name, whether Frank, Robert, Henry, Anna or Maria, I beg you to call to mind the table covered with your last Christmas gifts, as in their newest gloss they first appeared to your delighted vision. You will then be able to imagine the astonishment of the children, as they stood with sparkling eyes, unable to utter a word, for joy at the sight before them. At last Maria called out with a deep sigh, "Ah, how beautiful! ah, how beautiful!" and Frederic gave two or three leaps in the air higher than he had ever done before. The children must have been very obedient and good children during the past year, for never on any Christmas Eve before, had so many beautiful things been given to them. A tall fir tree stood in the middle of the room, covered with gold and silver apples, while sugar almonds, comfits, lemon drops, and every kind of confectionery, hung like buds and blossoms upon all its branches. But the greatest beauty about this wonderful tree, was the many little lights that sparkled amid its dark boughs, which like stars illuminated its treasures, or like friendly eyes seemed to invite the children to partake of its blossoms and fruit.

The table under the tree shone and flushed with a thousand different colors—ah, what beautiful things were there! who can describe them? Maria spied the prettiest dolls, a tea set, all kinds of nice little furniture, and what eclipsed all the rest, a silk dress tastefully ornamented with gay ribbons, which hung upon a frame before her eyes, so that she could view it on every side. This she did too, and exclaimed over and over again, "Ah, the sweet—ah, the dear, dear frock! and may I put it on? Yes, yes—may I really, though, wear it?"

In the meanwhile Fred had been galloping round and round the room, trying his new bay horse, which, true enough, he had found, fastened by its bridle to the table. Dismounting again, he said it was a wild creature, but that was nothing; he would soon break him. He then reviewed his new regiment of hussars, who were very elegantly arrayed in red and gold, and carried silver weapons, and rode upon such bright shining horses, that you would almost believe these were of pure silver also. The children had now become somewhat more composed, and turned to the picture books, which lay open on the table, where all kinds of beautiful flowers, and gayly dressed people, and boys and girls at play, were painted as natural as if they were alive. Yes, the children had just turned to these singular books, when—kling, ling, kling, ling—the bell was heard again. They knew that Godfather Drosselmeier was now about to display his Christmas gift, and ran towards a table that stood against the wall, covered by a curtain reaching from the ceiling to the floor. The curtain behind which he had remained so long concealed, was quickly drawn aside, and what saw the children then?

Upon a green meadow, spangled with flowers, stood a noble castle, with clear glass windows and golden turrets. A musical clock began to play, when the doors and windows flew open, and little men and women, with feathers in their hats, and long flowing trains, were seen sauntering about in the rooms. In the middle hall, which seemed as if it were all on fire, so many little tapers were burning in silver chandeliers, there were children in white frocks and green jackets, dancing to the sound of the music. A man in an emerald-green cloak, at intervals put his head out of the window, nodded, and then disappeared; and Godfather Drosselmeier himself, only that he was not much bigger than Papa's thumb, came now and then to the door of the castle, looked about him, and then went in again. Fred, with his arms resting upon the table, gazed at the beautiful castle, and the little walking and dancing figures, and then said, "Godfather Drosselmeier, let me go into your castle."

The Counsellor gave him to understand that that could not be done. And he was right, for it was foolish in Fred to wish to go into a castle, which with all its golden turrets was not as high as his head. Fred saw that likewise himself. After a while as the men and women kept walking back and forth, and the children danced, and the emerald man looked out at his window, and Godfather Drosselmeier came to the door, and all without the least change; Fred called out impatiently, "Godfather Drosselmeier, come out this time at the other door."

"That can never be, dear Fred," said the Counsellor.

"Well then," continued Frederic, "let the green man who peeps out at the window walk about with the rest."

"And that can never be," rejoined the Counsellor.

"Then the children must come down," cried Fred, "I want to see them nearer."

"All that can never be, I say," replied the Counsellor, a little out of humor. "As the mechanism is made, so it must remain."

"So—o," cried Fred, in a drawling tone, "all that can never be! Listen, Godfather Drosselmeier. If your little dressed up figures in the castle there, can do nothing else but always the same thing, they are not good for much, and I care very little about them. No, give me my hussars, who can maneuver backward and forward, as I order them, and are not shut up in a house."

With this, he darted towards a large table, drew up his regiment upon their silver horses, and let them trot and gallop, and cut and slash, to his heart's content. Maria also had softly stolen away, for she too was soon tired of the sauntering and dancing puppets in the castle; but as she was very amiable and good, she did not wish it to be observed so plainly in her as it was in her brother Fred. Counsellor Drosselmeier turned to the parents, and said, somewhat angrily, "An ingenious work like this was not made for stupid children. I will put up my castle again, and carry it home." But their mother now stepped forward, and desired to see the secret mechanism and curious works by which the little figures were set in motion. The Counsellor took it all apart, and then put it together again. While he was employed in this manner he became good-natured once more, and gave the children some nice brown men and women, with gilt faces, hands, and feet. They were all made of sweet thorn, and smelt like gingerbread, at which Frederic and Maria were greatly delighted. At her mother's request, the elder sister, Louise, had put on the new dress which had been given to her, and she looked most charmingly in it, but Maria, when it came to her turn, thought she would like to look at hers a while longer as it hung. This was readily permitted.

THE FAVORITE

The truth is, Maria was unwilling to leave the table then, because she had discovered something upon it, which no one had yet remarked. By the marching out of Fred's hussars, who had been drawn up close to the tree, a curious little man came into view, who stood there silent and retired, as if he were waiting quietly for his turn to be noticed. It must be confessed, a great deal could not be said in favor of the beauty of his figure, for not only was his rather broad, stout body, out of all proportion to the little, slim legs that carried it, but his head was by far too large for either. A genteel dress went a great way to compensate for these defects, and led to the belief that he must be a man of taste and good breeding. He wore a hussar's jacket of beautiful bright violet, fastened together with white loops and buttons, pantaloons of exactly the same color, and the neatest boots that ever graced the foot of a student or an officer. They fitted as tight to his little legs as if they were painted upon them. It was laughable to see, that in addition to this handsome apparel, he had hung upon his back a narrow clumsy cloak, that looked as if it were made of wood, and upon his head he wore a woodman's cap; but Maria remembered that Godfather Drosselmeier wore an old shabby cloak and an ugly cap, and still he was a dear, dear godfather. Maria could not help thinking also, that even if Godfather Drosselmeier were in other respects as well dressed as this little fellow, yet after all he would not look half so handsome as he. The longer Maria gazed upon the little man whom she had taken a liking to at first sight, the more she was sensible how much good nature and friendliness was expressed in his features. Nothing but kindness and benevolence shone in his clear green, though somewhat too prominent eyes. It was very becoming to the man that he wore about his chin a nicely trimmed beard of white cotton, for by this the sweet smile upon his deep red lips was rendered much more striking. "Ah, dear father," exclaimed Maria at last, "to whom belongs that charming little man by the tree there?"

"He shall work industriously for you all, dear child," said her father. "He can crack the hardest nuts with his teeth, and he belongs as well to Louise as to you and Fred." With these words her father took him carefully from the table, and raised up his wooden cloak, whereupon the little man stretched his mouth wide open, and showed two rows of very white sharp teeth. At her father's bidding

Maria put in a nut, and—crack—the man had bitten it in two, so that the shell fell off, and Maria caught the sweet kernel in her hand. Maria and the other two children were now informed that this dainty little man came of the family of Nutcrackers, and practiced the profession of his forefathers. Maria was overjoyed at what she heard, and her father said, "Dear Maria, since friend Nutcracker is so great a favorite with you, I place him under your particular care and keeping, although, as I said before, Louise and Fred shall have as much right to his services as you."

Maria took him immediately in her arms, and set him to cracking nuts, but she picked out the smallest, that the little fellow need not stretch his mouth open so wide, which in truth was not very becoming to him. Louise sat down by her, and friend Nutcracker must perform the same service for her too, which he seemed to do quite willingly, for he kept smiling all the while very pleasantly. In the meantime Fred had become tired of riding and parading his hussars, and when he heard the nuts crack so merrily, he ran to his sister, and laughed very heartily at the droll little man, who now, since Fred must have a share in the sport, passed from hand to hand, and thus there was no end to his labor. Fred always chose the biggest and hardest nuts, when all at once—crack—crack—it went, and three teeth fell out of Nutcracker's mouth, and his whole under jaw became loose and rickety. "Ah, my poor dear Nutcracker!" said Maria, and snatched him out of Fred's hands.

"That's a stupid fellow," said Fred. "He wants to be a nutcracker, and has poor teeth—he don't understand his trade. Give him to me, Maria. He shall crack nuts for me if he loses all his teeth, and his whole chin into the bargain. Why make such a fuss about such a fellow?"

"No, no," exclaimed Maria, weeping; "you shall not have my dear Nutcracker. See how sorrowfully he looks at me, and shows me his poor mouth. But you are a hard-hearted fellow; you beat your horses; yes, and lately you had one of your soldiers shot through the head."

"That's all right," said Fred, "though you don't understand it. But Nutcracker belongs as much to me as to you, so let me have him."

Maria began to cry bitterly, and rolled up the sick Nutcracker as quickly as she could in her little pocket handkerchief. Their parents now came up with Godfather Drosselmeier. The latter, to Maria's great distress, took Fred's part. But their father said, "I have placed Nutcracker expressly under Maria's protection, and as I see that he is now greatly in need of it, I give her full authority over him, and no one must dispute it. Besides, I wonder at Fred, that he should require farther duty from one who has been maimed in the service. As a good soldier, he ought to know that the wounded are not expected to take their place in the ranks."

Fred was much ashamed, and without troubling himself farther about nuts or Nutcracker, stole around to the opposite end of the table, where his hussars, after stationing suitable outposts, had encamped for the night. Maria collected together Nutcracker's lost teeth, tied up his wounded chin with a nice white ribbon which she had taken from her dress, and then wrapped up the little fellow more carefully than ever in her handkerchief, for he looked very pale and frightened. Thus she held him, rocking him in her arms like a little child, while she looked over the beautiful pictures of the new picture-book, which she found among her other Christmas gifts. Contrary to her usual disposition, she showed some ill-temper towards Father Drosselmeier, who kept continually laughing at her, and asked again and again how it was that she liked to caress such an ugly little fellow. That singular comparison with Drosselmeier, which she made when her eyes first fell upon Nutcracker, now came again into her mind, and she said very seriously: "Who knows, dear godfather, if you were dressed like my sweet Nutcracker, and had on such bright little boots—who knows but you would then be as handsome as he is!" Maria could not tell why her parents laughed so loudly at this, and why the Counsellor's face turned so red, and he, for his part, did not laugh half so heartily this time as he had done more than once before. It is likely there was some particular reason for it.

WONDERS UPON WONDERS

In the sitting room of the Doctor's house, just as you enter the room, there stands on the left hand, close against the wall, a high glass-case, in which the children preserve all the beautiful things which are given to them every year. Louise was quite a little girl when her father had the case made by a skillful joiner, who set in it such large, clear panes of glass, and arranged all the parts so well together, that everything looked much brighter and handsomer when on its shelves than when it was held in the hands. On the upper shelf, which Maria and Fred were unable to reach, stood all Godfather Drosselmeier's curious machines. Immediately below this was a shelf for the picture-books; the two lower shelves Maria and Fred filled up as they pleased, but it always happened that Maria used the lower one as a house for her dolls, while Fred, on the contrary, cantoned his troops in the one above.

And so it happened today, for while Fred set his hussars in order above, Maria, having laid Miss Trutchen aside, and having installed the new and sweetly dressed doll in her best furnished chamber below, had invited herself to tea with her. I have said that the chamber was well furnished, and it is true; here was a nice chintz sofa and several tiny chairs, there stood a tea-table, but above all, there was a clean, white little bed for her doll to repose upon. All these things were arranged in one corner of the glass case, the sides of which were hung with gay pictures, and it will readily be supposed, that in such a chamber the new doll, Miss Clara, must have found herself very comfortable.

It was now late in the evening, and night, indeed, was close at hand, and Godfather Drosselmeier had long since gone home, yet still the children could not leave the glass-case, although their mother repeatedly told them that it was high time to go to bed. "It is true," cried Fred at last; "the poor fellows (meaning his hussars) would like to get a little rest, and as long as I am here, not one of them will dare to nod—I know that." With these words he went up to bed, but Maria begged very hard, "Only leave me here a little while, dear mother. I have two or three things to attend to, and when they are done I will go immediately to bed." Maria was a very good and sensible child, and therefore her mother could leave her alone with her playthings without anxiety. But for fear she might become so much interested in her new doll and other presents as to forget the lights which burned around the glass case, her mother blew them all out, and left only the lamp which hung down from the ceiling in the middle of the chamber, and which diffused a soft, pleasant light. "Come in soon, dear Maria, or you will not be up in time tomorrow morning," called her mother, as she went up to bed. There was something Maria had at heart to do, which she had not told her mother, though she knew not the reason why; and as soon as she found herself alone she went quickly about it. She still carried in her arms the wounded Nutcracker, rolled up in her pocket handkerchief. Now she laid him carefully upon the table, unrolled the handkerchief softly, and examined his wound. Nutcracker was very pale, but still he smiled so kindly and sorrowfully that it went straight to Maria's heart. "Ah! Nutcracker, Nutcracker, do not be angry at brother Fred because he hurt you so, he did not mean to be so rough; it is the wild soldier's life with his hussars that has made him a little hard-hearted, but otherwise he is a good fellow, I can assure you. Now I will tend you very carefully until you are well and merry again; as to fastening in your teeth and setting your shoulders, that Godfather Drosselmeier must do; he understands such things."

But Maria was hardly able to finish the sentence, for as she mentioned the name of Drosselmeier, friend Nutcracker made a terrible wry face, and there darted something out of his eyes like green sparkling flashes. Maria was just going to fall into a dreadful fright, when behold, it was the sad smiling face of the honest Nutcracker again, which she saw before her, and she knew now that it must be the glare of the lamp, which, stirred by the draught, had flared up, and distorted Nutcracker's features so strangely. "Am I not a foolish girl," she said, "to be so easily frightened, and to think that a wooden puppet could make faces at me? But I love Nutcracker too well, because he is so droll and so good tempered; therefore he shall be taken good care of as he deserves." With this Maria took friend Nutcracker in her arms, walked to the glass case, stooped down, and said to her new doll, "Pray, Miss Clara, be so good as to give up your bed to the sick and wounded Nutcracker, and make out as well as you can with the sofa. Remember that you are well and hearty, or you would not have such fat red cheeks, and very few little dolls have such nice sofas."

Miss Clara, in her gay Christmas attire, looked very grand and haughty, and would not even say "Muck." "But why should I stand upon ceremony?" said Maria, and she took out the bed, laid little Nutcracker down upon it softly, and gently rolled a nice ribbon which she wore around her waist, about his poor shoulders, and then drew the bedclothes over him snugly, so that there was nothing to be seen of him below the nose. "He shan't stay with the naughty Clara," she said, and raised the bed with Nutcracker in it to the shelf above, and placed it close by the pretty village, where Fred's hussars were quartered. She locked the case, and was about to go up to bed, when—listen children—when softly, softly it began to rustle, and to whisper, and to rattle round and round, under the hearth, behind the chairs, behind the cupboards and glass case. The great clock whirred louder and louder, but it could not strike. Maria turned towards it, and there the large gilt owl that sat on the top, had dropped down its wings, so that they covered the whole face, and it stretched out its ugly head with the short, crooked beak, and looked just like a cat. And the clock whirred louder in plain words. "Dick—ry, dick—ry, dock—whirr, softly clock, Mouse King has a fine ear—prr—prr—pum—pum—the old song let him hear—prr—prr—pum—pum—or he might—run away in a fright—now clock strike softly and light." And pum—pum, it went with a dull deadened sound twelve times. Maria began now to tremble with fear, and she was upon the point of running out of the room in terror, when she beheld Godfather Drosselmeier, who sat in the owl's place on the top of the clock, and had hung down the skirts of his brown coat just like wings. But she took courage, and cried out loudly, with sobs, "Godfather Drosselmeier, Godfather Drosselmeier, what are you doing up there? Come down, and do not frighten me so, you naughty Godfather Drosselmeier!"

Just then a wild squeaking and whimpering broke out on all sides, and then there was a running, trotting and galloping behind the walls, as if a thousand little feet were in motion, and a thousand little lights flashed out of the crevices in the floor. But they were not lights—no—they were sparkling little eyes, and Maria perceived that mice were all around, peeping out and working their way into the room. Presently it went trot—trot—hop—hop about the chamber, and more and more mice, in greater or smaller parties galloped across, and at last placed themselves in line and column, just as Fred was accustomed to place his soldiers when they went to battle. This Maria thought was very droll, and as she had not that aversion to mice which most children have, her terror was gradually leaving her, when all at once there arose a squeaking so terrible and piercing, that it seemed as if ice-cold water was poured down her back. Ah, what now did she see!

I know, my worthy reader Frederic, that thy heart, like that of the wise and brave soldier Frederic Stahlbaum, sits in the right place, but if thou hadst seen what Maria now beheld, thou wouldst certainly have run away; yes, I believe that thou wouldst have jumped as quickly as possible into bed, and then have drawn the covering over thine ears much farther than was necessary to keep thee warm. Alas! poor Maria could not do that now, for—listen children—close before her feet, there burst out sand and lime and crumbled wall stones, as if thrown up by some subterranean force, and seven mice-heads with seven sparkling crowns rose out of the floor, squeaking and squealing terribly. Presently the mouse's body to which these seven heads belonged, worked its way out, and the great mouse crowned with the seven diadems, squeaking loudly, huzzaed in full chorus, as he advanced to meet his army, which at once set itself in motion, and hott—hott—trot—trot it went—alas, straight towards the glass case—straight towards poor Maria who stood close before it!

Her heart had before beat so terribly from anxiety and fear, that she thought it would leap out of her bosom, and then she knew she must die; but now it seemed as if the blood stood still in her veins. Half fainting, she tottered backward, when clatter—clatter—rattle—rattle it went—and a glass pane which she had struck with her elbow fell in pieces at her feet. She felt at the moment a sharp pain in her left arm, but her heart all at once became much lighter, she heard no more squeaking and squealing, all had become still, and although she did not dare to look, yet she believed that the mice, frightened by the clatter of the broken glass, had retreated into their holes. But what was that again! Close behind her in the glass case a strange bustling and rustling began, and little fine voices were heard. "Up, up, awake—arms take—awake—to the fight—this night—up, up—to the fight." And all the while something rang out clear and sweet like little bells. "Ah, that is my dear musical clock!" exclaimed Maria joyfully, and turned quickly to look.

She then saw how it flashed and lightened strangely in the glass case, and there was a great stir and bustle upon the shelves. Many little figures crossed up and down by each other, and worked and stretched out their arms as if they were making ready. And now, Nutcracker raised himself all of a sudden, threw the bedclothes clear off, and leaped with both feet at once out of bed, crying aloud, "Crack—crack—crack—stupid pack—drive mouse back—stupid pack—crack—crack—mouse—back—crick—crack—stupid pack." With these words he drew his little sword, flourished it in the air, and exclaimed, "My loving vassals, friends and brothers, will you stand by me in the hard fight?" Straightway three Scaramouches, a Harlequin, four Chimney-sweepers, two Guitar-players and a drummer cried out, "Yes, my lord, we will follow you with fidelity and courage—we will march with you to battle—to victory or death," and then rushed after the fiery Nutcracker, who ventured the dangerous leap down from the upper shelf. Ah, it was easy enough for *them* to perform this feat, for beside the fine garments of thick cloth and silk which they wore, the inside of their bodies were made of cotton and tow, so that they came down plump, like bags of wool. But poor Nutcracker had certainly broken his arms or his legs, for remember, it was almost two feet from the shelf where he stood to the floor, and his body was as brittle as if it had been cut out of Linden wood. Yes, Nutcracker would certainly have broken his arms or his legs, if, at the moment when he leaped, Miss Clara had not sprung quickly from the sofa, and caught the hero with his drawn sword in her soft arms. "Ah, thou dear, good Clara," sobbed Maria, "how I have wronged thee! Thou didst certainly resign thy bed willingly to little Nutcracker."

But Miss Clara now spoke, as she softly pressed the young hero to her silken bosom. "You will not, oh, my lord! sick and wounded as you are, share the dangers of the fight. See how your brave vassals assemble themselves, eager for the affray, and certain of conquest. Scaramouch, Harlequin, Chimney-sweepers, Guitar-players, Drummer, are all ready drawn up below, and the china figures on the shelf stir and move strangely! Will you not, oh, my lord! repose upon the sofa, or from my arms look down upon your victory?" Thus spoke Clara, but Nutcracker demeaned himself very ungraciously, for he kicked and struggled so violently with his legs, that Clara was obliged to set him quickly down upon the floor. He then, however, dropped gracefully upon one knee, and said, "Fair lady, the recollection of thy favor and condescension will go with me into the battle and the strife."

Clara then stooped so low that she could take him by the arm, raised him gently from his knees, took off her bespangled girdle, and was about to throw it across his neck, but little Nutcracker stepped two paces backward, laid his hand upon his breast, and said very earnestly, "Not so, fair lady, lavish not thy favors thus upon me, for—" he stopped, sighed heavily, tore off the ribbon which Maria had bound about his shoulders, pressed it to his lips, hung it across him like a scarf, and then boldly flourishing his bright little blade, leaped like a bird over the edge of the glass case upon the floor. You understand my kind and good readers and listeners, that Nutcracker, even before he had thus come to life, had felt very sensibly the kindness and love which Maria had shown towards him, and it was because he had become so partial to her, that he would not receive and wear the girdle of Miss Clara, although it shone and sparkled so brightly. The true and faithful Nutcracker preferred to wear Maria's simple ribbon. But what will now happen? As soon as Nutcracker had leaped out, the squeaking and whistling was heard again. Ah, it is under the large table, that the hateful mice have concealed their countless bands, and high above them all towers the dreadful mouse with seven heads! What will now happen!

THE BATTLE

"Beat the march, true vassal Drummer!" screamed Nutcracker very loudly, and immediately the drummer began to rattle and to roll upon his drum so skillfully, that the windows of the glass case trembled and hummed again. Now it rustled and clattered therein, and Maria perceived that the covers of the little boxes in which Fred's army were quartered were bursting open, and now the soldiers leaped out, and then down again upon the lowest shelf, where they drew up in fine array. Nutcracker ran up and down, speaking inspiring words to the troops—"Let no dog of a trumpeter blow or stir!" he cried angrily, for he was afraid he should not be heard, and then turned quickly to Harlequin, who had grown a little pale, and chattered with his long chin. "General," he said, earnestly, "I know your courage and your experience; there is need now for a quick eye, and skill to seize the proper moment. I entrust to your command all the cavalry and artillery. You do not need a horse, for you have very long legs, and can gallop yourself tolerably well. I look to see you do your duty." Thereupon Harlequin put his long, thin fingers to his mouth, and crowed so piercingly, that it sounded as if a hundred shrill trumpets were blown merrily.

Then it stirred again in the glass case—a neighing, and a whinnying, and a stamping were heard, and see! Fred's cuirassiers and dragoons, but above all, his new splendid hussars marched out, and halted close by the case. Regiment after regiment now defiled before Nutcracker, with flying colors and warlike music, and ranged themselves in long rows across the floor of the chamber. Before them went Fred's cannon rattling along, surrounded by the cannoniers, and soon bom—bom it went, and Maria could see how the mice suffered by the fire, how the sugarplums plunged into their dark, heavy mass, covering them with white powder, and throwing them more than once into shameful disorder. But the greatest damage was done them by a heavy battery that was mounted upon mamma's footstool, which—pum, pum—kept up a steady fire of caraway seeds against the enemy, by which a great many of them fell. The mice, notwithstanding, came nearer and nearer, and at last mastered some of the cannon, but then it went prr—prr—and Maria could scarcely see what now happened for the smoke and dust. This however was certain, that each corps fought with the greatest animosity, and the victory was for a long time doubtful. The mice kept deploying more and more forces, and the little silver shot, which they fired very skillfully, struck now even into the glass case. Clara and Trutchen ran around in despair. "Must I die in the blossom of youth?" said Clara. "Have I so well preserved myself for this, to perish here in these walls?" cried Trutchen. Then they fell about each other's necks, and screamed so terribly, that they could be heard above the mad tumult of the battle.

Of the scene that now presented itself you can have no idea, good reader. It went prr—prr—puff—piff—clitter—clatter—bom, burum—bom, burum—bom—in the wildest confusion, while the Mouse King and mice squeaked and screamed, and now and then the mighty voice of Nutcracker was heard, as he gave the necessary orders, and he was seen striding along through the battalions in the hottest of the fire. Harlequin had made some splendid charges with his cavalry, and covered himself with honor, but Fred's hussars were battered by the enemy's artillery, with odious, offensive balls, which made dreadful spots in their red jackets, for which reason they would not move forward. Harlequin ordered them to draw off to the left, and in the enthusiasm of command headed the movement himself, and the cuirassiers and dragoons followed; that is, they all drew off to the left, and galloped home. By this step the battery upon the footstool was exposed to great danger, and it was not long before a strong body of very ugly mice pushed on with such determined bravery, that the footstool, cannons, cannoniers and all were overthrown by their headlong charge. Nutcracker seemed a little disturbed at this, and gave orders that the right wing should make a retreating movement. You know very well, oh my military reader Frederic, that to make such a movement is almost the same thing as to run away, and you are now grieving with me at the disaster which impends over the army of Maria's darling Nutcracker.

But turn your eyes from this scene, and view the left wing, where all is still in good order, and where there is yet great hope, both for the general and the army. During the hottest of the fight, large masses of mice cavalry had debouched softly from under the settee, and amid loud and hideous squeaking had thrown themselves with fury upon the left wing; but what an obstinate resistance did they meet with there! Slowly, as the difficult nature of the ground required—for the edge of the glass case had to be traversed—the china figures had advanced, headed by two Chinese emperors, and formed themselves into a hollow square. These brave, motley, but noble troops, which were composed of Gardeners, Tyrolese, Bonzes, Friseurs, Merry-andrews, Cupids, Lions, Tigers, Peacocks, and

Apes, fought with coolness, courage, and determination. By their Spartan bravery this battalion of picked men would have wrested the victory from the foe, had not a bold major rushed madly from the enemy's ranks, and bitten off the head of one of the Chinese emperors, who in falling dashed to the ground two Bonzes and a Cupid. Through this gap the enemy penetrated into the square, and in a few moments the whole battalion was torn to pieces. Their brave resistance, therefore, was of no avail to Nutcracker's army, which, once having begun to retreat, retired farther and farther, and at every step with diminished numbers, until the unfortunate Nutcracker halted with a little band close before the glass case. "Let the reserve advance! Harlequin—Scaramouch—Drummer—where are you?"

Thus cried Nutcracker, in hopes of new troops which should deploy out of the glass case. And there actually came forth a few brown men and women, made of sweet thorn, with golden faces, and caps, and helmets, but they fought around so awkwardly, that they did not hit one of the enemy, and at last knocked the cap off their own general's head. The enemies' chasseurs, too, bit off their legs before long, so that they tumbled over, and carried with them to the ground some of Nutcracker's best officers. Nutcracker, now completely surrounded by the foe, was in the greatest peril. He tried to leap over the edge, into the glass case, but found his legs too short. Clara and Trutchen lay each in a deep swoon—they could not help him—hussars, dragoons sprang merrily by him into safe quarters, and in wild despair, he cried, "A horse—a horse—a kingdom for a horse!" At this moment two of the enemies' tirailleurs seized him by his wooden mantle, and the Mouse King, squeaking from his seven throats, leaped in triumph towards him. Maria could no longer control herself. "Oh, my poor Nutcracker!" she cried, sobbing, and without being exactly conscious of what she did, grasped her left shoe, and threw it with all her strength into the thickest of the mice, straight at their king. In an instant, all seemed scattered and dispersed, but Maria felt in her left arm a still sharper pain than before, and sank in a swoon to the floor.

THE SICKNESS

When Maria woke out of her deep and deathlike slumber, she found herself lying in her own bed, with the sun shining bright and sparkling through the ice-covered windows into the chamber. Close beside her sat a stranger, whom she soon recognized, however, as the Surgeon Wendelstern. He said softly, "She is awake!" Her mother then came to the bedside, and gazed upon her with anxious and inquiring looks. "Ah, dear mother," lisped little Maria, "are all the hateful mice gone, and is the good Nutcracker safe?"

"Do not talk such foolish stuff," replied her mother; "what have the mice to do with Nutcracker? You naughty child, you have caused us a great deal of anxiety. But so it always is, when children are disobedient and do not mind their parents. You played last night with your dolls until it was very late. You became sleepy, probably, and a stray mouse may have jumped out and frightened you; at all events, you broke a pane of glass with your elbow, and cut your arm so severely, that neighbor Wendelstern, who has just taken the piece of glass out of the wound, declares that it came very near cutting a vein, in which case you might have had a stiff arm all your life, or perhaps have bled to death. It was fortunate that I woke about midnight, and not finding you in your bed, got up and went into the sitting-room. There you lay in a swoon upon the floor, close by the glass case, the blood flowing in a stream. I almost fainted away myself at the sight. There you lay, and scattered around, were many of Frederic's leaden soldiers, broken china figures, gingerbread men and women and other playthings, and not far off your left shoe."

"Ah! dear mother, dear mother," exclaimed Maria, interrupting her, "those were the traces of that dreadful battle between the puppets and the mice, and what frightened me so was the danger of poor Nutcracker, when the mice were going to take him prisoner. Then I threw my shoe at the mice, and after that I don't know what happened."

Surgeon Wendelstern here made a sign to the mother, and she said very softly to Maria, "Well, never mind about it, my dear child, the mice are all gone, and little Nutcracker stands safe and sound in the glass case." Doctor Stahlbaum now entered the chamber, and spoke for a while with Surgeon Wendelstern, then he felt Maria's pulse, and she could hear very plainly that he said something about a fever. She was obliged to remain in bed and take physic, and so it continued for some days, although except a slight pain in her arm, she felt quite well and comfortable. She knew little Nutcracker had escaped safe from the battle, and it seemed to her that she sometimes heard his voice quite plainly, as if in a dream, saying mournfully, "Maria, dearest lady, what thanks do I not owe you! but you can do still more for me." Maria tried to think what it could be, but in vain; nothing occurred to her. She could not play very well on account of the wound in her arm, and when she tried to read or look at her picture books, a strange glare came across her eyes, so that she was obliged to desist. The time, during the day, always seemed very long to her, and she waited impatiently for evening, as her mother then usually seated herself by her bedside, and read or related some pretty story to her.

One evening she had just finished the wonderful history of prince Fackardin, when the door opened, and Godfather Drosselmeier entered, saying, "I must see now for myself how it goes with the sick and wounded Maria." As soon as

Maria saw Godfather Drosselmeier in his brown coat, the image of that night in which Nutcracker lost the battle against the mice returned vividly to her mind, and she cried out involuntarily, "Oh Godfather Drosselmeier, you have been very naughty; I saw you as you sat upon the clock, and covered it with your wings, so that it should not strike loud, to scare away the mice. I heard how you called out to the Mouse King. Why did you not come to help us; me, and the poor Nutcracker? It is all your fault, naughty Godfather Drosselmeier, that I must be here sick in bed." Her mother was quite frightened at this, and said, "What is the matter with you, dear Maria?"

But Godfather Drosselmeier made very strange faces, and said in a grating, monotonous tone, "Pendulum must whirr—whirr—whirr—this way—that way—clock will strike—tired of ticking—all the day—softly whirr—whirr— whirr—strike kling—klang—strike klang—kling—bing and bang and bang and bing—'twill scare away the Mouse King. Then Owl in swift flight comes at dead of night. Pendulum must whirr—whirr—Clock will strike kling—klang—this way—that way—tired of ticking all the day—bing—bang—and Mouse King scare away—whirr—whirr—prr—prr." Maria stared at Godfather Drosselmeier, for he did not look at all as he usually did, but appeared much uglier, and he moved his right arm backward and forward, like a puppet pulled by wires. She would have been afraid of him, if her mother had not been present, and if Fred had not slipped in, in the meanwhile, and interrupted him with loud laughter. "Ha, ha! Godfather Drosselmeier," cried Fred, "you are today too droll again— you act just like my Harlequin that I threw into the lumber room long ago." But their mother was very serious, and said, "Dear Counsellor, this is very strange sport—what do you really mean by it?"

"Gracious me," replied Drosselmeier, laughing, "have you forgotten then my pretty watchmaker's song? I always sing it to such patients as Maria." With this he drew his chair close to her bed, and said, "Do not be angry that I did not pick out the Mouse King's fourteen eyes—that could not be—but instead, I have in store for you a very agreeable surprise." The Counsellor with these words put his hand in his pocket, drew something out slowly, and behold it was—Nutcracker with his lost teeth nicely fastened in, and his lame chin well set and sound. Maria cried aloud with joy, while her mother smiled, and said, "You see now, Maria, that Godfather Drosselmeier meant well by your little Nutcracker."

"But still you must confess, Maria," said the Counsellor, "that Nutcracker's figure is none of the finest, neither can his face be called exactly handsome. How this ugliness came to be hereditary in the family, I will now relate to you, if you will listen. Or perhaps you know already the story of the Princess Pirlipat and the Lady Mouserings, and the skilful Watchmaker?"

"Look here, Godfather Drosselmeier," interrupted Fred, "Nutcracker's teeth you have fastened in very well, and his chin is no longer lame and rickety, but why has he no sword? why have you not put on his sword?"

"Ah," replied the Counsellor, angrily, "you must always meddle and make, you rogue. What is Nutcracker's sword to me? I have cured his wounds, and he may find a sword for himself as he can."

"That's true," said Fred, "he is a brave fellow, and will know how to get one."

"Tell me then, Maria," continued the Counsellor, "have you heard the story of the Princess Pirlipat?"

"I hope, dear Counsellor," said the mother, "that your story will not be frightful, as those that you narrate usually are."

"By no means, dearest madam," replied Drosselmeier, "on the contrary, what I have this time the honor to relate is droll and merry."

"Begin, begin then, dear Godfather!" cried the children, and the Counsellor began as follows.

THE STORY OF THE HARD NUT

Pirlipat's mother was the wife of a king, and therefore a queen, and Pirlipat straightway at the moment of her birth a true princess. The king was beside himself with joy, when he saw his beautiful daughter, as she lay in the cradle. He shouted aloud, danced, jumped about upon one leg, and cried again and again, "Ha! ha! was there ever anything seen more beautiful than my little Pirlipat?" Thereupon all the ministers, generals, presidents and staff officers jumped about upon one leg like the king, and cried aloud, "No, never!" And it was so, in truth, for as long as the world has been standing, a lovelier child was never born, than this very Princess Pirlipat. Her little face seemed made of lilies and roses, delicate white and red; her eyes were of living sparkling azure, and it was charming to see how her little locks curled in bright golden ringlets. Besides this, Pirlipat had brought into the world two rows of little pearly teeth, with which two hours after her birth, she bit the high chancellor's finger, as he was examining her features too closely, so that he screamed out, "Oh, Gemini!" Others assert that he screamed out, "Oh, Crickee!" but on this point authorities are at the present day divided. Well, little Pirlipat bit the high chancellor's finger, and the enraptured land knew now that some sense dwelt in Pirlipat's beautiful body. As has been said, all were delighted. The queen alone was very anxious and uneasy, and no one knew wherefore, but everybody remarked with surprise, the care with which she watched Pirlipat's cradle. Besides that the doors were guarded by soldiers, and not counting the two nurses, who always remained close by the cradle, six maids night after night sat in the room to watch. But what seemed very foolish, and no one could understand the meaning of it, was this; each of these six maids must have a cat upon her lap, and stroke it the whole night through, and thus keep it continually purring. It is impossible that you, dear children, can guess why Pirlipat's mother made all these arrangements, but I know, and will straightway tell you.

It happened that once upon a time many great kings and fine princes were assembled at the court of Pirlipat's father, on which occasion much splendor was displayed, the theatres were crowded, balls were given, and tournaments held almost every day. The king, in order to show plainly that he was in no want of gold and silver, was resolved to take a good handful out of his royal treasury, and expend it in a suitable manner. Therefore as soon as he had been privately informed by the overseer of the kitchen, that the court astronomer had predicted the right time for killing, he ordered a great feast of sausages, leaped into his carriage, and went himself to invite the assembled kings and princes to take a little soup with him, in order to enjoy the agreeable surprise which he had prepared for them. Upon his return, he said very affectionately to the queen, "You know, my dear, how extremely fond I am of sausages." The queen knew at once what he meant by that, and it was this, that she should take upon herself, as she had often done before, the useful occupation of making sausages. The lord treasurer must straightway bring to the kitchen the great golden sausage kettle, and the silver chopping knives and stew-pans. A large fire of sandalwood was made, the queen put on her damask apron, and soon the sweet smell of the sausage meat began to steam up out of the kettle. The agreeable odor penetrated even to the royal council chamber, and the king, seized with a sudden transport, could no longer restrain himself. "With your permission, my lords," he cried, and leaped up, ran as fast as he could into the kitchen, embraced the queen, stirred a little with his golden sceptre in the kettle, and then his emotion being quieted, returned calmly to the council.

The important moment had now arrived when the fat was to be chopped into little pieces, and browned gently in the silver stew-pans. The maids of honor now retired, for the queen, out of true devotion and reverence for her royal spouse, wished to perform this duty alone. But just as the fat began to fry, a small wimpering, whispering voice was heard, "Give me a little of the fat, sister—I should like my part of the feast—I too am a queen—give me a little of the fat." The queen knew very well that it was Lady Mouserings who said this. Lady Mouserings had lived these many years in the king's palace. She maintained that she was related to the royal family, and that she was herself a queen in the kingdom of Mousalia, for which reason she held a great court under the hearth.

The queen was a kind and benevolent lady, and although she was not exactly willing to acknowledge Lady Mouserings as a true queen and sister, yet she was very ready to allow her a little banquet on this great holiday. She answered, therefore, "Come out, then, Lady Mouserings, you are welcome to a little of the fat." Upon this, Lady Mouserings leaped out very quickly and merrily, jumped upon the hearth, and seized with her dainty little paws, one piece of fat after the other as the queen reached it to her. But now, all the cousins and aunts of the Lady Mouserings came running out, besides her seven sons, rude and forward rogues, who all fell at once upon the fat, and the terrified queen could not drive them away. But as good fortune would have it, the chief maid of honor came in at this moment, and chased away the intruding guests, so that a little of the fat was left. The king's mathematician being summoned, demonstrated very clearly that there was enough remaining to season all the sausages, if distributed with the nicest judgment and skill.

Drums and trumpets were now heard without, and all the invited potentates and princes, some on white palfreys, some in crystal carriages, came in splendid apparel to the sausage-feast. The king received them kindly and graciously, and then, adorned with crown and sceptre, as became the monarch of the land, seated himself at the head of the table. Already in the first course, that of the sausage balls, it was observed that he grew pale and paler; raised his eyes to heaven; gentle sighs escaped from his bosom, and he seemed to undergo great inward suffering. But in the second course, which consisted of the long sausages, he sank back upon his throne, sobbing and moaning, held both bands to his face, and at last wept and groaned aloud. All sprang up from the table, the royal physician tried in vain to feel the pulse of the unhappy monarch, a deep-seated, unknown torture appeared to agitate him. At last, after much anxiety, and after the application of some very strong remedies, the king seemed to come a little to himself, and stammered out scarce audibly the words, "*Too little fat!*"

Then the queen threw herself in despair at his feet, and sobbed out, "Oh, my poor, unhappy, royal husband! Alas, how great must be the suffering which you endure! But see the guilty one at your feet; punish, punish her without mercy. Alas! Lady Mouserings with her seven sons, and aunts and cousins, *have eaten up the fat, and—*" with these words she fell right over backwards in a swoon. Then the king, full of rage, leaped up and cried out, "Chief maid of honor, how happened that?" The chief maid of honor told the story, as much as she knew of it, and the king resolved to take vengeance upon Lady Mouserings and her family for having eaten up the fat of his sausages. The privy council was called, and it was resolved to summon Lady Mouserings to trial, and confiscate all her estates. But as the king was of opinion that in the meanwhile she might eat up more of his sausage fat, the affair was placed at last in the hands of the royal watchmaker and mechanist.

This man (whose name was the same as mine, to wit, Christian Elias Drosselmeier) engaged, by means of a very singular and deep political scheme, to drive Lady Mouserings and her family from the palace forever. He invented therefore several curious little machines, in which a piece of toasted fat was fastened to a thread, and these Drosselmeier placed around Lady Mouserings' dwelling. Lady Mouserings was much too wise not to see through Drosselmeier's craft, but all her warnings, all her entreaties were of no avail, every one of her seven sons, and many of her cousins and aunts, went into Drosselmeier's machines, and, as they tried to snap away the fat, were caught by an iron grating, which fell suddenly down behind them, and were afterwards miserably slaughtered in the kitchen. Lady Mouserings, with the little remnant of her family, forsook the dreadful place. Grief, despair, revenge filled her bosom. The court revelled in joy at this event, but the queen was very anxious, for she knew the disposition of Lady Mouserings, and was very sure that she would not suffer the death of her sons to go unavenged. In fact, Lady Mouserings appeared one day, when the queen was in the kitchen, preparing a harslet hash for her royal husband, a dish of which he was very fond, and said, "My sons, my cousins and aunts are destroyed; take care queen, that Mouse-Queen does not bite thy little princess in two—take good care." With this she disappeared, and was not seen again; but the queen was so frightened that she let the hash fall into the fire; and thus a second time Lady Mouserings spoiled a favorite dish for the king, at which he was very angry.

"But this, dear children," said Drosselmeier, "is enough for tonight—the rest at another time."

Maria, who had her own thoughts about this story, begged Godfather Drosselmeier very hard to go on, but she could not prevail upon him. He rose, saying, "Too much at once is bad for the health—the rest tomorrow." As the Counsellor was just stepping out of the room, Fred called out, "Tell me, Godfather Drosselmeier, is it then really true that you invented mousetraps?"

"How can you ask such a silly question?" said his mother, but the Counsellor smiled mysteriously, and said in an under tone, "Am I a skilful watchmaker, and yet not able to invent a mousetrap?"

THE STORY OF THE HARD NUT CONTINUED

You know now, children, commenced Counsellor Drosselmeier, on the following evening, why the queen took such care in guarding the beautiful Princess Pirlipat. Was it not to be feared that Lady Mouserings would execute her threat, that she would come again, and bite the little princess to death? Drosselmeier's machines were not the least protection against the wise and prudent Lady Mouserings, but the court astronomer, who was at the same time private star-gazer and fortune-teller to his majesty, declared it to be his opinion that the family of Baron Purr would be able to keep Lady Mouserings from the cradle. Most of that name were secretaries of legation at court, with little to do, though always at hand for an embassy to a foreign power, but they must now render themselves useful at home. And thus it came that each of the waiting-women must hold a son of that family upon her lap, and by continual and attentive fondling, lighten the severe public duties which fell to their lot.

Late one night the two chief nurses who sat close by the cradle started up out of a deep sleep. All around lay in quiet slumber—no purring—the stillness of the grave! even the death-watch could be heard ticking! and what was the terror of the two chief waiting-women, as they just saw before them a large, dreadful mouse, which stood erect upon its hind feet, and had laid its ugly head close against the face of the princess. With a cry of terror they jumped up; all awoke, but in a moment Lady Mouserings (for the great mouse by Pirlipat's cradle was no one but she) ran as fast as she could to the corner of the chamber. The secretaries of legation leaped after her, but too late—she had disappeared through a hole in the chamber floor. Little Pirlipat awoke at the noise and wept bitterly. "Thank heaven," cried the nurse, "she lives—she lives!" But how great was their terror, when they looked at Pirlipat, and saw what a change had taken place in the sweet beautiful child. Instead of the white and red face with golden locks, a large, ill-shaped head sat upon her thin shrivelled body, her azure blue eyes were changed into green staring ones, and her little mouth had stretched itself from ear to ear. The queen was brought to death's door by grief and sorrow, and it was found necessary to hang the king's library with thick wadded tapestry, for again and again he ran his head against the wall, crying out at every time in lamentable tones, "Ah, me, unhappy monarch!" He might now have seen how much better it would have been to eat his sausages without fat, and to leave Lady Mouserings and her family at peace under the hearth; but Pirlipat's royal father did not think about this, he laid all the blame upon the court watchmaker and mechanist, Christian Elias Drosselmeier of Nuremburg. He therefore wisely decreed that Drosselmeier should restore the Princess Pirlipat to her former condition within four weeks, or at least find out some certain and infallible method of effecting this, otherwise he should suffer a shameful death under the axe of the executioner.

Drosselmeier was not a little terrified, but he had great confidence in his skill and good fortune, and began immediately the first operation which he thought useful. He took little Princess Pirlipat apart with great dexterity, unscrewed her little hands and feet, and carefully examined her inward structure; but he found, alas, that the princess would grow uglier as she grew bigger, and knew not what to do or what to advise. He put the princess carefully together again, and sank down by her cradle in despair, for he was not allowed to leave it. The fourth week had commenced—yes, Thursday had come, when the king looked in with flashing eyes, and shaking his sceptre at him, cried, "Christian Elias Drosselmeier, cure the princess, or thou must die." Drosselmeier began to weep bitterly, but the Princess Pirlipat lay as happy as the day, and cracked nuts. Pirlipat's uncommon appetite for nuts now occurred for the first time to the mechanist, and the fact likewise that she had come into the world with teeth.

In truth, immediately after her transformation, she had screamed continually until a nut accidentally came in her way, which she immediately put into her mouth, cracked it, ate the kernel, and then became quite composed. Since that time her nurses found that nothing pleased her so well as to be supplied with nuts. "Oh, sacred instinct of Nature! eternal, inexplicable sympathy of existence!" cried Christian Elias Drosselmeier. "Thou pointest me to the gates of this mystery. I will knock, and they will open." He begged straightway for permission to speak with the royal astronomer, and was led to his apartment under a strong guard. They embraced with many tears, for they had been warm friends, then retired into a private cabinet, and examined a great many books which treated of instinct, of sympathies, and antipathies, and other mysterious things. Night came on; the astronomer looked at the stars, and with the aid of Drosselmeier, who had great skill in such matters, set up the horoscope of Princess Pirlipat. It was a great deal of trouble, for the lines grew all the while more and more intricate; but at last— what joy!—at last it became clear, that the Princess Pirlipat, in order to be freed from the magic which had deformed her, and to regain her beauty, had nothing to do but to eat the kernel of the nut Crackatuck.

Now the nut Crackatuck had such a hard shell, that an eight-and-forty pounder might be wheeled over it without breaking it. This hard nut must be cracked with the teeth before the princess, by a man who had never been shaved, and had never worn boots. The young man must then hand her the kernel with closed eyes, and must not open them again until he had marched seven steps backward without stumbling. Drosselmeier and the astronomer had labored together, without cessation, for three days and nights, and the king was seated at dinner on Sunday afternoon, when the mechanist, who was to have been beheaded early Monday morning, rushed in with joy and transport, and proclaimed that he had found out a method of restoring to the Princess Pirlipat her lost beauty. The king embraced him with great kindness, and promised him a diamond sword, four orders of honor, and two new Sunday suits. "Immediately after dinner we will go to work," he added; "and see to it, dear mechanist, that the unshorn young man in shoes is ready at hand with the nut Crackatuck; and take care that he drinks no wine beforehand, for fear he should stumble as he goes the seven steps backward, like a crab; afterward he may drink like a fish." Drosselmeier was very much discomposed at these words; and, after much stuttering and stammering, said that the method was discovered, indeed, but that the nut Crackatuck and the young man to crack it were yet to be sought after, and that it was quite doubtful whether nut or nutcracker would ever be found.

The king in great anger swung his sceptre about his crowned head, and roared with the voice of a lion, "Then off goes thy head!" It was very fortunate for the unhappy Drosselmeier that the king's dinner had been cooked better than usual this day, so that he was in a pleasant humor, and disposed to listen to reason, while the good queen, who was moved by the hard fate of the mechanist, used her influence to soothe him. Drosselmeier then after a while took courage, and represented to the monarch that he had performed his task in discovering the means to restore the princess to her beauty, and thus by the terms of the royal decree had secured his safety. The king said that was all trash, stupid stuff and nonsense, but resolved at last, that the watchmaker should leave the court instantly, accompanied by the royal astronomer, and never return without the nut Crackatuck in his pocket. By the intercession of the queen, he consented that the nutcracker might be summoned by a notice in all the home and foreign newspapers and journals.

Here the Counsellor broke off again, and promised to narrate the rest on the following evening.

CONCLUSION OF THE STORY OF THE HARD NUT

The next evening as soon as the candles were lighted, Godfather Drosselmeier appeared, and continued his story as follows:

Drosselmeier and the astronomer had been fifteen years on their journey without seeing the least signs of the nut Crackatuck. It would take me a month, children, to tell where they went, and what strange things happened to them. I must pass them over, and commence where Drosselmeier sank at last into despondency, and felt a great desire to see his dear native city, Nuremburg. This desire came upon him all at once, as he was smoking a pipe of tobacco with his friend in the middle of a great wood in Asia. "Oh, sweet city," he cried, "sweet native city, sweet Nuremberg! He who has never seen thee, though he may have traveled to London, Paris, Rome, if his heart is not dead to emotion, must continually desire to visit thee—thee, oh Nuremberg, sweet city, where there are so many beautiful houses with windows!" As Drosselmeier grieved in such a sorrowful manner, the astronomer was moved with sympathy, and began to cry and howl so pitifully that it was heard far and wide through Asia. He soon composed himself again, wiped the tears out of his eyes, and said: "But why, my respected colleague, why sit here and howl? Why should we not go to Nuremberg? Is it not all the same, wherever we seek after this miserable nut, Crackatuck?"

"That is true," replied Drosselmeier, greatly consoled. Both arose, knocked out their pipes, and went straightforward out of the wood in the middle of Asia, right to Nuremburg. They had scarcely arrived there, when Drosselmeier ran to his brother, Christopher Zacharias Drosselmeier, puppet-maker, varnisher, and gilder, whom he had not seen for these many years. The watchmaker told him the whole story of the Princess Pirlipat, Lady Mouserings, and the nut Crackatuck, so that he struck his hands together, over and over again with astonishment, and exclaimed: "Ei, ei, brother, brother, what strange things are these!" Drosselmeier then related the history of his travels: how he had passed two years with King Date, how coldly he had been received by Prince Almond, and how he had sought information to no purpose of the Natural Society in Squirrelberg—in short, how his search everywhere had been in vain to find even the least signs of the nut Crackatuck.

During this account, Christopher Zacharias had often snapped his fingers, turned about on one foot, winked, laughed, clucked with his tongue, and then called out: "Hi—hem—ei—oh!—if it should!—" At last, he tossed his hat and wig up in the air, clasped his brother round the neck, and cried: "Brother, brother, you are safe!—safe, I say; for I must be wonderfully mistaken if I have not that nut Crackatuck at this very moment in my possession!" He then drew a little box from his pocket, and took out of it a gilded nut of moderate size. "See," he said, "this nut fell into my hands in this way. Many years ago, a stranger came here at Christmas time with a sack full of nuts, which he offered for sale cheap. Just as he passed my shop, he got into a quarrel with a nut-seller of this city, who did not like to see a stranger come hither to undersell him, and for this reason attacked him. The man put down his sack upon the ground, the better to defend himself, and at the same moment, a heavily laden wagon passed directly over it; all the nuts were cracked in pieces except this one, which the stranger, with a singular smile, offered me, for a bright dollar of the year 1720. I thought that strange, but as I found in my pocket just such a dollar as the man wanted, I bought the nut, and gilded it over, without exactly knowing why I bought the nut so dear, or why I set so much store by it.

All doubt, whether this nut was actually the long-sought nut, Crackatuck, was instantly removed when the astronomer was called, who carefully scraped off the gold, and found upon the rind the word Crackatuck, engraved in Chinese characters. The joy of the travelers was beyond bounds, and the brother the happiest man under the sun, for Drosselmeier assured him that his fortune was made, since he would have a considerable pension for the rest of his days, and then there was the gold which had been scraped off—he might keep that for gilding. The mechanist and the astronomer had both put on their nightcaps, and were getting into bed as the latter commenced: "My worthy colleague, good fortune never comes single. Take my word for it, we have found, not only the nut Crackatuck, but also the young man who is to crack it, and hand the kernel to the princess. I mean nobody else than your brother's son. I cannot sleep; no, this very night I must cast the youth's horoscope." With these words, he threw the night-cap off his head, and began straightway to take an observation.

The brother's son was in truth a handsome, well grown young man, who had never been shaved, and who had never worn boots. In his early youth he had on Christmas nights gone around as a Merry Andrew, but this could not be seen in his behavior in the least, so well had his manners been formed by his father's care. On Christmas days he wore a handsome red coat trimmed with gold, a sword, a hat under his arm, and a curling wig. In this fine dress he would stand in his father's shop, and out of gallantry crack nuts for the young girls, for which reason he was called the handsome Nutcracker.

On the following morning the astronomer was in raptures: he fell upon the mechanist's neck, and cried, "It is he—we have him—he is found! But there are two things, worthy colleague, which we must see to. In the first place, we must braid for your excellent nephew a stout wooden queue, which shall be joined in such a way to his lower jaw, that it can move it with great force. In the next place, when we arrive at the king's palace, we must let no one know that we have brought the young man with us who is to crack the nut Crackatuck. It is best that he should not be found for a long time. I read in his horoscope, that after many young men have broken their teeth to no purpose, the king will promise to him who cracks the nut, and restores to the princess her lost beauty, the princess herself, and the succession to the throne as a reward."

His brother, the puppet-maker, was highly delighted to think that his son might marry the Princess Pirlipat, and become a prince and king, and he gave him up entirely into the hands of the two travelers. The queue which Drosselmeier fastened upon his young and hopeful nephew, answered admirably, so that he made a series of the most successful experiments, even upon the hardest peach-stones. As Drosselmeier and the astronomer had sent immediate information to the palace, of the discovery of the nut Crackatuck, suitable notices had been published, and when the travelers arrived, many handsome young men, and among them some handsome princes, had appeared, who trusting to their sound teeth, were ready to undertake the disenchantment of the princess. The travelers were not a little terrified when they beheld the princess again. Her little body, with its tiny hands and feet, was hardly able to carry her great misshapen head, and the ugliness of her face was increased by a white cotton beard, which had spread itself around her mouth, and over her chin. All happened as the astronomer had read in the horoscope. One youth in shoes after another bit upon the nut Crackatuck until his teeth and jaws were sore, and as he was led away, half swooning, by the physician in attendance, sighed out, "That was a hard nut."

When the king, in the anguish of his heart, had promised his daughter and his kingdom to him who should effect the disenchantment, the handsome young Drosselmeier stepped forward, and begged for permission to begin the experiment. And no one had pleased the fancy of Princess Pirlipat as well as young Drosselmeier; she laid her little hand upon her heart, and sighed deeply, "Ah, if this might be the one who is to crack the nut Crackatuck, and become my husband!" After young Drosselmeier had gracefully saluted the king and queen, and then the Princess Pirlipat, he received the nut Crackatuck from the hands of the master of ceremonies, put it without hesitation between his teeth, pulled his queue very hard, and crack—crack—the shell broke into many pieces. He then nicely removed the little threads and broken bits of shell that hung to the kernel, and reached it with a low bow to the princess, after which he shut his eyes, and began to walk backwards. The princess straightway swallowed the kernel, and behold! her ugly shape was gone, and in its place appeared a most beautiful figure, with a face of roses and lilies, delicate white and red, eyes of living, sparkling azure, and locks curling in bright golden ringlets.

Drums and trumpets mingled their sounds with the loud rejoicings of the people. The king and his whole court danced, as at Pirlipat's birth, upon one leg; and the queen had to be carefully tended with Cologne water, because she had fallen into a swoon from delight and rapture. Young Drosselmeier, who had still his seven steps to perform, was a good deal discomposed by the tumult, but he kept firm, and was just stretching back his right foot for the seventh step, when Lady Mouserings rose squeaking and squealing out of the floor; down came his foot upon her head, and he stumbled, so that he hardly kept himself from falling. Alas! what a hard fate! As quick as thought, the youth was changed to the former figure of the princess. His body became shrivelled up, and was hardly able to support his great misshapen head, his eyes turned green and staring, and his mouth was stretched from ear to ear. Instead of his queue, a narrow wooden cloak hung down upon his back, with which he moved his lower jaw.

The watchmaker and astronomer were benumbed with terror and affright, while Lady Mouserings rolled bleeding and kicking upon the floor. Her malice did not go unpunished, for young Drosselmeier had trodden upon her neck so heavily with the sharp heel of his shoe that she could not survive. When Lady Mouserings lay in her last agonies, she squeaked and whimpered in a piteous tone: "Oh, Crackatuck! hard nut—hi, hi!—of thee I now must die!—que, que— son with seven crowns will bite—Nutcracker—at night—hi, hi—que, que— and revenge his mother's death—short breath—must I—hi, hi—die, die—so young—que, que—oh, agony!—queek!" With this cry, Lady Mouserings died, and the royal oven-heater carried out her body. As for young Drosselmeier, no one troubled himself any further about him, but the princess put the king in mind of his promise, and he commanded that they should bring the young hero before him. But when the unfortunate youth approached, the princess held both hands before her face, and cried, "Away, away with the ugly Nutcracker!" The court marshal immediately took him by the shoulders, and pushed him out of doors. The king was full of anger because they had wished to give him a Nutcracker for a son-in-law, and he put all the blame upon the mechanist and astronomer, and banished them forever from the kingdom. This did not stand in the horoscope which the astronomer had set up at Nuremberg, but he did not allow himself to be discouraged. He straightway took another observation, and declared that he could read in the stars, that young Drosselmeier would conduct himself so well in his new station, that in spite of his deformity, he would yet become a prince and a king; and that his former beauty would return, as soon as the son of Lady Mouserings, who had been born with seven heads, after the death of her seven sons, had fallen by his hand, and a maiden had loved him, notwithstanding his ugly shape. And they say that young Drosselmeier has actually been seen about Christmas time in his father's shop at Nuremberg, as a Nutcracker, it is true, but, at the same time, as a prince.

This, children, is the story of the Hard Nut; and you know now why people say so often, "That was a hard nut!" and whence it comes that Nutcrackers are so ugly.

The Counsellor thus concluded his narration. Maria thought that the Princess Pirlipat was an ill-natured, ungrateful thing; and Fred declared, that if Nutcracker were anything of a man, he would not be long in settling matters with the Mouse King, and would get his old shape again very soon.

THE UNCLE AND NEPHEW

If any one of my good readers has ever had the misfortune to cut himself with glass, he knows how it hurts, and how long a time it takes to heal. Whenever Maria tried to get up, she felt very dizzy, and so it continued for a whole week, during which time she was obliged to remain in bed; but at last she became entirely well, and could play about the chamber as merrily as ever. Everything in the glass case looked prettily, for the trees, flowers, and houses, and beautiful puppets stood there as new and bright as ever. But, best of all, Maria found her dear Nutcracker again. He stood on the second shelf, and smiled upon her with a good, sound set of teeth. In the midst of all the pleasure which she felt in gazing at her favorite, a pang went through her heart, when she thought that Godfather Drosselmeier's story had been nothing else but the history of the Nutcracker, and of his quarrel with Lady Mouserings and her son. She knew well enough that her Nutcracker could be none other than the young Drosselmeier of Nuremberg—Godfather Drosselmeier's agreeable, but now, alas! enchanted, nephew. For, that the skilful watchmaker at the court of Pirlipat's father was the Counsellor Drosselmeier himself, she did not doubt for an instant, even while he was telling the story.

"But why was it that your uncle did not help you?—why did he not help you?" complained Maria, as it became clearer and clearer to her mind, that in that battle which she saw, Nutcracker's crown and kingdom were at stake. "Were not all the other puppets subject to him, and is it not plain that the prophecy of the astronomer has been fulfilled, and that young Drosselmeier is prince and king of the puppets?" While the shrewd Maria explained and arranged all this so well in her mind, she believed, since she had seen Nutcracker and his vassals in life and motion, that they actually did live and move. But that was not so; everything in the glass case remained stiff and lifeless; yet Maria, far from giving up her conviction, cast all the blame upon the magic of Lady Mouserings and her seven-headed son. "But, if you are not able to move, or to talk to me, dear Master Drosselmeier," she said aloud to the Nutcracker, "yet I know well enough that you understand me, and know what a good friend I am to you. You may depend upon my help, and I will beg of your uncle to bring his skill to your assistance, whenever you have need of it." Nutcracker remained still and motionless, but it seemed to Maria as if a gentle sigh was breathed in the glass case, so that the panes trembled, scarce audibly indeed, but with a strange, sweet tone; and a voice rang out, like a little bell: "Maria mine—I'll be thine—and thou mine—Maria mine!" Maria felt, in the cold shuddering that crept over her, a singular pleasure.

Twilight had come on; the doctor, with Godfather Drosselmeier, entered the sitting-room; and it was not long before Louise had arranged the tea-table, and all sat around, talking cheerfully of various things. Maria had very quietly taken her little armchair, and seated herself close at Godfather Drosselmeier's feet. During a moment when they were all silent, she looked up with her large blue eyes in the Counsellor's face, and said: "I know, dear Godfather Drosselmeier, that my

Nutcracker is your nephew, the young Drosselmeier, of Nuremberg, and he has become a prince, or king rather, as your companion, the astronomer, foretold. All has turned out exactly so. You know now that he is at war with the son of Lady Mouserings—with the hateful Mouse King. Why do you not help him?" Maria then related the whole course of the battle, just as she had seen it, and was often interrupted by the loud laughter of her mother and Louise. Fred and Drosselmeier only remained serious. "Where does the child get all this strange stuff in her head?" said the doctor.

"She has a lively imagination," replied the mother; "in fact, they are nothing but dreams caused by her violent fever."

"That story is not true," said Fred. "My red hussars are not such cowards as that. If I thought so—swords and daggers!—I would make a stir among them!"

But Godfather Drosselmeier, with a strange smile, took little Maria upon his lap, and said in a softer tone than he was ever heard to speak in before: "Ah, dear Maria, more power is given to thee than to me, or to the rest of us. Thou, like Pirlipat, art a princess born, for thou dost reign in a bright and beautiful kingdom. But thou hast much to suffer, if thou wouldst take the part of the poor misshapen Nutcracker, for the Mouse King watches for him at every hole and corner. I cannot, thou—thou alone canst rescue him; be firm and true." Neither Maria nor anyone else knew what Drosselmeier meant by these words; and they appeared so singular to Doctor Stahlbaum, that he felt the Counsellor's pulse, and said: "Worthy friend, you have some violent congestion about the head; I will prescribe something for you." But the mother shook her head thoughtfully, and spoke: "I feel what it is that the Counsellor means, but I cannot express it in words."

THE VICTORY

Not long after, Maria was awaked one moonlight night by a strange rattling that seemed to come out of a corner of the chamber. It sounded as if little stones were thrown and rolled about; and every now and then there was a terrible squeaking and squealing. "Ah! the mice—the mice are coming again!" exclaimed Maria, in affright; and she was about to wake her mother, but her voice failed her, and she could stir neither hand nor foot, for she saw the Mouse King work his way out of a hole in the wall, then run, with sparkling eyes and crowns, around and around the chamber, when, at last, with a desperate leap, he sprang upon the little table that stood close by her bed. "Hi—hi—hi—must give me thy sugarplums—thy gingerbread—little thing—or I will bite thy Nutcracker—thy Nutcracker!" So squeaked the Mouse King, and snapped and grated hideously with his teeth, then sprang down again, and away through the hole in the wall. Maria was so distressed by this occurrence that she looked very pale in the morning, and was scarcely able to say a word. A hundred times she was going to inform her mother or Louise of what had happened, or at least to tell Fred, but she thought: "No one will believe me, and I shall only be laughed at." This, at least, was very clear, that if she wished to save little Nutcracker, she must give up her sugarplums and her gingerbread. So, in the evening, she laid all that she had—and she had a great deal—down before the foot of the glass case.

The next morning, her mother said: "It is strange what brings the mice all at once into the sitting-room. See, poor Maria, they have eaten up all your gingerbread." And so it was. The ravenous Mouse King had not found the sugarplums exactly to his taste, but he had gnawed them with his sharp teeth, so that they had to be thrown away. Maria did not grieve about her cake and sugarplums, for she was greatly delighted to think that she had saved little Nutcracker. But what was her terror, when the very next night she heard a squeaking and squealing close to her ear! Ah, the Mouse King was there again, and his eyes sparkled more dreadfully, and he whistled and squeaked much louder than before: "Must give me thy sugar puppets—chocolate figures—little thing—or I will bite thy Nutcracker—thy Nutcracker!" and with this, the terrible Mouse King sprang down, and ran away again. Maria was very sad; she went the next morning to the glass case, and gazed with the most sorrowful looks at her sugar and chocolate figures. And her grief was reasonable, for thou canst not imagine, my attentive reader, what beautiful figures of sugar and chocolate little Maria Stahlbaum possessed. A pretty shepherd and shepherdess watched a whole flock of milk-white lambs, while a little dog frisked about them; next came two letter-carriers, with letters in their hands; and then four neat pairs of nicely dressed boys and girls, with gay ribbons, rocked at see-saw upon as many boards, white and smooth as marble. Behind some dancers stood Farmer Caraway and the Maid of Orleans—these Maria did not care so much about; but close in a corner stood her darling, a little red-cheeked baby, and now the tears came into her eyes. "Ah, dear Master Drosselmeier," she said, turning to Nutcracker, "there is nothing that I will not do to save you, but this is very hard!" Nutcracker looked all the while so sorrowfully, that Maria, who felt as if she saw the Mouse King open his seven mouths, to devour the unhappy youth, resolved to sacrifice them all. So at evening she placed all her sugar figures down at the foot of the glass case, just as she had done before with her sugarplums and cake. She kissed the shepherd, and the shepherdess, and the lambs, and at last took her darling, the little red-cheeked baby out of the corner, and placed it down behind all the rest; Farmer Caraway and the Maid of Orleans must stand in the first row.

"Well, that is too bad!" said her mother, the next morning. "A mouse must have got into the glass case, for all poor Maria's sugar figures are gnawed and bitten in pieces." Maria could not keep from shedding tears, but she soon smiled again, and said to herself: "That is nothing, if Nutcracker is only saved." In the evening, her mother told the Counsellor of the mischief which the mouse had been doing in the glass case, and said: "It is provoking that we cannot destroy this fellow that makes such havoc with Maria's sugar toys."

"Ha!" cried Fred, merrily, "the baker opposite has a fine, gray secretary of legation; suppose I bring him over? He will soon make an end of the thing; he will have the mouse's head off, very quickly, even if it be Lady Mouserings herself, or her son, the Mouse King."

"And jump about the tables and chairs," said his mother, laughing, "and throw down cups and saucers, and do all kinds of mischief."

"Ah, no indeed," said Fred; "the baker's secretary of legation is a light, careful fellow. I wish I could walk on the roof of a house as well as he!"

"Let us have no cats in the night," said Louise, who could not bear them.

"Fred's plan is the best," said the doctor, "but we will try a trap first. Have we got one?"

"Godfather Drosselmeier can make them best," said Fred, "for he invented them."

All laughed; and, when the mother said that there was no mousetrap in the house, the Counsellor assured her that he had a number in his possession, and immediately sent for one. In a short time it was brought, and a very excellent mousetrap it seemed to be. The story of the Hard Nut now came vividly to the minds of the children. As the cook toasted the fat, Maria shook and trembled. Her head was full of the story and its wonders, and she said to her old friend Dora: "Ah, great Queen, take care of Lady Mouserings and her family!" But Fred had drawn his sword, and cried: "Let them come on! Let them come on! I will scatter them!" But all remained still and quiet under the hearth. As the Counsellor tied the fat to a fine piece of thread, and set the trap softly, softly down by the glass case, Fred cried out: "Take care, Godfather Mechanist, or Mouse King will play you a trick!"

Ah, but what a night did Maria pass! Something cold as ice tapped here and there against her arm; and crept, rough and hideous, upon her cheek, and squeaked and squealed in her ear. The hateful Mouse King sat upon her shoulder. He opened his seven blood-red mouths, and, grating and snapping his teeth, he squeaked and hissed in her ear: "Wise mouse—wise mouse—goes not into the house—goes not to the feast—likes sugar things best—craft set at naught—will not be caught—give, give all—new frock—picture books—all the best—or shall have no rest.—I will tear and bite—Nutcracker at night—hi, hi—que, que!" Maria was full of sorrow and anxiety. She looked very pale and disturbed on the following morning, when Fred told her that the mouse had not been caught, so that her mother thought that she was grieving for her sugar things, or perhaps was afraid of the mouse. "Do not grieve, dear child," she said; "we will soon get rid of him. If the trap does not answer, Fred shall bring his gray secretary of legation."

As soon as Maria was alone in the sitting-room, she stepped to the glass case, and said, sobbing, to Nutcracker: "Ah, my dear, good Mr. Drosselmeier, what can I—poor, unhappy maiden—do? for, if I should give up all my picture-books, and even my new, beautiful frock, to the hateful mouse, he will ask more and more. And, when I have nothing left to give him, he will at last want me, instead of you, to bite in pieces." As little Maria grieved and sorrowed in this way, she observed a large spot of blood on Nutcracker's neck, which had been there ever since the battle. Now, after Maria had known that her Nutcracker was young Drosselmeier, the Counsellor's nephew, she did not carry him any more in her arms, nor hug and kiss him, as she used to do; indeed, she would very seldom move or touch him; but when she saw the spot of blood, she took him carefully from the shelf, and commenced rubbing it with her pocket-handkerchief. But what was her astonishment, when she felt that he suddenly grew warm in her hand, and began to move! She put him quickly back upon the shelf again, when—behold!—his little mouth began to work and twist, and move up and down, and at last, with a great deal of labor, he lisped out: "Ah, dearest, best Miss Stahlbaum—excellent friend, how shall I thank you? No! No picture books, no Christmas frock! Get me a sword—a sword. For the rest, I—" Here speech left him, and his eyes, which had begun to express the deepest sympathy, became staring and motionless.

Maria did not feel the least terror; on the contrary, she leaped for joy, for she had now found a way to rescue Nutcracker without any more painful sacrifices. But where should she obtain a sword for him? Maria at last resolved to ask advice of Fred; and in the evening, when their parents had gone out, and they sat alone together in the chamber by the glass case, she told him all that had happened to Nutcracker and Mouse King, and then begged him to furnish the little fellow with a sword. Upon no part of this narration did Fred reflect so long and so earnestly as upon the poor account which she gave him of the bravery of his hussars. He asked once more very seriously, if it were so. Maria assured him of it upon her word, when Fred ran quickly to the glass case, addressed his hussars in a very moving speech, and then, as a punishment for their cowardice, cut their military badges from their caps, and forbade them for a year to play the Hussar's Grand March. After this, he turned again to Maria, and said: "As to a sword, I can easily supply the little fellow with one. I yesterday permitted an old colonel of the cuirassiers to retire upon a pension, and consequently he has no farther use for his fine sharp sabre." The aforesaid colonel was living on the pension which Fred had allowed him, in the farthest corner of the third shelf. He was brought out, his fine silver sabre taken from him, and buckled about Nutcracker.

Maria could scarcely get to sleep that night, she was so anxious and fearful. About midnight, it seemed to her as if she heard a strange rustling, and rattling, and slashing, in the sitting-room. All at once, it went "Queek!" "The Mouse King! The Mouse King!" cried Maria, and sprang in her fright out of bed. All was still; but presently she heard a gentle knocking at the door, and a soft voice was heard: "Worthiest, best, kindest Miss Stahlbaum, open the door without fear—good tidings!" Maria knew the voice of the young Drosselmeier, so she threw her frock about her, and opened the door. Little Nutcracker stood without, with a bloody sword in his right hand, and a wax taper in his left. As soon as he saw Maria, he bent down on one knee, and said: "You, oh lady—you alone it was, that filled me with knightly courage, and gave this arm strength to contend with the presumptuous foe who dared to disturb your slumber. The treacherous Mouse King is overcome; he lies bathed in his blood. Scorn not to receive the tokens of victory from a knight who will remain devoted to your service until death." With these words, Nutcracker took off the seven crowns of the Mouse King, which he had hung upon his left arm, and reached them to Maria, who received them with great joy. Nutcracker then arose, and said: "Best, kindest Miss Stahlbaum, you know not what beautiful things I could show you at this moment while my enemy lies vanquished, if you would have the condescension to follow me for a few steps. Oh, will you not be so kind? will you not be so good, best, kindest Miss Stahlbaum?"

THE PUPPET KINGDOM

I believe that none of you, children, would have hesitated for an instant to follow the good, honest Nutcracker, who could never have meditated any evil. Maria consented to follow him, so much the more readily, because she knew what claims she had upon his gratitude, and because she was convinced that he would keep his word, and show her many beautiful things. "I will go with you, Master Drosselmeier," she said; "but it must not be far, and it must not be long, for as yet I have hardly had any sleep."

"I will choose, then," replied Nutcracker, "the nearest, though a more difficult way." He went onward, and Maria followed him, until he stopped before a large, antique wardrobe, which stood in the hall. Maria perceived, to her astonishment, that the doors of this wardrobe, which were always kept locked, now stood wide open, so that she could see her father's fox-furred traveling coat, which hung in front. Nutcracker clambered very nimbly up by the carved figures and ornaments, until he could grasp the large tassel which hung down the back of the coat, and was fastened to it by a thick cord. As soon as Nutcracker pulled upon the tassel, a neat little stairs of cedarwood stretched down from the sleeve of the traveling-coat to the floor. "Ascend, if you please, dearest Miss," cried Nutcracker. Maria did so; but scarcely had she gone up the sleeve—scarcely had she seen her way out at the collar, when a dazzling light broke forth upon her, and all at once she stood upon a sweet-smelling meadow, surrounded by millions of sparks, which darted up like flashing jewels. "We are now upon Candy Meadow," said Nutcracker; "but we will directly pass through yonder gate." When Maria looked up, she saw the beautiful gate, which stood a few steps before them upon the meadow. It seemed built of variegated marble, of white, brown, and raisin color; but when Maria came nearer, she perceived that the whole mass consisted of sugar, almonds and raisins, kneaded and baked together, for which reason the gate, as Nutcracker assured her when they passed through it, was called the Almond and Raisin Gate. Upon a gallery built over the gate, made apparently of barley-sugar, there were six apes, in red jackets, who struck up the finest Turkish music which was ever heard, so that Maria scarcely observed that they were walking onward and onward, over a rich mosaic, which was nothing else than a pavement of nicely inlaid lozenges. Very soon the sweetest odors streamed around them, which were wafted from a wonderful little wood that opened on each side before them. There it shone and sparkled so, among the dark leaves, that the golden and silvery fruit could plainly be seen hanging from their gayly colored stems, while the trunks and branches were ornamented with ribbons and nosegays; and when the orange perfume stirred and moved like a soft breeze, how it rustled among the boughs and leaves, and the golden fruit rocked and rattled in merry music, to which the bright, dancing sparkles kept time! "Ah, how delightful it is here!" cried Maria, entranced in happiness.

"We are in Christmas Wood, best miss," said Nutcracker.

"Ah, if I could but linger here a while," cried Maria. "Oh, it is too, too charming!"

Nutcracker clapped his hands, and some little shepherds and shepherdesses, and hunters and huntresses came near, who were so delicate and white, that they seemed made of pure sugar. They brought a dainty little armchair, all of gold, laid upon it a green cushion of candied citron, and invited Maria very politely to sit down. She did so, and immediately the shepherds and shepherdesses danced a very pretty ballet, while the hunters very obligingly blew their horns, and then all disappeared again in the bushes. "Pardon, pardon, kindest Miss Stahlbaum," said Nutcracker, "the dance was miserably performed, but the people all belong to our company of wire dancers, and they can do nothing but the same, same thing; they are deficient in variety. And the hunters blew so dull and lazily—but shall we not walk a little farther?"

"Ah, it was all very pretty, and pleased me very much," said Maria, as she rose, and followed Nutcracker.

They now walked along by a soft, rustling brook, out of which all the sweet perfumes seemed to arise which filled the whole wood. "This is the Orange Brook," said Nutcracker, "but its fine perfume excepted, it cannot compare either in size or beauty with Lemonade River, which like it empties into Orgeat Lake." In fact Maria very soon heard a louder rustling and dashing, and then beheld the broad Lemonade River, which rolled in proud cream-colored billows, between banks covered with bright green bushes. A refreshing coolness arose out of its noble waves.

Not far off, a dark yellow stream dragged itself lazily along, but it gave forth a very sweet odor, and a great number of little children sat on the shore angling for little fish, which they ate up as soon as caught. When Maria came nearer she observed that these fish were shaped almost like peanuts. At a distance there was a very neat little village, on the borders of this stream; houses, churches, parsonages, barns were all dark brown, but many of the roofs were gilded, and some of the walls were painted so strangely, that it seemed as if little sugarplums and bits of citron were stuck upon them. "That is Gingerbreadville," said Nutcracker, "which lies on Molasses River. Very pretty people live in it, but they are a little ill-tempered, because they suffer a good deal from the toothache, and so we will not visit it."

At this moment Maria observed a little town in which the houses were clear and transparent, and of different colors, which was a very pretty sight to look at. Nutcracker went straight forward towards it, and now Maria heard a busy, merry clatter, and saw a thousand tiny little figures, collected around some heavily laden wagons, which had stopped in the market. These they unloaded, and what they took out looked like sheets of colored paper and chocolate cakes. "We are now in Bonbon Town," said Nutcracker. "An importation has just arrived from Paper Land, and from King Chocolate. The poor people of Bonbon Town are often terribly threatened by the armies of Generals Fly and Gnat, for which reason they fortify their houses with stout materials from Paper Land, and throw up fortifications of the strong bulwarks, which King Chocolate sends to them. But, worthiest Miss Stahlbaum, we will not visit all the little towns and villages of this land. To the capital—to the capital!"

Nutcracker hastened forward, and Maria followed full of curiosity. It was not long before a sweet odor of roses enveloped them, and everything around was touched with a soft rose-colored tint. Maria soon observed that this was the reflection of the red glancing lake, which rustled and danced before them, with charming and melodious tones in little rosy waves. Beautiful silver-white swans with golden collars swam over the lake singing sweet tunes, while little diamond fish dipped up and down in the rosy water, as if in the merriest dance. "Ah," exclaimed Maria, ardently, "this is then the lake which Godfather Drosselmeier was once going to make for me, and I myself am the maiden, who is to fondle and caress the dear swans."

Nutcracker laughed in a scornful manner, such as Maria had never observed in him before, and then said: "Godfather Drosselmeier can never make anything like this. You—you yourself, rather, sweetest Miss Stahlbaum—but we will not trouble our heads about that. Let us sail across the Rose Lake to the capital."

THE CAPITAL

Nutcracker clapped his little hands together again, when the Rose Lake began to dash louder, the waves rolled higher, and Maria perceived a car of shells, covered with bright, sparkling, gay-colored jewels, moving toward them in the distance, drawn by two golden-scaled dolphins. Twelve of the loveliest little Moors, with caps and aprons braided of hummingbird's feathers, leaped upon the shore, and carried, first Maria, and then Nutcracker, with a soft, gliding step, over the waves, and placed them in the car, which straightway began to move across the lake. Ah, how delightful it was as Maria sailed along, with the rosy air and the rosy waves breathing and dashing around her! The two golden-scaled dolphins raised up their heads, and spouted clear, crystal streams out of their nostrils, high, high in the air, which fell down again in a thousand quivering, flashing rainbows, and it seemed as if two small silver voices sang out: "Who sails upon the rosy lake? The little fairy—awake, awake! Music and song—bim-bim, fishes—sim-sim, swans—tweet-tweet, birds—whiz-whiz, breezes!—rustling, ringing, singing, blowing!—a fairy o'er the waves is going! Rosy billows, murmuring, playing, dashing, cooling the air!—roll along, along."

But the singing of the falling fountains did not seem to please the twelve little Moors, who were seated up behind the car, for they shook their parasols so hard that the palm-leaves of which they were made rattled and clattered, and they stamped with their feet in very strange time, and sang, "Klapp and klipp, and klipp and klapp, backward and forward, up and down!" "Moors are a merry folk," said Nutcracker, somewhat disturbed, "but they will make the whole lake rebellious." And very soon there arose a confused din of strange voices, which seemed to float in the sea and in the air; but Maria did not heed them, for she was gazing in the sweet-scented, rosy waves, out of which the face of a charming little maiden smiled up upon her. "Ah!" she cried joyfully, and struck her hands together. "Look, look, dear Master Drosselmeier! There is the Princess Pirlipat down in the water! Oh, how sweetly she smiles upon me!"

Nutcracker sighed quite sorrowfully, and said: "Oh, kindest Miss Stahlbaum, that is not the Princess Pirlipat—it is you, you—it is your own lovely face that smiles so sweetly out of the Rose Lake." Upon this, Maria drew her head back very quickly, put her hands before her face, and blushed very much. At this moment, she was lifted out of the car by the twelve Moors, and carried to the shore. They now found themselves in a little thicket, which was perhaps more beautiful even than the Christmas Wood, it was so bright and sparkling. What was most wonderful in it were the strange fruits that hung upon the trees, which were not only curiously colored, but gave out also every kind of sweet odor. "We are in Sweetmeat Grove," said Nutcracker, "but yonder is the Capital."

And what a sight! How can I venture, children, to describe the beauty and splendor of the city which now displayed itself to Maria's eyes, upon the broad, flowery meadow before them? Not only did the walls and towers glitter with the gayest colors, but the style of the buildings was like nothing else that is to be found in the world. Instead of roofs, the houses had diadems set upon them, braided and twisted in the daintiest manner; and the towers were crowned with variegated trelliswork, and hung with festoons the most beautiful that ever were seen. As they passed through the gate, which looked as if it were built of macaroons and candied fruits, silver soldiers presented arms, and a little man in a brocade dressing-gown threw himself upon Nutcracker's neck, with the words: "Welcome, best prince! Welcome to Confectionville!"

Maria was not a little astonished to hear young Drosselmeier called a prince by such a distinguished man. But she now heard such a hubbub of little voices, such a huzzaing and laughter, such a singing and playing, that she could think of nothing else, and turned to Nutcracker to ask him what it all meant. "Oh, worthiest Miss Stahlbaum, it is nothing uncommon. Confectionville is a populous and merry city; thus it goes here every day. Let us walk farther, if you please."

They had only gone a few steps, when they came to the great marketplace, which presented a wonderful sight. All the houses around were of sugared filagree work; gallery was built over gallery, and in the middle stood a tall obelisk of white and red sugared cream, while four curious, sweet fountains played in the air, of orgeat, lemonade, mead, and soda-water, and in the great basin were soft bruised fruits, mixed with sugar and cream, and touched a little by the frost.

But prettier than all this were the charming little people, who, by thousands, pushed and squeezed, knocked their heads together, huzzaed, laughed, jested, and sang—who had raised indeed that merry din which Maria had heard at a distance. Here were beautifully dressed men and women, Armenians and Greeks, Jews and Tyrolese, officers and soldiers, preachers, shepherds, and harlequins—in short, all the people that can possibly be found in the world. On one corner the tumult increased; the people rocked and reeled to clear the way, for just at that moment the Grand Mogul was carried by in a palanquin, attended by ninety-three grandees of the kingdom, and seven hundred slaves. Now, on the opposite corner, the fishermen, five hundred strong, were marching in procession; and it happened, very unfortunately, that the Grand Turk took it into his head just then to ride over the market-place with three thousand Janissaries, besides which a loner train came from the Festival of Sacrifices, with sounding music, singing: "Up, and thank the mighty sun!" and pushed straight on for the obelisk. Then what a squeezing, and a pushing, and a rattling, and a clattering. By and by, a screaming was heard, for a fisherman had knocked off a Brahmin's head in the crowd, and the Great Mogul was almost run over by a Harlequin. The tumult grew wilder and wilder, and they had commenced to beat and strike each other, when the man in the brocade dressing-gown, who had called Nutcracker a prince at the gate, clambered up by the obelisk, and having thrice pulled a little bell, called out three times: "Confiseur! Confiseur! Confiseur!"

The tumult was immediately appeased; each one tried to help himself as well as he could; and, after the confused trains and processions were set in order, and the dirt upon the Great Mogul's clothes was brushed off, and the Brahmin's head put on again, the former hubbub began anew. "What do they mean by 'Confiseur,' good Master Drosselmeier?" asked Maria.

"Ah, best Miss Stahlbaum," replied Nutcracker, "by 'Confiseur' is meant an unknown but very fearful power, which they believe can do with them as he pleases; it is the Fate that rules over this merry little people, and they fear it so much, that the mere mention of the name is able to still the greatest tumult. Each one then thinks no longer of anything earthly—of cuffs, and kicks, and broken heads, but retires within himself, and says: 'What are we, and what is our destiny?'"

Maria could not refrain from a loud exclamation of surprise and wonder, as all at once they stood before a castle glimmering with rosy light, and crowned with a hundred airy towers. Beautiful nosegays of violets, narcissuses, tulips, and dahlias were hung about the walls, and their dark, glowing colors only heightened the dazzling, rose-tinted, white ground upon which they were fastened. The large cupola of the center building and the sloping roofs of the towers were spangled with a thousand gold and silver stars. "We are now in front of Marchpane Castle," said Nutcracker. Maria was completely lost in admiration of this magic palace, yet it did not escape her that one of the large towers was without a roof, while little men were moving around it upon a scaffolding of cinnamon, as if busied in repairing it. But before she had time to inquire about it, Nutcracker continued: "Not long ago, this beautiful castle was threatened with serious injury, if not with entire destruction. The Giant Sweet-tooth came this way, and bit off the roof of yonder tower, and was gnawing upon the great cupola, when the people of Confectionville gave up to him a full quarter of the city, and a considerable portion of Sweetmeat Grove, as tribute, with which he contented himself, and went his way."

At this moment soft music was heard, the doors of the palace opened, and twelve little pages marched out with lighted cloves, which they carried in their hands like torches. Each of their heads was a pearl; their bodies were made of rubies and emeralds; and they walked upon feet cast out of pure gold. Four ladies followed them, almost as tall as Maria's Clara, but so richly and splendidly dressed, that she saw in a moment that they were princesses born. They embraced Nutcracker in the tenderest manner, and cried with joyful sobs: "Oh, my prince, my best prince! Oh, my brother!"

Nutcracker seemed very much moved; he wiped the tears out of his eyes; then took Maria by the hand, and said with great emotion: "This is Miss Maria Stahlbaum, the daughter of a much-respected and very worthy physician, and she is the preserver of my life. Had she not thrown her shoe at the right time— had she not supplied me with the sword of a pensioned colonel, I should now be lying in my grave, torn and bitten to pieces by the terrible Mouse King. View her—gaze upon her, and tell me, if Pirlipat, although a princess by birth, can compare with her in beauty, goodness, and virtue? No, I say no!"

And all the ladies cried out "No!" and then fell upon Maria's neck, exclaiming: "Ah, dear preserver of the prince, our beloved brother! charming Miss Maria Stahlbaum!" She now accompanied these ladies and Nutcracker into the castle, and entered a room, the walls of which were of bright, colored crystal. But of all the beautiful things which Maria saw here, what pleased her most were the nice little chairs, sofas, secretaries, and bureaus with which the room was furnished, and which were all made of cedar or brazilwood, and ornamented with golden flowers. The princesses made Maria and Nutcracker sit down, and said that they would immediately prepare something for them to eat. They then brought out a great many little cups and saucers, and plates and dishes, all of the finest porcelain, and spoons, knives, and forks, graters, kettles, pans, and other kitchen furniture, all of gold and silver.

Then they brought the finest fruits and sugar-things, such as Maria had never seen before, and began in the nicest manner to squeeze the fruits with their little snow-white hands, and to pound the spice, and grate the sugar-almonds, in short, so to turn and handle everything, that Maria could see how well the princesses had been brought up, and what a delicious meal they were preparing. As she desired very much to learn such things, she could not help wishing to herself that she might assist the princesses in their labor. The most beautiful of Nutcracker's sisters, as if she had guessed Maria's secret thoughts, reached her a little golden mortar, saying: "Oh, sweet friend, dear preserver of my brother, will you not pound a little of this sugar-candy?"

While Maria pounded in the mortar, Nutcracker began to give a full account of his adventures, of the dreadful battle between his army and that of the Mouse King, and how he had lost it by the cowardice of his troops; how the terrible Mouse King lay in wait to bite him in pieces, and how Maria, to preserve him, gave up many of his subjects, who had entered her service, and all just as it had happened. During this narration, it seemed to Maria, as if his words became less and less audible, and the pounding of her mortar also sounded more and more distant, until she could scarcely hear it; presently, she saw a silver gauze before her, in which the princesses, the pages, Nutcracker, and herself, too, were all enveloped. A singular humming, and rustling, and singing was heard, which seemed to die away in the distance; and now Maria was raised up, as if upon mounting waves, higher and higher—higher and higher—higher and higher!

THE CONCLUSION

Prr—puff it went! Maria fell down from an immeasurable height. That was a fall! But she opened her eyes, and there she lay upon her little bed; it was bright day, and her mother stood by her, saying: "How can you sleep so long? breakfast has been ready this great while." You now perceive, kind readers and listeners, that Maria, completely confused by the wonderful things which she had seen, had at last fallen asleep in the room at Marchpane Castle, and that the Moors, or the pages, or perhaps even the princesses themselves must have carried her home, and laid her softly in bed. "Oh, mother, dear mother, you cannot think where young Master Drosselmeier led me last night, and what beautiful things I have seen!" And then she began and told the whole, almost as accurately as I have related it, while her mother listened in astonishment.

When she had finished, her mother said: "You have had a long and very beautiful dream, but now drive it all out of your head." Maria insisted upon it that she had not dreamed, but had actually seen what she had related, when her mother led her into the sitting-room, to the glass case; took Nutcracker out, who was standing, as usual, upon the second shelf, and said: "Silly child, how can you believe that this wooden Nuremberg puppet can have life or motion?"

"But, dear mother," replied Maria, "I know little Nutcracker is young Master Drosselmeier, of Nuremberg, Godfather Drosselmeier's nephew." Then her father and mother both laughed very heartily. "Ah, dear father," said Maria, almost crying, "you should not laugh so at my Nutcracker; he has spoken very well of you; for when we entered Marchpane Castle, and he presented me to his sisters, the princesses, he said that you were a much respected and very worthy physician." At this the laughter was still louder, and Louise, and even Fred, joined in. Maria then ran into the other chamber, took the seven crowns of the Mouse King out of her little box, brought them in, and handed them to her mother, saying: "See here, dear mother, here are the seven crowns of the Mouse King, which young Master Drosselmeier gave me last night, as a token of his victory." Her mother examined the little crowns in great astonishment; they were made of a strange but very shining metal, and were so delicately worked, that it seemed impossible that mortal hands could have formed them. Her father, likewise, could not gaze enough at them, and he insisted very seriously that Maria should confess how she obtained them. But she could give no other account of them, and kept firm to what she had said; and, as her father spoke very harshly to her, and even called her a little storyteller, she began to cry bitterly, and said: "Oh, what, what then shall I say?"

At this moment the door opened. The Counsellor entered, and exclaimed: "What's this? what's this?" The doctor told him of all that had happened, and showed him the little crowns. As soon as the Counsellor cast his eyes on them, he laughed and cried: "Stupid pack—stupid pack! These are the very crowns which I used to wear on my watch-chain, years ago, and which I gave to little Maria, on her birthday, when she was two years old. Don't you remember them?" Neither father nor mother could remember them; but when Maria saw that her parents had forgotten their anger, she ran to Godfather Drosselmeier, and said: "Ah, you know all about it, Godfather Drosselmeier. Tell them yourself, that my Nutcracker is your nephew, young Master Drosselmeier, of Nuremberg, and that it was he who gave me the crowns!"

The Counsellor's face turned very dark and grave, and he muttered: "Stupid pack—stupid pack!" Upon this, the doctor took little Maria upon his knee, and said very seriously: "Listen to me, Maria. Once for all, drive your foolish dreams and nonsense out of your head. If I ever hear you say again that the silly, ugly Nutcracker is the nephew of your Godfather Drosselmeier, I will throw him out of the window, and all the rest of your puppets, Miss Clara not excepted."

Poor Maria durst not now speak of all these wonders, but she thought so much the more. Her whole soul was full of them; for you may imagine that things so fine and beautiful as those which she had seen are not easily forgotten. Even Fred turned his back upon his sister, whenever she spoke of the wonderful kingdom in which she had been so happy; and, it is said, that he sometimes would mutter between his teeth: "Silly goose!" But that I can hardly believe of so amiable and good-natured a fellow. This is certain, however, he no longer believed a word of what Maria had told him. He made a formal apology to his hussars, on public parade, for the injustice which he had done them; stuck in their caps feathers of goose-quill, much finer and taller than those of which they had been deprived; and permitted them again to blow the Hussar's Grand March. Ah, ha! We know best how it stood with their courage, when those hateful balls spotted their red coats!

Maria was not allowed, then, to speak any more of her adventures, but the images of that wonderful fairy kingdom played about her in sweet, rustling tones. She could bring them all back again, whenever she fixed her thoughts steadfastly upon them, and hence it came that, instead of playing, as she formerly did, she would sit silent and thoughtful, musing within herself, for which reason the rest would often scold her, and call her a little dreamer. Some time after this, it happened that the Counsellor was busy, repairing a clock in Doctor Stahlbaum's house. Maria sat close by the glass case, and, lost in her dreams, was gazing at Nutcracker, when the words broke from her lips involuntarily: "Ah, dear Master Drosselmeier, if you actually were living, I would not behave like Princess Pirlipat, and slight you, because for my sake you had ceased to be a handsome young man!"

At this, the Counsellor screamed: "Hey—hey—stupid pack!" Then there was a clap, and a knock, so loud that Maria sank from her chair in a swoon. When she came to herself, her mother was busied about her, and said: "How came such a great girl to fall from her chair? Here is Godfather Drosselmeier's nephew, just arrived from Nuremberg! Come—behave like a little woman!"

She looked up; the Counsellor had put on his glass wig again, and his brown coat; he was smiling very pleasantly, and he held by the hand a little but very well-shaped young man. His face was as white as milk, and as red as blood; he wore a handsome red coat, trimmed with gold, and shoes and white silk stockings; in his button-hole was stuck a nosegay; his hair was nicely powdered and curled; and down his back there hung a magnificent queue. The sword by his side seemed to be made of nothing but jewels, it flashed and sparkled so brightly, and the little hat which he carried under his arm looked as if it were overlaid with soft, silken flakes. It very soon appeared how polite and well-bred the young man was, for he had brought Maria a great many handsome playthings—the nicest gingerbread, and the same sugar figures which the Mouse King had bitten to pieces; and for

Fred he had brought a splendid sabre. At table, the little fellow cracked nuts for the whole company—the hardest could not resist him; with the right hand he put them in his mouth; with the left, he pulled hard upon his queue, and—crack— the nut fell in pieces! Maria had turned very red when she first saw the handsome young man; and she became still redder when, after dinner, young Drosselmeier invited her to go with him into the sitting-room to the glass case. "Play prettily together, children; I have nothing against it, since all my clocks are going," cried the Counsellor.

Scarcely was Maria alone with young Drosselmeier when he stooped upon one knee and said: "Oh, my very best Miss Stahlbaum, you see here at your feet the happy Drosselmeier, whose life you saved on this very spot. You said most amiably that you would not slight me, like the hateful Princess Pirlipat, if I had become ugly for your sake. From that moment, I ceased to be a miserable Nutcracker, and resumed again my old—and, I hope, not disagreeable—figure. Oh, excellent Miss Stahlbaum, make me happy with your dear hand; share with me crown and kingdom; rule with me in Marchpane Castle, for there I am still king!"

Maria raised the youth, and said softly: "Dear Master Drosselmeier, you are a kind, good-natured young man; and, since you rule in such a charming land, among such pretty, merry people, I will be your bride." With this, Maria immediately became Drosselmeier's betrothed bride.

After a year and a day, he came, as I have heard, and carried her away in a golden chariot, drawn by silver horses. There danced at the wedding two-and-twenty thousand of the most splendid figures, adorned with pearls and diamonds; and Maria, it is said, is at this hour queen of a land, where sparkling Christmas woods, transparent Marchpane Castles—in short, where the most beautiful, the most wonderful things can be seen by those who will only have eyes for them.

A Visit from St. Nicholas

Clement Clarke Moore

'Twas the night before Christmas, when all through the house
Not a creature was stirring, not even a mouse;
The stockings were hung by the chimney with care
In hopes that St. Nicholas soon would be there;

The children were nestled all snug in their beds,
While visions of sugar-plums danced in their heads;
And mamma in her 'kerchief, and I in my cap,
Had just settled our brains for a long winter's nap,

When out on the lawn there arose such a clatter,
I sprang from the bed to see what was the matter.
Away to the window I flew like a flash,
Tore open the shutters and threw up the sash.

The moon on the breast of the new-fallen snow
Gave the lustre of mid-day to objects below,
When, what to my wondering eyes should appear,
But a miniature sleigh, and eight tiny reindeer,

With a little old driver, so lively and quick,
I knew in a moment it must be St. Nick.
More rapid than eagles his coursers they came,
And he whistled, and shouted, and called them by name:

"Now, *Dasher!* now, *Dancer!* now, *Prancer* and *Vixen!*
On, *Comet!* on, *Cupid!* on, *Donder* and *Blitzen!*
To the top of the porch! to the top of the wall!
Now dash away! dash away! dash away all!"

As dry leaves that before the wild hurricane fly,
When they meet with an obstacle, mount to the sky;

So up to the house-top the coursers they flew,
With the sleigh full of toys, and St. Nicholas too.

And then, in a twinkling, I heard on the roof
The prancing and pawing of each little hoof.
As I drew in my head, and was turning around,
Down the chimney St. Nicholas came with a bound.

He was dressed all in fur, from his head to his foot,
And his clothes were all tarnished with ashes and soot;
A bundle of toys he had flung on his back,
And he looked like a pedler just opening his pack.

His eyes—how they twinkled! his dimples how merry!
His cheeks were like roses, his nose like a cherry!
His droll little mouth was drawn up like a bow,
And the beard of his chin was as white as the snow;

The stump of a pipe he held tight in his teeth,
And the smoke it encircled his head like a wreath;
He had a broad face and a little round belly,
That shook when he laughed, like a bowlful of jelly.

He was chubby and plump, a right jolly old elf,
And I laughed when I saw him, in spite of myself;
A wink of his eye and a twist of his head,
Soon gave me to know I had nothing to dread;

He spoke not a word, but went straight to his work,
And filled all the stockings; then turned with a jerk,
And laying his finger aside of his nose,
And giving a nod, up the chimney he rose;

He sprang to his sleigh, to his team gave a whistle,
And away they all flew like the down of a thistle.
But I heard him exclaim, ere he drove out of sight—
"Happy Christmas to all, and to all a good-night!"

The Fir Tree

Hans Christian Andersen

Out in the woods stood such a pretty little fir tree. It grew in a good place, where it had plenty of sun and plenty of fresh air. Around it stood many tall comrades, both fir trees and pines.

The little fir tree was in a headlong hurry to grow up. It didn't care a thing for the warm sunshine, or the fresh air, and it took no interest in the peasant children who ran about chattering when they came to pick strawberries or raspberries. Often when the children had picked their pails full, or had gathered long strings of berries threaded on straws, they would sit down to rest near the little fir. "Oh, isn't it a nice little tree?" they would say. "It's the baby of the woods." The little tree didn't like their remarks at all.

Next year, it shot up a long joint of new growth, and the following year, another joint, still longer. You can always tell how old a fir tree is by counting the number of joints it has.

"I wish I were a grown-up tree, like my comrades," the little tree sighed. "Then I could stretch out my branches and see from my top what the world is like. The birds would make me their nesting place, and when the wind blew, I could bow back and forth with all the great trees."

It took no pleasure in the sunshine, nor in the birds. The glowing clouds that sailed overhead at sunrise and sunset meant nothing to it.

In winter, when the snow lay sparkling on the ground, a hare would often come hopping along and jump right over the little tree. Oh, how irritating that was! That happened for two winters, but when the third winter came, the tree was so tall that the hare had to turn aside and hop around it.

"Oh, to grow, grow! To get older and taller," the little tree thought. "That is the most wonderful thing in this world."

In the autumn, woodcutters came and cut down a few of the largest trees. This happened every year. The young fir was no longer a baby tree, and it trembled to see how those stately great trees crashed to the ground, how their limbs were lopped off, and how lean they looked as the naked trunks were loaded into carts. It could hardly recognize the trees it had known when the horses pulled them out of the woods.

Where were they going? What would become of them?

In the springtime, when swallows and storks came back, the tree asked them, "Do you know where the other trees went? Have you met them?"

The swallows knew nothing about it, but the stork looked thoughtful and nodded his head. "Yes, I think I met them," he said. "On my way from Egypt, I met many new ships, and some had tall, stately masts. They may well have been the trees you mean, for I remember the smell of fir. They wanted to be remembered to you."

"Oh, I wish I were old enough to travel on the sea. Please tell me what it really is, and how it looks."

"That would take too long to tell," said the stork, and off he strode.

"Rejoice in your youth," said the sunbeams. "Take pride in your growing strength and in the stir of life within you."

And the wind kissed the tree, and the dew wept over it, for the tree was young and without understanding.

When Christmas came near, many young trees were cut down. Some were not even as old or as tall as this fir tree of ours, who was in such a hurry and fret to go traveling. These young trees, which were always the handsomest ones, had their branches left on them when they were loaded on carts and the horses drew them out of the woods.

"Where can they be going?" the fir tree wondered. "They are no taller than I am. One was really much smaller than I am. And why are they allowed to keep all their branches? Where can they be going?"

"We know! We know!" the sparrows chirped. "We have been to town and peeped in the windows. We know where they are going. The greatest splendor and glory you can imagine awaits them. We've peeped through windows. We've seen them planted right in the middle of a warm room and decked out with the most splendid things—gold apples, good gingerbread, gay toys, and many hundreds of candles."

"And then?" asked the fir tree, trembling in every twig. "And then? What happens then?"

"We saw nothing more. And never have we seen anything that could match it."

"I wonder if I was created for such a glorious future?" The fir tree rejoiced. "Why, that is better than to cross the sea. I'm tormented with longing. Oh, if Christmas would only come! I'm just as tall and grown-up as the trees they chose last year. How I wish I were already in the cart, on my way to the warm room where there's so much splendor and glory. Then—then something even better, something still more important is bound to happen, or why should they deck me so fine? Yes, there must be something still grander! But what? Oh, how I long: I don't know what's the matter with me."

"Enjoy us while you may," the air and sunlight told him. "Rejoice in the days of your youth, out here in the open."

But the tree did not rejoice at all. It just grew. It grew and was green both winter and summer—dark evergreen. People who passed it said, "There's a beautiful tree!" And when Christmas time came again, they cut it down first. The ax struck deep into its marrow. The tree sighed as it fell to the ground. It felt faint with pain. Instead of the happiness it had expected, the tree was sorry to leave the home where it had grown up. It knew that never again would it see its dear old comrades, the little bushes and the flowers about it—and perhaps not even the birds. The departure was anything but pleasant.

The tree did not get over it until all the trees were unloaded in the yard, and it heard a man say, "That's a splendid one. That's the tree for us." Then two servants came in fine livery, and carried the fir tree into a big splendid drawing room. Portraits were hung all around the walls. On either side of the white porcelain stove stood great Chinese vases with lions on their lids. There were easy chairs, silk-covered sofas, and long tables strewn with picture books and with toys that were worth a mint of money, or so the children said.

The fir tree was planted in a large tub filled with sand, but no one could see that it was a tub because it was wrapped in a gay green cloth and set on a many-colored carpet. How the tree quivered! What would come next? The servants and even the young ladies helped it on with its fine decorations. From its branches, they hung little nets cut out of colored paper, and each net was filled with candies. Gilded apples and walnuts hung in clusters as if they grew there, and a hundred little white, blue, and even red candles were fastened to its twigs. Among its green branches swayed dolls that it took to be real living people, for the tree had never seen their like before. And up at its very top was set a large gold tinsel star. It was splendid, I tell you, splendid beyond all words!

"Tonight," they all said, "ah, tonight how the tree will shine!"

"Oh," thought the tree, "if tonight would only come! If only the candles were lit! And after that, what happens then? Will the trees come trooping out of the woods to see me? Will the sparrows flock to the windows? Shall I take root here, and stand in fine ornaments all winter and summer long?"

That was how much it knew about it. All its longing had gone to its bark and set it to arching, which is as bad for a tree as a headache is for us.

Now the candles were lighted. What dazzling splendor! What a blaze of light! The tree quivered, so in every bough a candle set one of its twigs ablaze. It hurt terribly.

"Mercy me!" cried every young lady, and the fire was quickly put out. The tree no longer dared rustle a twig—it was awful! Wouldn't it be terrible if it were to drop one of its ornaments? Its own brilliance dazzled it.

Suddenly, the folding doors were thrown back, and a whole flock of children burst in as if they would overturn the tree completely. Their elders marched in after them, more sedately. For a moment, but only for a moment, the young ones were stricken speechless. Then they shouted till the rafters rang. They danced about the tree and plucked off one present after another.

"What are they up to?" the tree wondered. "What will happen next?"

As the candles burned down to the bark, they were snuffed out, one by one, and then the children had permission to plunder the tree. They went about it in such earnest that the branches crackled, and, if the tree had not been tied to the ceiling by the gold star at top, it would have tumbled headlong.

The children danced about with their splendid playthings. No one looked at the tree now, except an old nurse who peered in among the branches, but this was only to make sure that not an apple or fig had been overlooked.

"Tell us a story! Tell us a story!" the children clamored, as they towed a fat little man to the tree. He sat down beneath it and said, "Here we are in the woods, and it will do the tree a lot of good to listen to our story. Mind you, I'll tell only one. Which will you have, the story of Ivedy-Avedy, or the one about Humpty-Dumpty who tumbled downstairs, yet ascended the throne and married the princess?"

"Ivedy-Avedy," cried some. "Humpty-Dumpty," cried the others. And there was a great hullabaloo. Only the fir tree held its peace, though it thought to itself, "Am I to be left out of this? Isn't there anything I can do?" For all the fun of the evening had centered upon it, and it had played its part well.

The fat little man told them all about Humpty-Dumpty, who tumbled downstairs, yet ascended the throne and married the princess. And the children clapped and shouted, "Tell us another one! Tell us another one!" For they wanted to hear about Ivedy-Avedy too, but after Humpty-Dumpty, the storytelling stopped. The fir tree stood very still as it pondered how the birds in the woods had never told it a story to equal this.

"Humpty-Dumpty tumbled downstairs, yet he married the princess. Imagine! That must be how things happen in the world. You never can tell. Maybe I'll tumble downstairs and marry a princess too," thought the fir tree, who believed every word of the story because such a nice man had told it.

The tree looked forward to the following day, when they would deck it again with fruit and toys, candles and gold. "Tomorrow I shall not quiver," it decided. "I'll enjoy my splendor to the full. Tomorrow I shall hear about Humpty-Dumpty again, and perhaps about Ivedy-Avedy too." All night long, the tree stood silent as it dreamed its dreams, and next morning, the butler and the maid came in with their dusters.

"Now my splendor will be renewed," the fir tree thought. But they dragged it upstairs to the garret, and there they left it in a dark corner where no daylight ever came. "What's the meaning of this?" the tree wondered. "What am I going to do here? What stories shall I hear?" It leaned against the wall, lost in dreams. It had plenty of time for dreaming, as the days and the nights went by. Nobody came to the garret. And when at last someone did come, it was only to put many big boxes away in the corner. The tree was quite hidden. One might think it had been entirely forgotten.

"It's still winter outside," the tree thought. "The earth is too hard and covered with snow for them to plant me now. I must have been put here for shelter until springtime comes. How thoughtful of them! How good people are! Only, I wish it weren't so dark here, and so very, very lonely. There's not even a little hare. It was so friendly out in the woods when the snow was on the ground and the hare came hopping along. Yes, he was friendly even when he jumped right over me, though I did not think so then. Here it's all so terribly lonely."

"Squeak, squeak!" said a little mouse just then. He crept across the floor, and another one followed him. They sniffed the fir tree and rustled in and out among its branches.

"It is fearfully cold," one of them said. "Except for that, it would be very nice here, wouldn't it, you old fir tree?"

"I'm not at all old," said the fir tree. "Many trees are much older than I am."

"Where did you come from?" the mice asked him. "And what do you know?" They were most inquisitive creatures.

"Tell us about the most beautiful place in the world. Have you been there? Were you ever in the larder, where there are cheeses on shelves and hams that hang from the rafters? It's the place where you can dance upon tallow candles—where you can dart in thin and squeeze out fat."

"I know nothing of that place," said the tree. "But I know the woods where the sun shines and the little birds sing." Then it told them about its youth. The little mice had never heard the like of it. They listened very intently, and said, "My! How much you have seen! And how happy it must have made you."

"I?" the fir tree thought about it. "Yes, those days were rather amusing." And it went on to tell them about Christmas Eve, when it was decked out with candies and candles.

"Oh," said the little mice, "how lucky you have been, you old fir tree!"

"I am not at all old," it insisted. "I came out of the woods just this winter, and I'm really in the prime of life, though at the moment, my growth is suspended."

"How nicely you tell things," said the mice. The next night they came with four other mice to hear what the tree had to say. The more it talked, the more clearly it recalled things, and it thought, "Those were happy times. But they may still come back—they may come back again. Humpty-Dumpty fell downstairs, and yet he married the princess. Maybe the same thing will happen to me." It thought about a charming little birch tree that grew out in the woods. To the fir tree, she was a real and lovely princess.

"Who is Humpty-Dumpty?" the mice asked it. So the fir tree told them the whole story, for it could remember it word by word. The little mice were ready to jump to the top of the tree for joy. The next night, many more mice came to see the fir tree, and on Sunday, two rats paid it a call, but they said that the story was not very amusing. This made the little mice so sad that they began to find it not so very interesting either.

"Is that the only story you know?" the rats asked.

"Only that one," the tree answered. "I heard it on the happiest evening of my life, but I did not know then how happy I was."

"It's a very silly story. Don't you know one that tells about bacon and candles? Can't you tell us a good larder story?"

"No," said the tree.

"Then good-bye, and we won't be back," the rats said, and went away.

At last, the little mice took to staying away, too. The tree sighed, "Oh, wasn't it pleasant when those gay little mice sat around and listened to all that I had to say? Now that, too, is past and gone. But I will take good care to enjoy myself, once they let me out of here."

When would that be? Well, it came to pass on a morning when people came up to clean out the garret. The boxes were moved, the tree was pulled out and thrown—thrown hard—on the floor. But a servant dragged it at once to the stairway, where there was daylight again.

"Now my life will start all over," the tree thought. It felt the fresh air and the first sunbeam strike it as if it came out into the courtyard. This all happened so quickly, and there was so much going around it, that the tree forgot to give even a glance at itself. The courtyard adjoined a garden, where flowers were blooming. Great masses of fragrant roses hung over the picket fence. The linden trees were in blossom, and between them, the swallows skimmed past, calling, "Tilira-lira-lee, my love's come back to me." But it was not the fir tree of whom they spoke.

"Now I shall live again," it rejoiced, and tried to stretch out its branches. Alas, they were withered, and brown, and brittle. It was tossed into a corner, among weeds and nettles. But the gold star that was still tied to its top sparkled bravely in the sunlight.

Several of the merry children, who had danced around the tree and taken such pleasure in it at Christmas, were playing in the courtyard. One of the youngest seized upon it and tore off the tinsel star.

"Look what is still hanging on that ugly old Christmas tree," the child said, and stamped upon the branches until they cracked beneath his shoes.

The tree saw the beautiful flowers blooming freshly in the garden. It saw itself, and wished that they had left it in the darkest corner of the garret. It thought of its own young days in the deep woods, and of the merry Christmas Eve, and of the little mice who had been so pleased when it told them the story of Humpty-Dumpty.

"My days are over and past," said the poor tree. "Why didn't I enjoy them while I could? Now they are gone—all gone."

A servant came and chopped the tree into little pieces. These heaped together quite high. The wood blazed beautifully under the big copper kettle, and the fir tree moaned so deeply that each groan sounded like a muffled shot. That's why the children who were playing nearby ran to make a circle around the flames, staring into the fire and crying, "Pif! Paf!" But as each groans burst from it, the tree thought of a bright summer day in the woods, or a starlit winter night. It thought of Christmas Eve and thought of Humpty-Dumpty, which was the only story it ever heard and knew how to tell. And so the tree was burned completely away.

The children played on in the courtyard. The youngest child wore on his breast the gold star that had topped the tree on its happiest night of all. But that was no more, and the tree was no more, and there's no more to my story. No more, nothing more. All stories come to an end.

The Little Match Girl

Hans Christian Andersen

It was so terribly cold. Snow was falling, and it was almost dark. Evening came on, the last evening of the year. In the cold and gloom, a poor little girl, bareheaded and barefoot, was walking through the streets. Of course, when she had left her house she'd had slippers on, but what good had they been? They were very big slippers, way too big for her, for they belonged to her mother. The little girl had lost them running across the road, where two carriages had rattled by terribly fast. One slipper she'd not been able to find again, and a boy had run off with the other, saying he could use it very well as a cradle someday when he had children of his own. And so the little girl walked on her naked feet, which were quite red and blue with the cold. In an old apron, she carried several packages of matches, and she held a box of them in her hand. No one had bought any from her all day long, and no one had given her a cent.

Shivering with cold and hunger, she crept along, a picture of misery, poor little girl! The snowflakes fell on her long fair hair, which hung in pretty curls over her neck. In all the windows, lights were shining, and there was a wonderful smell of roast goose, for it was New Year's Eve. Yes, she thought of that!

In a corner formed by two houses, one of which projected farther out into the street than the other, she sat down and drew up her little feet under her. She was getting colder and colder, but did not dare to go home, for she had sold no matches, nor earned a single cent, and her father would surely beat her. Besides, it was cold at home, for they had nothing over them but a roof through which the wind whistled even though the biggest cracks had been stuffed with straw and rags.

Her hands were almost dead with cold. Oh, how much one little match might warm her! If she could only take one from the box and rub it against the wall and warm her hands. She drew one out. R-r-ratch! How it sputtered and burned! It made a warm, bright flame, like a little candle, as she held her hands over it; but it gave a strange light! It really seemed to the little girl as if she were sitting before a great iron stove with shining brass knobs and a brass cover. How wonderfully the fire burned! How comfortable it was! The youngster stretched out her feet to warm them too; then the little flame went out, the stove vanished, and she had only the remains of the burnt match in her hand.

She struck another match against the wall. It burned brightly, and when the light fell upon the wall, it became transparent like a thin veil, and she could see through it into a room. On the table a snow-white cloth was spread, and on it stood a shining dinner service. The roast goose steamed gloriously, stuffed with apples and prunes. And what was still better, the goose jumped down from the dish and waddled along the floor with a knife and fork in its breast, right over to the little girl. Then the match went out, and she could see only the thick, cold wall. She lighted another match. Then she was sitting under the most beautiful Christmas tree. It was much larger and much more beautiful than the one she had seen last Christmas through the glass door at the rich merchant's home. Thousands of candles burned on the green branches, and colored pictures like those in the printshops looked down at her. The little girl reached both her hands toward them. Then the match went out. But the Christmas lights mounted higher. She saw them now as bright stars in the sky. One of them fell down, forming a long line of fire.

"Now someone is dying," thought the little girl, for her old grandmother, the only person who had loved her and who was now dead, had told her that when a star fell down, a soul went up to God.

She rubbed another match against the wall. It became bright again, and in the glow, the old grandmother stood clear and shining, kind and lovely.

"Grandmother!" cried the child. "Oh, take me with you! I know you will disappear when the match is burned out. You will vanish like the warm stove, the wonderful roast goose, and the beautiful big Christmas tree!"

And she quickly struck the whole bundle of matches, for she wished to keep her grandmother with her. And the matches burned with such a glow that it became brighter than daylight. Grandmother had never been so grand and beautiful. She took the little girl in her arms, and both of them flew in brightness and joy above Earth, very, very high, and up there was neither cold, nor hunger, nor fear—they were with God.

But in the corner, leaning against the wall, sat the little girl with red cheeks and smiling mouth, frozen to death on the last evening of the old year. The New Year's sun rose upon a little pathetic figure. The child sat there, stiff and cold, holding the matches, of which one bundle was almost burned.

"She wanted to warm herself," the people said. No one imagined what beautiful things she had seen, and how happily she had gone with her old grandmother into the bright New Year.

A Christmas Carol

Charles Dickens

STAVE I: MARLEY'S GHOST

Marley was dead: to begin with. There is no doubt whatever about that. The register of his burial was signed by the clergyman, the clerk, the undertaker, and the chief mourner. Scrooge signed it: and Scrooge's name was good upon 'Change, for anything he chose to put his hand to.

Old Marley was as dead as a door-nail.

Mind! I don't mean to say that I know, of my own knowledge, what there is particularly dead about a door-nail. I might have been inclined, myself, to regard a coffin-nail as the deadest piece of ironmongery in the trade. But the wisdom of our ancestors is in the simile; and my unhallowed hands shall not disturb it, or the Country's done for. You will therefore permit me to repeat, emphatically, that Marley was as dead as a door-nail.

Scrooge knew he was dead? Of course he did. How could it be otherwise? Scrooge and he were partners for I don't know how many years. Scrooge was his sole executor, his sole administrator, his sole assign, his sole residuary legatee, his sole friend, and sole mourner. And even Scrooge was not so dreadfully cut up by the sad event, but that he was an excellent man of business on the very day of the funeral, and solemnised it with an undoubted bargain.

The mention of Marley's funeral brings me back to the point I started from. There is no doubt that Marley was dead. This must be distinctly understood, or nothing wonderful can come of the story I am going to relate. If we were not perfectly convinced that Hamlet's Father died before the play began, there would be nothing more remarkable in his taking a stroll at night, in an easterly wind, upon his own ramparts, than there would be in any other middle-aged gentleman rashly turning out after dark in a breezy spot—say Saint Paul's Churchyard for instance—literally to astonish his son's weak mind.

Scrooge never painted out Old Marley's name. There it stood, years afterwards, above the warehouse door: Scrooge and Marley. The firm was known as Scrooge and Marley. Sometimes people new to the business called Scrooge Scrooge, and sometimes Marley, but he answered to both names. It was all the same to him.

Oh! But he was a tight-fisted hand at the grindstone, Scrooge! a squeezing, wrenching, grasping, scraping, clutching, covetous, old sinner! Hard and sharp as flint, from which no steel had ever struck out generous fire; secret, and self-contained, and solitary as an oyster. The cold within him froze his old features, nipped his pointed nose, shrivelled his cheek, stiffened his gait; made his eyes red, his thin lips blue; and spoke out shrewdly in his grating voice. A frosty rime was on his head, and on his eyebrows, and his wiry chin. He carried his own low temperature always about with him; he iced his office in the dog-days; and didn't thaw it one degree at Christmas.

External heat and cold had little influence on Scrooge. No warmth could warm, no wintry weather chill him. No wind that blew was bitterer than he, no falling snow was more intent upon its purpose, no pelting rain less open to entreaty. Foul weather didn't know where to have him. The heaviest rain, and snow, and hail, and sleet, could boast of the advantage over him in only one respect. They often "came down" handsomely, and Scrooge never did.

Nobody ever stopped him in the street to say, with gladsome looks, "My dear Scrooge, how are you? When will you come to see me?" No beggars implored him to bestow a trifle, no children asked him what it was o'clock, no man or woman ever once in all his life inquired the way to such and such a place, of Scrooge. Even the blind men's dogs appeared to know him; and when they saw him coming on, would tug their owners into doorways and up courts; and then would wag their tails as though they said, "No eye at all is better than an evil eye, dark master!"

But what did Scrooge care! It was the very thing he liked. To edge his way along the crowded paths of life, warning all human sympathy to keep its distance, was what the knowing ones call "nuts" to Scrooge.

Once upon a time—of all the good days in the year, on Christmas Eve—old Scrooge sat busy in his counting-house. It was cold, bleak, biting weather: foggy withal: and he could hear the people in the court outside, go wheezing up and down, beating their hands upon their breasts, and stamping their feet upon the pavement stones to warm them. The city clocks had only just gone three, but it was quite dark already—it had not been light all day—and candles were flaring in the windows of the neighbouring offices, like ruddy smears upon the palpable brown air. The fog came pouring in at every chink and keyhole, and was so dense without, that although the court was of the narrowest, the houses opposite were mere phantoms. To see the dingy cloud come drooping down, obscuring everything, one might have thought that Nature lived hard by, and was brewing on a large scale.

The door of Scrooge's counting-house was open that he might keep his eye upon his clerk, who in a dismal little cell beyond, a sort of tank, was copying letters. Scrooge had a very small fire, but the clerk's fire was so very much smaller that it looked like one coal. But he couldn't replenish it, for Scrooge kept the coal-box in his own room; and so surely as the clerk came in with the shovel, the master predicted that it would be necessary for them to part. Wherefore the clerk put on his white comforter, and tried to warm himself at the candle; in which effort, not being a man of a strong imagination, he failed.

"A merry Christmas, uncle! God save you!" cried a cheerful voice. It was the voice of Scrooge's nephew, who came upon him so quickly that this was the first intimation he had of his approach.

"Bah!" said Scrooge, "Humbug!"

He had so heated himself with rapid walking in the fog and frost, this nephew of Scrooge's, that he was all in a glow; his face was ruddy and handsome; his eyes sparkled, and his breath smoked again.

"Christmas a humbug, uncle!" said Scrooge's nephew. "You don't mean that, I am sure?"

"I do," said Scrooge. "Merry Christmas! What right have you to be merry? What reason have you to be merry? You're poor enough."

"Come, then," returned the nephew gaily. "What right have you to be dismal? What reason have you to be morose? You're rich enough."

Scrooge having no better answer ready on the spur of the moment, said, "Bah!" again; and followed it up with "Humbug."

"Don't be cross, uncle!" said the nephew.

"What else can I be," returned the uncle, "when I live in such a world of fools as this? Merry Christmas! Out upon merry Christmas! What's Christmas time to you but a time for paying bills without money; a time for finding yourself a year older, but not an hour richer; a time for balancing your books and having every item in 'em through a round dozen of months presented dead against you? If I could work my will," said Scrooge indignantly, "every idiot who goes about with 'Merry Christmas' on his lips, should be boiled with his own pudding, and buried with a stake of holly through his heart. He should!"

"Uncle!" pleaded the nephew.

"Nephew!" returned the uncle sternly, "keep Christmas in your own way, and let me keep it in mine."

"Keep it!" repeated Scrooge's nephew. "But you don't keep it."

"Let me leave it alone, then," said Scrooge. "Much good may it do you! Much good it has ever done you!"

"There are many things from which I might have derived good, by which I have not profited, I dare say," returned the nephew. "Christmas among the rest. But I am sure I have always thought of Christmas time, when it has come round—apart from the veneration due to its sacred name and origin, if anything belonging to it can be apart from that—as a good time; a kind, forgiving, charitable, pleasant time; the only time I know of, in the long calendar of the year, when men and women seem by one consent to open their shut-up hearts freely, and to think of people below them as if they really were fellow-passengers to the grave, and not another race of creatures bound on other journeys. And therefore, uncle, though it has never put a scrap of gold or silver in my pocket, I believe that it has done me good, and will do me good; and I say, God bless it!"

The clerk in the Tank involuntarily applauded. Becoming immediately sensible of the impropriety, he poked the fire, and extinguished the last frail spark for ever.

"Let me hear another sound from you," said Scrooge, "and you'll keep your Christmas by losing your situation! You're quite a powerful speaker, sir," he added, turning to his nephew. "I wonder you don't go into Parliament."

"Don't be angry, uncle. Come! Dine with us tomorrow."

Scrooge said that he would see him—yes, indeed he did. He went the whole length of the expression, and said that he would see him in that extremity first.

"But why?" cried Scrooge's nephew. "Why?"

"Why did you get married?" said Scrooge.

"Because I fell in love."

"Because you fell in love!" growled Scrooge, as if that were the only one thing in the world more ridiculous than a merry Christmas. "Good afternoon!"

"Nay, uncle, but you never came to see me before that happened. Why give it as a reason for not coming now?"

"Good afternoon," said Scrooge.

"I want nothing from you; I ask nothing of you; why cannot we be friends?"

"Good afternoon," said Scrooge.

"I am sorry, with all my heart, to find you so resolute. We have never had any quarrel, to which I have been a party. But I have made the trial in homage to Christmas, and I'll keep my Christmas humour to the last. So A Merry Christmas, uncle!"

"Good afternoon!" said Scrooge.

"And A Happy New Year!"

"Good afternoon!" said Scrooge.

His nephew left the room without an angry word, notwithstanding. He stopped at the outer door to bestow the greetings of the season on the clerk, who, cold as he was, was warmer than Scrooge; for he returned them cordially.

"There's another fellow," muttered Scrooge; who overheard him: "my clerk, with fifteen shillings a week, and a wife and family, talking about a merry Christmas. I'll retire to Bedlam."

This lunatic, in letting Scrooge's nephew out, had let two other people in. They were portly gentlemen, pleasant to behold, and now stood, with their hats off, in Scrooge's office. They had books and papers in their hands, and bowed to him.

"Scrooge and Marley's, I believe," said one of the gentlemen, referring to his list. "Have I the pleasure of addressing Mr. Scrooge, or Mr. Marley?"

"Mr. Marley has been dead these seven years," Scrooge replied. "He died seven years ago, this very night."

"We have no doubt his liberality is well represented by his surviving partner," said the gentleman, presenting his credentials.

It certainly was; for they had been two kindred spirits. At the ominous word "liberality," Scrooge frowned, and shook his head, and handed the credentials back.

"At this festive season of the year, Mr. Scrooge," said the gentleman, taking up a pen, "it is more than usually desirable that we should make some slight provision for the Poor and destitute, who suffer greatly at the present time. Many thousands are in want of common necessaries; hundreds of thousands are in want of common comforts, sir."

"Are there no prisons?" asked Scrooge.

"Plenty of prisons," said the gentleman, laying down the pen again.

"And the Union workhouses?" demanded Scrooge. "Are they still in operation?"

"They are. Still," returned the gentleman, "I wish I could say they were not."

"The Treadmill and the Poor Law are in full vigour, then?" said Scrooge.

"Both very busy, sir."

"Oh! I was afraid, from what you said at first, that something had occurred to stop them in their useful course," said Scrooge. "I'm very glad to hear it."

"Under the impression that they scarcely furnish Christian cheer of mind or body to the multitude," returned the gentleman, "a few of us are endeavouring to raise a fund to buy the Poor some meat and drink, and means of warmth. We choose this time, because it is a time, of all others, when Want is keenly felt, and Abundance rejoices. What shall I put you down for?"

"Nothing!" Scrooge replied.

"You wish to be anonymous?"

"I wish to be left alone," said Scrooge. "Since you ask me what I wish, gentlemen, that is my answer. I don't make merry myself at Christmas and I can't afford to make idle people merry. I help to support the establishments I have mentioned— they cost enough; and those who are badly off must go there."

"Many can't go there; and many would rather die."

"If they would rather die," said Scrooge, "they had better do it, and decrease the surplus population. Besides—excuse me—I don't know that."

"But you might know it," observed the gentleman.

"It's not my business," Scrooge returned. "It's enough for a man to understand his own business, and not to interfere with other people's. Mine occupies me constantly. Good afternoon, gentlemen!"

Seeing clearly that it would be useless to pursue their point, the gentlemen withdrew. Scrooge resumed his labours with an improved opinion of himself, and in a more facetious temper than was usual with him.

Meanwhile the fog and darkness thickened so, that people ran about with flaring links, proffering their services to go before horses in carriages, and conduct them on their way. The ancient tower of a church, whose gruff old bell was always peeping slily down at Scrooge out of a gothic window in the wall, became invisible, and struck the hours and quarters in the clouds, with tremulous vibrations afterwards as if its teeth were chattering in its frozen head up there. The cold became intense. In the main street, at the corner of the court, some labourers were repairing the gas-pipes, and had lighted a great fire in a brazier, round which a party of ragged men and boys were gathered: warming their hands and winking their eyes before the blaze in rapture. The water-plug being left in solitude, its overflowings sullenly congealed, and turned to misanthropic ice. The brightness of the shops where holly sprigs and berries crackled in the lamp heat of the windows, made pale faces ruddy as they passed. Poulterers' and grocers' trades became a splendid joke: a glorious pageant, with which it was next to impossible to believe that such dull principles as bargain and sale had anything to do. The Lord Mayor, in the stronghold of the mighty Mansion House, gave orders to his fifty cooks and butlers to keep Christmas as a Lord Mayor's household should; and even the little tailor, whom he had fined five shillings on the previous Monday for being drunk and bloodthirsty in the streets, stirred up to-morrow's pudding in his garret, while his lean wife and the baby sallied out to buy the beef.

Foggier yet, and colder! Piercing, searching, biting cold. If the good Saint Dunstan had but nipped the Evil Spirit's nose with a touch of such weather as that, instead of using his familiar weapons, then indeed he would have roared to lusty purpose. The owner of one scant young nose, gnawed and mumbled by the hungry cold as bones are gnawed by dogs, stooped down at Scrooge's keyhole to regale him with a Christmas carol: but at the first sound of

"God bless you, merry gentleman!

May nothing you dismay!"

Scrooge seized the ruler with such energy of action, that the singer fled in terror, leaving the keyhole to the fog and even more congenial frost.

At length the hour of shutting up the counting-house arrived. With an ill-will Scrooge dismounted from his stool, and tacitly admitted the fact to the expectant clerk in the Tank, who instantly snuffed his candle out, and put on his hat.

"You'll want all day to-morrow, I suppose?" said Scrooge.

"If quite convenient, sir."

"It's not convenient," said Scrooge, "and it's not fair. If I was to stop half-a-crown for it, you'd think yourself ill-used, I'll be bound?"

The clerk smiled faintly.

"And yet," said Scrooge, "you don't think me ill-used, when I pay a day's wages for no work."

The clerk observed that it was only once a year.

"A poor excuse for picking a man's pocket every twenty-fifth of December!" said Scrooge, buttoning his great-coat to the chin. "But I suppose you must have the whole day. Be here all the earlier next morning."

The clerk promised that he would; and Scrooge walked out with a growl. The office was closed in a twinkling, and the clerk, with the long ends of his white comforter dangling below his waist (for he boasted no great-coat), went down a slide on Cornhill, at the end of a lane of boys, twenty times, in honour of its being Christmas Eve, and then ran home to Camden Town as hard as he could pelt, to play at blindman's-buff.

Scrooge took his melancholy dinner in his usual melancholy tavern; and having read all the newspapers, and beguiled the rest of the evening with his banker's-book, went home to bed. He lived in chambers which had once belonged to his deceased partner. They were a gloomy suite of rooms, in a lowering pile of building up a yard, where it had so little business to be, that one could scarcely help fancying it must have run there when it was a young house, playing at hide-and-seek with other houses, and forgotten the way out again. It was old enough now, and dreary enough, for nobody lived in it but Scrooge, the other rooms being all let out as offices. The yard was so dark that even Scrooge, who knew its every stone, was fain to grope with his hands. The fog and frost so hung about the black old gateway of the house, that it seemed as if the Genius of the Weather sat in mournful meditation on the threshold.

Now, it is a fact, that there was nothing at all particular about the knocker on the door, except that it was very large. It is also a fact, that Scrooge had seen it, night and morning, during his whole residence in that place; also that Scrooge had as little of what is called fancy about him as any man in the city of London, even including—which is a bold word—the corporation, aldermen, and livery. Let it also be borne in mind that Scrooge had not bestowed one thought on Marley, since his last mention of his seven years' dead partner that afternoon. And then let any man explain to me, if he can, how it happened that Scrooge, having his key in the lock of the door, saw in the knocker, without its undergoing any intermediate process of change—not a knocker, but Marley's face.

Marley's face. It was not in impenetrable shadow as the other objects in the yard were, but had a dismal light about it, like a bad lobster in a dark cellar. It was not angry or ferocious, but looked at Scrooge as Marley used to look: with ghostly spectacles turned up on its ghostly forehead. The hair was curiously stirred, as if by breath or hot air; and, though the eyes were wide open, they were perfectly motionless. That, and its livid colour, made it horrible; but its horror seemed to be in spite of the face and beyond its control, rather than a part of its own expression.

As Scrooge looked fixedly at this phenomenon, it was a knocker again.

To say that he was not startled, or that his blood was not conscious of a terrible sensation to which it had been a stranger from infancy, would be untrue. But he put his hand upon the key he had relinquished, turned it sturdily, walked in, and lighted his candle.

He did pause, with a moment's irresolution, before he shut the door; and he did look cautiously behind it first, as if he half expected to be terrified with the sight of Marley's pigtail sticking out into the hall. But there was nothing on the back of the door, except the screws and nuts that held the knocker on, so he said "Pooh, pooh!" and closed it with a bang.

The sound resounded through the house like thunder. Every room above, and every cask in the wine-merchant's cellars below, appeared to have a separate peal of echoes of its own. Scrooge was not a man to be frightened by echoes. He fastened the door, and walked across the hall, and up the stairs; slowly too: trimming his candle as he went.

You may talk vaguely about driving a coach-and-six up a good old flight of stairs, or through a bad young Act of Parliament; but I mean to say you might have got a hearse up that staircase, and taken it broadwise, with the splinter-bar towards the wall and the door towards the balustrades: and done it easy. There was plenty of width for that, and room to spare; which is perhaps the reason why Scrooge thought he saw a locomotive hearse going on before him in the gloom. Half-a-dozen gas-lamps out of the street wouldn't have lighted the entry too well, so you may suppose that it was pretty dark with Scrooge's dip.

Up Scrooge went, not caring a button for that. Darkness is cheap, and Scrooge liked it. But before he shut his heavy door, he walked through his rooms to see that all was right. He had just enough recollection of the face to desire to do that.

Sitting-room, bedroom, lumber-room. All as they should be. Nobody under the table, nobody under the sofa; a small fire in the grate; spoon and basin ready; and the little saucepan of gruel (Scrooge had a cold in his head) upon the hob. Nobody under the bed; nobody in the closet; nobody in his dressing-gown, which was hanging up in a suspicious attitude against the wall. Lumber-room as usual. Old fire-guard, old shoes, two fish-baskets, washing-stand on three legs, and a poker.

Quite satisfied, he closed his door, and locked himself in; double-locked himself in, which was not his custom. Thus secured against surprise, he took off his cravat; put on his dressing-gown and slippers, and his nightcap; and sat down before the fire to take his gruel.

It was a very low fire indeed; nothing on such a bitter night. He was obliged to sit close to it, and brood over it, before he could extract the least sensation of warmth from such a handful of fuel. The fireplace was an old one, built by some Dutch merchant long ago, and paved all round with quaint Dutch tiles, designed to illustrate the Scriptures. There were Cains and Abels, Pharaoh's daughters; Queens of Sheba, Angelic messengers descending through the air on clouds like feather-beds, Abrahams, Belshazzars, Apostles putting off to sea in butter-boats, hundreds of figures to attract his thoughts; and yet that face of Marley, seven years dead, came like the ancient Prophet's rod, and swallowed up the whole. If each smooth tile had been a blank at first, with power to shape some picture on its surface from the disjointed fragments of his thoughts, there would have been a copy of old Marley's head on every one.

"Humbug!" said Scrooge; and walked across the room.

After several turns, he sat down again. As he threw his head back in the chair, his glance happened to rest upon a bell, a disused bell, that hung in the room, and communicated for some purpose now forgotten with a chamber in the highest story of the building. It was with great astonishment, and with a strange, inexplicable dread, that as he looked, he saw this bell begin to swing. It swung so softly in the outset that it scarcely made a sound; but soon it rang out loudly, and so did every bell in the house.

This might have lasted half a minute, or a minute, but it seemed an hour. The bells ceased as they had begun, together. They were succeeded by a clanking noise, deep down below; as if some person were dragging a heavy chain over the casks in the wine-merchant's cellar. Scrooge then remembered to have heard that ghosts in haunted houses were described as dragging chains.

The cellar-door flew open with a booming sound, and then he heard the noise much louder, on the floors below; then coming up the stairs; then coming straight towards his door.

"It's humbug still!" said Scrooge. "I won't believe it."

His colour changed though, when, without a pause, it came on through the heavy door, and passed into the room before his eyes. Upon its coming in, the dying flame leaped up, as though it cried, "I know him; Marley's Ghost!" and fell again.

The same face: the very same. Marley in his pigtail, usual waistcoat, tights and boots; the tassels on the latter bristling, like his pigtail, and his coat-skirts, and the hair upon his head. The chain he drew was clasped about his middle. It was long, and wound about him like a tail; and it was made (for Scrooge observed it closely) of cash-boxes, keys, padlocks, ledgers, deeds, and heavy purses wrought in steel. His body was transparent; so that Scrooge, observing him, and looking through his waistcoat, could see the two buttons on his coat behind.

Scrooge had often heard it said that Marley had no bowels, but he had never believed it until now.

No, nor did he believe it even now. Though he looked the phantom through and through, and saw it standing before him; though he felt the chilling influence of its death-cold eyes; and marked the very texture of the folded kerchief bound about its head and chin, which wrapper he had not observed before; he was still incredulous, and fought against his senses.

"How now!" said Scrooge, caustic and cold as ever. "What do you want with me?"

"Much!"—Marley's voice, no doubt about it.

"Who are you?"

"Ask me who I was."

"Who were you then?" said Scrooge, raising his voice. "You're particular, for a shade." He was going to say "to a shade," but substituted this, as more appropriate.

"In life I was your partner, Jacob Marley."

"Can you—can you sit down?" asked Scrooge, looking doubtfully at him.

"I can."

"Do it, then."

Scrooge asked the question, because he didn't know whether a ghost so transparent might find himself in a condition to take a chair; and felt that in the event of its being impossible, it might involve the necessity of an embarrassing explanation. But the ghost sat down on the opposite side of the fireplace, as if he were quite used to it.

"You don't believe in me," observed the Ghost.

"I don't," said Scrooge.

"What evidence would you have of my reality beyond that of your senses?"

"I don't know," said Scrooge.

"Why do you doubt your senses?"

"Because," said Scrooge, "a little thing affects them. A slight disorder of the stomach makes them cheats. You may be an undigested bit of beef, a blot of mustard, a crumb of cheese, a fragment of an underdone potato. There's more of gravy than of grave about you, whatever you are!"

Scrooge was not much in the habit of cracking jokes, nor did he feel, in his heart, by any means waggish then. The truth is, that he tried to be smart, as a means of distracting his own attention, and keeping down his terror; for the spectre's voice disturbed the very marrow in his bones.

To sit, staring at those fixed glazed eyes, in silence for a moment, would play, Scrooge felt, the very deuce with him. There was something very awful, too, in the spectre's being provided with an infernal atmosphere of its own. Scrooge could not feel it himself, but this was clearly the case; for though the Ghost sat perfectly motionless, its hair, and skirts, and tassels, were still agitated as by the hot vapour from an oven.

"You see this toothpick?" said Scrooge, returning quickly to the charge, for the reason just assigned; and wishing, though it were only for a second, to divert the vision's stony gaze from himself.

"I do," replied the Ghost.

"You are not looking at it," said Scrooge.

"But I see it," said the Ghost, "notwithstanding."

"Well!" returned Scrooge, "I have but to swallow this, and be for the rest of my days persecuted by a legion of goblins, all of my own creation. Humbug, I tell you! humbug!"

At this the spirit raised a frightful cry, and shook its chain with such a dismal and appalling noise, that Scrooge held on tight to his chair, to save himself from falling in a swoon. But how much greater was his horror, when the phantom taking off the bandage round its head, as if it were too warm to wear indoors, its lower jaw dropped down upon its breast!

Scrooge fell upon his knees, and clasped his hands before his face.

"Mercy!" he said. "Dreadful apparition, why do you trouble me?"

"Man of the worldly mind!" replied the Ghost, "do you believe in me or not?"

"I do," said Scrooge. "I must. But why do spirits walk the earth, and why do they come to me?"

"It is required of every man," the Ghost returned, "that the spirit within him should walk abroad among his fellowmen, and travel far and wide; and if that spirit goes not forth in life, it is condemned to do so after death. It is doomed to wander through the world—oh, woe is me!—and witness what it cannot share, but might have shared on earth, and turned to happiness!"

Again the spectre raised a cry, and shook its chain and wrung its shadowy hands.

"You are fettered," said Scrooge, trembling. "Tell me why?"

"I wear the chain I forged in life," replied the Ghost. "I made it link by link, and yard by yard; I girded it on of my own free will, and of my own free will I wore it. Is its pattern strange to you?"

Scrooge trembled more and more.

"Or would you know," pursued the Ghost, "the weight and length of the strong coil you bear yourself? It was full as heavy and as long as this, seven Christmas Eves ago. You have laboured on it, since. It is a ponderous chain!"

Scrooge glanced about him on the floor, in the expectation of finding himself surrounded by some fifty or sixty fathoms of iron cable: but he could see nothing.

"Jacob," he said, imploringly. "Old Jacob Marley, tell me more. Speak comfort to me, Jacob!"

"I have none to give," the Ghost replied. "It comes from other regions, Ebenezer Scrooge, and is conveyed by other ministers, to other kinds of men. Nor can I tell you what I would. A very little more is all permitted to me. I cannot rest, I cannot stay, I cannot linger anywhere. My spirit never walked beyond our counting-house—mark me!—in life my spirit never roved beyond the narrow limits of our money-changing hole; and weary journeys lie before me!"

It was a habit with Scrooge, whenever he became thoughtful, to put his hands in his breeches pockets. Pondering on what the Ghost had said, he did so now, but without lifting up his eyes, or getting off his knees.

"You must have been very slow about it, Jacob," Scrooge observed, in a business-like manner, though with humility and deference.

"Slow!" the Ghost repeated.

"Seven years dead," mused Scrooge. "And travelling all the time!"

"The whole time," said the Ghost. "No rest, no peace. Incessant torture of remorse."

"You travel fast?" said Scrooge.

"On the wings of the wind," replied the Ghost.

"You might have got over a great quantity of ground in seven years," said Scrooge.

The Ghost, on hearing this, set up another cry, and clanked its chain so hideously in the dead silence of the night, that the Ward would have been justified in indicting it for a nuisance.

"Oh! captive, bound, and double-ironed," cried the phantom, "not to know, that ages of incessant labour by immortal creatures, for this earth must pass into eternity before the good of which it is susceptible is all developed. Not to know that any Christian spirit working kindly in its little sphere, whatever it may be, will find its mortal life too short for its vast means of usefulness. Not to know that no space of regret can make amends for one life's opportunity misused! Yet such was I! Oh! such was I!"

"But you were always a good man of business, Jacob," faltered Scrooge, who now began to apply this to himself.

"Business!" cried the Ghost, wringing its hands again. "Mankind was my business. The common welfare was my business; charity, mercy, forbearance, and benevolence, were, all, my business. The dealings of my trade were but a drop of water in the comprehensive ocean of my business!"

It held up its chain at arm's length, as if that were the cause of all its unavailing grief, and flung it heavily upon the ground again.

"At this time of the rolling year," the spectre said, "I suffer most. Why did I walk through crowds of fellow-beings with my eyes turned down, and never raise them to that blessed Star which led the Wise Men to a poor abode! Were there no poor homes to which its light would have conducted me!"

Scrooge was very much dismayed to hear the spectre going on at this rate, and began to quake exceedingly.

"Hear me!" cried the Ghost. "My time is nearly gone."

"I will," said Scrooge. "But don't be hard upon me! Don't be flowery, Jacob! Pray!"

"How it is that I appear before you in a shape that you can see, I may not tell. I have sat invisible beside you many and many a day."

It was not an agreeable idea. Scrooge shivered, and wiped the perspiration from his brow.

"That is no light part of my penance," pursued the Ghost. "I am here to-night to warn you, that you have yet a chance and hope of escaping my fate. A chance and hope of my procuring, Ebenezer."

"You were always a good friend to me," said Scrooge. "Thank 'ee!"

"You will be haunted," resumed the Ghost, "by Three Spirits."

Scrooge's countenance fell almost as low as the Ghost's had done.

"Is that the chance and hope you mentioned, Jacob?" he demanded, in a faltering voice.

"It is."

"I—I think I'd rather not," said Scrooge.

"Without their visits," said the Ghost, "you cannot hope to shun the path I tread. Expect the first to-morrow, when the bell tolls One."

"Couldn't I take 'em all at once, and have it over, Jacob?" hinted Scrooge.

"Expect the second on the next night at the same hour. The third upon the next night when the last stroke of Twelve has ceased to vibrate. Look to see me no more; and look that, for your own sake, you remember what has passed between us!"

When it had said these words, the spectre took its wrapper from the table, and bound it round its head, as before. Scrooge knew this, by the smart sound its teeth made, when the jaws were brought together by the bandage. He ventured to raise his eyes again, and found his supernatural visitor confronting him in an erect attitude, with its chain wound over and about its arm.

The apparition walked backward from him; and at every step it took, the window raised itself a little, so that when the spectre reached it, it was wide open.

It beckoned Scrooge to approach, which he did. When they were within two paces of each other, Marley's Ghost held up its hand, warning him to come no nearer. Scrooge stopped.

Not so much in obedience, as in surprise and fear: for on the raising of the hand, he became sensible of confused noises in the air; incoherent sounds of lamentation and regret; wailings inexpressibly sorrowful and self-accusatory. The spectre, after listening for a moment, joined in the mournful dirge; and floated out upon the bleak, dark night.

Scrooge followed to the window: desperate in his curiosity. He looked out.

The air was filled with phantoms, wandering hither and thither in restless haste, and moaning as they went. Every one of them wore chains like Marley's Ghost; some few (they might be guilty governments) were linked together; none were free. Many had been personally known to Scrooge in their lives. He had been quite familiar with one old ghost, in a white waistcoat, with a monstrous iron safe attached to its ankle, who cried piteously at being unable to assist a wretched woman with an infant, whom it saw below, upon a door-step. The misery with them all was, clearly, that they sought to interfere, for good, in human matters, and had lost the power forever.

Whether these creatures faded into mist, or mist enshrouded them, he could not tell. But they and their spirit voices faded together; and the night became as it had been when he walked home.

Scrooge closed the window, and examined the door by which the Ghost had entered. It was double-locked, as he had locked it with his own hands, and the bolts were undisturbed. He tried to say "Humbug!" but stopped at the first syllable. And being, from the emotion he had undergone, or the fatigues of the day, or his glimpse of the Invisible World, or the dull conversation of the Ghost, or the lateness of the hour, much in need of repose; went straight to bed, without undressing, and fell asleep upon the instant.

STAVE II: THE FIRST OF THE THREE SPIRITS

When Scrooge awoke, it was so dark, that looking out of bed, he could scarcely distinguish the transparent window from the opaque walls of his chamber. He was endeavouring to pierce the darkness with his ferret eyes, when the chimes of a neighbouring church struck the four quarters. So he listened for the hour.

To his great astonishment the heavy bell went on from six to seven, and from seven to eight, and regularly up to twelve; then stopped. Twelve! It was past two when he went to bed. The clock was wrong. An icicle must have got into the works. Twelve!

He touched the spring of his repeater, to correct this most preposterous clock. Its rapid little pulse beat twelve: and stopped.

"Why, it isn't possible," said Scrooge, "that I can have slept through a whole day and far into another night. It isn't possible that anything has happened to the sun, and this is twelve at noon!"

The idea being an alarming one, he scrambled out of bed, and groped his way to the window. He was obliged to rub the frost off with the sleeve of his dressing-gown before he could see anything; and could see very little then. All he could make out was, that it was still very foggy and extremely cold, and that there was no noise of people running to and fro, and making a great stir, as there unquestionably would have been if night had beaten off bright day, and taken possession of the world. This was a great relief, because "three days after sight of this First of Exchange pay to Mr. Ebenezer Scrooge or his order," and so forth, would have become a mere United States' security if there were no days to count by.

Scrooge went to bed again, and thought, and thought, and thought it over and over and over, and could make nothing of it. The more he thought, the more perplexed he was; and the more he endeavoured not to think, the more he thought.

Marley's Ghost bothered him exceedingly. Every time he resolved within himself, after mature inquiry, that it was all a dream, his mind flew back again, like a strong spring released, to its first position, and presented the same problem to be worked all through, "Was it a dream or not?"

Scrooge lay in this state until the chime had gone three quarters more, when he remembered, on a sudden, that the Ghost had warned him of a visitation when the bell tolled one. He resolved to lie awake until the hour was passed; and, considering that he could no more go to sleep than go to Heaven, this was perhaps the wisest resolution in his power.

The quarter was so long, that he was more than once convinced he must have sunk into a doze unconsciously, and missed the clock. At length it broke upon his listening ear.

"Ding, dong!"

"A quarter past," said Scrooge, counting.

"Ding, dong!"

"Half-past!" said Scrooge.

"Ding, dong!"

"A quarter to it," said Scrooge.

"Ding, dong!"

"The hour itself," said Scrooge, triumphantly, "and nothing else!"

He spoke before the hour bell sounded, which it now did with a deep, dull, hollow, melancholy One. Light flashed up in the room upon the instant, and the curtains of his bed were drawn.

The curtains of his bed were drawn aside, I tell you, by a hand. Not the curtains at his feet, nor the curtains at his back, but those to which his face was addressed. The curtains of his bed were drawn aside; and Scrooge, starting up into a half-recumbent attitude, found himself face to face with the unearthly visitor who drew them: as close to it as I am now to you, and I am standing in the spirit at your elbow.

It was a strange figure—like a child: yet not so like a child as like an old man, viewed through some supernatural medium, which gave him the appearance of having receded from the view, and being diminished to a child's proportions. Its hair, which hung about its neck and down its back, was white as if with age; and yet the face had not a wrinkle in it, and the tenderest bloom was on the skin. The arms were very long and muscular; the hands the same, as if its hold were of uncommon strength. Its legs and feet, most delicately formed, were, like those upper members, bare. It wore a tunic of the purest white; and round its waist was bound a lustrous belt, the sheen of which was beautiful. It held a branch of fresh green holly in its hand; and, in singular contradiction of that wintry emblem, had its dress trimmed with summer flowers. But the strangest thing about it was, that from the crown of its head there sprung a bright clear jet of light, by which all this was visible; and which was doubtless the occasion of its using, in its duller moments, a great extinguisher for a cap, which it now held under its arm.

Even this, though, when Scrooge looked at it with increasing steadiness, was not its strangest quality. For as its belt sparkled and glittered now in one part and now in another, and what was light one instant, at another time was dark, so the figure itself fluctuated in its distinctness: being now a thing with one arm, now with one leg, now with twenty legs, now a pair of legs without a head, now a head without a body: of which dissolving parts, no outline would be visible in the dense gloom wherein they melted away. And in the very wonder of this, it would be itself again; distinct and clear as ever.

"Are you the Spirit, sir, whose coming was foretold to me?" asked Scrooge.

"I am!"

The voice was soft and gentle. Singularly low, as if instead of being so close beside him, it were at a distance.

"Who, and what are you?" Scrooge demanded.

"I am the Ghost of Christmas Past."

"Long Past?" inquired Scrooge: observant of its dwarfish stature.

"No. Your past."

Perhaps, Scrooge could not have told anybody why, if anybody could have asked him; but he had a special desire to see the Spirit in his cap; and begged him to be covered.

"What!" exclaimed the Ghost, "would you so soon put out, with worldly hands, the light I give? Is it not enough that you are one of those whose passions made this cap, and force me through whole trains of years to wear it low upon my brow!"

Scrooge reverently disclaimed all intention to offend or any knowledge of having wilfully "bonneted" the Spirit at any period of his life. He then made bold to inquire what business brought him there.

"Your welfare!" said the Ghost.

Scrooge expressed himself much obliged, but could not help thinking that a night of unbroken rest would have been more conducive to that end. The Spirit must have heard him thinking, for it said immediately:

"Your reclamation, then. Take heed!"

It put out its strong hand as it spoke, and clasped him gently by the arm.

"Rise! and walk with me!"

It would have been in vain for Scrooge to plead that the weather and the hour were not adapted to pedestrian purposes; that bed was warm, and the thermometer a long way below freezing; that he was clad but lightly in his slippers, dressing-gown, and nightcap; and that he had a cold upon him at that time. The grasp, though gentle as a woman's hand, was not to be resisted. He rose: but finding that the Spirit made towards the window, clasped his robe in supplication.

"I am a mortal," Scrooge remonstrated, "and liable to fall."

"Bear but a touch of my hand there," said the Spirit, laying it upon his heart, "and you shall be upheld in more than this!"

As the words were spoken, they passed through the wall, and stood upon an open country road, with fields on either hand. The city had entirely vanished. Not a vestige of it was to be seen. The darkness and the mist had vanished with it, for it was a clear, cold, winter day, with snow upon the ground.

"Good Heaven!" said Scrooge, clasping his hands together, as he looked about him. "I was bred in this place. I was a boy here!"

The Spirit gazed upon him mildly. Its gentle touch, though it had been light and instantaneous, appeared still present to the old man's sense of feeling. He was conscious of a thousand odours floating in the air, each one connected with a thousand thoughts, and hopes, and joys, and cares long, long, forgotten!

"Your lip is trembling," said the Ghost. "And what is that upon your cheek?"

Scrooge muttered, with an unusual catching in his voice, that it was a pimple; and begged the Ghost to lead him where he would.

"You recollect the way?" inquired the Spirit.

"Remember it!" cried Scrooge with fervour; "I could walk it blindfold."

"Strange to have forgotten it for so many years!" observed the Ghost. "Let us go on."

They walked along the road, Scrooge recognising every gate, and post, and tree; until a little market-town appeared in the distance, with its bridge, its church, and winding river. Some shaggy ponies now were seen trotting towards them with boys upon their backs, who called to other boys in country gigs and carts, driven by farmers. All these boys were in great spirits, and shouted to each other, until the broad fields were so full of merry music, that the crisp air laughed to hear it!

"These are but shadows of the things that have been," said the Ghost. "They have no consciousness of us."

The jocund travellers came on; and as they came, Scrooge knew and named them every one. Why was he rejoiced beyond all bounds to see them! Why did his cold eye glisten, and his heart leap up as they went past! Why was he filled with gladness when he heard them give each other Merry Christmas, as they parted at cross-roads and by-ways, for their several homes! What was merry Christmas to Scrooge? Out upon merry Christmas! What good had it ever done to him?

"The school is not quite deserted," said the Ghost. "A solitary child, neglected by his friends, is left there still."

Scrooge said he knew it. And he sobbed.

They left the high-road, by a well-remembered lane, and soon approached a mansion of dull red brick, with a little weathercock-surmounted cupola, on the roof, and a bell hanging in it. It was a large house, but one of broken fortunes; for the spacious offices were little used, their walls were damp and mossy, their windows broken, and their gates decayed. Fowls clucked and strutted in the stables; and the coach-houses and sheds were over-run with grass. Nor was it more retentive of its ancient state, within; for entering the dreary hall, and glancing through the open doors of many rooms, they found them poorly furnished, cold, and vast. There was an earthy savour in the air, a chilly bareness in the place, which associated itself somehow with too much getting up by candle-light, and not too much to eat.

They went, the Ghost and Scrooge, across the hall, to a door at the back of the house. It opened before them, and disclosed a long, bare, melancholy room, made barer still by lines of plain deal forms and desks. At one of these a lonely boy was reading near a feeble fire; and Scrooge sat down upon a form, and wept to see his poor forgotten self as he used to be.

Not a latent echo in the house, not a squeak and scuffle from the mice behind the panelling, not a drip from the half-thawed water-spout in the dull yard behind, not a sigh among the leafless boughs of one despondent poplar, not the idle swinging of an empty store-house door, no, not a clicking in the fire, but fell upon the heart of Scrooge with a softening influence, and gave a freer passage to his tears.

The Spirit touched him on the arm, and pointed to his younger self, intent upon his reading. Suddenly a man, in foreign garments: wonderfully real and distinct to look at: stood outside the window, with an axe stuck in his belt, and leading by the bridle an ass laden with wood.

"Why, it's Ali Baba!" Scrooge exclaimed in ecstasy. "It's dear old honest Ali Baba! Yes, yes, I know! One Christmas time, when yonder solitary child was left here all alone, he did come, for the first time, just like that. Poor boy! And Valentine," said Scrooge, "and his wild brother, Orson; there they go! And what's his name, who was put down in his drawers, asleep, at the Gate of Damascus; don't you see him! And the Sultan's Groom turned upside down by the Genii; there he is upon his head! Serve him right. I'm glad of it. What business had he to be married to the Princess!"

To hear Scrooge expending all the earnestness of his nature on such subjects, in a most extraordinary voice between laughing and crying; and to see his heightened and excited face; would have been a surprise to his business friends in the city, indeed.

"There's the Parrot!" cried Scrooge. "Green body and yellow tail, with a thing like a lettuce growing out of the top of his head; there he is! Poor Robin Crusoe, he called him, when he came home again after sailing round the island. 'Poor Robin Crusoe, where have you been, Robin Crusoe?' The man thought he was dreaming, but he wasn't. It was the Parrot, you know. There goes Friday, running for his life to the little creek! Halloa! Hoop! Halloo!"

Then, with a rapidity of transition very foreign to his usual character, he said, in pity for his former self, "Poor boy!" and cried again.

"I wish," Scrooge muttered, putting his hand in his pocket, and looking about him, after drying his eyes with his cuff: "but it's too late now."

"What is the matter?" asked the Spirit.

"Nothing," said Scrooge. "Nothing. There was a boy singing a Christmas Carol at my door last night. I should like to have given him something: that's all."

The Ghost smiled thoughtfully, and waved its hand: saying as it did so, "Let us see another Christmas!"

Scrooge's former self grew larger at the words, and the room became a little darker and more dirty. The panels shrunk, the windows cracked; fragments of plaster fell out of the ceiling, and the naked laths were shown instead; but how all this was brought about, Scrooge knew no more than you do. He only knew that it was quite correct; that everything had happened so; that there he was, alone again, when all the other boys had gone home for the jolly holidays.

He was not reading now, but walking up and down despairingly. Scrooge looked at the Ghost, and with a mournful shaking of his head, glanced anxiously towards the door.

It opened; and a little girl, much younger than the boy, came darting in, and putting her arms about his neck, and often kissing him, addressed him as her "Dear, dear brother."

"I have come to bring you home, dear brother!" said the child, clapping her tiny hands, and bending down to laugh. "To bring you home, home, home!"

"Home, little Fan?" returned the boy.

"Yes!" said the child, brimful of glee. "Home, for good and all. Home, forever and ever. Father is so much kinder than he used to be, that home's like Heaven! He spoke so gently to me one dear night when I was going to bed, that I was not afraid to ask him once more if you might come home; and he said Yes, you should; and sent me in a coach to bring you. And you're to be a man!" said the child, opening her eyes, "and are never to come back here; but first, we're to be together all the Christmas long, and have the merriest time in all the world."

"You are quite a woman, little Fan!" exclaimed the boy.

She clapped her hands and laughed, and tried to touch his head; but being too little, laughed again, and stood on tiptoe to embrace him. Then she began to drag him, in her childish eagerness, towards the door; and he, nothing loth to go, accompanied her.

A terrible voice in the hall cried, "Bring down Master Scrooge's box, there!" and in the hall appeared the schoolmaster himself, who glared on Master Scrooge with a ferocious condescension, and threw him into a dreadful state of mind by shaking hands with him. He then conveyed him and his sister into the veriest old well of a shivering best-parlour that ever was seen, where the maps upon the wall, and the celestial and terrestrial globes in the windows, were waxy with cold. Here he produced a decanter of curiously light wine, and a block of curiously heavy cake, and administered instalments of those dainties to the young people: at the same time, sending out a meagre servant to offer a glass of "something" to the postboy, who answered that he thanked the gentleman, but if it was the same tap as he had tasted before, he had rather not. Master Scrooge's trunk being by this time tied on to the top of the chaise, the children bade the schoolmaster good-bye right willingly; and getting into it, drove gaily down the garden-sweep: the quick wheels dashing the hoar-frost and snow from off the dark leaves of the evergreens like spray.

"Always a delicate creature, whom a breath might have withered," said the Ghost. "But she had a large heart!"

"So she had," cried Scrooge. "You're right. I will not gainsay it, Spirit. God forbid!"

"She died a woman," said the Ghost, "and had, as I think, children."

"One child," Scrooge returned.

"True," said the Ghost. "Your nephew!"

Scrooge seemed uneasy in his mind; and answered briefly, "Yes."

Although they had but that moment left the school behind them, they were now in the busy thoroughfares of a city, where shadowy passengers passed and repassed; where shadowy carts and coaches battled for the way, and all the strife and tumult of a real city were. It was made plain enough, by the dressing of the shops, that here too it was Christmas time again; but it was evening, and the streets were lighted up.

The Ghost stopped at a certain warehouse door, and asked Scrooge if he knew it.

"Know it!" said Scrooge. "Was I apprenticed here!"

They went in. At sight of an old gentleman in a Welsh wig, sitting behind such a high desk, that if he had been two inches taller he must have knocked his head against the ceiling, Scrooge cried in great excitement:

"Why, it's old Fezziwig! Bless his heart; it's Fezziwig alive again!"

Old Fezziwig laid down his pen, and looked up at the clock, which pointed to the hour of seven. He rubbed his hands; adjusted his capacious waistcoat; laughed all over himself, from his shoes to his organ of benevolence; and called out in a comfortable, oily, rich, fat, jovial voice:

"Yo ho, there! Ebenezer! Dick!"

Scrooge's former self, now grown a young man, came briskly in, accompanied by his fellow-'prentice.

"Dick Wilkins, to be sure!" said Scrooge to the Ghost. "Bless me, yes. There he is. He was very much attached to me, was Dick. Poor Dick! Dear, dear!"

"Yo ho, my boys!" said Fezziwig. "No more work to-night. Christmas Eve, Dick. Christmas, Ebenezer! Let's have the shutters up," cried old Fezziwig, with a sharp clap of his hands, "before a man can say Jack Robinson!"

You wouldn't believe how those two fellows went at it! They charged into the street with the shutters—one, two, three—had 'em up in their places—four, five, six—barred 'em and pinned 'em—seven, eight, nine—and came back before you could have got to twelve, panting like race-horses.

"Hilli-ho!" cried old Fezziwig, skipping down from the high desk, with wonderful agility. "Clear away, my lads, and let's have lots of room here! Hilli-ho, Dick! Chirrup, Ebenezer!"

Clear away! There was nothing they wouldn't have cleared away, or couldn't have cleared away, with old Fezziwig looking on. It was done in a minute. Every movable was packed off, as if it were dismissed from public life for evermore; the floor was swept and watered, the lamps were trimmed, fuel was heaped upon the fire; and the warehouse was as snug, and warm, and dry, and bright a ball-room, as you would desire to see upon a winter's night.

In came a fiddler with a music-book, and went up to the lofty desk, and made an orchestra of it, and tuned like fifty stomach-aches. In came Mrs. Fezziwig, one vast substantial smile. In came the three Miss Fezziwigs, beaming and lovable. In came the six young followers whose hearts they broke. In came all the young men and women employed in the business. In came the housemaid, with her cousin, the baker. In came the cook, with her brother's particular friend, the milkman. In came the boy from over the way, who was suspected of not having board enough from his master; trying to hide himself behind the girl from next door but one, who was proved to have had her ears pulled by her mistress. In they all came, one after another; some shyly, some boldly, some gracefully, some awkwardly, some pushing, some pulling; in they all came, anyhow and everyhow. Away they all went, twenty couple at once; hands half round and back again the other way; down the middle and up again; round and round in various stages of affectionate grouping; old top couple always turning up in the wrong place; new top couple starting off again, as soon as they got there; all top couples at last, and not a bottom one to help them! When this result was brought about, old Fezziwig, clapping his hands to stop the dance, cried out, "Well done!" and the fiddler plunged his hot face into a pot of porter, especially provided for that purpose. But scorning rest, upon his reappearance, he instantly began again, though there were no dancers yet, as if the other fiddler had been carried home, exhausted, on a shutter, and he were a bran-new man resolved to beat him out of sight, or perish.

There were more dances, and there were forfeits, and more dances, and there was cake, and there was negus, and there was a great piece of Cold Roast, and there was a great piece of Cold Boiled, and there were mince-pies, and plenty of beer. But the great effect of the evening came after the Roast and Boiled, when the fiddler (an artful dog, mind! The sort of man who knew his business better than you or I could have told it him!) struck up "Sir Roger de Coverley." Then old Fezziwig stood out to dance with Mrs. Fezziwig. Top couple, too; with a good stiff piece of work cut out for them; three or four and twenty pair of partners; people who were not to be trifled with; people who would dance, and had no notion of walking.

But if they had been twice as many—ah, four times—old Fezziwig would have been a match for them, and so would Mrs. Fezziwig. As to her, she was worthy to be his partner in every sense of the term. If that's not high praise, tell me higher, and I'll use it. A positive light appeared to issue from Fezziwig's calves. They shone in every part of the dance like moons. You couldn't have predicted, at any given time, what would have become of them next. And when old Fezziwig and Mrs. Fezziwig had gone all through the dance; advance and retire, both hands to your partner, bow and curtsey, corkscrew, thread-the-needle, and back again to your place; Fezziwig "cut"—cut so deftly, that he appeared to wink with his legs, and came upon his feet again without a stagger.

When the clock struck eleven, this domestic ball broke up. Mr. and Mrs. Fezziwig took their stations, one on either side of the door, and shaking hands with every person individually as he or she went out, wished him or her a Merry Christmas. When everybody had retired but the two 'prentices, they did the same to them; and thus the cheerful voices died away, and the lads were left to their beds; which were under a counter in the back-shop.

During the whole of this time, Scrooge had acted like a man out of his wits. His heart and soul were in the scene, and with his former self. He corroborated everything, remembered everything, enjoyed everything, and underwent the strangest agitation. It was not until now, when the bright faces of his former self and Dick were turned from them, that he remembered the Ghost, and became conscious that it was looking full upon him, while the light upon its head burnt very clear.

"A small matter," said the Ghost, "to make these silly folks so full of gratitude."

"Small!" echoed Scrooge.

The Spirit signed to him to listen to the two apprentices, who were pouring out their hearts in praise of Fezziwig: and when he had done so, said,

"Why! Is it not? He has spent but a few pounds of your mortal money: three or four perhaps. Is that so much that he deserves this praise?"

"It isn't that," said Scrooge, heated by the remark, and speaking unconsciously like his former, not his latter, self. "It isn't that, Spirit. He has the power to render us happy or unhappy; to make our service light or burdensome; a pleasure or a toil. Say that his power lies in words and looks; in things so slight and insignificant that it is impossible to add and count 'em up: what then? The happiness he gives, is quite as great as if it cost a fortune."

He felt the Spirit's glance, and stopped.

"What is the matter?" asked the Ghost.

"Nothing particular," said Scrooge.

"Something, I think?" the Ghost insisted.

"No," said Scrooge, "No. I should like to be able to say a word or two to my clerk just now. That's all."

His former self turned down the lamps as he gave utterance to the wish; and Scrooge and the Ghost again stood side by side in the open air.

"My time grows short," observed the Spirit. "Quick!"

This was not addressed to Scrooge, or to any one whom he could see, but it produced an immediate effect. For again Scrooge saw himself. He was older now; a man in the prime of life. His face had not the harsh and rigid lines of later years; but it had begun to wear the signs of care and avarice. There was an eager, greedy, restless motion in the eye, which showed the passion that had taken root, and where the shadow of the growing tree would fall.

He was not alone, but sat by the side of a fair young girl in a mourning-dress: in whose eyes there were tears, which sparkled in the light that shone out of the Ghost of Christmas Past.

"It matters little," she said, softly. "To you, very little. Another idol has displaced me; and if it can cheer and comfort you in time to come, as I would have tried to do, I have no just cause to grieve."

"What Idol has displaced you?" he rejoined.

"A golden one."

"This is the even-handed dealing of the world!" he said. "There is nothing on which it is so hard as poverty; and there is nothing it professes to condemn with such severity as the pursuit of wealth!"

"You fear the world too much," she answered, gently. "All your other hopes have merged into the hope of being beyond the chance of its sordid reproach. I have seen your nobler aspirations fall off one by one, until the master-passion, Gain, engrosses you. Have I not?"

"What then?" he retorted. "Even if I have grown so much wiser, what then? I am not changed towards you."

She shook her head.

"Am I?"

"Our contract is an old one. It was made when we were both poor and content to be so, until, in good season, we could improve our worldly fortune by our patient industry. You are changed. When it was made, you were another man."

"I was a boy," he said impatiently.

"Your own feeling tells you that you were not what you are," she returned. "I am. That which promised happiness when we were one in heart, is fraught with misery now that we are two. How often and how keenly I have thought of this, I will not say. It is enough that I have thought of it, and can release you."

"Have I ever sought release?"

"In words. No. Never."

"In what, then?"

"In a changed nature; in an altered spirit; in another atmosphere of life; another Hope as its great end. In everything that made my love of any worth or value in your sight. If this had never been between us," said the girl, looking mildly, but with steadiness, upon him; "tell me, would you seek me out and try to win me now? Ah, no!"

He seemed to yield to the justice of this supposition, in spite of himself. But he said with a struggle, "You think not."

"I would gladly think otherwise if I could," she answered, "Heaven knows! When I have learned a Truth like this, I know how strong and irresistible it must be. But if you were free to-day, to-morrow, yesterday, can even I believe that you would choose a dowerless girl—you who, in your very confidence with her, weigh everything by Gain: or, choosing her, if for a moment you were false enough to your one guiding principle to do so, do I not know that your repentance and regret would surely follow? I do; and I release you. With a full heart, for the love of him you once were."

He was about to speak; but with her head turned from him, she resumed.

"You may—the memory of what is past half makes me hope you will—have pain in this. A very, very brief time, and you will dismiss the recollection of it, gladly, as an unprofitable dream, from which it happened well that you awoke. May you be happy in the life you have chosen!"

She left him, and they parted.

"Spirit!" said Scrooge, "show me no more! Conduct me home. Why do you delight to torture me?"

"One shadow more!" exclaimed the Ghost.

"No more!" cried Scrooge. "No more. I don't wish to see it. Show me no more!"

But the relentless Ghost pinioned him in both his arms, and forced him to observe what happened next.

They were in another scene and place; a room, not very large or handsome, but full of comfort. Near to the winter fire sat a beautiful young girl, so like that last that Scrooge believed it was the same, until he saw her, now a comely matron, sitting opposite her daughter. The noise in this room was perfectly tumultuous, for there were more children there, than Scrooge in his agitated state of mind could count; and, unlike the celebrated herd in the poem, they were not forty children conducting themselves like one, but every child was conducting itself like forty. The consequences were uproarious beyond belief; but no one seemed to care; on the contrary, the mother and daughter laughed heartily, and enjoyed it very much; and the latter, soon beginning to mingle in the sports, got pillaged by the young brigands most ruthlessly. What would I not have given to be one of them! Though I never could have been so rude, no, no! I wouldn't for the wealth of all the world have crushed that braided hair, and torn it down; and for the precious little shoe, I wouldn't have plucked it off, God bless my soul! to save my life. As to measuring her waist in sport, as they did, bold young brood, I couldn't have done it; I should have expected my arm to have grown round it for a punishment, and never come straight again. And yet I should have dearly liked, I own, to have touched her lips; to have questioned her, that she might have opened them; to have looked upon the lashes of her downcast eyes, and never raised a blush; to have let loose waves of hair, an inch of which would be a keepsake beyond price: in short, I should have liked, I do confess, to have had the lightest licence of a child, and yet to have been man enough to know its value.

But now a knocking at the door was heard, and such a rush immediately ensued that she with laughing face and plundered dress was borne towards it the centre of a flushed and boisterous group, just in time to greet the father, who came home attended by a man laden with Christmas toys and presents. Then the shouting and the struggling, and the onslaught that was made on the defenceless porter! The scaling him with chairs for ladders to dive into his pockets, despoil him of brown-paper parcels, hold on tight by his cravat, hug him round his neck, pommel his back, and kick his legs in irrepressible affection! The shouts of wonder and delight with which the development of every package was received! The terrible announcement that the baby had been taken in the act of putting a doll's frying-pan into his mouth, and was more than suspected of having swallowed a fictitious turkey, glued on a wooden platter! The immense relief of finding this a false alarm! The joy, and gratitude, and ecstasy! They are all indescribable alike. It is enough that by degrees the children and their emotions got out of the parlour, and by one stair at a time, up to the top of the house; where they went to bed, and so subsided.

And now Scrooge looked on more attentively than ever, when the master of the house, having his daughter leaning fondly on him, sat down with her and her mother at his own fireside; and when he thought that such another creature, quite as graceful and as full of promise, might have called him father, and been a spring-time in the haggard winter of his life, his sight grew very dim indeed.

"Belle," said the husband, turning to his wife with a smile, "I saw an old friend of yours this afternoon."

"Who was it?"

"Guess!"

"How can I? Tut, don't I know?" she added in the same breath, laughing as he laughed. "Mr. Scrooge."

"Mr. Scrooge it was. I passed his office window; and as it was not shut up, and he had a candle inside, I could scarcely help seeing him. His partner lies upon the point of death, I hear; and there he sat alone. Quite alone in the world, I do believe."

"Spirit!" said Scrooge in a broken voice, "remove me from this place."

"I told you these were shadows of the things that have been," said the Ghost. "That they are what they are, do not blame me!"

"Remove me!" Scrooge exclaimed, "I cannot bear it!"

He turned upon the Ghost, and seeing that it looked upon him with a face, in which in some strange way there were fragments of all the faces it had shown him, wrestled with it.

"Leave me! Take me back. Haunt me no longer!"

In the struggle, if that can be called a struggle in which the Ghost with no visible resistance on its own part was undisturbed by any effort of its adversary, Scrooge observed that its light was burning high and bright; and dimly connecting that with its influence over him, he seized the extinguisher-cap, and by a sudden action pressed it down upon its head.

The Spirit dropped beneath it, so that the extinguisher covered its whole form; but though Scrooge pressed it down with all his force, he could not hide the light: which streamed from under it, in an unbroken flood upon the ground.

He was conscious of being exhausted, and overcome by an irresistible drowsiness; and, further, of being in his own bedroom. He gave the cap a parting squeeze, in which his hand relaxed; and had barely time to reel to bed, before he sank into a heavy sleep.

STAVE III: THE SECOND OF THE THREE SPIRITS

Awaking in the middle of a prodigiously tough snore, and sitting up in bed to get his thoughts together, Scrooge had no occasion to be told that the bell was again upon the stroke of One. He felt that he was restored to consciousness in the right nick of time, for the especial purpose of holding a conference with the second messenger despatched to him through Jacob Marley's intervention. But, finding that he turned uncomfortably cold when he began to wonder which of his curtains this new spectre would draw back, he put them every one aside with his own hands; and lying down again, established a sharp look-out all round the bed. For he wished to challenge the Spirit on the moment of its appearance, and did not wish to be taken by surprise, and made nervous.

Gentlemen of the free-and-easy sort, who plume themselves on being acquainted with a move or two, and being usually equal to the time-of-day, express the wide range of their capacity for adventure by observing that they are good for anything from pitch-and-toss to manslaughter; between which opposite extremes, no doubt, there lies a tolerably wide and comprehensive range of subjects. Without venturing for Scrooge quite as hardily as this, I don't mind calling on you to believe that he was ready for a good broad field of strange appearances, and that nothing between a baby and rhinoceros would have astonished him very much.

Now, being prepared for almost anything, he was not by any means prepared for nothing; and, consequently, when the Bell struck One, and no shape appeared, he was taken with a violent fit of trembling. Five minutes, ten minutes, a quarter of an hour went by, yet nothing came. All this time, he lay upon his bed, the very core and centre of a blaze of ruddy light, which streamed upon it when the clock proclaimed the hour; and which, being only light, was more alarming than a dozen ghosts, as he was powerless to make out what it meant, or would be at; and was sometimes apprehensive that he might be at that very moment an interesting case of spontaneous combustion, without having the consolation of knowing it. At last, however, he began to think—as you or I would have thought at first; for it is always the person not in the predicament who knows what ought to have been done in it, and would unquestionably have done it too—at last, I say, he began to think that the source and secret of this ghostly light might be in the adjoining room, from whence, on further tracing it, it seemed to shine. This idea taking full possession of his mind, he got up softly and shuffled in his slippers to the door.

The moment Scrooge's hand was on the lock, a strange voice called him by his name, and bade him enter. He obeyed.

It was his own room. There was no doubt about that. But it had undergone a surprising transformation. The walls and ceiling were so hung with living green, that it looked a perfect grove; from every part of which, bright gleaming berries glistened. The crisp leaves of holly, mistletoe, and ivy reflected back the light, as if so many little mirrors had been scattered there; and such a mighty blaze went roaring up the chimney, as that dull petrification of a hearth had never known in Scrooge's time, or Marley's, or for many and many a winter season gone. Heaped up on the floor, to form a kind of throne, were turkeys, geese, game, poultry, brawn, great joints of meat, sucking-pigs, long wreaths of sausages, mince-pies, plum-puddings, barrels of oysters, red-hot chestnuts, cherry-cheeked apples, juicy oranges, luscious pears, immense twelfth-cakes, and seething bowls of punch, that made the chamber dim with their delicious steam. In easy state upon this couch, there sat a jolly Giant, glorious to see; who bore a glowing torch, in shape not unlike Plenty's horn, and held it up, high up, to shed its light on Scrooge, as he came peeping round the door.

"Come in!" exclaimed the Ghost. "Come in! and know me better, man!"

Scrooge entered timidly, and hung his head before this Spirit. He was not the dogged Scrooge he had been; and though the Spirit's eyes were clear and kind, he did not like to meet them.

"I am the Ghost of Christmas Present," said the Spirit. "Look upon me!"

Scrooge reverently did so. It was clothed in one simple green robe, or mantle, bordered with white fur. This garment hung so loosely on the figure, that its capacious breast was bare, as if disdaining to be warded or concealed by any artifice. Its feet, observable beneath the ample folds of the garment, were also bare; and on its head it wore no other covering than a holly wreath, set here and there with shining icicles. Its dark brown curls were long and free; free as its genial face, its sparkling eye, its open hand, its cheery voice, its unconstrained demeanour, and its joyful air. Girded round its middle was an antique scabbard; but no sword was in it, and the ancient sheath was eaten up with rust.

"You have never seen the like of me before!" exclaimed the Spirit.

"Never," Scrooge made answer to it.

"Have never walked forth with the younger members of my family; meaning (for I am very young) my elder brothers born in these later years?" pursued the Phantom.

"I don't think I have," said Scrooge. "I am afraid I have not. Have you had many brothers, Spirit?"

"More than eighteen hundred," said the Ghost.

"A tremendous family to provide for!" muttered Scrooge.

The Ghost of Christmas Present rose.

"Spirit," said Scrooge submissively, "conduct me where you will. I went forth last night on compulsion, and I learnt a lesson which is working now. To-night, if you have aught to teach me, let me profit by it."

"Touch my robe!"

Scrooge did as he was told, and held it fast.

Holly, mistletoe, red berries, ivy, turkeys, geese, game, poultry, brawn, meat, pigs, sausages, oysters, pies, puddings, fruit, and punch, all vanished instantly. So did the room, the fire, the ruddy glow, the hour of night, and they stood in the city streets on Christmas morning, where (for the weather was severe) the people made a rough, but brisk and not unpleasant kind of music, in scraping the snow from the pavement in front of their dwellings, and from the tops of their houses, whence it was mad delight to the boys to see it come plumping down into the road below, and splitting into artificial little snow-storms.

The house fronts looked black enough, and the windows blacker, contrasting with the smooth white sheet of snow upon the roofs, and with the dirtier snow upon the ground; which last deposit had been ploughed up in deep furrows by the heavy wheels of carts and waggons; furrows that crossed and re-crossed each other hundreds of times where the great streets branched off; and made intricate channels, hard to trace in the thick yellow mud and icy water. The sky was gloomy, and the shortest streets were choked up with a dingy mist, half thawed, half frozen, whose heavier particles descended in a shower of sooty atoms, as if all the chimneys in Great Britain had, by one consent, caught fire, and were blazing away to their dear hearts' content. There was nothing very cheerful in the climate or the town, and yet was there an air of cheerfulness abroad that the clearest summer air and brightest summer sun might have endeavoured to diffuse in vain.

For, the people who were shovelling away on the housetops were jovial and full of glee; calling out to one another from the parapets, and now and then exchanging a facetious snowball better-natured missile far than many a wordy jest—laughing heartily if it went right and not less heartily if it went wrong. The poulterers' shops were still half open, and the fruiterers' were radiant in their glory. There were great, round, pot-bellied baskets of chestnuts, shaped like the waistcoats of jolly old gentlemen, lolling at the doors, and tumbling out into the street in their apoplectic opulence. There were ruddy, brown-faced, broad-girthed Spanish Onions, shining in the fatness of their growth like Spanish Friars, and winking from their shelves in wanton slyness at the girls as they went by, and glanced demurely at the hung-up mistletoe. There were pears and apples, clustered high in blooming pyramids; there were bunches of grapes, made, in the shopkeepers' benevolence to dangle from conspicuous hooks, that people's mouths might water gratis as they passed; there were piles of filberts, mossy and brown, recalling, in their fragrance, ancient walks among the woods, and pleasant shufflings ankle deep through withered leaves; there were Norfolk Biffins, squab and swarthy, setting off the yellow of the oranges and lemons, and, in the great compactness of their juicy persons, urgently entreating and beseeching to be carried home in paper bags and eaten after dinner. The very gold and silver fish, set forth among these choice fruits in a bowl, though members of a dull and stagnant-blooded race, appeared to know that there was something going on; and, to a fish, went gasping round and round their little world in slow and passionless excitement.

The Grocers'! oh, the Grocers'! nearly closed, with perhaps two shutters down, or one; but through those gaps such glimpses! It was not alone that the scales descending on the counter made a merry sound, or that the twine and roller parted company so briskly, or that the canisters were rattled up and down like juggling tricks, or even that the blended scents of tea and coffee were so grateful to the nose, or even that the raisins were so plentiful and rare, the almonds so extremely white, the sticks of cinnamon so long and straight, the other spices so delicious, the candied fruits so caked and spotted with molten sugar as to make the coldest lookers-on feel faint and subsequently bilious. Nor was it that the figs were moist and pulpy, or that the French plums blushed in modest tartness from their highly-decorated boxes, or that everything was good to eat and in its Christmas dress; but the customers were all so hurried and so eager in the hopeful promise of the day, that they tumbled up against each other at the door, crashing their wicker baskets wildly, and left their purchases upon the counter, and came running back to fetch them, and committed hundreds of the like mistakes, in the best humour possible; while the Grocer and his people were so frank and fresh that the polished hearts with which they fastened their aprons behind might have been their own, worn outside for general inspection, and for Christmas daws to peck at if they chose.

But soon the steeples called good people all, to church and chapel, and away they came, flocking through the streets in their best clothes, and with their gayest faces. And at the same time there emerged from scores of by-streets, lanes, and nameless turnings, innumerable people, carrying their dinners to the bakers' shops. The sight of these poor revellers appeared to interest the Spirit very much, for he stood with Scrooge beside him in a baker's doorway, and taking off the covers as their bearers passed, sprinkled incense on their dinners from his torch. And it was a very uncommon kind of torch, for once or twice when there were angry words between some dinner-carriers who had jostled each other, he shed a few drops of water on them from it, and their good humour was restored directly. For they said, it was a shame to quarrel upon Christmas Day. And so it was! God love it, so it was!

In time the bells ceased, and the bakers were shut up; and yet there was a genial shadowing forth of all these dinners and the progress of their cooking, in the thawed blotch of wet above each baker's oven; where the pavement smoked as if its stones were cooking too.

"Is there a peculiar flavour in what you sprinkle from your torch?" asked Scrooge.

"There is. My own."

"Would it apply to any kind of dinner on this day?" asked Scrooge.

"To any kindly given. To a poor one most."

"Why to a poor one most?" asked Scrooge.

"Because it needs it most."

"Spirit," said Scrooge, after a moment's thought, "I wonder you, of all the beings in the many worlds about us, should desire to cramp these people's opportunities of innocent enjoyment."

"I!" cried the Spirit.

"You would deprive them of their means of dining every seventh day, often the only day on which they can be said to dine at all," said Scrooge. "Wouldn't you?"

"I!" cried the Spirit.

"You seek to close these places on the Seventh Day?" said Scrooge. "And it comes to the same thing."

"I seek!" exclaimed the Spirit.

"Forgive me if I am wrong. It has been done in your name, or at least in that of your family," said Scrooge.

"There are some upon this earth of yours," returned the Spirit, "who lay claim to know us, and who do their deeds of passion, pride, ill-will, hatred, envy, bigotry, and selfishness in our name, who are as strange to us and all our kith and kin, as if they had never lived. Remember that, and charge their doings on themselves, not us."

Scrooge promised that he would; and they went on, invisible, as they had been before, into the suburbs of the town. It was a remarkable quality of the Ghost (which Scrooge had observed at the baker's), that notwithstanding his gigantic size, he could accommodate himself to any place with ease; and that he stood beneath a low roof quite as gracefully and like a supernatural creature, as it was possible he could have done in any lofty hall.

And perhaps it was the pleasure the good Spirit had in showing off this power of his, or else it was his own kind, generous, hearty nature, and his sympathy with all poor men, that led him straight to Scrooge's clerk's; for there he went, and took Scrooge with him, holding to his robe; and on the threshold of the door the Spirit smiled, and stopped to bless Bob Cratchit's dwelling with the sprinkling of his torch. Think of that! Bob had but fifteen "Bob" a-week himself; he pocketed on Saturdays but fifteen copies of his Christian name; and yet the Ghost of Christmas Present blessed his four-roomed house!

Then up rose Mrs. Cratchit, Cratchit's wife, dressed out but poorly in a twice-turned gown, but brave in ribbons, which are cheap and make a goodly show for sixpence; and she laid the cloth, assisted by Belinda Cratchit, second of her daughters, also brave in ribbons; while Master Peter Cratchit plunged a fork into the saucepan of potatoes, and getting the corners of his monstrous shirt collar (Bob's private property, conferred upon his son and heir in honour of the day) into his mouth, rejoiced to find himself so gallantly attired, and yearned to show his linen in the fashionable Parks. And now two smaller Cratchits, boy and girl, came tearing in, screaming that outside the baker's they had smelt the goose, and known it for their own; and basking in luxurious thoughts of sage and onion, these young Cratchits danced about the table, and exalted Master Peter Cratchit to the skies, while he (not proud, although his collars nearly choked him) blew the fire, until the slow potatoes bubbling up, knocked loudly at the saucepan-lid to be let out and peeled.

"What has ever got your precious father then?" said Mrs. Cratchit. "And your brother, Tiny Tim! And Martha warn't as late last Christmas Day by half an hour?"

"Here's Martha, mother!" said a girl, appearing as she spoke.

"Here's Martha, mother!" cried the two young Cratchits. "Hurrah! There's such a goose, Martha!"

"Why, bless your heart alive, my dear, how late you are!" said Mrs. Cratchit, kissing her a dozen times, and taking off her shawl and bonnet for her with officious zeal.

"We'd a deal of work to finish up last night," replied the girl, "and had to clear away this morning, mother!"

"Well! Never mind so long as you are come," said Mrs. Cratchit. "Sit ye down before the fire, my dear, and have a warm, Lord bless ye!"

"No, no! There's father coming," cried the two young Cratchits, who were everywhere at once. "Hide, Martha, hide!"

So Martha hid herself, and in came little Bob, the father, with at least three feet of comforter exclusive of the fringe, hanging down before him; and his threadbare clothes darned up and brushed, to look seasonable; and Tiny Tim upon his shoulder. Alas for Tiny Tim, he bore a little crutch, and had his limbs supported by an iron frame!

"Why, where's our Martha?" cried Bob Cratchit, looking round.

"Not coming," said Mrs. Cratchit.

"Not coming!" said Bob, with a sudden declension in his high spirits; for he had been Tim's blood horse all the way from church, and had come home rampant. "Not coming upon Christmas Day!"

Martha didn't like to see him disappointed, if it were only in joke; so she came out prematurely from behind the closet door, and ran into his arms, while the two young Cratchits hustled Tiny Tim, and bore him off into the wash-house, that he might hear the pudding singing in the copper.

"And how did little Tim behave?" asked Mrs. Cratchit, when she had rallied Bob on his credulity, and Bob had hugged his daughter to his heart's content.

"As good as gold," said Bob, "and better. Somehow he gets thoughtful, sitting by himself so much, and thinks the strangest things you ever heard. He told me, coming home, that he hoped the people saw him in the church, because he was a cripple, and it might be pleasant to them to remember upon Christmas Day, who made lame beggars walk, and blind men see."

Bob's voice was tremulous when he told them this, and trembled more when he said that Tiny Tim was growing strong and hearty.

His active little crutch was heard upon the floor, and back came Tiny Tim before another word was spoken, escorted by his brother and sister to his stool before the fire; and while Bob, turning up his cuffs—as if, poor fellow, they were capable of being made more shabby—compounded some hot mixture in a jug with gin and lemons, and stirred it round and round and put it on the hob to simmer; Master Peter, and the two ubiquitous young Cratchits went to fetch the goose, with which they soon returned in high procession.

Such a bustle ensued that you might have thought a goose the rarest of all birds; a feathered phenomenon, to which a black swan was a matter of course and in truth it was something very like it in that house. Mrs. Cratchit made the gravy (ready beforehand in a little saucepan) hissing hot; Master Peter mashed the potatoes with incredible vigour; Miss Belinda sweetened up the apple-sauce; Martha dusted the hot plates; Bob took Tiny Tim beside him in a tiny corner at the table; the two young Cratchits set chairs for everybody, not forgetting themselves, and mounting guard upon their posts, crammed spoons into their mouths, lest they should shriek for goose before their turn came to be helped. At last the dishes were set on, and grace was said. It was succeeded by a breathless pause, as Mrs. Cratchit, looking slowly all along the carving-knife, prepared to plunge it in the breast; but when she did, and when the long expected gush of stuffing issued forth, one murmur of delight arose all round the board, and even Tiny Tim, excited by the two young Cratchits, beat on the table with the handle of his knife, and feebly cried Hurrah!

There never was such a goose. Bob said he didn't believe there ever was such a goose cooked. Its tenderness and flavour, size and cheapness, were the themes of universal admiration. Eked out by apple-sauce and mashed potatoes, it was a sufficient dinner for the whole family; indeed, as Mrs. Cratchit said with great delight (surveying one small atom of a bone upon the dish), they hadn't ate it all at last! Yet every one had had enough, and the youngest Cratchits in particular, were steeped in sage and onion to the eyebrows! But now, the plates being changed by Miss Belinda, Mrs. Cratchit left the room alone—too nervous to bear witnesses—to take the pudding up and bring it in.

Suppose it should not be done enough! Suppose it should break in turning out! Suppose somebody should have got over the wall of the back-yard, and stolen it, while they were merry with the goose—a supposition at which the two young Cratchits became livid! All sorts of horrors were supposed.

Hallo! A great deal of steam! The pudding was out of the copper. A smell like a washing-day! That was the cloth. A smell like an eating-house and a pastrycook's next door to each other, with a laundress's next door to that! That was the pudding! In half a minute Mrs. Cratchit entered—flushed, but smiling proudly—with the pudding, like a speckled cannon-ball, so hard and firm, blazing in half of half-a-quartern of ignited brandy, and bedight with Christmas holly stuck into the top.

"Oh, a wonderful pudding!" Bob Cratchit said, and calmly too, that he regarded it as the greatest success achieved by Mrs. Cratchit since their marriage. Mrs. Cratchit said that now the weight was off her mind, she would confess she had had her doubts about the quantity of flour. Everybody had something to say about it, but nobody said or thought it was at all a small pudding for a large family. It would have been flat heresy to do so. Any Cratchit would have blushed to hint at such a thing.

At last the dinner was all done, the cloth was cleared, the hearth swept, and the fire made up. The compound in the jug being tasted, and considered perfect, apples and oranges were put upon the table, and a shovel-full of chestnuts on the fire. Then all the Cratchit family drew round the hearth, in what Bob Cratchit called a circle, meaning half a one; and at Bob Cratchit's elbow stood the family display of glass. Two tumblers, and a custard-cup without a handle.

These held the hot stuff from the jug, however, as well as golden goblets would have done; and Bob served it out with beaming looks, while the chestnuts on the fire sputtered and cracked noisily. Then Bob proposed:

"A Merry Christmas to us all, my dears. God bless us!"

Which all the family re-echoed.

"God bless us every one!" said Tiny Tim, the last of all.

He sat very close to his father's side upon his little stool. Bob held his withered little hand in his, as if he loved the child, and wished to keep him by his side, and dreaded that he might be taken from him.

"Spirit," said Scrooge, with an interest he had never felt before, "tell me if Tiny Tim will live."

"I see a vacant seat," replied the Ghost, "in the poor chimney-corner, and a crutch without an owner, carefully preserved. If these shadows remain unaltered by the Future, the child will die."

"No, no," said Scrooge. "Oh, no, kind Spirit! say he will be spared."

"If these shadows remain unaltered by the Future, none other of my race," returned the Ghost, "will find him here. What then? If he be like to die, he had better do it, and decrease the surplus population."

Scrooge hung his head to hear his own words quoted by the Spirit, and was overcome with penitence and grief.

"Man," said the Ghost, "if man you be in heart, not adamant, forbear that wicked cant until you have discovered What the surplus is, and Where it is. Will you decide what men shall live, what men shall die? It may be, that in the sight of Heaven, you are more worthless and less fit to live than millions like this poor man's child. Oh God! to hear the Insect on the leaf pronouncing on the too much life among his hungry brothers in the dust!"

Scrooge bent before the Ghost's rebuke, and trembling cast his eyes upon the ground. But he raised them speedily, on hearing his own name.

"Mr. Scrooge!" said Bob; "I'll give you Mr. Scrooge, the Founder of the Feast!"

"The Founder of the Feast indeed!" cried Mrs. Cratchit, reddening. "I wish I had him here. I'd give him a piece of my mind to feast upon, and I hope he'd have a good appetite for it."

"My dear," said Bob, "the children! Christmas Day."

"It should be Christmas Day, I am sure," said she, "on which one drinks the health of such an odious, stingy, hard, unfeeling man as Mr. Scrooge. You know he is, Robert! Nobody knows it better than you do, poor fellow!"

"My dear," was Bob's mild answer, "Christmas Day."

"I'll drink his health for your sake and the Day's," said Mrs. Cratchit, "not for his. Long life to him! A merry Christmas and a happy new year! He'll be very merry and very happy, I have no doubt!"

The children drank the toast after her. It was the first of their proceedings which had no heartiness. Tiny Tim drank it last of all, but he didn't care twopence for it. Scrooge was the Ogre of the family. The mention of his name cast a dark shadow on the party, which was not dispelled for full five minutes.

After it had passed away, they were ten times merrier than before, from the mere relief of Scrooge the Baleful being done with. Bob Cratchit told them how he had a situation in his eye for Master Peter, which would bring in, if obtained, full five-and-sixpence weekly. The two young Cratchits laughed tremendously at the idea of Peter's being a man of business; and Peter himself looked thoughtfully at the fire from between his collars, as if he were deliberating what particular investments he should favour when he came into the receipt of that bewildering income. Martha, who was a poor apprentice at a milliner's, then told them what kind of work she had to do, and how many hours she worked at a stretch, and how she meant to lie abed to-morrow morning for a good long rest; tomorrow being a holiday she passed at home. Also how she had seen a countess and a lord some days before, and how the lord "was much about as tall as Peter"; at which Peter pulled up his collars so high that you couldn't have seen his head if you had been there. All this time the chestnuts and the jug went round and round; and by and by they had a song, about a lost child travelling in the snow, from Tiny Tim, who had a plaintive little voice, and sang it very well indeed.

There was nothing of high mark in this. They were not a handsome family; they were not well dressed; their shoes were far from being water-proof; their clothes were scanty; and Peter might have known, and very likely did, the inside of a pawnbroker's. But, they were happy, grateful, pleased with one another, and contented with the time; and when they faded, and looked happier yet in the bright sprinklings of the Spirit's torch at parting, Scrooge had his eye upon them, and especially on Tiny Tim, until the last.

By this time it was getting dark, and snowing pretty heavily; and as Scrooge and the Spirit went along the streets, the brightness of the roaring fires in kitchens, parlours, and all sorts of rooms, was wonderful. Here, the flickering of the blaze showed preparations for a cosy dinner, with hot plates baking through and through before the fire, and deep red curtains, ready to be drawn to shut out cold and darkness. There all the children of the house were running out into the snow to meet their married sisters, brothers, cousins, uncles, aunts, and be the first to greet them. Here, again, were shadows on the window-blind of guests assembling; and there a group of handsome girls, all hooded and fur-booted, and all chattering at once, tripped lightly off to some near neighbour's house; where, woe upon the single man who saw them enter—artful witches, well they knew it—in a glow!

But, if you had judged from the numbers of people on their way to friendly gatherings, you might have thought that no one was at home to give them welcome when they got there, instead of every house expecting company, and piling up its fires half-chimney high. Blessings on it, how the Ghost exulted! How it bared its breadth of breast, and opened its capacious palm, and floated on, outpouring, with a generous hand, its bright and harmless mirth on everything within its reach! The very lamplighter, who ran on before, dotting the dusky street with specks of light, and who was dressed to spend the evening somewhere, laughed out loudly as the Spirit passed, though little kenned the lamplighter that he had any company but Christmas!

And now, without a word of warning from the Ghost, they stood upon a bleak and desert moor, where monstrous masses of rude stone were cast about, as though it were the burial-place of giants; and water spread itself wheresoever it listed, or would have done so, but for the frost that held it prisoner; and nothing grew but moss and furze, and coarse rank grass. Down in the west the setting sun had left a streak of fiery red, which glared upon the desolation for an instant, like a sullen eye, and frowning lower, lower, lower yet, was lost in the thick gloom of darkest night.

"What place is this?" asked Scrooge.

"A place where Miners live, who labour in the bowels of the earth," returned the Spirit. "But they know me. See!"

A light shone from the window of a hut, and swiftly they advanced towards it. Passing through the wall of mud and stone, they found a cheerful company assembled round a glowing fire. An old, old man and woman, with their children and their children's children, and another generation beyond that, all decked out gaily in their holiday attire. The old man, in a voice that seldom rose above the howling of the wind upon the barren waste, was singing them a Christmas song— it had been a very old song when he was a boy—and from time to time they all joined in the chorus. So surely as they raised their voices, the old man got quite blithe and loud; and so surely as they stopped, his vigour sank again.

The Spirit did not tarry here, but bade Scrooge hold his robe, and passing on above the moor, sped—whither? Not to sea? To sea. To Scrooge's horror, looking back, he saw the last of the land, a frightful range of rocks, behind them; and his ears were deafened by the thundering of water, as it rolled and roared, and raged among the dreadful caverns it had worn, and fiercely tried to undermine the earth.

Built upon a dismal reef of sunken rocks, some league or so from shore, on which the waters chafed and dashed, the wild year through, there stood a solitary lighthouse. Great heaps of sea-weed clung to its base, and storm-birds—born of the wind one might suppose, as sea-weed of the water—rose and fell about it, like the waves they skimmed.

But even here, two men who watched the light had made a fire, that through the loophole in the thick stone wall shed out a ray of brightness on the awful sea. Joining their horny hands over the rough table at which they sat, they wished each other Merry Christmas in their can of grog; and one of them: the elder, too, with his face all damaged and scarred with hard weather, as the figure-head of an old ship might be: struck up a sturdy song that was like a Gale in itself.

Again the Ghost sped on, above the black and heaving sea on, on until, being far away, as he told Scrooge, from any shore, they lighted on a ship. They stood beside the helmsman at the wheel, the look-out in the bow, the officers who had the watch; dark, ghostly figures in their several stations; but every man among them hummed a Christmas tune, or had a Christmas thought, or spoke below his breath to his companion of some bygone Christmas Day, with homeward hopes belonging to it. And every man on board, waking or sleeping, good or bad, had had a kinder word for another on that day than on any day in the year; and had shared to some extent in its festivities; and had remembered those he cared for at a distance, and had known that they delighted to remember him.

It was a great surprise to Scrooge, while listening to the moaning of the wind, and thinking what a solemn thing it was to move on through the lonely darkness over an unknown abyss, whose depths were secrets as profound as Death: it was a great surprise to Scrooge, while thus engaged, to hear a hearty laugh. It was a much greater surprise to Scrooge to recognise it as his own nephew's and to find himself in a bright, dry, gleaming room, with the Spirit standing smiling by his side, and looking at that same nephew with approving affability!

"Ha, ha!" laughed Scrooge's nephew. "Ha, ha, ha!"

If you should happen, by any unlikely chance, to know a man more blest in a laugh than Scrooge's nephew, all I can say is, I should like to know him too. Introduce him to me, and I'll cultivate his acquaintance.

It is a fair, even-handed, noble adjustment of things, that while there is infection in disease and sorrow, there is nothing in the world so irresistibly contagious as laughter and good-humour. When Scrooge's nephew laughed in this way: holding his sides, rolling his head, and twisting his face into the most extravagant contortions: Scrooge's niece, by marriage, laughed as heartily as he. And their assembled friends being not a bit behindhand, roared out lustily.

"Ha, ha! Ha, ha, ha, ha!"

"He said that Christmas was a humbug, as I live!" cried Scrooge's nephew. "He believed it too!"

"More shame for him, Fred!" said Scrooge's niece, indignantly. Bless those women; they never do anything by halves. They are always in earnest.

She was very pretty: exceedingly pretty. With a dimpled, surprised-looking, capital face; a ripe little mouth, that seemed made to be kissed—as no doubt it was; all kinds of good little dots about her chin, that melted into one another when she laughed; and the sunniest pair of eyes you ever saw in any little creature's head. Altogether she was what you would have called provoking, you know; but satisfactory, too. Oh, perfectly satisfactory.

"He's a comical old fellow," said Scrooge's nephew, "that's the truth: and not so pleasant as he might be. However, his offences carry their own punishment, and I have nothing to say against him."

"I'm sure he is very rich, Fred," hinted Scrooge's niece. "At least you always tell me so."

"What of that, my dear!" said Scrooge's nephew. "His wealth is of no use to him. He don't do any good with it. He don't make himself comfortable with it. He hasn't the satisfaction of thinking—ha, ha, ha!—that he is ever going to benefit Us with it."

"I have no patience with him," observed Scrooge's niece. Scrooge's niece's sisters, and all the other ladies, expressed the same opinion.

"Oh, I have!" said Scrooge's nephew. "I am sorry for him; I couldn't be angry with him if I tried. Who suffers by his ill whims! Himself, always. Here, he takes it into his head to dislike us, and he won't come and dine with us. What's the consequence? He don't lose much of a dinner."

"Indeed, I think he loses a very good dinner," interrupted Scrooge's niece. Everybody else said the same, and they must be allowed to have been competent judges, because they had just had dinner; and, with the dessert upon the table, were clustered round the fire, by lamplight.

"Well! I'm very glad to hear it," said Scrooge's nephew, "because I haven't great faith in these young housekeepers. What do you say, Topper?"

Topper had clearly got his eye upon one of Scrooge's niece's sisters, for he answered that a bachelor was a wretched outcast, who had no right to express an opinion on the subject. Whereat Scrooge's niece's sister—the plump one with the lace tucker: not the one with the roses—blushed.

"Do go on, Fred," said Scrooge's niece, clapping her hands. "He never finishes what he begins to say! He is such a ridiculous fellow!"

Scrooge's nephew revelled in another laugh, and as it was impossible to keep the infection off; though the plump sister tried hard to do it with aromatic vinegar; his example was unanimously followed.

"I was only going to say," said Scrooge's nephew, "that the consequence of his taking a dislike to us, and not making merry with us, is, as I think, that he loses some pleasant moments, which could do him no harm. I am sure he loses pleasanter companions than he can find in his own thoughts, either in his mouldy old office, or his dusty chambers. I mean to give him the same chance every year, whether he likes it or not, for I pity him. He may rail at Christmas till he dies, but he can't help thinking better of it—I defy him—if he finds me going there, in good temper, year after year, and saying 'Uncle Scrooge, how are you?' If it only puts him in the vein to leave his poor clerk fifty pounds, that's something; and I think I shook him yesterday."

It was their turn to laugh now at the notion of his shaking Scrooge. But being thoroughly good-natured, and not much caring what they laughed at, so that they laughed at any rate, he encouraged them in their merriment, and passed the bottle joyously.

After tea, they had some music. For they were a musical family, and knew what they were about, when they sung a Glee or Catch, I can assure you: especially Topper, who could growl away in the bass like a good one, and never swell the large veins in his forehead, or get red in the face over it. Scrooge's niece played well upon the harp; and played among other tunes a simple little air (a mere nothing: you might learn to whistle it in two minutes), which had been familiar to the child who fetched Scrooge from the boarding-school, as he had been reminded by the Ghost of Christmas Past. When this strain of music sounded, all the things that Ghost had shown him, came upon his mind; he softened more and more; and thought that if he could have listened to it often, years ago, he might have cultivated the kindnesses of life for his own happiness with his own hands, without resorting to the sexton's spade that buried Jacob Marley.

But they didn't devote the whole evening to music. After a while they played at forfeits; for it is good to be children sometimes, and never better than at Christmas, when its mighty Founder was a child himself. Stop! There was first a game at blind-man's buff. Of course there was. And I no more believe Topper was really blind than I believe he had eyes in his boots. My opinion is, that it was a done thing between him and Scrooge's nephew; and that the Ghost of Christmas Present knew it. The way he went after that plump sister in the lace tucker, was an outrage on the credulity of human nature. Knocking down the fire-irons, tumbling over the chairs, bumping against the piano, smothering himself among the curtains, wherever she went, there went he! He always knew where the plump sister was. He wouldn't catch anybody else. If you had fallen up against him (as some of them did), on purpose, he would have made a feint of endeavouring to seize you, which would have been an affront to your understanding, and would instantly have sidled off in the direction of the plump sister. She often cried out that it wasn't fair; and it really was not. But when at last, he caught her; when, in spite of all her silken rustlings, and her rapid flutterings past him, he got her into a corner whence there was no escape; then his conduct was the most execrable. For his pretending not to know her; his pretending that it was necessary to touch her head-dress, and further to assure himself of her identity by pressing a certain ring upon her finger, and a certain chain about her neck; was vile, monstrous! No doubt she told him her opinion of it, when, another blind man being in office, they were so very confidential together, behind the curtains.

Scrooge's niece was not one of the blind-man's buff party, but was made comfortable with a large chair and a footstool, in a snug corner, where the Ghost and Scrooge were close behind her. But she joined in the forfeits, and loved her love to admiration with all the letters of the alphabet. Likewise at the game of How, When, and Where, she was very great, and to the secret joy of Scrooge's nephew, beat her sisters hollow: though they were sharp girls too, as Topper could have told you. There might have been twenty people there, young and old, but they all played, and so did Scrooge; for wholly forgetting in the interest he had in what was going on, that his voice made no sound in their ears, he sometimes came out with his guess quite loud, and very often guessed quite right, too; for the sharpest needle, best Whitechapel, warranted not to cut in the eye, was not sharper than Scrooge; blunt as he took it in his head to be.

The Ghost was greatly pleased to find him in this mood, and looked upon him with such favour, that he begged like a boy to be allowed to stay until the guests departed. But this the Spirit said could not be done.

"Here is a new game," said Scrooge. "One half hour, Spirit, only one!"

It was a Game called Yes and No, where Scrooge's nephew had to think of something, and the rest must find out what; he only answering to their questions yes or no, as the case was. The brisk fire of questioning to which he was exposed, elicited from him that he was thinking of an animal, a live animal, rather a disagreeable animal, a savage animal, an animal that growled and grunted sometimes, and talked sometimes, and lived in London, and walked about the streets, and wasn't made a show of, and wasn't led by anybody, and didn't live in a menagerie, and was never killed in a market, and was not a horse, or an ass, or a cow, or a bull, or a tiger, or a dog, or a pig, or a cat, or a bear. At every fresh question that was put to him, this nephew burst into a fresh roar of laughter; and was so inexpressibly tickled, that he was obliged to get up off the sofa and stamp. At last the plump sister, falling into a similar state, cried out:

"I have found it out! I know what it is, Fred! I know what it is!"

"What is it?" cried Fred.

"It's your Uncle Scro-o-o-o-oge!"

Which it certainly was. Admiration was the universal sentiment, though some objected that the reply to "Is it a bear?" ought to have been "Yes"; inasmuch as an answer in the negative was sufficient to have diverted their thoughts from Mr. Scrooge, supposing they had ever had any tendency that way.

"He has given us plenty of merriment, I am sure," said Fred, "and it would be ungrateful not to drink his health. Here is a glass of mulled wine ready to our hand at the moment; and I say, 'Uncle Scrooge!'?"

"Well! Uncle Scrooge!" they cried.

"A Merry Christmas and a Happy New Year to the old man, whatever he is!" said Scrooge's nephew. "He wouldn't take it from me, but may he have it, nevertheless. Uncle Scrooge!"

Uncle Scrooge had imperceptibly become so gay and light of heart, that he would have pledged the unconscious company in return, and thanked them in an inaudible speech, if the Ghost had given him time. But the whole scene passed off in the breath of the last word spoken by his nephew; and he and the Spirit were again upon their travels.

Much they saw, and far they went, and many homes they visited, but always with a happy end. The Spirit stood beside sick beds, and they were cheerful; on foreign lands, and they were close at home; by struggling men, and they were patient in their greater hope; by poverty, and it was rich. In almshouse, hospital, and jail, in misery's every refuge, where vain man in his little brief authority had not made fast the door, and barred the Spirit out, he left his blessing, and taught Scrooge his precepts.

It was a long night, if it were only a night; but Scrooge had his doubts of this, because the Christmas Holidays appeared to be condensed into the space of time they passed together. It was strange, too, that while Scrooge remained unaltered in his outward form, the Ghost grew older, clearly older. Scrooge had observed this change, but never spoke of it, until they left a children's Twelfth Night party, when, looking at the Spirit as they stood together in an open place, he noticed that its hair was grey.

"Are spirits' lives so short?" asked Scrooge.

"My life upon this globe, is very brief," replied the Ghost. "It ends to-night."

"To-night!" cried Scrooge.

"To-night at midnight. Hark! The time is drawing near."

The chimes were ringing the three quarters past eleven at that moment.

"Forgive me if I am not justified in what I ask," said Scrooge, looking intently at the Spirit's robe, "but I see something strange, and not belonging to yourself, protruding from your skirts. Is it a foot or a claw?"

"It might be a claw, for the flesh there is upon it," was the Spirit's sorrowful reply. "Look here."

From the foldings of its robe, it brought two children; wretched, abject, frightful, hideous, miserable. They knelt down at its feet, and clung upon the outside of its garment.

"Oh, Man! look here. Look, look, down here!" exclaimed the Ghost.

They were a boy and girl. Yellow, meagre, ragged, scowling, wolfish; but prostrate, too, in their humility. Where graceful youth should have filled their features out, and touched them with its freshest tints, a stale and shrivelled hand, like that of age, had pinched, and twisted them, and pulled them into shreds. Where angels might have sat enthroned, devils lurked, and glared out menacing. No change, no degradation, no perversion of humanity, in any grade, through all the mysteries of wonderful creation, has monsters half so horrible and dread.

Scrooge started back, appalled. Having them shown to him in this way, he tried to say they were fine children, but the words choked themselves, rather than be parties to a lie of such enormous magnitude.

"Spirit! are they yours?" Scrooge could say no more.

"They are Man's," said the Spirit, looking down upon them. "And they cling to me, appealing from their fathers. This boy is Ignorance. This girl is Want. Beware them both, and all of their degree, but most of all beware this boy, for on his brow I see that written which is Doom, unless the writing be erased. Deny it!" cried the Spirit, stretching out its hand towards the city. "Slander those who tell it ye! Admit it for your factious purposes, and make it worse. And bide the end!"

"Have they no refuge or resource?" cried Scrooge.

"Are there no prisons?" said the Spirit, turning on him for the last time with his own words. "Are there no workhouses?"

The bell struck twelve.

Scrooge looked about him for the Ghost, and saw it not. As the last stroke ceased to vibrate, he remembered the prediction of old Jacob Marley, and lifting up his eyes, beheld a solemn Phantom, draped and hooded, coming, like a mist along the ground, towards him.

STAVE IV: THE LAST OF THE SPIRITS

The Phantom slowly, gravely, silently, approached. When it came near him, Scrooge bent down upon his knee; for in the very air through which this Spirit moved it seemed to scatter gloom and mystery.

It was shrouded in a deep black garment, which concealed its head, its face, its form, and left nothing of it visible save one outstretched hand. But for this it would have been difficult to detach its figure from the night, and separate it from the darkness by which it was surrounded.

He felt that it was tall and stately when it came beside him, and that its mysterious presence filled him with a solemn dread. He knew no more, for the Spirit neither spoke nor moved.

"I am in the presence of the Ghost of Christmas Yet To Come?" said Scrooge.

The Spirit answered not, but pointed onward with its hand.

"You are about to show me shadows of the things that have not happened, but will happen in the time before us," Scrooge pursued. "Is that so, Spirit?"

The upper portion of the garment was contracted for an instant in its folds, as if the Spirit had inclined its head. That was the only answer he received.

Although well used to ghostly company by this time, Scrooge feared the silent shape so much that his legs trembled beneath him, and he found that he could hardly stand when he prepared to follow it. The Spirit paused a moment, as observing his condition, and giving him time to recover.

But Scrooge was all the worse for this. It thrilled him with a vague uncertain horror, to know that behind the dusky shroud, there were ghostly eyes intently fixed upon him, while he, though he stretched his own to the utmost, could see nothing but a spectral hand and one great heap of black.

"Ghost of the Future!" he exclaimed, "I fear you more than any spectre I have seen. But as I know your purpose is to do me good, and as I hope to live to be another man from what I was, I am prepared to bear you company, and do it with a thankful heart. Will you not speak to me?"

It gave him no reply. The hand was pointed straight before them.

"Lead on!" said Scrooge. "Lead on! The night is waning fast, and it is precious time to me, I know. Lead on, Spirit!"

The Phantom moved away as it had come towards him. Scrooge followed in the shadow of its dress, which bore him up, he thought, and carried him along.

They scarcely seemed to enter the city; for the city rather seemed to spring up about them, and encompass them of its own act. But there they were, in the heart of it; on 'Change, amongst the merchants; who hurried up and down, and chinked the money in their pockets, and conversed in groups, and looked at their watches, and trifled thoughtfully with their great gold seals; and so forth, as Scrooge had seen them often.

The Spirit stopped beside one little knot of business men. Observing that the hand was pointed to them, Scrooge advanced to listen to their talk.

"No," said a great fat man with a monstrous chin, "I don't know much about it, either way. I only know he's dead."

"When did he die?" inquired another.

"Last night, I believe."

"Why, what was the matter with him?" asked a third, taking a vast quantity of snuff out of a very large snuff-box. "I thought he'd never die."

"God knows," said the first, with a yawn.

"What has he done with his money?" asked a red-faced gentleman with a pendulous excrescence on the end of his nose, that shook like the gills of a turkey-cock.

"I haven't heard," said the man with the large chin, yawning again. "Left it to his company, perhaps. He hasn't left it to me. That's all I know."

This pleasantry was received with a general laugh.

"It's likely to be a very cheap funeral," said the same speaker; "for upon my life I don't know of anybody to go to it. Suppose we make up a party and volunteer?"

"I don't mind going if a lunch is provided," observed the gentleman with the excrescence on his nose. "But I must be fed, if I make one."

Another laugh.

"Well, I am the most disinterested among you, after all," said the first speaker, "for I never wear black gloves, and I never eat lunch. But I'll offer to go, if anybody else will. When I come to think of it, I'm not at all sure that I wasn't his most particular friend; for we used to stop and speak whenever we met. Bye, bye!"

Speakers and listeners strolled away, and mixed with other groups. Scrooge knew the men, and looked towards the Spirit for an explanation.

The Phantom glided on into a street. Its finger pointed to two persons meeting. Scrooge listened again, thinking that the explanation might lie here.

He knew these men, also, perfectly. They were men of business: very wealthy, and of great importance. He had made a point always of standing well in their esteem: in a business point of view, that is; strictly in a business point of view.

"How are you?" said one.

"How are you?" returned the other.

"Well!" said the first. "Old Scratch has got his own at last, hey?"

"So I am told," returned the second. "Cold, isn't it?"

"Seasonable for Christmas time. You're not a skater, I suppose?"

"No. No. Something else to think of. Good morning!"

Not another word. That was their meeting, their conversation, and their parting.

Scrooge was at first inclined to be surprised that the Spirit should attach importance to conversations apparently so trivial; but feeling assured that they must have some hidden purpose, he set himself to consider what it was likely to be. They could scarcely be supposed to have any bearing on the death of Jacob, his old partner, for that was Past, and this Ghost's province was the Future. Nor could he think of any one immediately connected with himself, to whom he could apply them. But nothing doubting that to whomsoever they applied they had some latent moral for his own improvement, he resolved to treasure up every word he heard, and everything he saw; and especially to observe the shadow of himself when it appeared. For he had an expectation that the conduct of his future self would give him the clue he missed, and would render the solution of these riddles easy.

He looked about in that very place for his own image; but another man stood in his accustomed corner, and though the clock pointed to his usual time of day for being there, he saw no likeness of himself among the multitudes that poured in through the porch. It gave him little surprise, however; for he had been revolving in his mind a change of life, and thought and hoped he saw his new-born resolutions carried out in this.

Quiet and dark, beside him stood the Phantom, with its outstretched hand. When he roused himself from his thoughtful quest, he fancied from the turn of the hand, and its situation in reference to himself, that the Unseen Eyes were looking at him keenly. It made him shudder, and feel very cold.

They left the busy scene, and went into an obscure part of the town, where Scrooge had never penetrated before, although he recognised its situation, and its bad repute. The ways were foul and narrow; the shops and houses wretched; the people half-naked, drunken, slipshod, ugly. Alleys and archways, like so many cesspools, disgorged their offences of smell, and dirt, and life, upon the straggling streets; and the whole quarter reeked with crime, with filth, and misery.

Far in this den of infamous resort, there was a low-browed, beetling shop, below a pent-house roof, where iron, old rags, bottles, bones, and greasy offal, were bought. Upon the floor within, were piled up heaps of rusty keys, nails, chains, hinges, files, scales, weights, and refuse iron of all kinds. Secrets that few would like to scrutinise were bred and hidden in mountains of unseemly rags, masses of corrupted fat, and sepulchres of bones. Sitting in among the wares he dealt in, by a charcoal stove, made of old bricks, was a grey-haired rascal, nearly seventy years of age; who had screened himself from the cold air without, by a frousy curtaining of miscellaneous tatters, hung upon a line; and smoked his pipe in all the luxury of calm retirement.

Scrooge and the Phantom came into the presence of this man, just as a woman with a heavy bundle slunk into the shop. But she had scarcely entered, when another woman, similarly laden, came in too; and she was closely followed by a man in faded black, who was no less startled by the sight of them, than they had been upon the recognition of each other. After a short period of blank astonishment, in which the old man with the pipe had joined them, they all three burst into a laugh.

"Let the charwoman alone to be the first!" cried she who had entered first. "Let the laundress alone to be the second; and let the undertaker's man alone to be the third. Look here, old Joe, here's a chance! If we haven't all three met here without meaning it!"

"You couldn't have met in a better place," said old Joe, removing his pipe from his mouth. "Come into the parlour. You were made free of it long ago, you know; and the other two an't strangers. Stop till I shut the door of the shop. Ah! How it skreeks! There an't such a rusty bit of metal in the place as its own hinges, I believe; and I'm sure there's no such old bones here, as mine. Ha, ha! We're all suitable to our calling, we're well matched. Come into the parlour. Come into the parlour."

The parlour was the space behind the screen of rags. The old man raked the fire together with an old stair-rod, and having trimmed his smoky lamp (for it was night), with the stem of his pipe, put it in his mouth again.

While he did this, the woman who had already spoken threw her bundle on the floor, and sat down in a flaunting manner on a stool; crossing her elbows on her knees, and looking with a bold defiance at the other two.

"What odds then! What odds, Mrs. Dilber?" said the woman. "Every person has a right to take care of themselves. He always did."

"That's true, indeed!" said the laundress. "No man more so."

"Why then, don't stand staring as if you was afraid, woman; who's the wiser? We're not going to pick holes in each other's coats, I suppose?"

"No, indeed!" said Mrs. Dilber and the man together. "We should hope not."

"Very well, then!" cried the woman. "That's enough. Who's the worse for the loss of a few things like these? Not a dead man, I suppose."

"No, indeed," said Mrs. Dilber, laughing.

"If he wanted to keep 'em after he was dead, a wicked old screw," pursued the woman, "why wasn't he natural in his lifetime? If he had been, he'd have had somebody to look after him when he was struck with Death, instead of lying gasping out his last there, alone by himself."

"It's the truest word that ever was spoke," said Mrs. Dilber. "It's a judgment on him."

"I wish it was a little heavier judgment," replied the woman; "and it should have been, you may depend upon it, if I could have laid my hands on anything else. Open that bundle, old Joe, and let me know the value of it. Speak out plain. I'm not afraid to be the first, nor afraid for them to see it. We know pretty well that we were helping ourselves, before we met here, I believe. It's no sin. Open the bundle, Joe."

But the gallantry of her friends would not allow of this; and the man in faded black, mounting the breach first, produced his plunder. It was not extensive. A seal or two, a pencil-case, a pair of sleeve-buttons, and a brooch of no great value, were all. They were severally examined and appraised by old Joe, who chalked the sums he was disposed to give for each, upon the wall, and added them up into a total when he found there was nothing more to come.

"That's your account," said Joe, "and I wouldn't give another sixpence, if I was to be boiled for not doing it. Who's next?"

Mrs. Dilber was next. Sheets and towels, a little wearing apparel, two old-fashioned silver teaspoons, a pair of sugar-tongs, and a few boots. Her account was stated on the wall in the same manner.

"I always give too much to ladies. It's a weakness of mine, and that's the way I ruin myself," said old Joe. "That's your account. If you asked me for another penny, and made it an open question, I'd repent of being so liberal and knock off half-a-crown."

"And now undo my bundle, Joe," said the first woman.

Joe went down on his knees for the greater convenience of opening it, and having unfastened a great many knots, dragged out a large and heavy roll of some dark stuff.

"What do you call this?" said Joe. "Bed-curtains!"

"Ah!" returned the woman, laughing and leaning forward on her crossed arms. "Bed-curtains!"

"You don't mean to say you took 'em down, rings and all, with him lying there?" said Joe.

"Yes I do," replied the woman. "Why not?"

"You were born to make your fortune," said Joe, "and you'll certainly do it."

"I certainly shan't hold my hand, when I can get anything in it by reaching it out, for the sake of such a man as He was, I promise you, Joe," returned the woman coolly. "Don't drop that oil upon the blankets, now."

"His blankets?" asked Joe.

"Whose else's do you think?" replied the woman. "He isn't likely to take cold without 'em, I dare say."

"I hope he didn't die of anything catching? Eh?" said old Joe, stopping in his work, and looking up.

"Don't you be afraid of that," returned the woman. "I an't so fond of his company that I'd loiter about him for such things, if he did. Ah! you may look through that shirt till your eyes ache; but you won't find a hole in it, nor a threadbare place. It's the best he had, and a fine one too. They'd have wasted it, if it hadn't been for me."

"What do you call wasting of it?" asked old Joe.

"Putting it on him to be buried in, to be sure," replied the woman with a laugh. "Somebody was fool enough to do it, but I took it off again. If calico an't good enough for such a purpose, it isn't good enough for anything. It's quite as becoming to the body. He can't look uglier than he did in that one."

Scrooge listened to this dialogue in horror. As they sat grouped about their spoil, in the scanty light afforded by the old man's lamp, he viewed them with a detestation and disgust, which could hardly have been greater, though they had been obscene demons, marketing the corpse itself.

"Ha, ha!" laughed the same woman, when old Joe, producing a flannel bag with money in it, told out their several gains upon the ground. "This is the end of it, you see! He frightened every one away from him when he was alive, to profit us when he was dead! Ha, ha, ha!"

"Spirit!" said Scrooge, shuddering from head to foot. "I see, I see. The case of this unhappy man might be my own. My life tends that way, now. Merciful Heaven, what is this!"

He recoiled in terror, for the scene had changed, and now he almost touched a bed: a bare, uncurtained bed: on which, beneath a ragged sheet, there lay a something covered up, which, though it was dumb, announced itself in awful language.

The room was very dark, too dark to be observed with any accuracy, though Scrooge glanced round it in obedience to a secret impulse, anxious to know what kind of room it was. A pale light, rising in the outer air, fell straight upon the bed; and on it, plundered and bereft, unwatched, unwept, uncared for, was the body of this man.

Scrooge glanced towards the Phantom. Its steady hand was pointed to the head. The cover was so carelessly adjusted that the slightest raising of it, the motion of a finger upon Scrooge's part, would have disclosed the face. He thought of it, felt how easy it would be to do, and longed to do it; but had no more power to withdraw the veil than to dismiss the spectre at his side.

Oh cold, cold, rigid, dreadful Death, set up thine altar here, and dress it with such terrors as thou hast at thy command: for this is thy dominion! But of the loved, revered, and honoured head, thou canst not turn one hair to thy dread purposes, or make one feature odious. It is not that the hand is heavy and will fall down when released; it is not that the heart and pulse are still; but that the hand was open, generous, and true; the heart brave, warm, and tender; and the pulse a man's. Strike, Shadow, strike! And see his good deeds springing from the wound, to sow the world with life immortal!

No voice pronounced these words in Scrooge's ears, and yet he heard them when he looked upon the bed. He thought, if this man could be raised up now, what would be his foremost thoughts? Avarice, hard-dealing, griping cares? They have brought him to a rich end, truly!

He lay, in the dark empty house, with not a man, a woman, or a child, to say that he was kind to me in this or that, and for the memory of one kind word I will be kind to him. A cat was tearing at the door, and there was a sound of gnawing rats beneath the hearth-stone. What they wanted in the room of death, and why they were so restless and disturbed, Scrooge did not dare to think.

"Spirit!" he said, "this is a fearful place. In leaving it, I shall not leave its lesson, trust me. Let us go!"

Still the Ghost pointed with an unmoved finger to the head.

"I understand you," Scrooge returned, "and I would do it, if I could. But I have not the power, Spirit. I have not the power."

Again it seemed to look upon him.

"If there is any person in the town, who feels emotion caused by this man's death," said Scrooge quite agonised, "show that person to me, Spirit, I beseech you!"

The Phantom spread its dark robe before him for a moment, like a wing; and withdrawing it, revealed a room by daylight, where a mother and her children were.

She was expecting some one, and with anxious eagerness; for she walked up and down the room; started at every sound; looked out from the window; glanced at the clock; tried, but in vain, to work with her needle; and could hardly bear the voices of the children in their play.

At length the long-expected knock was heard. She hurried to the door, and met her husband; a man whose face was careworn and depressed, though he was young. There was a remarkable expression in it now; a kind of serious delight of which he felt ashamed, and which he struggled to repress.

He sat down to the dinner that had been hoarding for him by the fire; and when she asked him faintly what news (which was not until after a long silence), he appeared embarrassed how to answer.

"Is it good?" she said, "or bad?" to help him.

"Bad," he answered.

"We are quite ruined?"

"No. There is hope yet, Caroline."

"If he relents," she said, amazed, "there is! Nothing is past hope, if such a miracle has happened."

"He is past relenting," said her husband. "He is dead."

She was a mild and patient creature if her face spoke truth; but she was thankful in her soul to hear it, and she said so, with clasped hands. She prayed forgiveness the next moment, and was sorry; but the first was the emotion of her heart.

"What the half-drunken woman whom I told you of last night, said to me, when I tried to see him and obtain a week's delay; and what I thought was a mere excuse to avoid me; turns out to have been quite true. He was not only very ill, but dying, then."

"To whom will our debt be transferred?"

"I don't know. But before that time we shall be ready with the money; and even though we were not, it would be a bad fortune indeed to find so merciless a creditor in his successor. We may sleep to-night with light hearts, Caroline!"

Yes. Soften it as they would, their hearts were lighter. The children's faces, hushed and clustered round to hear what they so little understood, were brighter; and it was a happier house for this man's death! The only emotion that the Ghost could show him, caused by the event, was one of pleasure.

"Let me see some tenderness connected with a death," said Scrooge; "or that dark chamber, Spirit, which we left just now, will be forever present to me."

The Ghost conducted him through several streets familiar to his feet; and as they went along, Scrooge looked here and there to find himself, but nowhere was he to be seen. They entered poor Bob Cratchit's house; the dwelling he had visited before; and found the mother and the children seated round the fire.

Quiet. Very quiet. The noisy little Cratchits were as still as statues in one corner, and sat looking up at Peter, who had a book before him. The mother and her daughters were engaged in sewing. But surely they were very quiet!

"And He took a child, and set him in the midst of them."

Where had Scrooge heard those words? He had not dreamed them. The boy must have read them out, as he and the Spirit crossed the threshold. Why did he not go on?

The mother laid her work upon the table, and put her hand up to her face.

"The colour hurts my eyes," she said.

The colour? Ah, poor Tiny Tim!

"They're better now again," said Cratchit's wife. "It makes them weak by candle-light; and I wouldn't show weak eyes to your father when he comes home, for the world. It must be near his time."

"Past it rather," Peter answered, shutting up his book. "But I think he has walked a little slower than he used, these few last evenings, mother."

They were very quiet again. At last she said, and in a steady, cheerful voice, that only faltered once:

"I have known him walk with—I have known him walk with Tiny Tim upon his shoulder, very fast indeed."

"And so have I," cried Peter. "Often."

"And so have I," exclaimed another. So had all.

"But he was very light to carry," she resumed, intent upon her work, "and his father loved him so, that it was no trouble: no trouble. And there is your father at the door!"

She hurried out to meet him; and little Bob in his comforter—he had need of it, poor fellow—came in. His tea was ready for him on the hob, and they all tried who should help him to it most. Then the two young Cratchits got upon his knees and laid, each child a little cheek, against his face, as if they said, "Don't mind it, father. Don't be grieved!"

Bob was very cheerful with them, and spoke pleasantly to all the family. He looked at the work upon the table, and praised the industry and speed of Mrs. Cratchit and the girls. They would be done long before Sunday, he said.

"Sunday! You went to-day, then, Robert?" said his wife.

"Yes, my dear," returned Bob. "I wish you could have gone. It would have done you good to see how green a place it is. But you'll see it often. I promised him that I would walk there on a Sunday. My little, little child!" cried Bob. "My little child!"

He broke down all at once. He couldn't help it. If he could have helped it, he and his child would have been farther apart perhaps than they were.

He left the room, and went upstairs into the room above, which was lighted cheerfully, and hung with Christmas. There was a chair set close beside the child, and there were signs of some one having been there, lately. Poor Bob sat down in it, and when he had thought a little and composed himself, he kissed the little face. He was reconciled to what had happened, and went down again quite happy.

They drew about the fire, and talked; the girls and mother working still. Bob told them of the extraordinary kindness of Mr. Scrooge's nephew, whom he had scarcely seen but once, and who, meeting him in the street that day, and seeing that he looked a little—"just a little down you know," said Bob, inquired what had happened to distress him. "On which," said Bob, "for he is the pleasantest-spoken gentleman you ever heard, I told him. 'I am heartily sorry for it, Mr. Cratchit,' he said, 'and heartily sorry for your good wife.' By the bye, how he ever knew that, I don't know."

"Knew what, my dear?"

"Why, that you were a good wife," replied Bob.

"Everybody knows that!" said Peter.

"Very well observed, my boy!" cried Bob. "I hope they do. 'Heartily sorry,' he said, 'for your good wife. If I can be of service to you in any way,' he said, giving me his card, 'that's where I live. Pray come to me.' Now, it wasn't," cried Bob, "for the sake of anything he might be able to do for us, so much as for his kind way, that this was quite delightful. It really seemed as if he had known our Tiny Tim, and felt with us."

"I'm sure he's a good soul!" said Mrs. Cratchit.

"You would be surer of it, my dear," returned Bob, "if you saw and spoke to him. I shouldn't be at all surprised mark what I say! if he got Peter a better situation."

"Only hear that, Peter," said Mrs. Cratchit.

"And then," cried one of the girls, "Peter will be keeping company with some one, and setting up for himself."

"Get along with you!" retorted Peter, grinning.

"It's just as likely as not," said Bob, "one of these days; though there's plenty of time for that, my dear. But however and whenever we part from one another, I am sure we shall none of us forget poor Tiny Tim—shall we—or this first parting that there was among us?"

"Never, father!" cried they all.

"And I know," said Bob, "I know, my dears, that when we recollect how patient and how mild he was; although he was a little, little child; we shall not quarrel easily among ourselves, and forget poor Tiny Tim in doing it."

"No, never, father!" they all cried again.

"I am very happy," said little Bob, "I am very happy!"

Mrs. Cratchit kissed him, his daughters kissed him, the two young Cratchits kissed him, and Peter and himself shook hands. Spirit of Tiny Tim, thy childish essence was from God!

"Spectre," said Scrooge, "something informs me that our parting moment is at hand. I know it, but I know not how. Tell me what man that was whom we saw lying dead?"

The Ghost of Christmas Yet To Come conveyed him, as before—though at a different time, he thought: indeed, there seemed no order in these latter visions, save that they were in the Future—into the resorts of business men, but showed him not himself. Indeed, the Spirit did not stay for anything, but went straight on, as to the end just now desired, until besought by Scrooge to tarry for a moment.

"This court," said Scrooge, "through which we hurry now, is where my place of occupation is, and has been for a length of time. I see the house. Let me behold what I shall be, in days to come!"

The Spirit stopped; the hand was pointed elsewhere.

"The house is yonder," Scrooge exclaimed. "Why do you point away?"

The inexorable finger underwent no change.

Scrooge hastened to the window of his office, and looked in. It was an office still, but not his. The furniture was not the same, and the figure in the chair was not himself. The Phantom pointed as before.

He joined it once again, and wondering why and whither he had gone, accompanied it until they reached an iron gate. He paused to look round before entering.

A churchyard. Here, then; the wretched man whose name he had now to learn, lay underneath the ground. It was a worthy place. Walled in by houses; overrun by grass and weeds, the growth of vegetation's death, not life; choked up with too much burying; fat with repleted appetite. A worthy place!

The Spirit stood among the graves, and pointed down to One. He advanced towards it trembling. The Phantom was exactly as it had been, but he dreaded that he saw new meaning in its solemn shape.

"Before I draw nearer to that stone to which you point," said Scrooge, "answer me one question. Are these the shadows of the things that Will be, or are they shadows of things that May be, only?"

Still the Ghost pointed downward to the grave by which it stood.

"Men's courses will foreshadow certain ends, to which, if persevered in, they must lead," said Scrooge. "But if the courses be departed from, the ends will change. Say it is thus with what you show me!"

The Spirit was immovable as ever.

Scrooge crept towards it, trembling as he went; and following the finger, read upon the stone of the neglected grave his own name, EBENEZER SCROOGE.

"Am I that man who lay upon the bed?" he cried, upon his knees.

The finger pointed from the grave to him, and back again.

"No, Spirit! Oh no, no!"

The finger still was there.

"Spirit!" he cried, tight clutching at its robe, "hear me! I am not the man I was. I will not be the man I must have been but for this intercourse. Why show me this, if I am past all hope!"

For the first time the hand appeared to shake.

"Good Spirit," he pursued, as down upon the ground he fell before it: "Your nature intercedes for me, and pities me. Assure me that I yet may change these shadows you have shown me, by an altered life!"

The kind hand trembled.

"I will honour Christmas in my heart, and try to keep it all the year. I will live in the Past, the Present, and the Future. The Spirits of all Three shall strive within me. I will not shut out the lessons that they teach. Oh, tell me I may sponge away the writing on this stone!"

In his agony, he caught the spectral hand. It sought to free itself, but he was strong in his entreaty, and detained it. The Spirit, stronger yet, repulsed him.

Holding up his hands in a last prayer to have his fate reversed, he saw an alteration in the Phantom's hood and dress. It shrunk, collapsed, and dwindled down into a bedpost.

STAVE V: THE END OF IT

Yes! and the bedpost was his own. The bed was his own, the room was his own. Best and happiest of all, the Time before him was his own, to make amends in!

"I will live in the Past, the Present, and the Future!" Scrooge repeated, as he scrambled out of bed. "The Spirits of all Three shall strive within me. Oh Jacob Marley! Heaven, and the Christmas Time be praised for this! I say it on my knees, old Jacob; on my knees!"

He was so fluttered and so glowing with his good intentions, that his broken voice would scarcely answer to his call. He had been sobbing violently in his conflict with the Spirit, and his face was wet with tears.

"They are not torn down," cried Scrooge, folding one of his bed-curtains in his arms, "they are not torn down, rings and all. They are here—I am here—the shadows of the things that would have been, may be dispelled. They will be. I know they will!"

His hands were busy with his garments all this time; turning them inside out, putting them on upside down, tearing them, mislaying them, making them parties to every kind of extravagance.

"I don't know what to do!" cried Scrooge, laughing and crying in the same breath; and making a perfect Laocoön of himself with his stockings. "I am as light as a feather, I am as happy as an angel, I am as merry as a schoolboy. I am as giddy as a drunken man. A merry Christmas to everybody! A happy New Year to all the world. Hallo here! Whoop! Hallo!"

He had frisked into the sitting-room, and was now standing there: perfectly winded.

"There's the saucepan that the gruel was in!" cried Scrooge, starting off again, and going round the fireplace. "There's the door, by which the Ghost of Jacob Marley entered! There's the corner where the Ghost of Christmas Present, sat! There's the window where I saw the wandering Spirits! It's all right, it's all true, it all happened. Ha ha ha!"

Really, for a man who had been out of practice for so many years, it was a splendid laugh, a most illustrious laugh. The father of a long, long line of brilliant laughs!

"I don't know what day of the month it is!" said Scrooge. "I don't know how long I've been among the Spirits. I don't know anything. I'm quite a baby. Never mind. I don't care. I'd rather be a baby. Hallo! Whoop! Hallo here!"

He was checked in his transports by the churches ringing out the lustiest peals he had ever heard. Clash, clang, hammer; ding, dong, bell. Bell, dong, ding; hammer, clang, clash! Oh, glorious, glorious!

Running to the window, he opened it, and put out his head. No fog, no mist; clear, bright, jovial, stirring, cold; cold, piping for the blood to dance to; Golden sunlight; Heavenly sky; sweet fresh air; merry bells. Oh, glorious! Glorious!

"What's to-day!" cried Scrooge, calling downward to a boy in Sunday clothes, who perhaps had loitered in to look about him.

"Eh?" returned the boy, with all his might of wonder.

"What's to-day, my fine fellow?" said Scrooge.

"To-day!" replied the boy. "Why, Christmas Day."

"It's Christmas Day!" said Scrooge to himself. "I haven't missed it. The Spirits have done it all in one night. They can do anything they like. Of course they can. Of course they can. Hallo, my fine fellow!"

"Hallo!" returned the boy.

"Do you know the Poulterer's, in the next street but one, at the corner?" Scrooge inquired.

"I should hope I did," replied the lad.

"An intelligent boy!" said Scrooge. "A remarkable boy! Do you know whether they've sold the prize Turkey that was hanging up there? Not the little prize Turkey: the big one?"

"What, the one as big as me?" returned the boy.

"What a delightful boy!" said Scrooge. "It's a pleasure to talk to him. Yes, my buck!"

"It's hanging there now," replied the boy.

"Is it?" said Scrooge. "Go and buy it."

"Walk-er!" exclaimed the boy.

"No, no," said Scrooge, "I am in earnest. Go and buy it, and tell 'em to bring it here, that I may give them the direction where to take it. Come back with the man, and I'll give you a shilling. Come back with him in less than five minutes and I'll give you half-a-crown!"

The boy was off like a shot. He must have had a steady hand at a trigger who could have got a shot off half so fast.

"I'll send it to Bob Cratchit's!" whispered Scrooge, rubbing his hands, and splitting with a laugh. "He shan't know who sends it. It's twice the size of Tiny Tim. Joe Miller never made such a joke as sending it to Bob's will be!"

The hand in which he wrote the address was not a steady one, but write it he did, somehow, and went downstairs to open the street door, ready for the coming of the poulterer's man. As he stood there, waiting his arrival, the knocker caught his eye.

"I shall love it, as long as I live!" cried Scrooge, patting it with his hand. "I scarcely ever looked at it before. What an honest expression it has in its face! It's a wonderful knocker!—Here's the Turkey! Hallo! Whoop! How are you! Merry Christmas!"

It was a Turkey! He never could have stood upon his legs, that bird. He would have snapped 'em short off in a minute, like sticks of sealing-wax.

"Why, it's impossible to carry that to Camden Town," said Scrooge. "You must have a cab."

The chuckle with which he said this, and the chuckle with which he paid for the Turkey, and the chuckle with which he paid for the cab, and the chuckle with which he recompensed the boy, were only to be exceeded by the chuckle with which he sat down breathless in his chair again, and chuckled till he cried.

Shaving was not an easy task, for his hand continued to shake very much; and shaving requires attention, even when you don't dance while you are at it. But if he had cut the end of his nose off, he would have put a piece of sticking-plaister over it, and been quite satisfied.

He dressed himself "all in his best," and at last got out into the streets. The people were by this time pouring forth, as he had seen them with the Ghost of Christmas Present; and walking with his hands behind him, Scrooge regarded every one with a delighted smile. He looked so irresistibly pleasant, in a word, that three or four good-humoured fellows said, "Good morning, sir! A merry Christmas to you!" And Scrooge said often afterwards, that of all the blithe sounds he had ever heard, those were the blithest in his ears.

He had not gone far, when coming on towards him he beheld the portly gentleman, who had walked into his counting-house the day before, and said, "Scrooge and Marley's, I believe?" It sent a pang across his heart to think how this old gentleman would look upon him when they met; but he knew what path lay straight before him, and he took it.

"My dear sir," said Scrooge, quickening his pace, and taking the old gentleman by both his hands. "How do you do? I hope you succeeded yesterday. It was very kind of you. A merry Christmas to you, sir!"

"Mr. Scrooge?"

"Yes," said Scrooge. "That is my name, and I fear it may not be pleasant to you. Allow me to ask your pardon. And will you have the goodness"—here Scrooge whispered in his ear.

"Lord bless me!" cried the gentleman, as if his breath were taken away. "My dear Mr. Scrooge, are you serious?"

"If you please," said Scrooge. "Not a farthing less. A great many back-payments are included in it, I assure you. Will you do me that favour?"

"My dear sir," said the other, shaking hands with him. "I don't know what to say to such munifi—"

"Don't say anything, please," retorted Scrooge. "Come and see me. Will you come and see me?"

"I will!" cried the old gentleman. And it was clear he meant to do it.

"Thank 'ee," said Scrooge. "I am much obliged to you. I thank you fifty times. Bless you!"

He went to church, and walked about the streets, and watched the people hurrying to and fro, and patted children on the head, and questioned beggars, and looked down into the kitchens of houses, and up to the windows, and found that everything could yield him pleasure. He had never dreamed that any walk that anything could give him so much happiness. In the afternoon he turned his steps towards his nephew's house.

He passed the door a dozen times, before he had the courage to go up and knock. But he made a dash, and did it:

"Is your master at home, my dear?" said Scrooge to the girl. Nice girl! Very.

"Yes, sir."

"Where is he, my love?" said Scrooge.

"He's in the dining-room, sir, along with mistress. I'll show you upstairs, if you please."

"Thank 'ee. He knows me," said Scrooge, with his hand already on the dining-room lock. "I'll go in here, my dear."

He turned it gently, and sidled his face in, round the door. They were looking at the table (which was spread out in great array); for these young housekeepers are always nervous on such points, and like to see that everything is right.

"Fred!" said Scrooge.

Dear heart alive, how his niece by marriage started! Scrooge had forgotten, for the moment, about her sitting in the corner with the footstool, or he wouldn't have done it, on any account.

"Why bless my soul!" cried Fred, "who's that?"

"It's I. Your uncle Scrooge. I have come to dinner. Will you let me in, Fred?"

Let him in! It is a mercy he didn't shake his arm off. He was at home in five minutes. Nothing could be heartier. His niece looked just the same. So did Topper when he came. So did the plump sister when she came. So did every one when they came. Wonderful party, wonderful games, wonderful unanimity, wonderful happiness!

But he was early at the office next morning. Oh, he was early there. If he could only be there first, and catch Bob Cratchit coming late! That was the thing he had set his heart upon.

And he did it; yes, he did! The clock struck nine. No Bob. A quarter past. No Bob. He was full eighteen minutes and a half behind his time. Scrooge sat with his door wide open, that he might see him come into the Tank.

His hat was off, before he opened the door; his comforter too. He was on his stool in a jiffy; driving away with his pen, as if he were trying to overtake nine o'clock.

"Hallo!" growled Scrooge, in his accustomed voice, as near as he could feign it. "What do you mean by coming here at this time of day?"

"I am very sorry, sir," said Bob. "I am behind my time."

"You are?" repeated Scrooge. "Yes. I think you are. Step this way, sir, if you please."

"It's only once a year, sir," pleaded Bob, appearing from the Tank. "It shall not be repeated. I was making rather merry yesterday, sir."

"Now, I'll tell you what, my friend," said Scrooge, "I am not going to stand this sort of thing any longer. And therefore," he continued, leaping from his stool, and giving Bob such a dig in the waistcoat that he staggered back into the Tank again; "and therefore I am about to raise your salary!"

Bob trembled, and got a little nearer to the ruler. He had a momentary idea of knocking Scrooge down with it, holding him, and calling to the people in the court for help and a strait-waistcoat.

"A merry Christmas, Bob!" said Scrooge, with an earnestness that could not be mistaken, as he clapped him on the back. "A merrier Christmas, Bob, my good fellow, than I have given you, for many a year! I'll raise your salary, and endeavour to assist your struggling family, and we will discuss your affairs this very afternoon, over a Christmas bowl of smoking bishop, Bob! Make up the fires, and buy another coal-scuttle before you dot another i, Bob Cratchit!"

Scrooge was better than his word. He did it all, and infinitely more; and to Tiny Tim, who did not die, he was a second father. He became as good a friend, as good a master, and as good a man, as the good old city knew, or any other good old city, town, or borough, in the good old world. Some people laughed to see the alteration in him, but he let them laugh, and little heeded them; for he was wise enough to know that nothing ever happened on this globe, for good, at which some people did not have their fill of laughter in the outset; and knowing that such as these would be blind anyway, he thought it quite as well that they should wrinkle up their eyes in grins, as have the malady in less attractive forms. His own heart laughed: and that was quite enough for him.

He had no further intercourse with Spirits, but lived upon the Total Abstinence Principle, ever afterwards; and it was always said of him, that he knew how to keep Christmas well, if any man alive possessed the knowledge. May that be truly said of us, and all of us! And so, as Tiny Tim observed, God bless Us, Every One!

The Chimes

Charles Dickens

CHAPTER I. FIRST QUARTER

There are not many people—and as it is desirable that a story-teller and a story-reader should establish a mutual understanding as soon as possible, I beg it to be noticed that I confine this observation neither to young people nor to little people, but extend it to all conditions of people: little and big, young and old: yet growing up, or already growing down again—there are not, I say, many people who would care to sleep in a church. I don't mean at sermon-time in warm weather (when the thing has actually been done, once or twice), but in the night, and alone. A great multitude of persons will be violently astonished, I know, by this position, in the broad bold Day. But it applies to Night. It must be argued by night, and I will undertake to maintain it successfully on any gusty winter's night appointed for the purpose, with any one opponent chosen from the rest, who will meet me singly in an old churchyard, before an old church-door; and will previously empower me to lock him in, if needful to his satisfaction, until morning.

For the night-wind has a dismal trick of wandering round and round a building of that sort, and moaning as it goes; and of trying, with its unseen hand, the windows and the doors; and seeking out some crevices by which to enter. And when it has got in; as one not finding what it seeks, whatever that may be, it wails and howls to issue forth again: and not content with stalking through the aisles, and gliding round and round the pillars, and tempting the deep organ, soars up to the roof, and strives to rend the rafters: then flings itself despairingly upon the stones below, and passes, muttering, into the vaults. Anon, it comes up stealthily, and creeps along the walls, seeming to read, in whispers, the Inscriptions sacred to the Dead. At some of these, it breaks out shrilly, as with laughter; and at others, moans and cries as if it were lamenting. It has a ghostly sound too, lingering within the altar; where it seems to chaunt, in its wild way, of Wrong and Murder done, and false Gods worshipped, in defiance of the Tables of the Law, which look so fair and smooth, but are so flawed and broken. Ugh! Heaven preserve us, sitting snugly round the fire! It has an awful voice, that wind at Midnight, singing in a church!

But, high up in the steeple! There the foul blast roars and whistles! High up in the steeple, where it is free to come and go through many an airy arch and loophole, and to twist and twine itself about the giddy stair, and twirl the groaning weathercock, and make the very tower shake and shiver! High up in the steeple, where the belfry is, and iron rails are ragged with rust, and sheets of lead and copper, shrivelled by the changing weather, crackle and heave beneath the unaccustomed tread; and birds stuff shabby nests into corners of old oaken joists and beams; and dust grows old and grey; and speckled spiders, indolent and fat with long security, swing idly to and fro in the vibration of the bells, and never loose their hold upon their thread-spun castles in the air, or climb up sailor-like in quick alarm, or drop upon the ground and ply a score of nimble legs to save one life! High up in the steeple of an old church, far above the light and murmur of the town and far below the flying clouds that shadow it, is the wild and dreary place at night: and high up in the steeple of an old church, dwelt the Chimes I tell of.

They were old Chimes, trust me. Centuries ago, these Bells had been baptized by bishops: so many centuries ago, that the register of their baptism was lost long, long before the memory of man, and no one knew their names. They had had their Godfathers and Godmothers, these Bells (for my own part, by the way, I would rather incur the responsibility of being Godfather to a Bell than a Boy), and had their silver mugs no doubt, besides. But Time had mowed down their sponsors, and Henry the Eighth had melted down their mugs; and they now hung, nameless and mugless, in the church-tower.

Not speechless, though. Far from it. They had clear, loud, lusty, sounding voices, had these Bells; and far and wide they might be heard upon the wind. Much too sturdy Chimes were they, to be dependent on the pleasure of the wind, moreover; for, fighting gallantly against it when it took an adverse whim, they would pour their cheerful notes into a listening ear right royally; and bent on being heard on stormy nights, by some poor mother watching a sick child, or some lone wife whose husband was at sea, they had been sometimes known to beat a blustering Nor' Wester; aye, "all to fits," as Toby Veck said;—for though they chose to call him Trotty Veck, his name was Toby, and nobody could make it anything else either (except Tobias) without a special act of parliament; he having been as lawfully christened in his day as the Bells had been in theirs, though with not quite so much of solemnity or public rejoicing.

For my part, I confess myself of Toby Veck's belief, for I am sure he had opportunities enough of forming a correct one. And whatever Toby Veck said, I say. And I take my stand by Toby Veck, although he did stand all day long (and weary work it was) just outside the church-door. In fact he was a ticket-porter, Toby Veck, and waited there for jobs.

And a breezy, goose-skinned, blue-nosed, red-eyed, stony-toed, tooth-chattering place it was, to wait in, in the winter-time, as Toby Veck well knew. The wind came tearing round the corner—especially the east wind—as if it had sallied forth, express, from the confines of the earth, to have a blow at Toby. And oftentimes it seemed to come upon him sooner than it had expected, for bouncing round the corner, and passing Toby, it would suddenly wheel round again, as if it cried "Why, here he is!" Incontinently his little white apron would be caught up over his head like a naughty boy's garments, and his feeble little cane would be seen to wrestle and struggle unavailingly in his hand, and his legs would undergo tremendous agitation, and Toby himself all aslant, and facing now in this direction, now in that, would be so banged and buffeted, and touzled, and worried, and hustled, and lifted off his feet, as to render it a state of things but one degree removed from a positive miracle, that he wasn't carried up bodily into the air as a colony of frogs or snails or other very portable creatures sometimes are, and rained down again, to the great astonishment of the natives, on some strange corner of the world where ticket-porters are unknown.

But, windy weather, in spite of its using him so roughly, was, after all, a sort of holiday for Toby. That's the fact. He didn't seem to wait so long for a sixpence in the wind, as at other times; the having to fight with that boisterous element took off his attention, and quite freshened him up, when he was getting hungry and low-spirited. A hard frost too, or a fall of snow, was an Event; and it seemed to do him good, somehow or other—it would have been hard to say in what respect though, Toby! So wind and frost and snow, and perhaps a good stiff storm of hail, were Toby Veck's red-letter days.

Wet weather was the worst; the cold, damp, clammy wet, that wrapped him up like a moist great-coat—the only kind of great-coat Toby owned, or could have added to his comfort by dispensing with. Wet days, when the rain came slowly, thickly, obstinately down; when the street's throat, like his own, was choked with mist; when smoking umbrellas passed and re-passed, spinning round and round like so many teetotums, as they knocked against each other on the crowded footway, throwing off a little whirlpool of uncomfortable sprinklings; when gutters brawled and waterspouts were full and noisy; when the wet from the projecting stones and ledges of the church fell drip, drip, drip, on Toby, making the wisp of straw on which he stood mere mud in no time; those were the days that tried him. Then, indeed, you might see Toby looking anxiously out from his shelter in an angle of the church wall—such a meagre shelter that in summer time it never cast a shadow thicker than a good-sized walking stick upon the sunny pavement—with a disconsolate and lengthened face. But coming out, a minute afterwards, to warm himself by exercise, and trotting up and down some dozen times, he would brighten even then, and go back more brightly to his niche.

They called him Trotty from his pace, which meant speed if it didn't make it. He could have walked faster perhaps; most likely; but rob him of his trot, and Toby would have taken to his bed and died. It bespattered him with mud in dirty weather; it cost him a world of trouble; he could have walked with infinitely greater ease; but that was one reason for his clinging to it so tenaciously. A weak, small, spare old man, he was a very Hercules, this Toby, in his good intentions. He loved to earn his money. He delighted to believe—Toby was very poor, and couldn't well afford to part with a delight—that he was worth his salt. With a shilling or an eighteen-penny message or small parcel in hand, his courage always high, rose higher. As he trotted on, he would call out to fast Postmen ahead of him, to get out of the way; devoutly believing that in the natural course of things he must inevitably overtake and run them down; and he had perfect faith—not often tested—in his being able to carry anything that man could lift.

Thus, even when he came out of his nook to warm himself on a wet day, Toby trotted. Making, with his leaky shoes, a crooked line of slushy footprints in the mire; and blowing on his chilly hands and rubbing them against each other, poorly defended from the searching cold by threadbare mufflers of grey worsted, with a private apartment only for the thumb, and a common room or tap for the rest of the fingers; Toby, with his knees bent and his cane beneath his arm, still trotted. Falling out into the road to look up at the belfry when the Chimes resounded, Toby trotted still.

He made this last excursion several times a day, for they were company to him; and when he heard their voices, he had an interest in glancing at their lodging-place, and thinking how they were moved, and what hammers beat upon them. Perhaps he was the more curious about these Bells, because there were points of resemblance between themselves and him. They hung there, in all weathers, with the wind and rain driving in upon them; facing only the outsides of all those houses; never getting any nearer to the blazing fires that gleamed and shone upon the windows, or came puffing out of the chimney tops; and incapable of participation in any of the good things that were constantly being handled, through the street doors and the area railings, to prodigious cooks. Faces came and went at many windows: sometimes pretty faces, youthful faces, pleasant faces: sometimes the reverse: but Toby knew no more (though he often speculated on these trifles, standing idle in the streets) whence they came, or where they went, or whether, when the lips moved, one kind word was said of him in all the year, than did the Chimes themselves.

Toby was not a casuist—that he knew of, at least—and I don't mean to say that when he began to take to the Bells, and to knit up his first rough acquaintance with them into something of a closer and more delicate woof, he passed through these considerations one by one, or held any formal review or great field-day in his thoughts. But what I mean to say, and do say is, that as the functions of Toby's body, his digestive organs for example, did of their own cunning, and by a great many operations of which he was altogether ignorant, and the knowledge of which would have astonished him very much, arrive at a certain end; so his mental faculties, without his privity or concurrence, set all these wheels and springs in motion, with a thousand others, when they worked to bring about his liking for the Bells.

And though I had said his love, I would not have recalled the word, though it would scarcely have expressed his complicated feeling. For, being but a simple man, he invested them with a strange and solemn character. They were so mysterious, often heard and never seen; so high up, so far off, so full of such a deep strong melody, that he regarded them with a species of awe; and sometimes when he looked up at the dark arched windows in the tower, he half expected to be beckoned to by something which was not a Bell, and yet was what he had heard so often sounding in the Chimes. For all this, Toby scouted with indignation a certain flying rumour that the Chimes were haunted, as implying the possibility of their being connected with any Evil thing. In short, they were very often in his ears, and very often in his thoughts, but always in his good opinion; and he very often got such a crick in his neck by staring with his mouth wide open, at the steeple where they hung, that he was fain to take an extra trot or two, afterwards, to cure it.

The very thing he was in the act of doing one cold day, when the last drowsy sound of Twelve o'clock, just struck, was humming like a melodious monster of a Bee, and not by any means a busy bee, all through the steeple!

"Dinner-time, eh!" said Toby, trotting up and down before the church. "Ah!"

Toby's nose was very red, and his eyelids were very red, and he winked very much, and his shoulders were very near his ears, and his legs were very stiff, and altogether he was evidently a long way upon the frosty side of cool.

"Dinner-time, eh!" repeated Toby, using his right-hand muffler like an infantine boxing-glove, and punishing his chest for being cold. "Ah-h-h-h!"

He took a silent trot, after that, for a minute or two.

"There's nothing," said Toby, breaking forth afresh—but here he stopped short in his trot, and with a face of great interest and some alarm, felt his nose carefully all the way up. It was but a little way (not being much of a nose) and he had soon finished.

"I thought it was gone," said Toby, trotting off again. "It's all right, however. I am sure I couldn't blame it if it was to go. It has a precious hard service of it in the bitter weather, and precious little to look forward to; for I don't take snuff myself.

It's a good deal tried, poor creetur, at the best of times; for when it does get hold of a pleasant whiff or so (which an't too often) it's generally from somebody else's dinner, a-coming home from the baker's."

The reflection reminded him of that other reflection, which he had left unfinished.

"There's nothing," said Toby, "more regular in its coming round than dinner-time, and nothing less regular in its coming round than dinner. That's the great difference between 'em. It's took me a long time to find it out. I wonder whether it would be worth any gentleman's while, now, to buy that obserwation for the Papers; or the Parliament!"

Toby was only joking, for he gravely shook his head in self-depreciation.

"Why! Lord!" said Toby. "The Papers is full of obserwations as it is; and so's the Parliament. Here's last week's paper, now"; taking a very dirty one from his pocket, and holding it from him at arm's length; "full of obserwations! Full of obserwations! I like to know the news as well as any man," said Toby, slowly; folding it a little smaller, and putting it in his pocket again: "but it almost goes against the grain with me to read a paper now. It frightens me almost. I don't know what we poor people are coming to. Lord send we may be coming to something better in the New Year nigh upon us!"

"Why, father, father!" said a pleasant voice, hard by.

But Toby, not hearing it, continued to trot backwards and forwards: musing as he went, and talking to himself.

"It seems as if we can't go right, or do right, or be righted," said Toby. "I hadn't much schooling, myself, when I was young; and I can't make out whether we have any business on the face of the earth, or not. Sometimes I think we must have—a little; and sometimes I think we must be intruding. I get so puzzled sometimes that I am not even able to make up my mind whether there is any good at all in us, or whether we are born bad. We seem to be dreadful things; we seem to give a deal of trouble; we are always being complained of and guarded against. One way or other, we fill the papers. Talk of a New Year!" said Toby, mournfully. "I can bear up as well as another man at most times; better than a good many, for I am as strong as a lion, and all men an't; but supposing it should really be that we have no right to a New Year—supposing we really are intruding—"

"Why, father, father!" said the pleasant voice again.

Toby heard it this time; started; stopped; and shortening his sight, which had been directed a long way off as seeking the enlightenment in the very heart of the approaching year, found himself face to face with his own child, and looking close into her eyes.

Bright eyes they were. Eyes that would bear a world of looking in, before their depth was fathomed. Dark eyes, that reflected back the eyes which searched them; not flashingly, or at the owner's will, but with a clear, calm, honest, patient radiance, claiming kindred with that light which Heaven called into being. Eyes that were beautiful and true, and beaming with Hope. With Hope so young and fresh; with Hope so buoyant, vigorous, and bright, despite the twenty years of work and poverty on which they had looked; that they became a voice to Trotty Veck, and said: "I think we have some business here—a little!"

Trotty kissed the lips belonging to the eyes, and squeezed the blooming face between his hands.

"Why, Pet," said Trotty. "What's to do? I didn't expect you to-day, Meg."

"Neither did I expect to come, father," cried the girl, nodding her head and smiling as she spoke. "But here I am! And not alone; not alone!"

"Why you don't mean to say," observed Trotty, looking curiously at a covered basket which she carried in her hand, "that you—"

"Smell it, father dear," said Meg. "Only smell it!"

Trotty was going to lift up the cover at once, in a great hurry, when she gaily interposed her hand.

"No, no, no," said Meg, with the glee of a child. "Lengthen it out a little. Let me just lift up the corner; just the lit-tle ti-ny cor-ner, you know," said Meg, suiting the action to the word with the utmost gentleness, and speaking very softly, as if she were afraid of being overheard by something inside the basket; "there. Now. What's that?"

Toby took the shortest possible sniff at the edge of the basket, and cried out in a rapture:

"Why, it's hot!"

"It's burning hot!" cried Meg. "Ha, ha, ha! It's scalding hot!"

"Ha, ha, ha!" roared Toby, with a sort of kick. "It's scalding hot!"

"But what is it, father?" said Meg. "Come. You haven't guessed what it is. And you must guess what it is. I can't think of taking it out, till you guess what it is. Don't be in such a hurry! Wait a minute! A little bit more of the cover. Now guess!"

Meg was in a perfect fright lest he should guess right too soon; shrinking away, as she held the basket towards him; curling up her pretty shoulders; stopping her ear with her hand, as if by so doing she could keep the right word out of Toby's lips; and laughing softly the whole time.

Meanwhile Toby, putting a hand on each knee, bent down his nose to the basket, and took a long inspiration at the lid; the grin upon his withered face expanding in the process, as if he were inhaling laughing gas.

"Ah! It's very nice," said Toby. "It an't—I suppose it an't Polonies?"

"No, no, no!" cried Meg, delighted. "Nothing like Polonies!"

"No," said Toby, after another sniff. "It's—it's mellower than Polonies. It's very nice. It improves every moment. It's too decided for Trotters. An't it?"

Meg was in an ecstasy. He could not have gone wider of the mark than Trotters—except Polonies.

"Liver?" said Toby, communing with himself. "No. There's a mildness about it that don't answer to liver. Pettitoes? No. It an't faint enough for pettitoes. It wants the stringiness of Cocks' heads. And I know it an't sausages. I'll tell you what it is. It's chitterlings!"

"No, it an't!" cried Meg, in a burst of delight. "No, it an't!"

"Why, what am I a-thinking of!" said Toby, suddenly recovering a position as near the perpendicular as it was possible for him to assume. "I shall forget my own name next. It's tripe!"

Tripe it was; and Meg, in high joy, protested he should say, in half a minute more, it was the best tripe ever stewed.

"And so," said Meg, busying herself exultingly with the basket, "I'll lay the cloth at once, father; for I have brought the tripe in a basin, and tied the basin up in a pocket-handkerchief; and if I like to be proud for once, and spread that for a cloth, and call it a cloth, there's no law to prevent me; is there, father?"

"Not that I know of, my dear," said Toby. "But they're always a-bringing up some new law or other."

"And according to what I was reading you in the paper the other day, father; what the Judge said, you know; we poor people are supposed to know them all. Ha ha! What a mistake! My goodness me, how clever they think us!"

"Yes, my dear," cried Trotty; "and they'd be very fond of any one of us that did know 'em all. He'd grow fat upon the work he'd get, that man, and be popular with the gentlefolks in his neighbourhood. Very much so!"

"He'd eat his dinner with an appetite, whoever he was, if it smelt like this," said Meg, cheerfully. "Make haste, for there's a hot potato besides, and half a pint of fresh-drawn beer in a bottle. Where will you dine, father? On the Post, or on the Steps? Dear, dear, how grand we are. Two places to choose from!"

"The steps to-day, my Pet," said Trotty. "Steps in dry weather. Post in wet. There's a greater conveniency in the steps at all times, because of the sitting down; but they're rheumatic in the damp."

"Then here," said Meg, clapping her hands, after a moment's bustle; "here it is, all ready! And beautiful it looks! Come, father. Come!"

Since his discovery of the contents of the basket, Trotty had been standing looking at her—and had been speaking too—in an abstracted manner, which showed that though she was the object of his thoughts and eyes, to the exclusion even of tripe, he neither saw nor thought about her as she was at that moment, but had before him some imaginary rough sketch or drama of her future life. Roused, now, by her cheerful summons, he shook off a melancholy shake of the head which was just coming upon him, and trotted to her side. As he was stooping to sit down, the Chimes rang.

"Amen!" said Trotty, pulling off his hat and looking up towards them.

"Amen to the Bells, father?" cried Meg.

"They broke in like a grace, my dear," said Trotty, taking his seat. "They'd say a good one, I am sure, if they could. Many's the kind thing they say to me."

"The Bells do, father!" laughed Meg, as she set the basin, and a knife and fork, before him. "Well!"

"Seem to, my Pet," said Trotty, falling to with great vigour. "And where's the difference? If I hear 'em, what does it matter whether they speak it or not? Why bless you, my dear," said Toby, pointing at the tower with his fork, and becoming more animated under the influence of dinner, "how often have I heard them bells say, "Toby Veck, Toby Veck, keep a good heart, Toby! Toby Veck, Toby Veck, keep a good heart, Toby!" A million times? More!"

"Well, I never!" cried Meg.

She had, though—over and over again. For it was Toby's constant topic.

"When things is very bad," said Trotty; "very bad indeed, I mean; almost at the worst; then it's 'Toby Veck, Toby Veck, job coming soon, Toby! Toby Veck, Toby Veck, job coming soon, Toby!' That way."

"And it comes—at last, father," said Meg, with a touch of sadness in her pleasant voice.

"Always," answered the unconscious Toby. "Never fails."

While this discourse was holding, Trotty made no pause in his attack upon the savoury meat before him, but cut and ate, and cut and drank, and cut and chewed, and dodged about, from tripe to hot potato, and from hot potato back again to tripe, with an unctuous and unflagging relish. But happening now to look all round the street—in case anybody should be beckoning from any door or window, for a porter—his eyes, in coming back again, encountered Meg: sitting opposite to him, with her arms folded and only busy in watching his progress with a smile of happiness.

"Why, Lord forgive me!" said Trotty, dropping his knife and fork. "My dove! Meg! why didn't you tell me what a beast I was?"

"Father?"

"Sitting here," said Trotty, in penitent explanation, "cramming, and stuffing, and gorging myself; and you before me there, never so much as breaking your precious fast, nor wanting to, when—"

"But I have broken it, father," interposed his daughter, laughing, "all to bits. I have had my dinner."

"Nonsense," said Trotty. "Two dinners in one day! It an't possible! You might as well tell me that two New Year's Days will come together, or that I have had a gold head all my life, and never changed it."

"I have had my dinner, father, for all that," said Meg, coming nearer to him. "And if you'll go on with yours, I'll tell you how and where; and how your dinner came to be brought; and—and something else besides."

Toby still appeared incredulous; but she looked into his face with her clear eyes, and laying her hand upon his shoulder, motioned him to go on while the meat was hot. So Trotty took up his knife and fork again, and went to work. But much more slowly than before, and shaking his head, as if he were not at all pleased with himself.

"I had my dinner, father," said Meg, after a little hesitation, "with—with Richard. His dinner-time was early; and as he brought his dinner with him when he came to see me, we—we had it together, father."

Trotty took a little beer, and smacked his lips. Then he said, "Oh!"—because she waited.

"And Richard says, father—" Meg resumed. Then stopped.

"What does Richard say, Meg?" asked Toby.

"Richard says, father—" Another stoppage.

"Richard's a long time saying it," said Toby.

"He says then, father," Meg continued, lifting up her eyes at last, and speaking in a tremble, but quite plainly; "another year is nearly gone, and where is the use of waiting on from year to year, when it is so unlikely we shall ever be better off than we are now? He says we are poor now, father, and we shall be poor then, but we are young now, and years will make us old before we know it. He says that if we wait: people in our condition: until we see our way quite clearly, the way will be a narrow one indeed—the common way—the Grave, father."

A bolder man than Trotty Veck must needs have drawn upon his boldness largely, to deny it. Trotty held his peace.

"And how hard, father, to grow old, and die, and think we might have cheered and helped each other! How hard in all our lives to love each other; and to grieve, apart, to see each other working, changing, growing old and grey. Even if I got the better of it, and forgot him (which I never could), oh father dear, how hard to have a heart so full as mine is now, and live to have it slowly drained out every drop, without the recollection of one happy moment of a woman's life, to stay behind and comfort me, and make me better!"

Trotty sat quite still. Meg dried her eyes, and said more gaily: that is to say, with here a laugh, and there a sob, and here a laugh and sob together:

"So Richard says, father; as his work was yesterday made certain for some time to come, and as I love him, and have loved him full three years—ah! longer than that, if he knew it!—will I marry him on New Year's Day; the best and happiest day, he says, in the whole year, and one that is almost sure to bring good fortune with it. It's a short notice, father—isn't it?—but I haven't my fortune to be settled, or my wedding dresses to be made, like the great ladies, father, have I? And he said so much, and said it in his way; so strong and earnest, and all the time so kind and gentle; that I said I'd come and talk to you, father. And as they paid the money for that work of mine this morning (unexpectedly, I am sure!) and as you have fared very poorly for a whole week, and as I couldn't help wishing there should be something to make this day a sort of holiday to you as well as a dear and happy day to me, father, I made a little treat and brought it to surprise you."

"And see how he leaves it cooling on the step!" said another voice.

It was the voice of this same Richard, who had come upon them unobserved, and stood before the father and daughter; looking down upon them with a face as glowing as the iron on which his stout sledge-hammer daily rung. A handsome, well-made, powerful youngster he was; with eyes that sparkled like the red-hot droppings from a furnace fire; black hair that curled about his swarthy temples rarely; and a smile—a smile that bore out Meg's eulogium on his style of conversation.

"See how he leaves it cooling on the step!" said Richard. "Meg don't know what he likes. Not she!"

Trotty, all action and enthusiasm, immediately reached up his hand to Richard, and was going to address him in great hurry, when the house-door opened without any warning, and a footman very nearly put his foot into the tripe.

"Out of the vays here, will you! You must always go and be a-settin on our steps, must you! You can't go and give a turn to none of the neighbours never, can't you! Will you clear the road, or won't you?"

Strictly speaking, the last question was irrelevant, as they had already done it.

"What's the matter, what's the matter!" said the gentleman for whom the door was opened; coming out of the house at that kind of light-heavy pace—that peculiar compromise between a walk and a jog-trot—with which a gentleman upon the smooth down-hill of life, wearing creaking boots, a watch-chain, and clean linen, may come out of his house: not only without any abatement of his dignity, but with an expression of having important and wealthy engagements elsewhere. "What's the matter! What's the matter!"

"You're always a-being begged, and prayed, upon your bended knees you are," said the footman with great emphasis to Trotty Veck, "to let our door-steps be. Why don't you let 'em be? Can't you let 'em be?"

"There! That'll do, that'll do!" said the gentleman. "Halloa there! Porter!" beckoning with his head to Trotty Veck. "Come here. What's that? Your dinner?"

"Yes, sir," said Trotty, leaving it behind him in a corner.

"Don't leave it there," exclaimed the gentleman. "Bring it here, bring it here. So! This is your dinner, is it?"

"Yes, sir," repeated Trotty, looking with a fixed eye and a watery mouth, at the piece of tripe he had reserved for a last delicious tit-bit; which the gentleman was now turning over and over on the end of the fork.

Two other gentlemen had come out with him. One was a low-spirited gentleman of middle age, of a meagre habit, and a disconsolate face; who kept his hands continually in the pockets of his scanty pepper-and-salt trousers, very large and dog's-eared from that custom; and was not particularly well brushed or washed. The other, a full-sized, sleek, well-conditioned gentleman, in a blue coat with bright buttons, and a white cravat. This gentleman had a very red face, as if an undue proportion of the blood in his body were squeezed up into his head; which perhaps accounted for his having also the appearance of being rather cold about the heart.

He who had Toby's meat upon the fork, called to the first one by the name of Filer; and they both drew near together. Mr. Filer being exceedingly short-sighted, was obliged to go so close to the remnant of Toby's dinner before he could make out what it was, that Toby's heart leaped up into his mouth. But Mr. Filer didn't eat it.

"This is a description of animal food, Alderman," said Filer, making little punches in it with a pencil-case, "commonly known to the labouring population of this country, by the name of tripe."

The Alderman laughed, and winked; for he was a merry fellow, Alderman Cute. Oh, and a sly fellow too! A knowing fellow. Up to everything. Not to be imposed upon. Deep in the people's hearts! He knew them, Cute did. I believe you!

"But who eats tripe?" said Mr. Filer, looking round. "Tripe is without an exception the least economical, and the most wasteful article of consumption that the markets of this country can by possibility produce. The loss upon a pound of tripe has been found to be, in the boiling, seven-eights of a fifth more than the loss upon a pound of any other animal substance whatever. Tripe is more expensive, properly understood, than the hothouse pine-apple. Taking into account the number of animals slaughtered yearly within the bills of mortality alone; and forming a low estimate of the quantity of tripe which the carcases of those animals, reasonably well butchered, would yield; I find that the waste on that amount of tripe, if boiled, would victual a garrison of five hundred men for five months of thirty-one days each, and a February over. The Waste, the Waste!"

Trotty stood aghast, and his legs shook under him. He seemed to have starved a garrison of five hundred men with his own hand.

"Who eats tripe?" said Mr. Filer, warmly. "Who eats tripe?"

Trotty made a miserable bow.

"You do, do you?" said Mr. Filer. "Then I'll tell you something. You snatch your tripe, my friend, out of the mouths of widows and orphans."

"I hope not, sir," said Trotty, faintly. "I'd sooner die of want!"

"Divide the amount of tripe before-mentioned, Alderman," said Mr. Filer, "by the estimated number of existing widows and orphans, and the result will be one pennyweight of tripe to each. Not a grain is left for that man. Consequently, he's a robber."

Trotty was so shocked, that it gave him no concern to see the Alderman finish the tripe himself. It was a relief to get rid of it, anyhow.

"And what do you say?" asked the Alderman, jocosely, of the red-faced gentleman in the blue coat. "You have heard friend Filer. What do you say?"

"What's it possible to say?" returned the gentleman. "What is to be said? Who can take any interest in a fellow like this," meaning Trotty; "in such degenerate times as these? Look at him. What an object! The good old times, the grand old times, the great old times! Those were the times for a bold peasantry, and all that sort of thing. Those were the times for every sort of thing, in fact. There's nothing now-a-days. Ah!" sighed the red-faced gentleman. "The good old times, the good old times!"

The gentleman didn't specify what particular times he alluded to; nor did he say whether he objected to the present times, from a disinterested consciousness that they had done nothing very remarkable in producing himself.

"The good old times, the good old times," repeated the gentleman. "What times they were! They were the only times. It's of no use talking about any other times, or discussing what the people are in these times. You don't call these, times, do you? I don't. Look into Strutt's Costumes, and see what a Porter used to be, in any of the good old English reigns."

"He hadn't, in his very best circumstances, a shirt to his back, or a stocking to his foot; and there was scarcely a vegetable in all England for him to put into his mouth," said Mr. Filer. "I can prove it, by tables."

But still the red-faced gentleman extolled the good old times, the grand old times, the great old times. No matter what anybody else said, he still went turning round and round in one set form of words concerning them; as a poor squirrel turns and turns in its revolving cage; touching the mechanism, and trick of which, it has probably quite as distinct perceptions, as ever this red-faced gentleman had of his deceased Millennium.

It is possible that poor Trotty's faith in these very vague Old Times was not entirely destroyed, for he felt vague enough at that moment. One thing, however, was plain to him, in the midst of his distress; to wit, that however these gentlemen might differ in details, his misgivings of that morning, and of many other mornings, were well founded. "No, no. We can't go right or do right," thought Trotty in despair. "There is no good in us. We are born bad!"

But Trotty had a father's heart within him; which had somehow got into his breast in spite of this decree; and he could not bear that Meg, in the blush of her brief joy, should have her fortune read by these wise gentlemen. "God help her," thought poor Trotty. "She will know it soon enough."

He anxiously signed, therefore, to the young smith, to take her away. But he was so busy, talking to her softly at a little distance, that he only became conscious of this desire, simultaneously with Alderman Cute. Now, the Alderman had not yet had his say, but he was a philosopher, too—practical, though! Oh, very practical—and, as he had no idea of losing any portion of his audience, he cried "Stop!"

"Now, you know," said the Alderman, addressing his two friends, with a self-complacent smile upon his face which was habitual to him, "I am a plain man, and a practical man; and I go to work in a plain practical way. That's my way. There is not the least mystery or difficulty in dealing with this sort of people if you only understand 'em, and can talk to 'em in their own manner. Now, you Porter! Don't you ever tell me, or anybody else, my friend, that you haven't always enough to eat, and of the best; because I know better. I have tasted your tripe, you know, and you can't 'chaff' me. You understand what 'chaff' means, eh? That's the right word, isn't it? Ha, ha, ha! Lord bless you," said the Alderman, turning to his friends again, "it's the easiest thing on earth to deal with this sort of people, if you understand 'em."

Famous man for the common people, Alderman Cute! Never out of temper with them! Easy, affable, joking, knowing gentleman!

"You see, my friend," pursued the Alderman, "there's a great deal of nonsense talked about Want—'hard up,' you know; that's the phrase, isn't it? ha! ha! ha!—and I intend to Put it Down. There's a certain amount of cant in vogue about Starvation, and I mean to Put it Down. That's all! Lord bless you," said the Alderman, turning to his friends again, "you may Put Down anything among this sort of people, if you only know the way to set about it."

Trotty took Meg's hand and drew it through his arm. He didn't seem to know what he was doing though.

"Your daughter, eh?" said the Alderman, chucking her familiarly under the chin.

Always affable with the working classes, Alderman Cute! Knew what pleased them! Not a bit of pride!

"Where's her mother?" asked that worthy gentleman.

"Dead," said Toby. "Her mother got up linen; and was called to Heaven when She was born."

"Not to get up linen there, I suppose," remarked the Alderman pleasantly.

Toby might or might not have been able to separate his wife in Heaven from her old pursuits. But query: If Mrs. Alderman Cute had gone to Heaven, would Mr. Alderman Cute have pictured her as holding any state or station there?

"And you're making love to her, are you?" said Cute to the young smith.

"Yes," returned Richard quickly, for he was nettled by the question. "And we are going to be married on New Year's Day."

"What do you mean!" cried Filer sharply. "Married!"

"Why, yes, we're thinking of it, Master," said Richard. "We're rather in a hurry, you see, in case it should be Put Down first."

"Ah!" cried Filer, with a groan. "Put that down indeed, Alderman, and you'll do something. Married! Married! The ignorance of the first principles of political economy on the part of these people; their improvidence; their wickedness; is, by Heavens! enough to— Now look at that couple, will you!"

Well? They were worth looking at. And marriage seemed as reasonable and fair a deed as they need have in contemplation.

"A man may live to be as old as Methuselah," said Mr. Filer, "and may labour all his life for the benefit of such people as those; and may heap up facts on figures, facts on figures, facts on figures, mountains high and dry; and he can no more hope to persuade 'em that they have no right or business to be married, than he can hope to persuade 'em that they have no earthly right or business to be born. And that we know they haven't. We reduced it to a mathematical certainty long ago!"

Alderman Cute was mightily diverted, and laid his right forefinger on the side of his nose, as much as to say to both his friends, "Observe me, will you! Keep your eye on the practical man!"—and called Meg to him.

"Come here, my girl!" said Alderman Cute.

The young blood of her lover had been mounting, wrathfully, within the last few minutes; and he was indisposed to let her come. But, setting a constraint upon himself, he came forward with a stride as Meg approached, and stood beside her. Trotty kept her hand within his arm still, but looked from face to face as wildly as a sleeper in a dream.

"Now, I'm going to give you a word or two of good advice, my girl," said the Alderman, in his nice easy way. "It's my place to give advice, you know, because I'm a Justice. You know I'm a Justice, don't you?"

Meg timidly said, "Yes." But everybody knew Alderman Cute was a Justice! Oh dear, so active a Justice always! Who such a mote of brightness in the public eye, as Cute!

"You are going to be married, you say," pursued the Alderman. "Very unbecoming and indelicate in one of your sex! But never mind that. After you are married, you'll quarrel with your husband and come to be a distressed wife. You may think not; but you will, because I tell you so. Now, I give you fair warning, that I have made up my mind to Put distressed wives Down. So, don't be brought before me. You'll have children—boys. Those boys will grow up bad, of course, and run wild in the streets, without shoes and stockings. Mind, my young friend! I'll convict 'em summarily, every one, for I am determined to Put boys without shoes and stockings, Down. Perhaps your husband will die young (most likely) and leave you with a baby. Then you'll be turned out of doors, and wander up and down the streets. Now, don't wander near me, my dear, for I am resolved, to Put all wandering mothers Down. All young mothers, of all sorts and kinds, it's my determination to Put Down. Don't think to plead illness as an excuse with me; or babies as an excuse with me; for all sick persons and young children (I hope you know the church-service, but I'm afraid not) I am determined to Put Down. And if you attempt, desperately, and ungratefully, and impiously, and fraudulently attempt, to drown yourself, or hang yourself, I'll have no pity for you, for I have made up my mind to Put all suicide Down! If there is one thing," said the Alderman, with his self-satisfied smile, "on which I can be said to have made up my mind more than on another, it is to Put suicide Down. So don't try it on. That's the phrase, isn't it? Ha, ha! now we understand each other."

Toby knew not whether to be agonised or glad, to see that Meg had turned a deadly white, and dropped her lover's hand.

"And as for you, you dull dog," said the Alderman, turning with even increased cheerfulness and urbanity to the young smith, "what are you thinking of being married for? What do you want to be married for, you silly fellow? If I was a fine, young, strapping chap like you, I should be ashamed of being milksop enough to pin myself to a woman's apron-strings! Why, she'll be an old woman before you're a middle-aged man! And a pretty figure you'll cut then, with a draggle-tailed wife and a crowd of squalling children crying after you wherever you go!"

O, he knew how to banter the common people, Alderman Cute!

"There! Go along with you," said the Alderman, "and repent. Don't make such a fool of yourself as to get married on New Year's Day. You'll think very differently of it, long before next New Year's Day: a trim young fellow like you, with all the girls looking after you. There! Go along with you!"

They went along. Not arm in arm, or hand in hand, or interchanging bright glances; but, she in tears; he, gloomy and down-looking. Were these the hearts that had so lately made old Toby's leap up from its faintness? No, no. The Alderman (a blessing on his head!) had Put them Down.

"As you happen to be here," said the Alderman to Toby, "you shall carry a letter for me. Can you be quick? You're an old man."

Toby, who had been looking after Meg, quite stupidly, made shift to murmur out that he was very quick, and very strong.

"How old are you?" inquired the Alderman.

"I'm over sixty, sir," said Toby.

"O! This man's a great deal past the average age, you know," cried Mr. Filer breaking in as if his patience would bear some trying, but this really was carrying matters a little too far.

"I feel I'm intruding, sir," said Toby. "I—I misdoubted it this morning. Oh dear me!"

The Alderman cut him short by giving him the letter from his pocket. Toby would have got a shilling too; but Mr. Filer clearly showing that in that case he would rob a certain given number of persons of ninepence-halfpenny a-piece, he only got sixpence; and thought himself very well off to get that.

Then the Alderman gave an arm to each of his friends, and walked off in high feather; but, he immediately came hurrying back alone, as if he had forgotten something.

"Porter!" said the Alderman.

"Sir!" said Toby.

"Take care of that daughter of yours. She's much too handsome."

"Even her good looks are stolen from somebody or other, I suppose," thought Toby, looking at the sixpence in his hand, and thinking of the tripe. "She's been and robbed five hundred ladies of a bloom a-piece, I shouldn't wonder. It's very dreadful!"

"She's much too handsome, my man," repeated the Alderman. "The chances are, that she'll come to no good, I clearly see. Observe what I say. Take care of her!" With which, he hurried off again.

"Wrong every way. Wrong every way!" said Trotty, clasping his hands. "Born bad. No business here!"

The Chimes came clashing in upon him as he said the words. Full, loud, and sounding—but with no encouragement. No, not a drop.

"The tune's changed," cried the old man, as he listened. "There's not a word of all that fancy in it. Why should there be? I have no business with the New Year nor with the old one neither. Let me die!"

Still the Bells, pealing forth their changes, made the very air spin. Put 'em down, Put 'em down! Good old Times, Good old Times! Facts and Figures, Facts and Figures! Put 'em down, Put 'em down! If they said anything they said this, until the brain of Toby reeled.

He pressed his bewildered head between his hands, as if to keep it from splitting asunder. A well-timed action, as it happened; for finding the letter in one of them, and being by that means reminded of his charge, he fell, mechanically, into his usual trot, and trotted off.

CHAPTER II. SECOND QUARTER

The letter Toby had received from Alderman Cute, was addressed to a great man in the great district of the town. The greatest district of the town. It must have been the greatest district of the town, because it was commonly called "the world" by its inhabitants. The letter positively seemed heavier in Toby's hand, than another letter. Not because the Alderman had sealed it with a very large coat of arms and no end of wax, but because of the weighty name on the superscription, and the ponderous amount of gold and silver with which it was associated.

"How different from us!" thought Toby, in all simplicity and earnestness, as he looked at the direction. "Divide the lively turtles in the bills of mortality, by the number of gentlefolks able to buy 'em; and whose share does he take but his own! As to snatching tripe from anybody's mouth—he'd scorn it!"

With the involuntary homage due to such an exalted character, Toby interposed a corner of his apron between the letter and his fingers.

"His children," said Trotty, and a mist rose before his eyes; "his daughters— Gentlemen may win their hearts and marry them; they may be happy wives and mothers; they may be handsome like my darling M-e-."

He couldn't finish the name. The final letter swelled in his throat, to the size of the whole alphabet.

"Never mind," thought Trotty. "I know what I mean. That's more than enough for me." And with this consolatory rumination, trotted on.

It was a hard frost, that day. The air was bracing, crisp, and clear. The wintry sun, though powerless for warmth, looked brightly down upon the ice it was too weak to melt, and set a radiant glory there. At other times, Trotty might have learned a poor man's lesson from the wintry sun; but, he was past that, now.

The Year was Old, that day. The patient Year had lived through the reproaches and misuses of its slanderers, and faithfully performed its work. Spring, summer, autumn, winter. It had laboured through the destined round, and now laid down its weary head to die. Shut out from hope, high impulse, active happiness, itself, but active messenger of many joys to others, it made appeal in its decline to have its toiling days and patient hours remembered, and to die in peace. Trotty might have read a poor man's allegory in the fading year; but he was past that, now.

And only he? Or has the like appeal been ever made, by seventy years at once upon an English labourer's head, and made in vain!

The streets were full of motion, and the shops were decked out gaily. The New Year, like an Infant Heir to the whole world, was waited for, with welcomes, presents, and rejoicings. There were books and toys for the New Year, glittering trinkets for the New Year, dresses for the New Year, schemes of fortune for the New Year; new inventions to beguile it. Its life was parcelled out in almanacks and pocket-books; the coming of its moons, and stars, and tides, was known beforehand to the moment; all the workings of its seasons in their days and nights, were calculated with as much precision as Mr. Filer could work sums in men and women.

The New Year, the New Year. Everywhere the New Year! The Old Year was already looked upon as dead; and its effects were selling cheap, like some drowned mariner's aboardship. Its patterns were Last Year's, and going at a sacrifice, before its breath was gone. Its treasures were mere dirt, beside the riches of its unborn successor!

Trotty had no portion, to his thinking, in the New Year or the Old.

"Put 'em down, Put 'em down! Facts and Figures, Facts and Figures! Good old Times, Good old Times! Put 'em down, Put 'em down!"—his trot went to that measure, and would fit itself to nothing else.

But, even that one, melancholy as it was, brought him, in due time, to the end of his journey. To the mansion of Sir Joseph Bowley, Member of Parliament.

The door was opened by a Porter. Such a Porter! Not of Toby's order. Quite another thing. His place was the ticket though; not Toby's.

This Porter underwent some hard panting before he could speak; having breathed himself by coming incautiously out of his chair, without first taking time to think about it and compose his mind. When he had found his voice—which it took him a long time to do, for it was a long way off, and hidden under a load of meat—he said in a fat whisper,

"Who's it from?"

Toby told him.

"You're to take it in, yourself," said the Porter, pointing to a room at the end of a long passage, opening from the hall. "Everything goes straight in, on this day of the year. You're not a bit too soon; for the carriage is at the door now, and they have only come to town for a couple of hours, a' purpose."

Toby wiped his feet (which were quite dry already) with great care, and took the way pointed out to him; observing as he went that it was an awfully grand house, but hushed and covered up, as if the family were in the country. Knocking at the room-door, he was told to enter from within; and doing so found himself in a spacious library, where, at a table strewn with files and papers, were a stately lady in a bonnet; and a not very stately gentleman in black who wrote from her dictation; while another, and an older, and a much statelier gentleman, whose hat and cane were on the table, walked up and down, with one hand in his breast, and looked complacently from time to time at his own picture—a full length; a very full length—hanging over the fireplace.

"What is this?" said the last-named gentleman. "Mr. Fish, will you have the goodness to attend?"

Mr. Fish begged pardon, and taking the letter from Toby, handed it, with great respect.

"From Alderman Cute, Sir Joseph."

"Is this all? Have you nothing else, Porter?" inquired Sir Joseph.

Toby replied in the negative.

"You have no bill or demand upon me—my name is Bowley, Sir Joseph Bowley—of any kind from anybody, have you?" said Sir Joseph. "If you have, present it. There is a cheque-book by the side of Mr. Fish. I allow nothing to be carried into the New Year. Every description of account is settled in this house at the close of the old one. So that if death was to—to—"

"To cut," suggested Mr. Fish.

"To sever, sir," returned Sir Joseph, with great asperity, "the cord of existence—my affairs would be found, I hope, in a state of preparation."

"My dear Sir Joseph!" said the lady, who was greatly younger than the gentleman. "How shocking!"

"My lady Bowley," returned Sir Joseph, floundering now and then, as in the great depth of his observations, "at this season of the year we should think of—of—ourselves. We should look into our—our accounts. We should feel that every return of so eventful a period in human transactions, involves a matter of deep moment between a man and his—and his banker."

Sir Joseph delivered these words as if he felt the full morality of what he was saying; and desired that even Trotty should have an opportunity of being improved by such discourse. Possibly he had this end before him in still forbearing to break the seal of the letter, and in telling Trotty to wait where he was, a minute.

"You were desiring Mr. Fish to say, my lady—" observed Sir Joseph.

"Mr. Fish has said that, I believe," returned his lady, glancing at the letter. "But, upon my word, Sir Joseph, I don't think I can let it go after all. It is so very dear."

"What is dear?" inquired Sir Joseph.

"That Charity, my love. They only allow two votes for a subscription of five pounds. Really monstrous!"

"My lady Bowley," returned Sir Joseph, "you surprise me. Is the luxury of feeling in proportion to the number of votes; or is it, to a rightly constituted mind, in proportion to the number of applicants, and the wholesome state of mind to which their canvassing reduces them? Is there no excitement of the purest kind in having two votes to dispose of among fifty people?"

"Not to me, I acknowledge," replied the lady. "It bores one. Besides, one can't oblige one's acquaintance. But you are the Poor Man's Friend, you know, Sir Joseph. You think otherwise."

"I am the Poor Man's Friend," observed Sir Joseph, glancing at the poor man present. "As such I may be taunted. As such I have been taunted. But I ask no other title."

"Bless him for a noble gentleman!" thought Trotty.

"I don't agree with Cute here, for instance," said Sir Joseph, holding out the letter. "I don't agree with the Filer party. I don't agree with any party. My friend the Poor Man, has no business with anything of that sort, and nothing of that sort has any business with him. My friend the Poor Man, in my district, is my business. No man or body of men has any right to interfere between my friend and me. That is the ground I take. I assume a—a paternal character towards my friend. I say, 'My good fellow, I will treat you paternally.'"

Toby listened with great gravity, and began to feel more comfortable.

"Your only business, my good fellow," pursued Sir Joseph, looking abstractedly at Toby; "your only business in life is with me. You needn't trouble yourself to think about anything. I will think for you; I know what is good for you; I am your perpetual parent. Such is the dispensation of an all-wise Providence! Now, the design of your creation is—not that you should swill, and guzzle, and associate your enjoyments, brutally, with food"; Toby thought remorsefully of the tripe; "but that you should feel the Dignity of Labour. Go forth erect into the cheerful morning air, and—and stop there. Live hard and temperately, be respectful, exercise your self-denial, bring up your family on next to nothing, pay your rent as regularly as the clock strikes, be punctual in your dealings (I set you a good example; you will find Mr. Fish, my confidential secretary, with a cash-box before him at all times); and you may trust to me to be your Friend and Father."

"Nice children, indeed, Sir Joseph!" said the lady, with a shudder. "Rheumatisms, and fevers, and crooked legs, and asthmas, and all kinds of horrors!"

"My lady," returned Sir Joseph, with solemnity, "not the less am I the Poor Man's Friend and Father. Not the less shall he receive encouragement at my hands. Every quarter-day he will be put in communication with Mr. Fish. Every New Year's Day, myself and friends will drink his health. Once every year, myself and friends will address him with the deepest feeling. Once in his life, he may even perhaps receive; in public, in the presence of the gentry; a Trifle from a Friend. And when, upheld no more by these stimulants, and the Dignity of Labour, he sinks into his comfortable grave, then, my lady"—here Sir Joseph blew his nose—"I will be a Friend and a Father—on the same terms—to his children."

Toby was greatly moved.

"O! You have a thankful family, Sir Joseph!" cried his wife.

"My lady," said Sir Joseph, quite majestically, "Ingratitude is known to be the sin of that class. I expect no other return."

"Ah! Born bad!" thought Toby. "Nothing melts us."

"What man can do, I do," pursued Sir Joseph. "I do my duty as the Poor Man's Friend and Father; and I endeavour to educate his mind, by inculcating on all occasions the one great moral lesson which that class requires. That is, entire Dependence on myself. They have no business whatever with—with themselves. If wicked and designing persons tell them otherwise, and they become impatient and discontented, and are guilty of insubordinate conduct and black-hearted ingratitude; which is undoubtedly the case; I am their Friend and Father still. It is so Ordained. It is in the nature of things."

With that great sentiment, he opened the Alderman's letter; and read it.

"Very polite and attentive, I am sure!" exclaimed Sir Joseph. "My lady, the Alderman is so obliging as to remind me that he has had "the distinguished honour"—he is very good—of meeting me at the house of our mutual friend Deedles, the banker; and he does me the favour to inquire whether it will be agreeable to me to have Will Fern put down."

"Most agreeable!" replied my Lady Bowley. "The worst man among them! He has been committing a robbery, I hope?"

"Why no," said Sir Joseph," referring to the letter. "Not quite. Very near. Not quite. He came up to London, it seems, to look for employment (trying to better himself—that's his story), and being found at night asleep in a shed, was taken into custody, and carried next morning before the Alderman. The Alderman observes (very properly) that he is determined to put this sort of thing down; and that if it will be agreeable to me to have Will Fern put down, he will be happy to begin with him."

"Let him be made an example of, by all means," returned the lady. "Last winter, when I introduced pinking and eyelet-holing among the men and boys in the village, as a nice evening employment, and had the lines,

O let us love our occupations,
Bless the squire and his relations,
Live upon our daily rations,
And always know our proper stations,

set to music on the new system, for them to sing the while; this very Fern—I see him now—touched that hat of his, and said, 'I humbly ask your pardon, my lady, but an't I something different from a great girl?' I expected it, of course; who can expect anything but insolence and ingratitude from that class of people! That is not to the purpose, however. Sir Joseph! Make an example of him!"

"Hem!" coughed Sir Joseph. "Mr. Fish, if you'll have the goodness to attend—"

Mr. Fish immediately seized his pen, and wrote from Sir Joseph's dictation.

"Private. My dear Sir. I am very much indebted to you for your courtesy in the matter of the man William Fern, of whom, I regret to add, I can say nothing favourable. I have uniformly considered myself in the light of his Friend and Father, but have been repaid (a common case, I grieve to say) with ingratitude, and constant opposition to my plans. He is a turbulent and rebellious spirit. His character will not bear investigation. Nothing will persuade him to be happy when he might. Under these circumstances, it appears to me, I own, that when he comes before you again (as you informed me he promised to do to-morrow, pending your inquiries, and I think he may be so far relied upon), his committal for some short term as a Vagabond, would be a service to society, and would be a salutary example in a country where—for the sake of those who are, through good and evil report, the Friends and Fathers of the Poor, as well as with a view to that, generally speaking, misguided class themselves—examples are greatly needed. And I am," and so forth.

"It appears," remarked Sir Joseph when he had signed this letter, and Mr. Fish was sealing it, "as if this were Ordained: really. At the close of the year, I wind up my account and strike my balance, even with William Fern!"

Trotty, who had long ago relapsed, and was very low-spirited, stepped forward with a rueful face to take the letter.

"With my compliments and thanks," said Sir Joseph. "Stop!"

"Stop!" echoed Mr. Fish.

"You have heard, perhaps," said Sir Joseph, oracularly, "certain remarks into which I have been led respecting the solemn period of time at which we have arrived, and the duty imposed upon us of settling our affairs, and being prepared. You have observed that I don't shelter myself behind my superior standing in society, but that Mr. Fish—that gentleman—has a cheque-book at his elbow, and is in fact here, to enable me to turn over a perfectly new leaf, and enter on the epoch before us with a clean account. Now, my friend, can you lay your hand upon your heart, and say, that you also have made preparations for a New Year?"

"I am afraid, sir," stammered Trotty, looking meekly at him, "that I am a—a— little behind-hand with the world."

"Behind-hand with the world!" repeated Sir Joseph Bowley, in a tone of terrible distinctness.

"I am afraid, sir," faltered Trotty, "that there's a matter of ten or twelve shillings owing to Mrs. Chickenstalker."

"To Mrs. Chickenstalker!" repeated Sir Joseph, in the same tone as before.

"A shop, sir," exclaimed Toby, "in the general line. Also a—a little money on account of rent. A very little, sir. It oughtn't to be owing, I know, but we have been hard put to it, indeed!"

Sir Joseph looked at his lady, and at Mr. Fish, and at Trotty, one after another, twice all round. He then made a despondent gesture with both hands at once, as if he gave the thing up altogether.

"How a man, even among this improvident and impracticable race; an old man; a man grown grey; can look a New Year in the face, with his affairs in this condition; how he can lie down on his bed at night, and get up again in the morning, and— There!" he said, turning his back on Trotty. "Take the letter. Take the letter!"

"I heartily wish it was otherwise, sir," said Trotty, anxious to excuse himself. "We have been tried very hard."

Sir Joseph still repeating "Take the letter, take the letter!" and Mr. Fish not only saying the same thing, but giving additional force to the request by motioning the bearer to the door, he had nothing for it but to make his bow and leave the house. And in the street, poor Trotty pulled his worn old hat down on his head, to hide the grief he felt at getting no hold on the New Year, anywhere.

He didn't even lift his hat to look up at the Bell tower when he came to the old church on his return. He halted there a moment, from habit: and knew that it was growing dark, and that the steeple rose above him, indistinct and faint, in the murky air. He knew, too, that the Chimes would ring immediately; and that they sounded to his fancy, at such a time, like voices in the clouds. But he only made the more haste to deliver the Alderman's letter, and get out of the way before they began; for he dreaded to hear them tagging "Friends and Fathers, Friends and Fathers," to the burden they had rung out last.

Toby discharged himself of his commission, therefore, with all possible speed, and set off trotting homeward. But what with his pace, which was at best an awkward one in the street; and what with his hat, which didn't improve it; he trotted against somebody in less than no time, and was sent staggering out into the road.

"I beg your pardon, I'm sure!" said Trotty, pulling up his hat in great confusion, and between the hat and the torn lining, fixing his head into a kind of bee-hive. "I hope I haven't hurt you."

As to hurting anybody, Toby was not such an absolute Samson, but that he was much more likely to be hurt himself: and indeed, he had flown out into the road, like a shuttlecock. He had such an opinion of his own strength, however, that he was in real concern for the other party: and said again,

"I hope I haven't hurt you?"

The man against whom he had run; a sun-browned, sinewy, country-looking man, with grizzled hair, and a rough chin; stared at him for a moment, as if he suspected him to be in jest. But, satisfied of his good faith, he answered:

"No, friend. You have not hurt me."

"Nor the child, I hope?" said Trotty.

"Nor the child," returned the man. "I thank you kindly."

As he said so, he glanced at a little girl he carried in his arms, asleep: and shading her face with the long end of the poor handkerchief he wore about his throat, went slowly on.

The tone in which he said "I thank you kindly," penetrated Trotty's heart. He was so jaded and foot-sore, and so soiled with travel, and looked about him so forlorn and strange, that it was a comfort to him to be able to thank any one: no matter for how little. Toby stood gazing after him as he plodded wearily away, with the child's arm clinging round his neck.

At the figure in the worn shoes—now the very shade and ghost of shoes— rough leather leggings, common frock, and broad slouched hat, Trotty stood gazing, blind to the whole street. And at the child's arm, clinging round its neck.

Before he merged into the darkness the traveller stopped; and looking round, and seeing Trotty standing there yet, seemed undecided whether to return or go on. After doing first the one and then the other, he came back, and Trotty went half-way to meet him.

"You can tell me, perhaps," said the man with a faint smile, "and if you can I am sure you will, and I'd rather ask you than another—where Alderman Cute lives."

"Close at hand," replied Toby. "I'll show you his house with pleasure."

"I was to have gone to him elsewhere to-morrow," said the man, accompanying Toby, "but I'm uneasy under suspicion, and want to clear myself, and to be free to go and seek my bread—I don't know where. So, maybe he'll forgive my going to his house to-night."

"It's impossible," cried Toby with a start, "that your name's Fern!"

"Eh!" cried the other, turning on him in astonishment.

"Fern! Will Fern!" said Trotty.

"That's my name," replied the other.

"Why then," said Trotty, seizing him by the arm, and looking cautiously round, "for Heaven's sake don't go to him! Don't go to him! He'll put you down as sure as ever you were born. Here! come up this alley, and I'll tell you what I mean. Don't go to him."

His new acquaintance looked as if he thought him mad; but he bore him company nevertheless. When they were shrouded from observation, Trotty told him what he knew, and what character he had received, and all about it.

The subject of his history listened to it with a calmness that surprised him. He did not contradict or interrupt it, once. He nodded his head now and then—more in corroboration of an old and worn-out story, it appeared, than in refutation of it; and once or twice threw back his hat, and passed his freckled hand over a brow, where every furrow he had ploughed seemed to have set its image in little. But he did no more.

"It's true enough in the main," he said, "master, I could sift grain from husk here and there, but let it be as 'tis. What odds? I have gone against his plans; to my misfortun'. I can't help it; I should do the like to-morrow. As to character, them gentlefolks will search and search, and pry and pry, and have it as free from spot or speck in us, afore they'll help us to a dry good word!—Well! I hope they don't lose good opinion as easy as we do, or their lives is strict indeed, and hardly worth the keeping. For myself, master, I never took with that hand"—holding it before him—"what wasn't my own; and never held it back from work, however hard, or poorly paid. Whoever can deny it, let him chop it off! But when work won't maintain me like a human creetur; when my living is so bad, that I am Hungry, out of doors and in; when I see a whole working life begin that way, go on that way, and end that way, without a chance or change; then I say to the gentlefolks 'Keep away from me! Let my cottage be. My doors is dark enough without your darkening of 'em more. Don't look for me to come up into the Park to help the show when there's a Birthday, or a fine Speechmaking, or what not. Act your Plays and Games without me, and be welcome to 'em, and enjoy 'em. We've nowt to do with one another. I'm best let alone!'"

Seeing that the child in his arms had opened her eyes, and was looking about her in wonder, he checked himself to say a word or two of foolish prattle in her ear, and stand her on the ground beside him. Then slowly winding one of her long tresses round and round his rough forefinger like a ring, while she hung about his dusty leg, he said to Trotty:

"I'm not a cross-grained man by natur', I believe; and easy satisfied, I'm sure. I bear no ill-will against none of 'em. I only want to live like one of the Almighty's creeturs. I can't—I don't—and so there's a pit dug between me, and them that can and do. There's others like me. You might tell 'em off by hundreds and by thousands, sooner than by ones."

Trotty knew he spoke the Truth in this, and shook his head to signify as much.

"I've got a bad name this way," said Fern; "and I'm not likely, I'm afeared, to get a better. 'Tan't lawful to be out of sorts, and I am out of sorts, though God knows I'd sooner bear a cheerful spirit if I could. Well! I don't know as this Alderman could hurt me much by sending me to jail; but without a friend to speak a word for me, he might do it; and you see—!" pointing downward with his finger, at the child.

"She has a beautiful face," said Trotty.

"Why yes!" replied the other in a low voice, as he gently turned it up with both his hands towards his own, and looked upon it steadfastly. "I've thought so, many times. I've thought so, when my hearth was very cold, and cupboard very bare. I thought so t'other night, when we were taken like two thieves. But they—they shouldn't try the little face too often, should they, Lilian? That's hardly fair upon a man!"

He sunk his voice so low, and gazed upon her with an air so stern and strange, that Toby, to divert the current of his thoughts, inquired if his wife were living.

"I never had one," he returned, shaking his head. "She's my brother's child: a orphan. Nine year old, though you'd hardly think it; but she's tired and worn out now. They'd have taken care on her, the Union—eight-and-twenty mile away from where we live—between four walls (as they took care of my old father when he couldn't work no more, though he didn't trouble 'em long); but I took her instead, and she's lived with me ever since. Her mother had a friend once, in London here. We are trying to find her, and to find work too; but it's a large place. Never mind. More room for us to walk about in, Lilly!"

Meeting the child's eyes with a smile which melted Toby more than tears, he shook him by the hand.

"I don't so much as know your name," he said, "but I've opened my heart free to you, for I'm thankful to you; with good reason. I'll take your advice, and keep clear of this—"

"Justice," suggested Toby.

"Ah!" he said. "If that's the name they give him. This Justice. And to-morrow will try whether there's better fortun' to be met with, somewheres near London. Good night. A Happy New Year!"

"Stay!" cried Trotty, catching at his hand, as he relaxed his grip. "Stay! The New Year never can be happy to me, if we part like this. The New Year never can be happy to me, if I see the child and you go wandering away, you don't know where, without a shelter for your heads. Come home with me! I'm a poor man, living in a poor place; but I can give you lodging for one night and never miss it. Come home with me! Here! I'll take her!" cried Trotty, lifting up the child. "A pretty one! I'd carry twenty times her weight, and never know I'd got it. Tell me if I go too quick for you. I'm very fast. I always was!" Trotty said this, taking about six of his trotting paces to one stride of his fatigued companion; and with his thin legs quivering again, beneath the load he bore.

"Why, she's as light," said Trotty, trotting in his speech as well as in his gait; for he couldn't bear to be thanked, and dreaded a moment's pause; "as light as a feather. Lighter than a Peacock's feather—a great deal lighter. Here we are and here we go! Round this first turning to the right, Uncle Will, and past the pump, and sharp off up the passage to the left, right opposite the public-house. Here we are and here we go! Cross over, Uncle Will, and mind the kidney pieman at the corner! Here we are and here we go! Down the Mews here, Uncle Will, and stop at the black door, with "T. Veck, Ticket Porter," wrote upon a board; and here we are and here we go, and here we are indeed, my precious. Meg, surprising you!"

With which words Trotty, in a breathless state, set the child down before his daughter in the middle of the floor. The little visitor looked once at Meg; and doubting nothing in that face, but trusting everything she saw there; ran into her arms.

"Here we are and here we go!" cried Trotty, running round the room, and choking audibly. "Here, Uncle Will, here's a fire you know! Why don't you come to the fire? Oh here we are and here we go! Meg, my precious darling, where's the kettle? Here it is and here it goes, and it'll bile in no time!"

Trotty really had picked up the kettle somewhere or other in the course of his wild career and now put it on the fire: while Meg, seating the child in a warm corner, knelt down on the ground before her, and pulled off her shoes, and dried her wet feet on a cloth. Ay, and she laughed at Trotty too—so pleasantly, so cheerfully, that Trotty could have blessed her where she knelt; for he had seen that, when they entered, she was sitting by the fire in tears.

"Why, father!" said Meg. "You're crazy to-night, I think. I don't know what the Bells would say to that. Poor little feet. How cold they are!"

"Oh, they're warmer now!" exclaimed the child. "They're quite warm now!"

"No, no, no," said Meg. "We haven't rubbed 'em half enough. We're so busy. So busy! And when they're done, we'll brush out the damp hair; and when that's done, we'll bring some colour to the poor pale face with fresh water; and when that's done, we'll be so gay, and brisk, and happy—!"

The child, in a burst of sobbing, clasped her round the neck; caressed her fair cheek with its hand; and said, "Oh Meg! oh dear Meg!"

Toby's blessing could have done no more. Who could do more!

"Why, father!" cried Meg, after a pause.

"Here I am and here I go, my dear!" said Trotty.

"Good Gracious me!" cried Meg. "He's crazy! He's put the dear child's bonnet on the kettle, and hung the lid behind the door!"

"I didn't go for to do it, my love," said Trotty, hastily repairing this mistake. "Meg, my dear?"

Meg looked towards him and saw that he had elaborately stationed himself behind the chair of their male visitor, where with many mysterious gestures he was holding up the sixpence he had earned.

"I see, my dear," said Trotty, "as I was coming in, half an ounce of tea lying somewhere on the stairs; and I'm pretty sure there was a bit of bacon too. As I don't remember where it was exactly, I'll go myself and try to find 'em."

With this inscrutable artifice, Toby withdrew to purchase the viands he had spoken of, for ready money, at Mrs. Chickenstalker's; and presently came back, pretending he had not been able to find them, at first, in the dark.

"But here they are at last," said Trotty, setting out the tea-things, "all correct! I was pretty sure it was tea, and a rasher. So it is. Meg, my pet, if you'll just make the tea, while your unworthy father toasts the bacon, we shall be ready, immediate. It's a curious circumstance," said Trotty, proceeding in his cookery, with the assistance of the toasting-fork, "curious, but well known to my friends, that I never care, myself, for rashers, nor for tea. I like to see other people enjoy 'em," said Trotty, speaking very loud, to impress the fact upon his guest, "but to me, as food, they're disagreeable."

Yet Trotty sniffed the savour of the hissing bacon—ah!—as if he liked it; and when he poured the boiling water in the tea-pot, looked lovingly down into the depths of that snug cauldron, and suffered the fragrant steam to curl about his nose, and wreathe his head and face in a thick cloud. However, for all this, he neither ate nor drank, except at the very beginning, a mere morsel for form's sake, which he appeared to eat with infinite relish, but declared was perfectly uninteresting to him.

No. Trotty's occupation was, to see Will Fern and Lilian eat and drink; and so was Meg's. And never did spectators at a city dinner or court banquet find such high delight in seeing others feast: although it were a monarch or a pope: as those two did, in looking on that night. Meg smiled at Trotty, Trotty laughed at Meg. Meg shook her head, and made belief to clap her hands, applauding Trotty; Trotty conveyed, in dumb-show, unintelligible narratives of how and when and where he had found their visitors, to Meg; and they were happy. Very happy.

"Although," thought Trotty, sorrowfully, as he watched Meg's face; "that match is broken off, I see!"

"Now, I'll tell you what," said Trotty after tea. "The little one, she sleeps with Meg, I know."

"With good Meg!" cried the child, caressing her. "With Meg."

"That's right," said Trotty. "And I shouldn't wonder if she kiss Meg's father, won't she? I'm Meg's father."

Mightily delighted Trotty was, when the child went timidly towards him, and having kissed him, fell back upon Meg again.

"She's as sensible as Solomon," said Trotty. "Here we come and here we—no, we don't—I don't mean that—I—what was I saying, Meg, my precious?"

Meg looked towards their guest, who leaned upon her chair, and with his face turned from her, fondled the child's head, half hidden in her lap.

"To be sure," said Toby. "To be sure! I don't know what I'm rambling on about, to-night. My wits are wool-gathering, I think. Will Fern, you come along with me. You're tired to death, and broken down for want of rest. You come along with me." The man still played with the child's curls, still leaned upon Meg's chair, still turned away his face. He didn't speak, but in his rough coarse fingers, clenching and expanding in the fair hair of the child, there was an eloquence that said enough.

"Yes, yes," said Trotty, answering unconsciously what he saw expressed in his daughter's face. "Take her with you, Meg. Get her to bed. There! Now, Will, I'll show you where you lie. It's not much of a place: only a loft; but, having a loft, I always say, is one of the great conveniences of living in a mews; and till this coach-house and stable gets a better let, we live here cheap. There's plenty of sweet hay up there, belonging to a neighbour; and it's as clean as hands, and Meg, can make it. Cheer up! Don't give way. A new heart for a New Year, always!"

The hand released from the child's hair, had fallen, trembling, into Trotty's hand. So Trotty, talking without intermission, led him out as tenderly and easily as if he had been a child himself.

Returning before Meg, he listened for an instant at the door of her little chamber; an adjoining room. The child was murmuring a simple Prayer before lying down to sleep; and when she had remembered Meg's name, "Dearly, Dearly"—so her words ran—Trotty heard her stop and ask for his.

It was some short time before the foolish little old fellow could compose himself to mend the fire, and draw his chair to the warm hearth. But, when he had done so, and had trimmed the light, he took his newspaper from his pocket, and began to read. Carelessly at first, and skimming up and down the columns; but with an earnest and a sad attention, very soon.

For this same dreaded paper re-directed Trotty's thoughts into the channel they had taken all that day, and which the day's events had so marked out and shaped. His interest in the two wanderers had set him on another course of thinking, and a happier one, for the time; but being alone again, and reading of the crimes and violences of the people, he relapsed into his former train.

In this mood, he came to an account (and it was not the first he had ever read) of a woman who had laid her desperate hands not only on her own life but on that of her young child. A crime so terrible, and so revolting to his soul, dilated with the love of Meg, that he let the journal drop, and fell back in his chair, appalled!

"Unnatural and cruel!" Toby cried. "Unnatural and cruel! None but people who were bad at heart, born bad, who had no business on the earth, could do such deeds. It's too true, all I've heard to-day; too just, too full of proof. We're Bad!"

The Chimes took up the words so suddenly—burst out so loud, and clear, and sonorous—that the Bells seemed to strike him in his chair.

And what was that, they said?

"Toby Veck, Toby Veck, waiting for you Toby! Toby Veck, Toby Veck, waiting for you Toby! Come and see us, come and see us, Drag him to us, drag him to us, Haunt and hunt him, haunt and hunt him, Break his slumbers, break his slumbers! Toby Veck Toby Veck, door open wide Toby, Toby Veck Toby Veck, door open wide Toby—" then fiercely back to their impetuous strain again, and ringing in the very bricks and plaster on the walls.

Toby listened. Fancy, fancy! His remorse for having run away from them that afternoon! No, no. Nothing of the kind. Again, again, and yet a dozen times again. "Haunt and hunt him, haunt and hunt him, Drag him to us, drag him to us!" Deafening the whole town!

"Meg," said Trotty softly: tapping at her door. "Do you hear anything?"

"I hear the Bells, father. Surely they're very loud to-night."

"Is she asleep?" said Toby, making an excuse for peeping in.

"So peacefully and happily! I can't leave her yet though, father. Look how she holds my hand!"

"Meg," whispered Trotty. "Listen to the Bells!"

She listened, with her face towards him all the time. But it underwent no change. She didn't understand them.

Trotty withdrew, resumed his seat by the fire, and once more listened by himself. He remained here a little time.

It was impossible to bear it; their energy was dreadful.

"If the tower-door is really open," said Toby, hastily laying aside his apron, but never thinking of his hat, "what's to hinder me from going up into the steeple and satisfying myself? If it's shut, I don't want any other satisfaction. That's enough."

He was pretty certain as he slipped out quietly into the street that he should find it shut and locked, for he knew the door well, and had so rarely seen it open, that he couldn't reckon above three times in all. It was a low arched portal, outside the church, in a dark nook behind a column; and had such great iron hinges, and such a monstrous lock, that there was more hinge and lock than door.

But what was his astonishment when, coming bare-headed to the church; and putting his hand into this dark nook, with a certain misgiving that it might be unexpectedly seized, and a shivering propensity to draw it back again; he found that the door, which opened outwards, actually stood ajar!

He thought, on the first surprise, of going back; or of getting a light, or a companion, but his courage aided him immediately, and he determined to ascend alone.

"What have I to fear?" said Trotty. "It's a church! Besides, the ringers may be there, and have forgotten to shut the door." So he went in, feeling his way as he went, like a blind man; for it was very dark. And very quiet, for the Chimes were silent.

The dust from the street had blown into the recess; and lying there, heaped up, made it so soft and velvet-like to the foot, that there was something startling, even in that. The narrow stair was so close to the door, too, that he stumbled at the very first; and shutting the door upon himself, by striking it with his foot, and causing it to rebound back heavily, he couldn't open it again.

This was another reason, however, for going on. Trotty groped his way, and went on. Up, up, up, and round, and round; and up, up, up; higher, higher, higher up!

It was a disagreeable staircase for that groping work; so low and narrow, that his groping hand was always touching something; and it often felt so like a man or ghostly figure standing up erect and making room for him to pass without discovery, that he would rub the smooth wall upward searching for its face, and downward searching for its feet, while a chill tingling crept all over him. Twice or thrice, a door or niche broke the monotonous surface; and then it seemed a gap as wide as the whole church; and he felt on the brink of an abyss, and going to tumble headlong down, until he found the wall again.

Still up, up, up; and round and round; and up, up, up; higher, higher, higher up!

At length, the dull and stifling atmosphere began to freshen: presently to feel quite windy: presently it blew so strong, that he could hardly keep his legs. But, he got to an arched window in the tower, breast high, and holding tight, looked down upon the house-tops, on the smoking chimneys, on the blurr and blotch of lights (towards the place where Meg was wondering where he was and calling to him perhaps), all kneaded up together in a leaven of mist and darkness.

This was the belfry, where the ringers came. He had caught hold of one of the frayed ropes which hung down through apertures in the oaken roof. At first he started, thinking it was hair; then trembled at the very thought of waking the deep Bell. The Bells themselves were higher. Higher, Trotty, in his fascination, or in working out the spell upon him, groped his way. By ladders now, and toilsomely, for it was steep, and not too certain holding for the feet.

Up, up, up; and climb and clamber; up, up, up; higher, higher, higher up!

Until, ascending through the floor, and pausing with his head just raised above its beams, he came among the Bells. It was barely possible to make out their great shapes in the gloom; but there they were. Shadowy, and dark, and dumb.

A heavy sense of dread and loneliness fell instantly upon him, as he climbed into this airy nest of stone and metal. His head went round and round. He listened, and then raised a wild "Holloa!" Holloa! was mournfully protracted by the echoes.

Giddy, confused, and out of breath, and frightened, Toby looked about him vacantly, and sunk down in a swoon.

CHAPTER III. THIRD QUARTER

Black are the brooding clouds and troubled the deep waters, when the Sea of Thought, first heaving from a calm, gives up its Dead. Monsters uncouth and wild, arise in premature, imperfect resurrection; the several parts and shapes of different things are joined and mixed by chance; and when, and how, and by what wonderful degrees, each separates from each, and every sense and object of the mind resumes its usual form and lives again, no man—though every man is every day the casket of this type of the Great Mystery—can tell.

So, when and how the darkness of the night-black steeple changed to shining light; when and how the solitary tower was peopled with a myriad figures; when and how the whispered "Haunt and hunt him," breathing monotonously through his sleep or swoon, became a voice exclaiming in the waking ears of Trotty, "Break his slumbers"; when and how he ceased to have a sluggish and confused idea that such things were, companioning a host of others that were not; there are no dates or means to tell. But, awake and standing on his feet upon the boards where he had lately lain, he saw this Goblin Sight.

He saw the tower, whither his charmed footsteps had brought him, swarming with dwarf phantoms, spirits, elfin creatures of the Bells. He saw them leaping, flying, dropping, pouring from the Bells without a pause. He saw them, round him on the ground; above him, in the air; clambering from him, by the ropes below; looking down upon him, from the massive iron-girded beams; peeping in upon him, through the chinks and loopholes in the walls; spreading away and away from him in enlarging circles, as the water ripples give way to a huge stone that suddenly comes plashing in among them. He saw them, of all aspects and all shapes. He saw them ugly, handsome, crippled, exquisitely formed. He saw them young, he saw them old, he saw them kind, he saw them cruel, he saw them merry, he saw them grim; he saw them dance, and heard them sing; he saw them tear their hair, and heard them howl. He saw the air thick with them. He saw them come and go, incessantly. He saw them riding downward, soaring upward, sailing off afar, perching near at hand, all restless and all violently active. Stone, and brick, and slate, and tile, became transparent to him as to them. He saw them in the houses, busy at the sleepers' beds. He saw them soothing people in their dreams; he saw them beating them with knotted whips; he saw them yelling in their ears; he saw them playing softest music on their pillows; he saw them cheering some with the songs of birds and the perfume of flowers; he saw them flashing awful faces on the troubled rest of others, from enchanted mirrors which they carried in their hands.

He saw these creatures, not only among sleeping men but waking also, active in pursuits irreconcilable with one another, and possessing or assuming natures the most opposite. He saw one buckling on innumerable wings to increase his speed; another loading himself with chains and weights, to retard his. He saw some putting the hands of clocks forward, some putting the hands of clocks backward, some endeavouring to stop the clock entirely. He saw them representing, here a marriage ceremony, there a funeral; in this chamber an election, in that a ball he saw, everywhere, restless and untiring motion.

Bewildered by the host of shifting and extraordinary figures, as well as by the uproar of the Bells, which all this while were ringing, Trotty clung to a wooden pillar for support, and turned his white face here and there, in mute and stunned astonishment.

As he gazed, the Chimes stopped. Instantaneous change! The whole swarm fainted! their forms collapsed, their speed deserted them; they sought to fly, but in the act of falling died and melted into air. No fresh supply succeeded them. One straggler leaped down pretty briskly from the surface of the Great Bell, and alighted on his feet, but he was dead and gone before he could turn round. Some few of the late company who had gambolled in the tower, remained there, spinning over and over a little longer; but these became at every turn more faint, and few, and feeble, and soon went the way of the rest. The last of all was one small hunchback, who had got into an echoing corner, where he twirled and twirled, and floated by himself a long time; showing such perseverance, that at last he dwindled to a leg and even to a foot, before he finally retired; but he vanished in the end, and then the tower was silent.

Then and not before, did Trotty see in every Bell a bearded figure of the bulk and stature of the Bell—incomprehensibly, a figure and the Bell itself. Gigantic, grave, and darkly watchful of him, as he stood rooted to the ground.

Mysterious and awful figures! Resting on nothing; poised in the night air of the tower, with their draped and hooded heads merged in the dim roof; motionless and shadowy. Shadowy and dark, although he saw them by some light belonging to themselves—none else was there—each with its muffled hand upon its goblin mouth.

He could not plunge down wildly through the opening in the floor; for all power of motion had deserted him. Otherwise he would have done so—aye, would have thrown himself, headforemost, from the steeple-top, rather than have seen them watching him with eyes that would have waked and watched although the pupils had been taken out.

Again, again, the dread and terror of the lonely place, and of the wild and fearful night that reigned there, touched him like a spectral hand. His distance from all help; the long, dark, winding, ghost-beleaguered way that lay between him and the earth on which men lived; his being high, high, high, up there, where it had made him dizzy to see the birds fly in the day; cut off from all good people, who at such an hour were safe at home and sleeping in their beds; all this struck coldly through him, not as a reflection but a bodily sensation. Meantime his eyes and thoughts and fears, were fixed upon the watchful figures; which, rendered unlike any figures of this world by the deep gloom and shade enwrapping and enfolding them, as well as by their looks and forms and supernatural hovering above the floor, were nevertheless as plainly to be seen as were the stalwart oaken frames, cross-pieces, bars and beams, set up there to support the Bells. These hemmed them, in a very forest of hewn timber; from the entanglements, intricacies, and depths of which, as from among the boughs of a dead wood blighted for their phantom use, they kept their darksome and unwinking watch.

A blast of air—how cold and shrill!—came moaning through the tower. As it died away, the Great Bell, or the Goblin of the Great Bell, spoke.

"What visitor is this!" it said. The voice was low and deep, and Trotty fancied that it sounded in the other figures as well.

"I thought my name was called by the Chimes!" said Trotty, raising his hands in an attitude of supplication. "I hardly know why I am here, or how I came. I have listened to the Chimes these many years. They have cheered me often."

"And you have thanked them?" said the Bell.

"A thousand times!" cried Trotty.

"How?"

"I am a poor man," faltered Trotty, "and could only thank them in words."

"And always so?" inquired the Goblin of the Bell. "Have you never done us wrong in words?"

"No!" cried Trotty eagerly.

"Never done us foul, and false, and wicked wrong, in words?" pursued the Goblin of the Bell.

Trotty was about to answer, "Never!" But he stopped, and was confused.

"The voice of Time," said the Phantom, "cries to man, Advance! Time is for his advancement and improvement; for his greater worth, his greater happiness, his better life; his progress onward to that goal within its knowledge and its view, and set there, in the period when Time and He began. Ages of darkness, wickedness, and violence, have come and gone—millions uncountable, have suffered, lived, and died—to point the way before him. Who seeks to turn him back, or stay him on his course, arrests a mighty engine which will strike the meddler dead; and be the fiercer and the wilder, ever, for its momentary check!"

"I never did so to my knowledge, sir," said Trotty. "It was quite by accident if I did. I wouldn't go to do it, I'm sure."

"Who puts into the mouth of Time, or of its servants," said the Goblin of the Bell, "a cry of lamentation for days which have had their trial and their failure, and have left deep traces of it which the blind may see—a cry that only serves the present time, by showing men how much it needs their help when any ears can listen to regrets for such a past—who does this, does a wrong. And you have done that wrong, to us, the Chimes."

Trotty's first excess of fear was gone. But he had felt tenderly and gratefully towards the Bells, as you have seen; and when he heard himself arraigned as one who had offended them so weightily, his heart was touched with penitence and grief.

"If you knew," said Trotty, clasping his hands earnestly—"or perhaps you do know—if you know how often you have kept me company; how often you have cheered me up when I've been low; how you were quite the plaything of my little daughter Meg (almost the only one she ever had) when first her mother died, and she and me were left alone; you won't bear malice for a hasty word!"

"Who hears in us, the Chimes, one note bespeaking disregard, or stern regard, of any hope, or joy, or pain, or sorrow, of the many-sorrowed throng; who hears us make response to any creed that gauges human passions and affections, as it gauges the amount of miserable food on which humanity may pine and wither; does us wrong. That wrong you have done us!" said the Bell.

"I have!" said Trotty. "Oh forgive me!"

"Who hears us echo the dull vermin of the earth: the Putters Down of crushed and broken natures, formed to be raised up higher than such maggots of the time can crawl or can conceive," pursued the Goblin of the Bell; "who does so, does us wrong. And you have done us wrong!"

"Not meaning it," said Trotty. "In my ignorance. Not meaning it!"

"Lastly, and most of all," pursued the Bell. "Who turns his back upon the fallen and disfigured of his kind; abandons them as vile; and does not trace and track with pitying eyes the unfenced precipice by which they fell from good—grasping in their fall some tufts and shreds of that lost soil, and clinging to them still when bruised and dying in the gulf below; does wrong to Heaven and man, to time and to eternity. And you have done that wrong!"

"Spare me!" cried Trotty, falling on his knees; "for Mercy's sake!"

"Listen!" said the Shadow.

"Listen!" cried the other Shadows.

"Listen!" said a clear and childlike voice, which Trotty thought he recognised as having heard before.

The organ sounded faintly in the church below. Swelling by degrees, the melody ascended to the roof, and filled the choir and nave. Expanding more and more, it rose up, up; up, up; higher, higher, higher up; awakening agitated hearts within the burly piles of oak: the hollow bells, the iron-bound doors, the stairs of solid stone; until the tower walls were insufficient to contain it, and it soared into the sky.

No wonder that an old man's breast could not contain a sound so vast and mighty. It broke from that weak prison in a rush of tears; and Trotty put his hands before his face.

"Listen!" said the Shadow.

"Listen!" said the other Shadows.

"Listen!" said the child's voice.

A solemn strain of blended voices, rose into the tower.

It was a very low and mournful strain—a Dirge—and as he listened, Trotty heard his child among the singers.

"She is dead!" exclaimed the old man. "Meg is dead! Her Spirit calls to me. I hear it!"

"The Spirit of your child bewails the dead, and mingles with the dead—dead hopes, dead fancies, dead imaginings of youth," returned the Bell, "but she is living. Learn from her life, a living truth. Learn from the creature dearest to your heart, how bad the bad are born. See every bud and leaf plucked one by one from off the fairest stem, and know how bare and wretched it may be. Follow her! To desperation!"

Each of the shadowy figures stretched its right arm forth, and pointed downward.

"The Spirit of the Chimes is your companion," said the figure.

"Go! It stands behind you!"

Trotty turned, and saw—the child! The child Will Fern had carried in the street; the child whom Meg had watched, but now, asleep!

"I carried her myself, to-night," said Trotty. "In these arms!"

"Show him what he calls himself," said the dark figures, one and all.

The tower opened at his feet. He looked down, and beheld his own form, lying at the bottom, on the outside: crushed and motionless.

"No more a living man!" cried Trotty. "Dead!"

"Dead!" said the figures all together.

"Gracious Heaven! And the New Year—"

"Past," said the figures.

"What!" he cried, shuddering. "I missed my way, and coming on the outside of this tower in the dark, fell down—a year ago?"

"Nine years ago!" replied the figures.

As they gave the answer, they recalled their outstretched hands; and where their figures had been, there the Bells were.

And they rung; their time being come again. And once again, vast multitudes of phantoms sprung into existence; once again, were incoherently engaged, as they had been before; once again, faded on the stopping of the Chimes; and dwindled into nothing.

"What are these?" he asked his guide. "If I am not mad, what are these?"

"Spirits of the Bells. Their sound upon the air," returned the child. "They take such shapes and occupations as the hopes and thoughts of mortals, and the recollections they have stored up, give them."

"And you," said Trotty wildly. "What are you?"

"Hush, hush!" returned the child. "Look here!"

In a poor, mean room; working at the same kind of embroidery which he had often, often seen before her; Meg, his own dear daughter, was presented to his view. He made no effort to imprint his kisses on her face; he did not strive to clasp her to his loving heart; he knew that such endearments were, for him, no more. But, he held his trembling breath, and brushed away the blinding tears, that he might look upon her; that he might only see her.

Ah! Changed. Changed. The light of the clear eye, how dimmed. The bloom, how faded from the cheek. Beautiful she was, as she had ever been, but Hope, Hope, Hope, oh where was the fresh Hope that had spoken to him like a voice!

She looked up from her work, at a companion. Following her eyes, the old man started back.

In the woman grown, he recognised her at a glance. In the long silken hair, he saw the self-same curls; around the lips, the child's expression lingering still. See! In the eyes, now turned inquiringly on Meg, there shone the very look that scanned those features when he brought her home!

Then what was this, beside him!

Looking with awe into its face, he saw a something reigning there: a lofty something, undefined and indistinct, which made it hardly more than a remembrance of that child—as yonder figure might be—yet it was the same: the same: and wore the dress.

Hark. They were speaking!

"Meg," said Lilian, hesitating. "How often you raise your head from your work to look at me!"

"Are my looks so altered, that they frighten you?" asked Meg.

"Nay, dear! But you smile at that, yourself! Why not smile, when you look at me, Meg?"

"I do so. Do I not?" she answered: smiling on her.

"Now you do," said Lilian, "but not usually. When you think I'm busy, and don't see you, you look so anxious and so doubtful, that I hardly like to raise my eyes. There is little cause for smiling in this hard and toilsome life, but you were once so cheerful."

"Am I not now!" cried Meg, speaking in a tone of strange alarm, and rising to embrace her. "Do I make our weary life more weary to you, Lilian!"

"You have been the only thing that made it life," said Lilian, fervently kissing her; "sometimes the only thing that made me care to live so, Meg. Such work, such work! So many hours, so many days, so many long, long nights of hopeless, cheerless, never-ending work—not to heap up riches, not to live grandly or gaily, not to live upon enough, however coarse; but to earn bare bread; to scrape together just enough to toil upon, and want upon, and keep alive in us the consciousness of our hard fate! Oh Meg, Meg!" she raised her voice and twined her arms about her as she spoke, like one in pain. "How can the cruel world go round, and bear to look upon such lives!"

"Lilly!" said Meg, soothing her, and putting back her hair from her wet face. "Why, Lilly! You! So pretty and so young!"

"Oh Meg!" she interrupted, holding her at arm's-length, and looking in her face imploringly. "The worst of all, the worst of all! Strike me old, Meg! Wither me, and shrivel me, and free me from the dreadful thoughts that tempt me in my youth!"

Trotty turned to look upon his guide. But the Spirit of the child had taken flight. Was gone.

Neither did he himself remain in the same place; for, Sir Joseph Bowley, Friend and Father of the Poor, held a great festivity at Bowley Hall, in honour of the natal day of Lady Bowley. And as Lady Bowley had been born on New Year's Day (which the local newspapers considered an especial pointing of the finger of Providence to number One, as Lady Bowley's destined figure in Creation), it was on a New Year's Day that this festivity took place.

Bowley Hall was full of visitors. The red-faced gentleman was there, Mr. Filer was there, the great Alderman Cute was there—Alderman Cute had a sympathetic feeling with great people, and had considerably improved his acquaintance with Sir Joseph Bowley on the strength of his attentive letter: indeed had become quite a friend of the family since then—and many guests were there. Trotty's ghost was there, wandering about, poor phantom, drearily; and looking for its guide.

There was to be a great dinner in the Great Hall. At which Sir Joseph Bowley, in his celebrated character of Friend and Father of the Poor, was to make his great speech. Certain plum-puddings were to be eaten by his Friends and Children in another Hall first; and, at a given signal, Friends and Children flocking in among their Friends and Fathers, were to form a family assemblage, with not one manly eye therein unmoistened by emotion.

But, there was more than this to happen. Even more than this. Sir Joseph Bowley, Baronet and Member of Parliament, was to play a match at skittles—real skittles—with his tenants!

"Which quite reminds me," said Alderman Cute, "of the days of old King Hal, stout King Hal, bluff King Hal. Ah! Fine character!"

"Very," said Mr. Filer, dryly. "For marrying women and murdering 'em. Considerably more than the average number of wives by the bye."

"You'll marry the beautiful ladies, and not murder 'em, eh?" said Alderman Cute to the heir of Bowley, aged twelve. "Sweet boy! We shall have this little gentleman in Parliament now," said the Alderman, holding him by the shoulders, and looking as reflective as he could, "before we know where we are. We shall hear of his successes at the poll; his speeches in the House; his overtures from Governments; his brilliant achievements of all kinds; ah! we shall make our little orations about him in the Common Council, I'll be bound; before we have time to look about us!"

"Oh, the difference of shoes and stockings!" Trotty thought. But his heart yearned towards the child, for the love of those same shoeless and stockingless boys, predestined (by the Alderman) to turn out bad, who might have been the children of poor Meg.

"Richard," moaned Trotty, roaming among the company, to and fro; "where is he? I can't find Richard! Where is Richard?" Not likely to be there, if still alive! But Trotty's grief and solitude confused him; and he still went wandering among the gallant company, looking for his guide, and saying, "Where is Richard? Show me Richard!"

He was wandering thus, when he encountered Mr. Fish, the confidential Secretary: in great agitation.

"Bless my heart and soul!" cried Mr. Fish. "Where's Alderman Cute? Has anybody seen the Alderman?"

Seen the Alderman? Oh dear! Who could ever help seeing the Alderman? He was so considerate, so affable, he bore so much in mind the natural desires of folks to see him, that if he had a fault, it was the being constantly On View. And wherever the great people were, there, to be sure, attracted by the kindred sympathy between great souls, was Cute.

Several voices cried that he was in the circle round Sir Joseph. Mr. Fish made way there; found him; and took him secretly into a window near at hand. Trotty joined them. Not of his own accord. He felt that his steps were led in that direction.

"My dear Alderman Cute," said Mr. Fish. "A little more this way. The most dreadful circumstance has occurred. I have this moment received the intelligence. I think it will be best not to acquaint Sir Joseph with it till the day is over. You understand Sir Joseph, and will give me your opinion. The most frightful and deplorable event!"

"Fish!" returned the Alderman. "Fish! My good fellow, what is the matter? Nothing revolutionary, I hope! No—no attempted interference with the magistrates?"

"Deedles, the banker," gasped the Secretary. "Deedles Brothers—who was to have been here to-day—high in office in the Goldsmiths' Company—"

"Not stopped!" exclaimed the Alderman, "It can't be!"

"Shot himself."

"Good God!"

"Put a double-barrelled pistol to his mouth, in his own counting house," said Mr. Fish, "and blew his brains out. No motive. Princely circumstances!"

"Circumstances!" exclaimed the Alderman. "A man of noble fortune. One of the most respectable of men. Suicide, Mr. Fish! By his own hand!"

"This very morning," returned Mr. Fish.

"Oh the brain, the brain!" exclaimed the pious Alderman, lifting up his hands. "Oh the nerves, the nerves; the mysteries of this machine called Man! Oh the little that unhinges it: poor creatures that we are! Perhaps a dinner, Mr. Fish. Perhaps the conduct of his son, who, I have heard, ran very wild, and was in the habit of drawing bills upon him without the least authority! A most respectable man. One of the most respectable men I ever knew! A lamentable instance, Mr.

Fish. A public calamity! I shall make a point of wearing the deepest mourning. A most respectable man! But there is One above. We must submit, Mr. Fish. We must submit!"

What, Alderman! No word of Putting Down? Remember, Justice, your high moral boast and pride. Come, Alderman! Balance those scales. Throw me into this, the empty one, no dinner, and Nature's founts in some poor woman, dried by starving misery and rendered obdurate to claims for which her offspring has authority in holy mother Eve. Weigh me the two, you Daniel, going to judgment, when your day shall come! Weigh them, in the eyes of suffering thousands, audience (not unmindful) of the grim farce you play. Or supposing that you strayed from your five wits—it's not so far to go, but that it might be—and laid hands upon that throat of yours, warning your fellows (if you have a fellow) how they croak their comfortable wickedness to raving heads and stricken hearts. What then?

The words rose up in Trotty's breast, as if they had been spoken by some other voice within him. Alderman Cute pledged himself to Mr. Fish that he would assist him in breaking the melancholy catastrophe to Sir Joseph when the day was over. Then, before they parted, wringing Mr. Fish's hand in bitterness of soul, he said, "The most respectable of men!" And added that he hardly knew (not even he), why such afflictions were allowed on earth.

"It's almost enough to make one think, if one didn't know better," said Alderman Cute, "that at times some motion of a capsizing nature was going on in things, which affected the general economy of the social fabric. Deedles Brothers!"

The skittle-playing came off with immense success. Sir Joseph knocked the pins about quite skilfully; Master Bowley took an innings at a shorter distance also; and everybody said that now, when a Baronet and the Son of a Baronet played at skittles, the country was coming round again, as fast as it could come.

At its proper time, the Banquet was served up. Trotty involuntarily repaired to the Hall with the rest, for he felt himself conducted thither by some stronger impulse than his own free will. The sight was gay in the extreme; the ladies were very handsome; the visitors delighted, cheerful, and good-tempered. When the lower doors were opened, and the people flocked in, in their rustic dresses, the beauty of the spectacle was at its height; but Trotty only murmured more and more, "Where is Richard! He should help and comfort her! I can't see Richard!"

There had been some speeches made; and Lady Bowley's health had been proposed; and Sir Joseph Bowley had returned thanks, and had made his great speech, showing by various pieces of evidence that he was the born Friend and Father, and so forth; and had given as a Toast, his Friends and Children, and the Dignity of Labour; when a slight disturbance at the bottom of the Hall attracted

Toby's notice. After some confusion, noise, and opposition, one man broke through the rest, and stood forward by himself.

Not Richard. No. But one whom he had thought of, and had looked for, many times. In a scantier supply of light, he might have doubted the identity of that worn man, so old, and grey, and bent; but with a blaze of lamps upon his gnarled and knotted head, he knew Will Fern as soon as he stepped forth.

"What is this!" exclaimed Sir Joseph, rising. "Who gave this man admittance? This is a criminal from prison! Mr. Fish, sir, will you have the goodness—"

"A minute!" said Will Fern. "A minute! My Lady, you was born on this day along with a New Year. Get me a minute's leave to speak."

She made some intercession for him. Sir Joseph took his seat again, with native dignity.

The ragged visitor—for he was miserably dressed—looked round upon the company, and made his homage to them with a humble bow.

"Gentlefolks!" he said. "You've drunk the Labourer. Look at me!"

"Just come from jail," said Mr. Fish.

"Just come from jail," said Will. "And neither for the first time, nor the second, nor the third, nor yet the fourth."

Mr. Filer was heard to remark testily, that four times was over the average; and he ought to be ashamed of himself.

"Gentlefolks!" repeated Will Fern. "Look at me! You see I'm at the worst. Beyond all hurt or harm; beyond your help; for the time when your kind words or kind actions could have done me good,"—he struck his hand upon his breast, and shook his head, "is gone, with the scent of last year's beans or clover on the air. Let me say a word for these," pointing to the labouring people in the Hall; "and when you're met together, hear the real Truth spoke out for once."

"There's not a man here," said the host, "who would have him for a spokesman."

"Like enough, Sir Joseph. I believe it. Not the less true, perhaps, is what I say. Perhaps that's a proof on it. Gentlefolks, I've lived many a year in this place. You may see the cottage from the sunk fence over yonder. I've seen the ladies draw it in their books, a hundred times. It looks well in a picter, I've heerd say; but there an't weather in picters, and maybe 'tis fitter for that, than for a place to live in. Well! I lived there. How hard—how bitter hard, I lived there, I won't say. Any day in the year, and every day, you can judge for your own selves."

He spoke as he had spoken on the night when Trotty found him in the street. His voice was deeper and more husky, and had a trembling in it now and then; but he never raised it passionately, and seldom lifted it above the firm stern level of the homely facts he stated.

"'Tis harder than you think for, gentlefolks, to grow up decent, commonly decent, in such a place. That I growed up a man and not a brute, says something for me—as I was then. As I am now, there's nothing can be said for me or done for me. I'm past it."

"I am glad this man has entered," observed Sir Joseph, looking round serenely. "Don't disturb him. It appears to be Ordained. He is an example: a living example. I hope and trust, and confidently expect, that it will not be lost upon my Friends here."

"I dragged on," said Fern, after a moment's silence, "somehow. Neither me nor any other man knows how; but so heavy, that I couldn't put a cheerful face upon it, or make believe that I was anything but what I was. Now, gentlemen—you gentlemen that sits at Sessions—when you see a man with discontent writ on his face, you says to one another, 'He's suspicious. I has my doubts,' says you, 'about Will Fern. Watch that fellow!' I don't say, gentlemen, it ain't quite nat'ral, but I say 'tis so; and from that hour, whatever Will Fern does, or lets alone—all one—it goes against him."

Alderman Cute stuck his thumbs in his waistcoat-pockets, and leaning back in his chair, and smiling, winked at a neighbouring chandelier. As much as to say, "Of course! I told you so. The common cry! Lord bless you, we are up to all this sort of thing—myself and human nature."

"Now, gentlemen," said Will Fern, holding out his hands, and flushing for an instant in his haggard face, "see how your laws are made to trap and hunt us when we're brought to this. I tries to live elsewhere. And I'm a vagabond. To jail with him! I comes back here. I goes a-nutting in your woods, and breaks—who don't?—a limber branch or two. To jail with him! One of your keepers sees me in the broad day, near my own patch of garden, with a gun. To jail with him! I has a nat'ral angry word with that man, when I'm free again. To jail with him! I cuts a stick. To jail with him! I eats a rotten apple or a turnip. To jail with him! It's twenty mile away; and coming back I begs a trifle on the road. To jail with him! At last, the constable, the keeper—anybody—finds me anywhere, a-doing anything. To jail with him, for he's a vagrant, and a jail-bird known; and jail's the only home he's got."

The Alderman nodded sagaciously, as who should say, "A very good home too!"

"Do I say this to serve my cause!" cried Fern. "Who can give me back my liberty, who can give me back my good name, who can give me back my innocent niece? Not all the Lords and Ladies in wide England. But, gentlemen, gentlemen, dealing with other men like me, begin at the right end. Give us, in mercy, better homes when we're a-lying in our cradles; give us better food when we're a-working for our lives; give us kinder laws to bring us back when we're a-going wrong; and don't set Jail, Jail, Jail, afore us, everywhere we turn. There an't a condescension you can show the Labourer then, that he won't take, as ready and as grateful as a man can be; for, he has a patient, peaceful, willing heart. But you must put his rightful spirit in him first; for, whether he's a wreck and ruin such as me, or is like one of them that stand here now, his spirit is divided from you at this time. Bring it back, gentlefolks, bring it back! Bring it back, afore the day comes when even his Bible changes in his altered mind, and the words seem to him to read, as they have sometimes read in my own eyes—in Jail: 'Whither thou goest, I can Not go; where thou lodgest, I do Not lodge; thy people are Not my people; Nor thy God my God!'"

A sudden stir and agitation took place in Hall. Trotty thought at first, that several had risen to eject the man; and hence this change in its appearance. But, another moment showed him that the room and all the company had vanished from his sight, and that his daughter was again before him, seated at her work. But in a poorer, meaner garret than before; and with no Lilian by her side.

The frame at which she had worked, was put away upon a shelf and covered up. The chair in which she had sat, was turned against the wall. A history was written in these little things, and in Meg's grief-worn face. Oh! who could fail to read it!

Meg strained her eyes upon her work until it was too dark to see the threads; and when the night closed in, she lighted her feeble candle and worked on. Still her old father was invisible about her; looking down upon her; loving her—how dearly loving her!—and talking to her in a tender voice about the old times, and the Bells. Though he knew, poor Trotty, though he knew she could not hear him.

A great part of the evening had worn away, when a knock came at her door. She opened it. A man was on the threshold. A slouching, moody, drunken sloven, wasted by intemperance and vice, and with his matted hair and unshorn beard in wild disorder; but, with some traces on him, too, of having been a man of good proportion and good features in his youth.

He stopped until he had her leave to enter; and she, retiring a pace of two from the open door, silently and sorrowfully looked upon him. Trotty had his wish. He saw Richard.

"May I come in, Margaret?"

"Yes! Come in. Come in!"

It was well that Trotty knew him before he spoke; for with any doubt remaining on his mind, the harsh discordant voice would have persuaded him that it was not Richard but some other man.

There were but two chairs in the room. She gave him hers, and stood at some short distance from him, waiting to hear what he had to say.

He sat, however, staring vacantly at the floor; with a lustreless and stupid smile. A spectacle of such deep degradation, of such abject hopelessness, of such a miserable downfall, that she put her hands before her face and turned away, lest he should see how much it moved her.

Roused by the rustling of her dress, or some such trifling sound, he lifted his head, and began to speak as if there had been no pause since he entered.

"Still at work, Margaret? You work late."

"I generally do."

"And early?"

"And early."

"So she said. She said you never tired; or never owned that you tired. Not all the time you lived together. Not even when you fainted, between work and fasting. But I told you that, the last time I came."

"You did," she answered. "And I implored you to tell me nothing more; and you made me a solemn promise, Richard, that you never would."

"A solemn promise," he repeated, with a drivelling laugh and vacant stare. "A solemn promise. To be sure. A solemn promise!" Awakening, as it were, after a time; in the same manner as before; he said with sudden animation:

"How can I help it, Margaret? What am I to do? She has been to me again!"

"Again!" cried Meg, clasping her hands. "O, does she think of me so often! Has she been again!"

"Twenty times again," said Richard. "Margaret, she haunts me. She comes behind me in the street, and thrusts it in my hand. I hear her foot upon the ashes when I'm at my work (ha, ha! that an't often), and before I can turn my head, her voice is in my ear, saying, 'Richard, don't look round. For Heaven's love, give her this!' She brings it where I live: she sends it in letters; she taps at the window and lays it on the sill. What can I do? Look at it!"

He held out in his hand a little purse, and chinked the money it enclosed.

"Hide it," sad Meg. "Hide it! When she comes again, tell her, Richard, that I love her in my soul. That I never lie down to sleep, but I bless her, and pray for her. That, in my solitary work, I never cease to have her in my thoughts. That she is with me, night and day. That if I died to-morrow, I would remember her with my last breath. But, that I cannot look upon it!"

He slowly recalled his hand, and crushing the purse together, said with a kind of drowsy thoughtfulness:

"I told her so. I told her so, as plain as words could speak. I've taken this gift back and left it at her door, a dozen times since then. But when she came at last, and stood before me, face to face, what could I do?"

"You saw her!" exclaimed Meg. "You saw her! O, Lilian, my sweet girl! O, Lilian, Lilian!"

"I saw her," he went on to say, not answering, but engaged in the same slow pursuit of his own thoughts. "There she stood: trembling! 'How does she look, Richard? Does she ever speak of me? Is she thinner? My old place at the table: what's in my old place? And the frame she taught me our old work on—has she burnt it, Richard!' There she was. I heard her say it."

Meg checked her sobs, and with the tears streaming from her eyes, bent over him to listen. Not to lose a breath.

With his arms resting on his knees; and stooping forward in his chair, as if what he said were written on the ground in some half legible character, which it was his occupation to decipher and connect; he went on.

" 'Richard, I have fallen very low; and you may guess how much I have suffered in having this sent back, when I can bear to bring it in my hand to you. But you loved her once, even in my memory, dearly. Others stepped in between you; fears, and jealousies, and doubts, and vanities, estranged you from her; but you did love her, even in my memory!"

"I suppose I did," he said, interrupting himself for a moment. "I did! That's neither here nor there—'O Richard, if you ever did; if you have any memory for what is gone and lost, take it to her once more. Once more! Tell her how I laid my head upon your shoulder, where her own head might have lain, and was so humble to you, Richard. Tell her that you looked into my face, and saw the beauty which she used to praise, all gone: all gone: and in its place, a poor, wan, hollow cheek, that she would weep to see. Tell her everything, and take it back, and she will not refuse again. She will not have the heart!' "

So he sat musing, and repeating the last words, until he woke again, and rose.

"You won't take it, Margaret?"

She shook her head, and motioned an entreaty to him to leave her.

"Good night, Margaret."

"Good night!"

He turned to look upon her; struck by her sorrow, and perhaps by the pity for himself which trembled in her voice. It was a quick and rapid action; and for the moment some flash of his old bearing kindled in his form. In the next he went as he had come. Nor did this glimmer of a quenched fire seem to light him to a quicker sense of his debasement.

In any mood, in any grief, in any torture of the mind or body, Meg's work must be done. She sat down to her task, and plied it. Night, midnight. Still she worked.

She had a meagre fire, the night being very cold; and rose at intervals to mend it. The Chimes rang half-past twelve while she was thus engaged; and when they ceased she heard a gentle knocking at the door. Before she could so much as wonder who was there, at that unusual hour, it opened.

O Youth and Beauty, happy as ye should be, look at this. O Youth and Beauty, blest and blessing all within your reach, and working out the ends of your Beneficent Creator, look at this!

She saw the entering figure; screamed its name; cried "Lilian!"

It was swift, and fell upon its knees before her: clinging to her dress.

"Up, dear! Up! Lilian! My own dearest!"

"Never more, Meg; never more! Here! Here! Close to you, holding to you, feeling your dear breath upon my face!"

"Sweet Lilian! Darling Lilian! Child of my heart—no mother's love can be more tender—lay your head upon my breast!"

"Never more, Meg. Never more! When I first looked into your face, you knelt before me. On my knees before you, let me die. Let it be here!"

"You have come back. My Treasure! We will live together, work together, hope together, die together!"

"Ah! Kiss my lips, Meg; fold your arms about me; press me to your bosom; look kindly on me; but don't raise me. Let it be here. Let me see the last of your dear face upon my knees!"

O Youth and Beauty, happy as ye should be, look at this! O Youth and Beauty, working out the ends of your Beneficent Creator, look at this!

"Forgive me, Meg! So dear, so dear! Forgive me! I know you do, I see you do, but say so, Meg!"

She said so, with her lips on Lilian's cheek. And with her arms twined round— she knew it now—a broken heart.

"His blessing on you, dearest love. Kiss me once more! He suffered her to sit beside His feet, and dry them with her hair. O Meg, what Mercy and Compassion!"

As she died, the Spirit of the child returning, innocent and radiant, touched the old man with its hand, and beckoned him away.

CHAPTER IV. FOURTH QUARTER

Some new remembrance of the ghostly figures in the Bells; some faint impression of the ringing of the Chimes; some giddy consciousness of having seen the swarm of phantoms reproduced and reproduced until the recollection of them lost itself in the confusion of their numbers; some hurried knowledge, how conveyed to him he knew not, that more years had passed; and Trotty, with the Spirit of the child attending him, stood looking on at mortal company.

Fat company, rosy-cheeked company, comfortable company. They were but two, but they were red enough for ten. They sat before a bright fire, with a small low table between them; and unless the fragrance of hot tea and muffins lingered longer in that room than in most others, the table had seen service very lately. But all the cups and saucers being clean, and in their proper places in the corner-cupboard; and the brass toasting-fork hanging in its usual nook and spreading its four idle fingers out as if it wanted to be measured for a glove; there remained no other visible tokens of the meal just finished, than such as purred and washed their whiskers in the person of the basking cat, and glistened in the gracious, not to say the greasy, faces of her patrons.

This cosy couple (married, evidently) had made a fair division of the fire between them, and sat looking at the glowing sparks that dropped into the grate; now nodding off into a doze; now waking up again when some hot fragment, larger than the rest, came rattling down, as if the fire were coming with it.

It was in no danger of sudden extinction, however; for it gleamed not only in the little room, and on the panes of window-glass in the door, and on the curtain half drawn across them, but in the little shop beyond. A little shop, quite crammed and choked with the abundance of its stock; a perfectly voracious little shop, with a maw as accommodating and full as any shark's. Cheese, butter, firewood, soap, pickles, matches, bacon, table-beer, peg-tops, sweetmeats, boys' kites, bird-seed, cold ham, birch brooms, hearth-stones, salt, vinegar, blacking, red-herrings, stationery, lard, mushroom-ketchup, staylaces, loaves of bread, shuttlecocks, eggs, and slate pencil; everything was fish that came to the net of this greedy little shop, and all articles were in its net. How many other kinds of petty merchandise were there, it would be difficult to say; but balls of packthread, ropes of onions, pounds of candles, cabbage-nets, and brushes, hung in bunches from the ceiling, like extraordinary fruit; while various odd canisters emitting aromatic smells, established the veracity of the inscription over the outer door, which informed the public that the keeper of this little shop was a licensed dealer in tea, coffee, tobacco, pepper, and snuff.

Glancing at such of these articles as were visible in the shining of the blaze, and the less cheerful radiance of two smoky lamps which burnt but dimly in the shop itself, as though its plethora sat heavy on their lungs; and glancing, then, at one of the two faces by the parlour-fire; Trotty had small difficulty in recognising in the stout old lady, Mrs. Chickenstalker: always inclined to corpulency, even in the days when he had known her as established in the general line, and having a small balance against him in her books.

The features of her companion were less easy to him. The great broad chin, with creases in it large enough to hide a finger in; the astonished eyes, that seemed to expostulate with themselves for sinking deeper and deeper into the yielding fat of the soft face; the nose afflicted with that disordered action of its functions which is generally termed The Snuffles; the short thick throat and labouring chest, with other beauties of the like description; though calculated to impress the memory, Trotty could at first allot to nobody he had ever known: and yet he had some recollection of them too. At length, in Mrs. Chickenstalker's partner in the general line, and in the crooked and eccentric line of life, he recognised the former porter of Sir Joseph Bowley; an apoplectic innocent, who had connected himself in Trotty's mind with Mrs. Chickenstalker years ago, by giving him admission to the mansion where he had confessed his obligations to that lady, and drawn on his unlucky head such grave reproach.

Trotty had little interest in a change like this, after the changes he had seen; but association is very strong sometimes; and he looked involuntarily behind the parlour-door, where the accounts of credit customers were usually kept in chalk. There was no record of his name. Some names were there, but they were strange to him, and infinitely fewer than of old; from which he argued that the porter was an advocate of ready-money transactions, and on coming into the business had looked pretty sharp after the Chickenstalker defaulters.

So desolate was Trotty, and so mournful for the youth and promise of his blighted child, that it was a sorrow to him, even to have no place in Mrs. Chickenstalker's ledger.

"What sort of a night is it, Anne?" inquired the former porter of Sir Joseph Bowley, stretching out his legs before the fire, and rubbing as much of them as his short arms could reach; with an air that added, "Here I am if it's bad, and I don't want to go out if it's good."

"Blowing and sleeting hard," returned his wife; "and threatening snow. Dark. And very cold."

"I'm glad to think we had muffins," said the former porter, in the tone of one who had set his conscience at rest. "It's a sort of night that's meant for muffins. Likewise crumpets. Also Sally Lunns."

The former porter mentioned each successive kind of eatable, as if he were musingly summing up his good actions. After which he rubbed his fat legs as before, and jerking them at the knees to get the fire upon the yet unroasted parts, laughed as if somebody had tickled him.

"You're in spirits, Tugby, my dear," observed his wife.

The firm was Tugby, late Chickenstalker.

"No," said Tugby. "No. Not particular. I'm a little elewated. The muffins came so pat!"

With that he chuckled until he was black in the face; and had so much ado to become any other colour, that his fat legs took the strangest excursions into the air. Nor were they reduced to anything like decorum until Mrs. Tugby had thumped him violently on the back, and shaken him as if he were a great bottle.

"Good gracious, goodness, lord-a-mercy bless and save the man!" cried Mrs. Tugby, in great terror. "What's he doing?"

Mr. Tugby wiped his eyes, and faintly repeated that he found himself a little elewated.

"Then don't be so again, that's a dear good soul," said Mrs. Tugby, "if you don't want to frighten me to death, with your struggling and fighting!"

Mr. Tugby said he wouldn't; but, his whole existence was a fight, in which, if any judgment might be founded on the constantly-increasing shortness of his breath, and the deepening purple of his face, he was always getting the worst of it.

"So it's blowing, and sleeting, and threatening snow; and it's dark, and very cold, is it, my dear?" said Mr. Tugby, looking at the fire, and reverting to the cream and marrow of his temporary elevation.

"Hard weather indeed," returned his wife, shaking her head.

"Aye, aye! Years," said Mr. Tugby, "are like Christians in that respect. Some of 'em die hard; some of 'em die easy. This one hasn't many days to run, and is making a fight for it. I like him all the better. There's a customer, my love!"

Attentive to the rattling door, Mrs. Tugby had already risen.

"Now then!" said that lady, passing out into the little shop. "What's wanted? Oh! I beg your pardon, sir, I'm sure. I didn't think it was you."

She made this apology to a gentleman in black, who, with his wristbands tucked up, and his hat cocked loungingly on one side, and his hands in his pockets, sat down astride on the table-beer barrel, and nodded in return.

"This is a bad business up-stairs, Mrs. Tugby," said the gentleman. "The man can't live."

"Not the back-attic can't!" cried Tugby, coming out into the shop to join the conference.

"The back-attic, Mr. Tugby," said the gentleman, "is coming down-stairs fast, and will be below the basement very soon."

Looking by turns at Tugby and his wife, he sounded the barrel with his knuckles for the depth of beer, and having found it, played a tune upon the empty part.

"The back-attic, Mr. Tugby," said the gentleman: Tugby having stood in silent consternation for some time: "is Going."

"Then," said Tugby, turning to his wife, "he must Go, you know, before he's Gone."

"I don't think you can move him," said the gentleman, shaking his head. "I wouldn't take the responsibility of saying it could be done, myself. You had better leave him where he is. He can't live long."

"It's the only subject," said Tugby, bringing the butter-scale down upon the counter with a crash, by weighing his fist on it, "that we've ever had a word upon; she and me; and look what it comes to! He's going to die here, after all. Going to die upon the premises. Going to die in our house!"

"And where should he have died, Tugby?" cried his wife.

"In the workhouse," he returned. "What are workhouses made for?"

"Not for that," said Mrs. Tugby, with great energy. "Not for that! Neither did I marry you for that. Don't think it, Tugby. I won't have it. I won't allow it. I'd be separated first, and never see your face again. When my widow's name stood over that door, as it did for many years: this house being known as Mrs. Chickenstalker's far and wide, and never known but to its honest credit and its good report: when my widow's name stood over that door, Tugby, I knew him as a handsome, steady, manly, independent youth; I knew her as the sweetest-looking, sweetest-tempered girl, eyes ever saw; I knew her father (poor old creetur, he fell down from the steeple walking in his sleep, and killed himself), for the simplest, hardest-working, childest-hearted man, that ever drew the breath of life; and when I turn them out of house and home, may angels turn me out of Heaven. As they would! And serve me right!"

Her old face, which had been a plump and dimpled one before the changes which had come to pass, seemed to shine out of her as she said these words; and when she dried her eyes, and shook her head and her handkerchief at Tugby, with an expression of firmness which it was quite clear was not to be easily resisted, Trotty said, "Bless her! Bless her!"

Then he listened, with a panting heart, for what should follow. Knowing nothing yet, but that they spoke of Meg.

If Tugby had been a little elevated in the parlour, he more than balanced that account by being not a little depressed in the shop, where he now stood staring at his wife, without attempting a reply; secretly conveying, however—either in a fit of abstraction or as a precautionary measure—all the money from the till into his own pockets, as he looked at her.

The gentleman upon the table-beer cask, who appeared to be some authorised medical attendant upon the poor, was far too well accustomed, evidently, to little differences of opinion between man and wife, to interpose any remark in this instance. He sat softly whistling, and turning little drops of beer out of the tap upon the ground, until there was a perfect calm: when he raised his head, and said to Mrs. Tugby, late Chickenstalker:

"There's something interesting about the woman, even now. How did she come to marry him?"

"Why that," said Mrs. Tugby, taking a seat near him, "is not the least cruel part of her story, sir. You see they kept company, she and Richard, many years ago. When they were a young and beautiful couple, everything was settled, and they were to have been married on a New Year's Day. But, somehow, Richard got it into his head, through what the gentlemen told him, that he might do better, and that he'd soon repent it, and that she wasn't good enough for him, and that a young man of spirit had no business to be married. And the gentlemen frightened her, and made her melancholy, and timid of his deserting her, and of her children coming to the gallows, and of its being wicked to be man and wife, and a good deal more of it. And in short, they lingered and lingered, and their trust in one another was broken, and so at last was the match. But the fault was his. She would have married him, sir, joyfully. I've seen her heart swell many times afterwards, when he passed her in a proud and careless way; and never did a woman grieve more truly for a man, than she for Richard when he first went wrong."

"Oh! he went wrong, did he?" said the gentleman, pulling out the vent-peg of the table-beer, and trying to peep down into the barrel through the hole.

"Well, sir, I don't know that he rightly understood himself, you see. I think his mind was troubled by their having broke with one another; and that but for being ashamed before the gentlemen, and perhaps for being uncertain too, how she might take it, he'd have gone through any suffering or trial to have had Meg's promise and Meg's hand again. That's my belief. He never said so; more's the pity! He took to drinking, idling, bad companions: all the fine resources that were to be so much better for him than the Home he might have had. He lost his looks, his character, his health, his strength, his friends, his work: everything!"

"He didn't lose everything, Mrs. Tugby," returned the gentleman, "because he gained a wife; and I want to know how he gained her."

"I'm coming to it, sir, in a moment. This went on for years and years; he sinking lower and lower; she enduring, poor thing, miseries enough to wear her life away. At last, he was so cast down, and cast out, that no one would employ or notice him; and doors were shut upon him, go where he would. Applying from place to place, and door to door; and coming for the hundredth time to one gentleman who had often and often tried him (he was a good workman to the very end); that gentleman, who knew his history, said, "I believe you are incorrigible; there is only one person in the world who has a chance of reclaiming you; ask me to trust you no more, until she tries to do it." Something like that, in his anger and vexation."

"Ah!" said the gentleman. "Well?"

"Well, sir, he went to her, and kneeled to her; said it was so; said it ever had been so; and made a prayer to her to save him."

"And she?—Don't distress yourself, Mrs. Tugby."

"She came to me that night to ask me about living here. 'What he was once to me,' she said, 'is buried in a grave, side by side with what I was to him. But I have thought of this; and I will make the trial. In the hope of saving him; for the love of the light-hearted girl (you remember her) who was to have been married on a New Year's Day; and for the love of her Richard.' And she said he had come to her from Lilian, and Lilian had trusted to him, and she never could forget that. So they were married; and when they came home here, and I saw them, I hoped that such prophecies as parted them when they were young, may not often fulfil themselves as they did in this case, or I wouldn't be the makers of them for a Mine of Gold."

The gentleman got off the cask, and stretched himself, observing:

"I suppose he used her ill, as soon as they were married?"

"I don't think he ever did that," said Mrs. Tugby, shaking her head, and wiping her eyes. "He went on better for a short time; but, his habits were too old and strong to be got rid of; he soon fell back a little; and was falling fast back, when his illness came so strong upon him. I think he has always felt for her. I am sure he has. I have seen him, in his crying fits and tremblings, try to kiss her hand; and I have heard him call her 'Meg,' and say it was her nineteenth birthday. There he has been lying, now, these weeks and months. Between him and her baby, she has not been able to do her old work; and by not being able to be regular, she has lost it, even if she could have done it. How they have lived, I hardly know!"

"I know," muttered Mr. Tugby; looking at the till, and round the shop, and at his wife; and rolling his head with immense intelligence. "Like Fighting Cocks!"

He was interrupted by a cry—a sound of lamentation—from the upper story of the house. The gentleman moved hurriedly to the door.

"My friend," he said, looking back, "you needn't discuss whether he shall be removed or not. He has spared you that trouble, I believe."

Saying so, he ran up-stairs, followed by Mrs. Tugby; while Mr. Tugby panted and grumbled after them at leisure: being rendered more than commonly short-winded by the weight of the till, in which there had been an inconvenient quantity of copper. Trotty, with the child beside him, floated up the staircase like mere air.

"Follow her! Follow her! Follow her!" He heard the ghostly voices in the Bells repeat their words as he ascended. "Learn it, from the creature dearest to your heart!"

It was over. It was over. And this was she, her father's pride and joy! This haggard, wretched woman, weeping by the bed, if it deserved that name, and pressing to her breast, and hanging down her head upon, an infant. Who can tell how spare, how sickly, and how poor an infant! Who can tell how dear!

"Thank God!" cried Trotty, holding up his folded hands. "O, God be thanked! She loves her child!"

The gentleman, not otherwise hard-hearted or indifferent to such scenes, than that he saw them every day, and knew that they were figures of no moment in the Filer sums—mere scratches in the working of these calculations—laid his hand upon the heart that beat no more, and listened for the breath, and said, "His pain is over. It's better as it is!" Mrs. Tugby tried to comfort her with kindness. Mr. Tugby tried philosophy.

"Come, come!" he said, with his hands in his pockets, "you mustn't give way, you know. That won't do. You must fight up. What would have become of me if I had given way when I was porter, and we had as many as six runaway carriage-doubles at our door in one night! But, I fell back upon my strength of mind, and didn't open it!"

Again Trotty heard the voices saying, "Follow her!" He turned towards his guide, and saw it rising from him, passing through the air. "Follow her!" it said. And vanished.

He hovered round her; sat down at her feet; looked up into her face for one trace of her old self; listened for one note of her old pleasant voice. He flitted round the child: so wan, so prematurely old, so dreadful in its gravity, so plaintive in its feeble, mournful, miserable wail. He almost worshipped it. He clung to it as her only safeguard; as the last unbroken link that bound her to endurance. He set his father's hope and trust on the frail baby; watched her every look upon it as she held it in her arms; and cried a thousand times, "She loves it! God be thanked, she loves it!"

He saw the woman tend her in the night; return to her when her grudging husband was asleep, and all was still; encourage her, shed tears with her, set nourishment before her. He saw the day come, and the night again; the day, the night; the time go by; the house of death relieved of death; the room left to herself and to the child; he heard it moan and cry; he saw it harass her, and tire her out, and when she slumbered in exhaustion, drag her back to consciousness, and hold her with its little hands upon the rack; but she was constant to it, gentle with it, patient with it. Patient! Was its loving mother in her inmost heart and soul, and had its Being knitted up with hers as when she carried it unborn.

All this time, she was in want: languishing away, in dire and pining want. With the baby in her arms, she wandered here and there, in quest of occupation; and with its thin face lying in her lap, and looking up in hers, did any work for any wretched sum; a day and night of labour for as many farthings as there were figures on the dial. If she had quarrelled with it; if she had neglected it; if she had looked upon it with a moment's hate; if, in the frenzy of an instant, she had struck it! No. His comfort was, She loved it always.

She told no one of her extremity, and wandered abroad in the day lest she should be questioned by her only friend: for any help she received from her hands, occasioned fresh disputes between the good woman and her husband; and it was new bitterness to be the daily cause of strife and discord, where she owed so much.

She loved it still. She loved it more and more. But a change fell on the aspect of her love. One night.

She was singing faintly to it in its sleep, and walking to and fro to hush it, when her door was softly opened, and a man looked in.

"For the last time," he said.

"William Fern!"

"For the last time."

He listened like a man pursued: and spoke in whispers.

"Margaret, my race is nearly run. I couldn't finish it, without a parting word with you. Without one grateful word."

"What have you done?" she asked: regarding him with terror.

He looked at her, but gave no answer.

After a short silence, he made a gesture with his hand, as if he set her question by; as if he brushed it aside; and said:

"It's long ago, Margaret, now: but that night is as fresh in my memory as ever 'twas. We little thought, then," he added, looking round, "that we should ever meet like this. Your child, Margaret? Let me have it in my arms. Let me hold your child."

He put his hat upon the floor, and took it. And he trembled as he took it, from head to foot.

"Is it a girl?"

"Yes."

He put his hand before its little face.

"See how weak I'm grown, Margaret, when I want the courage to look at it! Let her be, a moment. I won't hurt her. It's long ago, but— What's her name?"

"Margaret," she answered, quickly.

"I'm glad of that," he said. "I'm glad of that!" He seemed to breathe more freely; and after pausing for an instant, took away his hand, and looked upon the infant's face. But covered it again, immediately.

"Margaret!" he said; and gave her back the child. "It's Lilian's."

"Lilian's!"

"I held the same face in my arms when Lilian's mother died and left her."

"When Lilian's mother died and left her!" she repeated, wildly.

"How shrill you speak! Why do you fix your eyes upon me so? Margaret!"

She sunk down in a chair, and pressed the infant to her breast, and wept over it. Sometimes, she released it from her embrace, to look anxiously in its face: then strained it to her bosom again. At those times, when she gazed upon it, then it was that something fierce and terrible began to mingle with her love. Then it was that her old father quailed.

"Follow her!" was sounded through the house. "Learn it, from the creature dearest to your heart!"

"Margaret," said Fern, bending over her, and kissing her upon the brow: "I thank you for the last time. Good night. Good bye! Put your hand in mine, and tell me you'll forget me from this hour, and try to think the end of me was here."

"What have you done?" she asked again.

"There'll be a Fire to-night," he said, removing from her. "There'll be Fires this winter-time, to light the dark nights, East, West, North, and South. When you see the distant sky red, they'll be blazing. When you see the distant sky red, think of me no more; or, if you do, remember what a Hell was lighted up inside of me, and think you see its flames reflected in the clouds. Good night. Good bye!" She called to him; but he was gone. She sat down stupefied, until her infant roused her to a sense of hunger, cold, and darkness. She paced the room with it the livelong night, hushing it and soothing it. She said at intervals, "Like Lilian, when her mother died and left her!" Why was her step so quick, her eye so wild, her love so fierce and terrible, whenever she repeated those words?

"But, it is Love," said Trotty. "It is Love. She'll never cease to love it. My poor Meg!"

She dressed the child next morning with unusual care—ah, vain expenditure of care upon such squalid robes!—and once more tried to find some means of life. It was the last day of the Old Year. She tried till night, and never broke her fast. She tried in vain.

She mingled with an abject crowd, who tarried in the snow, until it pleased some officer appointed to dispense the public charity (the lawful charity; not that once preached upon a Mount), to call them in, and question them, and say to this one, "Go to such a place," to that one, "Come next week"; to make a football of another wretch, and pass him here and there, from hand to hand, from house to house, until he wearied and lay down to die; or started up and robbed, and so became a higher sort of criminal, whose claims allowed of no delay. Here, too, she failed.

She loved her child, and wished to have it lying on her breast. And that was quite enough.

It was night: a bleak, dark, cutting night: when, pressing the child close to her for warmth, she arrived outside the house she called her home. She was so faint and giddy, that she saw no one standing in the doorway until she was close upon it, and about to enter. Then, she recognised the master of the house, who had so disposed himself—with his person it was not difficult—as to fill up the whole entry.

"O!" he said softly. "You have come back?"

She looked at the child, and shook her head.

"Don't you think you have lived here long enough without paying any rent? Don't you think that, without any money, you've been a pretty constant customer at this shop, now?" said Mr. Tugby.

She repeated the same mute appeal.

"Suppose you try and deal somewhere else," he said. "And suppose you provide yourself with another lodging. Come! Don't you think you could manage it?"

She said in a low voice, that it was very late. To-morrow.

"Now I see what you want," said Tugby; "and what you mean. You know there are two parties in this house about you, and you delight in setting 'em by the ears. I don't want any quarrels; I'm speaking softly to avoid a quarrel; but if you don't go away, I'll speak out loud, and you shall cause words high enough to please you. But you shan't come in. That I am determined."

She put her hair back with her hand, and looked in a sudden manner at the sky, and the dark lowering distance.

"This is the last night of an Old Year, and I won't carry ill-blood and quarrellings and disturbances into a New One, to please you nor anybody else," said Tugby, who was quite a retail Friend and Father. "I wonder you an't ashamed of yourself, to carry such practices into a New Year. If you haven't any business in the world, but to be always giving way, and always making disturbances between man and wife, you'd be better out of it. Go along with you."

"Follow her! To desperation!"

Again the old man heard the voices. Looking up, he saw the figures hovering in the air, and pointing where she went, down the dark street.

"She loves it!" he exclaimed, in agonised entreaty for her. "Chimes! she loves it still!"

"Follow her!" The shadow swept upon the track she had taken, like a cloud.

He joined in the pursuit; he kept close to her; he looked into her face. He saw the same fierce and terrible expression mingling with her love, and kindling in her eyes. He heard her say, "Like Lilian! To be changed like Lilian!" and her speed redoubled.

O, for something to awaken her! For any sight, or sound, or scent, to call up tender recollections in a brain on fire! For any gentle image of the Past, to rise before her!

"I was her father! I was her father!" cried the old man, stretching out his hands to the dark shadows flying on above. "Have mercy on her, and on me! Where does she go? Turn her back! I was her father!"

But they only pointed to her, as she hurried on; and said, "To desperation! Learn it from the creature dearest to your heart!" A hundred voices echoed it. The air was made of breath expended in those words. He seemed to take them in, at every gasp he drew. They were everywhere, and not to be escaped. And still she hurried on; the same light in her eyes, the same words in her mouth, "Like Lilian! To be changed like Lilian!" All at once she stopped.

"Now, turn her back!" exclaimed the old man, tearing his white hair. "My child! Meg! Turn her back! Great Father, turn her back!"

In her own scanty shawl, she wrapped the baby warm. With her fevered hands, she smoothed its limbs, composed its face, arranged its mean attire. In her wasted arms she folded it, as though she never would resign it more. And with her dry lips, kissed it in a final pang, and last long agony of Love.

Putting its tiny hand up to her neck, and holding it there, within her dress, next to her distracted heart, she set its sleeping face against her: closely, steadily, against her: and sped onward to the River.

To the rolling River, swift and dim, where Winter Night sat brooding like the last dark thoughts of many who had sought a refuge there before her. Where scattered lights upon the banks gleamed sullen, red, and dull, as torches that were burning there, to show the way to Death. Where no abode of living people cast its shadow, on the deep, impenetrable, melancholy shade.

To the River! To that portal of Eternity, her desperate footsteps tended with the swiftness of its rapid waters running to the sea. He tried to touch her as she passed him, going down to its dark level: but, the wild distempered form, the fierce and terrible love, the desperation that had left all human check or hold behind, swept by him like the wind.

He followed her. She paused a moment on the brink, before the dreadful plunge. He fell down on his knees, and in a shriek addressed the figures in the Bells now hovering above them.

"I have learnt it!" cried the old man. "From the creature dearest to my heart! O, save her, save her!"

He could wind his fingers in her dress; could hold it! As the words escaped his lips, he felt his sense of touch return, and knew that he detained her.

The figures looked down steadfastly upon him.

"I have learnt it!" cried the old man. "O, have mercy on me in this hour, if, in my love for her, so young and good, I slandered Nature in the breasts of mothers rendered desperate! Pity my presumption, wickedness, and ignorance, and save her." He felt his hold relaxing. They were silent still.

"Have mercy on her!" he exclaimed, "as one in whom this dreadful crime has sprung from Love perverted; from the strongest, deepest Love we fallen creatures know! Think what her misery must have been, when such seed bears such fruit! Heaven meant her to be good. There is no loving mother on the earth who might not come to this, if such a life had gone before. O, have mercy on my child, who, even at this pass, means mercy to her own, and dies herself, and perils her immortal soul, to save it!"

She was in his arms. He held her now. His strength was like a giant's.

"I see the Spirit of the Chimes among you!" cried the old man, singling out the child, and speaking in some inspiration, which their looks conveyed to him. "I know that our inheritance is held in store for us by Time. I know there is a sea of Time to rise one day, before which all who wrong us or oppress us will be swept away like leaves. I see it, on the flow! I know that we must trust and hope, and neither doubt ourselves, nor doubt the good in one another. I have learnt it from the creature dearest to my heart. I clasp her in my arms again. O Spirits, merciful and good, I take your lesson to my breast along with her! O Spirits, merciful and good, I am grateful!"

He might have said more; but, the Bells, the old familiar Bells, his own dear, constant, steady friends, the Chimes, began to ring the joy-peals for a New Year: so lustily, so merrily, so happily, so gaily, that he leapt upon his feet, and broke the spell that bound him.

"And whatever you do, father," said Meg, "don't eat tripe again, without asking some doctor whether it's likely to agree with you; for how you have been going on, Good gracious!"

She was working with her needle, at the little table by the fire; dressing her simple gown with ribbons for her wedding. So quietly happy, so blooming and youthful, so full of beautiful promise, that he uttered a great cry as if it were an Angel in his house; then flew to clasp her in his arms.

But, he caught his feet in the newspaper, which had fallen on the hearth; and somebody came rushing in between them.

"No!" cried the voice of this same somebody; a generous and jolly voice it was! "Not even you. Not even you. The first kiss of Meg in the New Year is mine. Mine! I have been waiting outside the house, this hour, to hear the Bells and claim it. Meg, my precious prize, a happy year! A life of happy years, my darling wife!"

And Richard smothered her with kisses.

You never in all your life saw anything like Trotty after this. I don't care where you have lived or what you have seen; you never in all your life saw anything at all approaching him! He sat down in his chair and beat his knees and cried; he sat down in his chair and beat his knees and laughed; he sat down in his chair and beat his knees and laughed and cried together; he got out of his chair and hugged Meg; he got out of his chair and hugged Richard; he got out of his chair and hugged them both at once; he kept running up to Meg, and squeezing her fresh face between his hands and kissing it, going from her backwards not to lose sight of it, and running up again like a figure in a magic lantern; and whatever he did, he was constantly sitting himself down in his chair, and never stopping in it for one single moment; being—that's the truth—beside himself with joy.

"And to-morrow's your wedding-day, my pet!" cried Trotty. "Your real, happy wedding-day!"

"To-day!" cried Richard, shaking hands with him. "To-day. The Chimes are ringing in the New Year. Hear them!"

They were ringing! Bless their sturdy hearts, they were ringing! Great Bells as they were; melodious, deep-mouthed, noble Bells; cast in no common metal; made by no common founder; when had they ever chimed like that, before!

"But, to-day, my pet," said Trotty. "You and Richard had some words to-day."

"Because he's such a bad fellow, father," said Meg. "An't you, Richard? Such a headstrong, violent man! He'd have made no more of speaking his mind to that great Alderman, and putting him down I don't know where, than he would of—"

"—Kissing Meg," suggested Richard. Doing it too!

"No. Not a bit more," said Meg. "But I wouldn't let him, father. Where would have been the use!"

"Richard my boy!" cried Trotty. "You was turned up Trumps originally; and Trumps you must be, till you die! But, you were crying by the fire to-night, my pet, when I came home! Why did you cry by the fire?"

"I was thinking of the years we've passed together, father. Only that. And thinking that you might miss me, and be lonely."

Trotty was backing off to that extraordinary chair again, when the child, who had been awakened by the noise, came running in half-dressed.

"Why, here she is!" cried Trotty, catching her up. "Here's little Lilian! Ha ha ha! Here we are and here we go! O here we are and here we go again! And here we are and here we go! and Uncle Will too!" Stopping in his trot to greet him heartily. "O, Uncle Will, the vision that I've had to-night, through lodging you! O, Uncle Will, the obligations that you've laid me under, by your coming, my good friend!"

Before Will Fern could make the least reply, a band of music burst into the room, attended by a lot of neighbours, screaming "A Happy New Year, Meg!" "A Happy Wedding!" "Many of 'em!" and other fragmentary good wishes of that sort. The Drum (who was a private friend of Trotty's) then stepped forward, and said:

"Trotty Veck, my boy! It's got about, that your daughter is going to be married to-morrow. There an't a soul that knows you that don't wish you well, or that knows her and don't wish her well. Or that knows you both, and don't wish you both all the happiness the New Year can bring. And here we are, to play it in and dance it in, accordingly."

Which was received with a general shout. The Drum was rather drunk, by the bye; but, never mind.

"What a happiness it is, I'm sure," said Trotty, "to be so esteemed! How kind and neighbourly you are! It's all along of my dear daughter. She deserves it!"

They were ready for a dance in half a second (Meg and Richard at the top); and the Drum was on the very brink of feathering away with all his power; when a combination of prodigious sounds was heard outside, and a good-humoured comely woman of some fifty years of age, or thereabouts, came running in, attended by a man bearing a stone pitcher of terrific size, and closely followed by the marrow-bones and cleavers, and the bells; not the Bells, but a portable collection on a frame.

Trotty said, "It's Mrs. Chickenstalker!" And sat down and beat his knees again.

"Married, and not tell me, Meg!" cried the good woman. "Never! I couldn't rest on the last night of the Old Year without coming to wish you joy. I couldn't have done it, Meg. Not if I had been bed-ridden. So here I am; and as it's New Year's Eve, and the Eve of your wedding too, my dear, I had a little flip made, and brought it with me."

Mrs. Chickenstalker's notion of a little flip did honour to her character. The pitcher steamed and smoked and reeked like a volcano; and the man who had carried it, was faint.

"Mrs. Tugby!" said Trotty, who had been going round and round her, in an ecstasy.—"I should say, Chickenstalker— Bless your heart and soul! A Happy New Year, and many of 'em! Mrs. Tugby," said Trotty when he had saluted her;— "I should say, Chickenstalker— This is William Fern and Lilian."

The worthy dame, to his surprise, turned very pale and very red.

"Not Lilian Fern whose mother died in Dorsetshire!" said she.

Her uncle answered "Yes," and meeting hastily, they exchanged some hurried words together; of which the upshot was, that Mrs. Chickenstalker shook him by both hands; saluted Trotty on his cheek again of her own free will; and took the child to her capacious breast.

"Will Fern!" said Trotty, pulling on his right-hand muffler. "Not the friend you was hoping to find?"

"Ay!" returned Will, putting a hand on each of Trotty's shoulders. "And like to prove a'most as good a friend, if that can be, as one I found."

"O!" said Trotty. "Please to play up there. Will you have the goodness!"

To the music of the band, and the bells, the marrow-bones and cleavers, all at once; and while the Chimes were yet in lusty operation out of doors; Trotty, making Meg and Richard, second couple, led off Mrs. Chickenstalker down the dance, and danced it in a step unknown before or since; founded on his own peculiar trot.

Had Trotty dreamed? Or, are his joys and sorrows, and the actors in them, but a dream; himself a dream; the teller of this tale a dreamer, waking but now? If it be so, O listener, dear to him in all his visions, try to bear in mind the stern realities from which these shadows come; and in your sphere—none is too wide, and none too limited for such an end—endeavour to correct, improve, and soften them. So may the New Year be a happy one to you, happy to many more whose happiness depends on you! So may each year be happier than the last, and not the meanest of our brethren or sisterhood debarred their rightful share, in what our Great Creator formed them to enjoy.

The Cricket on the Hearth

Charles Dickens

CHAPTER I. CHIRP THE FIRST

The kettle began it! Don't tell me what Mrs. Peerybingle said. I know better. Mrs. Peerybingle may leave it on record to the end of time that she couldn't say which of them began it; but, I say the kettle did. I ought to know, I hope! The kettle began it, full five minutes by the little waxy-faced Dutch clock in the corner, before the Cricket uttered a chirp.

As if the clock hadn't finished striking, and the convulsive little Haymaker at the top of it, jerking away right and left with a scythe in front of a Moorish Palace, hadn't mowed down half an acre of imaginary grass before the Cricket joined in at all!

Why, I am not naturally positive. Every one knows that. I wouldn't set my own opinion against the opinion of Mrs. Peerybingle, unless I were quite sure, on any account whatever. Nothing should induce me. But, this is a question of fact. And the fact is, that the kettle began it, at least five minutes before the Cricket gave any sign of being in existence. Contradict me, and I'll say ten.

Let me narrate exactly how it happened. I should have proceeded to do so in my very first word, but for this plain consideration—if I am to tell a story I must begin at the beginning; and how is it possible to begin at the beginning, without beginning at the kettle?

It appeared as if there were a sort of match, or trial of skill, you must understand, between the kettle and the Cricket. And this is what led to it, and how it came about.

Mrs. Peerybingle, going out into the raw twilight, and clicking over the wet stones in a pair of pattens that worked innumerable rough impressions of the first proposition in Euclid all about the yard—Mrs. Peerybingle filled the kettle at the water-butt. Presently returning, less the pattens (and a good deal less, for they were tall and Mrs. Peerybingle was but short), she set the kettle on the fire. In doing which she lost her temper, or mislaid it for an instant; for, the water being uncomfortably cold, and in that slippy, slushy, sleety sort of state wherein it seems to penetrate through every kind of substance, patten rings included— had laid hold of Mrs. Peerybingle's toes, and even splashed her legs. And when we rather plume ourselves (with reason too) upon our legs, and keep ourselves particularly neat in point of stockings, we find this, for the moment, hard to bear.

Besides, the kettle was aggravating and obstinate. It wouldn't allow itself to be adjusted on the top bar; it wouldn't hear of accommodating itself kindly to the knobs of coal; it would lean forward with a drunken air, and dribble, a very Idiot of a kettle, on the hearth. It was quarrelsome, and hissed and spluttered morosely at the fire. To sum up all, the lid, resisting Mrs. Peerybingle's fingers, first of all turned topsy-turvy, and then, with an ingenious pertinacity deserving of a better cause, dived sideways in—down to the very bottom of the kettle. And the hull of the Royal George has never made half the monstrous resistance to coming out of the water, which the lid of that kettle employed against Mrs. Peerybingle, before she got it up again.

It looked sullen and pig-headed enough, even then; carrying its handle with an air of defiance, and cocking its spout pertly and mockingly at Mrs. Peerybingle, as if it said, "I won't boil. Nothing shall induce me!"

But Mrs. Peerybingle, with restored good humour, dusted her chubby little hands against each other, and sat down before the kettle, laughing. Meantime, the jolly blaze uprose and fell, flashing and gleaming on the little Haymaker at the top of the Dutch clock, until one might have thought he stood stock still before the Moorish Palace, and nothing was in motion but the flame.

He was on the move, however; and had his spasms, two to the second, all right and regular. But, his sufferings when the clock was going to strike, were frightful to behold; and, when a Cuckoo looked out of a trap-door in the Palace, and gave note six times, it shook him, each time, like a spectral voice—or like a something wiry, plucking at his legs.

It was not until a violent commotion and a whirring noise among the weights and ropes below him had quite subsided, that this terrified Haymaker became himself again. Nor was he startled without reason; for these rattling, bony skeletons of clocks are very disconcerting in their operation, and I wonder very much how any set of men, but most of all how Dutchmen, can have had a liking to invent them. There is a popular belief that Dutchmen love broad cases and much clothing for their own lower selves; and they might know better than to leave their clocks so very lank and unprotected, surely.

Now it was, you observe, that the kettle began to spend the evening. Now it was, that the kettle, growing mellow and musical, began to have irrepressible gurglings in its throat, and to indulge in short vocal snorts, which it checked in the bud, as if it hadn't quite made up its mind yet, to be good company. Now it was, that after two or three such vain attempts to stifle its convivial sentiments, it threw off all moroseness, all reserve, and burst into a stream of song so cosy and hilarious, as never maudlin nightingale yet formed the least idea of.

So plain too! Bless you, you might have understood it like a book—better than some books you and I could name, perhaps. With its warm breath gushing forth in a light cloud which merrily and gracefully ascended a few feet, then hung about the chimney-corner as its own domestic Heaven, it trolled its song with that strong energy of cheerfulness, that its iron body hummed and stirred upon the fire; and the lid itself, the recently rebellious lid—such is the influence of a bright example—performed a sort of jig, and clattered like a deaf and dumb young cymbal that had never known the use of its twin brother.

That this song of the kettle's was a song of invitation and welcome to somebody out of doors: to somebody at that moment coming on, towards the snug small home and the crisp fire: there is no doubt whatever. Mrs. Peerybingle knew it, perfectly, as she sat musing before the hearth. It's a dark night, sang the kettle, and the rotten leaves are lying by the way; and, above, all is mist and darkness, and, below, all is mire and clay; and there's only one relief in all the sad and murky air; and I don't know that it is one, for it's nothing but a glare; of deep and angry crimson, where the sun and wind together; set a brand upon the clouds for being guilty of such weather; and the widest open country is a long dull streak of black; and there's hoar-frost on the finger-post, and thaw upon the track; and the ice it isn't water, and the water isn't free; and you couldn't say that anything is what it ought to be; but he's coming, coming, coming!—

And here, if you like, the Cricket did chime in! with a Chirrup, Chirrup, Chirrup of such magnitude, by way of chorus; with a voice so astoundingly disproportionate to its size, as compared with the kettle; (size! you couldn't see it!) that if it had then and there burst itself like an overcharged gun, if it had fallen a victim on the spot, and chirruped its little body into fifty pieces, it would have seemed a natural and inevitable consequence, for which it had expressly laboured.

The kettle had had the last of its solo performance. It persevered with undiminished ardour; but the Cricket took first fiddle and kept it. Good Heaven, how it chirped! Its shrill, sharp, piercing voice resounded through the house, and seemed to twinkle in the outer darkness like a star. There was an indescribable little trill and tremble in it, at its loudest, which suggested its being carried off its legs, and made to leap again, by its own intense enthusiasm. Yet they went very well together, the Cricket and the kettle. The burden of the song was still the same; and louder, louder, louder still, they sang it in their emulation.

The fair little listener—for fair she was, and young: though something of what is called the dumpling shape; but I don't myself object to that—lighted a candle, glanced at the Haymaker on the top of the clock, who was getting in a pretty average crop of minutes; and looked out of the window, where she saw nothing, owing to the darkness, but her own face imaged in the glass. And my opinion is (and so would yours have been), that she might have looked a long way, and seen nothing half so agreeable. When she came back, and sat down in her former seat, the Cricket and the kettle were still keeping it up, with a perfect fury of competition. The kettle's weak side clearly being, that he didn't know when he was beat.

There was all the excitement of a race about it. Chirp, chirp, chirp! Cricket a mile ahead. Hum, hum, hum—m—m! Kettle making play in the distance, like a great top. Chirp, chirp, chirp! Cricket round the corner. Hum, hum, hum—m—m! Kettle sticking to him in his own way; no idea of giving in. Chirp, chirp, chirp! Cricket fresher than ever. Hum, hum, hum—m—m! Kettle slow and steady. Chirp, chirp, chirp! Cricket going in to finish him. Hum, hum, hum—m—m! Kettle not to be finished. Until at last they got so jumbled together, in the hurry-skurry, helter-skelter, of the match, that whether the kettle chirped and the Cricket hummed, or the Cricket chirped and the kettle hummed, or they both chirped and both hummed, it would have taken a clearer head than yours or mine to have decided with anything like certainty. But, of this, there is no doubt: that, the kettle and the Cricket, at one and the same moment, and by some power of amalgamation best known to themselves, sent, each, his fireside song of comfort streaming into a ray of the candle that shone out through the window, and a long way down the lane. And this light, bursting on a certain person who, on the instant, approached towards it through the gloom, expressed the whole thing to him, literally in a twinkling, and cried, "Welcome home, old fellow! Welcome home, my boy!"

This end attained, the kettle, being dead beat, boiled over, and was taken off the fire. Mrs. Peerybingle then went running to the door, where, what with the wheels of a cart, the tramp of a horse, the voice of a man, the tearing in and out of an excited dog, and the surprising and mysterious appearance of a baby, there was soon the very What's-his-name to pay.

Where the baby came from, or how Mrs. Peerybingle got hold of it in that flash of time, I don't know. But a live baby there was, in Mrs. Peerybingle's arms; and a pretty tolerable amount of pride she seemed to have in it, when she was drawn gently to the fire, by a sturdy figure of a man, much taller and much older than herself, who had to stoop a long way down, to kiss her. But she was worth the trouble. Six foot six, with the lumbago, might have done it.

"Oh goodness, John!" said Mrs. P. "What a state you are in with the weather!"

He was something the worse for it, undeniably. The thick mist hung in clots upon his eyelashes like candied thaw; and between the fog and fire together, there were rainbows in his very whiskers.

"Why, you see, Dot," John made answer, slowly, as he unrolled a shawl from about his throat; and warmed his hands; "it—it an't exactly summer weather. So, no wonder."

"I wish you wouldn't call me Dot, John. I don't like it," said Mrs. Peerybingle: pouting in a way that clearly showed she did like it, very much.

"Why what else are you?" returned John, looking down upon her with a smile, and giving her waist as light a squeeze as his huge hand and arm could give. "A dot and"—here he glanced at the baby—"a dot and carry—I won't say it, for fear I should spoil it; but I was very near a joke. I don't know as ever I was nearer."

He was often near to something or other very clever, by his own account: this lumbering, slow, honest John; this John so heavy, but so light of spirit; so rough upon the surface, but so gentle at the core; so dull without, so quick within; so stolid, but so good! Oh Mother Nature, give thy children the true poetry of heart that hid itself in this poor Carrier's breast—he was but a Carrier by the way—and we can bear to have them talking prose, and leading lives of prose; and bear to bless thee for their company!

It was pleasant to see Dot, with her little figure, and her baby in her arms: a very doll of a baby: glancing with a coquettish thoughtfulness at the fire, and inclining her delicate little head just enough on one side to let it rest in an odd, half-natural, half-affected, wholly nestling and agreeable manner, on the great rugged figure of the Carrier. It was pleasant to see him, with his tender awkwardness, endeavouring to adapt his rude support to her slight need, and make his burly middle-age a leaning-staff not inappropriate to her blooming youth. It was pleasant to observe how Tilly Slowboy, waiting in the background for the baby, took special cognizance (though in her earliest teens) of this grouping; and stood with her mouth and eyes wide open, and her head thrust forward, taking it in as if it were air. Nor was it less agreeable to observe how John the Carrier, reference being made by Dot to the aforesaid baby, checked his hand when on the point of touching the infant, as if he thought he might crack it; and bending down, surveyed it from a safe distance, with a kind of puzzled pride, such as an amiable mastiff might be supposed to show, if he found himself, one day, the father of a young canary.

"An't he beautiful, John? Don't he look precious in his sleep?"

"Very precious," said John. "Very much so. He generally is asleep, an't he?"

"Lor, John! Good gracious no!"

"Oh," said John, pondering. "I thought his eyes was generally shut. Halloa!"

"Goodness, John, how you startle one!"

"It an't right for him to turn 'em up in that way!" said the astonished Carrier, "is it? See how he's winking with both of 'em at once! And look at his mouth! Why he's gasping like a gold and silver fish!"

"You don't deserve to be a father, you don't," said Dot, with all the dignity of an experienced matron. "But how should you know what little complaints children are troubled with, John! You wouldn't so much as know their names, you stupid fellow." And when she had turned the baby over on her left arm, and had slapped its back as a restorative, she pinched her husband's ear, laughing.

"No," said John, pulling off his outer coat. "It's very true, Dot. I don't know much about it. I only know that I've been fighting pretty stiffly with the wind to-night. It's been blowing north-east, straight into the cart, the whole way home."

"Poor old man, so it has!" cried Mrs. Peerybingle, instantly becoming very active. "Here! Take the precious darling, Tilly, while I make myself of some use. Bless it, I could smother it with kissing it, I could! Hie then, good dog! Hie, Boxer, boy! Only let me make the tea first, John; and then I'll help you with the parcels, like a busy bee. 'How doth the little'—and all the rest of it, you know, John. Did you ever learn 'how doth the little,' when you went to school, John?"

"Not to quite know it," John returned. "I was very near it once. But I should only have spoilt it, I dare say."

"Ha ha," laughed Dot. She had the blithest little laugh you ever heard. "What a dear old darling of a dunce you are, John, to be sure!"

Not at all disputing this position, John went out to see that the boy with the lantern, which had been dancing to and fro before the door and window, like a Will of the Wisp, took due care of the horse; who was fatter than you would quite believe, if I gave you his measure, and so old that his birthday was lost in the mists of antiquity. Boxer, feeling that his attentions were due to the family in general, and must be impartially distributed, dashed in and out with bewildering inconstancy; now, describing a circle of short barks round the horse, where he was being rubbed down at the stable-door; now feigning to make savage rushes at his mistress, and facetiously bringing himself to sudden stops; now, eliciting a shriek from Tilly Slowboy, in the low nursing-chair near the fire, by the unexpected application of his moist nose to her countenance; now, exhibiting an obtrusive interest in the baby; now, going round and round upon the hearth, and lying down as if he had established himself for the night; now, getting up again, and taking that nothing of a fag-end of a tail of his, out into the weather, as if he had just remembered an appointment, and was off, at a round trot, to keep it.

"There! There's the teapot, ready on the hob!" said Dot; as briskly busy as a child at play at keeping house. "And there's the cold knuckle of ham; and there's the butter; and there's the crusty loaf, and all! Here's the clothes-basket for the small parcels, John, if you've got any there—where are you, John?"

"Don't let the dear child fall under the grate, Tilly, whatever you do!"

It may be noted of Miss Slowboy, in spite of her rejecting the caution with some vivacity, that she had a rare and surprising talent for getting this baby into difficulties and had several times imperilled its short life, in a quiet way peculiarly her own. She was of a spare and straight shape, this young lady, insomuch that her garments appeared to be in constant danger of sliding off those sharp pegs, her shoulders, on which they were loosely hung. Her costume was remarkable for the partial development, on all possible occasions, of some flannel vestment of a singular structure; also for affording glimpses, in the region of the back, of a corset, or pair of stays, in colour a dead-green. Being always in a state of gaping admiration at everything, and absorbed, besides, in the perpetual contemplation of her mistress's perfections and the baby's, Miss Slowboy, in her little errors of judgment, may be said to have done equal honour to her head and to her heart; and though these did less honour to the baby's head, which they were the occasional means of bringing into contact with deal doors, dressers, stair-rails, bed-posts, and other foreign substances, still they were the honest results of Tilly Slowboy's constant astonishment at finding herself so kindly treated, and installed in such a comfortable home. For, the maternal and paternal Slowboy were alike unknown to Fame, and Tilly had been bred by public charity, a foundling; which word, though only differing from fondling by one vowel's length, is very different in meaning, and expresses quite another thing.

To have seen little Mrs. Peerybingle come back with her husband, tugging at the clothes-basket, and making the most strenuous exertions to do nothing at all (for he carried it), would have amused you almost as much as it amused him. It may have entertained the Cricket too, for anything I know; but, certainly, it now began to chirp again, vehemently.

"Heyday!" said John, in his slow way. "It's merrier than ever, to-night, I think."

"And it's sure to bring us good fortune, John! It always has done so. To have a Cricket on the Hearth, is the luckiest thing in all the world!"

John looked at her as if he had very nearly got the thought into his head, that she was his Cricket in chief, and he quite agreed with her. But, it was probably one of his narrow escapes, for he said nothing.

"The first time I heard its cheerful little note, John, was on that night when you brought me home—when you brought me to my new home here; its little mistress. Nearly a year ago. You recollect, John?"

O yes. John remembered. I should think so!

"Its chirp was such a welcome to me! It seemed so full of promise and encouragement. It seemed to say, you would be kind and gentle with me, and would not expect (I had a fear of that, John, then) to find an old head on the shoulders of your foolish little wife."

John thoughtfully patted one of the shoulders, and then the head, as though he would have said No, no; he had had no such expectation; he had been quite content to take them as they were. And really he had reason. They were very comely.

"It spoke the truth, John, when it seemed to say so; for you have ever been, I am sure, the best, the most considerate, the most affectionate of husbands to me. This has been a happy home, John; and I love the Cricket for its sake!"

"Why so do I then," said the Carrier. "So do I, Dot."

"I love it for the many times I have heard it, and the many thoughts its harmless music has given me. Sometimes, in the twilight, when I have felt a little solitary and down-hearted, John—before baby was here to keep me company and make the house gay—when I have thought how lonely you would be if I should die; how lonely I should be if I could know that you had lost me, dear; its Chirp, Chirp, Chirp upon the hearth, has seemed to tell me of another little voice, so sweet, so very dear to me, before whose coming sound my trouble vanished like a dream. And when I used to fear—I did fear once, John, I was very young you know—that ours might prove to be an ill-assorted marriage, I being such a child, and you more like my guardian than my husband; and that you might not, however hard you tried, be able to learn to love me, as you hoped and prayed you might; its Chirp, Chirp, Chirp has cheered me up again, and filled me with new trust and confidence. I was thinking of these things to-night, dear, when I sat expecting you; and I love the Cricket for their sake!"

"And so do I," repeated John. "But, Dot? I hope and pray that I might learn to love you? How you talk! I had learnt that, long before I brought you here, to be the Cricket's little mistress, Dot!"

She laid her hand, an instant, on his arm, and looked up at him with an agitated face, as if she would have told him something. Next moment she was down upon her knees before the basket, speaking in a sprightly voice, and busy with the parcels.

"There are not many of them to-night, John, but I saw some goods behind the cart, just now; and though they give more trouble, perhaps, still they pay as well; so we have no reason to grumble, have we? Besides, you have been delivering, I dare say, as you came along?"

"Oh yes," John said. "A good many."

"Why what's this round box? Heart alive, John, it's a wedding-cake!"

"Leave a woman alone to find out that," said John, admiringly. "Now a man would never have thought of it. Whereas, it's my belief that if you was to pack a wedding-cake up in a tea-chest, or a turn-up bedstead, or a pickled salmon keg, or any unlikely thing, a woman would be sure to find it out directly. Yes; I called for it at the pastry-cook's."

"And it weighs I don't know what—whole hundredweights!" cried Dot, making a great demonstration of trying to lift it.

"Whose is it, John? Where is it going?"

"Read the writing on the other side," said John.

"Why, John! My Goodness, John!"

"Ah! who'd have thought it!" John returned.

"You never mean to say," pursued Dot, sitting on the floor and shaking her head at him, "that it's Gruff and Tackleton the toymaker!"

John nodded.

Mrs. Peerybingle nodded also, fifty times at least. Not in assent—in dumb and pitying amazement; screwing up her lips the while with all their little force (they were never made for screwing up; I am clear of that), and looking the good Carrier through and through, in her abstraction. Miss Slowboy, in the mean time, who had a mechanical power of reproducing scraps of current conversation for the delectation of the baby, with all the sense struck out of them, and all the nouns changed into the plural number, inquired aloud of that young creature, Was it Gruffs and Tackletons the toymakers then, and Would it call at Pastry-cooks for wedding-cakes, and Did its mothers know the boxes when its fathers brought them homes; and so on.

"And that is really to come about!" said Dot. "Why, she and I were girls at school together, John."

He might have been thinking of her, or nearly thinking of her, perhaps, as she was in that same school time. He looked upon her with a thoughtful pleasure, but he made no answer.

"And he's as old! As unlike her!—Why, how many years older than you, is Gruff and Tackleton, John?"

"How many more cups of tea shall I drink to-night at one sitting, than Gruff and Tackleton ever took in four, I wonder!" replied John, good-humouredly, as he drew a chair to the round table, and began at the cold ham. "As to eating, I eat but little; but that little I enjoy, Dot."

Even this, his usual sentiment at meal times, one of his innocent delusions (for his appetite was always obstinate, and flatly contradicted him), awoke no smile in the face of his little wife, who stood among the parcels, pushing the cake-box slowly from her with her foot, and never once looked, though her eyes were cast down too, upon the dainty shoe she generally was so mindful of. Absorbed in thought, she stood there, heedless alike of the tea and John (although he called to her, and rapped the table with his knife to startle her), until he rose and touched her on the arm; when she looked at him for a moment, and hurried to her place behind the teaboard, laughing at her negligence. But, not as she had laughed before. The manner and the music were quite changed.

The Cricket, too, had stopped. Somehow the room was not so cheerful as it had been. Nothing like it.

"So, these are all the parcels, are they, John?" she said, breaking a long silence, which the honest Carrier had devoted to the practical illustration of one part of his favourite sentiment—certainly enjoying what he ate, if it couldn't be admitted that he ate but little. "So, these are all the parcels; are they, John?"

"That's all," said John. "Why—no—I—" laying down his knife and fork, and taking a long breath. "I declare—I've clean forgotten the old gentleman!"

"The old gentleman?"

"In the cart," said John. "He was asleep, among the straw, the last time I saw him. I've very nearly remembered him, twice, since I came in; but he went out of my head again. Holloa! Yahip there! Rouse up! That's my hearty!"

John said these latter words outside the door, whither he had hurried with the candle in his hand.

Miss Slowboy, conscious of some mysterious reference to The Old Gentleman, and connecting in her mystified imagination certain associations of a religious nature with the phrase, was so disturbed, that hastily rising from the low chair by the fire to seek protection near the skirts of her mistress, and coming into contact as she crossed the doorway with an ancient Stranger, she instinctively made a charge or butt at him with the only offensive instrument within her reach. This instrument happening to be the baby, great commotion and alarm ensued, which the sagacity of Boxer rather tended to increase; for, that good dog, more thoughtful than its master, had, it seemed, been watching the old gentleman in his sleep, lest he should walk off with a few young poplar trees that were tied up behind the cart; and he still attended on him very closely, worrying his gaiters in fact, and making dead sets at the buttons.

"You're such an undeniable good sleeper, sir," said John, when tranquillity was restored; in the mean time the old gentleman had stood, bareheaded and motionless, in the centre of the room; "that I have half a mind to ask you where the other six are—only that would be a joke, and I know I should spoil it. Very near though," murmured the Carrier, with a chuckle; "very near!"

The Stranger, who had long white hair, good features, singularly bold and well defined for an old man, and dark, bright, penetrating eyes, looked round with a smile, and saluted the Carrier's wife by gravely inclining his head.

His garb was very quaint and odd—a long, long way behind the time. Its hue was brown, all over. In his hand he held a great brown club or walking-stick; and striking this upon the floor, it fell asunder, and became a chair. On which he sat down, quite composedly.

"There!" said the Carrier, turning to his wife. "That's the way I found him, sitting by the roadside! Upright as a milestone. And almost as deaf."

"Sitting in the open air, John!"

"In the open air," replied the Carrier, "just at dusk. 'Carriage Paid,' he said; and gave me eighteenpence. Then he got in. And there he is."

"He's going, John, I think!"

Not at all. He was only going to speak.

"If you please, I was to be left till called for," said the Stranger, mildly. "Don't mind me."

With that, he took a pair of spectacles from one of his large pockets, and a book from another, and leisurely began to read. Making no more of Boxer than if he had been a house lamb!

The Carrier and his wife exchanged a look of perplexity. The Stranger raised his head; and glancing from the latter to the former, said,

"Your daughter, my good friend?"

"Wife," returned John.

"Niece?" said the Stranger.

"Wife," roared John.

"Indeed?" observed the Stranger. "Surely? Very young!"

He quietly turned over, and resumed his reading. But, before he could have read two lines, he again interrupted himself to say:

"Baby, yours?"

John gave him a gigantic nod; equivalent to an answer in the affirmative, delivered through a speaking trumpet.

"Girl?"

"Bo-o-oy!" roared John.

"Also very young, eh?"

Mrs. Peerybingle instantly struck in. "Two months and three da-ays! Vaccinated just six weeks ago-o! Took very fine-ly! Considered, by the doctor, a remarkably beautiful chi-ild! Equal to the general run of children at five months o-old! Takes notice, in a way quite wonderful! May seem impossible to you, but feels his legs al-ready!"

Here the breathless little mother, who had been shrieking these short sentences into the old man's ear, until her pretty face was crimsoned, held up the Baby before him as a stubborn and triumphant fact; while Tilly Slowboy, with a melodious cry of "Ketcher, Ketcher"—which sounded like some unknown words, adapted to a popular Sneeze—performed some cow-like gambols round that all unconscious Innocent.

"Hark! He's called for, sure enough," said John. "There's somebody at the door. Open it, Tilly."

Before she could reach it, however, it was opened from without; being a primitive sort of door, with a latch, that any one could lift if he chose—and a good many people did choose, for all kinds of neighbours liked to have a cheerful word or two with the Carrier, though he was no great talker himself. Being opened, it gave admission to a little, meagre, thoughtful, dingy-faced man, who seemed to have made himself a great-coat from the sack-cloth covering of some old box; for, when he turned to shut the door, and keep the weather out, he disclosed upon the back of that garment, the inscription G & T in large black capitals. Also the word GLASS in bold characters.

"Good-evening, John!" said the little man. "Good-evening, Mum. Good-evening, Tilly. Good evening, Unbeknown! How's Baby, Mum? Boxer's pretty well I hope?"

"All thriving, Caleb," replied Dot. "I am sure you need only look at the dear child, for one, to know that."

"And I'm sure I need only look at you for another," said Caleb.

He didn't look at her though; he had a wandering and thoughtful eye which seemed to be always projecting itself into some other time and place, no matter what he said; a description which will equally apply to his voice.

"Or at John for another," said Caleb. "Or at Tilly, as far as that goes. Or certainly at Boxer."

"Busy just now, Caleb?" asked the Carrier.

"Why, pretty well, John," he returned, with the distraught air of a man who was casting about for the Philosopher's stone, at least. "Pretty much so. There's rather a run on Noah's Arks at present. I could have wished to improve upon the Family, but I don't see how it's to be done at the price. It would be a satisfaction to one's mind, to make it clearer which was Shems and Hams, and which was Wives. Flies an't on that scale neither, as compared with elephants you know! Ah! well! Have you got anything in the parcel line for me, John?"

The Carrier put his hand into a pocket of the coat he had taken off; and brought out, carefully preserved in moss and paper, a tiny flower-pot.

"There it is!" he said, adjusting it with great care. "Not so much as a leaf damaged. Full of buds!"

Caleb's dull eye brightened, as he took it, and thanked him.

"Dear, Caleb," said the Carrier. "Very dear at this season."

"Never mind that. It would be cheap to me, whatever it cost," returned the little man. "Anything else, John?"

"A small box," replied the Carrier. "Here you are!"

" 'For Caleb Plummer,' " said the little man, spelling out the direction. " 'With Cash.' With Cash, John? I don't think it's for me."

"With Care," returned the Carrier, looking over his shoulder. "Where do you make out cash?"

"Oh! To be sure!" said Caleb. "It's all right. With care! Yes, yes; that's mine.

It might have been with cash, indeed, if my dear Boy in the Golden South Americas had lived, John. You loved him like a son; didn't you? You needn't say you did. I know, of course. 'Caleb Plummer. With care.' Yes, yes, it's all right. It's a box of dolls' eyes for my daughter's work. I wish it was her own sight in a box, John."

"I wish it was, or could be!" cried the Carrier.

"Thank 'ee," said the little man. "You speak very hearty. To think that she should never see the Dolls—and them a-staring at her, so bold, all day long! That's where it cuts. What's the damage, John?"

"I'll damage you," said John, "if you inquire. Dot! Very near?"

"Well! it's like you to say so," observed the little man. "It's your kind way. Let me see. I think that's all."

"I think not," said the Carrier. "Try again."

"Something for our Governor, eh?" said Caleb, after pondering a little while. "To be sure. That's what I came for; but my head's so running on them Arks and things! He hasn't been here, has he?"

"Not he," returned the Carrier. "He's too busy, courting."

"He's coming round though," said Caleb; "for he told me to keep on the near side of the road going home, and it was ten to one he'd take me up. I had better go, by the bye.—You couldn't have the goodness to let me pinch Boxer's tail, Mum, for half a moment, could you?"

"Why, Caleb! what a question!"

"Oh never mind, Mum," said the little man. "He mightn't like it perhaps. There's a small order just come in, for barking dogs; and I should wish to go as close to Natur' as I could, for sixpence. That's all. Never mind, Mum."

It happened opportunely, that Boxer, without receiving the proposed stimulus, began to bark with great zeal. But, as this implied the approach of some new visitor, Caleb, postponing his study from the life to a more convenient season, shouldered the round box, and took a hurried leave. He might have spared himself the trouble, for he met the visitor upon the threshold.

"Oh! You are here, are you? Wait a bit. I'll take you home. John Peerybingle, my service to you. More of my service to your pretty wife. Handsomer every day! Better too, if possible! And younger," mused the speaker, in a low voice; "that's the Devil of it!"

"I should be astonished at your paying compliments, Mr. Tackleton," said Dot, not with the best grace in the world; "but for your condition."

"You know all about it then?"

"I have got myself to believe it, somehow," said Dot.

"After a hard struggle, I suppose?"

"Very."

Tackleton the Toy-merchant, pretty generally known as Gruff and Tackleton—for that was the firm, though Gruff had been bought out long ago; only leaving his name, and as some said his nature, according to its Dictionary meaning, in the business—Tackleton the Toy-merchant, was a man whose vocation had been quite misunderstood by his Parents and Guardians. If they had made him a Money Lender, or a sharp Attorney, or a Sheriff's Officer, or a Broker, he might have sown his discontented oats in his youth, and, after having had the full run of himself in ill-natured transactions, might have turned out amiable, at last, for the sake of a little freshness and novelty. But, cramped and chafing in the peaceable pursuit of toy-making, he was a domestic Ogre, who had been living on children all his life, and was their implacable enemy. He despised all toys; wouldn't have bought one for the world; delighted, in his malice, to insinuate grim expressions into the faces of brown-paper farmers who drove pigs to market, bellmen who advertised lost lawyers' consciences, movable old ladies who darned stockings or carved pies; and other like samples of his stock in trade. In appalling masks; hideous, hairy, red-eyed Jacks in Boxes; Vampire Kites; demoniacal Tumblers who wouldn't lie down, and were perpetually flying forward, to stare infants out of countenance; his soul perfectly revelled. They were his only relief, and safety-valve. He was great in such inventions. Anything suggestive of a Pony-nightmare was delicious to him. He had even lost money (and he took to that toy very kindly) by getting up Goblin slides for magic-lanterns, whereon the Powers of Darkness were depicted as a sort of supernatural shell-fish, with human faces. In intensifying the portraiture of Giants, he had sunk quite a little capital; and, though no painter himself, he could indicate, for the instruction of his artists, with a piece of chalk, a certain furtive leer for the countenances of those monsters, which was safe to destroy the peace of mind of any young gentleman between the ages of six and eleven, for the whole Christmas or Midsummer Vacation.

What he was in toys, he was (as most men are) in other things. You may easily suppose, therefore, that within the great green cape, which reached down to the calves of his legs, there was buttoned up to the chin an uncommonly pleasant fellow; and that he was about as choice a spirit, and as agreeable a companion, as ever stood in a pair of bull-headed-looking boots with mahogany-coloured tops.

Still, Tackleton, the toy-merchant, was going to be married. In spite of all this, he was going to be married. And to a young wife too, a beautiful young wife.

He didn't look much like a bridegroom, as he stood in the Carrier's kitchen, with a twist in his dry face, and a screw in his body, and his hat jerked over the bridge of his nose, and his hands tucked down into the bottoms of his pockets, and his whole sarcastic ill-conditioned self peering out of one little corner of one little eye, like the concentrated essence of any number of ravens. But, a Bridegroom he designed to be.

"In three days' time. Next Thursday. The last day of the first month in the year. That's my wedding-day," said Tackleton.

Did I mention that he had always one eye wide open, and one eye nearly shut; and that the one eye nearly shut, was always the expressive eye? I don't think I did.

"That's my wedding-day!" said Tackleton, rattling his money.

"Why, it's our wedding-day too," exclaimed the Carrier.

"Ha ha!" laughed Tackleton. "Odd! You're just such another couple. Just!"

The indignation of Dot at this presumptuous assertion is not to be described. What next? His imagination would compass the possibility of just such another Baby, perhaps. The man was mad.

"I say! A word with you," murmured Tackleton, nudging the Carrier with his elbow, and taking him a little apart. "You'll come to the wedding? We're in the same boat, you know."

"How in the same boat?" inquired the Carrier.

"A little disparity, you know," said Tackleton, with another nudge. "Come and spend an evening with us, beforehand."

"Why?" demanded John, astonished at this pressing hospitality.

"Why?" returned the other. "That's a new way of receiving an invitation. Why, for pleasure—sociability, you know, and all that!"

"I thought you were never sociable," said John, in his plain way.

"Tchah! It's of no use to be anything but free with you, I see," said Tackleton. "Why, then, the truth is you have a—what tea-drinking people call a sort of a comfortable appearance together, you and your wife. We know better, you know, but—"

"No, we don't know better," interposed John. "What are you talking about?"

"Well! We don't know better, then," said Tackleton. "We'll agree that we don't. As you like; what does it matter? I was going to say, as you have that sort of appearance, your company will produce a favourable effect on Mrs. Tackleton that will be. And, though I don't think your good lady's very friendly to me, in this matter, still she can't help herself from falling into my views, for there's a compactness and cosiness of appearance about her that always tells, even in an indifferent case. You'll say you'll come?"

"We have arranged to keep our Wedding-Day (as far as that goes) at home," said John. "We have made the promise to ourselves these six months. We think, you see, that home—"

"Bah! what's home?" cried Tackleton. "Four walls and a ceiling! (why don't you kill that Cricket? I would! I always do. I hate their noise.) There are four walls and a ceiling at my house. Come to me!"

"You kill your Crickets, eh?" said John.

"Scrunch 'em, sir," returned the other, setting his heel heavily on the floor. "You'll say you'll come? it's as much your interest as mine, you know, that the women should persuade each other that they're quiet and contented, and couldn't be better off. I know their way. Whatever one woman says, another woman is determined to clinch, always. There's that spirit of emulation among 'em, sir, that if your wife says to my wife, "I'm the happiest woman in the world, and mine's the best husband in the world, and I dote on him," my wife will say the same to yours, or more, and half believe it."

"Do you mean to say she don't, then?" asked the Carrier.

"Don't!" cried Tackleton, with a short, sharp laugh. "Don't what?"

The Carrier had some faint idea of adding, "dote upon you." But, happening to meet the half-closed eye, as it twinkled upon him over the turned-up collar of the cape, which was within an ace of poking it out, he felt it such an unlikely part and parcel of anything to be doted on, that he substituted, "that she don't believe it?"

"Ah you dog! You're joking," said Tackleton.

But the Carrier, though slow to understand the full drift of his meaning, eyed him in such a serious manner, that he was obliged to be a little more explanatory.

"I have the humour," said Tackleton: holding up the fingers of his left hand, and tapping the forefinger, to imply "there I am, Tackleton to wit": "I have the humour, sir, to marry a young wife, and a pretty wife": here he rapped his little finger, to express the Bride; not sparingly, but sharply; with a sense of power. "I'm able to gratify that humour and I do. It's my whim. But—now look there!"

He pointed to where Dot was sitting, thoughtfully, before the fire; leaning her dimpled chin upon her hand, and watching the bright blaze. The Carrier looked at her, and then at him, and then at her, and then at him again.

"She honours and obeys, no doubt, you know," said Tackleton; "and that, as I am not a man of sentiment, is quite enough for me. But do you think there's anything more in it?"

"I think," observed the Carrier, "that I should chuck any man out of window, who said there wasn't."

"Exactly so," returned the other with an unusual alacrity of assent. "To be sure! Doubtless you would. Of course. I'm certain of it. Good night. Pleasant dreams!"

The Carrier was puzzled, and made uncomfortable and uncertain, in spite of himself. He couldn't help showing it, in his manner.

"Good night, my dear friend!" said Tackleton, compassionately. "I'm off. We're exactly alike, in reality, I see. You won't give us to-morrow evening? Well! Next day you go out visiting, I know. I'll meet you there, and bring my wife that is to be. It'll do her good. You're agreeable? Thank 'ee. What's that!"

It was a loud cry from the Carrier's wife: a loud, sharp, sudden cry, that made the room ring, like a glass vessel. She had risen from her seat, and stood like one transfixed by terror and surprise. The Stranger had advanced towards the fire to warm himself, and stood within a short stride of her chair. But quite still.

"Dot!" cried the Carrier. "Mary! Darling! What's the matter?"

They were all about her in a moment. Caleb, who had been dozing on the cake-box, in the first imperfect recovery of his suspended presence of mind, seized Miss Slowboy by the hair of her head, but immediately apologised.

"Mary!" exclaimed the Carrier, supporting her in his arms. "Are you ill! What is it? Tell me, dear!"

She only answered by beating her hands together, and falling into a wild fit of laughter. Then, sinking from his grasp upon the ground, she covered her face with her apron, and wept bitterly. And then she laughed again, and then she cried again, and then she said how cold it was, and suffered him to lead her to the fire, where she sat down as before. The old man standing, as before, quite still.

"I'm better, John," she said. "I'm quite well now—I—"

"John!" But John was on the other side of her. Why turn her face towards the strange old gentleman, as if addressing him! Was her brain wandering?

"Only a fancy, John dear—a kind of shock—a something coming suddenly before my eyes—I don't know what it was. It's quite gone, quite gone."

"I'm glad it's gone," muttered Tackleton, turning the expressive eye all round the room. "I wonder where it's gone, and what it was. Humph! Caleb, come here! Who's that with the grey hair?"

"I don't know, sir," returned Caleb in a whisper. "Never see him before, in all my life. A beautiful figure for a nut-cracker; quite a new model. With a screw-jaw opening down into his waistcoat, he'd be lovely."

"Not ugly enough," said Tackleton.

"Or for a firebox, either," observed Caleb, in deep contemplation, "what a model! Unscrew his head to put the matches in; turn him heels up'ards for the light; and what a firebox for a gentleman's mantel-shelf, just as he stands!"

"Not half ugly enough," said Tackleton. "Nothing in him at all! Come! Bring that box! All right now, I hope?"

"Quite gone!" said the little woman, waving him hurriedly away. "Good night!"

"Good night," said Tackleton. "Good night, John Peerybingle! Take care how you carry that box, Caleb. Let it fall, and I'll murder you! Dark as pitch, and weather worse than ever, eh? Good night!"

So, with another sharp look round the room, he went out at the door; followed by Caleb with the wedding-cake on his head.

The Carrier had been so much astounded by his little wife, and so busily engaged in soothing and tending her, that he had scarcely been conscious of the Stranger's presence, until now, when he again stood there, their only guest.

"He don't belong to them, you see," said John. "I must give him a hint to go."

"I beg your pardon, friend," said the old gentleman, advancing to him; "the more so, as I fear your wife has not been well; but the Attendant whom my infirmity," he touched his ears and shook his head, "renders almost indispensable, not having arrived, I fear there must be some mistake. The bad night which made the shelter of your comfortable cart (may I never have a worse!) so acceptable, is still as bad as ever. Would you, in your kindness, suffer me to rent a bed here?"

"Yes, yes," cried Dot. "Yes! Certainly!"

"Oh!" said the Carrier, surprised by the rapidity of this consent.

"Well! I don't object; but, still I'm not quite sure that—"

"Hush!" she interrupted. "Dear John!"

"Why, he's stone deaf," urged John.

"I know he is, but— Yes, sir, certainly. Yes! certainly! I'll make him up a bed, directly, John."

As she hurried off to do it, the flutter of her spirits, and the agitation of her manner, were so strange that the Carrier stood looking after her, quite confounded.

"Did its mothers make it up a Beds then!" cried Miss Slowboy to the Baby; "and did its hair grow brown and curly, when its caps was lifted off, and frighten it, a precious Pets, a-sitting by the fires!"

With that unaccountable attraction of the mind to trifles, which is often incidental to a state of doubt and confusion, the Carrier as he walked slowly to and fro, found himself mentally repeating even these absurd words, many times. So many times that he got them by heart, and was still conning them over and over, like a lesson, when Tilly, after administering as much friction to the little bald head with her hand as she thought wholesome (according to the practice of nurses), had once more tied the Baby's cap on.

"And frighten it, a precious Pets, a-sitting by the fires. What frightened Dot, I wonder!" mused the Carrier, pacing to and fro.

He scouted, from his heart, the insinuations of the Toy-merchant, and yet they filled him with a vague, indefinite uneasiness. For, Tackleton was quick and sly; and he had that painful sense, himself, of being of slow perception, that a broken hint was always worrying to him. He certainly had no intention in his mind of linking anything that Tackleton had said, with the unusual conduct of his wife, but the two subjects of reflection came into his mind together, and he could not keep them asunder.

The bed was soon made ready; and the visitor, declining all refreshment but a cup of tea, retired. Then, Dot—quite well again, she said, quite well again—arranged the great chair in the chimney-corner for her husband; filled his pipe and gave it him; and took her usual little stool beside him on the hearth.

She always would sit on that little stool. I think she must have had a kind of notion that it was a coaxing, wheedling little stool.

She was, out and out, the very best filler of a pipe, I should say, in the four quarters of the globe. To see her put that chubby little finger in the bowl, and then blow down the pipe to clear the tube, and, when she had done so, affect to think that there was really something in the tube, and blow a dozen times, and hold it to her eye like a telescope, with a most provoking twist in her capital little face, as she looked down it, was quite a brilliant thing. As to the tobacco, she was perfect mistress of the subject; and her lighting of the pipe, with a wisp of paper, when the Carrier had it in his mouth—going so very near his nose, and yet not scorching it—was Art, high Art.

And the Cricket and the kettle, turning up again, acknowledged it! The bright fire, blazing up again, acknowledged it! The little Mower on the clock, in his unheeded work, acknowledged it! The Carrier, in his smoothing forehead and expanding face, acknowledged it, the readiest of all.

And as he soberly and thoughtfully puffed at his old pipe, and as the Dutch clock ticked, and as the red fire gleamed, and as the Cricket chirped; that Genius of his Hearth and Home (for such the Cricket was) came out, in fairy shape, into the room, and summoned many forms of Home about him. Dots of all ages, and all sizes, filled the chamber. Dots who were merry children, running on before him gathering flowers, in the fields; coy Dots, half shrinking from, half yielding to, the pleading of his own rough image; newly-married Dots, alighting at the door, and taking wondering possession of the household keys; motherly little Dots, attended by fictitious Slowboys, bearing babies to be christened; matronly Dots, still young and blooming, watching Dots of daughters, as they danced at rustic balls; fat Dots, encircled and beset by troops of rosy grandchildren; withered Dots, who leaned on sticks, and tottered as they crept along. Old Carriers too, appeared, with blind old Boxers lying at their feet; and newer carts with younger drivers ("Peerybingle Brothers" on the tilt); and sick old Carriers, tended by the gentlest hands; and graves of dead and gone old Carriers, green in the churchyard. And as the Cricket showed him all these things—he saw them plainly, though his eyes were fixed upon the fire—the Carrier's heart grew light and happy, and he thanked his Household Gods with all his might, and cared no more for Gruff and Tackleton than you do.

But, what was that young figure of a man, which the same Fairy Cricket set so near Her stool, and which remained there, singly and alone? Why did it linger still, so near her, with its arm upon the chimney-piece, ever repeating "Married! and not to me!"

O Dot! O failing Dot! There is no place for it in all your husband's visions; why has its shadow fallen on his hearth!

CHAPTER II. CHIRP THE SECOND

Caleb Plummer and his Blind Daughter lived all alone by themselves, as the Story-books say—and my blessing, with yours to back it I hope, on the Story-books, for saying anything in this workaday world!—Caleb Plummer and his Blind Daughter lived all alone by themselves, in a little cracked nutshell of a wooden house, which was, in truth, no better than a pimple on the prominent red-brick nose of Gruff and Tackleton. The premises of Gruff and Tackleton were the great feature of the street; but you might have knocked down Caleb Plummer's dwelling with a hammer or two, and carried off the pieces in a cart.

If any one had done the dwelling-house of Caleb Plummer the honour to miss it after such an inroad, it would have been, no doubt, to commend its demolition as a vast improvement. It stuck to the premises of Gruff and Tackleton, like a barnacle to a ship's keel, or a snail to a door, or a little bunch of toadstools to the stem of a tree.

But, it was the germ from which the full-grown trunk of Gruff and Tackleton had sprung; and, under its crazy roof, the Gruff before last, had, in a small way, made toys for a generation of old boys and girls, who had played with them, and found them out, and broken them, and gone to sleep.

I have said that Caleb and his poor Blind Daughter lived here. I should have said that Caleb lived here, and his poor Blind Daughter somewhere else—in an enchanted home of Caleb's furnishing, where scarcity and shabbiness were not, and trouble never entered. Caleb was no sorcerer, but in the only magic art that still remains to us, the magic of devoted, deathless love, Nature had been the mistress of his study; and from her teaching, all the wonder came.

The Blind Girl never knew that ceilings were discoloured, walls blotched and bare of plaster here and there, high crevices unstopped and widening every day, beams mouldering and tending downward. The Blind Girl never knew that iron was rusting, wood rotting, paper peeling off; the size, and shape, and true proportion of the dwelling, withering away. The Blind Girl never knew that ugly shapes of delf and earthenware were on the board; that sorrow and faintheartedness were in the house; that Caleb's scanty hairs were turning greyer and more grey, before her sightless face. The Blind Girl never knew they had a master, cold, exacting, and uninterested—never knew that Tackleton was Tackleton in short; but lived in the belief of an eccentric humourist who loved to have his jest with them, and who, while he was the Guardian Angel of their lives, disdained to hear one word of thankfulness.

And all was Caleb's doing; all the doing of her simple father! But he too had a Cricket on his Hearth; and listening sadly to its music when the motherless Blind Child was very young, that Spirit had inspired him with the thought that even her great deprivation might be almost changed into a blessing, and the girl made happy by these little means. For all the Cricket tribe are potent Spirits, even though the people who hold converse with them do not know it (which is frequently the case); and there are not in the unseen world, voices more gentle and more true, that may be so implicitly relied on, or that are so certain to give none but tenderest counsel, as the Voices in which the Spirits of the Fireside and the Hearth address themselves to human kind.

Caleb and his daughter were at work together in their usual working-room, which served them for their ordinary living-room as well; and a strange place it was. There were houses in it, finished and unfinished, for Dolls of all stations in life. Suburban tenements for Dolls of moderate means; kitchens and single apartments for Dolls of the lower classes; capital town residences for Dolls of high estate. Some of these establishments were already furnished according to estimate, with a view to the convenience of Dolls of limited income; others, could be fitted on the most expensive scale, at a moment's notice, from whole shelves of chairs and tables, sofas, bedsteads, and upholstery. The nobility and gentry, and public in general, for whose accommodation these tenements were designed, lay, here and there, in baskets, staring straight up at the ceiling; but, in denoting their degrees in society, and confining them to their respective stations (which experience shows to be lamentably difficult in real life), the makers of these Dolls had far improved on Nature, who is often froward and perverse; for, they, not resting on such arbitrary marks as satin, cotton-print, and bits of rag, had superadded striking personal differences which allowed of no mistake. Thus, the Doll-lady of distinction had wax limbs of perfect symmetry; but only she and her compeers. The next grade in the social scale being made of leather, and the next of coarse linen stuff. As to the common-people, they had just so many matches out of tinder-boxes, for their arms and legs, and there they were— established in their sphere at once, beyond the possibility of getting out of it.

There were various other samples of his handicraft, besides Dolls, in Caleb Plummer's room. There were Noah's Arks, in which the Birds and Beasts were an uncommonly tight fit, I assure you; though they could be crammed in, anyhow, at the roof, and rattled and shaken into the smallest compass. By a bold poetical licence, most of these Noah's Arks had knockers on the doors; inconsistent appendages, perhaps, as suggestive of morning callers and a Postman, yet a pleasant finish to the outside of the building. There were scores of melancholy little carts, which, when the wheels went round, performed most doleful music. Many small fiddles, drums, and other instruments of torture; no end of cannon, shields, swords, spears, and guns. There were little tumblers in red breeches, incessantly swarming up high obstacles of red-tape, and coming down, head first, on the other side; and there were innumerable old gentlemen of respectable, not to say venerable, appearance, insanely flying over horizontal pegs, inserted, for the purpose, in their own street doors. There were beasts of all sorts; horses, in particular, of every breed, from the spotted barrel on four pegs, with a small tippet for a mane, to the thoroughbred rocker on his highest mettle. As it would have been hard to count the dozens upon dozens of grotesque figures that were ever ready to commit all sorts of absurdities on the turning of a handle, so it would have been no easy task to mention any human folly, vice, or weakness, that had not its type, immediate or remote, in Caleb Plummer's room. And not in an exaggerated form, for very little handles will move men and women to as strange performances, as any Toy was ever made to undertake.

In the midst of all these objects, Caleb and his daughter sat at work. The Blind Girl busy as a Doll's dressmaker; Caleb painting and glazing the four-pair front of a desirable family mansion.

The care imprinted in the lines of Caleb's face, and his absorbed and dreamy manner, which would have sat well on some alchemist or abstruse student, were at first sight an odd contrast to his occupation, and the trivialities about him. But, trivial things, invented and pursued for bread, become very serious matters of fact; and, apart from this consideration, I am not at all prepared to say, myself, that if Caleb had been a Lord Chamberlain, or a Member of Parliament, or a lawyer, or even a great speculator, he would have dealt in toys one whit less whimsical, while I have a very great doubt whether they would have been as harmless.

"So you were out in the rain last night, father, in your beautiful new great-coat," said Caleb's daughter.

"In my beautiful new great-coat," answered Caleb, glancing towards a clothes-line in the room, on which the sack-cloth garment previously described, was carefully hung up to dry.

"How glad I am you bought it, father!"

"And of such a tailor, too," said Caleb. "Quite a fashionable tailor. It's too good for me."

The Blind Girl rested from her work, and laughed with delight. "Too good, father! What can be too good for you?"

"I'm half-ashamed to wear it though," said Caleb, watching the effect of what he said, upon her brightening face; "upon my word! When I hear the boys and people say behind me, 'Hal-loa! Here's a swell!' I don't know which way to look. And when the beggar wouldn't go away last night; and when I said I was a very common man, said 'No, your Honour! Bless your Honour, don't say that!' I was quite ashamed. I really felt as if I hadn't a right to wear it."

Happy Blind Girl! How merry she was, in her exultation!

"I see you, father," she said, clasping her hands, "as plainly, as if I had the eyes I never want when you are with me. A blue coat—"

"Bright blue," said Caleb.

"Yes, yes! Bright blue!" exclaimed the girl, turning up her radiant face; "the colour I can just remember in the blessed sky! You told me it was blue before! A bright blue coat—"

"Made loose to the figure," suggested Caleb.

"Made loose to the figure!" cried the Blind Girl, laughing heartily; "and in it, you, dear father, with your merry eye, your smiling face, your free step, and your dark hair—looking so young and handsome!"

"Halloa! Halloa!" said Caleb. "I shall be vain, presently!"

"I think you are, already," cried the Blind Girl, pointing at him, in her glee. "I know you, father! Ha, ha, ha! I've found you out, you see!"

How different the picture in her mind, from Caleb, as he sat observing her! She had spoken of his free step. She was right in that. For years and years, he had never once crossed that threshold at his own slow pace, but with a footfall counterfeited for her ear; and never had he, when his heart was heaviest, forgotten the light tread that was to render hers so cheerful and courageous!

Heaven knows! But I think Caleb's vague bewilderment of manner may have half originated in his having confused himself about himself and everything around him, for the love of his Blind Daughter. How could the little man be otherwise than bewildered, after labouring for so many years to destroy his own identity, and that of all the objects that had any bearing on it!

"There we are," said Caleb, falling back a pace or two to form the better judgment of his work; "as near the real thing as sixpenn'orth of halfpence is to sixpence. What a pity that the whole front of the house opens at once! If there was only a staircase in it, now, and regular doors to the rooms to go in at! But that's the worst of my calling, I'm always deluding myself, and swindling myself."

"You are speaking quite softly. You are not tired, father?"

"Tired!" echoed Caleb, with a great burst of animation, "what should tire me, Bertha? I was never tired. What does it mean?"

To give the greater force to his words, he checked himself in an involuntary imitation of two half-length stretching and yawning figures on the mantel-shelf, who were represented as in one eternal state of weariness from the waist upwards; and hummed a fragment of a song. It was a Bacchanalian song, something about a Sparkling Bowl. He sang it with an assumption of a Devil-may-care voice, that made his face a thousand times more meagre and more thoughtful than ever.

"What! You're singing, are you?" said Tackleton, putting his head in at the door. "Go it! I can't sing."

Nobody would have suspected him of it. He hadn't what is generally termed a singing face, by any means.

"I can't afford to sing," said Tackleton. "I'm glad you can. I hope you can afford to work too. Hardly time for both, I should think?"

"If you could only see him, Bertha, how he's winking at me!" whispered Caleb. "Such a man to joke! you'd think, if you didn't know him, he was in earnest— wouldn't you now?"

The Blind Girl smiled and nodded.

"The bird that can sing and won't sing, must be made to sing, they say," grumbled Tackleton. "What about the owl that can't sing, and oughtn't to sing, and will sing; is there anything that he should be made to do?"

"The extent to which he's winking at this moment!" whispered Caleb to his daughter. "O, my gracious!"

"Always merry and light-hearted with us!" cried the smiling Bertha.

"O, you're there, are you?" answered Tackleton. "Poor Idiot!"

He really did believe she was an Idiot; and he founded the belief, I can't say whether consciously or not, upon her being fond of him.

"Well! and being there,—how are you?" said Tackleton, in his grudging way.

"Oh! well; quite well. And as happy as even you can wish me to be. As happy as you would make the whole world, if you could!"

"Poor Idiot!" muttered Tackleton. "No gleam of reason. Not a gleam!"

The Blind Girl took his hand and kissed it; held it for a moment in her own two hands; and laid her cheek against it tenderly, before releasing it. There was such unspeakable affection and such fervent gratitude in the act, that Tackleton himself was moved to say, in a milder growl than usual:

"What's the matter now?"

"I stood it close beside my pillow when I went to sleep last night, and remembered it in my dreams. And when the day broke, and the glorious red sun—the red sun, father?"

"Red in the mornings and the evenings, Bertha," said poor Caleb, with a woeful glance at his employer.

"When it rose, and the bright light I almost fear to strike myself against in walking, came into the room, I turned the little tree towards it, and blessed Heaven for making things so precious, and blessed you for sending them to cheer me!"

"Bedlam broke loose!" said Tackleton under his breath. "We shall arrive at the strait-waistcoat and mufflers soon. We're getting on!"

Caleb, with his hands hooked loosely in each other, stared vacantly before him while his daughter spoke, as if he really were uncertain (I believe he was) whether Tackleton had done anything to deserve her thanks, or not. If he could have been a perfectly free agent, at that moment, required, on pain of death, to kick the Toy-merchant, or fall at his feet, according to his merits, I believe it would have been an even chance which course he would have taken. Yet, Caleb knew that with his own hands he had brought the little rose-tree home for her, so carefully, and that with his own lips he had forged the innocent deception which should help to keep her from suspecting how much, how very much, he every day, denied himself, that she might be the happier.

"Bertha!" said Tackleton, assuming, for the nonce, a little cordiality. "Come here."

"Oh! I can come straight to you! You needn't guide me!" she rejoined.

"Shall I tell you a secret, Bertha?"

"If you will!" she answered, eagerly.

How bright the darkened face! How adorned with light, the listening head!

"This is the day on which little what's-her-name, the spoilt child, Peerybingle's wife, pays her regular visit to you—makes her fantastic Pic-Nic here; an't it?" said Tackleton, with a strong expression of distaste for the whole concern.

"Yes," replied Bertha. "This is the day."

"I thought so," said Tackleton. "I should like to join the party."

"Do you hear that, father!" cried the Blind Girl in an ecstasy.

"Yes, yes, I hear it," murmured Caleb, with the fixed look of a sleep-walker; "but I don't believe it. It's one of my lies, I've no doubt."

"You see I—I want to bring the Peerybingles a little more into company with May Fielding," said Tackleton. "I am going to be married to May."

"Married!" cried the Blind Girl, starting from him.

"She's such a con-founded Idiot," muttered Tackleton, "that I was afraid she'd never comprehend me. Ah, Bertha! Married! Church, parson, clerk, beadle, glass-coach, bells, breakfast, bride-cake, favours, marrow-bones, cleavers, and all the rest of the tomfoolery. A wedding, you know; a wedding. Don't you know what a wedding is?"

"I know," replied the Blind Girl, in a gentle tone. "I understand!"

"Do you?" muttered Tackleton. "It's more than I expected. Well! On that account I want to join the party, and to bring May and her mother. I'll send in a little something or other, before the afternoon. A cold leg of mutton, or some comfortable trifle of that sort. You'll expect me?"

"Yes," she answered.

She had drooped her head, and turned away; and so stood, with her hands crossed, musing.

"I don't think you will," muttered Tackleton, looking at her; "for you seem to have forgotten all about it, already. Caleb!"

"I may venture to say I'm here, I suppose," thought Caleb. "Sir!"

"Take care she don't forget what I've been saying to her."

"She never forgets," returned Caleb. "It's one of the few things she an't clever in."

"Every man thinks his own geese swans," observed the Toy-merchant, with a shrug. "Poor devil!"

Having delivered himself of which remark, with infinite contempt, old Gruff and Tackleton withdrew.

Bertha remained where he had left her, lost in meditation. The gaiety had vanished from her downcast face, and it was very sad. Three or four times she shook her head, as if bewailing some remembrance or some loss; but her sorrowful reflections found no vent in words.

It was not until Caleb had been occupied, some time, in yoking a team of horses to a wagon by the summary process of nailing the harness to the vital parts of their bodies, that she drew near to his working-stool, and sitting down beside him, said:

"Father, I am lonely in the dark. I want my eyes, my patient, willing eyes."

"Here they are," said Caleb. "Always ready. They are more yours than mine, Bertha, any hour in the four-and-twenty. What shall your eyes do for you, dear?"

"Look round the room, father."

"All right," said Caleb. "No sooner said than done, Bertha."

"Tell me about it."

"It's much the same as usual," said Caleb. "Homely, but very snug. The gay colours on the walls; the bright flowers on the plates and dishes; the shining wood, where there are beams or panels; the general cheerfulness and neatness of the building; make it very pretty."

Cheerful and neat it was wherever Bertha's hands could busy themselves. But nowhere else, were cheerfulness and neatness possible, in the old crazy shed which Caleb's fancy so transformed.

"You have your working dress on, and are not so gallant as when you wear the handsome coat?" said Bertha, touching him.

"Not quite so gallant," answered Caleb. "Pretty brisk though."

"Father," said the Blind Girl, drawing close to his side, and stealing one arm round his neck, "tell me something about May. She is very fair?"

"She is indeed," said Caleb. And she was indeed. It was quite a rare thing to Caleb, not to have to draw on his invention.

"Her hair is dark," said Bertha, pensively, "darker than mine. Her voice is sweet and musical, I know. I have often loved to hear it. Her shape—"

"There's not a Doll's in all the room to equal it," said Caleb. "And her eyes!—"

He stopped; for Bertha had drawn closer round his neck, and from the arm that clung about him, came a warning pressure which he understood too well.

He coughed a moment, hammered for a moment, and then fell back upon the song about the sparkling bowl; his infallible resource in all such difficulties.

"Our friend, father, our benefactor. I am never tired, you know, of hearing about him.—Now, was I ever?" she said, hastily.

"Of course not," answered Caleb, "and with reason."

"Ah! With how much reason!" cried the Blind Girl. With such fervency, that Caleb, though his motives were so pure, could not endure to meet her face; but dropped his eyes, as if she could have read in them his innocent deceit.

"Then, tell me again about him, dear father," said Bertha. "Many times again! His face is benevolent, kind, and tender. Honest and true, I am sure it is. The manly heart that tries to cloak all favours with a show of roughness and unwillingness, beats in its every look and glance."

"And makes it noble!" added Caleb, in his quiet desperation.

"And makes it noble!" cried the Blind Girl. "He is older than May, father."

"Ye-es," said Caleb, reluctantly. "He's a little older than May. But that don't signify."

"Oh father, yes! To be his patient companion in infirmity and age; to be his gentle nurse in sickness, and his constant friend in suffering and sorrow; to know no weariness in working for his sake; to watch him, tend him, sit beside his bed and talk to him awake, and pray for him asleep; what privileges these would be! What opportunities for proving all her truth and devotion to him! Would she do all this, dear father?

"No doubt of it," said Caleb.

"I love her, father; I can love her from my soul!" exclaimed the Blind Girl. And saying so, she laid her poor blind face on Caleb's shoulder, and so wept and wept, that he was almost sorry to have brought that tearful happiness upon her.

In the mean time, there had been a pretty sharp commotion at John Peerybingle's, for little Mrs. Peerybingle naturally couldn't think of going anywhere without the Baby; and to get the Baby under weigh took time. Not that there was much of the Baby, speaking of it as a thing of weight and measure, but there was a vast deal to do about and about it, and it all had to be done by easy stages. For instance, when the Baby was got, by hook and by crook, to a certain point of dressing, and you might have rationally supposed that another touch or two would finish him off, and turn him out a tip-top Baby challenging the world, he was unexpectedly extinguished in a flannel cap, and hustled off to bed; where he simmered (so to speak) between two blankets for the best part of an hour. From this state of inaction he was then recalled, shining very much and roaring violently, to partake of—well? I would rather say, if you'll permit me to speak generally—of a slight repast. After which, he went to sleep again. Mrs. Peerybingle took advantage of this interval, to make herself as smart in a small way as ever you saw anybody in all your life; and, during the same short truce, Miss Slowboy insinuated herself into a spencer of a fashion so surprising and ingenious, that it had no connection with herself, or anything else in the universe, but was a shrunken, dog's-eared, independent fact, pursuing its lonely course without the least regard to anybody. By this time, the Baby, being all alive again, was invested, by the united efforts of Mrs. Peerybingle and Miss Slowboy, with a cream-coloured mantle for its body, and a sort of nankeen raised-pie for its head; and so in course of time they all three got down to the door, where the old horse had already taken more than the full value of his day's toll out of the Turnpike Trust, by tearing up the road with his impatient autographs; and whence Boxer might be dimly seen in the remote perspective, standing looking back, and tempting him to come on without orders.

As to a chair, or anything of that kind for helping Mrs. Peerybingle into the cart, you know very little of John, if you think that was necessary. Before you could have seen him lift her from the ground, there she was in her place, fresh and rosy, saying, "John! How can you! Think of Tilly!"

If I might be allowed to mention a young lady's legs, on any terms, I would observe of Miss Slowboy's that there was a fatality about them which rendered them singularly liable to be grazed; and that she never effected the smallest ascent or descent, without recording the circumstance upon them with a notch, as Robinson Crusoe marked the days upon his wooden calendar. But as this might be considered ungenteel, I'll think of it.

"John? You've got the Basket with the Veal and Ham-Pie and things, and the bottles of Beer?" said Dot. "If you haven't, you must turn round again, this very minute."

"You're a nice little article," returned the Carrier, "to be talking about turning round, after keeping me a full quarter of an hour behind my time."

"I am sorry for it, John," said Dot in a great bustle, "but I really could not think of going to Bertha's—I would not do it, John, on any account—without the Veal and Ham-Pie and things, and the bottles of Beer. Way!"

This monosyllable was addressed to the horse, who didn't mind it at all.

"Oh do way, John!" said Mrs. Peerybingle. "Please!"

"It'll be time enough to do that," returned John, "when I begin to leave things behind me. The basket's here, safe enough."

"What a hard-hearted monster you must be, John, not to have said so, at once, and save me such a turn! I declared I wouldn't go to Bertha's without the Veal and Ham-Pie and things, and the bottles of Beer, for any money. Regularly once a fortnight ever since we have been married, John, have we made our little Pic-Nic there. If anything was to go wrong with it, I should almost think we were never to be lucky again."

"It was a kind thought in the first instance," said the Carrier: "and I honour you for it, little woman."

"My dear John," replied Dot, turning very red, "don't talk about honouring me. Good Gracious!"

"By the bye—" observed the Carrier. "That old gentleman—"

Again so visibly, and instantly embarrassed!

"He's an odd fish," said the Carrier, looking straight along the road before them. "I can't make him out. I don't believe there's any harm in him."

"None at all. I'm—I'm sure there's none at all."

"Yes," said the Carrier, with his eyes attracted to her face by the great earnestness of her manner. "I am glad you feel so certain of it, because it's a confirmation to me. It's curious that he should have taken it into his head to ask leave to go on lodging with us; an't it? Things come about so strangely."

"So very strangely," she rejoined in a low voice, scarcely audible.

"However, he's a good-natured old gentleman," said John, "and pays as a gentleman, and I think his word is to be relied upon, like a gentleman's. I had quite a long talk with him this morning: he can hear me better already, he says, as he gets more used to my voice. He told me a great deal about himself, and I told him a great deal about myself, and a rare lot of questions he asked me. I gave him information about my having two beats, you know, in my business; one day to the right from our house and back again; another day to the left from our house and back again (for he's a stranger and don't know the names of places about here); and he seemed quite pleased. "Why, then I shall be returning home to-night your way," he says, "when I thought you'd be coming in an exactly opposite direction. That's capital! I may trouble you for another lift perhaps, but I'll engage not to fall so sound asleep again." He was sound asleep, sure-ly!—Dot! what are you thinking of?"

"Thinking of, John? I—I was listening to you."

"O! That's all right!" said the honest Carrier. "I was afraid, from the look of your face, that I had gone rambling on so long, as to set you thinking about something else. I was very near it, I'll be bound."

Dot making no reply, they jogged on, for some little time, in silence. But, it was not easy to remain silent very long in John Peerybingle's cart, for everybody on the road had something to say. Though it might only be "How are you!" and indeed it was very often nothing else, still, to give that back again in the right spirit of cordiality, required, not merely a nod and a smile, but as wholesome an action of the lungs withal, as a long-winded Parliamentary speech. Sometimes, passengers on foot, or horseback, plodded on a little way beside the cart, for the express purpose of having a chat; and then there was a great deal to be said, on both sides.

Then, Boxer gave occasion to more good-natured recognitions of, and by, the Carrier, than half-a-dozen Christians could have done! Everybody knew him, all along the road—especially the fowls and pigs, who when they saw him approaching, with his body all on one side, and his ears pricked up inquisitively, and that knob of a tail making the most of itself in the air, immediately withdrew into remote back settlements, without waiting for the honour of a nearer acquaintance. He had business everywhere; going down all the turnings, looking into all the wells, bolting in and out of all the cottages, dashing into the midst of all the Dame-Schools, fluttering all the pigeons, magnifying the tails of all the cats, and trotting into the public-houses like a regular customer. Wherever he went, somebody or other might have been heard to cry, "Halloa! Here's Boxer!" and out came that somebody forthwith, accompanied by at least two or three other somebodies, to give John Peerybingle and his pretty wife, Good Day.

The packages and parcels for the errand cart, were numerous; and there were many stoppages to take them in and give them out, which were not by any means the worst parts of the journey. Some people were so full of expectation about their parcels, and other people were so full of wonder about their parcels, and other people were so full of inexhaustible directions about their parcels, and John had such a lively interest in all the parcels, that it was as good as a play. Likewise, there were articles to carry, which required to be considered and discussed, and in reference to the adjustment and disposition of which, councils had to be holden by the Carrier and the senders: at which Boxer usually assisted, in short fits of the closest attention, and long fits of tearing round and round the assembled sages and barking himself hoarse. Of all these little incidents, Dot was the amused and open-eyed spectatress from her chair in the cart; and as she sat there, looking on—a charming little portrait framed to admiration by the tilt—there was no lack of nudgings and glancings and whisperings and envyings among the younger men. And this delighted John the Carrier, beyond measure; for he was proud to have his little wife admired, knowing that she didn't mind it—that, if anything, she rather liked it perhaps.

The trip was a little foggy, to be sure, in the January weather; and was raw and cold. But who cared for such trifles? Not Dot, decidedly. Not Tilly Slowboy, for she deemed sitting in a cart, on any terms, to be the highest point of human joys; the crowning circumstance of earthly hopes. Not the Baby, I'll be sworn; for it's not in Baby nature to be warmer or more sound asleep, though its capacity is great in both respects, than that blessed young Peerybingle was, all the way.

You couldn't see very far in the fog, of course; but you could see a great deal! It's astonishing how much you may see, in a thicker fog than that, if you will only take the trouble to look for it. Why, even to sit watching for the Fairy-rings in the fields, and for the patches of hoar-frost still lingering in the shade, near hedges and by trees, was a pleasant occupation: to make no mention of the unexpected shapes in which the trees themselves came starting out of the mist, and glided into it again. The hedges were tangled and bare, and waved a multitude of blighted garlands in the wind; but there was no discouragement in this. It was agreeable to contemplate; for it made the fireside warmer in possession, and the summer greener in expectancy. The river looked chilly; but it was in motion, and moving at a good pace—which was a great point. The canal was rather slow and torpid; that must be admitted. Never mind. It would freeze the sooner when the frost set fairly in, and then there would be skating, and sliding; and the heavy old barges, frozen up somewhere near a wharf, would smoke their rusty iron chimney pipes all day, and have a lazy time of it.

In one place, there was a great mound of weeds or stubble burning; and they watched the fire, so white in the daytime, flaring through the fog, with only here and there a dash of red in it, until, in consequence, as she observed, of the smoke "getting up her nose," Miss Slowboy choked—she could do anything of that sort, on the smallest provocation—and woke the Baby, who wouldn't go to sleep again. But, Boxer, who was in advance some quarter of a mile or so, had already passed the outposts of the town, and gained the corner of the street where Caleb and his daughter lived; and long before they had reached the door, he and the Blind Girl were on the pavement waiting to receive them.

Boxer, by the way, made certain delicate distinctions of his own, in his communication with Bertha, which persuade me fully that he knew her to be blind. He never sought to attract her attention by looking at her, as he often did with other people, but touched her invariably. What experience he could ever have had of blind people or blind dogs, I don't know. He had never lived with a blind master; nor had Mr. Boxer the elder, nor Mrs. Boxer, nor any of his respectable family on either side, ever been visited with blindness, that I am aware of. He may have found it out for himself, perhaps, but he had got hold of it somehow; and therefore he had hold of Bertha too, by the skirt, and kept hold, until Mrs. Peerybingle and the Baby, and Miss Slowboy, and the basket, were all got safely within doors.

May Fielding was already come; and so was her mother—a little querulous chip of an old lady with a peevish face, who, in right of having preserved a waist like a bedpost, was supposed to be a most transcendent figure; and who, in consequence of having once been better off, or of labouring under an impression that she might have been, if something had happened which never did happen, and seemed to have never been particularly likely to come to pass—but it's all the same—was very genteel and patronising indeed. Gruff and Tackleton was also there, doing the agreeable, with the evident sensation of being as perfectly at home, and as unquestionably in his own element, as a fresh young salmon on the top of the Great Pyramid.

"May! My dear old friend!" cried Dot, running up to meet her. "What a happiness to see you."

Her old friend was, to the full, as hearty and as glad as she; and it really was, if you'll believe me, quite a pleasant sight to see them embrace. Tackleton was a man of taste beyond all question. May was very pretty.

You know sometimes, when you are used to a pretty face, how, when it comes into contact and comparison with another pretty face, it seems for the moment to be homely and faded, and hardly to deserve the high opinion you have had of it. Now, this was not at all the case, either with Dot or May; for May's face set off Dot's, and Dot's face set off May's, so naturally and agreeably, that, as John Peerybingle was very near saying when he came into the room, they ought to have been born sisters—which was the only improvement you could have suggested.

Tackleton had brought his leg of mutton, and, wonderful to relate, a tart besides—but we don't mind a little dissipation when our brides are in the case; we don't get married every day—and in addition to these dainties, there were the Veal and Ham-Pie, and "things," as Mrs. Peerybingle called them; which were chiefly nuts and oranges, and cakes, and such small deer. When the repast was set forth on the board, flanked by Caleb's contribution, which was a great wooden bowl of smoking potatoes (he was prohibited, by solemn compact, from producing any other viands), Tackleton led his intended mother-in-law to the post of honour. For the better gracing of this place at the high festival, the majestic old soul had adorned herself with a cap, calculated to inspire the thoughtless with sentiments of awe. She also wore her gloves. But let us be genteel, or die!

Caleb sat next his daughter; Dot and her old schoolfellow were side by side; the good Carrier took care of the bottom of the table. Miss Slowboy was isolated, for the time being, from every article of furniture but the chair she sat on, that she might have nothing else to knock the Baby's head against.

As Tilly stared about her at the dolls and toys, they stared at her and at the company. The venerable old gentlemen at the street doors (who were all in full action) showed especial interest in the party, pausing occasionally before leaping, as if they were listening to the conversation, and then plunging wildly over and over, a great many times, without halting for breath—as in a frantic state of delight with the whole proceedings.

Certainly, if these old gentlemen were inclined to have a fiendish joy in the contemplation of Tackleton's discomfiture, they had good reason to be satisfied. Tackleton couldn't get on at all; and the more cheerful his intended bride became in Dot's society, the less he liked it, though he had brought them together for that purpose. For he was a regular dog in the manger, was Tackleton; and when they laughed and he couldn't, he took it into his head, immediately, that they must be laughing at him.

"Ah, May!" said Dot. "Dear dear, what changes! To talk of those merry school-days makes one young again."

"Why, you an't particularly old, at any time; are you?" said Tackleton.

"Look at my sober plodding husband there," returned Dot. "He adds twenty years to my age at least. Don't you, John?"

"Forty," John replied.

"How many you'll add to May's, I am sure I don't know," said Dot, laughing. "But she can't be much less than a hundred years of age on her next birthday."

"Ha ha!" laughed Tackleton. Hollow as a drum, that laugh though. And he looked as if he could have twisted Dot's neck, comfortably.

"Dear dear!" said Dot. "Only to remember how we used to talk, at school, about the husbands we would choose. I don't know how young, and how handsome, and how gay, and how lively, mine was not to be! And as to May's!—Ah dear! I don't know whether to laugh or cry, when I think what silly girls we were."

May seemed to know which to do; for the colour flushed into her face, and tears stood in her eyes.

"Even the very persons themselves—real live young men—were fixed on sometimes," said Dot. "We little thought how things would come about. I never fixed on John I'm sure; I never so much as thought of him. And if I had told you, you were ever to be married to Mr. Tackleton, why you'd have slapped me. Wouldn't you, May?"

Though May didn't say yes, she certainly didn't say no, or express no, by any means.

Tackleton laughed—quite shouted, he laughed so loud. John Peerybingle laughed too, in his ordinary good-natured and contented manner; but his was a mere whisper of a laugh, to Tackleton's.

"You couldn't help yourselves, for all that. You couldn't resist us, you see," said Tackleton. "Here we are! Here we are!"

"Where are your gay young bridegrooms now!"

"Some of them are dead," said Dot; "and some of them forgotten. Some of them, if they could stand among us at this moment, would not believe we were the same creatures; would not believe that what they saw and heard was real, and we could forget them so. No! they would not believe one word of it!"

"Why, Dot!" exclaimed the Carrier. "Little woman!"

She had spoken with such earnestness and fire, that she stood in need of some recalling to herself, without doubt. Her husband's check was very gentle, for he merely interfered, as he supposed, to shield old Tackleton; but it proved effectual, for she stopped, and said no more. There was an uncommon agitation, even in her silence, which the wary Tackleton, who had brought his half-shut eye to bear upon her, noted closely, and remembered to some purpose too.

May uttered no word, good or bad, but sat quite still, with her eyes cast down, and made no sign of interest in what had passed. The good lady her mother now interposed, observing, in the first instance, that girls were girls, and byegones byegones, and that so long as young people were young and thoughtless, they would probably conduct themselves like young and thoughtless persons: with two or three other positions of a no less sound and incontrovertible character. She then remarked, in a devout spirit, that she thanked Heaven she had always found in her daughter May, a dutiful and obedient child; for which she took no credit to herself, though she had every reason to believe it was entirely owing to herself. With regard to Mr. Tackleton she said, That he was in a moral point of view an undeniable individual, and That he was in an eligible point of view a son-in-law to be desired, no one in their senses could doubt. (She was very emphatic here.) With regard to the family into which he was so soon about, after some solicitation, to be admitted, she believed Mr. Tackleton knew that, although reduced in purse, it had some pretensions to gentility; and if certain circumstances, not wholly unconnected, she would go so far as to say, with the Indigo Trade, but to which she would not more particularly refer, had happened differently, it might perhaps have been in possession of wealth. She then remarked that she would not allude to the past, and would not mention that her daughter had for some time rejected the suit of Mr. Tackleton; and that she would not say a great many other things which she did say, at great length. Finally, she delivered it as the general result of her observation and experience, that those marriages in which there was least of what was romantically and sillily called love, were always the happiest; and that she anticipated the greatest possible amount of bliss—not rapturous bliss; but the solid, steady-going article—from the approaching nuptials. She concluded by informing the company that to-morrow was the day she had lived for, expressly; and that when it was over, she would desire nothing better than to be packed up and disposed of, in any genteel place of burial.

As these remarks were quite unanswerable—which is the happy property of all remarks that are sufficiently wide of the purpose—they changed the current of the conversation, and diverted the general attention to the Veal and Ham-Pie, the cold mutton, the potatoes, and the tart. In order that the bottled beer might not be slighted, John Peerybingle proposed To-morrow: the Wedding-Day; and called upon them to drink a bumper to it, before he proceeded on his journey.

For you ought to know that he only rested there, and gave the old horse a bait. He had to go some four or five miles farther on; and when he returned in the evening, he called for Dot, and took another rest on his way home. This was the order of the day on all the Pic-Nic occasions, had been, ever since their institution.

There were two persons present, besides the bride and bridegroom elect, who did but indifferent honour to the toast. One of these was Dot, too flushed and discomposed to adapt herself to any small occurrence of the moment; the other, Bertha, who rose up hurriedly, before the rest, and left the table.

"Good bye!" said stout John Peerybingle, pulling on his dreadnought coat. "I shall be back at the old time. Good bye all!"

"Good bye, John," returned Caleb.

He seemed to say it by rote, and to wave his hand in the same unconscious manner; for he stood observing Bertha with an anxious wondering face, that never altered its expression.

"Good bye, young shaver!" said the jolly Carrier, bending down to kiss the child; which Tilly Slowboy, now intent upon her knife and fork, had deposited asleep (and strange to say, without damage) in a little cot of Bertha's furnishing; "good bye! Time will come, I suppose, when you'll turn out into the cold, my little friend, and leave your old father to enjoy his pipe and his rheumatics in the chimney-corner; eh? Where's Dot?"

"I'm here, John!" she said, starting.

"Come, come!" returned the Carrier, clapping his sounding hands. "Where's the pipe?"

"I quite forgot the pipe, John."

Forgot the pipe! Was such a wonder ever heard of! She! Forgot the pipe!

"I'll—I'll fill it directly. It's soon done."

But it was not so soon done, either. It lay in the usual place—the Carrier's dreadnought pocket—with the little pouch, her own work, from which she was used to fill it, but her hand shook so, that she entangled it (and yet her hand was small enough to have come out easily, I am sure), and bungled terribly. The filling of the pipe and lighting it, those little offices in which I have commended her discretion, were vilely done, from first to last. During the whole process, Tackleton stood looking on maliciously with the half-closed eye; which, whenever it met hers—or caught it, for it can hardly be said to have ever met another eye: rather being a kind of trap to snatch it up—augmented her confusion in a most remarkable degree.

"Why, what a clumsy Dot you are, this afternoon!" said John. "I could have done it better myself, I verily believe!"

With these good-natured words, he strode away, and presently was heard, in company with Boxer, and the old horse, and the cart, making lively music down the road. What time the dreamy Caleb still stood, watching his blind daughter, with the same expression on his face.

"Bertha!" said Caleb, softly. "What has happened? How changed you are, my darling, in a few hours—since this morning. You silent and dull all day! What is it? Tell me!"

"Oh father, father!" cried the Blind Girl, bursting into tears. "Oh my hard, hard fate!"

Caleb drew his hand across his eyes before he answered her.

"But think how cheerful and how happy you have been, Bertha! How good, and how much loved, by many people."

"That strikes me to the heart, dear father! Always so mindful of me! Always so kind to me!"

Caleb was very much perplexed to understand her.

"To be—to be blind, Bertha, my poor dear," he faltered, "is a great affliction; but—"

"I have never felt it!" cried the Blind Girl. "I have never felt it, in its fulness. Never! I have sometimes wished that I could see you, or could see him—only once, dear father, only for one little minute—that I might know what it is I treasure up," she laid her hands upon her breast, "and hold here! That I might be sure and have it right! And sometimes (but then I was a child) I have wept in my prayers at night, to think that when your images ascended from my heart to Heaven, they might not be the true resemblance of yourselves. But I have never had these feelings long. They have passed away and left me tranquil and contented."

"And they will again," said Caleb.

"But, father! Oh my good, gentle father, bear with me, if I am wicked!" said the Blind Girl. "This is not the sorrow that so weighs me down!"

Her father could not choose but let his moist eyes overflow; she was so earnest and pathetic, but he did not understand her, yet.

"Bring her to me," said Bertha. "I cannot hold it closed and shut within myself. Bring her to me, father!"

She knew he hesitated, and said, "May. Bring May!"

May heard the mention of her name, and coming quietly towards her, touched her on the arm. The Blind Girl turned immediately, and held her by both hands.

"Look into my face, Dear heart, Sweet heart!" said Bertha. "Read it with your beautiful eyes, and tell me if the truth is written on it."

"Dear Bertha, Yes!"

The Blind Girl still, upturning the blank sightless face, down which the tears were coursing fast, addressed her in these words:

"There is not, in my soul, a wish or thought that is not for your good, bright May! There is not, in my soul, a grateful recollection stronger than the deep remembrance which is stored there, of the many many times when, in the full pride of sight and beauty, you have had consideration for Blind Bertha, even when we two were children, or when Bertha was as much a child as ever blindness can be! Every blessing on your head! Light upon your happy course! Not the less, my dear May"; and she drew towards her, in a closer grasp; "not the less, my bird, because, to-day, the knowledge that you are to be His wife has wrung my heart almost to breaking! Father, May, Mary! oh forgive me that it is so, for the sake of all he has done to relieve the weariness of my dark life: and for the sake of the belief you have in me, when I call Heaven to witness that I could not wish him married to a wife more worthy of his goodness!"

While speaking, she had released May Fielding's hands, and clasped her garments in an attitude of mingled supplication and love. Sinking lower and lower down, as she proceeded in her strange confession, she dropped at last at the feet of her friend, and hid her blind face in the folds of her dress.

"Great Power!" exclaimed her father, smitten at one blow with the truth, "have I deceived her from the cradle, but to break her heart at last!"

It was well for all of them that Dot, that beaming, useful, busy little Dot—for such she was, whatever faults she had, and however you may learn to hate her, in good time—it was well for all of them, I say, that she was there: or where this would have ended, it were hard to tell. But Dot, recovering her self-possession, interposed, before May could reply, or Caleb say another word.

"Come, come, dear Bertha! come away with me! Give her your arm, May. So! How composed she is, you see, already; and how good it is of her to mind us," said the cheery little woman, kissing her upon the forehead. "Come away, dear Bertha. Come! and here's her good father will come with her; won't you, Caleb? To—be—sure!"

Well, well! she was a noble little Dot in such things, and it must have been an obdurate nature that could have withstood her influence. When she had got poor Caleb and his Bertha away, that they might comfort and console each other, as she knew they only could, she presently came bouncing back,—the saying is, as fresh as any daisy; I say fresher—to mount guard over that bridling little piece of consequence in the cap and gloves, and prevent the dear old creature from making discoveries.

"So bring me the precious Baby, Tilly," said she, drawing a chair to the fire; "and while I have it in my lap, here's Mrs. Fielding, Tilly, will tell me all about the management of Babies, and put me right in twenty points where I'm as wrong as can be. Won't you, Mrs. Fielding?"

Not even the Welsh Giant, who, according to the popular expression, was so "slow" as to perform a fatal surgical operation upon himself, in emulation of a juggling-trick achieved by his arch-enemy at breakfast-time; not even he fell half so readily into the snare prepared for him, as the old lady did into this artful pitfall. The fact of Tackleton having walked out; and furthermore, of two or three people having been talking together at a distance, for two minutes, leaving her to her own resources; was quite enough to have put her on her dignity, and the bewailment of that mysterious convulsion in the Indigo trade, for four-and-twenty hours. But this becoming deference to her experience, on the part of the young mother, was so irresistible, that after a short affectation of humility, she began to enlighten her with the best grace in the world; and sitting bolt upright before the wicked Dot, she did, in half an hour, deliver more infallible domestic recipes and precepts, than would (if acted on) have utterly destroyed and done up that Young Peerybingle, though he had been an Infant Samson.

To change the theme, Dot did a little needlework—she carried the contents of a whole workbox in her pocket; however she contrived it, I don't know—then did a little nursing; then a little more needlework; then had a little whispering chat with May, while the old lady dozed; and so in little bits of bustle, which was quite her manner always, found it a very short afternoon. Then, as it grew dark, and as it was a solemn part of this Institution of the Pic-Nic that she should perform all Bertha's household tasks, she trimmed the fire, and swept the hearth, and set the tea-board out, and drew the curtain, and lighted a candle. Then she played an air or two on a rude kind of harp, which Caleb had contrived for Bertha, and played them very well; for Nature had made her delicate little ear as choice a one for music as it would have been for jewels, if she had had any to wear. By this time it was the established hour for having tea; and Tackleton came back again, to share the meal, and spend the evening.

Caleb and Bertha had returned some time before, and Caleb had sat down to his afternoon's work. But he couldn't settle to it, poor fellow, being anxious and remorseful for his daughter. It was touching to see him sitting idle on his working-stool, regarding her so wistfully, and always saying in his face, "Have I deceived her from her cradle, but to break her heart!"

When it was night, and tea was done, and Dot had nothing more to do in washing up the cups and saucers; in a word—for I must come to it, and there is no use in putting it off—when the time drew nigh for expecting the Carrier's return in every sound of distant wheels, her manner changed again, her colour came and went, and she was very restless. Not as good wives are, when listening for their husbands. No, no, no. It was another sort of restlessness from that.

Wheels heard. A horse's feet. The barking of a dog. The gradual approach of all the sounds. The scratching paw of Boxer at the door!

"Whose step is that!" cried Bertha, starting up.

"Whose step?" returned the Carrier, standing in the portal, with his brown face ruddy as a winter berry from the keen night air. "Why, mine."

"The other step," said Bertha. "The man's tread behind you!"

"She is not to be deceived," observed the Carrier, laughing. "Come along, sir. You'll be welcome, never fear!"

He spoke in a loud tone; and as he spoke, the deaf old gentleman entered.

"He's not so much a stranger, that you haven't seen him once, Caleb," said the Carrier. "You'll give him house-room till we go?"

"Oh surely, John, and take it as an honour."

"He's the best company on earth, to talk secrets in," said John. "I have reasonable good lungs, but he tries 'em, I can tell you. Sit down, sir. All friends here, and glad to see you!"

When he had imparted this assurance, in a voice that amply corroborated what he had said about his lungs, he added in his natural tone, "A chair in the chimney-corner, and leave to sit quite silent and look pleasantly about him, is all he cares for. He's easily pleased."

Bertha had been listening intently. She called Caleb to her side, when he had set the chair, and asked him, in a low voice, to describe their visitor. When he had done so (truly now; with scrupulous fidelity), she moved, for the first time since he had come in, and sighed, and seemed to have no further interest concerning him.

The Carrier was in high spirits, good fellow that he was, and fonder of his little wife than ever.

"A clumsy Dot she was, this afternoon!" he said, encircling her with his rough arm, as she stood, removed from the rest; "and yet I like her somehow. See yonder, Dot!"

He pointed to the old man. She looked down. I think she trembled.

"He's—ha ha ha!—he's full of admiration for you!" said the Carrier. "Talked of nothing else, the whole way here. Why, he's a brave old boy. I like him for it!"

"I wish he had had a better subject, John," she said, with an uneasy glance about the room. At Tackleton especially.

"A better subject!" cried the jovial John. "There's no such thing. Come, off with the great-coat, off with the thick shawl, off with the heavy wrappers! and a cosy half-hour by the fire! My humble service, Mistress. A game at cribbage, you and I? That's hearty. The cards and board, Dot. And a glass of beer here, if there's any left, small wife!"

His challenge was addressed to the old lady, who accepting it with gracious readiness, they were soon engaged upon the game. At first, the Carrier looked about him sometimes, with a smile, or now and then called Dot to peep over his shoulder at his hand, and advise him on some knotty point. But his adversary being a rigid disciplinarian, and subject to an occasional weakness in respect of pegging more than she was entitled to, required such vigilance on his part, as left him neither eyes nor ears to spare. Thus, his whole attention gradually became absorbed upon the cards; and he thought of nothing else, until a hand upon his shoulder restored him to a consciousness of Tackleton.

"I am sorry to disturb you—but a word, directly."

"I'm going to deal," returned the Carrier. "It's a crisis."

"It is," said Tackleton. "Come here, man!"

There was that in his pale face which made the other rise immediately, and ask him, in a hurry, what the matter was.

"Hush! John Peerybingle," said Tackleton. "I am sorry for this. I am indeed. I have been afraid of it. I have suspected it from the first."

"What is it?" asked the Carrier, with a frightened aspect.

"Hush! I'll show you, if you'll come with me."

The Carrier accompanied him, without another word. They went across a yard, where the stars were shining, and by a little side-door, into Tackleton's own counting-house, where there was a glass window, commanding the ware-room, which was closed for the night. There was no light in the counting-house itself, but there were lamps in the long narrow ware-room; and consequently the window was bright.

"A moment!" said Tackleton. "Can you bear to look through that window, do you think?"

"Why not?" returned the Carrier.

"A moment more," said Tackleton. "Don't commit any violence. It's of no use. It's dangerous too. You're a strong-made man; and you might do murder before you know it."

The Carrier looked him in the face, and recoiled a step as if he had been struck. In one stride he was at the window, and he saw—

Oh Shadow on the Hearth! Oh truthful Cricket! Oh perfidious Wife!

He saw her, with the old man—old no longer, but erect and gallant—bearing in his hand the false white hair that had won his way into their desolate and miserable home. He saw her listening to him, as he bent his head to whisper in her ear; and suffering him to clasp her round the waist, as they moved slowly down the dim wooden gallery towards the door by which they had entered it. He saw them stop, and saw her turn—to have the face, the face he loved so, so presented to his view!—and saw her, with her own hands, adjust the lie upon his head, laughing, as she did it, at his unsuspicious nature!

He clenched his strong right hand at first, as if it would have beaten down a lion. But opening it immediately again, he spread it out before the eyes of Tackleton (for he was tender of her, even then), and so, as they passed out, fell down upon a desk, and was as weak as any infant.

He was wrapped up to the chin, and busy with his horse and parcels, when she came into the room, prepared for going home.

"Now, John, dear! Good night, May! Good night, Bertha!"

Could she kiss them? Could she be blithe and cheerful in her parting? Could she venture to reveal her face to them without a blush? Yes. Tackleton observed her closely, and she did all this.

Tilly was hushing the Baby, and she crossed and re-crossed Tackleton, a dozen times, repeating drowsily:

"Did the knowledge that it was to be its wifes, then, wring its hearts almost to breaking; and did its fathers deceive it from its cradles but to break its hearts at last!"

"Now, Tilly, give me the Baby! Good night, Mr. Tackleton. Where's John, for goodness' sake?"

"He's going to walk beside the horse's head," said Tackleton; who helped her to her seat.

"My dear John. Walk? To-night?"

The muffled figure of her husband made a hasty sign in the affirmative; and the false stranger and the little nurse being in their places, the old horse moved off. Boxer, the unconscious Boxer, running on before, running back, running round and round the cart, and barking as triumphantly and merrily as ever.

When Tackleton had gone off likewise, escorting May and her mother home, poor Caleb sat down by the fire beside his daughter; anxious and remorseful at the core; and still saying in his wistful contemplation of her, "Have I deceived her from her cradle, but to break her heart at last!"

The toys that had been set in motion for the Baby, had all stopped, and run down, long ago. In the faint light and silence, the imperturbably calm dolls, the agitated rocking-horses with distended eyes and nostrils, the old gentlemen at the street-doors, standing half doubled up upon their failing knees and ankles, the wry-faced nut-crackers, the very Beasts upon their way into the Ark, in twos, like a Boarding School out walking, might have been imagined to be stricken motionless with fantastic wonder, at Dot being false, or Tackleton beloved, under any combination of circumstances.

CHAPTER III. CHIRP THE THIRD

The Dutch clock in the corner struck Ten, when the Carrier sat down by his fireside. So troubled and grief-worn, that he seemed to scare the Cuckoo, who, having cut his ten melodious announcements as short as possible, plunged back into the Moorish Palace again, and clapped his little door behind him, as if the unwonted spectacle were too much for his feelings.

If the little Haymaker had been armed with the sharpest of scythes, and had cut at every stroke into the Carrier's heart, he never could have gashed and wounded it, as Dot had done.

It was a heart so full of love for her; so bound up and held together by innumerable threads of winning remembrance, spun from the daily working of her many qualities of endearment; it was a heart in which she had enshrined herself so gently and so closely; a heart so single and so earnest in its Truth, so strong in right, so weak in wrong; that it could cherish neither passion nor revenge at first, and had only room to hold the broken image of its Idol.

But, slowly, slowly, as the Carrier sat brooding on his hearth, now cold and dark, other and fiercer thoughts began to rise within him, as an angry wind comes rising in the night. The Stranger was beneath his outraged roof. Three steps would take him to his chamber-door. One blow would beat it in. "You might do murder before you know it," Tackleton had said. How could it be murder, if he gave the villain time to grapple with him hand to hand! He was the younger man.

It was an ill-timed thought, bad for the dark mood of his mind. It was an angry thought, goading him to some avenging act, that should change the cheerful house into a haunted place which lonely travellers would dread to pass by night; and where the timid would see shadows struggling in the ruined windows when the moon was dim, and hear wild noises in the stormy weather.

He was the younger man! Yes, yes; some lover who had won the heart that he had never touched. Some lover of her early choice, of whom she had thought and dreamed, for whom she had pined and pined, when he had fancied her so happy by his side. O agony to think of it!

She had been above-stairs with the Baby, getting it to bed. As he sat brooding on the hearth, she came close beside him, without his knowledge—in the turning of the rack of his great misery, he lost all other sounds—and put her little stool at his feet. He only knew it, when he felt her hand upon his own, and saw her looking up into his face.

With wonder? No. It was his first impression, and he was fain to look at her again, to set it right. No, not with wonder. With an eager and inquiring look; but not with wonder. At first it was alarmed and serious; then, it changed into a strange, wild, dreadful smile of recognition of his thoughts; then, there was nothing but her clasped hands on her brow, and her bent head, and falling hair.

Though the power of Omnipotence had been his to wield at that moment, he had too much of its diviner property of Mercy in his breast, to have turned one feather's weight of it against her. But he could not bear to see her crouching down upon the little seat where he had often looked on her, with love and pride, so innocent and gay; and, when she rose and left him, sobbing as she went, he felt it a relief to have the vacant place beside him rather than her so long-cherished presence. This in itself was anguish keener than all, reminding him how desolate he was become, and how the great bond of his life was rent asunder.

The more he felt this, and the more he knew he could have better borne to see her lying prematurely dead before him with their little child upon her breast, the higher and the stronger rose his wrath against his enemy. He looked about him for a weapon.

There was a gun, hanging on the wall. He took it down, and moved a pace or two towards the door of the perfidious Stranger's room. He knew the gun was loaded. Some shadowy idea that it was just to shoot this man like a wild beast, seized him, and dilated in his mind until it grew into a monstrous demon in complete possession of him, casting out all milder thoughts and setting up its undivided empire.

That phrase is wrong. Not casting out his milder thoughts, but artfully transforming them. Changing them into scourges to drive him on. Turning water into blood, love into hate, gentleness into blind ferocity. Her image, sorrowing, humbled, but still pleading to his tenderness and mercy with resistless power, never left his mind; but, staying there, it urged him to the door; raised the weapon to his shoulder; fitted and nerved his finger to the trigger; and cried "Kill him! In his bed!"

He reversed the gun to beat the stock up the door; he already held it lifted in the air; some indistinct design was in his thoughts of calling out to him to fly, for God's sake, by the window—

When, suddenly, the struggling fire illumined the whole chimney with a glow of light; and the Cricket on the Hearth began to Chirp!

No sound he could have heard, no human voice, not even hers, could so have moved and softened him. The artless words in which she had told him of her love for this same Cricket, were once more freshly spoken; her trembling, earnest manner at the moment, was again before him; her pleasant voice—O what a voice it was, for making household music at the fireside of an honest man!— thrilled through and through his better nature, and awoke it into life and action.

He recoiled from the door, like a man walking in his sleep, awakened from a frightful dream; and put the gun aside. Clasping his hands before his face, he then sat down again beside the fire, and found relief in tears.

The Cricket on the Hearth came out into the room, and stood in Fairy shape before him.

" 'I love it,' " said the Fairy Voice, repeating what he well remembered, "for the many times I have heard it, and the many thoughts its harmless music has given me."

"She said so!" cried the Carrier. "True!"

" 'This has been a happy home, John; and I love the Cricket for its sake!' "

"It has been, Heaven knows," returned the Carrier. "She made it happy, always,—until now."

"So gracefully sweet-tempered; so domestic, joyful, busy, and light-hearted!" said the Voice.

"Otherwise I never could have loved her as I did," returned the Carrier.

The Voice, correcting him, said "do."

The Carrier repeated "as I did." But not firmly. His faltering tongue resisted his control, and would speak in its own way, for itself and him.

The Figure, in an attitude of invocation, raised its hand and said:

"Upon your own hearth—"

"The hearth she has blighted," interposed the Carrier.

"The hearth she has—how often!—blessed and brightened," said the Cricket; "the hearth which, but for her, were only a few stones and bricks and rusty bars, but which has been, through her, the Altar of your Home; on which you have nightly sacrificed some petty passion, selfishness, or care, and offered up the homage of a tranquil mind, a trusting nature, and an overflowing heart; so that the smoke from this poor chimney has gone upward with a better fragrance than the richest incense that is burnt before the richest shrines in all the gaudy temples of this world!—Upon your own hearth; in its quiet sanctuary; surrounded by its gentle influences and associations; hear her! Hear me! Hear everything that speaks the language of your hearth and home!"

"And pleads for her?" inquired the Carrier.

"All things that speak the language of your hearth and home, must plead for her!" returned the Cricket. "For they speak the truth."

And while the Carrier, with his head upon his hands, continued to sit meditating in his chair, the Presence stood beside him, suggesting his reflections by its power, and presenting them before him, as in a glass or picture. It was not a solitary Presence. From the hearthstone, from the chimney, from the clock, the pipe, the kettle, and the cradle; from the floor, the walls, the ceiling, and the stairs; from the cart without, and the cupboard within, and the household implements; from every thing and every place with which she had ever been familiar, and with which she had ever entwined one recollection of herself in her unhappy husband's mind; Fairies came trooping forth. Not to stand beside him as the Cricket did, but to busy and bestir themselves. To do all honour to her image. To pull him by the skirts, and point to it when it appeared. To cluster round it, and embrace it, and strew flowers for it to tread on. To try to crown its fair head with their tiny hands. To show that they were fond of it and loved it; and that there was not one ugly, wicked or accusatory creature to claim knowledge of it—none but their playful and approving selves.

His thoughts were constant to her image. It was always there.

She sat plying her needle, before the fire, and singing to herself. Such a blithe, thriving, steady little Dot! The fairy figures turned upon him all at once, by one consent, with one prodigious concentrated stare, and seemed to say, "Is this the light wife you are mourning for!"

There were sounds of gaiety outside, musical instruments, and noisy tongues, and laughter. A crowd of young merry-makers came pouring in, among whom were May Fielding and a score of pretty girls. Dot was the fairest of them all; as young as any of them too. They came to summon her to join their party. It was a dance. If ever little foot were made for dancing, hers was, surely. But she laughed, and shook her head, and pointed to her cookery on the fire, and her table ready spread: with an exulting defiance that rendered her more charming than she was before. And so she merrily dismissed them, nodding to her would-be partners, one by one, as they passed, but with a comical indifference, enough to make them go and drown themselves immediately if they were her admirers—and they must have been so, more or less; they couldn't help it. And yet indifference was not her character. O no! For presently, there came a certain Carrier to the door; and bless her what a welcome she bestowed upon him!

Again the staring figures turned upon him all at once, and seemed to say, "Is this the wife who has forsaken you!"

A shadow fell upon the mirror or the picture: call it what you will. A great shadow of the Stranger, as he first stood underneath their roof; covering its surface, and blotting out all other objects. But the nimble Fairies worked like bees to clear it off again. And Dot again was there. Still bright and beautiful.

Rocking her little Baby in its cradle, singing to it softly, and resting her head upon a shoulder which had its counterpart in the musing figure by which the Fairy Cricket stood.

The night—I mean the real night: not going by Fairy clocks—was wearing now; and in this stage of the Carrier's thoughts, the moon burst out, and shone brightly in the sky. Perhaps some calm and quiet light had risen also, in his mind; and he could think more soberly of what had happened.

Although the shadow of the Stranger fell at intervals upon the glass—always distinct, and big, and thoroughly defined—it never fell so darkly as at first. Whenever it appeared, the Fairies uttered a general cry of consternation, and plied their little arms and legs, with inconceivable activity, to rub it out. And whenever they got at Dot again, and showed her to him once more, bright and beautiful, they cheered in the most inspiring manner.

They never showed her, otherwise than beautiful and bright, for they were Household Spirits to whom falsehood is annihilation; and being so, what Dot was there for them, but the one active, beaming, pleasant little creature who had been the light and sun of the Carrier's Home!

The Fairies were prodigiously excited when they showed her, with the Baby, gossiping among a knot of sage old matrons, and affecting to be wondrous old and matronly herself, and leaning in a staid, demure old way upon her husband's arm, attempting—she! such a bud of a little woman—to convey the idea of having abjured the vanities of the world in general, and of being the sort of person to whom it was no novelty at all to be a mother; yet in the same breath, they showed her, laughing at the Carrier for being awkward, and pulling up his shirt-collar to make him smart, and mincing merrily about that very room to teach him how to dance!

They turned, and stared immensely at him when they showed her with the Blind Girl; for, though she carried cheerfulness and animation with her wheresoever she went, she bore those influences into Caleb Plummer's home, heaped up and running over. The Blind Girl's love for her, and trust in her, and gratitude to her; her own good busy way of setting Bertha's thanks aside; her dexterous little arts for filling up each moment of the visit in doing something useful to the house, and really working hard while feigning to make holiday; her bountiful provision of those standing delicacies, the Veal and Ham-Pie and the bottles of Beer; her radiant little face arriving at the door, and taking leave; the wonderful expression in her whole self, from her neat foot to the crown of her head, of being a part of the establishment—a something necessary to it, which it couldn't be without; all this the Fairies revelled in, and loved her for. And once again they looked upon him all at once, appealingly, and seemed to say, while some among them nestled in her dress and fondled her, "Is this the wife who has betrayed your confidence!"

More than once, or twice, or thrice, in the long thoughtful night, they showed her to him sitting on her favourite seat, with her bent head, her hands clasped on her brow, her falling hair. As he had seen her last. And when they found her thus, they neither turned nor looked upon him, but gathered close round her, and comforted and kissed her, and pressed on one another to show sympathy and kindness to her, and forgot him altogether.

Thus the night passed. The moon went down; the stars grew pale; the cold day broke; the sun rose. The Carrier still sat, musing, in the chimney corner. He had sat there, with his head upon his hands, all night. All night the faithful Cricket had been Chirp, Chirp, Chirping on the Hearth. All night he had listened to its voice. All night the household Fairies had been busy with him. All night she had been amiable and blameless in the glass, except when that one shadow fell upon it.

He rose up when it was broad day, and washed and dressed himself. He couldn't go about his customary cheerful avocations—he wanted spirit for them—but it mattered the less, that it was Tackleton's wedding-day, and he had arranged to make his rounds by proxy. He thought to have gone merrily to church with Dot. But such plans were at an end. It was their own wedding-day too. Ah! how little he had looked for such a close to such a year!

The Carrier had expected that Tackleton would pay him an early visit; and he was right. He had not walked to and fro before his own door, many minutes, when he saw the Toy-merchant coming in his chaise along the road. As the chaise drew nearer, he perceived that Tackleton was dressed out sprucely for his marriage, and that he had decorated his horse's head with flowers and favours.

The horse looked much more like a bridegroom than Tackleton, whose half-closed eye was more disagreeably expressive than ever. But the Carrier took little heed of this. His thoughts had other occupation.

"John Peerybingle!" said Tackleton, with an air of condolence. "My good fellow, how do you find yourself this morning?"

"I have had but a poor night, Master Tackleton," returned the Carrier, shaking his head: "for I have been a good deal disturbed in my mind. But it's over now! Can you spare me half an hour or so, for some private talk?"

"I came on purpose," returned Tackleton, alighting. "Never mind the horse. He'll stand quiet enough, with the reins over this post, if you'll give him a mouthful of hay."

The Carrier having brought it from his stable, and set it before him, they turned into the house.

"You are not married before noon," he said, "I think?"

"No," answered Tackleton. "Plenty of time. Plenty of time."

When they entered the kitchen, Tilly Slowboy was rapping at the Stranger's door; which was only removed from it by a few steps. One of her very red eyes (for Tilly had been crying all night long, because her mistress cried) was at the keyhole; and she was knocking very loud; and seemed frightened.

"If you please I can't make nobody hear," said Tilly, looking round. "I hope nobody an't gone and been and died if you please!"

This philanthropic wish, Miss Slowboy emphasised with various new raps and kicks at the door; which led to no result whatever.

"Shall I go?" said Tackleton. "It's curious."

The Carrier, who had turned his face from the door, signed to him to go if he would.

So Tackleton went to Tilly Slowboy's relief; and he too kicked and knocked; and he too failed to get the least reply. But he thought of trying the handle of the door; and as it opened easily, he peeped in, looked in, went in, and soon came running out again.

"John Peerybingle," said Tackleton, in his ear. "I hope there has been nothing— nothing rash in the night?"

The Carrier turned upon him quickly.

"Because he's gone!" said Tackleton; "and the window's open. I don't see any marks—to be sure it's almost on a level with the garden: but I was afraid there might have been some—some scuffle. Eh?"

He nearly shut up the expressive eye altogether; he looked at him so hard. And he gave his eye, and his face, and his whole person, a sharp twist. As if he would have screwed the truth out of him.

"Make yourself easy," said the Carrier. "He went into that room last night, without harm in word or deed from me, and no one has entered it since. He is away of his own free will. I'd go out gladly at that door, and beg my bread from house to house, for life, if I could so change the past that he had never come. But he has come and gone. And I have done with him!"

"Oh!—Well, I think he has got off pretty easy," said Tackleton, taking a chair.

The sneer was lost upon the Carrier, who sat down too, and shaded his face with his hand, for some little time, before proceeding.

"You showed me last night," he said at length, "my wife; my wife that I love; secretly—"

"And tenderly," insinuated Tackleton.

"Conniving at that man's disguise, and giving him opportunities of meeting her alone. I think there's no sight I wouldn't have rather seen than that. I think there's no man in the world I wouldn't have rather had to show it me."

"I confess to having had my suspicions always," said Tackleton. "And that has made me objectionable here, I know."

"But as you did show it me," pursued the Carrier, not minding him; "and as you saw her, my wife, my wife that I love"—his voice, and eye, and hand, grew steadier and firmer as he repeated these words: evidently in pursuance of a steadfast purpose—"as you saw her at this disadvantage, it is right and just that you should also see with my eyes, and look into my breast, and know what my mind is, upon the subject. For it's settled," said the Carrier, regarding him attentively. "And nothing can shake it now."

Tackleton muttered a few general words of assent, about its being necessary to vindicate something or other; but he was overawed by the manner of his companion. Plain and unpolished as it was, it had a something dignified and noble in it, which nothing but the soul of generous honour dwelling in the man could have imparted.

"I am a plain, rough man," pursued the Carrier, "with very little to recommend me. I am not a clever man, as you very well know. I am not a young man. I loved my little Dot, because I had seen her grow up, from a child, in her father's house; because I knew how precious she was; because she had been my life, for years and years. There's many men I can't compare with, who never could have loved my little Dot like me, I think!"

He paused, and softly beat the ground a short time with his foot, before resuming.

"I often thought that though I wasn't good enough for her, I should make her a kind husband, and perhaps know her value better than another; and in this way I reconciled it to myself, and came to think it might be possible that we should be married. And in the end it came, and we were married."

"Hah!" said Tackleton, with a significant shake of the head.

"I had studied myself; I had had experience of myself; I knew how much I loved her, and how happy I should be," pursued the Carrier. "But I had not—I feel it now—sufficiently considered her."

"To be sure," said Tackleton. "Giddiness, frivolity, fickleness, love of admiration! Not considered! All left out of sight! Hah!"

"You had best not interrupt me," said the Carrier, with some sternness, "till you understand me; and you're wide of doing so. If, yesterday, I'd have struck that man down at a blow, who dared to breathe a word against her, to-day I'd set my foot upon his face, if he was my brother!"

The Toy-merchant gazed at him in astonishment. He went on in a softer tone:

"Did I consider," said the Carrier, "that I took her—at her age, and with her beauty—from her young companions, and the many scenes of which she was the ornament; in which she was the brightest little star that ever shone, to shut her up from day to day in my dull house, and keep my tedious company? Did I consider how little suited I was to her sprightly humour, and how wearisome a plodding man like me must be, to one of her quick spirit? Did I consider that it was no merit in me, or claim in me, that I loved her, when everybody must, who knew her? Never. I took advantage of her hopeful nature and her cheerful disposition; and I married her. I wish I never had! For her sake; not for mine!"

The Toy-merchant gazed at him, without winking. Even the half-shut eye was open now.

"Heaven bless her!" said the Carrier, "for the cheerful constancy with which she tried to keep the knowledge of this from me! And Heaven help me, that, in my slow mind, I have not found it out before! Poor child! Poor Dot! I not to find it out, who have seen her eyes fill with tears, when such a marriage as our own was spoken of! I, who have seen the secret trembling on her lips a hundred times, and never suspected it till last night! Poor girl! That I could ever hope she would be fond of me! That I could ever believe she was!"

"She made a show of it," said Tackleton. "She made such a show of it, that to tell you the truth it was the origin of my misgivings."

And here he asserted the superiority of May Fielding, who certainly made no sort of show of being fond of him.

"She has tried," said the poor Carrier, with greater emotion than he had exhibited yet; "I only now begin to know how hard she has tried, to be my dutiful and zealous wife. How good she has been; how much she has done; how brave and strong a heart she has; let the happiness I have known under this roof bear witness! It will be some help and comfort to me, when I am here alone."

"Here alone?" said Tackleton. "Oh! Then you do mean to take some notice of this?"

"I mean," returned the Carrier, "to do her the greatest kindness, and make her the best reparation, in my power. I can release her from the daily pain of an unequal marriage, and the struggle to conceal it. She shall be as free as I can render her."

"Make her reparation!" exclaimed Tackleton, twisting and turning his great ears with his hands. "There must be something wrong here. You didn't say that, of course."

The Carrier set his grip upon the collar of the Toy-merchant, and shook him like a reed.

"Listen to me!" he said. "And take care that you hear me right. Listen to me. Do I speak plainly?"

"Very plainly indeed," answered Tackleton.

"As if I meant it?"

"Very much as if you meant it."

"I sat upon that hearth, last night, all night," exclaimed the Carrier. "On the spot where she has often sat beside me, with her sweet face looking into mine. I called up her whole life, day by day. I had her dear self, in its every passage, in review before me. And upon my soul she is innocent, if there is One to judge the innocent and guilty!"

Staunch Cricket on the Hearth! Loyal household Fairies!

"Passion and distrust have left me!" said the Carrier; "and nothing but my grief remains. In an unhappy moment some old lover, better suited to her tastes and years than I; forsaken, perhaps, for me, against her will; returned. In an unhappy moment, taken by surprise, and wanting time to think of what she did, she made herself a party to his treachery, by concealing it. Last night she saw him, in the interview we witnessed. It was wrong. But otherwise than this she is innocent if there is truth on earth!"

"If that is your opinion"—Tackleton began.

"So, let her go!" pursued the Carrier. "Go, with my blessing for the many happy hours she has given me, and my forgiveness for any pang she has caused me. Let her go, and have the peace of mind I wish her! She'll never hate me. She'll learn to like me better, when I'm not a drag upon her, and she wears the chain I have riveted, more lightly. This is the day on which I took her, with so little thought for her enjoyment, from her home. To-day she shall return to it, and I will trouble her no more. Her father and mother will be here to-day—we had made a little plan for keeping it together—and they shall take her home. I can trust her, there, or anywhere. She leaves me without blame, and she will live so I am sure. If I should die—I may perhaps while she is still young; I have lost some courage in a few hours—she'll find that I remembered her, and loved her to the last! This is the end of what you showed me. Now, it's over!"

"O no, John, not over. Do not say it's over yet! Not quite yet. I have heard your noble words. I could not steal away, pretending to be ignorant of what has affected me with such deep gratitude. Do not say it's over, till the clock has struck again!"

She had entered shortly after Tackleton, and had remained there. She never looked at Tackleton, but fixed her eyes upon her husband. But she kept away from him, setting as wide a space as possible between them; and though she spoke with most impassioned earnestness, she went no nearer to him even then. How different in this from her old self!

"No hand can make the clock which will strike again for me the hours that are gone," replied the Carrier, with a faint smile. "But let it be so, if you will, my dear. It will strike soon. It's of little matter what we say. I'd try to please you in a harder case than that."

"Well!" muttered Tackleton. "I must be off, for when the clock strikes again, it'll be necessary for me to be upon my way to church. Good morning, John Peerybingle. I'm sorry to be deprived of the pleasure of your company. Sorry for the loss, and the occasion of it too!"

"I have spoken plainly?" said the Carrier, accompanying him to the door.

"Oh quite!"

"And you'll remember what I have said?"

"Why, if you compel me to make the observation," said Tackleton, previously taking the precaution of getting into his chaise; "I must say that it was so very unexpected, that I'm far from being likely to forget it."

"The better for us both," returned the Carrier. "Good bye. I give you joy!"

"I wish I could give it to you," said Tackleton. "As I can't; thank 'ee. Between ourselves, (as I told you before, eh?) I don't much think I shall have the less joy in my married life, because May hasn't been too officious about me, and too demonstrative. Good bye! Take care of yourself."

The Carrier stood looking after him until he was smaller in the distance than his horse's flowers and favours near at hand; and then, with a deep sigh, went strolling like a restless, broken man, among some neighbouring elms; unwilling to return until the clock was on the eve of striking.

His little wife, being left alone, sobbed piteously; but often dried her eyes and checked herself, to say how good he was, how excellent he was! and once or twice she laughed; so heartily, triumphantly, and incoherently (still crying all the time), that Tilly was quite horrified.

"Ow if you please don't!" said Tilly. "It's enough to dead and bury the Baby, so it is if you please."

"Will you bring him sometimes, to see his father, Tilly," inquired her mistress, drying her eyes; "when I can't live here, and have gone to my old home?"

"Ow if you please don't!" cried Tilly, throwing back her head, and bursting out into a howl—she looked at the moment uncommonly like Boxer. "Ow if you please don't! Ow, what has everybody gone and been and done with everybody, making everybody else so wretched! Ow-w-w-w!"

The soft-hearted Slowboy trailed off at this juncture, into such a deplorable howl, the more tremendous from its long suppression, that she must infallibly have awakened the Baby, and frightened him into something serious (probably convulsions), if her eyes had not encountered Caleb Plummer, leading in his daughter. This spectacle restoring her to a sense of the proprieties, she stood for some few moments silent, with her mouth wide open; and then, posting off to the bed on which the Baby lay asleep, danced in a weird, Saint Vitus manner on the floor, and at the same time rummaged with her face and head among the bedclothes, apparently deriving much relief from those extraordinary operations.

"Mary!" said Bertha. "Not at the marriage!"

"I told her you would not be there, mum," whispered Caleb. "I heard as much last night. But bless you," said the little man, taking her tenderly by both hands, "I don't care for what they say. I don't believe them. There an't much of me, but that little should be torn to pieces sooner than I'd trust a word against you!"

He put his arms about her and hugged her, as a child might have hugged one of his own dolls.

"Bertha couldn't stay at home this morning," said Caleb. "She was afraid, I know, to hear the bells ring, and couldn't trust herself to be so near them on their wedding-day. So we started in good time, and came here. I have been thinking of what I have done," said Caleb, after a moment's pause; "I have been blaming myself till I hardly knew what to do or where to turn, for the distress of mind I have caused her; and I've come to the conclusion that I'd better, if you'll stay with me, mum, the while, tell her the truth. You'll stay with me the while?" he inquired, trembling from head to foot. "I don't know what effect it may have upon her; I don't know what she'll think of me; I don't know that she'll ever care for her poor father afterwards. But it's best for her that she should be undeceived, and I must bear the consequences as I deserve!"

"Mary," said Bertha, "where is your hand! Ah! Here it is here it is!" pressing it to her lips, with a smile, and drawing it through her arm. "I heard them speaking softly among themselves, last night, of some blame against you. They were wrong."

The Carrier's Wife was silent. Caleb answered for her.

"They were wrong," he said.

"I knew it!" cried Bertha, proudly. "I told them so. I scorned to hear a word! Blame her with justice!" she pressed the hand between her own, and the soft cheek against her face. "No! I am not so blind as that."

Her father went on one side of her, while Dot remained upon the other: holding her hand.

"I know you all," said Bertha, "better than you think. But none so well as her. Not even you, father. There is nothing half so real and so true about me, as she is. If I could be restored to sight this instant, and not a word were spoken, I could choose her from a crowd! My sister!"

"Bertha, my dear!" said Caleb, "I have something on my mind I want to tell you, while we three are alone. Hear me kindly! I have a confession to make to you, my darling."

"A confession, father?"

"I have wandered from the truth and lost myself, my child," said Caleb, with a pitiable expression in his bewildered face. "I have wandered from the truth, intending to be kind to you; and have been cruel."

She turned her wonder-stricken face towards him, and repeated "Cruel!"

"He accuses himself too strongly, Bertha," said Dot. "You'll say so, presently. You'll be the first to tell him so."

"He cruel to me!" cried Bertha, with a smile of incredulity.

"Not meaning it, my child," said Caleb. "But I have been; though I never suspected it, till yesterday. My dear blind daughter, hear me and forgive me! The world you live in, heart of mine, doesn't exist as I have represented it. The eyes you have trusted in, have been false to you."

She turned her wonder-stricken face towards him still; but drew back, and clung closer to her friend.

"Your road in life was rough, my poor one," said Caleb, "and I meant to smooth it for you. I have altered objects, changed the characters of people, invented many things that never have been, to make you happier. I have had concealments from you, put deceptions on you, God forgive me! and surrounded you with fancies."

"But living people are not fancies!" she said hurriedly, and turning very pale, and still retiring from him. "You can't change them."

"I have done so, Bertha," pleaded Caleb. "There is one person that you know, my dove—"

"Oh father! why do you say, I know?" she answered, in a term of keen reproach. "What and whom do I know! I who have no leader! I so miserably blind."

In the anguish of her heart, she stretched out her hands, as if she were groping her way; then spread them, in a manner most forlorn and sad, upon her face.

"The marriage that takes place to-day," said Caleb, "is with a stern, sordid, grinding man. A hard master to you and me, my dear, for many years. Ugly in his looks, and in his nature. Cold and callous always. Unlike what I have painted him to you in everything, my child. In everything."

"Oh why," cried the Blind Girl, tortured, as it seemed, almost beyond endurance, "why did you ever do this! Why did you ever fill my heart so full, and then come in like Death, and tear away the objects of my love! O Heaven, how blind I am! How helpless and alone!"

Her afflicted father hung his head, and offered no reply but in his penitence and sorrow.

She had been but a short time in this passion of regret, when the Cricket on the Hearth, unheard by all but her, began to chirp. Not merrily, but in a low, faint, sorrowing way. It was so mournful that her tears began to flow; and when the Presence which had been beside the Carrier all night, appeared behind her, pointing to her father, they fell down like rain.

She heard the Cricket-voice more plainly soon, and was conscious, through her blindness, of the Presence hovering about her father.

"Mary," said the Blind Girl, "tell me what my home is. What it truly is."

"It is a poor place, Bertha; very poor and bare indeed. The house will scarcely keep out wind and rain another winter. It is as roughly shielded from the weather, Bertha," Dot continued in a low, clear voice, "as your poor father in his sack-cloth coat."

The Blind Girl, greatly agitated, rose, and led the Carrier's little wife aside.

"Those presents that I took such care of; that came almost at my wish, and were so dearly welcome to me," she said, trembling; "where did they come from? Did you send them?"

"No."

"Who then?"

Dot saw she knew, already, and was silent. The Blind Girl spread her hands before her face again. But in quite another manner now.

"Dear Mary, a moment. One moment? More this way. Speak softly to me. You are true, I know. You'd not deceive me now; would you?"

"No, Bertha, indeed!"

"No, I am sure you would not. You have too much pity for me. Mary, look across the room to where we were just now—to where my father is—my father, so compassionate and loving to me—and tell me what you see."

"I see," said Dot, who understood her well, "an old man sitting in a chair, and leaning sorrowfully on the back, with his face resting on his hand. As if his child should comfort him, Bertha."

THE CRICKET ON THE HEARTH

"Yes, yes. She will. Go on."

"He is an old man, worn with care and work. He is a spare, dejected, thoughtful, grey-haired man. I see him now, despondent and bowed down, and striving against nothing. But, Bertha, I have seen him many times before, and striving hard in many ways for one great sacred object. And I honour his grey head, and bless him!"

The Blind Girl broke away from her; and throwing herself upon her knees before him, took the grey head to her breast.

"It is my sight restored. It is my sight!" she cried. "I have been blind, and now my eyes are open. I never knew him! To think I might have died, and never truly seen the father who has been so loving to me!"

There were no words for Caleb's emotion.

"There is not a gallant figure on this earth," exclaimed the Blind Girl, holding him in her embrace, "that I would love so dearly, and would cherish so devotedly, as this! The greyer, and more worn, the dearer, father! Never let them say I am blind again. There's not a furrow in his face, there's not a hair upon his head, that shall be forgotten in my prayers and thanks to Heaven!"

Caleb managed to articulate "My Bertha!"

"And in my blindness, I believed him," said the girl, caressing him with tears of exquisite affection, "to be so different! And having him beside me, day by day, so mindful of me—always, never dreamed of this!"

"The fresh smart father in the blue coat, Bertha," said poor Caleb. "He's gone!"

"Nothing is gone," she answered. "Dearest father, no! Everything is here—in you. The father that I loved so well; the father that I never loved enough, and never knew; the benefactor whom I first began to reverence and love, because he had such sympathy for me; All are here in you. Nothing is dead to me. The soul of all that was most dear to me is here—here, with the worn face, and the grey head. And I am *not* blind, father, any longer!"

Dot's whole attention had been concentrated, during this discourse, upon the father and daughter; but looking, now, towards the little Haymaker in the Moorish meadow, she saw that the clock was within a few minutes of striking, and fell, immediately, into a nervous and excited state.

"Father," said Bertha, hesitating. "Mary."

"Yes, my dear," returned Caleb. "Here she is."

"There is no change in her. You never told me anything of her that was not true?"

"I should have done it, my dear, I am afraid," returned Caleb, "if I could have made her better than she was. But I must have changed her for the worse, if I had changed her at all. Nothing could improve her, Bertha."

Confident as the Blind Girl had been when she asked the question, her delight and pride in the reply and her renewed embrace of Dot, were charming to behold.

"More changes than you think for, may happen though, my dear," said Dot. "Changes for the better, I mean; changes for great joy to some of us. You mustn't let them startle you too much, if any such should ever happen, and affect you? Are those wheels upon the road? You've a quick ear, Bertha. Are they wheels?"

"Yes. Coming very fast."

"I—I—I know you have a quick ear," said Dot, placing her hand upon her heart, and evidently talking on, as fast as she could to hide its palpitating state, "because I have noticed it often, and because you were so quick to find out that strange step last night. Though why you should have said, as I very well recollect you did say, Bertha, "Whose step is that!" and why you should have taken any greater observation of it than of any other step, I don't know. Though as I said just now, there are great changes in the world: great changes: and we can't do better than prepare ourselves to be surprised at hardly anything."

Caleb wondered what this meant; perceiving that she spoke to him, no less than to his daughter. He saw her, with astonishment, so fluttered and distressed that she could scarcely breathe; and holding to a chair, to save herself from falling.

"They are wheels indeed!" she panted. "Coming nearer! Nearer! Very close! And now you hear them stopping at the garden-gate! And now you hear a step outside the door—the same step, Bertha, is it not!—and now!"—

She uttered a wild cry of uncontrollable delight; and running up to Caleb put her hands upon his eyes, as a young man rushed into the room, and flinging away his hat into the air, came sweeping down upon them.

"Is it over?" cried Dot.

"Yes!"

"Happily over?"

"Yes!"

"Do you recollect the voice, dear Caleb? Did you ever hear the like of it before?" cried Dot.

"If my boy in the Golden South Americas was alive"—said Caleb, trembling.

"He is alive!" shrieked Dot, removing her hands from his eyes, and clapping them in ecstasy; "look at him! See where he stands before you, healthy and strong! Your own dear son! Your own dear living, loving brother, Bertha!"

All honour to the little creature for her transports! All honour to her tears and laughter, when the three were locked in one another's arms! All honour to the heartiness with which she met the sunburnt sailor-fellow, with his dark streaming hair, half-way, and never turned her rosy little mouth aside, but suffered him to kiss it, freely, and to press her to his bounding heart!

And honour to the Cuckoo too—why not!—for bursting out of the trap-door in the Moorish Palace like a house-breaker, and hiccoughing twelve times on the assembled company, as if he had got drunk for joy!

The Carrier, entering, started back. And well he might, to find himself in such good company.

"Look, John!" said Caleb, exultingly, "look here! My own boy from the Golden South Americas! My own son! Him that you fitted out, and sent away yourself! Him that you were always such a friend to!"

The Carrier advanced to seize him by the hand; but, recoiling, as some feature in his face awakened a remembrance of the Deaf Man in the Cart, said:

"Edward! Was it you?"

"Now tell him all!" cried Dot. "Tell him all, Edward; and don't spare me, for nothing shall make me spare myself in his eyes, ever again."

"I was the man," said Edward.

"And could you steal, disguised, into the house of your old friend?" rejoined the Carrier. "There was a frank boy once—how many years is it, Caleb, since we heard that he was dead, and had it proved, we thought?—who never would have done that."

"There was a generous friend of mine, once; more a father to me than a friend"; said Edward, "who never would have judged me, or any other man, unheard. You were he. So I am certain you will hear me now."

The Carrier, with a troubled glance at Dot, who still kept far away from him, replied, "Well! that's but fair. I will."

"You must know that when I left here, a boy," said Edward, "I was in love, and my love was returned. She was a very young girl, who perhaps (you may tell me) didn't know her own mind. But I knew mine, and I had a passion for her."

"You had!" exclaimed the Carrier. "You!"

"Indeed I had," returned the other. "And she returned it. I have ever since believed she did, and now I am sure she did."

"Heaven help me!" said the Carrier. "This is worse than all."

"Constant to her," said Edward, "and returning, full of hope, after many hardships and perils, to redeem my part of our old contract, I heard, twenty miles away, that she was false to me; that she had forgotten me; and had bestowed herself upon another and a richer man. I had no mind to reproach her; but I wished to see her, and to prove beyond dispute that this was true. I hoped she might have been forced into it, against her own desire and recollection. It would be small comfort, but it would be some, I thought, and on I came. That I might have the truth, the real truth; observing freely for myself, and judging for myself, without obstruction on the one hand, or presenting my own influence (if I had any) before her, on the other; I dressed myself unlike myself—you know how; and waited on the road—you know where. You had no suspicion of me; neither had—had she," pointing to Dot, "until I whispered in her ear at that fireside, and she so nearly betrayed me."

"But when she knew that Edward was alive, and had come back," sobbed Dot, now speaking for herself, as she had burned to do, all through this narrative; "and when she knew his purpose, she advised him by all means to keep his secret close; for his old friend John Peerybingle was much too open in his nature, and too clumsy in all artifice—being a clumsy man in general," said Dot, half laughing and half crying—"to keep it for him. And when she—that's me, John," sobbed the little woman—"told him all, and how his sweetheart had believed him to be dead; and how she had at last been over-persuaded by her mother into a marriage which the silly, dear old thing called advantageous; and when she—that's me again, John—told him they were not yet married (though close upon it), and that it would be nothing but a sacrifice if it went on, for there was no love on her side; and when he went nearly mad with joy to hear it; then she—that's me again—said she would go between them, as she had often done before in old times, John, and would sound his sweetheart and be sure that what she—me again, John—said and thought was right. And it was right, John! And they were brought together, John! And they were married, John, an hour ago! And here's the Bride! And Gruff and Tackleton may die a bachelor! And I'm a happy little woman, May, God bless you!"

She was an irresistible little woman, if that be anything to the purpose; and never so completely irresistible as in her present transports. There never were congratulations so endearing and delicious, as those she lavished on herself and on the Bride.

Amid the tumult of emotions in his breast, the honest Carrier had stood, confounded. Flying, now, towards her, Dot stretched out her hand to stop him, and retreated as before.

"No, John, no! Hear all! Don't love me any more, John, till you've heard every word I have to say. It was wrong to have a secret from you, John. I'm very sorry. I didn't think it any harm, till I came and sat down by you on the little stool last night. But when I knew by what was written in your face, that you had seen me walking in the gallery with Edward, and when I knew what you thought, I felt how giddy and how wrong it was. But oh, dear John, how could you, could you, think so!"

Little woman, how she sobbed again! John Peerybingle would have caught her in his arms. But no; she wouldn't let him.

"Don't love me yet, please, John! Not for a long time yet! When I was sad about this intended marriage, dear, it was because I remembered May and Edward such young lovers; and knew that her heart was far away from Tackleton. You believe that, now. Don't you, John?"

John was going to make another rush at this appeal; but she stopped him again.

"No; keep there, please, John! When I laugh at you, as I sometimes do, John, and call you clumsy and a dear old goose, and names of that sort, it's because I love you, John, so well, and take such pleasure in your ways, and wouldn't see you altered in the least respect to have you made a King to-morrow."

"Hooroar!" said Caleb with unusual vigour. "My opinion!"

"And when I speak of people being middle-aged, and steady, John, and pretend that we are a humdrum couple, going on in a jog-trot sort of way, it's only because I'm such a silly little thing, John, that I like, sometimes, to act a kind of Play with Baby, and all that: and make believe."

She saw that he was coming; and stopped him again. But she was very nearly too late.

"No, don't love me for another minute or two, if you please, John! What I want most to tell you, I have kept to the last. My dear, good, generous John, when we were talking the other night about the Cricket, I had it on my lips to say, that at first I did not love you quite so dearly as I do now; that when I first came home here, I was half afraid I mightn't learn to love you every bit as well as I hoped and prayed I might—being so very young, John! But, dear John, every day and hour I loved you more and more. And if I could have loved you better than I do, the noble words I heard you say this morning, would have made me. But I can't. All the affection that I had (it was a great deal, John) I gave you, as you well deserve, long, long ago, and I have no more left to give. Now, my dear husband, take me to your heart again! That's my home, John; and never, never think of sending me to any other!"

You never will derive so much delight from seeing a glorious little woman in the arms of a third party, as you would have felt if you had seen Dot run into the Carrier's embrace. It was the most complete, unmitigated, soul-fraught little piece of earnestness that ever you beheld in all your days.

You may be sure the Carrier was in a state of perfect rapture; and you may be sure Dot was likewise; and you may be sure they all were, inclusive of Miss Slowboy, who wept copiously for joy, and wishing to include her young charge in the general interchange of congratulations, handed round the Baby to everybody in succession, as if it were something to drink.

But, now, the sound of wheels was heard again outside the door; and somebody exclaimed that Gruff and Tackleton was coming back. Speedily that worthy gentleman appeared, looking warm and flustered.

"Why, what the Devil's this, John Peerybingle!" said Tackleton. "There's some mistake. I appointed Mrs. Tackleton to meet me at the church, and I'll swear I passed her on the road, on her way here. Oh! here she is! I beg your pardon, sir; I haven't the pleasure of knowing you; but if you can do me the favour to spare this young lady, she has rather a particular engagement this morning."

"But I can't spare her," returned Edward. "I couldn't think of it."

"What do you mean, you vagabond?" said Tackleton.

"I mean, that as I can make allowance for your being vexed," returned the other, with a smile, "I am as deaf to harsh discourse this morning, as I was to all discourse last night."

The look that Tackleton bestowed upon him, and the start he gave!

"I am sorry, sir," said Edward, holding out May's left hand, and especially the third finger; "that the young lady can't accompany you to church; but as she has been there once, this morning, perhaps you'll excuse her."

Tackleton looked hard at the third finger, and took a little piece of silver-paper, apparently containing a ring, from his waistcoat-pocket.

"Miss Slowboy," said Tackleton. "Will you have the kindness to throw that in the fire? Thank 'ee."

"It was a previous engagement, quite an old engagement, that prevented my wife from keeping her appointment with you, I assure you," said Edward.

"Mr. Tackleton will do me the justice to acknowledge that I revealed it to him faithfully; and that I told him, many times, I never could forget it," said May, blushing.

"Oh certainly!" said Tackleton. "Oh to be sure. Oh it's all right. It's quite correct. Mrs. Edward Plummer, I infer?"

"That's the name," returned the bridegroom.

"Ah, I shouldn't have known you, sir," said Tackleton, scrutinising his face narrowly, and making a low bow. "I give you joy, sir!"

"Thank 'ee."

"Mrs. Peerybingle," said Tackleton, turning suddenly to where she stood with her husband; "I am sorry. You haven't done me a very great kindness, but, upon my life I am sorry. You are better than I thought you. John Peerybingle, I am sorry. You understand me; that's enough. It's quite correct, ladies and gentlemen all, and perfectly satisfactory. Good morning!"

With these words he carried it off, and carried himself off too: merely stopping at the door, to take the flowers and favours from his horse's head, and to kick that animal once, in the ribs, as a means of informing him that there was a screw loose in his arrangements.

Of course it became a serious duty now, to make such a day of it, as should mark these events for a high Feast and Festival in the Peerybingle Calendar for evermore. Accordingly, Dot went to work to produce such an entertainment, as should reflect undying honour on the house and on every one concerned; and in a very short space of time, she was up to her dimpled elbows in flour, and whitening the Carrier's coat, every time he came near her, by stopping him to give him a kiss. That good fellow washed the greens, and peeled the turnips, and broke the plates, and upset iron pots full of cold water on the fire, and made himself useful in all sorts of ways: while a couple of professional assistants, hastily called in from somewhere in the neighbourhood, as on a point of life or death, ran against each other in all the doorways and round all the corners, and everybody tumbled over Tilly Slowboy and the Baby, everywhere. Tilly never came out in such force before. Her ubiquity was the theme of general admiration. She was a stumbling-block in the passage at five-and-twenty minutes past two; a man-trap in the kitchen at half-past two precisely; and a pitfall in the garret at five-and-twenty minutes to three. The Baby's head was, as it were, a test and touchstone for every description of matter,—animal, vegetable, and mineral. Nothing was in use that day that didn't come, at some time or other, into close acquaintance with it.

Then, there was a great Expedition set on foot to go and find out Mrs. Fielding; and to be dismally penitent to that excellent gentlewoman; and to bring her back, by force, if needful, to be happy and forgiving. And when the Expedition first discovered her, she would listen to no terms at all, but said, an unspeakable number of times, that ever she should have lived to see the day! and couldn't be got to say anything else, except, "Now carry me to the grave": which seemed absurd, on account of her not being dead, or anything at all like it. After a time, she lapsed into a state of dreadful calmness, and observed, that when that unfortunate train of circumstances had occurred in the Indigo Trade, she had foreseen that she would be exposed, during her whole life, to every species of insult and contumely; and that she was glad to find it was the case; and begged they wouldn't trouble themselves about her,—for what was she? oh, dear! a nobody!—but would forget that such a being lived, and would take their course in life without her. From this bitterly sarcastic mood, she passed into an angry one, in which she gave vent to the remarkable expression that the worm would turn if trodden on; and, after that, she yielded to a soft regret, and said, if they had only given her their confidence, what might she not have had it in her power to suggest! Taking advantage of this crisis in her feelings, the Expedition embraced her; and she very soon had her gloves on, and was on her way to John Peerybingle's in a state of unimpeachable gentility; with a paper parcel at her side containing a cap of state, almost as tall, and quite as stiff, as a mitre.

Then, there were Dot's father and mother to come, in another little chaise;

and they were behind their time; and fears were entertained; and there was much looking out for them down the road; and Mrs. Fielding always would look in the wrong and morally impossible direction; and being apprised thereof, hoped she might take the liberty of looking where she pleased. At last they came: a chubby little couple, jogging along in a snug and comfortable little way that quite belonged to the Dot family; and Dot and her mother, side by side, were wonderful to see. They were so like each other.

Then, Dot's mother had to renew her acquaintance with May's mother; and May's mother always stood on her gentility; and Dot's mother never stood on anything but her active little feet. And old Dot—so to call Dot's father, I forgot it wasn't his right name, but never mind—took liberties, and shook hands at first sight, and seemed to think a cap but so much starch and muslin, and didn't defer himself at all to the Indigo Trade, but said there was no help for it now; and, in Mrs. Fielding's summing up, was a good-natured kind of man—but coarse, my dear.

I wouldn't have missed Dot, doing the honours in her wedding-gown, my benison on her bright face! for any money. No! nor the good Carrier, so jovial and so ruddy, at the bottom of the table. Nor the brown, fresh sailor-fellow, and his handsome wife. Nor any one among them. To have missed the dinner would have been to miss as jolly and as stout a meal as man need eat; and to have missed the overflowing cups in which they drank The Wedding-Day, would have been the greatest miss of all.

After dinner, Caleb sang the song about the Sparkling Bowl. As I'm a living man, hoping to keep so, for a year or two, he sang it through.

And, by the bye, a most unlooked-for incident occurred, just as he finished the last verse.

There was a tap at the door; and a man came staggering in, without saying with your leave, or by your leave, with something heavy on his head. Setting this down in the middle of the table, symmetrically in the centre of the nuts and apples, he said:

"Mr. Tackleton's compliments, and as he hasn't got no use for the cake himself, p'raps you'll eat it."

And with those words, he walked off.

There was some surprise among the company, as you may imagine. Mrs. Fielding, being a lady of infinite discernment, suggested that the cake was poisoned, and related a narrative of a cake, which, within her knowledge, had turned a seminary for young ladies, blue. But she was overruled by acclamation; and the cake was cut by May, with much ceremony and rejoicing.

I don't think any one had tasted it, when there came another tap at the door, and the same man appeared again, having under his arm a vast brown-paper parcel.

"Mr. Tackleton's compliments, and he's sent a few toys for the Babby. They ain't ugly."

After the delivery of which expressions, he retired again.

The whole party would have experienced great difficulty in finding words for their astonishment, even if they had had ample time to seek them. But they had none at all; for the messenger had scarcely shut the door behind him, when there came another tap, and Tackleton himself walked in.

"Mrs. Peerybingle!" said the Toy-merchant, hat in hand. "I'm sorry. I'm more sorry than I was this morning. I have had time to think of it. John Peerybingle! I'm sour by disposition; but I can't help being sweetened, more or less, by coming face to face with such a man as you. Caleb! This unconscious little nurse gave me a broken hint last night, of which I have found the thread. I blush to think how easily I might have bound you and your daughter to me, and what a miserable idiot I was, when I took her for one! Friends, one and all, my house is very lonely to-night. I have not so much as a Cricket on my Hearth. I have scared them all away. Be gracious to me; let me join this happy party!"

He was at home in five minutes. You never saw such a fellow. What had he been doing with himself all his life, never to have known, before, his great capacity of being jovial! Or what had the Fairies been doing with him, to have effected such a change!

"John! you won't send me home this evening; will you?" whispered Dot.

He had been very near it though!

There wanted but one living creature to make the party complete; and, in the twinkling of an eye, there he was, very thirsty with hard running, and engaged in hopeless endeavours to squeeze his head into a narrow pitcher. He had gone with the cart to its journey's end, very much disgusted with the absence of his master, and stupendously rebellious to the Deputy. After lingering about the stable for some little time, vainly attempting to incite the old horse to the mutinous act of returning on his own account, he had walked into the tap-room and laid himself down before the fire. But suddenly yielding to the conviction that the Deputy was a humbug, and must be abandoned, he had got up again, turned tail, and come home.

There was a dance in the evening. With which general mention of that recreation, I should have left it alone, if I had not some reason to suppose that it was quite an original dance, and one of a most uncommon figure. It was formed in an odd way; in this way.

Edward, that sailor-fellow—a good free dashing sort of a fellow he was—had been telling them various marvels concerning parrots, and mines, and Mexicans, and gold dust, when all at once he took it in his head to jump up from his seat and propose a dance; for Bertha's harp was there, and she had such a hand upon it as you seldom hear. Dot (sly little piece of affectation when she chose) said her dancing days were over; I think because the Carrier was smoking his pipe, and she liked sitting by him, best. Mrs. Fielding had no choice, of course, but to say her dancing days were over, after that; and everybody said the same, except May; May was ready.

So, May and Edward got up, amid great applause, to dance alone; and Bertha plays her liveliest tune.

Well! if you'll believe me, they have not been dancing five minutes, when suddenly the Carrier flings his pipe away, takes Dot round the waist, dashes out into the room, and starts off with her, toe and heel, quite wonderfully. Tackleton no sooner sees this, than he skims across to Mrs. Fielding, takes her round the waist, and follows suit. Old Dot no sooner sees this, than up he is, all alive, whisks off Mrs. Dot in the middle of the dance, and is the foremost there. Caleb no sooner sees this, than he clutches Tilly Slowboy by both hands and goes off at score; Miss Slowboy, firm in the belief that diving hotly in among the other couples, and effecting any number of concussions with them, is your only principle of footing it.

Hark! how the Cricket joins the music with its Chirp, Chirp, Chirp; and how the kettle hums!

But what is this! Even as I listen to them, blithely, and turn towards Dot, for one last glimpse of a little figure very pleasant to me, she and the rest have vanished into air, and I am left alone. A Cricket sings upon the Hearth; a broken child's-toy lies upon the ground; and nothing else remains.

The Battle of Life

Charles Dickens

CHAPTER I. PART THE FIRST

Once upon a time, it matters little when, and in stalwart England, it matters little where, a fierce battle was fought. It was fought upon a long summer day when the waving grass was green. Many a wild flower formed by the Almighty Hand to be a perfumed goblet for the dew, felt its enamelled cup filled high with blood that day, and shrinking dropped. Many an insect deriving its delicate colour from harmless leaves and herbs, was stained anew that day by dying men, and marked its frightened way with an unnatural track. The painted butterfly took blood into the air upon the edges of its wings. The stream ran red. The trodden ground became a quagmire, whence, from sullen pools collected in the prints of human feet and horses' hoofs, the one prevailing hue still lowered and glimmered at the sun.

Heaven keep us from a knowledge of the sights the moon beheld upon that field, when, coming up above the black line of distant rising-ground, softened and blurred at the edge by trees, she rose into the sky and looked upon the plain, strewn with upturned faces that had once at mothers' breasts sought mothers' eyes, or slumbered happily. Heaven keep us from a knowledge of the secrets whispered afterwards upon the tainted wind that blew across the scene of that day's work and that night's death and suffering! Many a lonely moon was bright upon the battle-ground, and many a star kept mournful watch upon it, and many a wind from every quarter of the earth blew over it, before the traces of the fight were worn away.

They lurked and lingered for a long time, but survived in little things; for, Nature, far above the evil passions of men, soon recovered Her serenity, and smiled upon the guilty battle-ground as she had done before, when it was innocent. The larks sang high above it; the swallows skimmed and dipped and flitted to and fro; the shadows of the flying clouds pursued each other swiftly, over grass and corn and turnip-field and wood, and over roof and church-spire in the nestling town among the trees, away into the bright distance on the borders of the sky and earth, where the red sunsets faded. Crops were sown, and grew up, and were gathered in; the stream that had been crimsoned, turned a watermill; men whistled at the plough; gleaners and haymakers were seen in quiet groups at work; sheep and oxen pastured; boys whooped and called, in fields, to scare away the birds; smoke rose from cottage chimneys; sabbath bells rang peacefully; old people lived and died; the timid creatures of the field, the simple flowers of the bush and garden, grew and withered in their destined terms: and all upon the fierce and bloody battle-ground, where thousands upon thousands had been killed in the great fight.

But, there were deep green patches in the growing corn at first, that people looked at awfully. Year after year they re-appeared; and it was known that underneath those fertile spots, heaps of men and horses lay buried, indiscriminately, enriching the ground. The husbandmen who ploughed those places, shrunk from the great worms abounding there; and the sheaves they yielded, were, for many a long year, called the Battle Sheaves, and set apart; and no one ever knew a Battle Sheaf to be among the last load at a Harvest Home. For a long time, every furrow that was turned, revealed some fragments of the fight. For a long time, there were wounded trees upon the battle-ground; and scraps of hacked and broken fence and wall, where deadly struggles had been made; and trampled parts where not a leaf or blade would grow. For a long time, no village girl would dress her hair or bosom with the sweetest flower from that field of death: and after many a year had come and gone, the berries growing there, were still believed to leave too deep a stain upon the hand that plucked them.

The Seasons in their course, however, though they passed as lightly as the summer clouds themselves, obliterated, in the lapse of time, even these remains of the old conflict; and wore away such legendary traces of it as the neighbouring people carried in their minds, until they dwindled into old wives' tales, dimly remembered round the winter fire, and waning every year. Where the wild flowers and berries had so long remained upon the stem untouched, gardens arose, and houses were built, and children played at battles on the turf. The wounded trees had long ago made Christmas logs, and blazed and roared away. The deep green patches were no greener now than the memory of those who lay in dust below. The ploughshare still turned up from time to time some rusty bits of metal, but it was hard to say what use they had ever served, and those who found them wondered and disputed. An old dinted corselet, and a helmet, had been hanging in the church so long, that the same weak half-blind old man who tried in vain to make them out above the whitewashed arch, had marvelled at them as a baby. If the host slain upon the field, could have been for a moment reanimated in the forms in which they fell, each upon the spot that was the bed of his untimely death, gashed and ghastly soldiers would have stared in, hundreds deep, at household door and window; and would have risen on the hearths of quiet homes; and would have been the garnered store of barns and granaries; and would have started up between the cradled infant and its nurse; and would have floated with the stream, and whirled round on the mill, and crowded the orchard, and burdened the meadow, and piled the rickyard high with dying men. So altered was the battle-ground, where thousands upon thousands had been killed in the great fight.

Nowhere more altered, perhaps, about a hundred years ago, than in one little orchard attached to an old stone house with a honeysuckle porch; where, on a bright autumn morning, there were sounds of music and laughter, and where two girls danced merrily together on the grass, while some half-dozen peasant women standing on ladders, gathering the apples from the trees, stopped in their work to look down, and share their enjoyment. It was a pleasant, lively, natural scene; a beautiful day, a retired spot; and the two girls, quite unconstrained and careless, danced in the freedom and gaiety of their hearts.

If there were no such thing as display in the world, my private opinion is, and I hope you agree with me, that we might get on a great deal better than we do, and might be infinitely more agreeable company than we are. It was charming to see how these girls danced. They had no spectators but the apple-pickers on the ladders. They were very glad to please them, but they danced to please themselves (or at least you would have supposed so); and you could no more help admiring, than they could help dancing. How they did dance!

Not like opera-dancers. Not at all. And not like Madame Anybody's finished pupils. Not the least. It was not quadrille dancing, nor minuet dancing, nor even country-dance dancing. It was neither in the old style, nor the new style, nor the French style, nor the English style: though it may have been, by accident, a trifle in the Spanish style, which is a free and joyous one, I am told, deriving a delightful air of off-hand inspiration, from the chirping little castanets. As they danced among the orchard trees, and down the groves of stems and back again, and twirled each other lightly round and round, the influence of their airy motion seemed to spread and spread, in the sun-lighted scene, like an expanding circle in the water. Their streaming hair and fluttering skirts, the elastic grass beneath their feet, the boughs that rustled in the morning air—the flashing leaves, the speckled shadows on the soft green ground—the balmy wind that swept along the landscape, glad to turn the distant windmill, cheerily—everything between the two girls, and the man and team at plough upon the ridge of land, where they showed against the sky as if they were the last things in the world—seemed dancing too.

At last, the younger of the dancing sisters, out of breath, and laughing gaily, threw herself upon a bench to rest. The other leaned against a tree hard by. The music, a wandering harp and fiddle, left off with a flourish, as if it boasted of its freshness; though the truth is, it had gone at such a pace, and worked itself to such a pitch of competition with the dancing, that it never could have held on, half a minute longer. The apple-pickers on the ladders raised a hum and murmur of applause, and then, in keeping with the sound, bestirred themselves to work again like bees.

The more actively, perhaps, because an elderly gentleman, who was no other than Doctor Jeddler himself—it was Doctor Jeddler's house and orchard, you should know, and these were Doctor Jeddler's daughters—came bustling out to see what was the matter, and who the deuce played music on his property, before breakfast. For he was a great philosopher, Doctor Jeddler, and not very musical.

"Music and dancing to-day" said the Doctor, stopping short, and speaking to himself. "I thought they dreaded to-day. But it's a world of contradictions. Why, Grace, why, Marion!" he added, aloud, "is the world more mad than usual this morning?"

"Make some allowance for it, father, if it be," replied his younger daughter, Marion, going close to him, and looking into his face, "for it's somebody's birth-day."

"Somebody's birth-day, Puss!" replied the Doctor. "Don't you know it's always somebody's birth-day? Did you never hear how many new performers enter on this—ha! ha! ha!—it's impossible to speak gravely of it—on this preposterous and ridiculous business called Life, every minute?"

"No, father!"

"No, not you, of course; you're a woman—almost," said the Doctor. "By the bye," and he looked into the pretty face, still close to his, "I suppose it's your birth-day."

"No! Do you really, father?" cried his pet daughter, pursing up her red lips to be kissed.

"There! Take my love with it," said the Doctor, imprinting his upon them; "and many happy returns of the—the idea!—of the day. The notion of wishing happy returns in such a farce as this," said the Doctor to himself, "is good! Ha! ha! ha!"

Doctor Jeddler was, as I have said, a great philosopher, and the heart and mystery of his philosophy was, to look upon the world as a gigantic practical joke; as something too absurd to be considered seriously, by any rational man. His system of belief had been, in the beginning, part and parcel of the battle-ground on which he lived, as you shall presently understand.

"Well! But how did you get the music?" asked the Doctor. "Poultry-stealers, of course! Where did the minstrels come from?"

"Alfred sent the music," said his daughter Grace, adjusting a few simple flowers in her sister's hair, with which, in her admiration of that youthful beauty, she had herself adorned it half-an-hour before, and which the dancing had disarranged.

"Oh! Alfred sent the music, did he?" returned the Doctor.

"Yes. He met it coming out of the town as he was entering early. The men are travelling on foot, and rested there last night; and as it was Marion's birth-day, and he thought it would please her, he sent them on, with a pencilled note to me, saying that if I thought so too, they had come to serenade her."

"Ay, ay," said the Doctor, carelessly, "he always takes your opinion."

"And my opinion being favourable," said Grace, good-humouredly; and pausing for a moment to admire the pretty head she decorated, with her own thrown back; "and Marion being in high spirits, and beginning to dance, I joined her. And so we danced to Alfred's music till we were out of breath. And we thought the music all the gayer for being sent by Alfred. Didn't we, dear Marion?"

"Oh, I don't know, Grace. How you tease me about Alfred."

"Tease you by mentioning your lover?" said her sister.

"I am sure I don't much care to have him mentioned," said the wilful beauty, stripping the petals from some flowers she held, and scattering them on the ground. "I am almost tired of hearing of him; and as to his being my lover—"

"Hush! Don't speak lightly of a true heart, which is all your own, Marion," cried her sister, "even in jest. There is not a truer heart than Alfred's in the world!"

"No—no," said Marion, raising her eyebrows with a pleasant air of careless consideration, "perhaps not. But I don't know that there's any great merit in that. I—I don't want him to be so very true. I never asked him. If he expects that I— But, dear Grace, why need we talk of him at all, just now!"

It was agreeable to see the graceful figures of the blooming sisters, twined together, lingering among the trees, conversing thus, with earnestness opposed to lightness, yet, with love responding tenderly to love. And it was very curious indeed to see the younger sister's eyes suffused with tears, and something fervently and deeply felt, breaking through the wilfulness of what she said, and striving with it painfully.

The difference between them, in respect of age, could not exceed four years at most; but Grace, as often happens in such cases, when no mother watches over both (the Doctor's wife was dead), seemed, in her gentle care of her young sister, and in the steadiness of her devotion to her, older than she was; and more removed, in course of nature, from all competition with her, or participation, otherwise than through her sympathy and true affection, in her wayward fancies, than their ages seemed to warrant. Great character of mother, that, even in this shadow and faint reflection of it, purifies the heart, and raises the exalted nature nearer to the angels!

The Doctor's reflections, as he looked after them, and heard the purport of their discourse, were limited at first to certain merry meditations on the folly of all loves and likings, and the idle imposition practised on themselves by young people, who believed for a moment, that there could be anything serious in such bubbles, and were always undeceived—always!

But, the home-adorning, self-denying qualities of Grace, and her sweet temper, so gentle and retiring, yet including so much constancy and bravery of spirit, seemed all expressed to him in the contrast between her quiet household figure and that of his younger and more beautiful child; and he was sorry for her sake—sorry for them both—that life should be such a very ridiculous business as it was.

The Doctor never dreamed of inquiring whether his children, or either of them, helped in any way to make the scheme a serious one. But then he was a Philosopher.

A kind and generous man by nature, he had stumbled, by chance, over that common Philosopher's stone (much more easily discovered than the object of the alchemist's researches), which sometimes trips up kind and generous men, and has the fatal property of turning gold to dross and every precious thing to poor account.

"Britain!" cried the Doctor. "Britain! Holloa!"

A small man, with an uncommonly sour and discontented face, emerged from the house, and returned to this call the unceremonious acknowledgment of "Now then!"

"Where's the breakfast table?" said the Doctor.

"In the house," returned Britain.

"Are you going to spread it out here, as you were told last night?" said the Doctor. "Don't you know that there are gentlemen coming? That there's business to be done this morning, before the coach comes by? That this is a very particular occasion?"

"I couldn't do anything, Dr. Jeddler, till the women had done getting in the apples, could I?" said Britain, his voice rising with his reasoning, so that it was very loud at last.

"Well, have they done now?" replied the Doctor, looking at his watch, and clapping his hands. "Come! make haste! where's Clemency?"

"Here am I, Mister," said a voice from one of the ladders, which a pair of clumsy feet descended briskly. "It's all done now. Clear away, gals. Everything shall be ready for you in half a minute, Mister."

With that she began to bustle about most vigorously; presenting, as she did so, an appearance sufficiently peculiar to justify a word of introduction.

She was about thirty years old, and had a sufficiently plump and cheerful face, though it was twisted up into an odd expression of tightness that made it comical. But, the extraordinary homeliness of her gait and manner, would have superseded any face in the world. To say that she had two left legs, and somebody else's arms, and that all four limbs seemed to be out of joint, and to start from perfectly wrong places when they were set in motion, is to offer the mildest outline of the reality. To say that she was perfectly content and satisfied with these arrangements, and regarded them as being no business of hers, and that she took her arms and legs as they came, and allowed them to dispose of themselves just as it happened, is to render faint justice to her equanimity. Her dress was a prodigious pair of self-willed shoes, that never wanted to go where her feet went; blue stockings; a printed gown of many colours, and the most hideous pattern procurable for money; and a white apron. She always wore short sleeves, and always had, by some accident, grazed elbows, in which she took so lively an interest, that she was continually trying to turn them round and get impossible views of them. In general, a little cap placed somewhere on her head; though it was rarely to be met with in the place usually occupied in other subjects, by that article of dress; but, from head to foot she was scrupulously clean, and maintained a kind of dislocated tidiness. Indeed, her laudable anxiety to be tidy and compact in her own conscience as well as in the public eye, gave rise to one of her most startling evolutions, which was to grasp herself sometimes by a sort of wooden handle (part of her clothing, and familiarly called a busk), and wrestle as it were with her garments, until they fell into a symmetrical arrangement.

Such, in outward form and garb, was Clemency Newcome; who was supposed to have unconsciously originated a corruption of her own Christian name, from Clementina (but nobody knew, for the deaf old mother, a very phenomenon of age, whom she had supported almost from a child, was dead, and she had no other relation); who now busied herself in preparing the table, and who stood, at intervals, with her bare red arms crossed, rubbing her grazed elbows with opposite hands, and staring at it very composedly, until she suddenly remembered something else she wanted, and jogged off to fetch it.

"Here are them two lawyers a-coming, Mister!" said Clemency, in a tone of no very great good-will.

"Ah!" cried the Doctor, advancing to the gate to meet them. "Good morning, good morning! Grace, my dear! Marion! Here are Messrs. Snitchey and Craggs. Where's Alfred!"

"He'll be back directly, father, no doubt," said Grace. "He had so much to do this morning in his preparations for departure, that he was up and out by daybreak. Good morning, gentlemen."

"Ladies!" said Mr. Snitchey, "for Self and Craggs," who bowed, "good morning! Miss," to Marion, "I kiss your hand." Which he did. "And I wish you"—which he might or might not, for he didn't look, at first sight, like a gentleman troubled with many warm outpourings of soul, in behalf of other people, "a hundred happy returns of this auspicious day."

"Ha ha ha!" laughed the Doctor thoughtfully, with his hands in his pockets. "The great farce in a hundred acts!"

"You wouldn't, I am sure," said Mr. Snitchey, standing a small professional blue bag against one leg of the table, "cut the great farce short for this actress, at all events, Doctor Jeddler."

"No," returned the Doctor. "God forbid! May she live to laugh at it, as long as she can laugh, and then say, with the French wit, 'The farce is ended; draw the curtain.'"

"The French wit," said Mr. Snitchey, peeping sharply into his blue bag, "was wrong, Doctor Jeddler, and your philosophy is altogether wrong, depend upon it, as I have often told you. Nothing serious in life! What do you call law?"

"A joke," replied the Doctor.

"Did you ever go to law?" asked Mr. Snitchey, looking out of the blue bag.

"Never," returned the Doctor.

"If you ever do," said Mr. Snitchey, "perhaps you'll alter that opinion."

Craggs, who seemed to be represented by Snitchey, and to be conscious of little or no separate existence or personal individuality, offered a remark of his own in this place. It involved the only idea of which he did not stand seized and possessed in equal moieties with Snitchey; but, he had some partners in it among the wise men of the world.

"It's made a great deal too easy," said Mr. Craggs.

"Law is?" asked the Doctor.

"Yes," said Mr. Craggs, "everything is. Everything appears to me to be made too easy, now-a-days. It's the vice of these times. If the world is a joke (I am not prepared to say it isn't), it ought to be made a very difficult joke to crack. It ought to be as hard a struggle, sir, as possible. That's the intention. But, it's being made far too easy. We are oiling the gates of life. They ought to be rusty. We shall have them beginning to turn, soon, with a smooth sound. Whereas they ought to grate upon their hinges, sir."

Mr. Craggs seemed positively to grate upon his own hinges, as he delivered this opinion; to which he communicated immense effect—being a cold, hard, dry, man, dressed in grey and white, like a flint; with small twinkles in his eyes, as if something struck sparks out of them. The three natural kingdoms, indeed, had each a fanciful representative among this brotherhood of disputants; for Snitchey was like a magpie or raven (only not so sleek), and the Doctor had a streaked face like a winter-pippin, with here and there a dimple to express the peckings of the birds, and a very little bit of pigtail behind that stood for the stalk.

As the active figure of a handsome young man, dressed for a journey, and followed by a porter bearing several packages and baskets, entered the orchard at a brisk pace, and with an air of gaiety and hope that accorded well with the morning, these three drew together, like the brothers of the sister Fates, or like the Graces most effectually disguised, or like the three weird prophets on the heath, and greeted him.

"Happy returns, Alf!" said the Doctor, lightly.

"A hundred happy returns of this auspicious day, Mr. Heathfield!" said Snitchey, bowing low.

"Returns!" Craggs murmured in a deep voice, all alone.

"Why, what a battery!" exclaimed Alfred, stopping short, "and one—two—three—all foreboders of no good, in the great sea before me. I am glad you are not the first I have met this morning: I should have taken it for a bad omen. But, Grace was the first—sweet, pleasant Grace—so I defy you all!"

"If you please, Mister, I was the first you know," said Clemency Newcome. "She was walking out here, before sunrise, you remember. I was in the house."

"That's true! Clemency was the first," said Alfred. "So I defy you with Clemency."

"Ha, ha, ha,—for Self and Craggs," said Snitchey. "What a defiance!"

"Not so bad a one as it appears, may be," said Alfred, shaking hands heartily with the Doctor, and also with Snitchey and Craggs, and then looking round. "Where are the— Good Heavens!"

With a start, productive for the moment of a closer partnership between Jonathan Snitchey and Thomas Craggs than the subsisting articles of agreement in that wise contemplated, he hastily betook himself to where the sisters stood together, and—however, I needn't more particularly explain his manner of saluting Marion first, and Grace afterwards, than by hinting that Mr. Craggs may possibly have considered it "too easy."

Perhaps to change the subject, Dr. Jeddler made a hasty move towards the breakfast, and they all sat down at table. Grace presided; but so discreetly stationed herself, as to cut off her sister and Alfred from the rest of the company. Snitchey and Craggs sat at opposite corners, with the blue bag between them for safety; the Doctor took his usual position, opposite to Grace. Clemency hovered galvanically about the table, as waitress; and the melancholy Britain, at another and a smaller board, acted as Grand Carver of a round of beef and a ham.

"Meat?" said Britain, approaching Mr. Snitchey, with the carving knife and fork in his hands, and throwing the question at him like a missile.

"Certainly," returned the lawyer.

"Do you want any?" to Craggs.

"Lean and well done," replied that gentleman.

Having executed these orders, and moderately supplied the Doctor (he seemed to know that nobody else wanted anything to eat), he lingered as near the Firm as he decently could, watching with an austere eye their disposition of the viands, and but once relaxing the severe expression of his face. This was on the occasion of Mr. Craggs, whose teeth were not of the best, partially choking, when he cried out with great animation, "I thought he was gone!"

"Now, Alfred," said the Doctor, "for a word or two of business, while we are yet at breakfast."

"While we are yet at breakfast," said Snitchey and Craggs, who seemed to have no present idea of leaving off.

Although Alfred had not been breakfasting, and seemed to have quite enough business on his hands as it was, he respectfully answered:

"If you please, sir."

"If anything could be serious," the Doctor began, "in such a—"

"Farce as this, sir," hinted Alfred.

"In such a farce as this," observed the Doctor, "it might be this recurrence, on the eve of separation, of a double birthday, which is connected with many associations pleasant to us four, and with the recollection of a long and amicable intercourse. That's not to the purpose."

"Ah! yes, yes, Dr. Jeddler," said the young man. "It is to the purpose. Much to the purpose, as my heart bears witness this morning; and as yours does too, I know, if you would let it speak. I leave your house to-day; I cease to be your ward to-day; we part with tender relations stretching far behind us, that never can be exactly renewed, and with others dawning—yet before us," he looked down at Marion beside him, "fraught with such considerations as I must not trust myself to speak of now. Come, come!" he added, rallying his spirits and the Doctor at once, "there's a serious grain in this large foolish dust-heap, Doctor. Let us allow to-day, that there is One."

"To-day!" cried the Doctor. "Hear him! Ha, ha, ha! Of all days in the foolish year. Why, on this day, the great battle was fought on this ground. On this ground where we now sit, where I saw my two girls dance this morning, where the fruit has just been gathered for our eating from these trees, the roots of which are struck in Men, not earth,—so many lives were lost, that within my recollection, generations afterwards, a churchyard full of bones, and dust of bones, and chips of cloven skulls, has been dug up from underneath our feet here. Yet not a hundred people in that battle knew for what they fought, or why; not a hundred of the inconsiderate rejoicers in the victory, why they rejoiced. Not half a hundred people were the better for the gain or loss. Not half-a-dozen men agree to this hour on the cause or merits; and nobody, in short, ever knew anything distinct about it, but the mourners of the slain. Serious, too!" said the Doctor, laughing. "Such a system!"

"But, all this seems to me," said Alfred, "to be very serious."

"Serious!" cried the Doctor. "If you allowed such things to be serious, you must go mad, or die, or climb up to the top of a mountain, and turn hermit."

"Besides—so long ago," said Alfred.

"Long ago!" returned the Doctor. "Do you know what the world has been doing, ever since? Do you know what else it has been doing? I don't!"

"It has gone to law a little," observed Mr. Snitchey, stirring his tea.

"Although the way out has been always made too easy," said his partner.

"And you'll excuse my saying, Doctor," pursued Mr. Snitchey, "having been already put a thousand times in possession of my opinion, in the course of our discussions, that, in its having gone to law, and in its legal system altogether, I do observe a serious side—now, really, a something tangible, and with a purpose and intention in it—"

Clemency Newcome made an angular tumble against the table, occasioning a sounding clatter among the cups and saucers.

"Heyday! what's the matter there?" exclaimed the Doctor.

"It's this evil-inclined blue bag," said Clemency, "always tripping up somebody!"

"With a purpose and intention in it, I was saying," resumed Snitchey, "that commands respect. Life a farce, Dr. Jeddler? With law in it?"

The Doctor laughed, and looked at Alfred.

"Granted, if you please, that war is foolish," said Snitchey. "There we agree. For example. Here's a smiling country," pointing it out with his fork, "once overrun by soldiers—trespassers every man of 'em—and laid waste by fire and sword. He, he, he! The idea of any man exposing himself, voluntarily, to fire and sword! Stupid, wasteful, positively ridiculous; you laugh at your fellow-creatures, you know, when you think of it! But take this smiling country as it stands. Think of the laws appertaining to real property; to the bequest and devise of real property; to the mortgage and redemption of real property; to leasehold, freehold, and copyhold estate; think," said Mr. Snitchey, with such great emotion that he actually smacked his lips, "of the complicated laws relating to title and proof of title, with all the contradictory precedents and numerous acts of parliament connected with them; think of the infinite number of ingenious and interminable chancery suits, to which this pleasant prospect may give rise; and acknowledge, Dr. Jeddler, that there is a green spot in the scheme about us! I believe," said Mr. Snitchey, looking at his partner, "that I speak for Self and Craggs?"

Mr. Craggs having signified assent, Mr. Snitchey, somewhat freshened by his recent eloquence, observed that he would take a little more beef and another cup of tea.

"I don't stand up for life in general," he added, rubbing his hands and chuckling, "it's full of folly; full of something worse. Professions of trust, and confidence, and unselfishness, and all that! Bah, bah, bah! We see what they're worth. But, you mustn't laugh at life; you've got a game to play; a very serious game indeed! Everybody's playing against you, you know, and you're playing against them. Oh! it's a very interesting thing. There are deep moves upon the board. You must only laugh, Dr. Jeddler, when you win—and then not much. He, he, he! And then not much," repeated Snitchey, rolling his head and winking his eye, as if he would have added, "you may do this instead!"

"Well, Alfred!" cried the Doctor, "what do you say now?"

"I say, sir," replied Alfred, "that the greatest favour you could do me, and yourself too, I am inclined to think, would be to try sometimes to forget this battle-field and others like it in that broader battle-field of Life, on which the sun looks every day."

"Really, I'm afraid that wouldn't soften his opinions, Mr. Alfred," said Snitchey. "The combatants are very eager and very bitter in that same battle of Life. There's a great deal of cutting and slashing, and firing into people's heads from behind. There is terrible treading down, and trampling on. It is rather a bad business."

"I believe, Mr. Snitchey," said Alfred, "there are quiet victories and struggles, great sacrifices of self, and noble acts of heroism, in it—even in many of its apparent lightnesses and contradictions—not the less difficult to achieve, because they have no earthly chronicle or audience—done every day in nooks and corners, and in little households, and in men's and women's hearts—any one of which might reconcile the sternest man to such a world, and fill him with belief and hope in it, though two-fourths of its people were at war, and another fourth at law; and that's a bold word."

Both the sisters listened keenly.

"Well, well!" said the Doctor, "I am too old to be converted, even by my friend Snitchey here, or my good spinster sister, Martha Jeddler; who had what she calls her domestic trials ages ago, and has led a sympathising life with all sorts of people ever since; and who is so much of your opinion (only she's less reasonable and more obstinate, being a woman), that we can't agree, and seldom meet. I was born upon this battle-field. I began, as a boy, to have my thoughts directed to the real history of a battle-field. Sixty years have gone over my head, and I have never seen the Christian world, including Heaven knows how many loving mothers and good enough girls like mine here, anything but mad for a battle-field. The same contradictions prevail in everything. One must either laugh or cry at such stupendous inconsistencies; and I prefer to laugh."

Britain, who had been paying the profoundest and most melancholy attention to each speaker in his turn, seemed suddenly to decide in favour of the same preference, if a deep sepulchral sound that escaped him might be construed into a demonstration of risibility. His face, however, was so perfectly unaffected by it, both before and afterwards, that although one or two of the breakfast party looked round as being startled by a mysterious noise, nobody connected the offender with it.

Except his partner in attendance, Clemency Newcome; who rousing him with one of those favourite joints, her elbows, inquired, in a reproachful whisper, what he laughed at.

"Not you!" said Britain.

"Who then?"

"Humanity," said Britain. "That's the joke!"

"What between master and them lawyers, he's getting more and more addle-headed every day!" cried Clemency, giving him a lunge with the other elbow, as a mental stimulant. "Do you know where you are? Do you want to get warning?"

"I don't know anything," said Britain, with a leaden eye and an immovable visage. "I don't care for anything. I don't make out anything. I don't believe anything. And I don't want anything."

Although this forlorn summary of his general condition may have been overcharged in an access of despondency, Benjamin Britain—sometimes called Little Britain, to distinguish him from Great; as we might say Young England, to express Old England with a decided difference—had defined his real state more accurately than might be supposed. For, serving as a sort of man Miles to the Doctor's Friar Bacon, and listening day after day to innumerable orations addressed by the Doctor to various people, all tending to shew that his very existence was at best a mistake and an absurdity, this unfortunate servitor had fallen, by degrees, into such an abyss of confused and contradictory suggestions from within and without, that Truth at the bottom of her well, was on the level surface as compared with Britain in the depths of his mystification. The only point he clearly comprehended, was, that the new element usually brought into these discussions by Snitchey and Craggs, never served to make them clearer, and always seemed to give the Doctor a species of advantage and confirmation. Therefore, he looked upon the Firm as one of the proximate causes of his state of mind, and held them in abhorrence accordingly.

"But, this is not our business, Alfred," said the Doctor. "Ceasing to be my ward (as you have said) to-day; and leaving us full to the brim of such learning as the Grammar School down here was able to give you, and your studies in London could add to that, and such practical knowledge as a dull old country Doctor like myself could graft upon both; you are away, now, into the world. The first term of probation appointed by your poor father, being over, away you go now, your own master, to fulfil his second desire. And long before your three years' tour among the foreign schools of medicine is finished, you'll have forgotten us. Lord, you'll forget us easily in six months!"

"If I do—But you know better; why should I speak to you!" said Alfred, laughing.

"I don't know anything of the sort," returned the Doctor. "What do you say, Marion?"

Marion, trifling with her teacup, seemed to say—but she didn't say it—that he was welcome to forget, if he could. Grace pressed the blooming face against her cheek, and smiled.

"I haven't been, I hope, a very unjust steward in the execution of my trust," pursued the Doctor; "but I am to be, at any rate, formally discharged, and released, and what not this morning; and here are our good friends Snitchey and Craggs, with a bagful of papers, and accounts, and documents, for the transfer of the balance of the trust fund to you (I wish it was a more difficult one to dispose of, Alfred, but you must get to be a great man and make it so), and other drolleries of that sort, which are to be signed, sealed, and delivered."

"And duly witnessed as by law required," said Snitchey, pushing away his plate, and taking out the papers, which his partner proceeded to spread upon the table; "and Self and Crags having been co-trustees with you, Doctor, in so far as the fund was concerned, we shall want your two servants to attest the signatures— can you read, Mrs. Newcome?"

"I an't married, Mister," said Clemency.

"Oh! I beg your pardon. I should think not," chuckled Snitchey, casting his eyes over her extraordinary figure. "You can read?"

"A little," answered Clemency.

"The marriage service, night and morning, eh?" observed the lawyer, jocosely.

"No," said Clemency. "Too hard. I only reads a thimble."

"Read a thimble!" echoed Snitchey. "What are you talking about, young woman?"

Clemency nodded. "And a nutmeg-grater."

"Why, this is a lunatic! a subject for the Lord High Chancellor!" said Snitchey, staring at her.

"—If possessed of any property," stipulated Craggs.

Grace, however, interposing, explained that each of the articles in question bore an engraved motto, and so formed the pocket library of Clemency Newcome, who was not much given to the study of books.

"Oh, that's it, is it, Miss Grace!" said Snitchey.

"Yes, yes. Ha, ha, ha! I thought our friend was an idiot. She looks uncommonly like it," he muttered, with a supercilious glance. "And what does the thimble say, Mrs. Newcome?"

"I an't married, Mister," observed Clemency.

"Well, Newcome. Will that do?" said the lawyer. "What does the thimble say, Newcome?"

How Clemency, before replying to this question, held one pocket open, and looked down into its yawning depths for the thimble which wasn't there,—and how she then held an opposite pocket open, and seeming to descry it, like a pearl of great price, at the bottom, cleared away such intervening obstacles as a handkerchief, an end of wax candle, a flushed apple, an orange, a lucky penny, a cramp bone, a padlock, a pair of scissors in a sheath more expressively describable as promising young shears, a handful or so of loose beads, several balls of cotton, a needle-case, a cabinet collection of curl-papers, and a biscuit, all of which articles she entrusted individually and separately to Britain to hold,—is of no consequence.

Nor how, in her determination to grasp this pocket by the throat and keep it prisoner (for it had a tendency to swing, and twist itself round the nearest corner), she assumed and calmly maintained, an attitude apparently inconsistent with the human anatomy and the laws of gravity. It is enough that at last she triumphantly produced the thimble on her finger, and rattled the nutmeg-grater: the literature of both those trinkets being obviously in course of wearing out and wasting away, through excessive friction.

"That's the thimble, is it, young woman?" said Mr. Snitchey, diverting himself at her expense. "And what does the thimble say?"

"It says," replied Clemency, reading slowly round as if it were a tower, "For-get and For-give."

Snitchey and Craggs laughed heartily. "So new!" said Snitchey. "So easy!" said Craggs. "Such a knowledge of human nature in it!" said Snitchey. "So applicable to the affairs of life!" said Craggs.

"And the nutmeg-grater?" inquired the head of the Firm.

"The grater says," returned Clemency, "Do as you—wold—be—done by."

"Do, or you'll be done brown, you mean," said Mr. Snitchey.

"I don't understand," retorted Clemency, shaking her head vaguely. "I an't no lawyer."

"I am afraid that if she was, Doctor," said Mr. Snitchey, turning to him suddenly, as if to anticipate any effect that might otherwise be consequent on this retort, "she'd find it to be the golden rule of half her clients. They are serious enough in that—whimsical as your world is—and lay the blame on us afterwards.

We, in our profession, are little else than mirrors after all, Mr. Alfred; but, we are generally consulted by angry and quarrelsome people who are not in their best looks, and it's rather hard to quarrel with us if we reflect unpleasant aspects. I think," said Mr. Snitchey, "that I speak for Self and Craggs?"

"Decidedly," said Craggs.

"And so, if Mr. Britain will oblige us with a mouthful of ink," said Mr. Snitchey, returning to the papers, "we'll sign, seal, and deliver as soon as possible, or the coach will be coming past before we know where we are."

If one might judge from his appearance, there was every probability of the coach coming past before Mr. Britain knew where he was; for he stood in a state of abstraction, mentally balancing the Doctor against the lawyers, and the lawyers against the Doctor, and their clients against both, and engaged in feeble attempts to make the thimble and nutmeg-grater (a new idea to him) square with anybody's system of philosophy; and, in short, bewildering himself as much as ever his great namesake has done with theories and schools. But, Clemency, who was his good Genius—though he had the meanest possible opinion of her understanding, by reason of her seldom troubling herself with abstract speculations, and being always at hand to do the right thing at the right time—having produced the ink in a twinkling, tendered him the further service of recalling him to himself by the application of her elbows; with which gentle flappers she so jogged his memory, in a more literal construction of that phrase than usual, that he soon became quite fresh and brisk.

How he laboured under an apprehension not uncommon to persons in his degree, to whom the use of pen and ink is an event, that he couldn't append his name to a document, not of his own writing, without committing himself in some shadowy manner, or somehow signing away vague and enormous sums of money; and how he approached the deeds under protest, and by dint of the Doctor's coercion, and insisted on pausing to look at them before writing (the cramped hand, to say nothing of the phraseology, being so much Chinese to him), and also on turning them round to see whether there was anything fraudulent underneath; and how, having signed his name, he became desolate as one who had parted with his property and rights; I want the time to tell. Also, how the blue bag containing his signature, afterwards had a mysterious interest for him, and he couldn't leave it; also, how Clemency Newcome, in an ecstasy of laughter at the idea of her own importance and dignity, brooded over the whole table with her two elbows, like a spread eagle, and reposed her head upon her left arm as a preliminary to the formation of certain cabalistic characters, which required a deal of ink, and imaginary counterparts whereof she executed at the same time with her tongue. Also, how, having once tasted ink, she became thirsty in that regard, as tame tigers are said to be after tasting another sort of fluid, and wanted to sign everything, and put her name in all kinds of places. In brief, the Doctor was discharged of his trust and all its responsibilities; and Alfred, taking it on himself, was fairly started on the journey of life.

"Britain!" said the Doctor. "Run to the gate, and watch for the coach. Time flies, Alfred."

"Yes, sir, yes," returned the young man, hurriedly. "Dear Grace! a moment! Marion—so young and beautiful, so winning and so much admired, dear to my heart as nothing else in life is—remember! I leave Marion to you!"

"She has always been a sacred charge to me, Alfred. She is doubly so, now. I will be faithful to my trust, believe me."

"I do believe it, Grace. I know it well. Who could look upon your face, and hear your voice, and not know it! Ah, Grace! If I had your well-governed heart, and tranquil mind, how bravely I would leave this place to-day!"

"Would you?" she answered with a quiet smile.

"And yet, Grace— Sister, seems the natural word."

"Use it!" she said quickly. "I am glad to hear it. Call me nothing else."

"And yet, sister, then," said Alfred, "Marion and I had better have your true and steadfast qualities serving us here, and making us both happier and better. I wouldn't carry them away, to sustain myself, if I could!"

"Coach upon the hill-top!" exclaimed Britain.

"Time flies, Alfred," said the Doctor.

Marion had stood apart, with her eyes fixed upon the ground; but, this warning being given, her young lover brought her tenderly to where her sister stood, and gave her into her embrace.

"I have been telling Grace, dear Marion," he said, "that you are her charge; my precious trust at parting. And when I come back and reclaim you, dearest, and the bright prospect of our married life lies stretched before us, it shall be one of our chief pleasures to consult how we can make Grace happy; how we can anticipate her wishes; how we can show our gratitude and love to her; how we can return her something of the debt she will have heaped upon us."

The younger sister had one hand in his; the other rested on her sister's neck. She looked into that sister's eyes, so calm, serene, and cheerful, with a gaze in which affection, admiration, sorrow, wonder, almost veneration, were blended. She looked into that sister's face, as if it were the face of some bright angel. Calm, serene, and cheerful, the face looked back on her and on her lover.

"And when the time comes, as it must one day," said Alfred,—"I wonder it has never come yet, but Grace knows best, for Grace is always right—when she will want a friend to open her whole heart to, and to be to her something of what she has been to us—then, Marion, how faithful we will prove, and what delight to us to know that she, our dear good sister, loves and is loved again, as we would have her!"

Still the younger sister looked into her eyes, and turned not—even towards him. And still those honest eyes looked back, so calm, serene, and cheerful, on herself and on her lover.

"And when all that is past, and we are old, and living (as we must!) together— close together—talking often of old times," said Alfred—"these shall be our favourite times among them—this day most of all; and, telling each other what we thought and felt, and hoped and feared at parting; and how we couldn't bear to say good bye—"

"Coach coming through the wood!" cried Britain.

"Yes! I am ready—and how we met again, so happily in spite of all; we'll make this day the happiest in all the year, and keep it as a treble birth-day. Shall we, dear?"

"Yes!" interposed the elder sister, eagerly, and with a radiant smile. "Yes! Alfred, don't linger. There's no time. Say good bye to Marion. And Heaven be with you!"

He pressed the younger sister to his heart. Released from his embrace, she again clung to her sister; and her eyes, with the same blended look, again sought those so calm, serene, and cheerful.

"Farewell, my boy!" said the Doctor. "To talk about any serious correspondence or serious affections, and engagements and so forth, in such a—ha ha ha!—you know what I mean—why that, of course, would be sheer nonsense. All I can say is, that if you and Marion should continue in the same foolish minds, I shall not object to have you for a son-in-law one of these days."

"Over the bridge!" cried Britain.

"Let it come!" said Alfred, wringing the Doctor's hand stoutly. "Think of me sometimes, my old friend and guardian, as seriously as you can! Adieu, Mr. Snitchey! Farewell, Mr. Craggs!"

"Coming down the road!" cried Britain.

"A kiss of Clemency Newcome for long acquaintance' sake! Shake hands, Britain! Marion, dearest heart, good bye! Sister Grace! remember!"

The quiet household figure, and the face so beautiful in its serenity, were turned towards him in reply; but Marion's look and attitude remained unchanged.

The coach was at the gate. There was a bustle with the luggage. The coach drove away. Marion never moved.

"He waves his hat to you, my love," said Grace. "Your chosen husband, darling. Look!"

The younger sister raised her head, and, for a moment, turned it. Then, turning back again, and fully meeting, for the first time, those calm eyes, fell sobbing on her neck.

"Oh, Grace. God bless you! But I cannot bear to see it, Grace! It breaks my heart."

CHAPTER II. PART THE SECOND

Snitchey and Craggs had a snug little office on the old Battle Ground, where they drove a snug little business, and fought a great many small pitched battles for a great many contending parties. Though it could hardly be said of these conflicts that they were running fights—for in truth they generally proceeded at a snail's pace—the part the Firm had in them came so far within the general denomination, that now they took a shot at this Plaintiff, and now aimed a chop at that Defendant, now made a heavy charge at an estate in Chancery, and now had some light skirmishing among an irregular body of small debtors, just as the occasion served, and the enemy happened to present himself. The Gazette was an important and profitable feature in some of their fields, as in fields of greater renown; and in most of the Actions wherein they showed their generalship, it was afterwards observed by the combatants that they had had great difficulty in making each other out, or in knowing with any degree of distinctness what they were about, in consequence of the vast amount of smoke by which they were surrounded.

The offices of Messrs. Snitchey and Craggs stood convenient, with an open door down two smooth steps, in the market-place; so that any angry farmer inclining towards hot water, might tumble into it at once. Their special council-chamber and hall of conference was an old back-room up-stairs, with a low dark ceiling, which seemed to be knitting its brows gloomily in the consideration of tangled points of law. It was furnished with some high-backed leathern chairs, garnished with great goggle-eyed brass nails, of which, every here and there, two or three had fallen out—or had been picked out, perhaps, by the wandering thumbs and forefingers of bewildered clients. There was a framed print of a great judge in it, every curl in whose dreadful wig had made a man's hair stand on end. Bales of papers filled the dusty closets, shelves, and tables; and round the wainscot there were tiers of boxes, padlocked and fireproof, with people's names painted outside, which anxious visitors felt themselves, by a cruel enchantment, obliged to spell backwards and forwards, and to make anagrams of, while they sat, seeming to listen to Snitchey and Craggs, without comprehending one word of what they said.

Snitchey and Craggs had each, in private life as in professional existence, a partner of his own. Snitchey and Craggs were the best friends in the world, and had a real confidence in one another; but Mrs. Snitchey, by a dispensation not uncommon in the affairs of life, was on principle suspicious of Mr. Craggs; and Mrs. Craggs was on principle suspicious of Mr. Snitchey. "Your Snitcheys indeed," the latter lady would observe, sometimes, to Mr. Craggs; using that imaginative plural as if in disparagement of an objectionable pair of pantaloons, or other articles not possessed of a singular number; "I don't see what you want with your Snitcheys, for my part. You trust a great deal too much to your Snitcheys, I think, and I hope you may never find my words come true." While Mrs. Snitchey would observe to Mr. Snitchey, of Craggs, "that if ever he was led away by man he was led away by that man, and that if ever she read a double purpose in a mortal eye, she read that purpose in Craggs's eye." Notwithstanding this, however, they were all very good friends in general: and Mrs. Snitchey and Mrs. Craggs maintained a close bond of alliance against "the office," which they both considered the Blue chamber, and common enemy, full of dangerous (because unknown) machinations.

In this office, nevertheless, Snitchey and Craggs made honey for their several hives. Here, sometimes, they would linger, of a fine evening, at the window of their council-chamber overlooking the old battle-ground, and wonder (but that was generally at assize time, when much business had made them sentimental) at the folly of mankind, who couldn't always be at peace with one another and go to law comfortably. Here, days, and weeks, and months, and years, passed over them: their calendar, the gradually diminishing number of brass nails in the leathern chairs, and the increasing bulk of papers on the tables. Here, nearly three years' flight had thinned the one and swelled the other, since the breakfast in the orchard; when they sat together in consultation at night.

Not alone; but, with a man of about thirty, or that time of life, negligently dressed, and somewhat haggard in the face, but well-made, well-attired, and well-looking, who sat in the armchair of state, with one hand in his breast, and the other in his dishevelled hair, pondering moodily. Messrs. Snitchey and Craggs sat opposite each other at a neighbouring desk. One of the fireproof boxes, unpadlocked and opened, was upon it; a part of its contents lay strewn upon the table, and the rest was then in course of passing through the hands of Mr. Snitchey; who brought it to the candle, document by document; looked at every paper singly, as he produced it; shook his head, and handed it to Mr. Craggs; who looked it over also, shook his head, and laid it down. Sometimes, they would stop, and shaking their heads in concert, look towards the abstracted client. And the name on the box being Michael Warden, Esquire, we may conclude from these premises that the name and the box were both his, and that the affairs of Michael Warden, Esquire, were in a bad way.

"That's all," said Mr. Snitchey, turning up the last paper. "Really there's no other resource. No other resource."

"All lost, spent, wasted, pawned, borrowed, and sold, eh?" said the client, looking up.

"All," returned Mr. Snitchey.

"Nothing else to be done, you say?"

"Nothing at all."

The client bit his nails, and pondered again.

"And I am not even personally safe in England? You hold to that, do you?"

"In no part of the United Kingdom of Great Britain and Ireland," replied Mr. Snitchey.

"A mere prodigal son with no father to go back to, no swine to keep, and no husks to share with them? Eh?" pursued the client, rocking one leg over the other, and searching the ground with his eyes.

Mr. Snitchey coughed, as if to deprecate the being supposed to participate in any figurative illustration of a legal position. Mr. Craggs, as if to express that it was a partnership view of the subject, also coughed.

"Ruined at thirty!" said the client. "Humph!"

"Not ruined, Mr. Warden," returned Snitchey. "Not so bad as that. You have done a good deal towards it, I must say, but you are not ruined. A little nursing—"

"A little Devil," said the client.

"Mr. Craggs," said Snitchey, "will you oblige me with a pinch of snuff? Thank you, sir."

As the imperturbable lawyer applied it to his nose with great apparent relish and a perfect absorption of his attention in the proceeding, the client gradually broke into a smile, and, looking up, said:

"You talk of nursing. How long nursing?"

"How long nursing?" repeated Snitchey, dusting the snuff from his fingers, and making a slow calculation in his mind. "For your involved estate, sir? In good hands? S. and C.'s, say? Six or seven years."

"To starve for six or seven years!" said the client with a fretful laugh, and an impatient change of his position.

"To starve for six or seven years, Mr. Warden," said Snitchey, "would be very uncommon indeed. You might get another estate by showing yourself, the while. But, we don't think you could do it—speaking for Self and Craggs—and consequently don't advise it."

"What do you advise?"

"Nursing, I say," repeated Snitchey. "Some few years of nursing by Self and Craggs would bring it round. But to enable us to make terms, and hold terms, and you to keep terms, you must go away; you must live abroad. As to starvation, we could ensure you some hundreds a-year to starve upon, even in the beginning—I dare say, Mr. Warden."

"Hundreds," said the client. "And I have spent thousands!"

"That," retorted Mr. Snitchey, putting the papers slowly back into the cast-iron box, "there is no doubt about. No doubt about," he repeated to himself, as he thoughtfully pursued his occupation.

The lawyer very likely knew his man; at any rate his dry, shrewd, whimsical manner, had a favourable influence on the client's moody state, and disposed him to be more free and unreserved. Or, perhaps the client knew his man, and had elicited such encouragement as he had received, to render some purpose he was about to disclose the more defensible in appearance. Gradually raising his head, he sat looking at his immovable adviser with a smile, which presently broke into a laugh.

"After all," he said, "my iron-headed friend—"

Mr. Snitchey pointed out his partner. "Self and—excuse me—Craggs."

"I beg Mr. Craggs's pardon," said the client. "After all, my iron-headed friends," he leaned forward in his chair, and dropped his voice a little, "you don't know half my ruin yet."

Mr. Snitchey stopped and stared at him. Mr. Craggs also stared.

"I am not only deep in debt," said the client, "but I am deep in—"

"Not in love!" cried Snitchey.

"Yes!" said the client, falling back in his chair, and surveying the Firm with his hands in his pockets. "Deep in love."

"And not with an heiress, sir?" said Snitchey.

"Not with an heiress."

"Nor a rich lady?"

"Nor a rich lady that I know of—except in beauty and merit."

"A single lady, I trust?" said Mr. Snitchey, with great expression.

"Certainly."

"It's not one of Dr. Jeddler's daughters?" said Snitchey, suddenly squaring his elbows on his knees, and advancing his face at least a yard.

"Yes!" returned the client.

"Not his younger daughter?" said Snitchey.

"Yes!" returned the client.

"Mr. Craggs," said Snitchey, much relieved, "will you oblige me with another pinch of snuff? Thank you! I am happy to say it don't signify, Mr. Warden; she's engaged, sir, she's bespoke. My partner can corroborate me. We know the fact."

"We know the fact," repeated Craggs.

"Why, so do I perhaps," returned the client quietly. "What of that! Are you men of the world, and did you never hear of a woman changing her mind?"

"There certainly have been actions for breach," said Mr. Snitchey, "brought against both spinsters and widows, but, in the majority of cases—"

"Cases!" interposed the client, impatiently. "Don't talk to me of cases. The general precedent is in a much larger volume than any of your law books. Besides, do you think I have lived six weeks in the Doctor's house for nothing?"

"I think, sir," observed Mr. Snitchey, gravely addressing himself to his partner, "that of all the scrapes Mr. Warden's horses have brought him into at one time and another—and they have been pretty numerous, and pretty expensive, as none know better than himself, and you, and I—the worst scrape may turn out to be, if he talks in this way, this having ever been left by one of them at the Doctor's garden wall, with three broken ribs, a snapped collar-bone, and the Lord knows how many bruises. We didn't think so much of it, at the time when we knew he was going on well under the Doctor's hands and roof; but it looks bad now, sir. Bad? It looks very bad. Doctor Jeddler too—our client, Mr. Craggs."

"Mr. Alfred Heathfield too—a sort of client, Mr. Snitchey," said Craggs.

"Mr. Michael Warden too, a kind of client," said the careless visitor, "and no bad one either: having played the fool for ten or twelve years. However, Mr. Michael Warden has sown his wild oats now—there's their crop, in that box; and he means to repent and be wise. And in proof of it, Mr. Michael Warden means, if he can, to marry Marion, the Doctor's lovely daughter, and to carry her away with him."

"Really, Mr. Craggs," Snitchey began.

"Really, Mr. Snitchey, and Mr. Craggs, partners both," said the client, interrupting him; "you know your duty to your clients, and you know well enough, I am sure, that it is no part of it to interfere in a mere love affair, which I am obliged to confide to you. I am not going to carry the young lady off, without her own consent. There's nothing illegal in it. I never was Mr. Heathfield's bosom friend. I violate no confidence of his. I love where he loves, and I mean to win where he would win, if I can."

"He can't, Mr. Craggs," said Snitchey, evidently anxious and discomfited. "He can't do it, sir. She dotes on Mr. Alfred."

"Does she?" returned the client.

"Mr. Craggs, she dotes on him, sir," persisted Snitchey.

"I didn't live six weeks, some few months ago, in the Doctor's house for nothing; and I doubted that soon," observed the client. "She would have doted on him, if her sister could have brought it about; but I watched them. Marion avoided his name, avoided the subject: shrunk from the least allusion to it, with evident distress."

"Why should she, Mr. Craggs, you know? Why should she, sir?" inquired Snitchey.

"I don't know why she should, though there are many likely reasons," said the client, smiling at the attention and perplexity expressed in Mr. Snitchey's shining eye, and at his cautious way of carrying on the conversation, and making himself informed upon the subject; "but I know she does. She was very young when she made the engagement—if it may be called one, I am not even sure of that—and has repented of it, perhaps. Perhaps—it seems a foppish thing to say, but upon my soul I don't mean it in that light—she may have fallen in love with me, as I have fallen in love with her."

"He, he! Mr. Alfred, her old playfellow too, you remember, Mr. Craggs," said Snitchey, with a disconcerted laugh; "knew her almost from a baby!"

"Which makes it the more probable that she may be tired of his idea," calmly pursued the client, "and not indisposed to exchange it for the newer one of another lover, who presents himself (or is presented by his horse) under romantic circumstances; has the not unfavourable reputation—with a country girl—of having lived thoughtlessly and gaily, without doing much harm to anybody; and who, for his youth and figure, and so forth—this may seem foppish again, but upon my soul I don't mean it in that light—might perhaps pass muster in a crowd with Mr. Alfred himself."

There was no gainsaying the last clause, certainly; and Mr. Snitchey, glancing at him, thought so. There was something naturally graceful and pleasant in the very carelessness of his air. It seemed to suggest, of his comely face and well-knit figure, that they might be greatly better if he chose: and that, once roused and made earnest (but he never had been earnest yet), he could be full of fire and purpose. "A dangerous sort of libertine," thought the shrewd lawyer, "to seem to catch the spark he wants, from a young lady's eyes."

"Now, observe, Snitchey," he continued, rising and taking him by the button, "and Craggs," taking him by the button also, and placing one partner on either side of him, so that neither might evade him. "I don't ask you for any advice. You are right to keep quite aloof from all parties in such a matter, which is not one in which grave men like you could interfere, on any side. I am briefly going to review in half-a-dozen words, my position and intention, and then I shall leave it to you to do the best for me, in money matters, that you can: seeing, that, if I run away with the Doctor's beautiful daughter (as I hope to do, and to become another man under her bright influence), it will be, for the moment, more chargeable than running away alone. But I shall soon make all that up in an altered life."

"I think it will be better not to hear this, Mr. Craggs?" said Snitchey, looking at him across the client.

THE BATTLE OF LIFE

"I think not," said Craggs.—Both listened attentively.

"Well! You needn't hear it," replied their client. "I'll mention it, however. I don't mean to ask the Doctor's consent, because he wouldn't give it me. But I mean to do the Doctor no wrong or harm, because (besides there being nothing serious in such trifles, as he says) I hope to rescue his child, my Marion, from what I see—I *know*—she dreads, and contemplates with misery: that is, the return of this old lover. If anything in the world is true, it is true that she dreads his return. Nobody is injured so far. I am so harried and worried here just now, that I lead the life of a flying-fish. I skulk about in the dark, I am shut out of my own house, and warned off my own grounds; but, that house, and those grounds, and many an acre besides, will come back to me one day, as you know and say; and Marion will probably be richer—on your showing, who are never sanguine—ten years hence as my wife, than as the wife of Alfred Heathfield, whose return she dreads (remember that), and in whom or in any man, my passion is not surpassed. Who is injured yet? It is a fair case throughout. My right is as good as his, if she decide in my favour; and I will try my right by her alone. You will like to know no more after this, and I will tell you no more. Now you know my purpose, and wants. When must I leave here?"

"In a week," said Snitchey. "Mr. Craggs?"

"In something less, I should say," responded Craggs.

"In a month," said the client, after attentively watching the two faces. "This day month. To-day is Thursday. Succeed or fail, on this day month I go."

"It's too long a delay," said Snitchey; "much too long. But let it be so. I thought he'd have stipulated for three," he murmured to himself. "Are you going? Good night, sir!"

"Good night!" returned the client, shaking hands with the Firm. "You'll live to see me making a good use of riches yet. Henceforth the star of my destiny is, Marion!"

"Take care of the stairs, sir," replied Snitchey; "for she don't shine there. Good night!"

"Good night!"

So they both stood at the stair-head with a pair of office-candles, watching him down. When he had gone away, they stood looking at each other.

"What do you think of all this, Mr. Craggs?" said Snitchey.

Mr. Craggs shook his head.

"It was our opinion, on the day when that release was executed, that there was something curious in the parting of that pair; I recollect," said Snitchey.

"It was," said Mr. Craggs.

"Perhaps he deceives himself altogether," pursued Mr. Snitchey, locking up the fireproof box, and putting it away; "or, if he don't, a little bit of fickleness and perfidy is not a miracle, Mr. Craggs. And yet I thought that pretty face was very true. I thought," said Mr. Snitchey, putting on his great-coat (for the weather was very cold), drawing on his gloves, and snuffing out one candle, "that I had even seen her character becoming stronger and more resolved of late. More like her sister's."

"Mrs. Craggs was of the same opinion," returned Craggs.

"I'd really give a trifle to-night," observed Mr. Snitchey, who was a good-natured man, "if I could believe that Mr. Warden was reckoning without his host; but, light-headed, capricious, and unballasted as he is, he knows something of the world and its people (he ought to, for he has bought what he does know, dear enough); and I can't quite think that. We had better not interfere: we can do nothing, Mr. Craggs, but keep quiet."

"Nothing," returned Craggs.

"Our friend the Doctor makes light of such things," said Mr. Snitchey, shaking his head. "I hope he mayn't stand in need of his philosophy. Our friend Alfred talks of the battle of life," he shook his head again, "I hope he mayn't be cut down early in the day. Have you got your hat, Mr. Craggs? I am going to put the other candle out." Mr. Craggs replying in the affirmative, Mr. Snitchey suited the action to the word, and they groped their way out of the council-chamber, now dark as the subject, or the law in general.

My story passes to a quiet little study, where, on that same night, the sisters and the hale old Doctor sat by a cheerful fireside. Grace was working at her needle. Marion read aloud from a book before her. The Doctor, in his dressing-gown and slippers, with his feet spread out upon the warm rug, leaned back in his easy-chair, and listened to the book, and looked upon his daughters.

They were very beautiful to look upon. Two better faces for a fireside, never made a fireside bright and sacred. Something of the difference between them had been softened down in three years' time; and enthroned upon the clear brow of the younger sister, looking through her eyes, and thrilling in her voice, was the same earnest nature that her own motherless youth had ripened in the elder sister long ago. But she still appeared at once the lovelier and weaker of the two; still seemed to rest her head upon her sister's breast, and put her trust in her, and look into her eyes for counsel and reliance. Those loving eyes, so calm, serene, and cheerful, as of old.

"'And being in her own home,'" read Marion, from the book; "'her home made exquisitely dear by these remembrances, she now began to know that the great trial of her heart must soon come on, and could not be delayed. O Home, our comforter and friend when others fall away, to part with whom, at any step between the cradle and the grave—'"

"Marion, my love!" said Grace.

"Why, Puss!" exclaimed her father, "what's the matter?"

She put her hand upon the hand her sister stretched towards her, and read on; her voice still faltering and trembling, though she made an effort to command it when thus interrupted.

" 'To part with whom, at any step between the cradle and the grave, is always sorrowful. O Home, so true to us, so often slighted in return, be lenient to them that turn away from thee, and do not haunt their erring footsteps too reproachfully! Let no kind looks, no well-remembered smiles, be seen upon thy phantom face. Let no ray of affection, welcome, gentleness, forbearance, cordiality, shine from thy white head. Let no old loving word, or tone, rise up in judgment against thy deserter; but if thou canst look harshly and severely, do, in mercy to the Penitent!' "

"Dear Marion, read no more to-night," said Grace for she was weeping.

"I cannot," she replied, and closed the book. "The words seem all on fire!"

The Doctor was amused at this; and laughed as he patted her on the head.

"What! overcome by a story-book!" said Doctor Jeddler. "Print and paper! Well, well, it's all one. It's as rational to make a serious matter of print and paper as of anything else. But, dry your eyes, love, dry your eyes. I dare say the heroine has got home again long ago, and made it up all round—and if she hasn't, a real home is only four walls; and a fictitious one, mere rags and ink. What's the matter now?"

"It's only me, Mister," said Clemency, putting in her head at the door.

"And what's the matter with you?" said the Doctor.

"Oh, bless you, nothing an't the matter with me," returned Clemency—and truly too, to judge from her well-soaped face, in which there gleamed as usual the very soul of good-humour, which, ungainly as she was, made her quite engaging. Abrasions on the elbows are not generally understood, it is true, to range within that class of personal charms called beauty-spots. But, it is better, going through the world, to have the arms chafed in that narrow passage, than the temper: and Clemency's was sound and whole as any beauty's in the land.

"Nothing an't the matter with me," said Clemency, entering, "but—come a little closer, Mister."

The Doctor, in some astonishment, complied with this invitation.

"You said I wasn't to give you one before them, you know," said Clemency.

A novice in the family might have supposed, from her extraordinary ogling as she said it, as well as from a singular rapture or ecstasy which pervaded her elbows, as if she were embracing herself, that "one," in its most favourable interpretation, meant a chaste salute. Indeed the Doctor himself seemed alarmed, for the moment; but quickly regained his composure, as Clemency, having had recourse to both her pockets—beginning with the right one, going away to the wrong one, and afterwards coming back to the right one again—produced a letter from the Post-office.

"Britain was riding by on a errand," she chuckled, handing it to the Doctor, "and see the mail come in, and waited for it. There's A. H. in the corner. Mr. Alfred's on his journey home, I bet. We shall have a wedding in the house—there was two spoons in my saucer this morning. Oh Luck, how slow he opens it!"

All this she delivered, by way of soliloquy, gradually rising higher and higher on tiptoe, in her impatience to hear the news, and making a corkscrew of her apron, and a bottle of her mouth. At last, arriving at a climax of suspense, and seeing the Doctor still engaged in the perusal of the letter, she came down flat upon the soles of her feet again, and cast her apron, as a veil, over her head, in a mute despair, and inability to bear it any longer.

"Here! Girls!" cried the Doctor. "I can't help it: I never could keep a secret in my life. There are not many secrets, indeed, worth being kept in such a—well! never mind that. Alfred's coming home, my dears, directly."

"Directly!" exclaimed Marion.

"What! The story-book is soon forgotten!" said the Doctor, pinching her cheek. "I thought the news would dry those tears. Yes. 'Let it be a surprise,' he says, here. But I can't let it be a surprise. He must have a welcome."

"Directly!" repeated Marion.

"Why, perhaps not what your impatience calls 'directly,'" returned the doctor; "but pretty soon too. Let us see. Let us see. To-day is Thursday, is it not? Then he promises to be here, this day month."

"This day month!" repeated Marion, softly.

"A gay day and a holiday for us," said the cheerful voice of her sister Grace, kissing her in congratulation. "Long looked forward to, dearest, and come at last."

She answered with a smile; a mournful smile, but full of sisterly affection. As she looked in her sister's face, and listened to the quiet music of her voice, picturing the happiness of this return, her own face glowed with hope and joy.

And with a something else; a something shining more and more through all the rest of its expression; for which I have no name. It was not exultation, triumph, proud enthusiasm. They are not so calmly shown. It was not love and gratitude alone, though love and gratitude were part of it. It emanated from no sordid thought, for sordid thoughts do not light up the brow, and hover on the lips, and move the spirit like a fluttered light, until the sympathetic figure trembles.

Dr. Jeddler, in spite of his system of philosophy—which he was continually contradicting and denying in practice, but more famous philosophers have done that—could not help having as much interest in the return of his old ward and pupil as if it had been a serious event. So he sat himself down in his easy-chair again, stretched out his slippered feet once more upon the rug, read the letter over and over a great many times, and talked it over more times still.

"Ah! The day was," said the Doctor, looking at the fire, "when you and he, Grace, used to trot about arm-in-arm, in his holiday time, like a couple of walking dolls. You remember?"

"I remember," she answered, with her pleasant laugh, and plying her needle busily.

"This day month, indeed!" mused the Doctor. "That hardly seems a twelve month ago. And where was my little Marion then!"

"Never far from her sister," said Marion, cheerily, "however little. Grace was everything to me, even when she was a young child herself."

"True, Puss, true," returned the Doctor. "She was a staid little woman, was Grace, and a wise housekeeper, and a busy, quiet, pleasant body; bearing with our humours and anticipating our wishes, and always ready to forget her own, even in those times. I never knew you positive or obstinate, Grace, my darling, even then, on any subject but one."

"I am afraid I have changed sadly for the worse, since," laughed Grace, still busy at her work. "What was that one, father?"

"Alfred, of course," said the Doctor. "Nothing would serve you but you must be called Alfred's wife; so we called you Alfred's wife; and you liked it better, I believe (odd as it seems now), than being called a Duchess, if we could have made you one."

"Indeed?" said Grace, placidly.

"Why, don't you remember?" inquired the Doctor.

"I think I remember something of it," she returned, "but not much. It's so long ago." And as she sat at work, she hummed the burden of an old song, which the Doctor liked.

"Alfred will find a real wife soon," she said, breaking off; "and that will be a happy time indeed for all of us. My three years' trust is nearly at an end, Marion. It has been a very easy one. I shall tell Alfred, when I give you back to him, that you have loved him dearly all the time, and that he has never once needed my good services. May I tell him so, love?"

"Tell him, dear Grace," replied Marion, "that there never was a trust so generously, nobly, steadfastly discharged; and that I have loved you, all the time, dearer and dearer every day; and O! how dearly now!"

"Nay," said her cheerful sister, returning her embrace, "I can scarcely tell him that; we will leave my deserts to Alfred's imagination. It will be liberal enough, dear Marion; like your own."

With that, she resumed the work she had for a moment laid down, when her sister spoke so fervently: and with it the old song the Doctor liked to hear. And the Doctor, still reposing in his easy-chair, with his slippered feet stretched out before him on the rug, listened to the tune, and beat time on his knee with Alfred's letter, and looked at his two daughters, and thought that among the many trifles of the trifling world, these trifles were agreeable enough.

Clemency Newcome, in the meantime, having accomplished her mission and lingered in the room until she had made herself a party to the news, descended to the kitchen, where her coadjutor, Mr. Britain, was regaling after supper, surrounded by such a plentiful collection of bright pot-lids, well-scoured saucepans, burnished dinner-covers, gleaming kettles, and other tokens of her industrious habits, arranged upon the walls and shelves, that he sat as in the centre of a hall of mirrors. The majority did not give forth very flattering portraits of him, certainly; nor were they by any means unanimous in their reflections; as some made him very long-faced, others very broad-faced, some tolerably well-looking, others vastly ill-looking, according to their several manners of reflecting: which were as various, in respect of one fact, as those of so many kinds of men. But they all agreed that in the midst of them sat, quite at his ease, an individual with a pipe in his mouth, and a jug of beer at his elbow, who nodded condescendingly to Clemency, when she stationed herself at the same table.

"Well, Clemmy," said Britain, "how are you by this time, and what's the news?"

Clemency told him the news, which he received very graciously. A gracious change had come over Benjamin from head to foot. He was much broader, much redder, much more cheerful, and much jollier in all respects. It seemed as if his face had been tied up in a knot before, and was now untwisted and smoothed out.

"There'll be another job for Snitchey and Craggs, I suppose," he observed, puffing slowly at his pipe. "More witnessing for you and me, perhaps, Clemmy!"

"Lor!" replied his fair companion, with her favourite twist of her favourite joints. "I wish it was me, Britain!"

"Wish what was you?"

"A-going to be married," said Clemency.

Benjamin took his pipe out of his mouth and laughed heartily. "Yes! you're a likely subject for that!" he said. "Poor Clem!" Clemency for her part laughed as heartily as he, and seemed as much amused by the idea. "Yes," she assented, "I'm a likely subject for that; an't I?"

"You'll never be married, you know," said Mr. Britain, resuming his pipe.

"Don't you think I ever shall though?" said Clemency, in perfect good faith. Mr. Britain shook his head. "Not a chance of it!"

"Only think!" said Clemency. "Well!—I suppose you mean to, Britain, one of these days; don't you?"

A question so abrupt, upon a subject so momentous, required consideration. After blowing out a great cloud of smoke, and looking at it with his head now on this side and now on that, as if it were actually the question, and he were surveying it in various aspects, Mr. Britain replied that he wasn't altogether clear about it, but—ye-es—he thought he might come to that at last.

"I wish her joy, whoever she may be!" cried Clemency.

"Oh she'll have that," said Benjamin, "safe enough."

"But she wouldn't have led quite such a joyful life as she will lead, and wouldn't have had quite such a sociable sort of husband as she will have," said Clemency, spreading herself half over the table, and staring retrospectively at the candle, "if it hadn't been for—not that I went to do it, for it was accidental, I am sure—if it hadn't been for me; now would she, Britain?"

"Certainly not," returned Mr. Britain, by this time in that high state of appreciation of his pipe, when a man can open his mouth but a very little way for speaking purposes; and sitting luxuriously immovable in his chair, can afford to turn only his eyes towards a companion, and that very passively and gravely. "Oh! I'm greatly beholden to you, you know, Clem."

"Lor, how nice that is to think of!" said Clemency.

At the same time, bringing her thoughts as well as her sight to bear upon the candle-grease, and becoming abruptly reminiscent of its healing qualities as a balsam, she anointed her left elbow with a plentiful application of that remedy.

"You see I've made a good many investigations of one sort and another in my time," pursued Mr. Britain, with the profundity of a sage, "having been always of an inquiring turn of mind; and I've read a good many books about the general Rights of things and Wrongs of things, for I went into the literary line myself, when I began life."

"Did you though!" cried the admiring Clemency.

"Yes," said Mr. Britain: "I was hid for the best part of two years behind a bookstall, ready to fly out if anybody pocketed a volume; and after that, I was light porter to a stay and mantua maker, in which capacity I was employed to carry about, in oilskin baskets, nothing but deceptions—which soured my spirits and disturbed my confidence in human nature; and after that, I heard a world of discussions in this house, which soured my spirits fresh; and my opinion after all is, that, as a safe and comfortable sweetener of the same, and as a pleasant guide through life, there's nothing like a nutmeg-grater."

Clemency was about to offer a suggestion, but he stopped her by anticipating it. "Com-bined," he added gravely, "with a thimble."

"Do as you wold, you know, and cetrer, eh!" observed Clemency, folding her arms comfortably in her delight at this avowal, and patting her elbows. "Such a short cut, an't it?"

"I'm not sure," said Mr. Britain, "that it's what would be considered good philosophy. I've my doubts about that; but it wears well, and saves a quantity of snarling, which the genuine article don't always."

"See how you used to go on once, yourself, you know!" said Clemency.

"Ah!" said Mr. Britain. "But the most extraordinary thing, Clemmy, is that I should live to be brought round, through you. That's the strange part of it. Through you! Why, I suppose you haven't so much as half an idea in your head."

Clemency, without taking the least offence, shook it, and laughed and hugged herself, and said, "No, she didn't suppose she had."

"I'm pretty sure of it," said Mr. Britain.

"Oh! I dare say you're right," said Clemency. "I don't pretend to none. I don't want any."

Benjamin took his pipe from his lips, and laughed till the tears ran down his face. "What a natural you are, Clemmy!" he said, shaking his head, with an infinite relish of the joke, and wiping his eyes. Clemency, without the smallest inclination to dispute it, did the like, and laughed as heartily as he.

"I can't help liking you," said Mr. Britain; "you're a regular good creature in your way, so shake hands, Clem. Whatever happens, I'll always take notice of you, and be a friend to you."

"Will you?" returned Clemency. "Well! that's very good of you."

"Yes, yes," said Mr. Britain, giving her his pipe to knock the ashes out of it; "I'll stand by you. Hark! That's a curious noise!"

"Noise!" repeated Clemency.

"A footstep outside. Somebody dropping from the wall, it sounded like," said Britain. "Are they all abed up-stairs?"

"Yes, all abed by this time," she replied.

"Didn't you hear anything?"

"No."

They both listened, but heard nothing.

"I tell you what," said Benjamin, taking down a lantern. "I'll have a look round, before I go to bed myself, for satisfaction's sake. Undo the door while I light this, Clemmy."

Clemency complied briskly; but observed as she did so, that he would only have his walk for his pains, that it was all his fancy, and so forth. Mr. Britain said "very likely"; but sallied out, nevertheless, armed with the poker, and casting the light of the lantern far and near in all directions.

"It's as quiet as a churchyard," said Clemency, looking after him; "and almost as ghostly too!"

Glancing back into the kitchen, she cried fearfully, as a light figure stole into her view, "What's that!"

"Hush!" said Marion in an agitated whisper. "You have always loved me, have you not!"

"Loved you, child! You may be sure I have."

"I am sure. And I may trust you, may I not? There is no one else just now, in whom I can trust."

"Yes," said Clemency, with all her heart.

"There is some one out there," pointing to the door, "whom I must see, and speak with, to-night. Michael Warden, for God's sake retire! Not now!"

Clemency started with surprise and trouble as, following the direction of the speaker's eyes, she saw a dark figure standing in the doorway.

"In another moment you may be discovered," said Marion. "Not now! Wait, if you can, in some concealment. I will come presently."

He waved his hand to her, and was gone. "Don't go to bed. Wait here for me!" said Marion, hurriedly. "I have been seeking to speak to you for an hour past. Oh, be true to me!"

Eagerly seizing her bewildered hand, and pressing it with both her own to her breast—an action more expressive, in its passion of entreaty, than the most eloquent appeal in words,—Marion withdrew; as the light of the returning lantern flashed into the room.

"All still and peaceable. Nobody there. Fancy, I suppose," said Mr. Britain, as he locked and barred the door. "One of the effects of having a lively imagination. Halloa! Why, what's the matter?"

Clemency, who could not conceal the effects of her surprise and concern, was sitting in a chair: pale, and trembling from head to foot.

"Matter!" she repeated, chafing her hands and elbows, nervously, and looking anywhere but at him. "That's good in you, Britain, that is! After going and frightening one out of one's life with noises and lanterns, and I don't know what all. Matter! Oh, yes!"

"If you're frightened out of your life by a lantern, Clemmy," said Mr. Britain, composedly blowing it out and hanging it up again, "that apparition's very soon got rid of. But you're as bold as brass in general," he said, stopping to observe her; "and were, after the noise and the lantern too. What have you taken into your head? Not an idea, eh?"

But, as Clemency bade him good night very much after her usual fashion, and began to bustle about with a show of going to bed herself immediately, Little Britain, after giving utterance to the original remark that it was impossible to account for a woman's whims, bade her good night in return, and taking up his candle strolled drowsily away to bed.

When all was quiet, Marion returned.

"Open the door," she said; "and stand there close beside me, while I speak to him, outside."

Timid as her manner was, it still evinced a resolute and settled purpose, such as Clemency could not resist. She softly unbarred the door: but before turning the key, looked round on the young creature waiting to issue forth when she should open it.

The face was not averted or cast down, but looking full upon her, in its pride of youth and beauty. Some simple sense of the slightness of the barrier that interposed itself between the happy home and honoured love of the fair girl, and what might be the desolation of that home, and shipwreck of its dearest treasure, smote so keenly on the tender heart of Clemency, and so filled it to overflowing with sorrow and compassion, that, bursting into tears, she threw her arms round Marion's neck.

"It's little that I know, my dear," cried Clemency, "very little; but I know that this should not be. Think of what you do!"

"I have thought of it many times," said Marion, gently.

"Once more," urged Clemency. "Till to-morrow." Marion shook her head.

"For Mr. Alfred's sake," said Clemency, with homely earnestness. "Him that you used to love so dearly, once!"

She hid her face, upon the instant, in her hands, repeating "Once!" as if it rent her heart.

"Let me go out," said Clemency, soothing her. "I'll tell him what you like. Don't cross the door-step to-night. I'm sure no good will come of it. Oh, it was an unhappy day when Mr. Warden was ever brought here! Think of your good father, darling—of your sister."

"I have," said Marion, hastily raising her head. "You don't know what I do. I must speak to him. You are the best and truest friend in all the world for what you have said to me, but I must take this step. Will you go with me, Clemency," she kissed her on her friendly face, "or shall I go alone?"

Sorrowing and wondering, Clemency turned the key, and opened the door. Into the dark and doubtful night that lay beyond the threshold, Marion passed quickly, holding by her hand.

In the dark night he joined her, and they spoke together earnestly and long;

and the hand that held so fast by Clemency's, now trembled, now turned deadly cold, now clasped and closed on hers, in the strong feeling of the speech it emphasised unconsciously. When they returned, he followed to the door, and pausing there a moment, seized the other hand, and pressed it to his lips. Then, stealthily withdrew.

The door was barred and locked again, and once again she stood beneath her father's roof. Not bowed down by the secret that she brought there, though so young; but, with that same expression on her face for which I had no name before, and shining through her tears.

Again she thanked and thanked her humble friend, and trusted to her, as she said, with confidence, implicitly. Her chamber safely reached, she fell upon her knees; and with her secret weighing on her heart, could pray!

Could rise up from her prayers, so tranquil and serene, and bending over her fond sister in her slumber, look upon her face and smile—though sadly: murmuring as she kissed her forehead, how that Grace had been a mother to her, ever, and she loved her as a child!

Could draw the passive arm about her neck when lying down to rest—it seemed to cling there, of its own will, protectingly and tenderly even in sleep— and breathe upon the parted lips, God bless her!

Could sink into a peaceful sleep, herself; but for one dream, in which she cried out, in her innocent and touching voice, that she was quite alone, and they had all forgotten her.

A month soon passes, even at its tardiest pace. The month appointed to elapse between that night and the return, was quick of foot, and went by, like a vapour.

The day arrived. A raging winter day, that shook the old house, sometimes, as if it shivered in the blast. A day to make home doubly home. To give the chimney-corner new delights. To shed a ruddier glow upon the faces gathered round the hearth, and draw each fireside group into a closer and more social league, against the roaring elements without. Such a wild winter day as best prepares the way for shut-out night; for curtained rooms, and cheerful looks; for music, laughter, dancing, light, and jovial entertainment!

All these the Doctor had in store to welcome Alfred back. They knew that he could not arrive till night; and they would make the night air ring, he said, as he approached. All his old friends should congregate about him. He should not miss a face that he had known and liked. No! They should every one be there!

So, guests were bidden, and musicians were engaged, and tables spread, and floors prepared for active feet, and bountiful provision made, of every hospitable kind. Because it was the Christmas season, and his eyes were all unused to English holly and its sturdy green, the dancing-room was garlanded and hung with it;

and the red berries gleamed an English welcome to him, peeping from among the leaves.

It was a busy day for all of them: a busier day for none of them than Grace, who noiselessly presided everywhere, and was the cheerful mind of all the preparations. Many a time that day (as well as many a time within the fleeting month preceding it), did Clemency glance anxiously, and almost fearfully, at Marion. She saw her paler, perhaps, than usual; but there was a sweet composure on her face that made it lovelier than ever.

At night when she was dressed, and wore upon her head a wreath that Grace had proudly twined about it—its mimic flowers were Alfred's favourites, as Grace remembered when she chose them—that old expression, pensive, almost sorrowful, and yet so spiritual, high, and stirring, sat again upon her brow, enhanced a hundred-fold.

"The next wreath I adjust on this fair head, will be a marriage wreath," said Grace; "or I am no true prophet, dear."

Her sister smiled, and held her in her arms.

"A moment, Grace. Don't leave me yet. Are you sure that I want nothing more?"

Her care was not for that. It was her sister's face she thought of, and her eyes were fixed upon it, tenderly.

"My art," said Grace, "can go no farther, dear girl; nor your beauty. I never saw you look so beautiful as now."

"I never was so happy," she returned.

"Ay, but there is a greater happiness in store. In such another home, as cheerful and as bright as this looks now," said Grace, "Alfred and his young wife will soon be living."

She smiled again. "It is a happy home, Grace, in your fancy. I can see it in your eyes. I know it will be happy, dear. How glad I am to know it."

"Well," cried the Doctor, bustling in. "Here we are, all ready for Alfred, eh? He can't be here until pretty late—an hour or so before midnight—so there'll be plenty of time for making merry before he comes. He'll not find us with the ice unbroken. Pile up the fire here, Britain! Let it shine upon the holly till it winks again. It's a world of nonsense, Puss; true lovers and all the rest of it—all nonsense; but we'll be nonsensical with the rest of 'em, and give our true lover a mad welcome. Upon my word!" said the old Doctor, looking at his daughters proudly, "I'm not clear to-night, among other absurdities, but that I'm the father of two handsome girls."

"All that one of them has ever done, or may do—may do, dearest father—to cause you pain or grief, forgive her," said Marion, "forgive her now, when her heart is full. Say that you forgive her. That you will forgive her. That she shall

THE BATTLE OF LIFE

always share your love, and—," and the rest was not said, for her face was hidden on the old man's shoulder.

"Tut, tut, tut," said the Doctor gently. "Forgive! What have I to forgive? Heyday, if our true lovers come back to flurry us like this, we must hold 'em at a distance; we must send expresses out to stop 'em short upon the road, and bring 'em on a mile or two a day, until we're properly prepared to meet 'em. Kiss me, Puss. Forgive! Why, what a silly child you are! If you had vexed and crossed me fifty times a day, instead of not at all, I'd forgive you everything, but such a supplication. Kiss me again, Puss. There! Prospective and retrospective—a clear score between us. Pile up the fire here! Would you freeze the people on this bleak December night! Let us be light, and warm, and merry, or I'll not forgive some of you!"

So gaily the old Doctor carried it! And the fire was piled up, and the lights were bright, and company arrived, and a murmuring of lively tongues began, and already there was a pleasant air of cheerful excitement stirring through all the house.

More and more company came flocking in. Bright eyes sparkled upon Marion; smiling lips gave her joy of his return; sage mothers fanned themselves, and hoped she mightn't be too youthful and inconstant for the quiet round of home; impetuous fathers fell into disgrace for too much exaltation of her beauty; daughters envied her; sons envied him; innumerable pairs of lovers profited by the occasion; all were interested, animated, and expectant.

Mr. and Mrs. Craggs came arm in arm, but Mrs. Snitchey came alone. "Why, what's become of him?" inquired the Doctor.

The feather of a Bird of Paradise in Mrs. Snitchey's turban, trembled as if the Bird of Paradise were alive again, when she said that doubtless Mr. Craggs knew. She was never told.

"That nasty office," said Mrs. Craggs.

"I wish it was burnt down," said Mrs. Snitchey.

"He's—he's—there's a little matter of business that keeps my partner rather late," said Mr. Craggs, looking uneasily about him.

"Oh-h! Business. Don't tell me!" said Mrs. Snitchey.

"We know what business means," said Mrs. Craggs.

But their not knowing what it meant, was perhaps the reason why Mrs. Snitchey's Bird of Paradise feather quivered so portentously, and why all the pendant bits on Mrs. Craggs's ear-rings shook like little bells.

"I wonder you could come away, Mr. Craggs," said his wife.

"Mr. Craggs is fortunate, I'm sure!" said Mrs. Snitchey.

"That office so engrosses 'em," said Mrs. Craggs.

"A person with an office has no business to be married at all," said Mrs. Snitchey.

Then, Mrs. Snitchey said, within herself, that that look of hers had pierced to Craggs's soul, and he knew it; and Mrs. Craggs observed to Craggs, that "his Snitcheys" were deceiving him behind his back, and he would find it out when it was too late.

Still, Mr. Craggs, without much heeding these remarks, looked uneasily about until his eye rested on Grace, to whom he immediately presented himself.

"Good evening, ma'am," said Craggs. "You look charmingly. Your—Miss—your sister, Miss Marion, is she—"

"Oh, she's quite well, Mr. Craggs."

"Yes—I—is she here?" asked Craggs.

"Here! Don't you see her yonder? Going to dance?" said Grace.

Mr. Craggs put on his spectacles to see the better; looked at her through them, for some time; coughed; and put them, with an air of satisfaction, in their sheath again, and in his pocket.

Now the music struck up, and the dance commenced. The bright fire crackled and sparkled, rose and fell, as though it joined the dance itself, in right good fellowship. Sometimes, it roared as if it would make music too. Sometimes, it flashed and beamed as if it were the eye of the old room: it winked too, sometimes, like a knowing patriarch, upon the youthful whisperers in corners. Sometimes, it sported with the holly-boughs; and, shining on the leaves by fits and starts, made them look as if they were in the cold winter night again, and fluttering in the wind. Sometimes its genial humour grew obstreperous, and passed all bounds; and then it cast into the room, among the twinkling feet, with a loud burst, a shower of harmless little sparks, and in its exultation leaped and bounded, like a mad thing, up the broad old chimney.

Another dance was near its close, when Mr. Snitchey touched his partner, who was looking on, upon the arm.

Mr. Craggs started, as if his familiar had been a spectre.

"Is he gone?" he asked.

"Hush! He has been with me," said Snitchey, "for three hours and more. He went over everything. He looked into all our arrangements for him, and was very particular indeed. He—Humph!"

The dance was finished. Marion passed close before him, as he spoke. She did not observe him, or his partner; but, looked over her shoulder towards her sister in the distance, as she slowly made her way into the crowd, and passed out of their view.

"You see! All safe and well," said Mr. Craggs. "He didn't recur to that subject, I suppose?"

"Not a word."

"And is he really gone? Is he safe away?"

"He keeps to his word. He drops down the river with the tide in that shell of a boat of his, and so goes out to sea on this dark night!—a dare-devil he is—before the wind. There's no such lonely road anywhere else. That's one thing. The tide flows, he says, an hour before midnight—about this time. I'm glad it's over." Mr. Snitchey wiped his forehead, which looked hot and anxious.

"What do you think," said Mr. Craggs, "about—"

"Hush!" replied his cautious partner, looking straight before him. "I understand you. Don't mention names, and don't let us, seem to be talking secrets. I don't know what to think; and to tell you the truth, I don't care now. It's a great relief. His self-love deceived him, I suppose. Perhaps the young lady coquetted a little. The evidence would seem to point that way. Alfred not arrived?"

"Not yet," said Mr. Craggs. "Expected every minute."

"Good." Mr. Snitchey wiped his forehead again. "It's a great relief. I haven't been so nervous since we've been in partnership. I intend to spend the evening now, Mr. Craggs."

Mrs. Craggs and Mrs. Snitchey joined them as he announced this intention. The Bird of Paradise was in a state of extreme vibration, and the little bells were ringing quite audibly.

"It has been the theme of general comment, Mr. Snitchey," said Mrs. Snitchey. "I hope the office is satisfied."

"Satisfied with what, my dear?" asked Mr. Snitchey.

"With the exposure of a defenceless woman to ridicule and remark," returned his wife. "That is quite in the way of the office, that is."

"I really, myself," said Mrs. Craggs, "have been so long accustomed to connect the office with everything opposed to domesticity, that I am glad to know it as the avowed enemy of my peace. There is something honest in that, at all events."

"My dear," urged Mr. Craggs, "your good opinion is invaluable, but I never avowed that the office was the enemy of your peace."

"No," said Mrs. Craggs, ringing a perfect peal upon the little bells. "Not you, indeed. You wouldn't be worthy of the office, if you had the candour to."

"As to my having been away to-night, my dear," said Mr. Snitchey, giving her his arm, "the deprivation has been mine, I'm sure; but, as Mr. Craggs knows—"

Mrs. Snitchey cut this reference very short by hitching her husband to a distance, and asking him to look at that man. To do her the favour to look at him!

"At which man, my dear?" said Mr. Snitchey.

"Your chosen companion; I'm no companion to you, Mr. Snitchey."

"Yes, yes, you are, my dear," he interposed.

"No, no, I'm not," said Mrs. Snitchey with a majestic smile. "I know my station. Will you look at your chosen companion, Mr. Snitchey; at your referee, at the keeper of your secrets, at the man you trust; at your other self, in short?"

The habitual association of Self with Craggs, occasioned Mr. Snitchey to look in that direction.

"If you can look that man in the eye this night," said Mrs. Snitchey, "and not know that you are deluded, practised upon, made the victim of his arts, and bent down prostrate to his will by some unaccountable fascination which it is impossible to explain and against which no warning of mine is of the least avail, all I can say is—I pity you!"

At the very same moment Mrs. Craggs was oracular on the cross subject. Was it possible, she said, that Craggs could so blind himself to his Snitcheys, as not to feel his true position? Did he mean to say that he had seen his Snitcheys come into that room, and didn't plainly see that there was reservation, cunning, treachery, in the man? Would he tell her that his very action, when he wiped his forehead and looked so stealthily about him, didn't show that there was something weighing on the conscience of his precious Snitcheys (if he had a conscience), that wouldn't bear the light? Did anybody but his Snitcheys come to festive entertainments like a burglar?—which, by the way, was hardly a clear illustration of the case, as he had walked in very mildly at the door. And would he still assert to her at noonday (it being nearly midnight), that his Snitcheys were to be justified through thick and thin, against all facts, and reason, and experience?

Neither Snitchey nor Craggs openly attempted to stem the current which had thus set in, but, both were content to be carried gently along it, until its force abated. This happened at about the same time as a general movement for a country dance; when Mr. Snitchey proposed himself as a partner to Mrs. Craggs, and Mr. Craggs gallantly offered himself to Mrs. Snitchey; and after some such slight evasions as "why don't you ask somebody else?" and "you'll be glad, I know, if I decline," and "I wonder you can dance out of the office" (but this jocosely now), each lady graciously accepted, and took her place.

It was an old custom among them, indeed, to do so, and to pair off, in like manner, at dinners and suppers; for they were excellent friends, and on a footing of easy familiarity. Perhaps the false Craggs and the wicked Snitchey were a recognised fiction with the two wives, as Doe and Roe, incessantly running up and down bailiwicks, were with the two husbands: or, perhaps the ladies had instituted, and taken upon themselves, these two shares in the business, rather than be left out of it altogether. But, certain it is, that each wife went as gravely and steadily to work in her vocation as her husband did in his, and would have considered it almost impossible for the Firm to maintain a successful and respectable existence, without her laudable exertions.

But, now, the Bird of Paradise was seen to flutter down the middle; and the little bells began to bounce and jingle in poussette; and the Doctor's rosy face spun round and round, like an expressive pegtop highly varnished; and breathless Mr. Craggs began to doubt already, whether country dancing had been made "too easy," like the rest of life; and Mr. Snitchey, with his nimble cuts and capers, footed it for Self and Craggs, and half-a-dozen more.

Now, too, the fire took fresh courage, favoured by the lively wind the dance awakened, and burnt clear and high. It was the Genius of the room, and present everywhere. It shone in people's eyes, it sparkled in the jewels on the snowy necks of girls, it twinkled at their ears as if it whispered to them slyly, it flashed about their waists, it flickered on the ground and made it rosy for their feet, it bloomed upon the ceiling that its glow might set off their bright faces, and it kindled up a general illumination in Mrs. Craggs's little belfry.

Now, too, the lively air that fanned it, grew less gentle as the music quickened and the dance proceeded with new spirit; and a breeze arose that made the leaves and berries dance upon the wall, as they had often done upon the trees; and the breeze rustled in the room as if an invisible company of fairies, treading in the foot-steps of the good substantial revellers, were whirling after them. Now, too, no feature of the Doctor's face could be distinguished as he spun and spun; and now there seemed a dozen Birds of Paradise in fitful flight; and now there were a thousand little bells at work; and now a fleet of flying skirts was ruffled by a little tempest, when the music gave in, and the dance was over.

Hot and breathless as the Doctor was, it only made him the more impatient for Alfred's coming.

"Anything been seen, Britain? Anything been heard?"

"Too dark to see far, sir. Too much noise inside the house to hear."

"That's right! The gayer welcome for him. How goes the time?"

"Just twelve, sir. He can't be long, sir."

"Stir up the fire, and throw another log upon it," said the Doctor. "Let him see his welcome blazing out upon the night—good boy!—as he comes along!"

He saw it—Yes! From the chaise he caught the light, as he turned the corner by the old church. He knew the room from which it shone. He saw the wintry branches of the old trees between the light and him. He knew that one of those trees rustled musically in the summer time at the window of Marion's chamber.

The tears were in his eyes. His heart throbbed so violently that he could hardly bear his happiness. How often he had thought of this time—pictured it under all circumstances—feared that it might never come—yearned, and wearied for it—far away!

Again the light! Distinct and ruddy; kindled, he knew, to give him welcome, and to speed him home. He beckoned with his hand, and waved his hat, and cheered out, loud, as if the light were they, and they could see and hear him, as he dashed towards them through the mud and mire, triumphantly.

Stop! He knew the Doctor, and understood what he had done. He would not let it be a surprise to them. But he could make it one, yet, by going forward on foot. If the orchard-gate were open, he could enter there; if not, the wall was easily climbed, as he knew of old; and he would be among them in an instant.

He dismounted from the chaise, and telling the driver—even that was not easy in his agitation—to remain behind for a few minutes, and then to follow slowly, ran on with exceeding swiftness, tried the gate, scaled the wall, jumped down on the other side, and stood panting in the old orchard.

There was a frosty rime upon the trees, which, in the faint light of the clouded moon, hung upon the smaller branches like dead garlands. Withered leaves crackled and snapped beneath his feet, as he crept softly on towards the house. The desolation of a winter night sat brooding on the earth, and in the sky. But, the red light came cheerily towards him from the windows; figures passed and repassed there; and the hum and murmur of voices greeted his ear sweetly.

Listening for hers: attempting, as he crept on, to detach it from the rest, and half believing that he heard it: he had nearly reached the door, when it was abruptly opened, and a figure coming out encountered his. It instantly recoiled with a half-suppressed cry.

"Clemency," he said, "don't you know me?"

"Don't come in!" she answered, pushing him back. "Go away. Don't ask me why. Don't come in."

"What is the matter?" he exclaimed.

"I don't know. I—I am afraid to think. Go back. Hark!"

There was a sudden tumult in the house. She put her hands upon her ears. A wild scream, such as no hands could shut out, was heard; and Grace—distraction in her looks and manner—rushed out at the door.

"Grace!" He caught her in his arms. "What is it! Is she dead!"

She disengaged herself, as if to recognise his face, and fell down at his feet.

A crowd of figures came about them from the house. Among them was her father, with a paper in his hand.

"What is it!" cried Alfred, grasping his hair with his hands, and looking in an agony from face to face, as he bent upon his knee beside the insensible girl. "Will no one look at me? Will no one speak to me? Does no one know me? Is there no voice among you all, to tell me what it is!"

There was a murmur among them. "She is gone."

"Gone!" he echoed.

"Fled, my dear Alfred!" said the Doctor, in a broken voice, and with his hands before his face. "Gone from her home and us. To-night! She writes that she has made her innocent and blameless choice—entreats that we will forgive her— prays that we will not forget her—and is gone."

"With whom? Where?"

He started up, as if to follow in pursuit; but, when they gave way to let him pass, looked wildly round upon them, staggered back, and sunk down in his former attitude, clasping one of Grace's cold hands in his own.

There was a hurried running to and fro, confusion, noise, disorder, and no purpose. Some proceeded to disperse themselves about the roads, and some took horse, and some got lights, and some conversed together, urging that there was no trace or track to follow. Some approached him kindly, with the view of offering consolation; some admonished him that Grace must be removed into the house, and that he prevented it. He never heard them, and he never moved.

The snow fell fast and thick. He looked up for a moment in the air, and thought that those white ashes strewn upon his hopes and misery, were suited to them well. He looked round on the whitening ground, and thought how Marion's foot-prints would be hushed and covered up, as soon as made, and even that remembrance of her blotted out. But he never felt the weather and he never stirred.

CHAPTER III. PART THE THIRD

The world had grown six years older since that night of the return. It was a warm autumn afternoon, and there had been heavy rain. The sun burst suddenly from among the clouds; and the old battle-ground, sparkling brilliantly and cheerfully at sight of it in one green place, flashed a responsive welcome there, which spread along the country side as if a joyful beacon had been lighted up, and answered from a thousand stations.

How beautiful the landscape kindling in the light, and that luxuriant influence passing on like a celestial presence, brightening everything! The wood, a sombre mass before, revealed its varied tints of yellow, green, brown, red: its different forms of trees, with raindrops glittering on their leaves and twinkling as they fell. The verdant meadow-land, bright and glowing, seemed as if it had been blind, a minute since, and now had found a sense of sight where-with to look up at the shining sky. Corn-fields, hedge-rows, fences, homesteads, and clustered roofs, the steeple of the church, the stream, the water-mill, all sprang out of the gloomy darkness smiling. Birds sang sweetly, flowers raised their drooping heads, fresh scents arose from the invigorated ground; the blue expanse above extended and diffused itself; already the sun's slanting rays pierced mortally the sullen bank of cloud that lingered in its flight; and a rainbow, spirit of all the colours that adorned the earth and sky, spanned the whole arch with its triumphant glory.

At such a time, one little roadside Inn, snugly sheltered behind a great elm-tree with a rare seat for idlers encircling its capacious bole, addressed a cheerful front towards the traveller, as a house of entertainment ought, and tempted him with many mute but significant assurances of a comfortable welcome. The ruddy sign-board perched up in the tree, with its golden letters winking in the sun, ogled the passer-by, from among the green leaves, like a jolly face, and promised good cheer. The horse-trough, full of clear fresh water, and the ground below it sprinkled with droppings of fragrant hay, made every horse that passed, prick up his ears. The crimson curtains in the lower rooms, and the pure white hangings in the little bed-chambers above, beckoned, Come in! with every breath of air. Upon the bright green shutters, there were golden legends about beer and ale, and neat wines, and good beds; and an affecting picture of a brown jug frothing over at the top. Upon the window-sills were flowering plants in bright red pots, which made a lively show against the white front of the house; and in the darkness of the doorway there were streaks of light, which glanced off from the surfaces of bottles and tankards.

On the door-step, appeared a proper figure of a landlord, too; for, though he was a short man, he was round and broad, and stood with his hands in his pockets, and his legs just wide enough apart to express a mind at rest upon the subject of the cellar, and an easy confidence—too calm and virtuous to become a swagger—in the general resources of the Inn. The superabundant moisture, trickling from everything after the late rain, set him off well. Nothing near him was thirsty. Certain top-heavy dahlias, looking over the palings of his neat well-ordered garden, had swilled as much as they could carry—perhaps a trifle more—and may have been the worse for liquor; but the sweet-briar, roses, wall-flowers, the plants at the windows, and the leaves on the old tree, were in the beaming state of moderate company that had taken no more than was wholesome for them, and had served to develop their best qualities. Sprinkling dewy drops about them on the ground, they seemed profuse of innocent and sparkling mirth, that did good where it lighted, softening neglected corners which the steady rain could seldom reach, and hurting nothing.

This village Inn had assumed, on being established, an uncommon sign. It was called The Nutmeg-Grater. And underneath that household word, was inscribed, up in the tree, on the same flaming board, and in the like golden characters, By Benjamin Britain.

At a second glance, and on a more minute examination of his face, you might have known that it was no other than Benjamin Britain himself who stood in the doorway—reasonably changed by time, but for the better; a very comfortable host indeed.

"Mrs. B.," said Mr. Britain, looking down the road, "is rather late. It's tea-time."

As there was no Mrs. Britain coming, he strolled leisurely out into the road and looked up at the house, very much to his satisfaction. "It's just the sort of house," said Benjamin, "I should wish to stop at, if I didn't keep it."

Then, he strolled towards the garden-paling, and took a look at the dahlias. They looked over at him, with a helpless drowsy hanging of their heads: which bobbed again, as the heavy drops of wet dripped off them.

"You must be looked after," said Benjamin. "Memorandum, not to forget to tell her so. She's a long time coming!"

Mr. Britain's better half seemed to be by so very much his better half, that his own moiety of himself was utterly cast away and helpless without her.

"She hadn't much to do, I think," said Ben. "There were a few little matters of business after market, but not many. Oh! here we are at last!"

A chaise-cart, driven by a boy, came clattering along the road: and seated in it, in a chair, with a large well-saturated umbrella spread out to dry behind her, was the plump figure of a matronly woman, with her bare arms folded across a basket which she carried on her knee, several other baskets and parcels lying crowded around her, and a certain bright good nature in her face and contented awkwardness in her manner, as she jogged to and fro with the motion of her carriage, which smacked of old times, even in the distance. Upon her nearer approach, this relish of by-gone days was not diminished; and when the cart stopped at the Nutmeg-Grater door, a pair of shoes, alighting from it, slipped nimbly through Mr. Britain's open arms, and came down with a substantial weight upon the pathway, which shoes could hardly have belonged to any one but Clemency Newcome.

In fact they did belong to her, and she stood in them, and a rosy comfortable-looking soul she was: with as much soap on her glossy face as in times of yore, but with whole elbows now, that had grown quite dimpled in her improved condition.

"You're late, Clemmy!" said Mr. Britain.

"Why, you see, Ben, I've had a deal to do!" she replied, looking busily after the safe removal into the house of all the packages and baskets: "eight, nine, ten—where's eleven? Oh! my basket's eleven! It's all right. Put the horse up, Harry, and if he coughs again give him a warm mash to-night. Eight, nine, ten. Why, where's eleven? Oh! forgot, it's all right. How's the children, Ben?"

"Hearty, Clemmy, hearty."

"Bless their precious faces!" said Mrs. Britain, unbonneting her own round countenance (for she and her husband were by this time in the bar), and smoothing her hair with her open hands. "Give us a kiss, old man!"

Mr. Britain promptly complied.

"I think," said Mrs. Britain, applying herself to her pockets and drawing forth an immense bulk of thin books and crumpled papers: a very kennel of dogs'-ears: "I've done everything. Bills all settled—turnips sold—brewer's account looked into and paid—'bacco pipes ordered—seventeen pound four, paid into the Bank—Doctor Heathfield's charge for little Clem—you'll guess what that is—Doctor Heathfield won't take nothing again, Ben."

"I thought he wouldn't," returned Ben.

"No. He says whatever family you was to have, Ben, he'd never put you to the cost of a halfpenny. Not if you was to have twenty."

Mr. Britain's face assumed a serious expression, and he looked hard at the wall.

"An't it kind of him?" said Clemency.

"Very," returned Mr. Britain. "It's the sort of kindness that I wouldn't presume upon, on any account."

"No," retorted Clemency. "Of course not. Then there's the pony—he fetched eight pound two; and that an't bad, is it?"

"It's very good," said Ben.

"I'm glad you're pleased!" exclaimed his wife. "I thought you would be; and I think that's all, and so no more at present from yours and cetrer, C. Britain. Ha ha ha! There! Take all the papers, and lock 'em up. Oh! Wait a minute. Here's a printed bill to stick on the wall. Wet from the printer's. How nice it smells!"

"What's this?" said Ben, looking over the document.

"I don't know," replied his wife. "I haven't read a word of it."

" 'To be sold by Auction,' " read the host of the Nutmeg-Grater, " 'unless previously disposed of by private contract.' "

"They always put that," said Clemency.

"Yes, but they don't always put this," he returned. "Look here, 'Mansion,' &c. 'offices,' &c., 'shrubberies,' &c., 'ring fence,' &c. 'Messrs. Snitchey and Craggs,' &c., 'ornamental portion of the unencumbered freehold property of Michael Warden, Esquire, intending to continue to reside abroad'!"

"Intending to continue to reside abroad!" repeated Clemency.

"Here it is," said Britain. "Look!"

"And it was only this very day that I heard it whispered at the old house, that better and plainer news had been half promised of her, soon!" said Clemency, shaking her head sorrowfully, and patting her elbows as if the recollection of old times unconsciously awakened her old habits. "Dear, dear, dear! There'll be heavy hearts, Ben, yonder."

Mr. Britain heaved a sigh, and shook his head, and said he couldn't make it out: he had left off trying long ago. With that remark, he applied himself to putting up the bill just inside the bar window. Clemency, after meditating in silence for a few moments, roused herself, cleared her thoughtful brow, and bustled off to look after the children.

Though the host of the Nutmeg-Grater had a lively regard for his good-wife, it was of the old patronising kind, and she amused him mightily. Nothing would have astonished him so much, as to have known for certain from any third party, that it was she who managed the whole house, and made him, by her plain straightforward thrift, good-humour, honesty, and industry, a thriving man. So easy it is, in any degree of life (as the world very often finds it), to take those cheerful natures that never assert their merit, at their own modest valuation; and to conceive a flippant liking of people for their outward oddities and eccentricities, whose innate worth, if we would look so far, might make us blush in the comparison!

It was comfortable to Mr. Britain, to think of his own condescension in having married Clemency. She was a perpetual testimony to him of the goodness of his heart, and the kindness of his disposition; and he felt that her being an excellent wife was an illustration of the old precept that virtue is its own reward.

He had finished wafering up the bill, and had locked the vouchers for her day's proceedings in the cupboard—chuckling all the time, over her capacity for business—when, returning with the news that the two Master Britains were playing in the coach-house under the superintendence of one Betsey, and that little Clem was sleeping "like a picture," she sat down to tea, which had awaited her arrival, on a little table. It was a very neat little bar, with the usual display of bottles and glasses; a sedate clock, right to the minute (it was half-past five); everything in its place, and everything furbished and polished up to the very utmost.

"It's the first time I've sat down quietly to-day, I declare," said Mrs. Britain, taking a long breath, as if she had sat down for the night; but getting up again immediately to hand her husband his tea, and cut him his bread-and-butter; "how that bill does set me thinking of old times!"

"Ah!" said Mr. Britain, handling his saucer like an oyster, and disposing of its contents on the same principle.

"That same Mr. Michael Warden," said Clemency, shaking her head at the notice of sale, "lost me my old place."

"And got you your husband," said Mr. Britain.

"Well! So he did," retorted Clemency, "and many thanks to him."

"Man's the creature of habit," said Mr. Britain, surveying her, over his saucer.

"I had somehow got used to you, Clem; and I found I shouldn't be able to get on without you. So we went and got made man and wife. Ha! ha! We! Who'd have thought it!"

"Who indeed!" cried Clemency. "It was very good of you, Ben."

"No, no, no," replied Mr. Britain, with an air of self-denial. "Nothing worth mentioning."

"Oh yes it was, Ben," said his wife, with great simplicity; "I'm sure I think so, and am very much obliged to you. Ah!" looking again at the bill; "when she was known to be gone, and out of reach, dear girl, I couldn't help telling—for her sake quite as much as theirs—what I knew, could I?"

"You told it, anyhow," observed her husband.

"And Dr. Jeddler," pursued Clemency, putting down her tea-cup, and looking thoughtfully at the bill, "in his grief and passion turned me out of house and home! I never have been so glad of anything in all my life, as that I didn't say an angry word to him, and hadn't any angry feeling towards him, even then; for he repented that truly, afterwards. How often he has sat in this room, and told me over and over again he was sorry for it!—the last time, only yesterday, when you were out. How often he has sat in this room, and talked to me, hour after hour, about one thing and another, in which he made believe to be interested!—but only for the sake of the days that are gone by, and because he knows she used to like me, Ben!"

"Why, how did you ever come to catch a glimpse of that, Clem?" asked her husband: astonished that she should have a distinct perception of a truth which had only dimly suggested itself to his inquiring mind.

"I don't know, I'm sure," said Clemency, blowing her tea, to cool it. "Bless you, I couldn't tell you, if you was to offer me a reward of a hundred pound."

He might have pursued this metaphysical subject but for her catching a glimpse of a substantial fact behind him, in the shape of a gentleman attired in mourning, and cloaked and booted like a rider on horseback, who stood at the bar-door. He seemed attentive to their conversation, and not at all impatient to interrupt it.

Clemency hastily rose at this sight. Mr. Britain also rose and saluted the guest. "Will you please to walk up-stairs, sir? There's a very nice room up-stairs, sir."

"Thank you," said the stranger, looking earnestly at Mr. Britain's wife. "May I come in here?"

"Oh, surely, if you like, sir," returned Clemency, admitting him.

"What would you please to want, sir?"

The bill had caught his eye, and he was reading it.

"Excellent property that, sir," observed Mr. Britain.

He made no answer; but, turning round, when he had finished reading, looked at Clemency with the same observant curiosity as before. "You were asking me,"—he said, still looking at her,—"What you would please to take, sir," answered Clemency, stealing a glance at him in return.

"If you will let me have a draught of ale," he said, moving to a table by the window, "and will let me have it here, without being any interruption to your meal, I shall be much obliged to you." He sat down as he spoke, without any further parley, and looked out at the prospect. He was an easy, well-knit figure of a man in the prime of life. His face, much browned by the sun, was shaded by a quantity of dark hair; and he wore a moustache. His beer being set before him, he filled out a glass, and drank, good-humouredly, to the house; adding, as he put the tumbler down again:

"It's a new house, is it not?"

"Not particularly new, sir," replied Mr. Britain.

"Between five and six years old," said Clemency; speaking very distinctly.

"I think I heard you mention Dr. Jeddler's name, as I came in," inquired the stranger. "That bill reminds me of him; for I happen to know something of that story, by hearsay, and through certain connexions of mine.—Is the old man living?"

"Yes, he's living, sir," said Clemency.

"Much changed?"

"Since when, sir?" returned Clemency, with remarkable emphasis and expression.

"Since his daughter—went away."

"Yes! he's greatly changed since then," said Clemency. "He's grey and old, and hasn't the same way with him at all; but, I think he's happy now. He has taken on with his sister since then, and goes to see her very often. That did him good, directly. At first, he was sadly broken down; and it was enough to make one's heart bleed, to see him wandering about, railing at the world; but a great change for the better came over him after a year or two, and then he began to like to talk about his lost daughter, and to praise her, ay and the world too! and was never tired of saying, with the tears in his poor eyes, how beautiful and good she was. He had forgiven her then. That was about the same time as Miss Grace's marriage. Britain, you remember?"

Mr. Britain remembered very well.

"The sister is married then," returned the stranger. He paused for some time before he asked, "To whom?"

Clemency narrowly escaped oversetting the tea-board, in her emotion at this question.

"Did you never hear?" she said.

"I should like to hear," he replied, as he filled his glass again, and raised it to his lips.

"Ah! It would be a long story, if it was properly told," said Clemency, resting her chin on the palm of her left hand, and supporting that elbow on her right hand, as she shook her head, and looked back through the intervening years, as if she were looking at a fire. "It would be a long story, I am sure."

"But told as a short one," suggested the stranger.

"Told as a short one," repeated Clemency in the same thoughtful tone, and without any apparent reference to him, or consciousness of having auditors, "what would there be to tell? That they grieved together, and remembered her together, like a person dead; that they were so tender of her, never would reproach her, called her back to one another as she used to be, and found excuses for her! Every one knows that. I'm sure I do. No one better," added Clemency, wiping her eyes with her hand.

"And so," suggested the stranger.

"And so," said Clemency, taking him up mechanically, and without any change in her attitude or manner, "they at last were married. They were married on her birth-day—it comes round again to-morrow—very quiet, very humble like, but very happy. Mr. Alfred said, one night when they were walking in the orchard, 'Grace, shall our wedding-day be Marion's birth-day?' And it was."

"And they have lived happily together?" said the stranger.

"Ay," said Clemency. "No two people ever more so. They have had no sorrow but this."

She raised her head as with a sudden attention to the circumstances under which she was recalling these events, and looked quickly at the stranger. Seeing that his face was turned toward the window, and that he seemed intent upon the prospect, she made some eager signs to her husband, and pointed to the bill, and moved her mouth as if she were repeating with great energy, one word or phrase to him over and over again. As she uttered no sound, and as her dumb motions like most of her gestures were of a very extraordinary kind, this unintelligible conduct reduced Mr. Britain to the confines of despair. He stared at the table, at the stranger, at the spoons, at his wife—followed her pantomime with looks of deep amazement and perplexity—asked in the same language, was it property in danger, was it he in danger, was it she—answered her signals with other signals expressive of the deepest distress and confusion—followed the motions of her lips—guessed half aloud "milk and water," "monthly warning," "mice and walnuts"—and couldn't approach her meaning.

Clemency gave it up at last, as a hopeless attempt; and moving her chair by very slow degrees a little nearer to the stranger, sat with her eyes apparently cast down but glancing sharply at him now and then, waiting until he should ask some other question. She had not to wait long; for he said, presently:

"And what is the after history of the young lady who went away? They know it, I suppose?"

Clemency shook her head. "I've heard," she said, "that Doctor Jeddler is thought to know more of it than he tells. Miss Grace has had letters from her sister, saying that she was well and happy, and made much happier by her being married to Mr. Alfred: and has written letters back. But there's a mystery about her life and fortunes, altogether, which nothing has cleared up to this hour, and which—"

She faltered here, and stopped.

"And which"—repeated the stranger.

"Which only one other person, I believe, could explain," said Clemency, drawing her breath quickly.

"Who may that be?" asked the stranger.

"Mr. Michael Warden!" answered Clemency, almost in a shriek: at once conveying to her husband what she would have had him understand before, and letting Michael Warden know that he was recognised.

"You remember me, sir?" said Clemency, trembling with emotion; "I saw just now you did! You remember me, that night in the garden. I was with her!"

"Yes. You were," he said.

"Yes, sir," returned Clemency. "Yes, to be sure. This is my husband, if you please. Ben, my dear Ben, run to Miss Grace—run to Mr. Alfred—run somewhere, Ben! Bring somebody here, directly!"

"Stay!" said Michael Warden, quietly interposing himself between the door and Britain. "What would you do?"

"Let them know that you are here, sir," answered Clemency, clapping her hands in sheer agitation. "Let them know that they may hear of her, from your own lips; let them know that she is not quite lost to them, but that she will come home again yet, to bless her father and her loving sister—even her old servant, even me," she struck herself upon the breast with both hands, "with a sight of her sweet face. Run, Ben, run!" And still she pressed him on towards the door, and still Mr. Warden stood before it, with his hand stretched out, not angrily, but sorrowfully.

"Or perhaps," said Clemency, running past her husband, and catching in her emotion at Mr. Warden's cloak, "perhaps she's here now; perhaps she's close by. I think from your manner she is. Let me see her, sir, if you please. I waited on her when she was a little child. I saw her grow to be the pride of all this place. I knew her when she was Mr. Alfred's promised wife. I tried to warn her when you tempted her away. I know what her old home was when she was like the soul of it, and how it changed when she was gone and lost. Let me speak to her, if you please!"

He gazed at her with compassion, not unmixed with wonder: but, he made no gesture of assent.

"I don't think she can know," pursued Clemency, "how truly they forgive her; how they love her; what joy it would be to them, to see her once more. She may be timorous of going home. Perhaps if she sees me, it may give her new heart. Only tell me truly, Mr. Warden, is she with you?"

"She is not," he answered, shaking his head.

This answer, and his manner, and his black dress, and his coming back so quietly, and his announced intention of continuing to live abroad, explained it all. Marion was dead.

He didn't contradict her; yes, she was dead! Clemency sat down, hid her face upon the table, and cried.

At that moment, a grey-headed old gentleman came running in: quite out of breath, and panting so much that his voice was scarcely to be recognised as the voice of Mr. Snitchey.

"Good Heaven, Mr. Warden!" said the lawyer, taking him aside, "what wind has blown—" He was so blown himself, that he couldn't get on any further until after a pause, when he added, feebly, "you here?"

"An ill-wind, I am afraid," he answered. "If you could have heard what has just passed—how I have been besought and entreated to perform impossibilities— what confusion and affliction I carry with me!"

"I can guess it all. But why did you ever come here, my good sir?" retorted Snitchey.

"Come! How should I know who kept the house? When I sent my servant on to you, I strolled in here because the place was new to me; and I had a natural curiosity in everything new and old, in these old scenes; and it was outside the town. I wanted to communicate with you, first, before appearing there. I wanted to know what people would say to me. I see by your manner that you can tell me. If it were not for your confounded caution, I should have been possessed of everything long ago."

"Our caution!" returned the lawyer, "speaking for Self and Craggs—deceased," here Mr. Snitchey, glancing at his hat-band, shook his head, "how can you reasonably blame us, Mr. Warden? It was understood between us that the subject was never to be renewed, and that it wasn't a subject on which grave and sober men like us (I made a note of your observations at the time) could interfere. Our caution too! When Mr. Craggs, sir, went down to his respected grave in the full belief—"

"I had given a solemn promise of silence until I should return, whenever that might be," interrupted Mr. Warden; "and I have kept it."

"Well, sir, and I repeat it," returned Mr. Snitchey, "we were bound to silence too. We were bound to silence in our duty towards ourselves, and in our duty towards a variety of clients, you among them, who were as close as wax. It was not our place to make inquiries of you on such a delicate subject. I had my suspicions, sir; but, it is not six months since I have known the truth, and been assured that you lost her."

"By whom?" inquired his client.

"By Doctor Jeddler himself, sir, who at last reposed that confidence in me voluntarily. He, and only he, has known the whole truth, years and years."

"And you know it?" said his client.

"I do, sir!" replied Snitchey; "and I have also reason to know that it will be broken to her sister to-morrow evening. They have given her that promise. In the meantime, perhaps you'll give me the honour of your company at my house; being unexpected at your own. But, not to run the chance of any more such difficulties as you have had here, in case you should be recognised—though you're a good deal changed; I think I might have passed you myself, Mr. Warden—we had better dine here, and walk on in the evening. It's a very good place to dine at, Mr. Warden: your own property, by the bye. Self and Craggs (deceased) took a chop here sometimes, and had it very comfortably served. Mr. Craggs, sir," said Snitchey, shutting his eyes tight for an instant, and opening them again, "was struck off the roll of life too soon."

"Heaven forgive me for not condoling with you," returned Michael Warden, passing his hand across his forehead, "but I'm like a man in a dream at present. I seem to want my wits. Mr. Craggs—yes—I am very sorry we have lost Mr. Craggs." But he looked at Clemency as he said it, and seemed to sympathise with Ben, consoling her.

"Mr. Craggs, sir," observed Snitchey, "didn't find life, I regret to say, as easy to have and to hold as his theory made it out, or he would have been among us now. It's a great loss to me. He was my right arm, my right leg, my right ear, my right eye, was Mr. Craggs. I am paralytic without him. He bequeathed his share of the business to Mrs. Craggs, her executors, administrators, and assigns. His name remains in the Firm to this hour. I try, in a childish sort of a way, to make believe, sometimes, he's alive. You may observe that I speak for Self and Craggs—deceased, sir—deceased," said the tender-hearted attorney, waving his pocket-handkerchief.

Michael Warden, who had still been observant of Clemency, turned to Mr. Snitchey when he ceased to speak, and whispered in his ear.

"Ah, poor thing!" said Snitchey, shaking his head. "Yes. She was always very faithful to Marion. She was always very fond of her. Pretty Marion! Poor Marion! Cheer up, Mistress—you are married now, you know, Clemency."

Clemency only sighed, and shook her head.

"Well, well! Wait till to-morrow," said the lawyer, kindly.

"To-morrow can't bring back the dead to life, Mister," said Clemency, sobbing.

"No. It can't do that, or it would bring back Mr. Craggs, deceased," returned the lawyer. "But it may bring some soothing circumstances; it may bring some comfort. Wait till to-morrow!"

So Clemency, shaking his proffered hand, said she would; and Britain, who had been terribly cast down at sight of his despondent wife (which was like the business hanging its head), said that was right; and Mr. Snitchey and Michael Warden went up-stairs; and there they were soon engaged in a conversation so cautiously conducted, that no murmur of it was audible above the clatter of plates and dishes, the hissing of the frying-pan, the bubbling of saucepans, the low monotonous waltzing of the jack—with a dreadful click every now and then as if it had met with some mortal accident to its head, in a fit of giddiness—and all the other preparations in the kitchen for their dinner.

To-morrow was a bright and peaceful day; and nowhere were the autumn tints more beautifully seen, than from the quiet orchard of the Doctor's house. The snows of many winter nights had melted from that ground, the withered leaves of many summer times had rustled there, since she had fled. The honey-suckle porch was green again, the trees cast bountiful and changing shadows on the grass, the landscape was as tranquil and serene as it had ever been; but where was she!

Not there. Not there. She would have been a stranger sight in her old home now, even than that home had been at first, without her. But, a lady sat in the familiar place, from whose heart she had never passed away; in whose true memory she lived, unchanging, youthful, radiant with all promise and all hope; in whose affection—and it was a mother's now, there was a cherished little daughter playing by her side—she had no rival, no successor; upon whose gentle lips her name was trembling then.

The spirit of the lost girl looked out of those eyes. Those eyes of Grace, her sister, sitting with her husband in the orchard, on their wedding-day, and his and Marion's birth-day.

He had not become a great man; he had not grown rich; he had not forgotten the scenes and friends of his youth; he had not fulfilled any one of the Doctor's old predictions. But, in his useful, patient, unknown visiting of poor men's homes; and in his watching of sick beds; and in his daily knowledge of the gentleness and goodness flowering the by-paths of this world, not to be trodden down beneath the heavy foot of poverty, but springing up, elastic, in its track, and making its way beautiful; he had better learned and proved, in each succeeding year, the truth of his old faith. The manner of his life, though quiet and remote, had shown him how often men still entertained angels, unawares, as in the olden time; and how the most unlikely forms—even some that were mean and ugly to the view, and poorly clad—became irradiated by the couch of sorrow, want, and pain, and changed to ministering spirits with a glory round their heads.

He lived to better purpose on the altered battle-ground, perhaps, than if he had contended restlessly in more ambitious lists; and he was happy with his wife, dear Grace.

And Marion. Had he forgotten her?

"The time has flown, dear Grace," he said, "since then"; they had been talking of that night; "and yet it seems a long long while ago. We count by changes and events within us. Not by years."

"Yet we have years to count by, too, since Marion was with us," returned Grace. "Six times, dear husband, counting to-night as one, we have sat here on her birthday, and spoken together of that happy return, so eagerly expected and so long deferred. Ah when will it be! When will it be!"

Her husband attentively observed her, as the tears collected in her eyes; and drawing nearer, said:

"But, Marion told you, in that farewell letter which she left for you upon your table, love, and which you read so often, that years must pass away before it could be. Did she not?"

She took a letter from her breast, and kissed it, and said "Yes."

"That through these intervening years, however happy she might be, she would look forward to the time when you would meet again, and all would be made clear; and that she prayed you, trustfully and hopefully to do the same. The letter runs so, does it not, my dear?"

"Yes, Alfred."

"And every other letter she has written since?"

"Except the last—some months ago—in which she spoke of you, and what you then knew, and what I was to learn to-night."

He looked towards the sun, then fast declining, and said that the appointed time was sunset.

"Alfred!" said Grace, laying her hand upon his shoulder earnestly, "there is something in this letter—this old letter, which you say I read so often—that I have never told you. But, to-night, dear husband, with that sunset drawing near, and all our life seeming to soften and become hushed with the departing day, I cannot keep it secret."

"What is it, love?"

"When Marion went away, she wrote me, here, that you had once left her a sacred trust to me, and that now she left you, Alfred, such a trust in my hands: praying and beseeching me, as I loved her, and as I loved you, not to reject the affection she believed (she knew, she said) you would transfer to me when the new wound was healed, but to encourage and return it."

"—And make me a proud, and happy man again, Grace. Did she say so?"

"She meant, to make myself so blest and honoured in your love," was his wife's answer, as he held her in his arms.

"Hear me, my dear!" he said.—"No. Hear me so!"—and as he spoke, he gently laid the head she had raised, again upon his shoulder. "I know why I have never heard this passage in the letter, until now. I know why no trace of it ever showed itself in any word or look of yours at that time. I know why Grace, although so true a friend to me, was hard to win to be my wife. And knowing it, my own! I know the priceless value of the heart I gird within my arms, and thank God for the rich possession!"

She wept, but not for sorrow, as he pressed her to his heart. After a brief space, he looked down at the child, who was sitting at their feet playing with a little basket of flowers, and bade her look how golden and how red the sun was.

"Alfred," said Grace, raising her head quickly at these words. "The sun is going down. You have not forgotten what I am to know before it sets."

"You are to know the truth of Marion's history, my love," he answered.

"All the truth," she said, imploringly. "Nothing veiled from me, any more. That was the promise. Was it not?"

"It was," he answered.

"Before the sun went down on Marion's birth-day. And you see it, Alfred? It is sinking fast."

He put his arm about her waist, and, looking steadily into her eyes, rejoined:

"That truth is not reserved so long for me to tell, dear Grace. It is to come from other lips."

"From other lips!" she faintly echoed.

"Yes. I know your constant heart, I know how brave you are, I know that to you a word of preparation is enough. You have said, truly, that the time is come. It is. Tell me that you have present fortitude to bear a trial—a surprise—a shock: and the messenger is waiting at the gate."

"What messenger?" she said. "And what intelligence does he bring?"

"I am pledged," he answered her, preserving his steady look, "to say no more. Do you think you understand me?"

"I am afraid to think," she said.

There was that emotion in his face, despite its steady gaze, which frightened her. Again she hid her own face on his shoulder, trembling, and entreated him to pause—a moment.

"Courage, my wife! When you have firmness to receive the messenger, the messenger is waiting at the gate. The sun is setting on Marion's birth-day. Courage, courage, Grace!"

She raised her head, and, looking at him, told him she was ready. As she stood, and looked upon him going away, her face was so like Marion's as it had been in her later days at home, that it was wonderful to see. He took the child with him. She called her back—she bore the lost girl's name—and pressed her to her bosom. The little creature, being released again, sped after him, and Grace was left alone.

She knew not what she dreaded, or what hoped; but remained there, motionless, looking at the porch by which they had disappeared.

Ah! what was that, emerging from its shadow; standing on its threshold! That figure, with its white garments rustling in the evening air; its head laid down upon her father's breast, and pressed against it to his loving heart! O God! was it a vision that came bursting from the old man's arms, and with a cry, and with a waving of its hands, and with a wild precipitation of itself upon her in its boundless love, sank down in her embrace!

"Oh, Marion, Marion! Oh, my sister! Oh, my heart's dear love! Oh, joy and happiness unutterable, so to meet again!"

It was no dream, no phantom conjured up by hope and fear, but Marion, sweet Marion! So beautiful, so happy, so unalloyed by care and trial, so elevated and exalted in her loveliness, that as the setting sun shone brightly on her upturned face, she might have been a spirit visiting the earth upon some healing mission.

Clinging to her sister, who had dropped upon a seat and bent down over her—and smiling through her tears—and kneeling, close before her, with both arms twining round her, and never turning for an instant from her face—and with the glory of the setting sun upon her brow, and with the soft tranquillity of evening gathering around them—Marion at length broke silence; her voice, so calm, low, clear, and pleasant, well-tuned to the time.

"When this was my dear home, Grace, as it will be now again—"

"Stay, my sweet love! A moment! O Marion, to hear you speak again."

She could not bear the voice she loved so well, at first.

"When this was my dear home, Grace, as it will be now again, I loved him from my soul. I loved him most devotedly. I would have died for him, though I was so young. I never slighted his affection in my secret breast for one brief instant. It was far beyond all price to me. Although it is so long ago, and past, and gone, and everything is wholly changed, I could not bear to think that you, who love so well, should think I did not truly love him once. I never loved him better, Grace, than when he left this very scene upon this very day. I never loved him better, dear one, than I did that night when I left here."

Her sister, bending over her, could look into her face, and hold her fast.

"But he had gained, unconsciously," said Marion, with a gentle smile, "another heart, before I knew that I had one to give him. That heart—yours, my sister!— was so yielded up, in all its other tenderness, to me; was so devoted, and so noble; that it plucked its love away, and kept its secret from all eyes but mine—Ah! what other eyes were quickened by such tenderness and gratitude!—and was content to sacrifice itself to me. But, I knew something of its depths. I knew the struggle it had made. I knew its high, inestimable worth to him, and his appreciation of it, let him love me as he would. I knew the debt I owed it. I had its great example every day before me. What you had done for me, I knew that I could do, Grace, if I would, for you. I never laid my head down on my pillow, but I prayed with tears to do it. I never laid my head down on my pillow, but I thought of Alfred's own words on the day of his departure, and how truly he had said (for I knew that, knowing you) that there were victories gained every day, in struggling hearts, to which these fields of battle were nothing. Thinking more and more upon the great endurance cheerfully sustained, and never known or cared for, that there must be, every day and hour, in that great strife of which he spoke, my trial seemed to grow light and easy. And He who knows our hearts, my dearest, at this moment, and who knows there is no drop of bitterness or grief—of anything but unmixed happiness—in mine, enabled me to make the resolution that I never would be Alfred's wife. That he should be my brother, and your husband, if the course I took could bring that happy end to pass; but that I never would (Grace, I then loved him dearly, dearly!) be his wife!"

"O Marion! O Marion!"

"I had tried to seem indifferent to him"; and she pressed her sister's face against her own; "but that was hard, and you were always his true advocate. I had tried to tell you of my resolution, but you would never hear me; you would never understand me. The time was drawing near for his return. I felt that I must act, before the daily intercourse between us was renewed. I knew that one great pang, undergone at that time, would save a lengthened agony to all of us. I knew that if I went away then, that end must follow which has followed, and which has made us both so happy, Grace! I wrote to good Aunt Martha, for a refuge in her house: I did not then tell her all, but something of my story, and she freely promised it. While I was contesting that step with myself, and with my love of you, and home, Mr. Warden, brought here by an accident, became, for some time, our companion."

"I have sometimes feared of late years, that this might have been," exclaimed her sister; and her countenance was ashy-pale. "You never loved him—and you married him in your self-sacrifice to me!"

"He was then," said Marion, drawing her sister closer to her, "on the eve of going secretly away for a long time. He wrote to me, after leaving here; told me what his condition and prospects really were; and offered me his hand. He told me he had seen I was not happy in the prospect of Alfred's return. I believe he thought my heart had no part in that contract; perhaps thought I might have loved him once, and did not then; perhaps thought that when I tried to seem indifferent, I tried to hide indifference—I cannot tell. But I wished that you should feel me wholly lost to Alfred—hopeless to him—dead. Do you understand me, love?"

Her sister looked into her face, attentively. She seemed in doubt.

"I saw Mr. Warden, and confided in his honour; charged him with my secret, on the eve of his and my departure. He kept it. Do you understand me, dear?"

Grace looked confusedly upon her. She scarcely seemed to hear.

"My love, my sister!" said Marion, "recall your thoughts a moment; listen to me. Do not look so strangely on me. There are countries, dearest, where those who would abjure a misplaced passion, or would strive, against some cherished feeling of their hearts and conquer it, retire into a hopeless solitude, and close the world against themselves and worldly loves and hopes for ever. When women do so, they assume that name which is so dear to you and me, and call each other Sisters. But, there may be sisters, Grace, who, in the broad world out of doors, and underneath its free sky, and in its crowded places, and among its busy life, and trying to assist and cheer it and to do some good,—learn the same lesson; and who, with hearts still fresh and young, and open to all happiness and means of happiness, can say the battle is long past, the victory long won. And such a one am I! You understand me now?"

Still she looked fixedly upon her, and made no reply.

"Oh Grace, dear Grace," said Marion, clinging yet more tenderly and fondly to that breast from which she had been so long exiled, "if you were not a happy wife and mother—if I had no little namesake here—if Alfred, my kind brother, were not your own fond husband—from whence could I derive the ecstasy I feel to-night! But, as I left here, so I have returned. My heart has known no other love, my hand has never been bestowed apart from it. I am still your maiden sister, unmarried, unbetrothed: your own loving old Marion, in whose affection you exist alone and have no partner, Grace!"

She understood her now. Her face relaxed: sobs came to her relief; and falling on her neck, she wept and wept, and fondled her as if she were a child again.

When they were more composed, they found that the Doctor, and his sister good Aunt Martha, were standing near at hand, with Alfred.

"This is a weary day for me," said good Aunt Martha, smiling through her tears, as she embraced her nieces; "for I lose my dear companion in making you all happy; and what can you give me, in return for my Marion?"

"A converted brother," said the Doctor.

"That's something, to be sure," retorted Aunt Martha, "in such a farce as—"

"No, pray don't," said the doctor penitently.

"Well, I won't," replied Aunt Martha. "But, I consider myself ill used. I don't know what's to become of me without my Marion, after we have lived together half-a-dozen years."

"You must come and live here, I suppose," replied the Doctor. "We shan't quarrel now, Martha."

"Or you must get married, Aunt," said Alfred.

"Indeed," returned the old lady, "I think it might be a good speculation if I were to set my cap at Michael Warden, who, I hear, is come home much the better for his absence in all respects. But as I knew him when he was a boy, and I was not a very young woman then, perhaps he mightn't respond. So I'll make up my mind to go and live with Marion, when she marries, and until then (it will not be very long, I dare say) to live alone. What do you say, Brother?"

"I've a great mind to say it's a ridiculous world altogether, and there's nothing serious in it," observed the poor old Doctor.

"You might take twenty affidavits of it if you chose, Anthony," said his sister; "but nobody would believe you with such eyes as those."

"It's a world full of hearts," said the Doctor, hugging his youngest daughter, and bending across her to hug Grace—for he couldn't separate the sisters; "and a serious world, with all its folly—even with mine, which was enough to have swamped the whole globe; and it is a world on which the sun never rises, but it looks upon a thousand bloodless battles that are some set-off against the miseries and wickedness of Battle-Fields; and it is a world we need be careful how we libel, Heaven forgive us, for it is a world of sacred mysteries, and its Creator only knows what lies beneath the surface of His lightest image!"

You would not be the better pleased with my rude pen, if it dissected and laid open to your view the transports of this family, long severed and now reunited. Therefore, I will not follow the poor Doctor through his humbled recollection of the sorrow he had had, when Marion was lost to him; nor, will I tell how serious he had found that world to be, in which some love, deep-anchored, is the portion of all human creatures; nor, how such a trifle as the absence of one little unit in the great absurd account, had stricken him to the ground. Nor, how, in compassion for his distress, his sister had, long ago, revealed the truth to him by slow degrees, and brought him to the knowledge of the heart of his self-banished daughter, and to that daughter's side.

Nor, how Alfred Heathfield had been told the truth, too, in the course of that then current year; and Marion had seen him, and had promised him, as her brother, that on her birth-day, in the evening, Grace should know it from her lips at last.

"I beg your pardon, Doctor," said Mr. Snitchey, looking into the orchard, "but have I liberty to come in?"

Without waiting for permission, he came straight to Marion, and kissed her hand, quite joyfully.

"If Mr. Craggs had been alive, my dear Miss Marion," said Mr. Snitchey, "he would have had great interest in this occasion. It might have suggested to him, Mr. Alfred, that our life is not too easy perhaps: that, taken altogether, it will bear any little smoothing we can give it; but Mr. Craggs was a man who could endure to be convinced, sir. He was always open to conviction. If he were open to conviction, now, I—this is weakness. Mrs. Snitchey, my dear,"—at his summons that lady appeared from behind the door, "you are among old friends."

Mrs. Snitchey having delivered her congratulations, took her husband aside.

"One moment, Mr. Snitchey," said that lady. "It is not in my nature to rake up the ashes of the departed."

"No, my dear," returned her husband.

"Mr. Craggs is—"

"Yes, my dear, he is deceased," said Snitchey.

"But I ask you if you recollect," pursued his wife, "that evening of the ball? I only ask you that. If you do; and if your memory has not entirely failed you, Mr. Snitchey; and if you are not absolutely in your dotage; I ask you to connect this time with that—to remember how I begged and prayed you, on my knees—"

"Upon your knees, my dear?" said Mr. Snitchey.

"Yes," said Mrs. Snitchey, confidently, "and you know it—to beware of that man—to observe his eye—and now to tell me whether I was right, and whether at that moment he knew secrets which he didn't choose to tell."

"Mrs. Snitchey," returned her husband, in her ear, "Madam. Did you ever observe anything in my eye?"

"No," said Mrs. Snitchey, sharply. "Don't flatter yourself."

"Because, Madam, that night," he continued, twitching her by the sleeve, "it happens that we both knew secrets which we didn't choose to tell, and both knew just the same professionally. And so the less you say about such things the better, Mrs. Snitchey; and take this as a warning to have wiser and more charitable eyes another time. Miss Marion, I brought a friend of yours along with me. Here! Mistress!"

Poor Clemency, with her apron to her eyes, came slowly in, escorted by her husband; the latter doleful with the presentiment, that if she abandoned herself to grief, the Nutmeg-Grater was done for.

"Now, Mistress," said the lawyer, checking Marion as she ran towards her, and interposing himself between them, "what's the matter with you?"

"The matter!" cried poor Clemency.—When, looking up in wonder, and in indignant remonstrance, and in the added emotion of a great roar from Mr. Britain, and seeing that sweet face so well remembered close before her, she stared, sobbed, laughed, cried, screamed, embraced her, held her fast, released her, fell on Mr. Snitchey and embraced him (much to Mrs. Snitchey's indignation), fell on the Doctor and embraced him, fell on Mr. Britain and embraced him, and concluded by embracing herself, throwing her apron over her head, and going into hysterics behind it.

A stranger had come into the orchard, after Mr. Snitchey, and had remained apart, near the gate, without being observed by any of the group; for they had little spare attention to bestow, and that had been monopolised by the ecstasies of Clemency. He did not appear to wish to be observed, but stood alone, with downcast eyes; and there was an air of dejection about him (though he was a gentleman of a gallant appearance) which the general happiness rendered more remarkable.

None but the quick eyes of Aunt Martha, however, remarked him at all; but, almost as soon as she espied him, she was in conversation with him. Presently, going to where Marion stood with Grace and her little namesake, she whispered something in Marion's ear, at which she started, and appeared surprised; but soon recovering from her confusion, she timidly approached the stranger, in Aunt Martha's company, and engaged in conversation with him too.

"Mr. Britain," said the lawyer, putting his hand in his pocket, and bringing out a legal-looking document, while this was going on, "I congratulate you. You are now the whole and sole proprietor of that freehold tenement, at present occupied and held by yourself as a licensed tavern, or house of public entertainment, and commonly called or known by the sign of the Nutmeg-Grater. Your wife lost one house, through my client Mr. Michael Warden; and now gains another. I shall have the pleasure of canvassing you for the county, one of these fine mornings."

"Would it make any difference in the vote if the sign was altered, sir?" asked Britain.

"Not in the least," replied the lawyer.

"Then," said Mr. Britain, handing him back the conveyance, "just clap in the words, 'and Thimble,' will you be so good; and I'll have the two mottoes painted up in the parlour instead of my wife's portrait."

"And let me," said a voice behind them; it was the stranger's—Michael Warden's; "let me claim the benefit of those inscriptions. Mr. Heathfield and Dr. Jeddler, I might have deeply wronged you both. That I did not, is no virtue of my own. I will not say that I am six years wiser than I was, or better. But I have known, at any rate, that term of self-reproach. I can urge no reason why you should deal gently with me. I abused the hospitality of this house; and learnt by my own demerits, with a shame I never have forgotten, yet with some profit too, I would fain hope, from one," he glanced at Marion, "to whom I made my humble supplication for forgiveness, when I knew her merit and my deep unworthiness. In a few days I shall quit this place for ever. I entreat your pardon. Do as you would be done by! Forget and Forgive!"

Time—from whom I had the latter portion of this story, and with whom I have the pleasure of a personal acquaintance of some five-and-thirty years' duration—informed me, leaning easily upon his scythe, that Michael Warden never went away again, and never sold his house, but opened it afresh, maintained a golden means of hospitality, and had a wife, the pride and honour of that countryside, whose name was Marion. But, as I have observed that Time confuses facts occasionally, I hardly know what weight to give to his authority.

The Haunted Man and the Ghost's Bargain

Charles Dickens

CHAPTER I. THE GIFT BESTOWED

Everybody said so. Far be it from me to assert that what everybody says must be true. Everybody is, often, as likely to be wrong as right. In the general experience, everybody has been wrong so often, and it has taken, in most instances, such a weary while to find out how wrong, that the authority is proved to be fallible. Everybody may sometimes be right; "but that's no rule," as the ghost of Giles Scroggins says in the ballad.

The dread word, Ghost, recalls me.

Everybody said he looked like a haunted man. The extent of my present claim for everybody is, that they were so far right. He did.

Who could have seen his hollow cheek; his sunken brilliant eye; his black-attired figure, indefinably grim, although well-knit and well-proportioned; his grizzled hair hanging, like tangled sea-weed, about his face,—as if he had been, through his whole life, a lonely mark for the chafing and beating of the great deep of humanity,—but might have said he looked like a haunted man?

Who could have observed his manner, taciturn, thoughtful, gloomy, shadowed by habitual reserve, retiring always and jocund never, with a distraught air of reverting to a bygone place and time, or of listening to some old echoes in his mind, but might have said it was the manner of a haunted man?

Who could have heard his voice, slow-speaking, deep, and grave, with a natural fulness and melody in it which he seemed to set himself against and stop, but might have said it was the voice of a haunted man?

Who that had seen him in his inner chamber, part library and part laboratory,—for he was, as the world knew, far and wide, a learned man in chemistry, and a teacher on whose lips and hands a crowd of aspiring ears and eyes hung daily,—who that had seen him there, upon a winter night, alone, surrounded by his drugs and instruments and books; the shadow of his shaded lamp a monstrous beetle on the wall, motionless among a crowd of spectral shapes raised there by the flickering of the fire upon the quaint objects around him; some of these phantoms (the reflection of glass vessels that held liquids), trembling at heart like things that knew his power to uncombine them, and to give back their component parts to fire and vapour;—who that had seen him then, his work done, and he pondering in his chair before the rusted grate and red flame, moving his thin mouth as if in speech, but silent as the dead, would not have said that the man seemed haunted and the chamber too?

Who might not, by a very easy flight of fancy, have believed that everything about him took this haunted tone, and that he lived on haunted ground?

His dwelling was so solitary and vault-like,—an old, retired part of an ancient endowment for students, once a brave edifice, planted in an open place, but now the obsolete whim of forgotten architects; smoke-age-and-weather-darkened, squeezed on every side by the overgrowing of the great city, and choked, like an old well, with stones and bricks; its small quadrangles, lying down in very pits formed by the streets and buildings, which, in course of time, had been constructed above its heavy chimney stalks; its old trees, insulted by the neighbouring smoke, which deigned to droop so low when it was very feeble and the weather very moody; its grass-plots, struggling with the mildewed earth to be grass, or to win any show of compromise; its silent pavements, unaccustomed to the tread of feet, and even to the observation of eyes, except when a stray face looked down from the upper world, wondering what nook it was; its sun-dial in a little bricked-up corner, where no sun had straggled for a hundred years, but where, in compensation for the sun's neglect, the snow would lie for weeks when it lay nowhere else, and the black east wind would spin like a huge humming-top, when in all other places it was silent and still.

His dwelling, at its heart and core—within doors—at his fireside—was so lowering and old, so crazy, yet so strong, with its worn-eaten beams of wood in the ceiling, and its sturdy floor shelving downward to the great oak chimney-piece; so environed and hemmed in by the pressure of the town yet so remote in fashion, age, and custom; so quiet, yet so thundering with echoes when a distant voice was raised or a door was shut,—echoes, not confined to the many low passages and empty rooms, but rumbling and grumbling till they were stifled in the heavy air of the forgotten Crypt where the Norman arches were half-buried in the earth.

You should have seen him in his dwelling about twilight, in the dead winter time.

When the wind was blowing, shrill and shrewd, with the going down of the blurred sun. When it was just so dark, as that the forms of things were indistinct and big—but not wholly lost. When sitters by the fire began to see wild faces and figures, mountains and abysses, ambuscades and armies, in the coals. When people in the streets bent down their heads and ran before the weather. When those who were obliged to meet it, were stopped at angry corners, stung by wandering snow-flakes alighting on the lashes of their eyes,—which fell too sparingly, and were blown away too quickly, to leave a trace upon the frozen ground. When windows of private houses closed up tight and warm. When lighted gas began to burst forth in the busy and the quiet streets, fast blackening otherwise. When stray pedestrians, shivering along the latter, looked down at the glowing fires in kitchens, and sharpened their sharp appetites by sniffing up the fragrance of whole miles of dinners.

When travellers by land were bitter cold, and looked wearily on gloomy landscapes, rustling and shuddering in the blast. When mariners at sea, outlying upon icy yards, were tossed and swung above the howling ocean dreadfully. When lighthouses, on rocks and headlands, showed solitary and watchful; and benighted sea-birds breasted on against their ponderous lanterns, and fell dead. When little readers of story-books, by the firelight, trembled to think of Cassim Baba cut into quarters, hanging in the Robbers' Cave, or had some small misgivings that the fierce little old woman, with the crutch, who used to start out of the box in the merchant Abudah's bedroom, might, one of these nights, be found upon the stairs, in the long, cold, dusky journey up to bed.

When, in rustic places, the last glimmering of daylight died away from the ends of avenues; and the trees, arching overhead, were sullen and black. When, in parks and woods, the high wet fern and sodden moss, and beds of fallen leaves, and trunks of trees, were lost to view, in masses of impenetrable shade. When mists arose from dyke, and fen, and river. When lights in old halls and in cottage windows, were a cheerful sight. When the mill stopped, the wheelwright and the blacksmith shut their workshops, the turnpike-gate closed, the plough and harrow were left lonely in the fields, the labourer and team went home, and the striking of the church clock had a deeper sound than at noon, and the churchyard wicket would be swung no more that night.

When twilight everywhere released the shadows, prisoned up all day, that now closed in and gathered like mustering swarms of ghosts. When they stood lowering, in corners of rooms, and frowned out from behind half-opened doors. When they had full possession of unoccupied apartments. When they danced upon the floors, and walls, and ceilings of inhabited chambers, while the fire was low, and withdrew like ebbing waters when it sprang into a blaze. When they fantastically mocked the shapes of household objects, making the nurse an ogress, the rocking-horse a monster, the wondering child, half-scared and half-amused, a stranger to itself,—the very tongs upon the hearth, a straddling giant with his arms a-kimbo, evidently smelling the blood of Englishmen, and wanting to grind people's bones to make his bread.

When these shadows brought into the minds of older people, other thoughts, and showed them different images. When they stole from their retreats, in the likenesses of forms and faces from the past, from the grave, from the deep, deep gulf, where the things that might have been, and never were, are always wandering.

When he sat, as already mentioned, gazing at the fire. When, as it rose and fell, the shadows went and came. When he took no heed of them, with his bodily eyes; but, let them come or let them go, looked fixedly at the fire. You should have seen him, then.

When the sounds that had arisen with the shadows, and come out of their lurking-places at the twilight summons, seemed to make a deeper stillness all about him. When the wind was rumbling in the chimney, and sometimes crooning, sometimes howling, in the house. When the old trees outside were so shaken and beaten, that one querulous old rook, unable to sleep, protested now and then, in a feeble, dozy, high-up "Caw!" When, at intervals, the window trembled, the rusty vane upon the turret-top complained, the clock beneath it recorded that another quarter of an hour was gone, or the fire collapsed and fell in with a rattle.

—When a knock came at his door, in short, as he was sitting so, and roused him.

"Who's that?" said he. "Come in!"

Surely there had been no figure leaning on the back of his chair; no face looking over it. It is certain that no gliding footstep touched the floor, as he lifted up his head, with a start, and spoke. And yet there was no mirror in the room on whose surface his own form could have cast its shadow for a moment; and, Something had passed darkly and gone!

"I'm humbly fearful, sir," said a fresh-coloured busy man, holding the door open with his foot for the admission of himself and a wooden tray he carried, and letting it go again by very gentle and careful degrees, when he and the tray had got in, lest it should close noisily, "that it's a good bit past the time to-night. But Mrs. William has been taken off her legs so often—"

"By the wind? Ay! I have heard it rising."

"—By the wind, sir—that it's a mercy she got home at all. Oh dear, yes. Yes. It was by the wind, Mr. Redlaw. By the wind."

He had, by this time, put down the tray for dinner, and was employed in lighting the lamp, and spreading a cloth on the table. From this employment he desisted in a hurry, to stir and feed the fire, and then resumed it; the lamp he had lighted, and the blaze that rose under his hand, so quickly changing the appearance of the room, that it seemed as if the mere coming in of his fresh red face and active manner had made the pleasant alteration.

"Mrs. William is of course subject at any time, sir, to be taken off her balance by the elements. She is not formed superior to that."

"No," returned Mr. Redlaw good-naturedly, though abruptly.

"No, sir. Mrs. William may be taken off her balance by Earth; as for example, last Sunday week, when sloppy and greasy, and she going out to tea with her newest sister-in-law, and having a pride in herself, and wishing to appear perfectly spotless though pedestrian. Mrs. William may be taken off her balance by Air; as being once over-persuaded by a friend to try a swing at Peckham Fair, which acted on her constitution instantly like a steam-boat. Mrs. William may be taken off her balance by Fire; as on a false alarm of engines at her mother's, when she went two miles in her nightcap. Mrs. William may be taken off her balance by Water; as at Battersea, when rowed into the piers by her young nephew, Charley Swidger junior, aged twelve, which had no idea of boats whatever. But these are elements. Mrs. William must be taken out of elements for the strength of her character to come into play."

As he stopped for a reply, the reply was "Yes," in the same tone as before.

"Yes, sir. Oh dear, yes!" said Mr. Swidger, still proceeding with his preparations, and checking them off as he made them. "That's where it is, sir. That's what I always say myself, sir. Such a many of us Swidgers!—Pepper. Why there's my father, sir, superannuated keeper and custodian of this Institution, eighty-seven year old. He's a Swidger!—Spoon."

"True, William," was the patient and abstracted answer, when he stopped again.

"Yes, sir," said Mr. Swidger. "That's what I always say, sir. You may call him the trunk of the tree!—Bread. Then you come to his successor, my unworthy self—Salt—and Mrs. William, Swidgers both.—Knife and fork. Then you come to all my brothers and their families, Swidgers, man and woman, boy and girl. Why, what with cousins, uncles, aunts, and relationships of this, that, and t'other degree, and whatnot degree, and marriages, and lyings-in, the Swidgers— Tumbler—might take hold of hands, and make a ring round England!"

Receiving no reply at all here, from the thoughtful man whom he addressed, Mr. William approached, him nearer, and made a feint of accidentally knocking the table with a decanter, to rouse him. The moment he succeeded, he went on, as if in great alacrity of acquiescence.

"Yes, sir! That's just what I say myself, sir. Mrs. William and me have often said so. 'There's Swidgers enough,' we say, 'without our voluntary contributions,'— Butter. In fact, sir, my father is a family in himself—Castors—to take care of; and it happens all for the best that we have no child of our own, though it's made Mrs. William rather quiet-like, too. Quite ready for the fowl and mashed potatoes, sir? Mrs. William said she'd dish in ten minutes when I left the Lodge."

"I am quite ready," said the other, waking as from a dream, and walking slowly to and fro.

"Mrs. William has been at it again, sir!" said the keeper, as he stood warming a plate at the fire, and pleasantly shading his face with it. Mr. Redlaw stopped in his walking, and an expression of interest appeared in him.

"What I always say myself, sir. She will do it! There's a motherly feeling in Mrs. William's breast that must and will have went."

"What has she done?"

"Why, sir, not satisfied with being a sort of mother to all the young gentlemen that come up from a variety of parts, to attend your courses of lectures at this ancient foundation—it's surprising how stone-chaney catches the heat this frosty weather, to be sure!" Here he turned the plate, and cooled his fingers.

"Well?" said Mr. Redlaw.

"That's just what I say myself, sir," returned Mr. William, speaking over his shoulder, as if in ready and delighted assent. "That's exactly where it is, sir! There ain't one of our students but appears to regard Mrs. William in that light. Every day, right through the course, they puts their heads into the Lodge, one after another, and have all got something to tell her, or something to ask her. 'Swidge' is the appellation by which they speak of Mrs. William in general, among themselves, I'm told; but that's what I say, sir. Better be called ever so far out of your name, if it's done in real liking, than have it made ever so much of, and not cared about! What's a name for? To know a person by. If Mrs. William is known by something better than her name—I allude to Mrs. William's qualities and disposition—never mind her name, though it is Swidger, by rights. Let 'em call her Swidge, Widge, Bridge—Lord! London Bridge, Blackfriars, Chelsea, Putney, Waterloo, or Hammersmith Suspension—if they like."

The close of this triumphant oration brought him and the plate to the table, upon which he half laid and half dropped it, with a lively sense of its being thoroughly heated, just as the subject of his praises entered the room, bearing another tray and a lantern, and followed by a venerable old man with long grey hair.

Mrs. William, like Mr. William, was a simple, innocent-looking person, in whose smooth cheeks the cheerful red of her husband's official waistcoat was very pleasantly repeated. But whereas Mr. William's light hair stood on end all over his head, and seemed to draw his eyes up with it in an excess of bustling readiness for anything, the dark brown hair of Mrs. William was carefully smoothed down, and waved away under a trim tidy cap, in the most exact and quiet manner imaginable. Whereas Mr. William's very trousers hitched themselves up at the ankles, as if it were not in their iron-grey nature to rest without looking about them, Mrs. William's neatly-flowered skirts—red and white, like her own pretty face—were as composed and orderly, as if the very wind that blew so hard out of doors could not disturb one of their folds. Whereas his coat had something of a fly-away and half-off appearance about the collar and breast, her little bodice was so placid and neat, that there should have been protection for her, in it, had she needed any, with the roughest people. Who could have had the heart to make so calm a bosom swell with grief, or throb with fear, or flutter with a thought of shame! To whom would its repose and peace have not appealed against disturbance, like the innocent slumber of a child!

"Punctual, of course, Milly," said her husband, relieving her of the tray, "or it wouldn't be you. Here's Mrs. William, sir!—He looks lonelier than ever to-night," whispering to his wife, as he was taking the tray, "and ghostlier altogether."

Without any show of hurry or noise, or any show of herself even, she was so calm and quiet, Milly set the dishes she had brought upon the table,—Mr. William, after much clattering and running about, having only gained possession of a butter-boat of gravy, which he stood ready to serve.

"What is that the old man has in his arms?" asked Mr. Redlaw, as he sat down to his solitary meal.

"Holly, sir," replied the quiet voice of Milly.

"That's what I say myself, sir," interposed Mr. William, striking in with the butter-boat. "Berries is so seasonable to the time of year!—Brown gravy!"

"Another Christmas come, another year gone!" murmured the Chemist, with a gloomy sigh. "More figures in the lengthening sum of recollection that we work and work at to our torment, till Death idly jumbles all together, and rubs all out. So, Philip!" breaking off, and raising his voice as he addressed the old man, standing apart, with his glistening burden in his arms, from which the quiet Mrs. William took small branches, which she noiselessly trimmed with her scissors, and decorated the room with, while her aged father-in-law looked on much interested in the ceremony.

"My duty to you, sir," returned the old man. "Should have spoke before, sir, but know your ways, Mr. Redlaw—proud to say—and wait till spoke to! Merry Christmas, sir, and Happy New Year, and many of 'em. Have had a pretty many of 'em myself—ha, ha!—and may take the liberty of wishing 'em. I'm eighty-seven!"

"Have you had so many that were merry and happy?" asked the other.

"Ay, sir, ever so many," returned the old man.

"Is his memory impaired with age? It is to be expected now," said Mr. Redlaw, turning to the son, and speaking lower.

"Not a morsel of it, sir," replied Mr. William. "That's exactly what I say myself, sir. There never was such a memory as my father's. He's the most wonderful man in the world. He don't know what forgetting means. It's the very observation I'm always making to Mrs. William, sir, if you'll believe me!"

Mr. Swidger, in his polite desire to seem to acquiesce at all events, delivered this as if there were no iota of contradiction in it, and it were all said in unbounded and unqualified assent.

The Chemist pushed his plate away, and, rising from the table, walked across the room to where the old man stood looking at a little sprig of holly in his hand.

"It recalls the time when many of those years were old and new, then?" he said, observing him attentively, and touching him on the shoulder. "Does it?"

"Oh many, many!" said Philip, half awaking from his reverie. "I'm eighty-seven!"

"Merry and happy, was it?" asked the Chemist in a low voice. "Merry and happy, old man?"

"Maybe as high as that, no higher," said the old man, holding out his hand a little way above the level of his knee, and looking retrospectively at his questioner, "when I first remember 'em! Cold, sunshiny day it was, out a-walking, when some one—it was my mother as sure as you stand there, though I don't know what her blessed face was like, for she took ill and died that Christmas-time—told me they were food for birds. The pretty little fellow thought—that's me, you understand—that birds' eyes were so bright, perhaps, because the berries that they lived on in the winter were so bright. I recollect that. And I'm eighty-seven!"

"Merry and happy!" mused the other, bending his dark eyes upon the stooping figure, with a smile of compassion. "Merry and happy—and remember well?"

"Ay, ay, ay!" resumed the old man, catching the last words. "I remember 'em well in my school time, year after year, and all the merry-making that used to come along with them. I was a strong chap then, Mr. Redlaw; and, if you'll believe me, hadn't my match at football within ten mile. Where's my son William? Hadn't my match at football, William, within ten mile!"

"That's what I always say, father!" returned the son promptly, and with great respect. "You are a Swidger, if ever there was one of the family!"

"Dear!" said the old man, shaking his head as he again looked at the holly. "His mother—my son William's my youngest son—and I, have sat among 'em all, boys and girls, little children and babies, many a year, when the berries like these were not shining half so bright all round us, as their bright faces. Many of 'em are gone; she's gone; and my son George (our eldest, who was her pride more than all the rest!) is fallen very low: but I can see them, when I look here, alive and healthy, as they used to be in those days; and I can see him, thank God, in his innocence. It's a blessed thing to me, at eighty-seven."

The keen look that had been fixed upon him with so much earnestness, had gradually sought the ground.

"When my circumstances got to be not so good as formerly, through not being honestly dealt by, and I first come here to be custodian," said the old man, "—which was upwards of fifty years ago—where's my son William? More than half a century ago, William!"

"That's what I say, father," replied the son, as promptly and dutifully as before, "that's exactly where it is. Two times ought's an ought, and twice five ten, and there's a hundred of 'em."

"It was quite a pleasure to know that one of our founders—or more correctly speaking," said the old man, with a great glory in his subject and his knowledge of it, "one of the learned gentlemen that helped endow us in Queen Elizabeth's time, for we were founded afore her day—left in his will, among the other bequests he made us, so much to buy holly, for garnishing the walls and windows, come Christmas. There was something homely and friendly in it. Being but strange here, then, and coming at Christmas time, we took a liking for his very picter that hangs in what used to be, anciently, afore our ten poor gentlemen commuted for an annual stipend in money, our great Dinner Hall.—A sedate gentleman in a peaked beard, with a ruff round his neck, and a scroll below him, in old English letters, 'Lord! keep my memory green!' You know all about him, Mr. Redlaw?"

"I know the portrait hangs there, Philip."

"Yes, sure, it's the second on the right, above the panelling. I was going to say—he has helped to keep my memory green, I thank him; for going round the building every year, as I'm a doing now, and freshening up the bare rooms with these branches and berries, freshens up my bare old brain. One year brings back another, and that year another, and those others numbers! At last, it seems to me as if the birth-time of our Lord was the birth-time of all I have ever had affection for, or mourned for, or delighted in,—and they're a pretty many, for I'm eighty-seven!"

"Merry and happy," murmured Redlaw to himself.

The room began to darken strangely.

"So you see, sir," pursued old Philip, whose hale wintry cheek had warmed into a ruddier glow, and whose blue eyes had brightened while he spoke, "I have plenty to keep, when I keep this present season. Now, where's my quiet Mouse? Chattering's the sin of my time of life, and there's half the building to do yet, if the cold don't freeze us first, or the wind don't blow us away, or the darkness don't swallow us up."

The quiet Mouse had brought her calm face to his side, and silently taken his arm, before he finished speaking.

"Come away, my dear," said the old man. "Mr. Redlaw won't settle to his dinner, otherwise, till it's cold as the winter. I hope you'll excuse me rambling on, sir, and I wish you good night, and, once again, a merry—"

"Stay!" said Mr. Redlaw, resuming his place at the table, more, it would have seemed from his manner, to reassure the old keeper, than in any remembrance of his own appetite. "Spare me another moment, Philip. William, you were going to tell me something to your excellent wife's honour. It will not be disagreeable to her to hear you praise her. What was it?"

"Why, that's where it is, you see, sir," returned Mr. William Swidger, looking towards his wife in considerable embarrassment. "Mrs. William's got her eye upon me."

"But you're not afraid of Mrs. William's eye?"

"Why, no, sir," returned Mr. Swidger, "that's what I say myself. It wasn't made to be afraid of. It wouldn't have been made so mild, if that was the intention. But I wouldn't like to—Milly!—him, you know. Down in the Buildings."

Mr. William, standing behind the table, and rummaging disconcertedly among the objects upon it, directed persuasive glances at Mrs. William, and secret jerks of his head and thumb at Mr. Redlaw, as alluring her towards him.

"Him, you know, my love," said Mr. William. "Down in the Buildings. Tell, my dear! You're the works of Shakespeare in comparison with myself. Down in the Buildings, you know, my love.—Student."

"Student?" repeated Mr. Redlaw, raising his head.

"That's what I say, sir!" cried Mr. William, in the utmost animation of assent. "If it wasn't the poor student down in the Buildings, why should you wish to hear it from Mrs. William's lips? Mrs. William, my dear—Buildings."

"I didn't know," said Milly, with a quiet frankness, free from any haste or confusion, "that William had said anything about it, or I wouldn't have come. I asked him not to. It's a sick young gentleman, sir—and very poor, I am afraid—who is too ill to go home this holiday-time, and lives, unknown to any one, in but a common kind of lodging for a gentleman, down in Jerusalem Buildings. That's all, sir."

"Why have I never heard of him?" said the Chemist, rising hurriedly. "Why has he not made his situation known to me? Sick!——give me my hat and cloak. Poor!—what house?—what number?"

"Oh, you mustn't go there, sir," said Milly, leaving her father-in-law, and calmly confronting him with her collected little face and folded hands.

"Not go there?"

"Oh dear, no!" said Milly, shaking her head as at a most manifest and self-evident impossibility. "It couldn't be thought of!"

"What do you mean? Why not?"

"Why, you see, sir," said Mr. William Swidger, persuasively and confidentially, "that's what I say. Depend upon it, the young gentleman would never have made his situation known to one of his own sex. Mrs. William has got into his confidence, but that's quite different. They all confide in Mrs. William; they all trust her. A man, sir, couldn't have got a whisper out of him; but woman, sir, and Mrs. William combined—!"

"There is good sense and delicacy in what you say, William," returned Mr. Redlaw, observant of the gentle and composed face at his shoulder. And laying his finger on his lip, he secretly put his purse into her hand.

"Oh dear no, sir!" cried Milly, giving it back again. "Worse and worse! Couldn't be dreamed of!"

Such a staid matter-of-fact housewife she was, and so unruffled by the momentary haste of this rejection, that, an instant afterwards, she was tidily picking up a few leaves which had strayed from between her scissors and her apron, when she had arranged the holly.

Finding, when she rose from her stooping posture, that Mr. Redlaw was still regarding her with doubt and astonishment, she quietly repeated—looking about, the while, for any other fragments that might have escaped her observation:

"Oh dear no, sir! He said that of all the world he would not be known to you, or receive help from you—though he is a student in your class. I have made no terms of secrecy with you, but I trust to your honour completely."

"Why did he say so?"

"Indeed I can't tell, sir," said Milly, after thinking a little, "because I am not at all clever, you know; and I wanted to be useful to him in making things neat and comfortable about him, and employed myself that way. But I know he is poor, and lonely, and I think he is somehow neglected too.—How dark it is!"

The room had darkened more and more. There was a very heavy gloom and shadow gathering behind the Chemist's chair.

"What more about him?" he asked.

"He is engaged to be married when he can afford it," said Milly, "and is studying, I think, to qualify himself to earn a living. I have seen, a long time, that he has studied hard and denied himself much.—How very dark it is!"

"It's turned colder, too," said the old man, rubbing his hands. "There's a chill and dismal feeling in the room. Where's my son William? William, my boy, turn the lamp, and rouse the fire!"

Milly's voice resumed, like quiet music very softly played:

"He muttered in his broken sleep yesterday afternoon, after talking to me" (this was to herself) "about some one dead, and some great wrong done that could never be forgotten; but whether to him or to another person, I don't know. Not by him, I am sure."

"And, in short, Mrs. William, you see—which she wouldn't say herself, Mr.

Redlaw, if she was to stop here till the new year after this next one—" said Mr. William, coming up to him to speak in his ear, "has done him worlds of good! Bless you, worlds of good! All at home just the same as ever—my father made as snug and comfortable—not a crumb of litter to be found in the house, if you were to offer fifty pound ready money for it—Mrs. William apparently never out of the way—yet Mrs. William backwards and forwards, backwards and forwards, up and down, up and down, a mother to him!"

The room turned darker and colder, and the gloom and shadow gathering behind the chair was heavier.

"Not content with this, sir, Mrs. William goes and finds, this very night, when she was coming home (why it's not above a couple of hours ago), a creature more like a young wild beast than a young child, shivering upon a door-step. What does Mrs. William do, but brings it home to dry it, and feed it, and keep it till our old Bounty of food and flannel is given away, on Christmas morning! If it ever felt a fire before, it's as much as ever it did; for it's sitting in the old Lodge chimney, staring at ours as if its ravenous eyes would never shut again. It's sitting there, at least," said Mr. William, correcting himself, on reflection, "unless it's bolted!"

"Heaven keep her happy!" said the Chemist aloud, "and you too, Philip! and you, William! I must consider what to do in this. I may desire to see this student, I'll not detain you any longer now. Good-night!"

"I thank'ee, sir, I thank'ee!" said the old man, "for Mouse, and for my son William, and for myself. Where's my son William? William, you take the lantern and go on first, through them long dark passages, as you did last year and the year afore. Ha ha! I remember—though I'm eighty-seven! 'Lord, keep my memory green!' It's a very good prayer, Mr. Redlaw, that of the learned gentleman in the peaked beard, with a ruff round his neck—hangs up, second on the right above the panelling, in what used to be, afore our ten poor gentlemen commuted, our great Dinner Hall. 'Lord, keep my memory green!' It's very good and pious, sir. Amen! Amen!"

As they passed out and shut the heavy door, which, however carefully withheld, fired a long train of thundering reverberations when it shut at last, the room turned darker.

As he fell a musing in his chair alone, the healthy holly withered on the wall, and dropped—dead branches.

As the gloom and shadow thickened behind him, in that place where it had been gathering so darkly, it took, by slow degrees,—or out of it there came, by some unreal, unsubstantial process—not to be traced by any human sense,—an awful likeness of himself!

Ghastly and cold, colourless in its leaden face and hands, but with his features, and his bright eyes, and his grizzled hair, and dressed in the gloomy shadow of his dress, it came into his terrible appearance of existence, motionless, without a sound. As he leaned his arm upon the elbow of his chair, ruminating before the fire, it leaned upon the chair-back, close above him, with its appalling copy of his face looking where his face looked, and bearing the expression his face bore.

This, then, was the Something that had passed and gone already. This was the dread companion of the haunted man!

It took, for some moments, no more apparent heed of him, than he of it. The Christmas Waits were playing somewhere in the distance, and, through his thoughtfulness, he seemed to listen to the music. It seemed to listen too.

At length he spoke; without moving or lifting up his face.

"Here again!" he said.

"Here again," replied the Phantom.

"I see you in the fire," said the haunted man; "I hear you in music, in the wind, in the dead stillness of the night."

The Phantom moved its head, assenting.

"Why do you come, to haunt me thus?"

"I come as I am called," replied the Ghost.

"No. Unbidden," exclaimed the Chemist.

"Unbidden be it," said the Spectre. "It is enough. I am here."

Hitherto the light of the fire had shone on the two faces—if the dread lineaments behind the chair might be called a face—both addressed towards it, as at first, and neither looking at the other. But, now, the haunted man turned, suddenly, and stared upon the Ghost. The Ghost, as sudden in its motion, passed to before the chair, and stared on him.

The living man, and the animated image of himself dead, might so have looked, the one upon the other. An awful survey, in a lonely and remote part of an empty old pile of building, on a winter night, with the loud wind going by upon its journey of mystery—whence or whither, no man knowing since the world began—and the stars, in unimaginable millions, glittering through it, from eternal space, where the world's bulk is as a grain, and its hoary age is infancy.

"Look upon me!" said the Spectre. "I am he, neglected in my youth, and miserably poor, who strove and suffered, and still strove and suffered, until I hewed out knowledge from the mine where it was buried, and made rugged steps thereof, for my worn feet to rest and rise on."

"I am that man," returned the Chemist.

"No mother's self-denying love," pursued the Phantom, "no father's counsel, aided me. A stranger came into my father's place when I was but a child, and I was easily an alien from my mother's heart. My parents, at the best, were of that sort whose care soon ends, and whose duty is soon done; who cast their offspring loose, early, as birds do theirs; and, if they do well, claim the merit; and, if ill, the pity."

It paused, and seemed to tempt and goad him with its look, and with the manner of its speech, and with its smile.

"I am he," pursued the Phantom, "who, in this struggle upward, found a friend. I made him—won him—bound him to me! We worked together, side by side. All the love and confidence that in my earlier youth had had no outlet, and found no expression, I bestowed on him."

"Not all," said Redlaw, hoarsely.

"No, not all," returned the Phantom. "I had a sister."

The haunted man, with his head resting on his hands, replied "I had!" The Phantom, with an evil smile, drew closer to the chair, and resting its chin upon its folded hands, its folded hands upon the back, and looking down into his face with searching eyes, that seemed instinct with fire, went on:

"Such glimpses of the light of home as I had ever known, had streamed from her. How young she was, how fair, how loving! I took her to the first poor roof that I was master of, and made it rich. She came into the darkness of my life, and made it bright.—She is before me!"

"I saw her, in the fire, but now. I hear her in music, in the wind, in the dead stillness of the night," returned the haunted man.

"Did he love her?" said the Phantom, echoing his contemplative tone. "I think he did, once. I am sure he did. Better had she loved him less—less secretly, less dearly, from the shallower depths of a more divided heart!"

"Let me forget it!" said the Chemist, with an angry motion of his hand. "Let me blot it from my memory!"

The Spectre, without stirring, and with its unwinking, cruel eyes still fixed upon his face, went on:

"A dream, like hers, stole upon my own life."

"It did," said Redlaw.

"A love, as like hers," pursued the Phantom, "as my inferior nature might cherish, arose in my own heart. I was too poor to bind its object to my fortune then, by any thread of promise or entreaty. I loved her far too well, to seek to do it. But, more than ever I had striven in my life, I strove to climb! Only an inch gained, brought me something nearer to the height. I toiled up! In the late pauses of my labour at that time,—my sister (sweet companion!) still sharing with me the expiring embers and the cooling hearth,—when day was breaking, what pictures of the future did I see!"

"I saw them, in the fire, but now," he murmured. "They come back to me in music, in the wind, in the dead stillness of the night, in the revolving years."

"—Pictures of my own domestic life, in aftertime, with her who was the inspiration of my toil. Pictures of my sister, made the wife of my dear friend, on equal terms—for he had some inheritance, we none—pictures of our sobered age and mellowed happiness, and of the golden links, extending back so far, that should bind us, and our children, in a radiant garland," said the Phantom.

"Pictures," said the haunted man, "that were delusions. Why is it my doom to remember them too well!"

"Delusions," echoed the Phantom in its changeless voice, and glaring on him with its changeless eyes. "For my friend (in whose breast my confidence was locked as in my own), passing between me and the centre of the system of my hopes and struggles, won her to himself, and shattered my frail universe. My sister, doubly dear, doubly devoted, doubly cheerful in my home, lived on to see me famous, and my old ambition so rewarded when its spring was broken, and then—"

"Then died," he interposed. "Died, gentle as ever; happy; and with no concern but for her brother. Peace!"

The Phantom watched him silently.

"Remembered!" said the haunted man, after a pause. "Yes. So well remembered, that even now, when years have passed, and nothing is more idle or more visionary to me than the boyish love so long outlived, I think of it with sympathy, as if it were a younger brother's or a son's. Sometimes I even wonder when her heart first inclined to him, and how it had been affected towards me.—Not lightly, once, I think.—But that is nothing. Early unhappiness, a wound from a hand I loved and trusted, and a loss that nothing can replace, outlive such fancies."

"Thus," said the Phantom, "I bear within me a Sorrow and a Wrong. Thus I prey upon myself. Thus, memory is my curse; and, if I could forget my sorrow and my wrong, I would!"

"Mocker!" said the Chemist, leaping up, and making, with a wrathful hand, at the throat of his other self. "Why have I always that taunt in my ears?"

"Forbear!" exclaimed the Spectre in an awful voice. "Lay a hand on Me, and die!"

He stopped midway, as if its words had paralysed him, and stood looking on it. It had glided from him; it had its arm raised high in warning; and a smile passed over its unearthly features, as it reared its dark figure in triumph.

"If I could forget my sorrow and wrong, I would," the Ghost repeated. "If I could forget my sorrow and my wrong, I would!"

"Evil spirit of myself," returned the haunted man, in a low, trembling tone, "my life is darkened by that incessant whisper."

"It is an echo," said the Phantom.

"If it be an echo of my thoughts—as now, indeed, I know it is," rejoined the haunted man, "why should I, therefore, be tormented? It is not a selfish thought. I suffer it to range beyond myself. All men and women have their sorrows,—most of them their wrongs; ingratitude, and sordid jealousy, and interest, besetting all degrees of life. Who would not forget their sorrows and their wrongs?"

"Who would not, truly, and be happier and better for it?" said the Phantom.

"These revolutions of years, which we commemorate," proceeded Redlaw, "what do they recall! Are there any minds in which they do not re-awaken some sorrow, or some trouble? What is the remembrance of the old man who was here to-night? A tissue of sorrow and trouble."

"But common natures," said the Phantom, with its evil smile upon its glassy face, "unenlightened minds and ordinary spirits, do not feel or reason on these things like men of higher cultivation and profounder thought."

"Tempter," answered Redlaw, "whose hollow look and voice I dread more than words can express, and from whom some dim foreshadowing of greater fear is stealing over me while I speak, I hear again an echo of my own mind."

"Receive it as a proof that I am powerful," returned the Ghost. "Hear what I offer! Forget the sorrow, wrong, and trouble you have known!"

"Forget them!" he repeated.

"I have the power to cancel their remembrance—to leave but very faint, confused traces of them, that will die out soon," returned the Spectre. "Say! Is it done?"

"Stay!" cried the haunted man, arresting by a terrified gesture the uplifted hand. "I tremble with distrust and doubt of you; and the dim fear you cast upon me deepens into a nameless horror I can hardly bear.—I would not deprive myself of any kindly recollection, or any sympathy that is good for me, or others. What shall I lose, if I assent to this? What else will pass from my remembrance?"

"No knowledge; no result of study; nothing but the intertwisted chain of feelings and associations, each in its turn dependent on, and nourished by, the banished recollections. Those will go."

"Are they so many?" said the haunted man, reflecting in alarm.

"They have been wont to show themselves in the fire, in music, in the wind, in the dead stillness of the night, in the revolving years," returned the Phantom scornfully.

"In nothing else?"

The Phantom held its peace.

But having stood before him, silent, for a little while, it moved towards the fire; then stopped.

"Decide!" it said, "before the opportunity is lost!"

"A moment! I call Heaven to witness," said the agitated man, "that I have never been a hater of any kind,—never morose, indifferent, or hard, to anything around me. If, living here alone, I have made too much of all that was and might have been, and too little of what is, the evil, I believe, has fallen on me, and not on others. But, if there were poison in my body, should I not, possessed of antidotes and knowledge how to use them, use them? If there be poison in my mind, and through this fearful shadow I can cast it out, shall I not cast it out?"

"Say," said the Spectre, "is it done?"

"A moment longer!" he answered hurriedly. "I would forget it if I could! Have I thought that, alone, or has it been the thought of thousands upon thousands, generation after generation? All human memory is fraught with sorrow and trouble. My memory is as the memory of other men, but other men have not this choice. Yes, I close the bargain. Yes! I will forget my sorrow, wrong, and trouble!"

"Say," said the Spectre, "is it done?"

"It is!"

"It is. And take this with you, man whom I here renounce! The gift that I have given, you shall give again, go where you will. Without recovering yourself the power that you have yielded up, you shall henceforth destroy its like in all whom you approach. Your wisdom has discovered that the memory of sorrow, wrong, and trouble is the lot of all mankind, and that mankind would be the happier, in its other memories, without it. Go! Be its benefactor! Freed from such remembrance, from this hour, carry involuntarily the blessing of such freedom with you. Its diffusion is inseparable and inalienable from you. Go! Be happy in the good you have won, and in the good you do!"

The Phantom, which had held its bloodless hand above him while it spoke, as if in some unholy invocation, or some ban; and which had gradually advanced its eyes so close to his, that he could see how they did not participate in the terrible smile upon its face, but were a fixed, unalterable, steady horror melted before him and was gone.

As he stood rooted to the spot, possessed by fear and wonder, and imagining he heard repeated in melancholy echoes, dying away fainter and fainter, the words, "Destroy its like in all whom you approach!" a shrill cry reached his ears. It came, not from the passages beyond the door, but from another part of the old building, and sounded like the cry of some one in the dark who had lost the way.

He looked confusedly upon his hands and limbs, as if to be assured of his identity, and then shouted in reply, loudly and wildly; for there was a strangeness and terror upon him, as if he too were lost.

The cry responding, and being nearer, he caught up the lamp, and raised a heavy curtain in the wall, by which he was accustomed to pass into and out of the theatre where he lectured,—which adjoined his room. Associated with youth and animation, and a high amphitheatre of faces which his entrance charmed to interest in a moment, it was a ghostly place when all this life was faded out of it, and stared upon him like an emblem of Death.

"Halloa!" he cried. "Halloa! This way! Come to the light!" When, as he held the curtain with one hand, and with the other raised the lamp and tried to pierce the gloom that filled the place, something rushed past him into the room like a wild-cat, and crouched down in a corner.

"What is it?" he said, hastily.

He might have asked "What is it?" even had he seen it well, as presently he did when he stood looking at it gathered up in its corner.

A bundle of tatters, held together by a hand, in size and form almost an infant's, but in its greedy, desperate little clutch, a bad old man's. A face rounded and smoothed by some half-dozen years, but pinched and twisted by the experiences of a life. Bright eyes, but not youthful. Naked feet, beautiful in their childish delicacy,—ugly in the blood and dirt that cracked upon them. A baby savage, a young monster, a child who had never been a child, a creature who might live to take the outward form of man, but who, within, would live and perish a mere beast.

Used, already, to be worried and hunted like a beast, the boy crouched down as he was looked at, and looked back again, and interposed his arm to ward off the expected blow.

"I'll bite," he said, "if you hit me!"

The time had been, and not many minutes since, when such a sight as this would have wrung the Chemist's heart. He looked upon it now, coldly; but with a heavy effort to remember something—he did not know what—he asked the boy what he did there, and whence he came.

"Where's the woman?" he replied. "I want to find the woman."

"Who?"

"The woman. Her that brought me here, and set me by the large fire. She was so long gone, that I went to look for her, and lost myself. I don't want you. I want the woman."

He made a spring, so suddenly, to get away, that the dull sound of his naked feet upon the floor was near the curtain, when Redlaw caught him by his rags.

"Come! you let me go!" muttered the boy, struggling, and clenching his teeth. "I've done nothing to you. Let me go, will you, to the woman!"

"That is not the way. There is a nearer one," said Redlaw, detaining him, in the same blank effort to remember some association that ought, of right, to bear upon this monstrous object. "What is your name?"

"Got none."

"Where do you live?

"Live! What's that?"

The boy shook his hair from his eyes to look at him for a moment, and then, twisting round his legs and wrestling with him, broke again into his repetition of "You let me go, will you? I want to find the woman."

The Chemist led him to the door. "This way," he said, looking at him still confusedly, but with repugnance and avoidance, growing out of his coldness. "I'll take you to her."

The sharp eyes in the child's head, wandering round the room, lighted on the table where the remnants of the dinner were.

"Give me some of that!" he said, covetously.

"Has she not fed you?"

"I shall be hungry again to-morrow, sha'n't I? Ain't I hungry every day?"

Finding himself released, he bounded at the table like some small animal of prey, and hugging to his breast bread and meat, and his own rags, all together, said:

"There! Now take me to the woman!"

As the Chemist, with a new-born dislike to touch him, sternly motioned him to follow, and was going out of the door, he trembled and stopped.

"The gift that I have given, you shall give again, go where you will!"

The Phantom's words were blowing in the wind, and the wind blew chill upon him.

"I'll not go there, to-night," he murmured faintly. "I'll go nowhere to-night. Boy! straight down this long-arched passage, and past the great dark door into the yard,—you see the fire shining on the window there."

"The woman's fire?" inquired the boy.

He nodded, and the naked feet had sprung away. He came back with his lamp, locked his door hastily, and sat down in his chair, covering his face like one who was frightened at himself.

For now he was, indeed, alone. Alone, alone.

CHAPTER II. THE GIFT DIFFUSED

A small man sat in a small parlour, partitioned off from a small shop by a small screen, pasted all over with small scraps of newspapers. In company with the small man, was almost any amount of small children you may please to name—at least it seemed so; they made, in that very limited sphere of action, such an imposing effect, in point of numbers.

Of these small fry, two had, by some strong machinery, been got into bed in a corner, where they might have reposed snugly enough in the sleep of innocence, but for a constitutional propensity to keep awake, and also to scuffle in and out of bed. The immediate occasion of these predatory dashes at the waking world, was the construction of an oyster-shell wall in a corner, by two other youths of tender age; on which fortification the two in bed made harassing descents (like those accursed Picts and Scots who beleaguer the early historical studies of most young Britons), and then withdrew to their own territory.

In addition to the stir attendant on these inroads, and the retorts of the invaded, who pursued hotly, and made lunges at the bed-clothes under which the marauders took refuge, another little boy, in another little bed, contributed his mite of confusion to the family stock, by casting his boots upon the waters; in other words, by launching these and several small objects, inoffensive in themselves, though of a hard substance considered as missiles, at the disturbers of his repose,—who were not slow to return these compliments.

Besides which, another little boy—the biggest there, but still little—was tottering to and fro, bent on one side, and considerably affected in his knees by the weight of a large baby, which he was supposed by a fiction that obtains sometimes in sanguine families, to be hushing to sleep. But oh! the inexhaustible regions of contemplation and watchfulness into which this baby's eyes were then only beginning to compose themselves to stare, over his unconscious shoulder!

It was a very Moloch of a baby, on whose insatiate altar the whole existence of this particular young brother was offered up a daily sacrifice. Its personality may be said to have consisted in its never being quiet, in any one place, for five consecutive minutes, and never going to sleep when required. "Tetterby's baby" was as well known in the neighbourhood as the postman or the pot-boy. It roved from door-step to door-step, in the arms of little Johnny Tetterby, and lagged heavily at the rear of troops of juveniles who followed the Tumblers or the Monkey, and came up, all on one side, a little too late for everything that was attractive, from Monday morning until Saturday night. Wherever childhood congregated to play, there was little Moloch making Johnny fag and toil. Wherever Johnny desired to stay, little Moloch became fractious, and would not remain. Whenever Johnny wanted to go out, Moloch was asleep, and must be watched. Whenever Johnny wanted to stay at home, Moloch was awake, and must be taken out. Yet Johnny was verily persuaded that it was a faultless baby, without its peer in the realm of England, and was quite content to catch meek glimpses of things in general from behind its skirts, or over its limp flapping bonnet, and to go staggering about with it like a very little porter with a very large parcel, which was not directed to anybody, and could never be delivered anywhere.

The small man who sat in the small parlour, making fruitless attempts to read his newspaper peaceably in the midst of this disturbance, was the father of the family, and the chief of the firm described in the inscription over the little shop front, by the name and title of A. Tetterby and Co., Newsmen. Indeed, strictly speaking, he was the only personage answering to that designation, as Co. was a mere poetical abstraction, altogether baseless and impersonal.

Tetterby's was the corner shop in Jerusalem Buildings. There was a good show of literature in the window, chiefly consisting of picture-newspapers out of date, and serial pirates, and footpads. Walking-sticks, likewise, and marbles, were included in the stock in trade. It had once extended into the light confectionery line; but it would seem that those elegancies of life were not in demand about Jerusalem Buildings, for nothing connected with that branch of commerce remained in the window, except a sort of small glass lantern containing a languishing mass of bull's-eyes, which had melted in the summer and congealed in the winter until all hope of ever getting them out, or of eating them without eating the lantern too, was gone for ever. Tetterby's had tried its hand at several things. It had once made a feeble little dart at the toy business; for, in another lantern, there was a heap of minute wax dolls, all sticking together upside down, in the direst confusion, with their feet on one another's heads, and a precipitate of broken arms and legs at the bottom. It had made a move in the millinery direction, which a few dry, wiry bonnet-shapes remained in a corner of the window to attest. It had fancied that a living might lie hidden in the tobacco trade, and had stuck up a representation of a native of each of the three integral portions of the British Empire, in the act of consuming that fragrant weed; with a poetic legend attached, importing that united in one cause they sat and joked, one chewed tobacco, one took snuff, one smoked: but nothing seemed to have come of it—except flies. Time had been when it had put a forlorn trust in imitative jewellery, for in one pane of glass there was a card of cheap seals, and another of pencil-cases, and a mysterious black amulet of inscrutable intention, labelled ninepence. But, to that hour, Jerusalem Buildings had bought none of them. In short, Tetterby's had tried so hard to get a livelihood out of Jerusalem Buildings in one way or other, and appeared to have done so indifferently in all, that the best position in the firm was too evidently Co.'s; Co., as a bodiless creation, being untroubled with the vulgar inconveniences of hunger and thirst, being chargeable neither to the poor's-rates nor the assessed taxes, and having no young family to provide for.

Tetterby himself, however, in his little parlour, as already mentioned, having the presence of a young family impressed upon his mind in a manner too clamorous to be disregarded, or to comport with the quiet perusal of a newspaper, laid down his paper, wheeled, in his distraction, a few times round the parlour, like an undecided carrier-pigeon, made an ineffectual rush at one or two flying little figures in bed-gowns that skimmed past him, and then, bearing suddenly down upon the only unoffending member of the family, boxed the ears of little Moloch's nurse.

"You bad boy!" said Mr. Tetterby, "haven't you any feeling for your poor father after the fatigues and anxieties of a hard winter's day, since five o'clock in the morning, but must you wither his rest, and corrode his latest intelligence, with your wicious tricks? Isn't it enough, sir, that your brother 'Dolphus is toiling and moiling in the fog and cold, and you rolling in the lap of luxury with a—with a baby, and everything you can wish for," said Mr. Tetterby, heaping this up as a great climax of blessings, "but must you make a wilderness of home, and maniacs of your parents? Must you, Johnny? Hey?" At each interrogation, Mr. Tetterby made a feint of boxing his ears again, but thought better of it, and held his hand.

"Oh, father!" whimpered Johnny, "when I wasn't doing anything, I'm sure, but taking such care of Sally, and getting her to sleep. Oh, father!"

"I wish my little woman would come home!" said Mr. Tetterby, relenting and repenting, "I only wish my little woman would come home! I ain't fit to deal with 'em. They make my head go round, and get the better of me. Oh, Johnny! Isn't it enough that your dear mother has provided you with that sweet sister?" indicating Moloch; "isn't it enough that you were seven boys before without a ray of gal, and that your dear mother went through what she did go through, on purpose that you might all of you have a little sister, but must you so behave yourself as to make my head swim?"

Softening more and more, as his own tender feelings and those of his injured son were worked on, Mr. Tetterby concluded by embracing him, and immediately breaking away to catch one of the real delinquents. A reasonably good start occurring, he succeeded, after a short but smart run, and some rather severe cross-country work under and over the bedsteads, and in and out among the intricacies of the chairs, in capturing this infant, whom he condignly punished, and bore to bed. This example had a powerful, and apparently, mesmeric influence on him of the boots, who instantly fell into a deep sleep, though he had been, but a moment before, broad awake, and in the highest possible feather. Nor was it lost upon the two young architects, who retired to bed, in an adjoining closet, with great privacy and speed. The comrade of the Intercepted One also shrinking into his nest with similar discretion, Mr. Tetterby, when he paused for breath, found himself unexpectedly in a scene of peace.

"My little woman herself," said Mr. Tetterby, wiping his flushed face, "could hardly have done it better! I only wish my little woman had had it to do, I do indeed!"

Mr. Tetterby sought upon his screen for a passage appropriate to be impressed upon his children's minds on the occasion, and read the following.

"'It is an undoubted fact that all remarkable men have had remarkable mothers, and have respected them in after life as their best friends.' Think of your own remarkable mother, my boys," said Mr. Tetterby, "and know her value while she is still among you!"

He sat down again in his chair by the fire, and composed himself, cross-legged, over his newspaper.

"Let anybody, I don't care who it is, get out of bed again," said Tetterby, as a general proclamation, delivered in a very soft-hearted manner, "and astonishment will be the portion of that respected contemporary!"—which expression Mr. Tetterby selected from his screen. "Johnny, my child, take care of your only sister, Sally; for she's the brightest gem that ever sparkled on your early brow."

Johnny sat down on a little stool, and devotedly crushed himself beneath the weight of Moloch.

"Ah, what a gift that baby is to you, Johnny!" said his father, "and how thankful you ought to be! 'It is not generally known, Johnny,'" he was now referring to the screen again, "'but it is a fact ascertained, by accurate calculations, that the following immense percentage of babies never attain to two years old; that is to say—'"

"Oh, don't, father, please!" cried Johnny. "I can't bear it, when I think of Sally."

Mr. Tetterby desisting, Johnny, with a profound sense of his trust, wiped his eyes, and hushed his sister.

"Your brother 'Dolphus," said his father, poking the fire, "is late to-night, Johnny, and will come home like a lump of ice. What's got your precious mother?"

"Here's mother, and 'Dolphus too, father!" exclaimed Johnny, "I think."

"You're right!" returned his father, listening. "Yes, that's the footstep of my little woman."

The process of induction, by which Mr. Tetterby had come to the conclusion that his wife was a little woman, was his own secret. She would have made two editions of himself, very easily. Considered as an individual, she was rather remarkable for being robust and portly; but considered with reference to her husband, her dimensions became magnificent. Nor did they assume a less imposing proportion, when studied with reference to the size of her seven sons, who were but diminutive. In the case of Sally, however, Mrs. Tetterby had asserted herself, at last; as nobody knew better than the victim Johnny, who weighed and measured that exacting idol every hour in the day.

Mrs. Tetterby, who had been marketing, and carried a basket, threw back her bonnet and shawl, and sitting down, fatigued, commanded Johnny to bring his sweet charge to her straightway, for a kiss. Johnny having complied, and gone back to his stool, and again crushed himself, Master Adolphus Tetterby, who had by this time unwound his torso out of a prismatic comforter, apparently interminable, requested the same favour. Johnny having again complied, and again gone back to his stool, and again crushed himself, Mr. Tetterby, struck by a sudden thought, preferred the same claim on his own parental part. The satisfaction of this third desire completely exhausted the sacrifice, who had hardly breath enough left to get back to his stool, crush himself again, and pant at his relations.

"Whatever you do, Johnny," said Mrs. Tetterby, shaking her head, "take care of her, or never look your mother in the face again."

"Nor your brother," said Adolphus.

"Nor your father, Johnny," added Mr. Tetterby.

Johnny, much affected by this conditional renunciation of him, looked down at Moloch's eyes to see that they were all right, so far, and skilfully patted her back (which was uppermost), and rocked her with his foot.

"Are you wet, 'Dolphus, my boy?" said his father. "Come and take my chair, and dry yourself."

"No, father, thank'ee," said Adolphus, smoothing himself down with his hands. "I an't very wet, I don't think. Does my face shine much, father?"

"Well, it does look waxy, my boy," returned Mr. Tetterby.

"It's the weather, father," said Adolphus, polishing his cheeks on the worn sleeve of his jacket. "What with rain, and sleet, and wind, and snow, and fog, my face gets quite brought out into a rash sometimes. And shines, it does—oh, don't it, though!"

Master Adolphus was also in the newspaper line of life, being employed, by a more thriving firm than his father and Co., to vend newspapers at a railway station, where his chubby little person, like a shabbily-disguised Cupid, and his shrill little voice (he was not much more than ten years old), were as well known as the hoarse panting of the locomotives, running in and out. His juvenility might have been at some loss for a harmless outlet, in this early application to traffic, but for a fortunate discovery he made of a means of entertaining himself, and of dividing the long day into stages of interest, without neglecting business. This ingenious invention, remarkable, like many great discoveries, for its simplicity, consisted in varying the first vowel in the word "paper," and substituting, in its stead, at different periods of the day, all the other vowels in grammatical succession. Thus, before daylight in the winter-time, he went to and fro, in his little oilskin cap and cape, and his big comforter, piercing the heavy air with his cry of "Morn-ing Pa-per!" which, about an hour before noon, changed to "Morn-ing Pepper!" which, at about two, changed to "Morn-ing Pip-per!" which in a couple of hours changed to "Morn-ing Pop-per!" and so declined with the sun into "Eve-ning Pup-per!" to the great relief and comfort of this young gentleman's spirits.

Mrs. Tetterby, his lady-mother, who had been sitting with her bonnet and shawl thrown back, as aforesaid, thoughtfully turning her wedding-ring round and round upon her finger, now rose, and divesting herself of her out-of-door attire, began to lay the cloth for supper.

"Ah, dear me, dear me, dear me!" said Mrs. Tetterby. "That's the way the world goes!"

"Which is the way the world goes, my dear?" asked Mr. Tetterby, looking round.

"Oh, nothing," said Mrs. Tetterby.

Mr. Tetterby elevated his eyebrows, folded his newspaper afresh, and carried his eyes up it, and down it, and across it, but was wandering in his attention, and not reading it.

Mrs. Tetterby, at the same time, laid the cloth, but rather as if she were punishing the table than preparing the family supper; hitting it unnecessarily hard with the knives and forks, slapping it with the plates, dinting it with the salt-cellar, and coming heavily down upon it with the loaf.

"Ah, dear me, dear me, dear me!" said Mrs. Tetterby. "That's the way the world goes!"

"My duck," returned her husband, looking round again, "you said that before. Which is the way the world goes?"

"Oh, nothing!" said Mrs. Tetterby.

"Sophia!" remonstrated her husband, "you said that before, too."

"Well, I'll say it again if you like," returned Mrs. Tetterby. "Oh nothing—there! And again if you like, oh nothing—there! And again if you like, oh nothing—now then!"

Mr. Tetterby brought his eye to bear upon the partner of his bosom, and said, in mild astonishment:

"My little woman, what has put you out?"

"I'm sure I don't know," she retorted. "Don't ask me. Who said I was put out at all? I never did."

Mr. Tetterby gave up the perusal of his newspaper as a bad job, and, taking a slow walk across the room, with his hands behind him, and his shoulders raised—his gait according perfectly with the resignation of his manner—addressed himself to his two eldest offspring.

"Your supper will be ready in a minute, 'Dolphus," said Mr. Tetterby. "Your mother has been out in the wet, to the cook's shop, to buy it. It was very good of your mother so to do. You shall get some supper too, very soon, Johnny. Your mother's pleased with you, my man, for being so attentive to your precious sister."

Mrs. Tetterby, without any remark, but with a decided subsidence of her animosity towards the table, finished her preparations, and took, from her ample basket, a substantial slab of hot pease pudding wrapped in paper, and a basin covered with a saucer, which, on being uncovered, sent forth an odour so agreeable, that the three pair of eyes in the two beds opened wide and fixed themselves upon the banquet. Mr. Tetterby, without regarding this tacit invitation to be seated, stood repeating slowly, "Yes, yes, your supper will be ready in a minute, 'Dolphus—your mother went out in the wet, to the cook's shop, to buy it. It was very good of your mother so to do"—until Mrs. Tetterby, who had been exhibiting sundry tokens of contrition behind him, caught him round the neck, and wept.

"Oh, 'Dolphus!" said Mrs. Tetterby, "how could I go and behave so?"

This reconciliation affected Adolphus the younger and Johnny to that degree, that they both, as with one accord, raised a dismal cry, which had the effect of immediately shutting up the round eyes in the beds, and utterly routing the two remaining little Tetterbys, just then stealing in from the adjoining closet to see what was going on in the eating way.

"I am sure, 'Dolphus," sobbed Mrs. Tetterby, "coming home, I had no more idea than a child unborn—"

Mr. Tetterby seemed to dislike this figure of speech, and observed, "Say than the baby, my dear."

"—Had no more idea than the baby," said Mrs. Tetterby.—"Johnny, don't look at me, but look at her, or she'll fall out of your lap and be killed, and then you'll die in agonies of a broken heart, and serve you right.—No more idea I hadn't than that darling, of being cross when I came home; but somehow, 'Dolphus—" Mrs. Tetterby paused, and again turned her wedding-ring round and round upon her finger.

"I see!" said Mr. Tetterby. "I understand! My little woman was put out. Hard times, and hard weather, and hard work, make it trying now and then. I see, bless your soul! No wonder! Dolf, my man," continued Mr. Tetterby, exploring the basin with a fork, "here's your mother been and bought, at the cook's shop, besides pease pudding, a whole knuckle of a lovely roast leg of pork, with lots of crackling left upon it, and with seasoning gravy and mustard quite unlimited. Hand in your plate, my boy, and begin while it's simmering."

Master Adolphus, needing no second summons, received his portion with eyes rendered moist by appetite, and withdrawing to his particular stool, fell upon his supper tooth and nail. Johnny was not forgotten, but received his rations on bread, lest he should, in a flush of gravy, trickle any on the baby. He was required, for similar reasons, to keep his pudding, when not on active service, in his pocket.

There might have been more pork on the knucklebone,—which knucklebone the carver at the cook's shop had assuredly not forgotten in carving for previous customers—but there was no stint of seasoning, and that is an accessory dreamily suggesting pork, and pleasantly cheating the sense of taste. The pease pudding, too, the gravy and mustard, like the Eastern rose in respect of the nightingale, if they were not absolutely pork, had lived near it; so, upon the whole, there was the flavour of a middle-sized pig. It was irresistible to the Tetterbys in bed, who, though professing to slumber peacefully, crawled out when unseen by their parents, and silently appealed to their brothers for any gastronomic token of fraternal affection. They, not hard of heart, presenting scraps in return, it resulted that a party of light skirmishers in nightgowns were careering about the parlour all through supper, which harassed Mr. Tetterby exceedingly, and once or twice imposed upon him the necessity of a charge, before which these guerilla troops retired in all directions and in great confusion.

Mrs. Tetterby did not enjoy her supper. There seemed to be something on Mrs. Tetterby's mind. At one time she laughed without reason, and at another time she cried without reason, and at last she laughed and cried together in a manner so very unreasonable that her husband was confounded.

"My little woman," said Mr. Tetterby, "if the world goes that way, it appears to go the wrong way, and to choke you."

"Give me a drop of water," said Mrs. Tetterby, struggling with herself, "and don't speak to me for the present, or take any notice of me. Don't do it!"

Mr. Tetterby having administered the water, turned suddenly on the unlucky Johnny (who was full of sympathy), and demanded why he was wallowing there, in gluttony and idleness, instead of coming forward with the baby, that the sight of her might revive his mother. Johnny immediately approached, borne down by its weight; but Mrs. Tetterby holding out her hand to signify that she was not in a condition to bear that trying appeal to her feelings, he was interdicted from advancing another inch, on pain of perpetual hatred from all his dearest connections; and accordingly retired to his stool again, and crushed himself as before.

After a pause, Mrs. Tetterby said she was better now, and began to laugh.

"My little woman," said her husband, dubiously, "are you quite sure you're better? Or are you, Sophia, about to break out in a fresh direction?"

"No, 'Dolphus, no," replied his wife. "I'm quite myself." With that, settling her hair, and pressing the palms of her hands upon her eyes, she laughed again.

"What a wicked fool I was, to think so for a moment!" said Mrs. Tetterby. "Come nearer, 'Dolphus, and let me ease my mind, and tell you what I mean. Let me tell you all about it."

Mr. Tetterby bringing his chair closer, Mrs. Tetterby laughed again, gave him a hug, and wiped her eyes.

"You know, 'Dolphus, my dear," said Mrs. Tetterby, "that when I was single, I might have given myself away in several directions. At one time, four after me at once; two of them were sons of Mars."

"We're all sons of Ma's, my dear," said Mr. Tetterby, "jointly with Pa's."

"I don't mean that," replied his wife, "I mean soldiers—serjeants."

"Oh!" said Mr. Tetterby.

"Well, 'Dolphus, I'm sure I never think of such things now, to regret them; and I'm sure I've got as good a husband, and would do as much to prove that I was fond of him, as—"

"As any little woman in the world," said Mr. Tetterby. "Very good. Very good."

If Mr. Tetterby had been ten feet high, he could not have expressed a gentler consideration for Mrs. Tetterby's fairy-like stature; and if Mrs. Tetterby had been two feet high, she could not have felt it more appropriately her due.

"But you see, 'Dolphus," said Mrs. Tetterby, "this being Christmas-time, when all people who can, make holiday, and when all people who have got money, like to spend some, I did, somehow, get a little out of sorts when I was in the streets just now. There were so many things to be sold—such delicious things to eat, such fine things to look at, such delightful things to have—and there was so much calculating and calculating necessary, before I durst lay out a sixpence for the commonest thing; and the basket was so large, and wanted so much in it; and my stock of money was so small, and would go such a little way;—you hate me, don't you, 'Dolphus?"

"Not quite," said Mr. Tetterby, "as yet."

"Well! I'll tell you the whole truth," pursued his wife, penitently, "and then perhaps you will. I felt all this, so much, when I was trudging about in the cold, and when I saw a lot of other calculating faces and large baskets trudging about, too, that I began to think whether I mightn't have done better, and been happier, if—I—hadn't—" the wedding-ring went round again, and Mrs. Tetterby shook her downcast head as she turned it.

"I see," said her husband quietly; "if you hadn't married at all, or if you had married somebody else?"

"Yes," sobbed Mrs. Tetterby. "That's really what I thought. Do you hate me now, 'Dolphus?"

"Why no," said Mr. Tetterby. "I don't find that I do, as yet."

Mrs. Tetterby gave him a thankful kiss, and went on.

"I begin to hope you won't, now, 'Dolphus, though I'm afraid I haven't told you the worst. I can't think what came over me. I don't know whether I was ill, or mad, or what I was, but I couldn't call up anything that seemed to bind us to each other, or to reconcile me to my fortune. All the pleasures and enjoyments we had ever had—they seemed so poor and insignificant, I hated them. I could have trodden on them. And I could think of nothing else, except our being poor, and the number of mouths there were at home."

"Well, well, my dear," said Mr. Tetterby, shaking her hand encouragingly, "that's truth, after all. We are poor, and there are a number of mouths at home here."

"Ah! but, Dolf, Dolf!" cried his wife, laying her hands upon his neck, "my good, kind, patient fellow, when I had been at home a very little while—how different! Oh, Dolf, dear, how different it was! I felt as if there was a rush of recollection on me, all at once, that softened my hard heart, and filled it up till it was bursting. All our struggles for a livelihood, all our cares and wants since we have been married, all the times of sickness, all the hours of watching, we have ever had, by one another, or by the children, seemed to speak to me, and say that they had made us one, and that I never might have been, or could have been, or would have been, any other than the wife and mother I am. Then, the cheap enjoyments that I could have trodden on so cruelly, got to be so precious to me—Oh so priceless, and dear!—that I couldn't bear to think how much I had wronged them; and I said, and say again a hundred times, how could I ever behave so, 'Dolphus, how could I ever have the heart to do it!"

The good woman, quite carried away by her honest tenderness and remorse, was weeping with all her heart, when she started up with a scream, and ran behind her husband. Her cry was so terrified, that the children started from their sleep and from their beds, and clung about her. Nor did her gaze belie her voice, as she pointed to a pale man in a black cloak who had come into the room.

"Look at that man! Look there! What does he want?"

"My dear," returned her husband, "I'll ask him if you'll let me go. What's the matter! How you shake!"

"I saw him in the street, when I was out just now. He looked at me, and stood near me. I am afraid of him."

"Afraid of him! Why?"

"I don't know why—I—stop! husband!" for he was going towards the stranger.

She had one hand pressed upon her forehead, and one upon her breast; and there was a peculiar fluttering all over her, and a hurried unsteady motion of her eyes, as if she had lost something.

"Are you ill, my dear?"

"What is it that is going from me again?" she muttered, in a low voice. "What is this that is going away?"

Then she abruptly answered: "Ill? No, I am quite well," and stood looking vacantly at the floor.

Her husband, who had not been altogether free from the infection of her fear at first, and whom the present strangeness of her manner did not tend to reassure, addressed himself to the pale visitor in the black cloak, who stood still, and whose eyes were bent upon the ground.

"What may be your pleasure, sir," he asked, "with us?"

"I fear that my coming in unperceived," returned the visitor, "has alarmed you; but you were talking and did not hear me."

"My little woman says—perhaps you heard her say it," returned Mr. Tetterby, "that it's not the first time you have alarmed her to-night."

"I am sorry for it. I remember to have observed her, for a few moments only, in the street. I had no intention of frightening her."

As he raised his eyes in speaking, she raised hers. It was extraordinary to see what dread she had of him, and with what dread he observed it—and yet how narrowly and closely.

"My name," he said, "is Redlaw. I come from the old college hard by. A young gentleman who is a student there, lodges in your house, does he not?"

"Mr. Denham?" said Tetterby.

"Yes."

It was a natural action, and so slight as to be hardly noticeable; but the little man, before speaking again, passed his hand across his forehead, and looked quickly round the room, as though he were sensible of some change in its atmosphere. The Chemist, instantly transferring to him the look of dread he had directed towards the wife, stepped back, and his face turned paler.

"The gentleman's room," said Tetterby, "is upstairs, sir. There's a more convenient private entrance; but as you have come in here, it will save your going out into the cold, if you'll take this little staircase," showing one communicating directly with the parlour, "and go up to him that way, if you wish to see him."

"Yes, I wish to see him," said the Chemist. "Can you spare a light?"

The watchfulness of his haggard look, and the inexplicable distrust that darkened it, seemed to trouble Mr. Tetterby. He paused; and looking fixedly at him in return, stood for a minute or so, like a man stupefied, or fascinated.

At length he said, "I'll light you, sir, if you'll follow me."

"No," replied the Chemist, "I don't wish to be attended, or announced to him. He does not expect me. I would rather go alone. Please to give me the light, if you can spare it, and I'll find the way."

In the quickness of his expression of this desire, and in taking the candle from the newsman, he touched him on the breast. Withdrawing his hand hastily, almost as though he had wounded him by accident (for he did not know in what part of himself his new power resided, or how it was communicated, or how the manner of its reception varied in different persons), he turned and ascended the stair.

But when he reached the top, he stopped and looked down. The wife was standing in the same place, twisting her ring round and round upon her finger. The husband, with his head bent forward on his breast, was musing heavily and sullenly. The children, still clustering about the mother, gazed timidly after the visitor, and nestled together when they saw him looking down.

"Come!" said the father, roughly. "There's enough of this. Get to bed here!"

"The place is inconvenient and small enough," the mother added, "without you. Get to bed!"

The whole brood, scared and sad, crept away; little Johnny and the baby lagging last. The mother, glancing contemptuously round the sordid room, and tossing from her the fragments of their meal, stopped on the threshold of her task of clearing the table, and sat down, pondering idly and dejectedly. The father betook himself to the chimney-corner, and impatiently raking the small fire together, bent over it as if he would monopolise it all. They did not interchange a word.

The Chemist, paler than before, stole upward like a thief; looking back upon the change below, and dreading equally to go on or return.

"What have I done!" he said, confusedly. "What am I going to do!"

"To be the benefactor of mankind," he thought he heard a voice reply.

He looked round, but there was nothing there; and a passage now shutting out the little parlour from his view, he went on, directing his eyes before him at the way he went.

"It is only since last night," he muttered gloomily, "that I have remained shut up, and yet all things are strange to me. I am strange to myself. I am here, as in a dream. What interest have I in this place, or in any place that I can bring to my remembrance? My mind is going blind!"

There was a door before him, and he knocked at it. Being invited, by a voice within, to enter, he complied.

"Is that my kind nurse?" said the voice. "But I need not ask her. There is no one else to come here."

It spoke cheerfully, though in a languid tone, and attracted his attention to a young man lying on a couch, drawn before the chimney-piece, with the back towards the door. A meagre scanty stove, pinched and hollowed like a sick man's cheeks, and bricked into the centre of a hearth that it could scarcely warm, contained the fire, to which his face was turned. Being so near the windy house-top, it wasted quickly, and with a busy sound, and the burning ashes dropped down fast.

"They chink when they shoot out here," said the student, smiling, "so, according to the gossips, they are not coffins, but purses. I shall be well and rich yet, some day, if it please God, and shall live perhaps to love a daughter Milly, in remembrance of the kindest nature and the gentlest heart in the world."

He put up his hand as if expecting her to take it, but, being weakened, he lay still, with his face resting on his other hand, and did not turn round.

The Chemist glanced about the room;—at the student's books and papers, piled upon a table in a corner, where they, and his extinguished reading-lamp, now prohibited and put away, told of the attentive hours that had gone before this illness, and perhaps caused it;—at such signs of his old health and freedom, as the out-of-door attire that hung idle on the wall;—at those remembrances of other and less solitary scenes, the little miniatures upon the chimney-piece, and the drawing of home;—at that token of his emulation, perhaps, in some sort, of his personal attachment too, the framed engraving of himself, the looker-on. The time had been, only yesterday, when not one of these objects, in its remotest association of interest with the living figure before him, would have been lost on Redlaw. Now, they were but objects; or, if any gleam of such connexion shot upon him, it perplexed, and not enlightened him, as he stood looking round with a dull wonder.

The student, recalling the thin hand which had remained so long untouched, raised himself on the couch, and turned his head.

"Mr. Redlaw!" he exclaimed, and started up.

Redlaw put out his arm.

"Don't come nearer to me. I will sit here. Remain you, where you are!"

He sat down on a chair near the door, and having glanced at the young man standing leaning with his hand upon the couch, spoke with his eyes averted towards the ground.

"I heard, by an accident, by what accident is no matter, that one of my class was ill and solitary. I received no other description of him, than that he lived in this street. Beginning my inquiries at the first house in it, I have found him."

"I have been ill, sir," returned the student, not merely with a modest hesitation, but with a kind of awe of him, "but am greatly better. An attack of fever—of the brain, I believe—has weakened me, but I am much better. I cannot say I have been solitary, in my illness, or I should forget the ministering hand that has been near me."

"You are speaking of the keeper's wife," said Redlaw.

"Yes." The student bent his head, as if he rendered her some silent homage.

The Chemist, in whom there was a cold, monotonous apathy, which rendered him more like a marble image on the tomb of the man who had started from his dinner yesterday at the first mention of this student's case, than the breathing man himself, glanced again at the student leaning with his hand upon the couch, and looked upon the ground, and in the air, as if for light for his blinded mind.

"I remembered your name," he said, "when it was mentioned to me down stairs, just now; and I recollect your face. We have held but very little personal communication together?"

"Very little."

"You have retired and withdrawn from me, more than any of the rest, I think?"

The student signified assent.

"And why?" said the Chemist; not with the least expression of interest, but with a moody, wayward kind of curiosity. "Why? How comes it that you have sought to keep especially from me, the knowledge of your remaining here, at this season, when all the rest have dispersed, and of your being ill? I want to know why this is?"

The young man, who had heard him with increasing agitation, raised his downcast eyes to his face, and clasping his hands together, cried with sudden earnestness and with trembling lips:

"Mr. Redlaw! You have discovered me. You know my secret!"

"Secret?" said the Chemist, harshly. "I know?"

"Yes! Your manner, so different from the interest and sympathy which endear you to so many hearts, your altered voice, the constraint there is in everything you say, and in your looks," replied the student, "warn me that you know me. That you would conceal it, even now, is but a proof to me (God knows I need none!) of your natural kindness and of the bar there is between us."

A vacant and contemptuous laugh, was all his answer.

"But, Mr. Redlaw," said the student, "as a just man, and a good man, think how innocent I am, except in name and descent, of participation in any wrong inflicted on you or in any sorrow you have borne."

"Sorrow!" said Redlaw, laughing. "Wrong! What are those to me?"

"For Heaven's sake," entreated the shrinking student, "do not let the mere interchange of a few words with me change you like this, sir! Let me pass again from your knowledge and notice. Let me occupy my old reserved and distant place among those whom you instruct. Know me only by the name I have assumed, and not by that of Longford—"

"Longford!" exclaimed the other.

He clasped his head with both his hands, and for a moment turned upon the young man his own intelligent and thoughtful face. But the light passed from it, like the sun-beam of an instant, and it clouded as before.

"The name my mother bears, sir," faltered the young man, "the name she took, when she might, perhaps, have taken one more honoured. Mr. Redlaw," hesitating, "I believe I know that history. Where my information halts, my guesses at what is wanting may supply something not remote from the truth. I am the child of a marriage that has not proved itself a well-assorted or a happy one. From infancy, I have heard you spoken of with honour and respect—with something that was almost reverence. I have heard of such devotion, of such fortitude and tenderness, of such rising up against the obstacles which press men down, that my fancy, since I learnt my little lesson from my mother, has shed a lustre on your name. At last, a poor student myself, from whom could I learn but you?"

Redlaw, unmoved, unchanged, and looking at him with a staring frown, answered by no word or sign.

"I cannot say," pursued the other, "I should try in vain to say, how much it has impressed me, and affected me, to find the gracious traces of the past, in that certain power of winning gratitude and confidence which is associated among us students (among the humblest of us, most) with Mr. Redlaw's generous name. Our ages and positions are so different, sir, and I am so accustomed to regard you from a distance, that I wonder at my own presumption when I touch, however lightly, on that theme. But to one who—I may say, who felt no common interest in my mother once—it may be something to hear, now that all is past, with what indescribable feelings of affection I have, in my obscurity, regarded him; with what pain and reluctance I have kept aloof from his encouragement, when a word of it would have made me rich; yet how I have felt it fit that I should hold my course, content to know him, and to be unknown. Mr. Redlaw," said the student, faintly, "what I would have said, I have said ill, for my strength is strange to me as yet; but for anything unworthy in this fraud of mine, forgive me, and for all the rest forget me!"

The staring frown remained on Redlaw's face, and yielded to no other expression until the student, with these words, advanced towards him, as if to touch his hand, when he drew back and cried to him:

"Don't come nearer to me!"

The young man stopped, shocked by the eagerness of his recoil, and by the sternness of his repulsion; and he passed his hand, thoughtfully, across his forehead.

"The past is past," said the Chemist. "It dies like the brutes. Who talks to me of its traces in my life? He raves or lies! What have I to do with your distempered dreams? If you want money, here it is. I came to offer it; and that is all I came for. There can be nothing else that brings me here," he muttered, holding his head again, with both his hands. "There can be nothing else, and yet—"

He had tossed his purse upon the table. As he fell into this dim cogitation with himself, the student took it up, and held it out to him.

"Take it back, sir," he said proudly, though not angrily. "I wish you could take from me, with it, the remembrance of your words and offer."

"You do?" he retorted, with a wild light in his eyes. "You do?"

"I do!"

The Chemist went close to him, for the first time, and took the purse, and turned him by the arm, and looked him in the face.

"There is sorrow and trouble in sickness, is there not?" he demanded, with a laugh.

The wondering student answered, "Yes."

"In its unrest, in its anxiety, in its suspense, in all its train of physical and mental miseries?" said the Chemist, with a wild unearthly exultation. "All best forgotten, are they not?"

The student did not answer, but again passed his hand, confusedly, across his forehead. Redlaw still held him by the sleeve, when Milly's voice was heard outside.

"I can see very well now," she said, "thank you, Dolf. Don't cry, dear. Father and mother will be comfortable again, to-morrow, and home will be comfortable too. A gentleman with him, is there!"

Redlaw released his hold, as he listened.

"I have feared, from the first moment," he murmured to himself, "to meet her. There is a steady quality of goodness in her, that I dread to influence. I may be the murderer of what is tenderest and best within her bosom."

She was knocking at the door.

"Shall I dismiss it as an idle foreboding, or still avoid her?" he muttered, looking uneasily around.

She was knocking at the door again.

"Of all the visitors who could come here," he said, in a hoarse alarmed voice, turning to his companion, "this is the one I should desire most to avoid. Hide me!"

The student opened a frail door in the wall, communicating where the garret-roof began to slope towards the floor, with a small inner room. Redlaw passed in hastily, and shut it after him.

The student then resumed his place upon the couch, and called to her to enter.

"Dear Mr. Edmund," said Milly, looking round, "they told me there was a gentleman here."

"There is no one here but I."

"There has been some one?"

"Yes, yes, there has been some one."

She put her little basket on the table, and went up to the back of the couch, as if to take the extended hand—but it was not there. A little surprised, in her quiet way, she leaned over to look at his face, and gently touched him on the brow.

"Are you quite as well to-night? Your head is not so cool as in the afternoon."

"Tut!" said the student, petulantly, "very little ails me."

A little more surprise, but no reproach, was expressed in her face, as she withdrew to the other side of the table, and took a small packet of needlework from her basket. But she laid it down again, on second thoughts, and going noiselessly about the room, set everything exactly in its place, and in the neatest order; even to the cushions on the couch, which she touched with so light a hand, that he hardly seemed to know it, as he lay looking at the fire. When all this was done, and she had swept the hearth, she sat down, in her modest little bonnet, to her work, and was quietly busy on it directly.

"It's the new muslin curtain for the window, Mr. Edmund," said Milly, stitching away as she talked. "It will look very clean and nice, though it costs very little, and will save your eyes, too, from the light. My William says the room should not be too light just now, when you are recovering so well, or the glare might make you giddy."

He said nothing; but there was something so fretful and impatient in his change of position, that her quick fingers stopped, and she looked at him anxiously.

"The pillows are not comfortable," she said, laying down her work and rising. "I will soon put them right."

"They are very well," he answered. "Leave them alone, pray. You make so much of everything."

He raised his head to say this, and looked at her so thanklessly, that, after he had thrown himself down again, she stood timidly pausing. However, she resumed her seat, and her needle, without having directed even a murmuring look towards him, and was soon as busy as before.

"I have been thinking, Mr. Edmund, that you have been often thinking of late, when I have been sitting by, how true the saying is, that adversity is a good teacher. Health will be more precious to you, after this illness, than it has ever been. And years hence, when this time of year comes round, and you remember the days when you lay here sick, alone, that the knowledge of your illness might not afflict those who are dearest to you, your home will be doubly dear and doubly blest. Now, isn't that a good, true thing?"

She was too intent upon her work, and too earnest in what she said, and too composed and quiet altogether, to be on the watch for any look he might direct towards her in reply; so the shaft of his ungrateful glance fell harmless, and did not wound her.

"Ah!" said Milly, with her pretty head inclining thoughtfully on one side, as she looked down, following her busy fingers with her eyes. "Even on me—and I am very different from you, Mr. Edmund, for I have no learning, and don't know how to think properly—this view of such things has made a great impression, since you have been lying ill. When I have seen you so touched by the kindness and attention of the poor people down stairs, I have felt that you thought even that experience some repayment for the loss of health, and I have read in your face, as plain as if it was a book, that but for some trouble and sorrow we should never know half the good there is about us."

His getting up from the couch, interrupted her, or she was going on to say more.

"We needn't magnify the merit, Mrs. William," he rejoined slightingly. "The people down stairs will be paid in good time I dare say, for any little extra service they may have rendered me; and perhaps they anticipate no less. I am much obliged to you, too."

Her fingers stopped, and she looked at him.

"I can't be made to feel the more obliged by your exaggerating the case," he said. "I am sensible that you have been interested in me, and I say I am much obliged to you. What more would you have?"

Her work fell on her lap, as she still looked at him walking to and fro with an intolerant air, and stopping now and then.

"I say again, I am much obliged to you. Why weaken my sense of what is your due in obligation, by preferring enormous claims upon me? Trouble, sorrow, affliction, adversity! One might suppose I had been dying a score of deaths here!"

"Do you believe, Mr. Edmund," she asked, rising and going nearer to him, "that I spoke of the poor people of the house, with any reference to myself? To me?" laying her hand upon her bosom with a simple and innocent smile of astonishment.

"Oh! I think nothing about it, my good creature," he returned. "I have had an indisposition, which your solicitude—observe! I say solicitude—makes a great deal more of, than it merits; and it's over, and we can't perpetuate it."

He coldly took a book, and sat down at the table.

She watched him for a little while, until her smile was quite gone, and then, returning to where her basket was, said gently:

"Mr. Edmund, would you rather be alone?"

"There is no reason why I should detain you here," he replied.

"Except—" said Milly, hesitating, and showing her work.

"Oh! the curtain," he answered, with a supercilious laugh. "That's not worth staying for."

She made up the little packet again, and put it in her basket. Then, standing before him with such an air of patient entreaty that he could not choose but look at her, she said:

"If you should want me, I will come back willingly. When you did want me, I was quite happy to come; there was no merit in it. I think you must be afraid, that, now you are getting well, I may be troublesome to you; but I should not have been, indeed. I should have come no longer than your weakness and confinement lasted. You owe me nothing; but it is right that you should deal as justly by me as if I was a lady—even the very lady that you love; and if you suspect me of meanly making much of the little I have tried to do to comfort your sick room, you do yourself more wrong than ever you can do me. That is why I am sorry. That is why I am very sorry."

If she had been as passionate as she was quiet, as indignant as she was calm, as angry in her look as she was gentle, as loud of tone as she was low and clear, she might have left no sense of her departure in the room, compared with that which fell upon the lonely student when she went away.

He was gazing drearily upon the place where she had been, when Redlaw came out of his concealment, and came to the door.

"When sickness lays its hand on you again," he said, looking fiercely back at him, "—may it be soon!—Die here! Rot here!"

"What have you done?" returned the other, catching at his cloak. "What change have you wrought in me? What curse have you brought upon me? Give me back myself!"

"Give me back myself!" exclaimed Redlaw like a madman. "I am infected! I am infectious! I am charged with poison for my own mind, and the minds of all mankind. Where I felt interest, compassion, sympathy, I am turning into stone. Selfishness and ingratitude spring up in my blighting footsteps. I am only so much less base than the wretches whom I make so, that in the moment of their transformation I can hate them."

As he spoke—the young man still holding to his cloak—he cast him off, and struck him: then, wildly hurried out into the night air where the wind was blowing, the snow falling, the cloud-drift sweeping on, the moon dimly shining; and where, blowing in the wind, falling with the snow, drifting with the clouds, shining in the moonlight, and heavily looming in the darkness, were the Phantom's words, "The gift that I have given, you shall give again, go where you will!"

Whither he went, he neither knew nor cared, so that he avoided company. The change he felt within him made the busy streets a desert, and himself a desert, and the multitude around him, in their manifold endurances and ways of life, a mighty waste of sand, which the winds tossed into unintelligible heaps and made a ruinous confusion of. Those traces in his breast which the Phantom had told him would "die out soon," were not, as yet, so far upon their way to death, but that he understood enough of what he was, and what he made of others, to desire to be alone.

This put it in his mind—he suddenly bethought himself, as he was going along, of the boy who had rushed into his room. And then he recollected, that of those with whom he had communicated since the Phantom's disappearance, that boy alone had shown no sign of being changed.

Monstrous and odious as the wild thing was to him, he determined to seek it out, and prove if this were really so; and also to seek it with another intention, which came into his thoughts at the same time.

So, resolving with some difficulty where he was, he directed his steps back to the old college, and to that part of it where the general porch was, and where, alone, the pavement was worn by the tread of the students' feet.

The keeper's house stood just within the iron gates, forming a part of the chief quadrangle. There was a little cloister outside, and from that sheltered place he knew he could look in at the window of their ordinary room, and see who was within. The iron gates were shut, but his hand was familiar with the fastening, and drawing it back by thrusting in his wrist between the bars, he passed through softly, shut it again, and crept up to the window, crumbling the thin crust of snow with his feet.

The fire, to which he had directed the boy last night, shining brightly through the glass, made an illuminated place upon the ground. Instinctively avoiding this, and going round it, he looked in at the window. At first, he thought that there was no one there, and that the blaze was reddening only the old beams in the ceiling and the dark walls; but peering in more narrowly, he saw the object of his search coiled asleep before it on the floor. He passed quickly to the door, opened it, and went in.

The creature lay in such a fiery heat, that, as the Chemist stooped to rouse him, it scorched his head. So soon as he was touched, the boy, not half awake, clutching his rags together with the instinct of flight upon him, half rolled and half ran into a distant corner of the room, where, heaped upon the ground, he struck his foot out to defend himself.

"Get up!" said the Chemist. "You have not forgotten me?"

"You let me alone!" returned the boy. "This is the woman's house— not yours."

The Chemist's steady eye controlled him somewhat, or inspired him with enough submission to be raised upon his feet, and looked at.

"Who washed them, and put those bandages where they were bruised and cracked?" asked the Chemist, pointing to their altered state.

"The woman did."

"And is it she who has made you cleaner in the face, too?"

"Yes, the woman."

Redlaw asked these questions to attract his eyes towards himself, and with the same intent now held him by the chin, and threw his wild hair back, though he loathed to touch him. The boy watched his eyes keenly, as if he thought it needful to his own defence, not knowing what he might do next; and Redlaw could see well that no change came over him.

"Where are they?" he inquired.

"The woman's out."

"I know she is. Where is the old man with the white hair, and his son?"

"The woman's husband, d'ye mean?" inquired the boy.

"Ay. Where are those two?"

"Out. Something's the matter, somewhere. They were fetched out in a hurry, and told me to stop here."

"Come with me," said the Chemist, "and I'll give you money."

"Come where? and how much will you give?"

"I'll give you more shillings than you ever saw, and bring you back soon. Do you know your way to where you came from?"

"You let me go," returned the boy, suddenly twisting out of his grasp. "I'm not a going to take you there. Let me be, or I'll heave some fire at you!"

He was down before it, and ready, with his savage little hand, to pluck the burning coals out.

What the Chemist had felt, in observing the effect of his charmed influence stealing over those with whom he came in contact, was not nearly equal to the cold vague terror with which he saw this baby-monster put it at defiance. It chilled his blood to look on the immovable impenetrable thing, in the likeness of a child, with its sharp malignant face turned up to his, and its almost infant hand, ready at the bars.

"Listen, boy!" he said. "You shall take me where you please, so that you take me where the people are very miserable or very wicked. I want to do them good, and not to harm them. You shall have money, as I have told you, and I will bring you back. Get up! Come quickly!" He made a hasty step towards the door, afraid of her returning.

"Will you let me walk by myself, and never hold me, nor yet touch me?" said the boy, slowly withdrawing the hand with which he threatened, and beginning to get up.

"I will!"

"And let me go, before, behind, or anyways I like?"

"I will!"

"Give me some money first, then, and go."

The Chemist laid a few shillings, one by one, in his extended hand. To count them was beyond the boy's knowledge, but he said "one," every time, and avariciously looked at each as it was given, and at the donor. He had nowhere to put them, out of his hand, but in his mouth; and he put them there.

Redlaw then wrote with his pencil on a leaf of his pocket-book, that the boy was with him; and laying it on the table, signed to him to follow. Keeping his rags together, as usual, the boy complied, and went out with his bare head and naked feet into the winter night.

Preferring not to depart by the iron gate by which he had entered, where they were in danger of meeting her whom he so anxiously avoided, the Chemist led the way, through some of those passages among which the boy had lost himself, and by that portion of the building where he lived, to a small door of which he had the key. When they got into the street, he stopped to ask his guide—who instantly retreated from him—if he knew where they were.

The savage thing looked here and there, and at length, nodding his head, pointed in the direction he designed to take. Redlaw going on at once, he followed, something less suspiciously; shifting his money from his mouth into his hand, and back again into his mouth, and stealthily rubbing it bright upon his shreds of dress, as he went along.

Three times, in their progress, they were side by side. Three times they stopped, being side by side. Three times the Chemist glanced down at his face, and shuddered as it forced upon him one reflection.

The first occasion was when they were crossing an old churchyard, and Redlaw stopped among the graves, utterly at a loss how to connect them with any tender, softening, or consolatory thought.

The second was, when the breaking forth of the moon induced him to look up at the Heavens, where he saw her in her glory, surrounded by a host of stars he still knew by the names and histories which human science has appended to them; but where he saw nothing else he had been wont to see, felt nothing he had been wont to feel, in looking up there, on a bright night.

The third was when he stopped to listen to a plaintive strain of music, but could only hear a tune, made manifest to him by the dry mechanism of the instruments and his own ears, with no address to any mystery within him, without a whisper in it of the past, or of the future, powerless upon him as the sound of last year's running water, or the rushing of last year's wind.

At each of these three times, he saw with horror that, in spite of the vast intellectual distance between them, and their being unlike each other in all physical respects, the expression on the boy's face was the expression on his own.

They journeyed on for some time—now through such crowded places, that he often looked over his shoulder thinking he had lost his guide, but generally finding him within his shadow on his other side; now by ways so quiet, that he could have counted his short, quick, naked footsteps coming on behind—until they arrived at a ruinous collection of houses, and the boy touched him and stopped.

"In there!" he said, pointing out one house where there were shattered lights in the windows, and a dim lantern in the doorway, with "Lodgings for Travellers" painted on it.

Redlaw looked about him; from the houses to the waste piece of ground on which the houses stood, or rather did not altogether tumble down, unfenced, undrained, unlighted, and bordered by a sluggish ditch; from that, to the sloping line of arches, part of some neighbouring viaduct or bridge with which it was surrounded, and which lessened gradually towards them, until the last but one was a mere kennel for a dog, the last a plundered little heap of bricks; from that, to the child, close to him, cowering and trembling with the cold, and limping on one little foot, while he coiled the other round his leg to warm it, yet staring at all these things with that frightful likeness of expression so apparent in his face, that Redlaw started from him.

"In there!" said the boy, pointing out the house again. "I'll wait."

"Will they let me in?" asked Redlaw.

"Say you're a doctor," he answered with a nod. "There's plenty ill here."

Looking back on his way to the house-door, Redlaw saw him trail himself upon the dust and crawl within the shelter of the smallest arch, as if he were a rat. He had no pity for the thing, but he was afraid of it; and when it looked out of its den at him, he hurried to the house as a retreat.

"Sorrow, wrong, and trouble," said the Chemist, with a painful effort at some more distinct remembrance, "at least haunt this place darkly. He can do no harm, who brings forgetfulness of such things here!"

With these words, he pushed the yielding door, and went in.

There was a woman sitting on the stairs, either asleep or forlorn, whose head was bent down on her hands and knees. As it was not easy to pass without treading on her, and as she was perfectly regardless of his near approach, he stopped, and touched her on the shoulder. Looking up, she showed him quite a young face, but one whose bloom and promise were all swept away, as if the haggard winter should unnaturally kill the spring.

With little or no show of concern on his account, she moved nearer to the wall to leave him a wider passage.

"What are you?" said Redlaw, pausing, with his hand upon the broken stair-rail.

"What do you think I am?" she answered, showing him her face again.

He looked upon the ruined Temple of God, so lately made, so soon disfigured; and something, which was not compassion—for the springs in which a true compassion for such miseries has its rise, were dried up in his breast—but which was nearer to it, for the moment, than any feeling that had lately struggled into the darkening, but not yet wholly darkened, night of his mind—mingled a touch of softness with his next words.

"I am come here to give relief, if I can," he said. "Are you thinking of any wrong?"

She frowned at him, and then laughed; and then her laugh prolonged itself into a shivering sigh, as she dropped her head again, and hid her fingers in her hair.

"Are you thinking of a wrong?" he asked once more.

"I am thinking of my life," she said, with a monetary look at him.

He had a perception that she was one of many, and that he saw the type of thousands, when he saw her, drooping at his feet.

"What are your parents?" he demanded.

"I had a good home once. My father was a gardener, far away, in the country."

"Is he dead?"

"He's dead to me. All such things are dead to me. You a gentleman, and not know that!" She raised her eyes again, and laughed at him.

"Girl!" said Redlaw, sternly, "before this death, of all such things, was brought about, was there no wrong done to you? In spite of all that you can do, does no remembrance of wrong cleave to you? Are there not times upon times when it is misery to you?"

So little of what was womanly was left in her appearance, that now, when she burst into tears, he stood amazed. But he was more amazed, and much disquieted, to note that in her awakened recollection of this wrong, the first trace of her old humanity and frozen tenderness appeared to show itself.

He drew a little off, and in doing so, observed that her arms were black, her face cut, and her bosom bruised.

"What brutal hand has hurt you so?" he asked.

"My own. I did it myself!" she answered quickly.

"It is impossible."

"I'll swear I did! He didn't touch me. I did it to myself in a passion, and threw myself down here. He wasn't near me. He never laid a hand upon me!"

In the white determination of her face, confronting him with this untruth, he saw enough of the last perversion and distortion of good surviving in that miserable breast, to be stricken with remorse that he had ever come near her.

"Sorrow, wrong, and trouble!" he muttered, turning his fearful gaze away. "All that connects her with the state from which she has fallen, has those roots! In the name of God, let me go by!"

Afraid to look at her again, afraid to touch her, afraid to think of having sundered the last thread by which she held upon the mercy of Heaven, he gathered his cloak about him, and glided swiftly up the stairs.

Opposite to him, on the landing, was a door, which stood partly open, and which, as he ascended, a man with a candle in his hand, came forward from within to shut. But this man, on seeing him, drew back, with much emotion in his manner, and, as if by a sudden impulse, mentioned his name aloud.

In the surprise of such a recognition there, he stopped, endeavouring to recollect the wan and startled face. He had no time to consider it, for, to his yet greater amazement, old Philip came out of the room, and took him by the hand.

"Mr. Redlaw," said the old man, "this is like you, this is like you, sir! you have heard of it, and have come after us to render any help you can. Ah, too late, too late!"

Redlaw, with a bewildered look, submitted to be led into the room. A man lay there, on a truckle-bed, and William Swidger stood at the bedside.

"Too late!" murmured the old man, looking wistfully into the Chemist's face; and the tears stole down his cheeks.

"That's what I say, father," interposed his son in a low voice. "That's where it is, exactly. To keep as quiet as ever we can while he's a dozing, is the only thing to do. You're right, father!"

Redlaw paused at the bedside, and looked down on the figure that was stretched upon the mattress. It was that of a man, who should have been in the vigour of his life, but on whom it was not likely the sun would ever shine again. The vices of his forty or fifty years' career had so branded him, that, in comparison with their effects upon his face, the heavy hand of Time upon the old man's face who watched him had been merciful and beautifying.

"Who is this?" asked the Chemist, looking round.

"My son George, Mr. Redlaw," said the old man, wringing his hands. "My eldest son, George, who was more his mother's pride than all the rest!"

Redlaw's eyes wandered from the old man's grey head, as he laid it down upon the bed, to the person who had recognised him, and who had kept aloof, in the remotest corner of the room. He seemed to be about his own age; and although he knew no such hopeless decay and broken man as he appeared to be, there was something in the turn of his figure, as he stood with his back towards him, and now went out at the door, that made him pass his hand uneasily across his brow.

"William," he said in a gloomy whisper, "who is that man?"

"Why you see, sir," returned Mr. William, "that's what I say, myself. Why should a man ever go and gamble, and the like of that, and let himself down inch by inch till he can't let himself down any lower!"

"Has he done so?" asked Redlaw, glancing after him with the same uneasy action as before.

"Just exactly that, sir," returned William Swidger, "as I'm told. He knows a little about medicine, sir, it seems; and having been wayfaring towards London with my unhappy brother that you see here," Mr. William passed his coat-sleeve across his eyes, "and being lodging up stairs for the night—what I say, you see, is that strange companions come together here sometimes—he looked in to attend upon him, and came for us at his request. What a mournful spectacle, sir! But that's where it is. It's enough to kill my father!"

Redlaw looked up, at these words, and, recalling where he was and with whom, and the spell he carried with him—which his surprise had obscured—retired a little, hurriedly, debating with himself whether to shun the house that moment, or remain.

Yielding to a certain sullen doggedness, which it seemed to be a part of his condition to struggle with, he argued for remaining.

"Was it only yesterday," he said, "when I observed the memory of this old man to be a tissue of sorrow and trouble, and shall I be afraid, to-night, to shake it? Are such remembrances as I can drive away, so precious to this dying man that I need fear for him? No! I'll stay here."

But he stayed in fear and trembling none the less for these words; and, shrouded in his black cloak with his face turned from them, stood away from the bedside, listening to what they said, as if he felt himself a demon in the place.

"Father!" murmured the sick man, rallying a little from stupor.

"My boy! My son George!" said old Philip.

"You spoke, just now, of my being mother's favourite, long ago. It's a dreadful thing to think now, of long ago!"

"No, no, no," returned the old man. "Think of it. Don't say it's dreadful. It's not dreadful to me, my son."

"It cuts you to the heart, father." For the old man's tears were falling on him.

"Yes, yes," said Philip, "so it does; but it does me good. It's a heavy sorrow to think of that time, but it does me good, George. Oh, think of it too, think of it too, and your heart will be softened more and more! Where's my son William? William, my boy, your mother loved him dearly to the last, and with her latest breath said, 'Tell him I forgave him, blessed him, and prayed for him.' Those were her words to me. I have never forgotten them, and I'm eighty-seven!"

"Father!" said the man upon the bed, "I am dying, I know. I am so far gone, that I can hardly speak, even of what my mind most runs on. Is there any hope for me beyond this bed?"

"There is hope," returned the old man, "for all who are softened and penitent. There is hope for all such. Oh!" he exclaimed, clasping his hands and looking up, "I was thankful, only yesterday, that I could remember this unhappy son when he was an innocent child. But what a comfort it is, now, to think that even God himself has that remembrance of him!"

Redlaw spread his hands upon his face, and shrank, like a murderer.

"Ah!" feebly moaned the man upon the bed. "The waste since then, the waste of life since then!"

"But he was a child once," said the old man. "He played with children. Before he lay down on his bed at night, and fell into his guiltless rest, he said his prayers at his poor mother's knee. I have seen him do it, many a time; and seen her lay his head upon her breast, and kiss him. Sorrowful as it was to her and me, to think of this, when he went so wrong, and when our hopes and plans for him were all broken, this gave him still a hold upon us, that nothing else could have given. Oh, Father, so much better than the fathers upon earth! Oh, Father, so much more afflicted by the errors of Thy children! take this wanderer back! Not as he is, but as he was then, let him cry to Thee, as he has so often seemed to cry to us!"

As the old man lifted up his trembling hands, the son, for whom he made the supplication, laid his sinking head against him for support and comfort, as if he were indeed the child of whom he spoke.

When did man ever tremble, as Redlaw trembled, in the silence that ensued! He knew it must come upon them, knew that it was coming fast.

"My time is very short, my breath is shorter," said the sick man, supporting himself on one arm, and with the other groping in the air, "and I remember there is something on my mind concerning the man who was here just now, Father and William—wait!—is there really anything in black, out there?"

"Yes, yes, it is real," said his aged father.

"Is it a man?"

"What I say myself, George," interposed his brother, bending kindly over him. "It's Mr. Redlaw."

"I thought I had dreamed of him. Ask him to come here."

The Chemist, whiter than the dying man, appeared before him. Obedient to the motion of his hand, he sat upon the bed.

"It has been so ripped up, to-night, sir," said the sick man, laying his hand upon his heart, with a look in which the mute, imploring agony of his condition was concentrated, "by the sight of my poor old father, and the thought of all the trouble I have been the cause of, and all the wrong and sorrow lying at my door, that—"

Was it the extremity to which he had come, or was it the dawning of another change, that made him stop?

"—that what I can do right, with my mind running on so much, so fast, I'll try to do. There was another man here. Did you see him?"

Redlaw could not reply by any word; for when he saw that fatal sign he knew so well now, of the wandering hand upon the forehead, his voice died at his lips. But he made some indication of assent.

"He is penniless, hungry, and destitute. He is completely beaten down, and has no resource at all. Look after him! Lose no time! I know he has it in his mind to kill himself."

It was working. It was on his face. His face was changing, hardening, deepening in all its shades, and losing all its sorrow.

"Don't you remember? Don't you know him?" he pursued.

He shut his face out for a moment, with the hand that again wandered over his forehead, and then it lowered on Redlaw, reckless, ruffianly, and callous.

"Why, d—n you!" he said, scowling round, "what have you been doing to me here! I have lived bold, and I mean to die bold. To the Devil with you!"

And so lay down upon his bed, and put his arms up, over his head and ears, as resolute from that time to keep out all access, and to die in his indifference.

If Redlaw had been struck by lightning, it could not have struck him from the bedside with a more tremendous shock. But the old man, who had left the bed while his son was speaking to him, now returning, avoided it quickly likewise, and with abhorrence.

"Where's my boy William?" said the old man hurriedly. "William, come away from here. We'll go home."

"Home, father!" returned William. "Are you going to leave your own son?"

"Where's my own son?" replied the old man.

"Where? why, there!"

"That's no son of mine," said Philip, trembling with resentment. "No such wretch as that, has any claim on me. My children are pleasant to look at, and they wait upon me, and get my meat and drink ready, and are useful to me. I've a right to it! I'm eighty-seven!"

"You're old enough to be no older," muttered William, looking at him grudgingly, with his hands in his pockets. "I don't know what good you are, myself. We could have a deal more pleasure without you."

"My son, Mr. Redlaw!" said the old man. "My son, too! The boy talking to me of my son! Why, what has he ever done to give me any pleasure, I should like to know?"

"I don't know what you have ever done to give me any pleasure," said William, sulkily.

"Let me think," said the old man. "For how many Christmas times running, have I sat in my warm place, and never had to come out in the cold night air; and have made good cheer, without being disturbed by any such uncomfortable, wretched sight as him there? Is it twenty, William?"

"Nigher forty, it seems," he muttered. "Why, when I look at my father, sir, and come to think of it," addressing Redlaw, with an impatience and irritation that were quite new, "I'm whipped if I can see anything in him but a calendar of ever so many years of eating and drinking, and making himself comfortable, over and over again."

"I—I'm eighty-seven," said the old man, rambling on, childishly and weakly, "and I don't know as I ever was much put out by anything. I'm not going to begin now, because of what he calls my son. He's not my son. I've had a power of pleasant times. I recollect once—no I don't—no, it's broken off. It was something about a game of cricket and a friend of mine, but it's somehow broken off. I wonder who he was—I suppose I liked him? And I wonder what became of him—I suppose he died? But I don't know. And I don't care, neither; I don't care a bit."

In his drowsy chuckling, and the shaking of his head, he put his hands into his waistcoat pockets. In one of them he found a bit of holly (left there, probably last night), which he now took out, and looked at.

"Berries, eh?" said the old man. "Ah! It's a pity they're not good to eat. I recollect, when I was a little chap about as high as that, and out a walking with—let me see—who was I out a walking with?—no, I don't remember how that was. I don't remember as I ever walked with any one particular, or cared for any one, or any one for me. Berries, eh? There's good cheer when there's berries. Well; I ought to have my share of it, and to be waited on, and kept warm and comfortable; for I'm eighty-seven, and a poor old man. I'm eigh-ty-seven. Eigh-ty-seven!"

The drivelling, pitiable manner in which, as he repeated this, he nibbled at the leaves, and spat the morsels out; the cold, uninterested eye with which his youngest son (so changed) regarded him; the determined apathy with which his eldest son lay hardened in his sin; impressed themselves no more on Redlaw's observation,—for he broke his way from the spot to which his feet seemed to have been fixed, and ran out of the house.

His guide came crawling forth from his place of refuge, and was ready for him before he reached the arches.

"Back to the woman's?" he inquired.

"Back, quickly!" answered Redlaw. "Stop nowhere on the way!"

For a short distance the boy went on before; but their return was more like a flight than a walk, and it was as much as his bare feet could do, to keep pace with the Chemist's rapid strides. Shrinking from all who passed, shrouded in his cloak, and keeping it drawn closely about him, as though there were mortal contagion in any fluttering touch of his garments, he made no pause until they reached the door by which they had come out. He unlocked it with his key, went in, accompanied by the boy, and hastened through the dark passages to his own chamber.

The boy watched him as he made the door fast, and withdrew behind the table, when he looked round.

"Come!" he said. "Don't you touch me! You've not brought me here to take my money away."

Redlaw threw some more upon the ground. He flung his body on it immediately, as if to hide it from him, lest the sight of it should tempt him to reclaim it; and not until he saw him seated by his lamp, with his face hidden in his hands, began furtively to pick it up. When he had done so, he crept near the fire, and, sitting down in a great chair before it, took from his breast some broken scraps of food, and fell to munching, and to staring at the blaze, and now and then to glancing at his shillings, which he kept clenched up in a bunch, in one hand.

"And this," said Redlaw, gazing on him with increased repugnance and fear, "is the only one companion I have left on earth!"

How long it was before he was aroused from his contemplation of this creature, whom he dreaded so—whether half-an-hour, or half the night—he knew not. But the stillness of the room was broken by the boy (whom he had seen listening) starting up, and running towards the door.

"Here's the woman coming!" he exclaimed.

The Chemist stopped him on his way, at the moment when she knocked.

"Let me go to her, will you?" said the boy.

"Not now," returned the Chemist. "Stay here. Nobody must pass in or out of the room now. Who's that?"

"It's I, sir," cried Milly. "Pray, sir, let me in!"

"No! not for the world!" he said.

"Mr. Redlaw, Mr. Redlaw, pray, sir, let me in."

"What is the matter?" he said, holding the boy.

"The miserable man you saw, is worse, and nothing I can say will wake him from his terrible infatuation. William's father has turned childish in a moment, William himself is changed. The shock has been too sudden for him; I cannot understand him; he is not like himself. Oh, Mr. Redlaw, pray advise me, help me!"

"No! No! No!" he answered.

"Mr. Redlaw! Dear sir! George has been muttering, in his doze, about the man you saw there, who, he fears, will kill himself."

"Better he should do it, than come near me!"

"He says, in his wandering, that you know him; that he was your friend once, long ago; that he is the ruined father of a student here—my mind misgives me, of the young gentleman who has been ill. What is to be done? How is he to be followed? How is he to be saved? Mr. Redlaw, pray, oh, pray, advise me! Help me!"

All this time he held the boy, who was half-mad to pass him, and let her in.

"Phantoms! Punishers of impious thoughts!" cried Redlaw, gazing round in anguish, "look upon me! From the darkness of my mind, let the glimmering of contrition that I know is there, shine up and show my misery! In the material world as I have long taught, nothing can be spared; no step or atom in the wondrous structure could be lost, without a blank being made in the great universe. I know, now, that it is the same with good and evil, happiness and sorrow, in the memories of men. Pity me! Relieve me!"

There was no response, but her "Help me, help me, let me in!" and the boy's struggling to get to her.

"Shadow of myself! Spirit of my darker hours!" cried Redlaw, in distraction, "come back, and haunt me day and night, but take this gift away! Or, if it must still rest with me, deprive me of the dreadful power of giving it to others. Undo what I have done. Leave me benighted, but restore the day to those whom I have cursed. As I have spared this woman from the first, and as I never will go forth again, but will die here, with no hand to tend me, save this creature's who is proof against me,—hear me!"

The only reply still was, the boy struggling to get to her, while he held him back; and the cry, increasing in its energy, "Help! let me in. He was your friend once, how shall he be followed, how shall he be saved? They are all changed, there is no one else to help me, pray, pray, let me in!"

CHAPTER III. THE GIFT REVERSED

Night was still heavy in the sky. On open plains, from hill-tops, and from the decks of solitary ships at sea, a distant low-lying line, that promised by and by to change to light, was visible in the dim horizon; but its promise was remote and doubtful, and the moon was striving with the night-clouds busily.

The shadows upon Redlaw's mind succeeded thick and fast to one another, and obscured its light as the night-clouds hovered between the moon and earth, and kept the latter veiled in darkness. Fitful and uncertain as the shadows which the night-clouds cast, were their concealments from him, and imperfect revelations to him; and, like the night-clouds still, if the clear light broke forth for a moment, it was only that they might sweep over it, and make the darkness deeper than before.

Without, there was a profound and solemn hush upon the ancient pile of building, and its buttresses and angles made dark shapes of mystery upon the ground, which now seemed to retire into the smooth white snow and now seemed to come out of it, as the moon's path was more or less beset. Within, the Chemist's room was indistinct and murky, by the light of the expiring lamp; a ghostly silence had succeeded to the knocking and the voice outside; nothing was audible but, now and then, a low sound among the whitened ashes of the fire, as of its yielding up its last breath. Before it on the ground the boy lay fast asleep. In his chair, the Chemist sat, as he had sat there since the calling at his door had ceased—like a man turned to stone.

At such a time, the Christmas music he had heard before, began to play. He listened to it at first, as he had listened in the church-yard; but presently—it playing still, and being borne towards him on the night air, in a low, sweet, melancholy strain—he rose, and stood stretching his hands about him, as if there were some friend approaching within his reach, on whom his desolate touch might rest, yet do no harm. As he did this, his face became less fixed and wondering; a gentle trembling came upon him; and at last his eyes filled with tears, and he put his hands before them, and bowed down his head.

His memory of sorrow, wrong, and trouble, had not come back to him; he knew that it was not restored; he had no passing belief or hope that it was. But some dumb stir within him made him capable, again, of being moved by what was hidden, afar off, in the music. If it were only that it told him sorrowfully the value of what he had lost, he thanked Heaven for it with a fervent gratitude.

As the last chord died upon his ear, he raised his head to listen to its lingering vibration. Beyond the boy, so that his sleeping figure lay at its feet, the Phantom stood, immovable and silent, with its eyes upon him.

Ghastly it was, as it had ever been, but not so cruel and relentless in its aspect—or he thought or hoped so, as he looked upon it trembling. It was not alone, but in its shadowy hand it held another hand.

And whose was that? Was the form that stood beside it indeed Milly's, or but her shade and picture? The quiet head was bent a little, as her manner was, and her eyes were looking down, as if in pity, on the sleeping child. A radiant light fell on her face, but did not touch the Phantom; for, though close beside her, it was dark and colourless as ever.

"Spectre!" said the Chemist, newly troubled as he looked, "I have not been stubborn or presumptuous in respect of her. Oh, do not bring her here. Spare me that!"

"This is but a shadow," said the Phantom; "when the morning shines seek out the reality whose image I present before you."

"Is it my inexorable doom to do so?" cried the Chemist.

"It is," replied the Phantom.

"To destroy her peace, her goodness; to make her what I am myself, and what I have made of others!"

"I have said seek her out," returned the Phantom. "I have said no more."

"Oh, tell me," exclaimed Redlaw, catching at the hope which he fancied might lie hidden in the words. "Can I undo what I have done?"

"No," returned the Phantom.

"I do not ask for restoration to myself," said Redlaw. "What I abandoned, I abandoned of my own free will, and have justly lost. But for those to whom I have transferred the fatal gift; who never sought it; who unknowingly received a curse of which they had no warning, and which they had no power to shun; can I do nothing?"

"Nothing," said the Phantom.

"If I cannot, can any one?"

The Phantom, standing like a statue, kept its gaze upon him for a while; then turned its head suddenly, and looked upon the shadow at its side.

"Ah! Can she?" cried Redlaw, still looking upon the shade.

The Phantom released the hand it had retained till now, and softly raised its own with a gesture of dismissal. Upon that, her shadow, still preserving the same attitude, began to move or melt away.

"Stay," cried Redlaw with an earnestness to which he could not give enough expression. "For a moment! As an act of mercy! I know that some change fell upon me, when those sounds were in the air just now. Tell me, have I lost the power of harming her? May I go near her without dread? Oh, let her give me any sign of hope!"

The Phantom looked upon the shade as he did—not at him—and gave no answer.

"At least, say this—has she, henceforth, the consciousness of any power to set right what I have done?"

"She has not," the Phantom answered.

"Has she the power bestowed on her without the consciousness?"

The phantom answered: "Seek her out."

And her shadow slowly vanished.

They were face to face again, and looking on each other, as intently and awfully as at the time of the bestowal of the gift, across the boy who still lay on the ground between them, at the Phantom's feet.

"Terrible instructor," said the Chemist, sinking on his knee before it, in an attitude of supplication, "by whom I was renounced, but by whom I am revisited (in which, and in whose milder aspect, I would fain believe I have a gleam of hope), I will obey without inquiry, praying that the cry I have sent up in the anguish of my soul has been, or will be, heard, in behalf of those whom I have injured beyond human reparation. But there is one thing—"

"You speak to me of what is lying here," the phantom interposed, and pointed with its finger to the boy.

"I do," returned the Chemist. "You know what I would ask. Why has this child alone been proof against my influence, and why, why, have I detected in its thoughts a terrible companionship with mine?"

"This," said the Phantom, pointing to the boy, "is the last, completest illustration of a human creature, utterly bereft of such remembrances as you have yielded up. No softening memory of sorrow, wrong, or trouble enters here, because this wretched mortal from his birth has been abandoned to a worse condition than the beasts, and has, within his knowledge, no one contrast, no humanising touch, to make a grain of such a memory spring up in his hardened breast. All within this desolate creature is barren wilderness. All within the man bereft of what you have resigned, is the same barren wilderness. Woe to such a man! Woe, tenfold, to the nation that shall count its monsters such as this, lying here, by hundreds and by thousands!"

Redlaw shrank, appalled, from what he heard.

"There is not," said the Phantom, "one of these—not one—but sows a harvest that mankind must reap. From every seed of evil in this boy, a field of ruin is grown that shall be gathered in, and garnered up, and sown again in many places in the world, until regions are overspread with wickedness enough to raise the waters of another Deluge. Open and unpunished murder in a city's streets would be less guilty in its daily toleration, than one such spectacle as this."

It seemed to look down upon the boy in his sleep. Redlaw, too, looked down upon him with a new emotion.

"There is not a father," said the Phantom, "by whose side in his daily or his nightly walk, these creatures pass; there is not a mother among all the ranks of loving mothers in this land; there is no one risen from the state of childhood, but shall be responsible in his or her degree for this enormity. There is not a country throughout the earth on which it would not bring a curse. There is no religion upon earth that it would not deny; there is no people upon earth it would not put to shame."

The Chemist clasped his hands, and looked, with trembling fear and pity, from the sleeping boy to the Phantom, standing above him with his finger pointing down.

"Behold, I say," pursued the Spectre, "the perfect type of what it was your choice to be. Your influence is powerless here, because from this child's bosom you can banish nothing. His thoughts have been in 'terrible companionship' with yours, because you have gone down to his unnatural level. He is the growth of man's indifference; you are the growth of man's presumption. The beneficent design of Heaven is, in each case, overthrown, and from the two poles of the immaterial world you come together."

The Chemist stooped upon the ground beside the boy, and, with the same kind of compassion for him that he now felt for himself, covered him as he slept, and no longer shrank from him with abhorrence or indifference.

Soon, now, the distant line on the horizon brightened, the darkness faded, the sun rose red and glorious, and the chimney stacks and gables of the ancient building gleamed in the clear air, which turned the smoke and vapour of the city into a cloud of gold. The very sun-dial in his shady corner, where the wind was used to spin with such unwindy constancy, shook off the finer particles of snow that had accumulated on his dull old face in the night, and looked out at the little white wreaths eddying round and round him. Doubtless some blind groping of the morning made its way down into the forgotten crypt so cold and earthy, where the Norman arches were half buried in the ground, and stirred the dull sap in the lazy vegetation hanging to the walls, and quickened the slow principle of life within the little world of wonderful and delicate creation which existed there, with some faint knowledge that the sun was up.

The Tetterbys were up, and doing. Mr. Tetterby took down the shutters of the shop, and, strip by strip, revealed the treasures of the window to the eyes, so proof against their seductions, of Jerusalem Buildings. Adolphus had been out so long already, that he was halfway on to "Morning Pepper." Five small Tetterbys, whose ten round eyes were much inflamed by soap and friction, were in the tortures of a cool wash in the back kitchen; Mrs. Tetterby presiding. Johnny, who was pushed and hustled through his toilet with great rapidity when Moloch chanced to be in an exacting frame of mind (which was always the case), staggered up and down with his charge before the shop door, under greater difficulties than usual; the weight of Moloch being much increased by a complication of defences against the cold, composed of knitted worsted-work, and forming a complete suit of chain-armour, with a head-piece and blue gaiters.

It was a peculiarity of this baby to be always cutting teeth. Whether they never came, or whether they came and went away again, is not in evidence; but it had certainly cut enough, on the showing of Mrs. Tetterby, to make a handsome dental provision for the sign of the Bull and Mouth. All sorts of objects were impressed for the rubbing of its gums, notwithstanding that it always carried, dangling at its waist (which was immediately under its chin), a bone ring, large enough to have represented the rosary of a young nun. Knife-handles, umbrella-tops, the heads of walking-sticks selected from the stock, the fingers of the family in general, but especially of Johnny, nutmeg-graters, crusts, the handles of doors, and the cool knobs on the tops of pokers, were among the commonest instruments indiscriminately applied for this baby's relief. The amount of electricity that must have been rubbed out of it in a week, is not to be calculated. Still Mrs. Tetterby always said "it was coming through, and then the child would be herself"; and still it never did come through, and the child continued to be somebody else.

The tempers of the little Tetterbys had sadly changed with a few hours. Mr. and Mrs. Tetterby themselves were not more altered than their offspring. Usually they were an unselfish, good-natured, yielding little race, sharing short commons when it happened (which was pretty often) contentedly and even generously, and taking a great deal of enjoyment out of a very little meat. But they were fighting now, not only for the soap and water, but even for the breakfast which was yet in perspective. The hand of every little Tetterby was against the other little Tetterbys; and even Johnny's hand—the patient, much-enduring, and devoted Johnny—rose against the baby! Yes, Mrs. Tetterby, going to the door by mere accident, saw him viciously pick out a weak place in the suit of armour where a slap would tell, and slap that blessed child.

Mrs. Tetterby had him into the parlour by the collar, in that same flash of time, and repaid him the assault with usury thereto.

"You brute, you murdering little boy," said Mrs. Tetterby. "Had you the heart to do it?"

"Why don't her teeth come through, then," retorted Johnny, in a loud rebellious voice, "instead of bothering me? How would you like it yourself?"

"Like it, sir!" said Mrs. Tetterby, relieving him of his dishonoured load.

"Yes, like it," said Johnny. "How would you? Not at all. If you was me, you'd go for a soldier. I will, too. There an't no babies in the Army."

Mr. Tetterby, who had arrived upon the scene of action, rubbed his chin thoughtfully, instead of correcting the rebel, and seemed rather struck by this view of a military life.

"I wish I was in the Army myself, if the child's in the right," said Mrs. Tetterby, looking at her husband, "for I have no peace of my life here. I'm a slave—a Virginia slave": some indistinct association with their weak descent on the tobacco trade perhaps suggested this aggravated expression to Mrs. Tetterby. "I never have a holiday, or any pleasure at all, from year's end to year's end! Why, Lord bless and save the child," said Mrs. Tetterby, shaking the baby with an irritability hardly suited to so pious an aspiration, "what's the matter with her now?"

Not being able to discover, and not rendering the subject much clearer by shaking it, Mrs. Tetterby put the baby away in a cradle, and, folding her arms, sat rocking it angrily with her foot.

"How you stand there, 'Dolphus," said Mrs. Tetterby to her husband. "Why don't you do something?"

"Because I don't care about doing anything," Mr. Tetterby replied.

"I am sure I don't," said Mrs. Tetterby.

"I'll take my oath I don't," said Mr. Tetterby.

A diversion arose here among Johnny and his five younger brothers, who, in preparing the family breakfast table, had fallen to skirmishing for the temporary possession of the loaf, and were buffeting one another with great heartiness; the smallest boy of all, with precocious discretion, hovering outside the knot of combatants, and harassing their legs. Into the midst of this fray, Mr. and Mrs. Tetterby both precipitated themselves with great ardour, as if such ground were the only ground on which they could now agree; and having, with no visible remains of their late soft-heartedness, laid about them without any lenity, and done much execution, resumed their former relative positions.

"You had better read your paper than do nothing at all," said Mrs. Tetterby.

"What's there to read in a paper?" returned Mr. Tetterby, with excessive discontent.

"What?" said Mrs. Tetterby. "Police."

"It's nothing to me," said Tetterby. "What do I care what people do, or are done to?"

"Suicides," suggested Mrs. Tetterby.

"No business of mine," replied her husband.

"Births, deaths, and marriages, are those nothing to you?" said Mrs. Tetterby.

"If the births were all over for good, and all to-day; and the deaths were all to begin to come off to-morrow; I don't see why it should interest me, till I thought it was a coming to my turn," grumbled Tetterby. "As to marriages, I've done it myself. I know quite enough about them."

To judge from the dissatisfied expression of her face and manner, Mrs. Tetterby appeared to entertain the same opinions as her husband; but she opposed him, nevertheless, for the gratification of quarrelling with him.

"Oh, you're a consistent man," said Mrs. Tetterby, "an't you? You, with the screen of your own making there, made of nothing else but bits of newspapers, which you sit and read to the children by the half-hour together!"

"Say used to, if you please," returned her husband. "You won't find me doing so any more. I'm wiser now."

"Bah! wiser, indeed!" said Mrs. Tetterby. "Are you better?"

The question sounded some discordant note in Mr. Tetterby's breast. He ruminated dejectedly, and passed his hand across and across his forehead.

"Better!" murmured Mr. Tetterby. "I don't know as any of us are better, or happier either. Better, is it?"

He turned to the screen, and traced about it with his finger, until he found a certain paragraph of which he was in quest.

"This used to be one of the family favourites, I recollect," said Tetterby, in a forlorn and stupid way, "and used to draw tears from the children, and make 'em good, if there was any little bickering or discontent among 'em, next to the story of the robin redbreasts in the wood. 'Melancholy case of destitution. Yesterday a small man, with a baby in his arms, and surrounded by half-a-dozen ragged little ones, of various ages between ten and two, the whole of whom were evidently in a famishing condition, appeared before the worthy magistrate, and made the following recital:'—Ha! I don't understand it, I'm sure," said Tetterby; "I don't see what it has got to do with us."

"How old and shabby he looks," said Mrs. Tetterby, watching him. "I never saw such a change in a man. Ah! dear me, dear me, dear me, it was a sacrifice!"

"What was a sacrifice?" her husband sourly inquired.

Mrs. Tetterby shook her head; and without replying in words, raised a complete sea-storm about the baby, by her violent agitation of the cradle.

"If you mean your marriage was a sacrifice, my good woman—" said her husband.

"I do mean it," said his wife.

"Why, then I mean to say," pursued Mr. Tetterby, as sulkily and surlily as she, "that there are two sides to that affair; and that I was the sacrifice; and that I wish the sacrifice hadn't been accepted."

"I wish it hadn't, Tetterby, with all my heart and soul I do assure you," said his wife. "You can't wish it more than I do, Tetterby."

"I don't know what I saw in her," muttered the newsman, "I'm sure;—certainly, if I saw anything, it's not there now. I was thinking so, last night, after supper, by the fire. She's fat, she's ageing, she won't bear comparison with most other women."

"He's common-looking, he has no air with him, he's small, he's beginning to stoop and he's getting bald," muttered Mrs. Tetterby.

"I must have been half out of my mind when I did it," muttered Mr. Tetterby.

"My senses must have forsook me. That's the only way in which I can explain it to myself," said Mrs. Tetterby with elaboration.

In this mood they sat down to breakfast. The little Tetterbys were not habituated to regard that meal in the light of a sedentary occupation, but discussed it as a dance or trot; rather resembling a savage ceremony, in the occasionally shrill whoops, and brandishings of bread and butter, with which it was accompanied, as well as in the intricate filings off into the street and back again, and the hoppings up and down the door-steps, which were incidental to the performance. In the present instance, the contentions between these Tetterby children for the milk-and-water jug, common to all, which stood upon the table, presented so lamentable an instance of angry passions risen very high indeed, that it was an outrage on the memory of Dr. Watts. It was not until Mr. Tetterby had driven the whole herd out at the front door, that a moment's peace was secured; and even that was broken by the discovery that Johnny had surreptitiously come back, and was at that instant choking in the jug like a ventriloquist, in his indecent and rapacious haste.

"These children will be the death of me at last!" said Mrs. Tetterby, after banishing the culprit. "And the sooner the better, I think."

"Poor people," said Mr. Tetterby, "ought not to have children at all. They give us no pleasure."

He was at that moment taking up the cup which Mrs. Tetterby had rudely pushed towards him, and Mrs. Tetterby was lifting her own cup to her lips, when they both stopped, as if they were transfixed.

"Here! Mother! Father!" cried Johnny, running into the room. "Here's Mrs. William coming down the street!"

And if ever, since the world began, a young boy took a baby from a cradle with the care of an old nurse, and hushed and soothed it tenderly, and tottered away with it cheerfully, Johnny was that boy, and Moloch was that baby, as they went out together!

Mr. Tetterby put down his cup; Mrs. Tetterby put down her cup. Mr. Tetterby rubbed his forehead; Mrs. Tetterby rubbed hers. Mr. Tetterby's face began to smooth and brighten; Mrs. Tetterby's began to smooth and brighten.

"Why, Lord forgive me," said Mr. Tetterby to himself, "what evil tempers have I been giving way to? What has been the matter here!"

"How could I ever treat him ill again, after all I said and felt last night!" sobbed Mrs. Tetterby, with her apron to her eyes.

"Am I a brute," said Mr. Tetterby, "or is there any good in me at all? Sophia! My little woman!"

" 'Dolphus dear," returned his wife.

"I—I've been in a state of mind," said Mr. Tetterby, "that I can't abear to think of, Sophy."

"Oh! It's nothing to what I've been in, Dolf," cried his wife in a great burst of grief.

"My Sophia," said Mr. Tetterby, "don't take on. I never shall forgive myself. I must have nearly broke your heart, I know."

"No, Dolf, no. It was me! Me!" cried Mrs. Tetterby.

"My little woman," said her husband, "don't. You make me reproach myself dreadful, when you show such a noble spirit. Sophia, my dear, you don't know what I thought. I showed it bad enough, no doubt; but what I thought, my little woman!—"

"Oh, dear Dolf, don't! Don't!" cried his wife.

"Sophia," said Mr. Tetterby, "I must reveal it. I couldn't rest in my conscience unless I mentioned it. My little woman—"

"Mrs. William's very nearly here!" screamed Johnny at the door.

"My little woman, I wondered how," gasped Mr. Tetterby, supporting himself by his chair, "I wondered how I had ever admired you—I forgot the precious children you have brought about me, and thought you didn't look as slim as I could wish. I—I never gave a recollection," said Mr. Tetterby, with severe self-accusation, "to the cares you've had as my wife, and along of me and mine, when you might have had hardly any with another man, who got on better and was luckier than me (anybody might have found such a man easily I am sure); and I quarrelled with you for having aged a little in the rough years you have lightened for me. Can you believe it, my little woman? I hardly can myself."

Mrs. Tetterby, in a whirlwind of laughing and crying, caught his face within her hands, and held it there.

"Oh, Dolf!" she cried. "I am so happy that you thought so; I am so grateful that you thought so! For I thought that you were common-looking, Dolf; and so you are, my dear, and may you be the commonest of all sights in my eyes, till you close them with your own good hands. I thought that you were small; and so you are, and I'll make much of you because you are, and more of you because I love my husband. I thought that you began to stoop; and so you do, and you shall lean on me, and I'll do all I can to keep you up. I thought there was no air about you; but there is, and it's the air of home, and that's the purest and the best there is, and God bless home once more, and all belonging to it, Dolf!"

"Hurrah! Here's Mrs. William!" cried Johnny.

So she was, and all the children with her; and so she came in, they kissed her, and kissed one another, and kissed the baby, and kissed their father and mother, and then ran back and flocked and danced about her, trooping on with her in triumph.

Mr. and Mrs. Tetterby were not a bit behind-hand in the warmth of their reception. They were as much attracted to her as the children were; they ran towards her, kissed her hands, pressed round her, could not receive her ardently or enthusiastically enough. She came among them like the spirit of all goodness, affection, gentle consideration, love, and domesticity.

"What! are you all so glad to see me, too, this bright Christmas morning?" said Milly, clapping her hands in a pleasant wonder. "Oh dear, how delightful this is!"

More shouting from the children, more kissing, more trooping round her, more happiness, more love, more joy, more honour, on all sides, than she could bear.

"Oh dear!" said Milly, "what delicious tears you make me shed. How can I ever have deserved this! What have I done to be so loved?"

"Who can help it!" cried Mr. Tetterby.

"Who can help it!" cried Mrs. Tetterby.

"Who can help it!" echoed the children, in a joyful chorus. And they danced and trooped about her again, and clung to her, and laid their rosy faces against her dress, and kissed and fondled it, and could not fondle it, or her, enough.

"I never was so moved," said Milly, drying her eyes, "as I have been this morning. I must tell you, as soon as I can speak.—Mr. Redlaw came to me at sunrise, and with a tenderness in his manner, more as if I had been his darling daughter than myself, implored me to go with him to where William's brother George is lying ill. We went together, and all the way along he was so kind, and so subdued, and seemed to put such trust and hope in me, that I could not help trying with pleasure. When we got to the house, we met a woman at the door (somebody had bruised and hurt her, I am afraid), who caught me by the hand, and blessed me as I passed."

"She was right!" said Mr. Tetterby. Mrs. Tetterby said she was right. All the children cried out that she was right.

"Ah, but there's more than that," said Milly. "When we got up stairs, into the room, the sick man who had lain for hours in a state from which no effort could rouse him, rose up in his bed, and, bursting into tears, stretched out his arms to me, and said that he had led a mis-spent life, but that he was truly repentant now, in his sorrow for the past, which was all as plain to him as a great prospect, from which a dense black cloud had cleared away, and that he entreated me to ask his poor old father for his pardon and his blessing, and to say a prayer beside his bed. And when I did so, Mr. Redlaw joined in it so fervently, and then so thanked and thanked me, and thanked Heaven, that my heart quite overflowed, and I could have done nothing but sob and cry, if the sick man had not begged me to sit down by him,—which made me quiet of course. As I sat there, he held my hand in his until he sank in a doze; and even then, when I withdrew my hand to leave him to come here (which Mr. Redlaw was very earnest indeed in wishing me to do), his hand felt for mine, so that some one else was obliged to take my place and make believe to give him my hand back. Oh dear, oh dear," said Milly, sobbing. "How thankful and how happy I should feel, and do feel, for all this!"

While she was speaking, Redlaw had come in, and, after pausing for a moment to observe the group of which she was the centre, had silently ascended the stairs. Upon those stairs he now appeared again; remaining there, while the young student passed him, and came running down.

"Kind nurse, gentlest, best of creatures," he said, falling on his knee to her, and catching at her hand, "forgive my cruel ingratitude!"

"Oh dear, oh dear!" cried Milly innocently, "here's another of them! Oh dear, here's somebody else who likes me. What shall I ever do!"

The guileless, simple way in which she said it, and in which she put her hands before her eyes and wept for very happiness, was as touching as it was delightful.

"I was not myself," he said. "I don't know what it was—it was some consequence of my disorder perhaps—I was mad. But I am so no longer. Almost as I speak, I am restored. I heard the children crying out your name, and the shade passed from me at the very sound of it. Oh, don't weep! Dear Milly, if you could read my heart, and only knew with what affection and what grateful homage it is glowing, you would not let me see you weep. It is such deep reproach."

"No, no," said Milly, "it's not that. It's not indeed. It's joy. It's wonder that you should think it necessary to ask me to forgive so little, and yet it's pleasure that you do."

"And will you come again? and will you finish the little curtain?"

"No," said Milly, drying her eyes, and shaking her head. "You won't care for my needlework now."

"Is it forgiving me, to say that?"

She beckoned him aside, and whispered in his ear.

"There is news from your home, Mr. Edmund."

"News? How?"

"Either your not writing when you were very ill, or the change in your handwriting when you began to be better, created some suspicion of the truth; however that is—but you're sure you'll not be the worse for any news, if it's not bad news?"

"Sure."

"Then there's some one come!" said Milly.

"My mother?" asked the student, glancing round involuntarily towards Redlaw, who had come down from the stairs.

"Hush! No," said Milly.

"It can be no one else."

"Indeed?" said Milly, "are you sure?"

"It is not—" Before he could say more, she put her hand upon his mouth.

"Yes it is!" said Milly. "The young lady (she is very like the miniature, Mr. Edmund, but she is prettier) was too unhappy to rest without satisfying her doubts, and came up, last night, with a little servant-maid. As you always dated your letters from the college, she came there; and before I saw Mr. Redlaw this morning, I saw her. She likes me too!" said Milly. "Oh dear, that's another!"

"This morning! Where is she now?"

"Why, she is now," said Milly, advancing her lips to his ear, "in my little parlour in the Lodge, and waiting to see you."

He pressed her hand, and was darting off, but she detained him.

"Mr. Redlaw is much altered, and has told me this morning that his memory is impaired. Be very considerate to him, Mr. Edmund; he needs that from us all."

The young man assured her, by a look, that her caution was not ill-bestowed; and as he passed the Chemist on his way out, bent respectfully and with an obvious interest before him.

Redlaw returned the salutation courteously and even humbly, and looked after him as he passed on. He dropped his head upon his hand too, as trying to reawaken something he had lost. But it was gone.

The abiding change that had come upon him since the influence of the music, and the Phantom's reappearance, was, that now he truly felt how much he had lost, and could compassionate his own condition, and contrast it, clearly, with the natural state of those who were around him. In this, an interest in those who were around him was revived, and a meek, submissive sense of his calamity was bred, resembling that which sometimes obtains in age, when its mental powers are weakened, without insensibility or sullenness being added to the list of its infirmities.

He was conscious that, as he redeemed, through Milly, more and more of the evil he had done, and as he was more and more with her, this change ripened itself within him. Therefore, and because of the attachment she inspired him with (but without other hope), he felt that he was quite dependent on her, and that she was his staff in his affliction.

So, when she asked him whether they should go home now, to where the old man and her husband were, and he readily replied "yes"—being anxious in that regard—he put his arm through hers, and walked beside her; not as if he were the wise and learned man to whom the wonders of Nature were an open book, and hers were the uninstructed mind, but as if their two positions were reversed, and he knew nothing, and she all.

He saw the children throng about her, and caress her, as he and she went away together thus, out of the house; he heard the ringing of their laughter, and their merry voices; he saw their bright faces, clustering around him like flowers; he witnessed the renewed contentment and affection of their parents; he breathed the simple air of their poor home, restored to its tranquillity; he thought of the unwholesome blight he had shed upon it, and might, but for her, have been diffusing then; and perhaps it is no wonder that he walked submissively beside her, and drew her gentle bosom nearer to his own.

When they arrived at the Lodge, the old man was sitting in his chair in the chimney-corner, with his eyes fixed on the ground, and his son was leaning against the opposite side of the fire-place, looking at him. As she came in at the door, both started, and turned round towards her, and a radiant change came upon their faces.

"Oh dear, dear, dear, they are all pleased to see me like the rest!" cried Milly, clapping her hands in an ecstasy, and stopping short. "Here are two more!"

Pleased to see her! Pleasure was no word for it. She ran into her husband's arms, thrown wide open to receive her, and he would have been glad to have her there, with her head lying on his shoulder, through the short winter's day. But the old man couldn't spare her. He had arms for her too, and he locked her in them.

"Why, where has my quiet Mouse been all this time?" said the old man. "She has been a long while away. I find that it's impossible for me to get on without Mouse. I—where's my son William?—I fancy I have been dreaming, William."

"That's what I say myself, father," returned his son. "I have been in an ugly sort of dream, I think.—How are you, father? Are you pretty well?"

"Strong and brave, my boy," returned the old man.

It was quite a sight to see Mr. William shaking hands with his father, and patting him on the back, and rubbing him gently down with his hand, as if he could not possibly do enough to show an interest in him.

"What a wonderful man you are, father!—How are you, father? Are you really pretty hearty, though?" said William, shaking hands with him again, and patting him again, and rubbing him gently down again.

"I never was fresher or stouter in my life, my boy."

"What a wonderful man you are, father! But that's exactly where it is," said Mr. William, with enthusiasm. "When I think of all that my father's gone through, and all the chances and changes, and sorrows and troubles, that have happened to him in the course of his long life, and under which his head has grown grey, and years upon years have gathered on it, I feel as if we couldn't do enough to honour the old gentleman, and make his old age easy.—How are you, father? Are you really pretty well, though?"

Mr. William might never have left off repeating this inquiry, and shaking hands with him again, and patting him again, and rubbing him down again, if the old man had not espied the Chemist, whom until now he had not seen.

"I ask your pardon, Mr. Redlaw," said Philip, "but didn't know you were here, sir, or should have made less free. It reminds me, Mr. Redlaw, seeing you here on a Christmas morning, of the time when you was a student yourself, and worked so hard that you were backwards and forwards in our Library even at Christmas time. Ha! ha! I'm old enough to remember that; and I remember it right well, I do, though I am eighty-seven. It was after you left here that my poor wife died. You remember my poor wife, Mr. Redlaw?"

The Chemist answered yes.

"Yes," said the old man. "She was a dear creetur.—I recollect you come here one Christmas morning with a young lady—I ask your pardon, Mr. Redlaw, but I think it was a sister you was very much attached to?"

The Chemist looked at him, and shook his head. "I had a sister," he said vacantly. He knew no more.

"One Christmas morning," pursued the old man, "that you come here with her—and it began to snow, and my wife invited the lady to walk in, and sit by the fire that is always a burning on Christmas Day in what used to be, before our ten poor gentlemen commuted, our great Dinner Hall. I was there; and I recollect, as I was stirring up the blaze for the young lady to warm her pretty feet by, she read the scroll out loud, that is underneath that pictur, 'Lord, keep my memory green!' She and my poor wife fell a talking about it; and it's a strange thing to think of, now, that they both said (both being so unlike to die) that it was a good prayer, and that it was one they would put up very earnestly, if they were called away young, with reference to those who were dearest to them. 'My brother,' says the young lady—'My husband,' says my poor wife.—'Lord, keep his memory of me, green, and do not let me be forgotten!'"

Tears more painful, and more bitter than he had ever shed in all his life, coursed down Redlaw's face. Philip, fully occupied in recalling his story, had not observed him until now, nor Milly's anxiety that he should not proceed.

"Philip!" said Redlaw, laying his hand upon his arm, "I am a stricken man, on whom the hand of Providence has fallen heavily, although deservedly. You speak to me, my friend, of what I cannot follow; my memory is gone."

"Merciful power!" cried the old man.

"I have lost my memory of sorrow, wrong, and trouble," said the Chemist, "and with that I have lost all man would remember!"

To see old Philip's pity for him, to see him wheel his own great chair for him to rest in, and look down upon him with a solemn sense of his bereavement, was to know, in some degree, how precious to old age such recollections are.

The boy came running in, and ran to Milly.

"Here's the man," he said, "in the other room. I don't want him."

"What man does he mean?" asked Mr. William.

"Hush!" said Milly.

Obedient to a sign from her, he and his old father softly withdrew. As they went out, unnoticed, Redlaw beckoned to the boy to come to him.

"I like the woman best," he answered, holding to her skirts.

"You are right," said Redlaw, with a faint smile. "But you needn't fear to come to me. I am gentler than I was. Of all the world, to you, poor child!"

The boy still held back at first, but yielding little by little to her urging, he consented to approach, and even to sit down at his feet. As Redlaw laid his hand upon the shoulder of the child, looking on him with compassion and a fellow-feeling, he put out his other hand to Milly. She stooped down on that side of him, so that she could look into his face, and after silence, said:

"Mr. Redlaw, may I speak to you?"

"Yes," he answered, fixing his eyes upon her. "Your voice and music are the same to me."

"May I ask you something?"

"What you will."

"Do you remember what I said, when I knocked at your door last night? About one who was your friend once, and who stood on the verge of destruction?"

"Yes. I remember," he said, with some hesitation.

"Do you understand it?"

He smoothed the boy's hair—looking at her fixedly the while, and shook his head.

"This person," said Milly, in her clear, soft voice, which her mild eyes, looking at him, made clearer and softer, "I found soon afterwards. I went back to the house, and, with Heaven's help, traced him. I was not too soon. A very little and I should have been too late."

He took his hand from the boy, and laying it on the back of that hand of hers, whose timid and yet earnest touch addressed him no less appealingly than her voice and eyes, looked more intently on her.

"He is the father of Mr. Edmund, the young gentleman we saw just now. His real name is Longford.—You recollect the name?"

"I recollect the name."

"And the man?"

"No, not the man. Did he ever wrong me?"

"Yes!"

"Ah! Then it's hopeless—hopeless."

He shook his head, and softly beat upon the hand he held, as though mutely asking her commiseration.

"I did not go to Mr. Edmund last night," said Milly,—"You will listen to me just the same as if you did remember all?"

"To every syllable you say."

"Both, because I did not know, then, that this really was his father, and because I was fearful of the effect of such intelligence upon him, after his illness, if it should be. Since I have known who this person is, I have not gone either; but that is for another reason. He has long been separated from his wife and son—has been a stranger to his home almost from this son's infancy, I learn from him— and has abandoned and deserted what he should have held most dear. In all that time he has been falling from the state of a gentleman, more and more, until—" she rose up, hastily, and going out for a moment, returned, accompanied by the wreck that Redlaw had beheld last night.

"Do you know me?" asked the Chemist.

"I should be glad," returned the other, "and that is an unwonted word for me to use, if I could answer no."

The Chemist looked at the man, standing in self-abasement and degradation before him, and would have looked longer, in an ineffectual struggle for enlightenment, but that Milly resumed her late position by his side, and attracted his attentive gaze to her own face.

"See how low he is sunk, how lost he is!" she whispered, stretching out her arm towards him, without looking from the Chemist's face. "If you could remember all that is connected with him, do you not think it would move your pity to reflect that one you ever loved (do not let us mind how long ago, or in what belief that he has forfeited), should come to this?"

"I hope it would," he answered. "I believe it would."

His eyes wandered to the figure standing near the door, but came back speedily to her, on whom he gazed intently, as if he strove to learn some lesson from every tone of her voice, and every beam of her eyes.

"I have no learning, and you have much," said Milly; "I am not used to think, and you are always thinking. May I tell you why it seems to me a good thing for us, to remember wrong that has been done us?"

"Yes."

"That we may forgive it."

"Pardon me, great Heaven!" said Redlaw, lifting up his eyes, "for having thrown away thine own high attribute!"

"And if," said Milly, "if your memory should one day be restored, as we will hope and pray it may be, would it not be a blessing to you to recall at once a wrong and its forgiveness?"

He looked at the figure by the door, and fastened his attentive eyes on her again; a ray of clearer light appeared to him to shine into his mind, from her bright face.

"He cannot go to his abandoned home. He does not seek to go there. He knows that he could only carry shame and trouble to those he has so cruelly neglected; and that the best reparation he can make them now, is to avoid them. A very little money carefully bestowed, would remove him to some distant place, where he might live and do no wrong, and make such atonement as is left within his power for the wrong he has done. To the unfortunate lady who is his wife, and to his son, this would be the best and kindest boon that their best friend could give them—one too that they need never know of; and to him, shattered in reputation, mind, and body, it might be salvation."

He took her head between her hands, and kissed it, and said: "It shall be done. I trust to you to do it for me, now and secretly; and to tell him that I would forgive him, if I were so happy as to know for what."

As she rose, and turned her beaming face towards the fallen man, implying that her mediation had been successful, he advanced a step, and without raising his eyes, addressed himself to Redlaw.

"You are so generous," he said, "—you ever were—that you will try to banish your rising sense of retribution in the spectacle that is before you. I do not try to banish it from myself, Redlaw. If you can, believe me."

The Chemist entreated Milly, by a gesture, to come nearer to him; and, as he listened looked in her face, as if to find in it the clue to what he heard.

"I am too decayed a wretch to make professions; I recollect my own career too well, to array any such before you. But from the day on which I made my first step downward, in dealing falsely by you, I have gone down with a certain, steady, doomed progression. That, I say."

Redlaw, keeping her close at his side, turned his face towards the speaker, and there was sorrow in it. Something like mournful recognition too.

"I might have been another man, my life might have been another life, if I had avoided that first fatal step. I don't know that it would have been. I claim nothing for the possibility. Your sister is at rest, and better than she could have been with me, if I had continued even what you thought me: even what I once supposed myself to be."

Redlaw made a hasty motion with his hand, as if he would have put that subject on one side.

"I speak," the other went on, "like a man taken from the grave. I should have made my own grave, last night, had it not been for this blessed hand."

"Oh dear, he likes me too!" sobbed Milly, under her breath. "That's another!"

"I could not have put myself in your way, last night, even for bread. But, to-day, my recollection of what has been is so strongly stirred, and is presented to me, I don't know how, so vividly, that I have dared to come at her suggestion, and to take your bounty, and to thank you for it, and to beg you, Redlaw, in your dying hour, to be as merciful to me in your thoughts, as you are in your deeds."

He turned towards the door, and stopped a moment on his way forth.

"I hope my son may interest you, for his mother's sake. I hope he may deserve to do so. Unless my life should be preserved a long time, and I should know that I have not misused your aid, I shall never look upon him more."

Going out, he raised his eyes to Redlaw for the first time. Redlaw, whose steadfast gaze was fixed upon him, dreamily held out his hand. He returned and touched it—little more—with both his own; and bending down his head, went slowly out.

In the few moments that elapsed, while Milly silently took him to the gate, the Chemist dropped into his chair, and covered his face with his hands. Seeing him thus, when she came back, accompanied by her husband and his father (who were both greatly concerned for him), she avoided disturbing him, or permitting him to be disturbed; and kneeled down near the chair to put some warm clothing on the boy.

"That's exactly where it is. That's what I always say, father!" exclaimed her admiring husband. "There's a motherly feeling in Mrs. William's breast that must and will have went!"

"Ay, ay," said the old man; "you're right. My son William's right!"

"It happens all for the best, Milly dear, no doubt," said Mr. William, tenderly, "that we have no children of our own; and yet I sometimes wish you had one to love and cherish. Our little dead child that you built such hopes upon, and that never breathed the breath of life—it has made you quiet-like, Milly."

"I am very happy in the recollection of it, William dear," she answered. "I think of it every day."

"I was afraid you thought of it a good deal."

"Don't say, afraid; it is a comfort to me; it speaks to me in so many ways. The innocent thing that never lived on earth, is like an angel to me, William."

"You are like an angel to father and me," said Mr. William, softly. "I know that."

"When I think of all those hopes I built upon it, and the many times I sat and pictured to myself the little smiling face upon my bosom that never lay there, and the sweet eyes turned up to mine that never opened to the light," said Milly, "I can feel a greater tenderness, I think, for all the disappointed hopes in which there is no harm. When I see a beautiful child in its fond mother's arms, I love it all the better, thinking that my child might have been like that, and might have made my heart as proud and happy."

Redlaw raised his head, and looked towards her.

"All through life, it seems by me," she continued, "to tell me something. For poor neglected children, my little child pleads as if it were alive, and had a voice I knew, with which to speak to me. When I hear of youth in suffering or shame, I think that my child might have come to that, perhaps, and that God took it from me in His mercy. Even in age and grey hair, such as father's, it is present: saying that it too might have lived to be old, long and long after you and I were gone, and to have needed the respect and love of younger people."

Her quiet voice was quieter than ever, as she took her husband's arm, and laid her head against it.

"Children love me so, that sometimes I half fancy—it's a silly fancy, William—they have some way I don't know of, of feeling for my little child, and me, and understanding why their love is precious to me. If I have been quiet since, I have been more happy, William, in a hundred ways. Not least happy, dear, in this—that even when my little child was born and dead but a few days, and I was weak and sorrowful, and could not help grieving a little, the thought arose, that if I tried to lead a good life, I should meet in Heaven a bright creature, who would call me, Mother!"

Redlaw fell upon his knees, with a loud cry.

"O Thou, he said, "who through the teaching of pure love, hast graciously restored me to the memory which was the memory of Christ upon the Cross, and of all the good who perished in His cause, receive my thanks, and bless her!"

Then, he folded her to his heart; and Milly, sobbing more than ever, cried, as she laughed, "He is come back to himself! He likes me very much indeed, too! Oh, dear, dear, dear me, here's another!"

Then, the student entered, leading by the hand a lovely girl, who was afraid to come. And Redlaw so changed towards him, seeing in him and his youthful choice, the softened shadow of that chastening passage in his own life, to which, as to a shady tree, the dove so long imprisoned in his solitary ark might fly for rest and company, fell upon his neck, entreating them to be his children.

Then, as Christmas is a time in which, of all times in the year, the memory of every remediable sorrow, wrong, and trouble in the world around us, should be active with us, not less than our own experiences, for all good, he laid his hand upon the boy, and, silently calling Him to witness who laid His hand on children in old time, rebuking, in the majesty of His prophetic knowledge, those who kept them from Him, vowed to protect him, teach him, and reclaim him.

Then, he gave his right hand cheerily to Philip, and said that they would that day hold a Christmas dinner in what used to be, before the ten poor gentlemen commuted, their great Dinner Hall; and that they would bid to it as many of that Swidger family, who, his son had told him, were so numerous that they might join hands and make a ring round England, as could be brought together on so short a notice.

And it was that day done. There were so many Swidgers there, grown up and children, that an attempt to state them in round numbers might engender doubts, in the distrustful, of the veracity of this history. Therefore the attempt shall not be made. But there they were, by dozens and scores—and there was good news and good hope there, ready for them, of George, who had been visited again by his father and brother, and by Milly, and again left in a quiet sleep. There, present at the dinner, too, were the Tetterbys, including young Adolphus, who arrived in his prismatic comforter, in good time for the beef. Johnny and the baby were too late, of course, and came in all on one side, the one exhausted, the other in a supposed state of double-tooth; but that was customary, and not alarming.

It was sad to see the child who had no name or lineage, watching the other children as they played, not knowing how to talk with them, or sport with them, and more strange to the ways of childhood than a rough dog. It was sad, though in a different way, to see what an instinctive knowledge the youngest children there had of his being different from all the rest, and how they made timid approaches to him with soft words and touches, and with little presents, that he might not be unhappy. But he kept by Milly, and began to love her—that was another, as she said!—and, as they all liked her dearly, they were glad of that, and when they saw him peeping at them from behind her chair, they were pleased that he was so close to it.

All this, the Chemist, sitting with the student and his bride that was to be, Philip, and the rest, saw.

Some people have said since, that he only thought what has been herein set down; others, that he read it in the fire, one winter night about the twilight time; others, that the Ghost was but the representation of his gloomy thoughts, and Milly the embodiment of his better wisdom. I say nothing.

—Except this. That as they were assembled in the old Hall, by no other light than that of a great fire (having dined early), the shadows once more stole out of their hiding-places, and danced about the room, showing the children marvellous shapes and faces on the walls, and gradually changing what was real and familiar there, to what was wild and magical. But that there was one thing in the Hall, to which the eyes of Redlaw, and of Milly and her husband, and of the old man, and of the student, and his bride that was to be, were often turned, which the shadows did not obscure or change. Deepened in its gravity by the fire-light, and gazing from the darkness of the panelled wall like life, the sedate face in the portrait, with the beard and ruff, looked down at them from under its verdant wreath of holly, as they looked up at it; and, clear and plain below, as if a voice had uttered them, were the words.

Lord keep my Memory green.

The Christmas Gift that Came to Rupert: A Story for Little Soldiers

Bret Harte

It was the Christmas season in California—a season of falling rain and springing grasses. There were intervals when, through driving clouds and flying scud, the sun visited the haggard hills with a miracle, and death and resurrection were as one, and out of the very throes of decay a joyous life struggled outward and upward. Even the storms that swept down the dead leaves nurtured the tender buds that took their places. There were no episodes of snowy silence; over the quickening fields the farmer's ploughshare hard followed the furrows left by the latest rains. Perhaps it was for this reason that the Christmas evergreens which decorated the drawing-room took upon themselves a foreign aspect, and offered a weird contrast to the roses, seen dimly through the windows, as the southwest wind beat their soft faces against the panes.

"Now," said the doctor, drawing his chair closer to the fire, and looking mildly but firmly at the semicircle of flaxen heads around him, "I want it distinctly understood before I begin my story, that I am not to be interrupted by any ridiculous questions. At the first one I shall stop. At the second, I shall feel it my duty to administer a dose of castor-oil all round. The boy that moves his legs or arms will be understood to invite amputation. I have brought my instruments with me, and never allow pleasure to interfere with my business. Do you promise?"

"Yes, sir," said six small voices simultaneously. The volley was, however, followed by half a dozen dropping questions.

"Silence! Bob, put your feet down, and stop rattling that sword. Flora shall sit by my side, like a little lady, and be an example to the rest. Fung Tang shall stay, too, if he likes. Now, turn down the gas a little; there, that will do—just enough to make the fire look brighter, and to show off the Christmas candles. Silence, everybody! The boy who cracks an almond, or breathes too loud over his raisins, will be put out of the room."

There was a profound silence. Bob laid his sword tenderly aside and nursed his leg thoughtfully. Flora, after coquettishly adjusting the pockets of her little apron, put her arm upon the doctor's shoulder, and permitted herself to be drawn beside him. Fung Tang, the little heathen page, who was permitted, on this rare occasion, to share the Christmas revels in the drawing-room, surveyed the group with a smile that was at once sweet and philosophical. The light ticking of a French clock on the mantel, supported by a young shepherdess of bronze complexion and great symmetry of limb, was the only sound that disturbed the Christmas-like peace of the apartment—a peace which held the odors of evergreens, new toys, cedar boxes, glue, and varnish in a harmonious combination that passed all understanding.

"About four years ago at this time," began the doctor, "I attended a course of lectures in a certain city. One of the professors, who was a sociable, kindly man—though somewhat practical and hard-headed—invited me to his house on Christmas night. I was very glad to go, as I was anxious to see one of his sons, who, though only twelve years old, was said to be very clever. I dare not tell you how many Latin verses this little fellow could recite, or how many English ones he had composed. In the first place, you'd want me to repeat them; secondly, I'm not a judge of poetry—Latin or English. But there were judges who said they were wonderful for a boy, and everybody predicted a splendid future for him. Everybody but his father. He shook his head doubtingly whenever it was mentioned, for, as I have told you, he was a practical, matter-of-fact man.

"There was a pleasant party at the professor's that night. All the children of the neighborhood were there, and among them the professor's clever son, Rupert, as they called him—a thin little chap, about as tall as Bobby there, and fair and delicate as Flora by my side. His health was feeble, his father said; he seldom ran about and played with other boys—preferring to stay at home and brood over his books, and compose what he called his verses.

"Well, we had a Christmas-tree just like this, and we had been laughing and talking, calling the names of the children who had presents on the tree, and everybody was very happy and joyous, when one of the children suddenly uttered a cry of mingled surprise and hilarity, and said, 'Here's something for Rupert— and what do you think it is?'

"We all guessed. 'A desk'; 'A copy of Milton'; 'A gold pen'; 'A rhyming dictionary.' 'No? What then?'

" 'A drum!'

" 'A what?' asked everybody.

" 'A drum! With Rupert's name on it.'

"Sure enough, there it was. A good-sized, bright, new, brass-bound drum, with a slip of paper on it, with the inscription, 'FOR RUPERT.'

"Of course we all laughed, and thought it a good joke. 'You see you're to make a noise in the world, Rupert!' said one. 'Here's parchment for the poet,' said another. 'Rupert's last work in sheepskin covers,' said a third. 'Give us a classical tune, Rupert,' said a fourth, and so on. But Rupert seemed too mortified to speak; he changed color, bit his lips, and finally burst into a passionate fit of crying and left the room. Then those who had joked him felt ashamed, and everybody began to ask who had put the drum there. But no one knew, or, if they did, the unexpected sympathy awakened for the sensitive boy kept them silent. Even the servants were called up and questioned, but no one could give any idea where it came from. And what was still more singular, everybody declared that up to the moment it was produced, no one had seen it hanging on the tree. What do I think? Well, I have my own opinion. But no questions! Enough for you to know that Rupert did not come downstairs again that night, and the party soon after broke up.

"I had almost forgotten those things, for the war of the Rebellion broke out the next spring, and I was appointed surgeon in one of the new regiments, and was on my way to the seat of war. But I had to pass through the city where the professor lived, and there I met him. My first question was about Rupert. The professor shook his head sadly. 'He's not so well' he said; 'he has been declining since last Christmas, when you saw him. A very strange case,' he added, giving it a long Latin name, 'a very singular case. But go and see him yourself' he urged; 'it may distract his mind and do him good.'

"I went accordingly to the professor's house, and found Rupert lying on a sofa propped up with pillows. Around him were scattered his books, and, what seemed in singular contrast, that drum I told you about was hanging on a nail just above his head. His face was thin and wasted; there was a red spot on either cheek, and his eyes were very bright and widely opened. He was glad to see me, and when I told him where I was going, he asked a thousand questions about the war. I thought I had thoroughly diverted his mind from its sick and languid fancies, when he suddenly grasped my hand and drew me towards him.

"'Doctor,' said he, in a low whisper, 'you won't laugh at me if I tell you something?'

"'No, certainly not,' I said.

"'You remember that drum?' he said, pointing to the glittering toy that hung against the wall. 'You know, too, how it came to me. A few weeks after Christmas I was lying half asleep here, and the drum was hanging on the wall, when suddenly I heard it beaten; at first low and slowly, then faster and louder, until its rolling filled the house. In the middle of the night I heard it again. I did not dare to tell anybody about it, but I have heard it every night ever since.'

"He paused and looked anxiously in my face. 'Sometimes,' he continued, 'it is played softly, sometimes loudly, but always quickening to a long roll, so loud and alarming that I have looked to see people coming into my room to ask what was the matter. But I think, doctor—I think,' he repeated slowly, looking up with painful interest into my face, 'that no one hears it but myself.'

"I thought so, too, but I asked him if he had heard it at any other time.

"'Once or twice in the daytime,' he replied, 'when I have been reading or writing; then very loudly, as though it were angry, and tried in that way to attract my attention away from my books.'

"I looked into his face and placed my hand upon his pulse. His eyes were very bright and his pulse a little flurried and quick. I then tried to explain to him that he was very weak, and that his senses were very acute, as most weak people's are; and how that when he read, or grew interested and excited, or when he was tired at night, the throbbing of a big artery made the beating sound he heard. He listened to me with a sad smile of unbelief, but thanked me, and in a little while I went away. But as I was going downstairs I met the professor. I gave him my opinion of the case—well, no matter what it was.

"'He wants fresh air and exercise,' said the professor, 'and some practical experience of life, sir.' The professor was not a bad man, but he was a little worried and impatient, and thought—as clever people are apt to think—that things which he didn't understand were either silly or improper.

"I left the city that very day, and in the excitement of battlefields and hospitals I forgot all about little Rupert, nor did I hear of him again, until one day, meeting an old classmate in the army, who had known the professor, he told me that Rupert had become quite insane, and that in one of his paroxysms he had escaped from the house, and as he had never been found, it was feared that he had fallen into the river and was drowned. I was terribly shocked for the moment, as you may imagine; but, dear me, I was living just then among scenes as terrible and shocking, and I had little time to spare to mourn over poor Rupert.

"It was not long after receiving this intelligence that we had a terrible battle, in which a portion of our army was slaughtered. I was detached from my brigade to ride over to the battlefield and assist the surgeons of the beaten division, who had more on their hands than they could attend to. When I reached the barn that served for a temporary hospital, I went at once to work. Ah! Bob," said the doctor thoughtfully, taking the bright sword from the hands of the half-frightened Bob, and holding it gravely before him, "these pretty playthings are symbols of cruel, ugly realities.

"I turned to a tall, stout Vermonter," he continued, very slowly, tracing a pattern on the rug with the point of the scabbard, "who was badly wounded in both thighs, but he held up his hands and begged me to help others first who needed it more than he. I did not at first heed his request, for this kind of unselfishness was very common in the army; but he went on, 'For God's sake, doctor, leave me here; there is a drummer boy of our regiment—a mere child— dying, if he isn't dead now. Go and see him first. He lies over there. He saved more than one life. He was at his post in the panic of this morning, and saved the honor of the regiment.' I was so much more impressed by the man's manner than by the substance of his speech, which was, however, corroborated by the other poor fellows stretched around me, that I passed over to where the drummer lay, with his drum beside him. I gave one glance at his face—and—yes, Bob—yes, my children—it *was* Rupert.

"Well! well! it needed not the chalked cross which my brother surgeons had left upon the rough board whereon he lay to show how urgent was the relief he sought; it needed not the prophetic words of the Vermonter, nor the damp that mingled with the brown curls that clung to his pale forehead, to show how hopeless it was now. I called him by name. He opened his eyes—larger, I thought, in the new vision that was beginning to dawn upon him—and recognized me. He whispered, 'I'm glad you are come, but I don't think you can do me any good.'

"I could not tell him a lie. I could not say anything. I only pressed his hand in mine as he went on.

"'But you will see father, and ask him to forgive me. Nobody is to blame but myself. It was a long time before I understood why the drum came to me that Christmas night, and why it kept calling to me every night, and what it said. I know it now. The work is done, and I am content. Tell father it is better as it is. I should have lived only to worry and perplex him, and something in me tells me this is right.'

"He lay still for a moment, and then grasping my hand, said,—

"'Hark!'

"I listened, but heard nothing but the suppressed moans of the wounded men around me. 'The drum,' he said faintly; 'don't you hear it?—the drum is calling me.'

"He reached out his arm to where it lay, as though he would embrace it.

"'Listen'—he went on—'it's the reveille. There are the ranks drawn up in review. Don't you see the sunlight flash down the long line of bayonets? Their faces are shining—they present arms—there comes the General—but his face I cannot look at for the glory round his head. He sees me; he smiles, it is—' and with a name upon his lips that he had learned long ago, he stretched himself wearily upon the planks and lay quite still.

"That's all.

"No questions now—never mind what became of the drum.

"Who's that sniveling?

"Bless my soul! where's my pill-box?"

The First Christmas of New England

Harriet Beecher Stowe

CHAPTER I

The shores of the Atlantic coast of America may well be a terror to navigators. They present an inexorable wall, against which forbidding and angry waves incessantly dash, and around which shifting winds continually rave. The approaches to safe harbors are few in number, intricate and difficult, requiring the skill of practiced pilots.

But, as if with a pitying spirit of hospitality, old Cape Cod, breaking from the iron line of the coast, like a generous-hearted sailor intent on helpfulness, stretches an hundred miles outward, and, curving his sheltering arms in a protective circle, gives a noble harborage. Of this harbor of Cape Cod the report of our governmental Coast Survey thus speaks: "It is one of the finest harbors for ships of war on the whole of our Atlantic coast. The width and freedom from obstruction of every kind at its entrance and the extent of sea room upon the bay side make it accessible to vessels of the largest class in almost all winds. This advantage, its capacity, depth of water, excellent anchorage, and the complete shelter it affords from all winds, render it one of the most valuable ship harbors upon our coast."

We have been thus particular in our mention of this place, because here, in this harbor, opened the first scene in the most wonderful drama of modern history.

Let us look into the magic mirror of the past and see this harbor of Cape Cod on the morning of the 11th of November, in the year of our Lord 1620, as described to us in the simple words of the pilgrims: "A pleasant bay, circled round, except the entrance, which is about four miles over from land to land, *compassed about to the very sea* with oaks, pines, junipers, sassafras, and other sweet weeds. It is a harbor wherein a thousand sail of ship may safely ride."

Such are the woody shores of Cape Cod as we look back upon them in that distant November day, and the harbor lies like a great crystal gem on the bosom of a virgin wilderness. The "fir trees, the pine trees, and the bay," rejoice together in freedom, for as yet the axe has spared them; in the noble bay no shipping has found shelter; no voice or sound of civilized man has broken the sweet calm of the forest. The oak leaves, now turned to crimson and maroon by the autumn frosts, reflect themselves in flushes of color on the still waters. The golden leaves of the sassafras yet cling to the branches, though their life has passed, and every brushing wind bears showers of them down to the water. Here and there the dark spires of the cedar and the green leaves and red berries of the holly contrast with these lighter tints. The forest foliage grows down to the water's edge, so that the dash of the rising and falling tide washes into the shaggy cedar boughs which here and there lean over and dip in the waves.

No voice or sound from earth or sky proclaims that anything unwonted is coming or doing on these shores to-day. The wandering Indians, moving their hunting-camps along the woodland paths, saw no sign in the stars that morning, and no different color in the sunrise from what had been in the days of their fathers. Panther and wild-cat under their furry coats felt no thrill of coming dispossession, and saw nothing through their great golden eyes but the dawning of a day just like all other days—when "the sun ariseth and they gather themselves into their dens and lay them down." And yet alike to Indian, panther, and wild-cat, to every oak of the forest, to every foot of land in America, from the stormy Atlantic to the broad Pacific, that day was a day of days.

There had been stormy and windy weather, but now dawned on the earth one of those still, golden times of November, full of dreamy rest and tender calm. The skies above were blue and fair, and the waters of the curving bay were a downward sky—a magical under-world, wherein the crimson oaks, and the dusk plumage of the pine, and the red holly-berries, and yellow sassafras leaves, all flickered and glinted in wavering bands of color as soft winds swayed the glassy floor of waters.

In a moment, there is heard in the silent bay a sound of a rush and ripple, different from the lap of the many-tongued waves on the shore; and, silently as a cloud, with white wings spread, a little vessel glides into the harbor.

A little craft is she—not larger than the fishing-smacks that ply their course along our coasts in summer; but her decks are crowded with men, women, and children, looking out with joyous curiosity on the beautiful bay, where, after many dangers and storms, they first have found safe shelter and hopeful harbor.

That small, unknown ship was the *Mayflower*; those men and women who crowded her decks were that little handful of God's own wheat which had been flailed by adversity, tossed and winnowed till every husk of earthly selfishness and self-will had been beaten away from them and left only pure seed, fit for the planting of a new world. It was old Master Cotton Mather who said of them, "The Lord sifted three countries to find seed wherewith to plant America."

Hark now to the hearty cry of the sailors, as with a plash and a cheer the anchor goes down, just in the deep water inside of Long Point; and then, says their journal, "being now passed the vast ocean and sea of troubles, before their preparation unto further proceedings as to seek out a place for habitation, they fell down on their knees and blessed the Lord, the God of heaven, who had brought them over the vast and furious ocean, and delivered them from all perils and miseries thereof."

Let us draw nigh and mingle with this singular act of worship. Elder Brewster, with his well-worn Geneva Bible in hand, leads the thanksgiving in words which, though thousands of years old, seem as if written for the occasion of that hour:

"Praise the Lord because he is good, for his mercy endureth forever. Let them which have been redeemed of the Lord show how he delivereth them from the hand of the oppressor, and gathered them out of the lands: from the east, and from the west, from the north, and from the south, when they wandered in deserts and wildernesses out of the way and found no city to dwell in. Both hungry and thirsty, their soul failed in them. Then they cried unto the Lord in their troubles, and he delivered them in their distresses. And led them forth by the right way, that they might go unto a city of habitation. They that go down to the sea and occupy by the great waters: they see the works of the Lord and his wonders in the deep. For he commandeth and raiseth the stormy wind, and it lifteth up the waves thereof. They mount up to heaven, and descend to the deep: so that their soul melteth for trouble. They are tossed to and fro, and stagger like a drunken man, and all their cunning is gone. Then they cry unto the Lord in their trouble, and he bringeth them out of their distresses. He turneth the storm to a calm, so that the waves thereof are still. When they are quieted they are glad, and he bringeth them unto the haven where they would be."

As yet, the treasures of sacred song which are the liturgy of modern Christians had not arisen in the church. There was no Watts, and no Wesley, in the days of the Pilgrims; they brought with them in each family, as the most precious of household possessions, a thick volume containing, first, the Book of Common Prayer, with the Psalter appointed to be read in churches; second, the whole Bible in the Geneva translation, which was the basis on which our present English translation was made; and, third, the Psalms of David, in meter, by Sternhold and Hopkins, with the music notes of the tunes, adapted to singing. Therefore it was that our little band were able to lift up their voices together in song and that the noble tones of Old Hundred for the first time floated over the silent bay and mingled with the sound of winds and waters, consecrating our American shores.

> All people that on earth do dwell,
>   Sing to the Lord with cheerful voice:
> Him serve with fear, His praise forthtell;
>   Come ye before Him and rejoice.

The Lord, ye know, is God indeed;
  Without our aid He did us make;
We are His flock, He doth us feed,
  And for his sheep He doth us take.

O enter then His gates with praise,
  Approach with joy His courts unto:
Praise, laud, and bless His name always,
  For it is seemly so to do.

For why? The Lord our God is good,
  His mercy is forever sure;
His truth at all times firmly stood,
  And shall from age to age endure.

This grand hymn rose and swelled and vibrated in the still November air; while in between the pauses came the warble of birds, the scream of the jay, the hoarse call of hawk and eagle, going on with their forest ways all unmindful of the new era which had been ushered in with those solemn sounds.

CHAPTER II. THE FIRST DAY ON SHORE

The sound of prayer and psalm-singing died away on the shore, and the little band, rising from their knees, saluted each other in that genial humor which always possesses a ship's company when they have weathered the ocean and come to land together.

"Well, Master Jones, here we are," said Elder Brewster cheerily to the ship-master.

"Aye, aye, sir, here we be sure enough; but I've had many a shrewd doubt of this upshot. I tell you, sirs, when that beam amidships sprung and cracked Master Coppin here said we must give over—hands couldn't bring her through. Thou rememberest, Master Coppin?"

"That I do," replied Master Coppin, the first mate, a stocky, cheery sailor, with a face red and shining as a glazed bun. "I said then that praying might save her, perhaps, but nothing else would."

"Praying wouldn't have saved her," said Master Brown, the carpenter, "if I had not put in that screw and worked the beam to her place again."

"Aye, aye, Master Carpenter," said Elder Brewster, "the Lord hath abundance of the needful ever to his hand. When He wills to answer prayer, there will be found both carpenter and screws in their season, I trow."

"Well, Deb," said Master Coppin, pinching the ear of a great mastiff bitch who sat by him, "what sayest thou? Give us thy mind on it, old girl; say, wilt thou go deer-hunting with us yonder?"

The dog, who was full of the excitement of all around, wagged her tail and gave three tremendous barks, whereat a little spaniel with curly ears, that stood by Rose Standish, barked aloud.

"Well done!" said Captain Miles Standish. "Why, here is a salute of ordnance! Old Deb is in the spirit of the thing and opens out like a cannon. The old girl is spoiling for a chase in those woods."

"Father, may I go ashore? I want to see the country," said Wrestling Brewster, a bright, sturdy boy, creeping up to Elder Brewster and touching his father's elbow.

Thereat there was a crying to the different mothers of girls and boys tired of being cooped up,—"Oh, mother, mother, ask that we may all go ashore."

"For my part," said old Margery the serving-maid to Elder Brewster, "I want to go ashore to wash and be decent, for there isn't a soul of us hath anything fit for Christians. There be springs of water, I trow."

"Never doubt it, my woman," said Elder Brewster; "but all things in their order. How say you, Mr. Carver? You are our governor. What order shall we take?"

"We must have up the shallop," said Carver, "and send a picked company to see what entertainment there may be for us on shore."

"And I counsel that all go well armed," quoth Captain Miles Standish, "for these men of the forest are sharper than a thorn-hedge. What! what!" he said, looking over to the eager group of girls and boys, "ye would go ashore, would ye? Why, the lions and bears will make one mouthful of ye."

"I'm not afraid of lions," said young Wrestling Brewster in an aside to little Love Winslow, a golden-haired, pale-cheeked child, of a tender and spiritual beauty of face. "I'd like to meet a lion," he added, "and serve him as Samson did. I'd get honey out of him, I promise."

"Oh, there you are, young Master Boastful!" said old Margery. "Mind the old saying, 'Brag is a good dog, but holdfast is better.'"

"Dear husband," said Rose Standish, "wilt thou go ashore in this company?"

"Why, aye, sweetheart, what else am I come for—and who should go if not I?"

"Thou art so very venturesome, Miles."

"Even so, my Rose of the wilderness. Why else am I come on this quest? Not being good enough to be in your church nor one of the saints, I come for an arm of flesh to them, and so, here goes on my armor."

And as he spoke, he buried his frank, good-natured countenance in an iron headpiece, and Rose hastened to help him adjust his corselet.

The clang of armor, the bustle and motion of men and children, the barking of dogs, and the cheery Heave-o! of the sailors marked the setting off of the party which comprised some of the gravest, and wisest, as well as the youngest and most able-bodied of the ship's company. The impatient children ran in a group and clustered on the side of the ship to see them go. Old Deb, with her two half-grown pups, barked and yelped after her master in the boat, running up and down the vessel's deck with piteous cries of impatience.

"Come hither, dear old Deb," said little Love Winslow, running up and throwing her arms round the dog's rough neck; "thou must not take on so; thy master will be back again; so be a good dog now, and lie down."

And the great rough mastiff quieted down under her caresses, and sitting down by her she patted and played with her, with her little thin hands.

"See the darling," said Rose Standish, "what a way that baby hath! In all the roughness and the terrors of the sea she hath been like a little sunbeam to us—yet she is so frail!"

"She hath been marked in the womb by the troubles her mother bore," said old Margery, shaking her head. "She never had the ways of other babies, but hath ever that wistful look—and her eyes are brighter than they should be. Mistress Winslow will never raise that child—now mark me!"

"Take care!" said Rose, "let not her mother hear you."

"Why, look at her beside of Wrestling Brewster, or Faith Carver. They are flesh and blood, and she looks as if she had been made out of sunshine. 'Tis a sweet babe as ever was; but fitter for the kingdom of heaven than our rough life—deary me! a hard time we have had of it. I suppose it's all best, but I don't know."

"Oh, never talk that way, Margery," said Rose Standish; "we must all keep up heart, our own and one another's."

"Ah, well a day—I suppose so, but then I look at my good Master Brewster and remember how, when I was a girl, he was at our good Queen Elizabeth's court, ruffling it with the best, and everybody said that there wasn't a young man that had good fortune to equal his. Why, Master Davidson, the Queen's Secretary of State, thought all the world of him; and when he went to Holland on the Queen's business, he must take him along; and when he took the keys of the cities there, it was my master that he trusted them to, who used to sleep with them under his pillow. I remember when he came home to the Queen's court, wearing the great gold chain that the States had given him. Ah me! I little thought he would ever come to a poor man's coat, then!"

"Well, good Margery," said Rose, "it isn't the coat, but the heart under it—that's the thing. Thou hast more cause of pride in thy master's poverty than in his riches."

"Maybe so—I don't know," said Margery, "but he hath had many a sore trouble in worldly things—driven and hunted from place to place in England, clapt into prison, and all he had eaten up with fines and charges and costs."

"All that is because he chose rather to suffer affliction with the people of God than to enjoy the pleasures of sin for a season," said Rose; "he shall have his reward by and by."

"Well, there be good men and godly in Old England that get to heaven in better coats and with easy carriages and fine houses and servants, and I would my master had been of such. But if he must come to the wilderness I will come with him. Gracious me! what noise is that?" she exclaimed, as a sudden report of firearms from below struck her ear. "I do believe there is that Frank Billington at the gunpowder; that boy will never leave, I do believe, till he hath blown up the ship's company."

In fact, it appeared that young master Frank, impatient of the absence of his father, had toled Wrestling Brewster and two other of the boys down into the cabin to show them his skill in managing his father's fowling-piece, had burst the gun, scattering the pieces about the cabin.

Margery soon appeared, dragging the culprit after her. "Look here now, Master Malapert, see what you'll get when your father comes home! Lord a mercy! here was half a keg of powder standing open! Enough to have blown us all up! Here, Master Clarke, Master Clarke, come and keep this boy with you till his father come back, or we be all sent sky high before we know."

At even tide the boat came back laden to the water's edge with the first gettings and givings from the new soil of America. There is a richness and sweetness gleaming through the brief records of these men in their journals, which shows how the new land was seen through a fond and tender medium, half poetic; and its new products lend a savor to them of somewhat foreign and rare.

Of this day's expedition the record is thus:

"That day, so soon as we could, we set ashore some fifteen or sixteen men well armed, with some to fetch wood, for we had none left; as also to see what the land was and what inhabitants they could meet with. They found it to be a small neck of land on this side where we lay in the bay, and on the further side the sea, the ground or earth, sand-hills, much like the downs in Holland, but much better; the crust of the earth a spit's depth of excellent black earth; all wooded with oaks, pines, sassafras, juniper, birch, holly, vines, some ash and walnut; the wood for the most part open and without underwood, fit either to walk or to ride in. At night our people returned and found not any people or inhabitants, and laded their boat with juniper, which smelled very sweet and strong, and of which we burned for the most part while we were there."

"See there," said little Love Winslow, "what fine red berries Captain Miles Standish hath brought."

"Yea, my little maid, there is a brave lot of holly berries for thee to dress the cabin withal. We shall not want for Christmas greens here, though the houses and churches are yet to come."

"Yea, Brother Miles," said Elder Brewster, "the trees of the Lord are full of sap in this land, even the cedars of Lebanon, which he hath planted. It hath the look to me of a land which the Lord our God hath blessed."

"There is a most excellent depth of black, rich earth," said Carver, "and a great tangle of grapevines, whereon the leaves in many places yet hung, and we picked up stores of walnuts under a tree—not so big as our English ones—but sweet and well-flavored."

"Know ye, brethren, what in this land smelleth sweetest to me?" said Elder Brewster. "It is the smell of liberty. The soil is free—no man hath claim thereon. In Old England a poor man may starve right on his mother's bosom; there may be stores of fish in the river, and bird and fowl flying, and deer running by, and yet though a man's children be crying for bread, an' he catch a fish or snare a bird, he shall be snatched up and hanged. This is a sore evil in Old England; but we will make a country here for the poor to dwell in, where the wild fruits and fish and fowl shall be the inheritance of whosoever will have them; and every man shall have his portion of our good mother earth, with no lords and no bishops to harry and distrain, and worry with taxes and tythes."

"Amen, brother!" said Miles Standish, "and thereto I give my best endeavors with sword and buckler."

CHAPTER III. CHRISTMAS TIDE IN PLYMOUTH HARBOR

For the rest of that month of November the *Mayflower* lay at anchor in Cape Cod harbor, and formed a floating home for the women and children, while the men were out exploring the country, with a careful and steady shrewdness and good sense, to determine where should be the site of the future colony. The record of their adventures is given in their journals with that sweet homeliness of phrase which hangs about the Old English of that period like the smell of rosemary in an ancient cabinet.

We are told of a sort of picnic day, when "our women went on shore to wash and all to refresh themselves"; and fancy the times there must have been among the little company, while the mothers sorted and washed and dried the linen, and the children, under the keeping of the old mastiffs and with many cautions against the wolves and wild cubs, once more had liberty to play in the green wood. For it appears in these journals how, in one case, the little spaniel of John Goodman was chased by two wolves, and was fain to take refuge between his master's legs for shelter. Goodman "had nothing in hand," says the journal, "but took up a stick and threw at one of them and hit him, and they presently ran away, but came again. He got a pale-board in his hand, but they both sat on their tails a good while, grinning at him, and then went their way and left him."

Such little touches show what the care of families must have been in the woodland picnics, and why the ship was, on the whole, the safest refuge for the women and children.

We are told, moreover, how the party who had struck off into the wilderness, "having marched through boughs and bushes and under hills and valleys which tore our very armor in pieces, yet could meet with no inhabitants nor find any fresh water which we greatly stood in need of, for we brought neither beer nor water with us, and our victual was only biscuit and Holland cheese, and a little bottle of aqua vitae. So we were sore athirst. About ten o'clock we came into a deep valley full of brush, sweet gaile and long grass, through which we found little paths or tracks; and we saw there a deer and found springs of water, of which we were heartily glad, and sat us down and drunk our first New England water with as much delight as we ever drunk drink in all our lives."

Three such expeditions through the country, with all sorts of haps and mishaps and adventures, took up the time until near the 15th of December, when, having selected a spot for their colony, they weighed anchor to go to their future home.

Plymouth Harbor, as they found it, is thus described:

"This harbor is a bay greater than Cape Cod, compassed with a goodly land, and in the bay two fine islands uninhabited, wherein are nothing but woods, oaks, pines, walnuts, beeches, sassafras, vines, and other trees which we know not. The bay is a most hopeful place, innumerable stores of fowl, and excellent good; and it cannot but be of fish in their season. Skate, cod, and turbot, and herring we have tasted of—abundance of mussels (clams) the best we ever saw; and crabs and lobsters in their time, infinite."

On the main land they write:

"The land is, for a spit's depth, excellent black mould and fat in some places. Two or three great oaks, pines, walnut, beech, ash, birch, hazel, holly, and sassafras in abundance, and vines everywhere, with cherry-trees, plum-trees, and others which we know not. Many kind of herbs we found here in winter, as strawberry leaves innumerable, sorrel, yarrow, carvel, brook-lime, liver-wort, water-cresses, with great store of leeks and onions, and an excellent strong kind of flax and hemp."

It is evident from this description that the season was a mild one even thus late into December, that there was still sufficient foliage hanging upon the trees to determine the species, and that the pilgrims viewed their new mother-land through eyes of cheerful hope.

And now let us look in the glass at them once more, on Saturday morning of the 23d of December.

The little *Mayflower* lies swinging at her moorings in the harbor, while every man and boy who could use a tool has gone on shore to cut down and prepare timber for future houses.

Mary Winslow and Rose Standish are sitting together on deck, fashioning garments, while little Love Winslow is playing at their feet with such toys as the new world afforded her—strings of acorns and scarlet holly-berries and some bird-claws and arrowheads and bright-colored ears of Indian corn, which Captain Miles Standish has brought home to her from one of their explorations.

Through the still autumnal air may now and then be heard the voices of men calling to one another on shore, the quick, sharp ring of axes, and anon the crash of falling trees, with shouts from juveniles as the great forest monarch is laid low. Some of the women are busy below, sorting over and arranging their little household stores and stuff with a view to moving on shore, and holding domestic consultations with each other.

A sadness hangs over the little company, for since their arrival the stroke of death has more than once fallen; we find in Bradford's brief record that by the 24th of December six had died.

What came nearest to the hearts of all was the loss of Dorothea Bradford, who, when all the men of the party were absent on an exploring tour, accidentally fell over the side of the vessel and sunk in the deep waters. What this loss was to the husband and the little company of brothers and sisters appears by no note or word of wailing, merely by a simple entry which says no more than the record on a gravestone, that, "on the 7th of December, Dorothy, wife of William Bradford, fell over and was drowned."

That much-enduring company could afford themselves few tears. Earthly having and enjoying was a thing long since dismissed from their calculations. They were living on the primitive Christian platform; they "rejoiced as though they rejoiced not," and they "wept as though they wept not," and they "had wives and children as though they had them not," or, as one of themselves expressed it, "We are in all places strangers, pilgrims, travelers and sojourners; our dwelling is but a wandering, our abiding but as a fleeting, our home is nowhere but in the heavens, in that house not made with hands, whose builder and maker is God."

When one of their number fell they were forced to do as soldiers in the stress of battle—close up the ranks and press on.

But Mary Winslow, as she sat over her sewing, dropped now and then a tear down on her work for the loss of her sister and counselor and long-tried friend. From the lower part of the ship floated up, at intervals, snatches of an old English ditty that Margery was singing while she moved to and fro about her work, one of those genuine English melodies, full of a rich, strange mournfulness blent with a soothing pathos:

> *Fear no more the heat o' the sun*
> *Nor the furious winter rages,*
> *Thou thy worldly task hast done,*
> *Home art gone and ta'en thy wages.*

The air was familiar, and Mary Winslow, dropping her work in her lap, involuntarily joined in it:

> *Fear no more the frown of the great,*
> *Thou art past the tyrant's stroke;*
> *Care no more to clothe and eat,*
> *To thee the reed is as the oak.*

"There goes a great tree on shore!" quoth little Love Winslow, clapping her hands. "Dost hear, mother? I've been counting the strokes—fifteen—and then crackle! crackle! crackle! and down it comes!"

"Peace, darling," said Mary Winslow; "hear what old Margery is singing below."

> *Fear no more the lightning's flash,*
> *Nor the all-dreaded thunder stone;*
> *Fear not slander, censure rash—*
> *Thou hast finished joy and moan.*
> *All lovers young—all lovers must*
> *Consign to thee, and come to dust.*

"Why do you cry, mother?" said the little one, climbing on her lap and wiping her tears.

"I was thinking of dear Auntie, who is gone from us."

"She is not gone from us, mother."

"My darling, she is with Jesus."

"Well, mother, Jesus is ever with us—you tell me that—and if she is with him she is with us too—I know she is—for sometimes I see her. She sat by me last night and stroked my head when that ugly, stormy wind waked me—she looked so sweet, oh, ever so beautiful!—and she made me go to sleep so quiet—it is sweet to be as she is, mother—not away from us but with Jesus."

"These little ones see further in the kingdom than we," said Rose Standish. "If we would be like them, we should take things easier. When the Lord would show who was greatest in his kingdom, he took a little child on his lap."

"Ah me, Rose!" said Mary Winslow, "I am aweary in spirit with this tossing sea-life. I long to have a home on dry land once more, be it ever so poor. The sea wearies me. Only think, it is almost Christmas time, only two days now to Christmas. How shall we keep it in these woods?"

"Aye, aye," said old Margery, coming up at the moment, "a brave muster and to do is there now in old England; and men and boys going forth singing and bearing home branches of holly, and pine, and mistletoe for Christmas greens. Oh! I remember I used to go forth with them and help dress the churches. God help the poor children, they will grow up in the wilderness and never see such brave sights as I have. They will never know what a church is, such as they are in old England, with fine old windows like the clouds, and rainbows, and great wonderful arches like the very skies above us, and the brave music with the old organs rolling and the boys marching in white garments and singing so as should draw the very heart out of one. All this we have left behind in old England—ah! well a day! well a day!"

"Oh, but, Margery," said Mary Winslow, "we have a 'better country' than old England, where the saints and angels are keeping Christmas; we confess that we are strangers and pilgrims on earth."

And Rose Standish immediately added the familiar quotation from the Geneva Bible:

"For they that say such things declare plainly that they seek a country. For if they had been mindful of that country from whence they came out they had leisure to have returned. But now they desire a better—that is, an heavenly; wherefore God is not ashamed of them to be called their God."

The fair young face glowed as she repeated the heroic words, for already, though she knew it not, Rose Standish was feeling the approaching sphere of the angel life. Strong in spirit, as delicate in frame, she had given herself and drawn her martial husband to the support of a great and noble cause; but while the spirit was ready, the flesh was weak, and even at that moment her name was written in the Lamb's Book to enter the higher life, in one short month's time from that Christmas.

Only one month of sweetness and perfume was that sweet rose to shed over the hard and troubled life of the pilgrims, for the saints and angels loved her, and were from day to day gently untying mortal bands to draw her to themselves. Yet was there nothing about her of mournfulness; on the contrary, she was ever alert and bright, with a ready tongue to cheer and a helpful hand to do; and, seeing the sadness that seemed stealing over Mary Winslow, she struck another key, and, catching little Love up in her arms, said cheerily,

"Come hither, pretty one, and Rose will sing thee a brave carol for Christmas. We won't be down-hearted, will we? Hark now to what the minstrels used to sing under my window when I was a little girl:

I saw three ships come sailing in
On Christmas day, on Christmas day,
I saw three ships come sailing in
On Christmas day in the morning.

And what was in those ships all three
On Christmas day, on Christmas day,
And what was in those ships all three
On Christmas day in the morning?

Our Saviour Christ and his laydie,
On Christmas day, on Christmas day,
Our Saviour Christ and his laydie
On Christmas day in the morning.

Pray, whither sailed those ships all three,
On Christmas day, on Christmas day?
Oh, they sailed into Bethlehem,
On Christmas day in the morning.

And all the bells on earth shall ring
On Christmas day, on Christmas day;
And all the angels in heaven shall sing
On Christmas day in the morning.

Then let us all rejoice amain,
On Christmas day, on Christmas day;
Then let us all rejoice amain
On Christmas day in the morning.

"Now, isn't that a brave ballad?" said Rose. "Yea, and thou singest like a real English robin," said Margery, "to do the heart good to hear thee."

CHAPTER IV. ELDER BREWSTER'S CHRISTMAS SERMON

Sunday morning found the little company gathered once more on the ship, with nothing to do but rest and remember their homes, temporal and spiritual—homes backward, in old England, and forward, in Heaven. They were, every man and woman of them, English to the back-bone. From Captain Jones who commanded the ship to Elder Brewster who ruled and guided in spiritual affairs, all alike were of that stock and breeding which made the Englishman of the days of Bacon and Shakespeare, and in those days Christmas was knit into the heart of every one of them by a thousand threads, which no after years could untie.

Christmas carols had been sung to them by nurses and mothers and grandmothers; the Christmas holly spoke to them from every berry and prickly leaf, full of dearest household memories. Some of them had been men of substance among the English gentry, and in their prosperous days had held high festival in ancestral halls in the season of good cheer. Elder Brewster himself had been a rising young diplomat in the court of Elizabeth, in the days when the Lord Keeper of the Seals led the revels of Christmas as Lord of Misrule.

So that, though this Sunday morning arose gray and lowering, with snow-flakes hovering through the air, there was Christmas in the thoughts of every man and woman among them—albeit it was the Christmas of wanderers and exiles in a wilderness looking back to bright home-fires across stormy waters.

The men had come back from their work on shore with branches of green pine and holly, and the women had stuck them about the ship, not without tearful thoughts of old home-places, where their childhood fathers and mothers did the same.

Bits and snatches of Christmas carols were floating all around the ship, like land-birds blown far out to sea. In the forecastle Master Coppin was singing:

Come, bring with a noise,
My merry boys,
  The Christmas log to the firing;
While my good dame, she
Bids ye all be free,
  And drink to your hearts' desiring.
Drink now the strong beer,
Cut the white loaf here.

> *The while the meat is shredding*
> *For the rare minced pie,*
> *And the plums stand by*
>   *To fill the paste that's a-kneading.*

"Ah, well-a-day, Master Jones, it is dull cheer to sing Christmas songs here in the woods, with only the owls and the bears for choristers. I wish I could hear the bells of merry England once more."

And down in the cabin Rose Standish was hushing little Peregrine, the first American-born baby, with a Christmas lullaby:

> *This winter's night*
> *I saw a sight—*
>   *A star as bright as day;*
> *And ever among*
> *A maiden sung,*
>   *Lullay, by-by, lullay!*

> *This lovely laydie sat and sung,*
>   *And to her child she said,*
> *My son, my brother, and my father dear,*
>   *Why lyest thou thus in hayd?*
> *My sweet bird,*
> *Tho' it betide*
>   *Thou be not king veray;*
> *But nevertheless I will not cease*
>   *To sing, by-by, lullay!*

> *The child then spake in his talking,*
>   *And to his mother he said,*
> *It happeneth, mother, I am a king,*
>   *In crib though I be laid,*
> *For angels bright*
> *Did down alight,*
>   *Thou knowest it is no nay;*
> *And of that sight*
> *Thou may'st be light*
>   *To sing, by-by, lullay!*

Now, sweet son, since thou art a king,
  Why art thou laid in stall?
Why not ordain thy bedding
  In some great king his hall?
We thinketh 'tis right
That king or knight
  Should be in good array;
And them among,
It were no wrong
  To sing, by-by, lullay!

Mary, mother, I am thy child,
  Tho' I be laid in stall;
Lords and dukes shall worship me,
  And so shall kinges all.
And ye shall see
That kinges three
  Shall come on the twelfth day;
For this behest
Give me thy breast,
  And sing, by-by, lullay!"

"See here," quoth Miles Standish, "when my Rose singeth, the children gather round her like bees round a flower. Come, let us all strike up a goodly carol together. Sing one, sing all, girls and boys, and get a bit of Old England's Christmas before to-morrow, when we must to our work on shore."

Thereat Rose struck up a familiar ballad-meter of a catching rhythm, and every voice of young and old was soon joining in it:

Behold a silly,* tender Babe,
  In freezing winter night,
In homely manger trembling lies;
  Alas! a piteous sight,
The inns are full, no man will yield
  This little Pilgrim bed;
But forced He is, with silly beasts
  In crib to shroud His head.

---

* Old English: simple.

Despise Him not for lying there,
  First what He is inquire:
An orient pearl is often found
  In depth of dirty mire.

Weigh not His crib, His wooden dish,
  Nor beasts that by Him feed;
Weigh not His mother's poor attire,
  Nor Joseph's simple weed.
This stable is a Prince's court,
  The crib His chair of state,
The beasts are parcel of His pomp,
  The wooden dish His plate.
The persons in that poor attire
  His royal liveries wear;
The Prince Himself is come from Heaven,
  This pomp is prized there.
With joy approach, O Christian wight,
  Do homage to thy King;
And highly praise His humble pomp,
  Which He from Heaven doth bring.

The cheerful sounds spread themselves through the ship like the flavor of some rare perfume, bringing softness of heart through a thousand tender memories.

Anon, the hour of Sabbath morning worship drew on, and Elder Brewster read from the New Testament the whole story of the Nativity, and then gave a sort of Christmas homily from the words of St. Paul, in the eighth chapter of Romans, the sixth and seventh verses, which the Geneva version thus renders:

For the wisdom of the flesh is death, but the wisdom of the spirit is life and peace.

For the wisdom of the flesh is enmity against God, for it is not subject to the law of God, neither indeed can be.

"Ye know full well, dear brethren, what the wisdom of the flesh sayeth. The wisdom of the flesh sayeth to each one, 'Take care of thyself; look after thyself, to get and to have and to hold and to enjoy.' The wisdom of the flesh sayeth, 'So thou art warm, full, and in good liking, take thine ease, eat, drink, and be merry, and care not how many go empty and be lacking.' But ye have seen in the Gospel this morning that this was not the wisdom of our Lord Jesus Christ, who, though he was Lord of all, became poorer than any, that we, through His poverty, might become rich. When our Lord Jesus Christ came, the wisdom of the flesh despised Him; the wisdom of the flesh had no room for Him at the inn.

"There was room enough always for Herod and his concubines, for the wisdom of the flesh set great store by them; but a poor man and woman were thrust out to a stable; and there was a poor baby born whom the wisdom of the flesh knew not, because the wisdom of the flesh is enmity against God.

"The wisdom of the flesh, brethren, ever despiseth the wisdom of God, because it knoweth it not. The wisdom of the flesh looketh at the thing that is great and strong and high; it looketh at riches, at kings' courts, at fine clothes and fine jewels and fine feastings, and it despiseth the little and the poor and the weak.

"But the wisdom of the Spirit goeth to worship the poor babe in the manger, and layeth gold and myrrh and frankincense at his feet while he lieth in weakness and poverty, as did the wise men who were taught of God.

"Now, forasmuch as our Saviour Christ left His riches and throne in glory and came in weakness and poverty to this world, that he might work out a mighty salvation that shall be to all people, how can we better keep Christmas than to follow in his steps? We be a little company who have forsaken houses and lands and possessions, and come here unto the wilderness that we may prepare a resting-place whereto others shall come to reap what we shall sow. And to-morrow we shall keep our first Christmas, not in flesh-pleasing, and in reveling and in fullness of bread, but in small beginning and great weakness, as our Lord Christ kept it when He was born in a stable and lay in a manger.

"To-morrow, God willing, we will all go forth to do good, honest Christian work, and begin the first house-building in this our New England—it may be roughly fashioned, but as good a house, I'll warrant me, as our Lord Christ had on the Christmas Day we wot of. And let us not faint in heart because the wisdom of the world despiseth what we do. Though Sanballat the Horonite, and Tobias the Ammonite, and Geshem the Arabian make scorn of us, and say, 'What do these weak Jews? If a fox go up, he shall break down their stone wall'; yet the Lord our God is with us, and He can cause our work to prosper.

"The wisdom of the Spirit seeth the grain of mustard-seed, that is the least of all seeds, how it shall become a great tree, and the fowls of heaven shall lodge in its branches. Let us, then, lift up the hands that hang down and the feeble knees, and let us hope that, like as great salvation to all people came out of small beginnings of Bethlehem, so the work which we shall begin to-morrow shall be for the good of many nations.

"It is a custom on this Christmas Day to give love-presents. What love-gift giveth our Lord Jesus on this day? Brethren, it is a great one and a precious; as St. Paul said to the Philippians: 'For unto you it is given for Christ, not only that ye should believe on Him, but also that ye should suffer for His sake'; and St. Peter also saith, 'Behold, we count them blessed which endure.' And the holy Apostles rejoiced that they were counted worthy to suffer rebuke for the name of Jesus.

"Our Lord Christ giveth us of His cup and His baptism; He giveth of the manger and the straw; He giveth of persecutions and afflictions; He giveth of the crown of thorns, and right dear unto us be these gifts.

"And now will I tell these children a story, which a cunning playwright, whom I once knew in our Queen's court, hath made concerning gifts:

"A great king would marry his daughter worthily, and so he caused three caskets to be made, in one of which he hid her picture. The one casket was of gold set with diamonds, the second of silver set with pearls, and the third a poor casket of lead.

"Now it was given out that each comer should have but one choice, and if he chose the one with the picture he should have the lady to wife.

"Divers kings, knights, and gentlemen came from far, but they never won, because they always snatched at the gold and the silver caskets, with the pearls and diamonds. So, when they opened these, they found only a grinning death's-head or a fool's cap.

"But anon cometh a true, brave knight and gentleman, who chooseth for love alone the old leaden casket; and, behold, within is the picture of her he loveth! and they were married with great feasting and content.

"So our Lord Jesus doth not offer himself to us in silver and gold and jewels, but in poverty and hardness and want; but whoso chooseth them for His love's sake shall find Him therein whom his soul loveth, and shall enter with joy to the marriage supper of the Lamb.

"And when the Lord shall come again in his glory, then he shall bring worthy gifts with him, for he saith: 'Be thou faithful unto death, and I will give thee a crown of life; to him that overcometh I will give to eat of the hidden manna, and I will give him a white stone with a new name that no man knoweth save he that receiveth it. He that overcometh and keepeth my words, I will give power over the nations and I will give him the morning star.'

"Let us then take joyfully Christ's Christmas gifts of labors and adversities and crosses to-day, that when he shall appear we may have these great and wonderful gifts at his coming; for if we suffer with him we shall also reign; but if we deny him, he also will deny us."

And so it happens that the only record of Christmas Day in the pilgrims' journal is this:

"Monday, the 25th, being Christmas Day, we went ashore, some to fell timber, some to saw, some to rive, and some to carry; and so no man rested all that day. But towards night some, as they were at work, heard a noise of Indians, which caused us all to go to our muskets; but we heard no further, so we came aboard again, leaving some to keep guard. That night we had a sore storm of wind and rain. But at night the ship-master caused us to have some beer aboard."

So worthily kept they the first Christmas, from which comes all the Christmas cheer of New England to-day. There is no record how Mary Winslow and Rose Standish and others, with women and children, came ashore and walked about encouraging the builders; and how little Love gathered stores of bright checker-berries and partridge plums, and was made merry in seeing squirrels and wild rabbits; nor how old Margery roasted certain wild geese to a turn at a woodland fire, and conserved wild cranberries with honey for sauce. In their journals the good pilgrims say they found bushels of strawberries in the meadows in December. But we, knowing the nature of things, know that these must have been cranberries, which grow still abundantly around Plymouth harbor.

And at the very time that all this was doing in the wilderness, and the men were working yeomanly to build a new nation, in King James's court the ambassadors of the French King were being entertained with maskings and mummerings, wherein the staple subject of merriment was the Puritans!

So goes the wisdom of the world and its ways—and so goes the wisdom of God!

Betty's Bright Idea

Harriet Beecher Stowe

"When He ascended up on high, He led captivity captive, and
gave gifts unto men."—Eph. iv. 8.

Some say that ever, 'gainst that season comes
Wherein our Saviour's birth is celebrate,
The bird of dawning singeth all night long.
And then, they say, no evil spirit walks;
The nights are wholesome; then no planets strike,
No fairy takes, no witch hath power to charm,—
So hallowed and so gracious is the time.

And this holy time, so hallowed and so gracious, was settling down over the great roaring, rattling, seething life-world of New York in the good year 1875. Who does not feel its on-coming in the shops and streets, in the festive air of trade and business, in the thousand garnitures by which every store hangs out triumphal banners and solicits you to buy something for a Christmas gift? For it is the peculiarity of all this array of prints, confectionery, dry goods, and manufactures of all kinds, that their bravery and splendor at Christmas tide is all to seduce you into generosity, and importune you to give something to others. It says to you, "The dear God gave you an unspeakable gift; give you a lesser gift to your brother!"

Do we ever think, when we walk those busy, bustling streets, all alive with Christmas shoppers, and mingle with the rushing tides that throng and jostle through the stores, that unseen spirits may be hastening to and fro along those same ways bearing Christ's Christmas gifts to men—gifts whose value no earthly gold or gems can represent?

Yet, on this morning of the day before Christmas, were these Shining Ones, moving to and fro with the crowd, whose faces were loving and serene as the invisible stars, whose robes took no defilement from the spatter and the rush of earth, whose coming and going was still as the falling snow-flakes. They entered houses without ringing door-bells, they passed through apartments without opening doors, and everywhere they were bearing Christ's Christmas presents, and silently offering them to whoever would open their souls to receive. Like themselves, their gifts were invisible—incapable of weight and measurement in gross earthly scales. To mourners they carried joy; to weary and perplexed hearts, peace; to souls stifling in luxury and self-indulgence they carried that noble discontent that rises to aspiration for higher things. Sometimes they took away an earthly treasure to make room for a heavenly one. They took health, but left resignation and cheerful faith, They took the babe from the dear cradle, but left in its place a heart full of pity for the suffering on earth and a fellowship with the blessed in heaven. Let us follow their footsteps awhile.

SCENE I

A young girl's boudoir in one of our American palaces of luxury, built after the choicest fancy of the architect, and furnished in all the latest devices of household decoration. Pictures, statuettes, and every form of *bijouterie* make the room a miracle of beauty, and the little princess of all sits in an easy chair before the fire, and thus revolves with herself:

"O, dear me! Christmas is a bore! Such a rush and crush in the streets, such a jam in the shops, and then *such* a fuss thinking up presents for everybody! All for nothing, too; for nobody wants anything. I'm sure *I* don't. I'm surfeited now with pictures and jewelry, and bon-bon boxes, and little china dogs and cats—and all these things that get so thick you can't move without upsetting some of them. There's papa, he don't want anything. He never uses any of my Christmas presents when I get them; and mamma, she has every earthly thing I can think of, and said the other day she did hope nobody'd give her any more worsted work! Then Aunt Maria and Uncle John, they don't want the things I give them; they have more than they know what to do with, now. All the boys say they don't want any more cigar cases or slippers, or smoking caps. Oh, dear!"

Here the Shining Ones came and stood over the little lady, and looked down on her with faces of pity, which seemed blent with a serene and half-amused indulgence. It was a heavenly amusement, such as that with which mothers listen to the foolish-wise prattle of children just learning to talk.

As the grave, sweet eyes rested tenderly on her, the girl somehow grew graver, leaned back in her chair, and sighed a little.

"I wish I knew how to be better!" she said to herself. "I remember last Sunday's text, 'It is more blessed to give than to receive.' That must mean something! Well, isn't there something, too, in the Bible about not giving to your rich neighbors that can give again, but giving to the poor that cannot recompense you? I don't know any poor people. Papa says there are very few deserving poor people. Well, for the matter of that, there aren't many *deserving rich* people. I, for example, how much do I *deserve* to have all these nice things? I'm no better than the poor shop-girls that go trudging by in the cold at six o'clock in the morning—ugh! it makes me shiver to think of it. I know if I had to do that *I* shouldn't be good at all. Well, I'd like to give to poor people, if I knew any."

At this moment the door opened and the maid entered.

"Betty, do you know any poor people I ought to get things for, this Christmas?"

"Poor folks is always plenty, miss," said Betty.

"O yes, of course, beggars; but I mean people that I could do something for besides just give cold victuals or money. I don't know where to hunt them up, and should be afraid to go if I did. O dear! it's no use. I'll give it up."

"Why, Miss Florence, that 'ud be too bad, afther bein' that good in yer heart, to let the poor folks alone for fear of goin' to them. But ye needn't do that, for, now I think of it, there's John Morley's wife."

"What, the gardener father turned off for drinking?"

"The same, miss. Poor boy, he's not so bad, and he's got a wife and two as pretty children as ever you see."

"I always liked John," said the young lady. "But papa is so strict about some things! He says he never will keep a man a day if he finds out that he drinks."

She was quite silent for a minute, and then broke out:

"I don't care; it's a good idea! I say, Betty, do you know where John's wife lives?"

"Yes, miss, I've been there often."

"Well, then, this afternoon I'll go with you and see if I can do anything for them."

SCENE II

An attic room, neat and clean, but poorly furnished; a bed and a trundle-bed, a small cooking-stove, a shelf with a few dishes, one or two chairs and stools, a pale, thin woman working on a vest.

Her face is anxious; her thin hands tremble with weakness, and now and then, as she works, quiet tears drop, which she wipes quickly. Poor people cannot afford to shed tears; it takes time and injures eyesight.

This is John Morley's wife. This morning he has risen and gone out in a desperate mood. "No use to try," he says. "Didn't I go a whole year and never touch a drop? And now just because I fell once I'm kicked out! No use to try. When a fellow once trips, everybody gives him a kick. Talk about love of Christ! Who believes it? Don't see much love of Christ where I go. Your Christians hit a fellow that's down as hard as anybody. It's everybody for himself and devil take the hindmost. Well, I'll trudge up to the Brooklyn Navy Yard and see if they'll take me on there—if they won't I might as well go to sea, or to the devil," and out he flings.

"Mamma!" says a little voice, "what are we going to have for our Christmas?"

It is a little girl, with soft curly hair and bright, earnest eyes, that speaks.

A sturdy little fellow of four presses up to the mother's knee and repeats the question, "Sha'n't we have a Christmas, mother?"

It overcomes the poor woman; she leans forward and breaks into sobbing,— a tempest of sorrow, long suppressed, that shakes her weak frame as she thinks that her husband is out of work, desperate, discouraged, and tempted of the devil, that the rent is falling due, and only the poor pay of her needle to meet it with. In one of those quick flashes which concentrate through the imagination the sorrows of years, she seems to see her little home broken up, her husband in the gutter, her children turned into the street. At this moment there goes up from her heart a despairing cry, such as a poor, hunted, tired-out creature gives when brought to the last gasp of endurance. It was like the shriek of the hare when the hounds are upon it. She clasps her hands and cries out, "O my God, help me."

There was no voice of any that answered; there was no sound of foot-fall on the staircase; no one entered the door; and yet that agonized cry had reached the heart it was meant for. The Shining Ones were with her; they stood, with faces full of tenderness, beaming down upon her; they brought her a Christmas gift from Christ—the gift of trust. She knew not from whence came the courage and rest that entered her soul; but while her little ones stood wondering and silent, she turned and drew to herself her well-worn Bible. Hands that she did not see guided her as she turned the pages, and pointed the words: *He shall deliver the needy when he crieth; the poor also and him that hath no helper. He shall spare the poor and needy, and shall save the souls of the needy. He shall redeem their soul from deceit and violence, and precious shall their blood be in his sight.*

She laid down her poor wan cheek on the merciful old book, as on her mother's breast, and gave up all the tangled skein of life into the hands of Infinite Pity. There seemed a consoling presence in the room, and her tired heart found rest.

She wiped away her tears, kissed her children, and smiled upon them. Then she rose, gathered up her finished work, and attired herself to go forth and carry it back to the shop.

"Mother," said the children softly, "they are dressing the church, and the gates are open, and people are going in and out; mayn't we play there by the church?"

The mother looked out on the ivy-grown walls of the church, with its flocks of twittering sparrows, and said:

"Yes, my little birds; you may play there if you'll be very good and quiet."

The mother had only her small, close attic room for her darlings, and to satisfy all their childish desire for variety and motion, she had only the refuge of the streets. She was a decent, godly woman, and the bold manners and evil words of street vagrants were terrible to her; and so, when the church gates were open for daily morning and evening prayers, she had often begged the sexton to let her little ones come in and hear the singing, and wander hand in hand around the old church walls. He was a kindly old man, and the children, stealing round like two still, bright-eyed little mice, had gained upon his heart, and he made them welcome there. It gave the mother a feeling of protection to have them play near the church, as if it were a father's house.

So she put on their little hoods and tippets, and led them forth, and saw them into the yard; and as she looked to the old gray church, with its rustling ivy bowers and flocks of birds, her heart swelled within her. "Yea, the sparrow hath found a house and the swallow a nest where she may lay her young, even thine altars, O Lord of hosts, my king and my God!" And the Shining Ones walking with her said, "Fear not; ye are of more value than many sparrows."

SCENE III

The little ones went gayly into the yard. They had been scared by their mother's tears; but she had smiled again, and that had made all right with them. The sun was shining brightly, and they were on the sunny side of the old church, and they laughed and chirped and chittered to each other as merrily as the little birds in the ivy boughs.

The old sexton came to the side door and threw out an armful of refuse greens, and then stopped a moment and nodded kindly at them.

"May we play with them, please, sir?" said the little Elsie, looking up with great reverence.

"Oh, yes, to be sure; these are done with—they are no good now."

"Oh, Tottie!" cried Elsie, rapturously, "just think, he says we may play with all these. Why, here's ever and ever so much green, enough to play house. Let's play build a house for father and mother."

"I'm going to build a big house for 'em when I grow up," said Tottie, "and I mean to have glass bead windows in it."

Tottie had once had presented to him a box of colored glass beads to string, and he could think of nothing finer in the future than unlimited glass beads.

Meanwhile, his sister began planting pine branches upright in the snow, to make her house.

"You see we can make believe there are windows and doors and a roof," she said, "and it's just as good. Now, let's make believe there is a bed in this corner, and we will lie down to sleep."

And Tottie obediently couched himself in the allotted corner and shut his eyes very hard, though after a moment he remarked that the snow got into his neck.

"You must play it isn't snow—play it's feathers," said Elsie.

"But I don't like it," persisted Tottie, "it don't feel a bit like feathers."

"Oh, well, then," said Elsie, accommodating herself to circumstances, "let's play get up now and I'll get breakfast."

Just now the door opened again, and the sexton began sweeping the refuse out of the church. There were bits of ivy and holly, and ruffles of ground-pine, and lots of bright red berries that came flying forth into the yard, and the children screamed for joy. "O Tottie!" "O Elsie!" "Only see how many pretty things—lots and lots!"

The sexton stood and looked and laughed as he saw the little ones so eager for the scraps and remnants.

"Don't you want to come in and see the church?" he said. "It's all done now, and a brave sight it is. You may come in."

They tipped in softly, with large bright, wondering eyes. The light through the stained glass windows fell blue and crimson and yellow on the pillars all ruffled with ground-pine and brightened with scarlet bitter-sweet berries, and there were stars and crosses and mottoes in green all through the bowery aisles, while the organist, hid in a thicket of verdure, was practicing softly, and sweet voices sung:

"Hark! the herald angels sing Glory to the new-born King."

The little ones wandered up and down the long aisles in a dream of awe and wonder. "Hush, Tottie!" said Elsie when he broke into an eager exclamation, "don't make a noise. I do believe it's something like heaven," she said, under her breath.

They made the course of the church and came round by the door again, where the sexton stood smiling on them.

"You can find lots of pretty Christmas greens out there," he said, pointing to the door; "perhaps your folks would like to have some."

"Oh, thank you, sir," exclaimed Elsie, rapturously. "Oh, Tottie, only think! Let's gather a good lot and go home and dress our room for Christmas. Oh, *won't* mother be astonished when she comes home, we'll make it so pretty!"

And forthwith the children began gathering into their little aprons wreaths of ground-pine, sprigs of holly, and twigs of crimson bitter-sweet. The sexton, seeing their zeal, brought out to them a little cross, fancifully made of red alder-berries and pine.

Then he said, "A lady took that down to put up a bigger one, and she gave it to me; you may have it if you want it."

"Oh, how beautiful," said Elsie. "How glad I am to have this for mother! When she comes back she won't know our room; it will be as fine as the church."

Soon the little gleaners were toddling off out of the yard—moving masses of green with all that their aprons and their little hands could carry.

The sexton looked after them. "Take heed that ye despise not these little ones," he said to himself, "for in heaven their angels—"

A ray of tenderness fell on the old man's head; it was from the Shining One who watched the children. He thought it was an afternoon sunbeam. His heart grew gentle and peaceful, and his thoughts went far back to a distant green grove where his own little one was sleeping. "Seems to me I've loved all little ones ever since," he said, thinking far back to the Christmas week when his lamb was laid to rest. "Well, she shall not return to me, but I shall go to her." The smile of the Shining One made a warm glow in his heart, which followed him all the way home.

The children had a merry time dressing the room. They stuck good big bushes of pine in each window; they put a little ruffle of ground-pine round mother's Bible, and they fastened the beautiful red cross up over the table, and they stuck sprigs of pine or holly into every crack that could be made, by fair means or foul, to accept it, and they were immensely satisfied and delighted. Tottie insisted on hanging up his string of many-colored beads in the window to imitate the effect of the stained glass of the great church window.

"It looks pretty when the light comes through," he remarked; and Elsie admitted that they might play they were painted windows, with some show of propriety. When everything had been stuck somewhere, Elsie swept the floor, and made up a fire, and put on the tea-kettle, to have everything ready to strike mother favorably on her return.

SCENE IV

A freezing, bright, cold afternoon. "Cold as Christmas!" say cheery voices, as the crowds rush to and fro into shops and stores, and come out with hands full of presents.

"Yes, cold as Christmas," says John Morley. "I should think so! Cold enough for a fellow that can't get in anywhere—that nobody wants and nobody helps! I should think so."

John had been trudging all day from point to point, only to hear the old story: times were hard, work was dull, nobody wanted him, and he felt morose and surly—out of humor with himself and with everybody else.

It is true that his misfortunes were from his own fault; but that consideration never makes a man a particle more patient or good-natured—indeed, it is an additional bitterness in his cup. John was an Englishman. When he first landed in New York from the old country, he had been wild and dissipated and given to drinking. But by his wife's earnest entreaties he had been persuaded to sign the temperance pledge, and had gone on prosperously keeping it for a year. He had a good place and good wages, and all went well with him till in an evil hour he met some of his former boon-companions, and was induced to have a social evening with them.

In the first half hour of that evening were lost the fruits of the whole year's self-denial and self-control. He was not only drunk that night, but he went off for a fortnight, and was drunk night after night, and came back to find that his master had discharged him in indignation. John thinks this over bitterly, as he thuds about in the cold and calls himself a fool.

Yet, if the truth must be confessed, John had not much "sense of sin," so called. He looked on himself as an unfortunate and rather ill-used man, for had he not tried very hard to be good, and gone a great while against the stream of evil inclination? and now, just for one yielding, he was pitched out of place, and everybody was turned against him! He thought this was hard measure. Didn't everybody hit wrong sometimes? Didn't rich fellows have their wine, and drink a little too much now and then? Yet nobody was down on *them*.

"It's only because I'm poor," said John. "Poor folks' sins are never pardoned. There's my good wife—poor girl!" and John's heart felt as if it were breaking, for he was an affectionate creature, and loved his wife and babies, and in his deepest consciousness he knew that he was the one at fault. We have heard much about the sufferings of the wives and children of men who are overtaken with drink; but what is not so well understood is the sufferings of the men themselves in their sober moments, when they feel that they are becoming a curse to all that are dearest to them. John's very soul was wrung within him to think of the misery he had brought on his wife and children—the greater miseries that might be in store for them. He was faint of heart; he was tired; he had eaten nothing for hours, and on ahead he saw a drinking saloon. Why shouldn't he go and take one good drink, and then pitch off a ferry-boat into the East River, and so end the whole miserable muddle of life altogether?

John's steps were turning that way, when one of the Shining Ones, who had watched him all day, came nearer and took his hand. He felt no touch; but at that moment there darted into his soul a thought of his mother, long dead, and he stopped irresolute, then turned to walk another way. The hand that was guiding him led him to turn a corner, and his curiosity was excited by a stream of people who seemed to be pressing into a building. A distant sound of singing was heard as he drew nearer, and soon he found himself passing with the multitude into a great prayer-meeting. The music grew more distinct as he went in. A man was singing in clear, penetrating tones:

> What means this eager, anxious throng,
> Which moves with busy haste along;
> These wondrous gatherings day by day;
> What means this strange commotion, say?
> In accents hushed the throng reply,
> "Jesus of Nazareth passeth by!'"

John had but a vague idea of religion, yet something in the singing affected him; and, weary and footsore and heartsore as he was, he sank into a seat and listened with absorbed attention:

> Jesus! 'tis he who once below
> Man's pathway trod in toil and woe;
> And burdened ones where'er he came
> Brought out their sick and deaf and lame.
> The blind rejoiced to hear the cry,
> "Jesus of Nazareth passeth by!"
>
> Ho, all ye heavy-laden, come!
> Here's pardon, comfort, rest, and home.
> Ye wanderers from a Father's face,
> Return, accept his proffered grace.
> Ye tempted ones, there's refuge nigh—
> "Jesus of Nazareth passeth by!"

A plain man, who spoke the language of plain working-men, now arose and read from his Bible the words which the angel of old spoke to the shepherds of Bethlehem:

"Fear not, for behold, I bring you tidings of great joy, which shall be to all people, for unto you is born this day a Saviour, which is Christ the Lord."

The man went on to speak of this with an intense practical earnestness that soon made John feel as if *he*, individually, were being talked to; and the purport of the speech was this: that God had sent to him, John Morley, a Saviour to save him from his sins, to lift him above his weakness, to help him overcome his bad habits; that His name was called Jesus, because he shall save his people *from their sins*. John listened with a strange new thrill. This was what he needed—a Friend, all-powerful, all-pitiful, who would undertake for him and help him to overcome himself—for he sorely felt how weak he was. Here was a Friend that could have compassion on the ignorant and them that were out of the way. The thought brought tears to his eyes and a glow of hope to his heart. What if He *would* help him? for deep down in John's heart, worse than cold or hunger or weariness, was the dreadful conviction that he was a doomed man, that he should drink again as he had drunk, and never come to good, but fall lower and lower, and drag all who loved him down with him.

And was this mighty Saviour given to him?

"Yes," cried the man who was speaking; "to *you*; to you, who have lost name and place; to you, that nobody cares for; to you, who have been down in the gutter. God has sent you a Saviour to take you up out of the mud and mire, to wash you clean, to give you strength to overcome your sins, and lead you home to his blessed kingdom. This is the glad tidings of great joy that the angels brought on the first Christmas day. Christ was *God's Christmas gift* to a poor, lost world, and you may have him now, to-day. He may be your own Saviour—yours as much as if there were no other one on earth to be saved. He is looking for you to-day, coming after you, seeking you; he calls you by me. Oh, accept him now!"

There was a deep breathing of suppressed emotion as the speaker sat down, a pause of solemn stillness.

A faint strain of music was heard, and the singer began singing a pathetic ballad of a lost sheep and of the Shepherd going forth to seek it:

> *There were ninety and nine that safely lay*
> *In the shelter of the fold,*
> *But one was out on the hills away,*
> *Far off from the gates of gold—*
> *Away on the mountains wild and bare,*
> *Away from the tender Shepherd's care.*
>
> *"Lord, Thou hast here Thy ninety and nine;*
> *Are they not enough for Thee?"*
> *But the Shepherd made answer: "'Tis of mine*
> *Has wandered away from me;*
> *And although the road be rough and steep*
> *I go to the desert to find my sheep."*

John heard with an absorbed interest. All around him were eager listeners, breathless, leaning forward with intense attention. The song went on:

> But none of the ransomed ever knew
> How deep were the waters crossed;
> Nor how dark was the night that the Lord went through
> Ere He found His sheep that was lost.
> Out in the desert He heard its cry—
> Sick and helpless, and ready to die.

There was a throbbing pathos in the intonation, and the verse floated over the weeping throng; when, after a pause, the strain was taken up triumphantly:

> But all through the mountains thunder-riven,
> And up from the rocky steep,
> There rose a cry to the gates of heaven,
> "Rejoice! I have found my sheep!"
> And the angels echoed around the throne,
> "Rejoice, for the Lord brings back His own!"

All day long, poor John had felt so lonesome! Nobody cared for him; nobody wanted him; everything was against him; and, worst of all, he had no faith in himself. But here was this Friend, *seeking* him, following him through the cold alleys and crowded streets. In heaven they would be glad to hear that he had become a good man. The thought broke down all his pride, all his bitterness; he wept like a little child; and the Christmas gift of Christ—the sense of a real, present, loving, pitying Saviour—came into his very *soul*.

He went homeward as one in a dream. He passed the drinking-saloon without a thought or wish of drinking. The expulsive force of a new emotion had for the time driven out all temptation. Raised above weakness, he thought only of this Jesus, this Saviour from sin, who he now believed had followed him and found him, and he longed to go home and tell his wife what great things the Lord had done for him.

SCENE V

Meanwhile a little drama had been acting in John's humble home. His wife had been to the shop that day and come home with the pittance for her work in her hands.

"I'll pay you full price to-day, but we can't pay such prices any longer," the man had said over the counter as he paid her. "Hard times—work dull—we are cutting down all our work-folks; you'll have to take a third less next time."

"I'll do my best," she said meekly, as she took her bundle of work and turned wearily away, but the invisible arm of the Shining One was round her, and the words again thrilled through her that she had read that morning: "He shall redeem their soul from deceit and violence, and precious shall their blood be in his sight." She saw no earthly helper; she heard none and felt none, and yet her soul was sustained, and she came home in peace.

When she opened the door of her little room she drew back astonished at the sight that presented itself. A brisk fire was roaring in the stove, and the tea-kettle was sputtering and sending out clouds of steam. A table with a white cloth on it was drawn out before the fire, and a new tea set of pure white cups and saucers, with teapot, sugar-bowl, and creamer, complete, gave a festive air to the whole. There were bread, and butter, and ham-sandwiches, and a Christmas cake all frosted, with little blue and red and green candles round it ready to be lighted, and a bunch of hot-house flowers in a pretty little vase in the centre.

A new stuffed rocking-chair stood on one side of the stove, and there sat Miss Florence De Witt, our young princess of Scene First, holding little Elsie in her lap, while the broad, honest countenance of Betty was beaming with kindness down on the delighted face of Tottie. Both children were dressed from head to foot in complete new suits of clothes, and Elsie was holding with tender devotion a fine doll, while Tottie rejoiced in a horse and cart which he was maneuvering under Betty's superintendence.

The little princess had pleased herself in getting up all this tableau. Doing good was a novelty to her, and she plunged into it with the zest of a new amusement. The amazed look of the poor woman, her dazed expressions of rapture and incredulous joy, the shrieks and cries of confused delight with which the little ones met their mother, delighted her more than any scene she had ever witnessed at the opera—with this added grace, unknown to her, that at this scene the invisible Shining Ones were pleased witnesses.

She had been out with Betty, buying here and there whatever was wanted,— and what was *not* wanted for those who had been living so long without work or money?

She had their little coal-bin filled, and a nice pile of wood and kindlings put behind the stove. She had bought a nice rocking-chair for the mother to rest in. She had dressed the children from head to foot at a ready-made clothing store, and bought them toys to their hearts' desire, while Betty had set the table for a Christmas feast.

And now she said to the poor woman at last:

"I'm so sorry John lost his place at father's. He was so kind and obliging, and I always liked him; and I've been thinking, if you'd get him to sign the pledge over again from Christmas Eve, never to touch another drop, I'll get papa to take him back. I always do get papa to do what I want, and the fact is, he hasn't got anybody that suited him so well since John left. So you tell John that I mean to go surety for him; he certainly won't fail *me*. Tell him *I trust him*." And Miss Florence pulled out a paper wherein, in her best round hand, she had written out again the temperance pledge, and dated it "*Christmas Eve, 1875*."

"Now, you come with John to-morrow morning, and bring this with his name to it, and you'll see what I'll do!" and, with a kiss to the children, the little good fairy departed, leaving the family to their Christmas Eve.

What that Christmas Eve was, when the husband and father came home with the new and softened heart that had been given him, who can say? There were joyful tears and solemn prayers, and earnest vows and purposes of a new life heard by the Shining Ones in the room that night.

"And the angels echoed around the throne, Rejoice! for the Lord brings back his own."

SCENE VI

Now, papa, I want you to give me something special to-day, because it's Christmas," said the little princess to her father, as she kissed and wished him "Merry Christmas" next morning.

"What is it, Pussy—half of my kingdom?"

"No, no, papa; not so much as that. It's a little bit of my own way that I want."

"Of course; well, what is it?"

"Well, I want you to take John back again."

Her father's face grew hard.

"Now, please, papa, don't say a word till you have heard me. John was a capital gardener; he kept the green-house looking beautiful; and this Mike that we've got now, he's nothing but an apprentice, and stupid as an owl at that! He'll never do in the world."

"All that is very true," said Mr. De Witt, "but *John drinks*, and I *won't* have a drinking man."

"But, papa, *I* mean to take care of that. I've written out the temperance pledge, and dated it, and got John to sign it, and *here it is*," and she handed the paper to her father, who read it carefully, and sat turning it in his hands while his daughter went on:

"You ought to have seen how poor, how very poor they were. His wife is such a nice, quiet, hardworking woman, and has two such pretty children. I went to see them and carry them Christmas things yesterday, but it's no good doing anything if John can't get work. She told me how the poor fellow had been walking the streets in the cold, day after day, trying everywhere, and nobody would take him. It's a dreadful time now for a man to be out of work, and it isn't fair his poor wife and children should suffer. Do try him again, papa!"

"John always did better with the pineapples than anybody we have tried," said Mrs. De Witt at this point. "He is the only one who really understands pineapples."

At this moment the door opened, and there was a sound of chirping voices in the hall. "Please, Miss Florence," said Betty, "the little folks says they wants to give you a Christmas." She added in a whisper: "They thinks much of giving you something, poor little things—plaze take it of 'em." And little Tottie at the word marched in and offered the young princess his dear, beautiful, beloved string of glass beads, and Elsie presented the cross of red berries—most dear to her heart and fair to her eyes. "We wanted to give *you something*," she said bashfully.

"Oh, you lovely dears!" cried Florence; "how sweet of you! I shall keep these beautiful glass beads always, and put the cross up over my dressing-table. I thank you *ever* so much!"

"Are those John's children?" asked Mr. De Witt, winking a tear out of his eye—he was at bottom a soft-hearted old gentleman.

"Yes, papa," said Florence, caressing Elsie's curly hair,—"see how sweet they are!"

"Well—you may tell John I'll try him again." And so passed Florence's Christmas, with a new, warm sense of joy in her heart, a feeling of something in the world to be done, worth doing.

"How much joy one can give with a little money!" she said to herself as she counted over what she had spent on her Christmas. Ah yes! and how true that "It *is* more blessed to give than to receive." A shining, invisible hand was laid on her head in blessing as she lay down that night, and a sweet sense of a loving presence stole like music into her soul. Unknown to herself, she had that day taken the first step out of self-life into that life of love and care for others which brought the King of Glory down to share earth's toils and sorrows. And that precious experience was Christ's Christmas gift to her.

The Beggar Boy at Christ's Christmas Tree

Fyodor Dostoyevsky

I am a novelist, and I suppose I have made up this story. I write "I suppose," though I know for a fact that I have made it up, but yet I keep fancying that it must have happened on Christmas Eve in some great town in a time of terrible frost.

I have a vision of a boy, a little boy, six years old or even younger. This boy woke up that morning in a cold damp cellar. He was dressed in a sort of little dressing-gown and was shivering with cold. There was a cloud of white steam from his breath, and sitting on a box in the corner, he blew the steam out of his mouth and amused himself in his dullness watching it float away. But he was terribly hungry. Several times that morning he went up to the plank bed where his sick mother was lying on a mattress as thin as a pancake, with some sort of bundle under her head for a pillow. How had she come here? She must have come with her boy from some other town and suddenly fallen ill. The landlady who let the "concerns" had been taken two days before the police station, the lodgers were out and about as the holiday was so near, and the only one left had been lying for the last twenty-four hours dead drunk, not having waited for Christmas. In another corner of the room a wretched old woman of eighty, who had once been a children's nurse but was now left to die friendless, was moaning and groaning with rheumatism, scolding and grumbling at the boy so that he was afraid to go near her corner. He had got a drink of water in the outer room, but could not find a crust anywhere, and had been on the point of waking his mother a dozen times. He felt frightened at last in the darkness: it had long been dusk, but no light was kindled. Touching his mother's face, he was surprised that she did not move at all, and that she was as cold as the wall. "It is very cold here," he thought. He stood a little, unconsciously letting his hands rest on the dead woman's shoulders, then he breathed on his fingers to warm them, and then quietly fumbling for his cap on the bed, he went out of the cellar. He would have gone earlier, but was afraid of the big dog which had been howling all day at the neighbor's door at the top of the stairs. But the dog was not there now, and he went out into the street.

Mercy on us, what a town! He had never seen anything like it before. In the town he had come from, it was always such black darkness at night. There was one lamp for the whole street, the little, low-pitched, wooden houses were closed up with shutters, there was no one to be seen in the street after dusk, all the people shut themselves up in their houses, and there was nothing but the howling all night. But there it was so warm and he was given food, while here—oh, dear, if he only had something to eat! And what a noise and rattle here, what light and what people, horses and carriages, and what a frost! The frozen steam hung in clouds over the horses, over their warmly breathing mouths; their hoofs clanged against the stones through the powdery snow, and everyone pushed so, and—oh, dear, how he longed for some morsel to eat, and how wretched he suddenly felt. A policeman walked by and turned away to avoid seeing the boy.

There was another street—oh, what a wide one, here he would be run over for certain; how everyone was shouting, racing and driving along, and the light, the light! And what was this? A huge glass window, and through the window a tree reaching up to the ceiling; it was a fir tree, and on it were ever so many lights, gold papers and apples and little dolls and horses; and there were children clean and dressed in their best running about the room, laughing and playing and eating and drinking something. And then a little girl began dancing with one of the boys, what a pretty little girl! And he could hear the music through the window. The boy looked and wondered and laughed, though his toes were aching with the cold and his fingers were red and stiff so that it hurt him to move them. And all at once the boy remembered how his toes and fingers hurt him, and began crying, and ran on; and again through another window-pane he saw another Christmas tree, and on a table cakes of all sorts—almond cakes, red cakes and yellow cakes, and three grand young ladies were sitting there, and they gave the cakes to anyone who went up to them, and the door kept opening, lots of gentlemen and ladies went in from the street. The boy crept up, suddenly opened the door and went in. Oh, how they shouted at him and waved him back! One lady went up to him hurriedly and slipped a kopeck into his hand, and with her own hands opened the door into the street for him! How frightened he was. And the kopeck rolled away and clinked upon the steps; he could not bend his red fingers to hold it right. The boy ran away and went on, where he did not know. He was ready to cry again but he was afraid, and ran on and on and blew his fingers. And he was miserable because he felt suddenly so lonely and terrified, and all at once, mercy on us! What was this again? People were standing in a crowd admiring. Behind a glass window there were three little dolls, dressed in red and green dresses, and exactly, exactly as though they were alive. One was a little old man sitting and playing a big violin, the two others were standing close by and playing little violins, and nodding in time, and looking at one another, and their lips moved, they were speaking, actually speaking, only one couldn't hear through the glass. And at first the boy thought they were alive, and when he grasped that they were dolls he laughed. He had never seen such dolls before, and had no idea there were such dolls! All at once he fancied that someone caught at his smock behind: a wicked big boy was standing beside him and suddenly hit him on the head, snatched off his cap and tripped him up. The boy fell down on the ground, at once there was a shout, he was numb with fright, he jumped up and ran away. He ran, and not knowing where he was going, ran in at the gate of someone's courtyard, and sat down behind a stack of wood: "They won't find me here, besides it's dark!"

He sat huddled up and was breathless from fright, and all at once, quite suddenly, he felt so happy: his hands and feet suddenly left off aching and grew so warm, as warm as though he were on a stove; then he shivered all over, then he gave a start, why, he must have been asleep. How nice to have a sleep here! "I'll sit here a little and go and look at the dolls again," said the boy, and smiled thinking of them. "Just as though they were alive! . . ." and suddenly he heard his mother singing over him. "Mammy, I am asleep; how nice it is to sleep here!"

"Come to my Christmas tree, little one," a soft voice suddenly whispered over his head.

He thought that this was still his mother, but no, it was not she. Who it was calling him, he could not see, but someone bent over to him, and . . . and all at once—oh, what a bright light! Oh, what a Christmas tree! And yet it was not a fir tree, he had never seen a tree like that! Where was he now? Everything was bright and shining, and all around him were dolls; but no, they were not dolls, they were little boys and girls, only so bright and shining. They all came flying round him, they all kissed him, took him and carried him along with them, and he was flying himself, and he saw that his mother was looking at him and laughing joyfully. "Mammy, Mammy; oh, how nice it is here, Mammy!" and again he kissed the children and wanted to tell them at once of those dolls in the shop windows.

"Who are you, boys? Who are you, girls?" he asked, laughing and admiring them.

"This is Christ's Christmas tree," they answered. "Christ always has a Christmas tree on this day, for the little children who have no tree of their own . . ." and he found out that all these little boys and girls were children just like himself; that some had been frozen in the baskets in which they had as babies been laid on the doorsteps of well-to-do Petersburg people, others had been boarded out with Finnish women by the Foundling and had been suffocated, others had died at their starved mothers' breasts (in the Samara famine), others had died in the third-class railway carriages from the foul air; and yet they were all here, they were all like angels about Christmas, and He was in the midst of them and held out His hands to them and blessed them and their sinful mothers . . . and the mothers of these children stood on one side weeping; each one knew her boy or girl, and the children flew up to them and kissed them and wiped away their tears with their little hands, and begged them not to weep because they were so happy.

And down below in the morning the porter found the little dead body of the frozen child on the woodstack; they sought out his mother too . . . she had died before him. They met before the Lord God in heaven.

Why have I made up such a story, so out of keeping with an ordinary diary, and a writer's above all? And I promised two stories dealing with real events! But that is just it, I keep fancying that all this may have happened really—that is, what took place in the cellar and on the woodstack; but as for Christ's Christmas tree, I cannot tell you whether that could have happened or not.

The Three Kings

Henry Wadsworth Longfellow

Three Kings came riding from far away,
    Melchior and Gaspar and Baltasar;
Three Wise Men out of the East were they,
And they travelled by night and they slept by day,
    For their guide was a beautiful, wonderful star.

The star was so beautiful, large and clear,
    That all the other stars of the sky
Became a white mist in the atmosphere,
And by this they knew that the coming was near
    Of the Prince foretold in the prophecy.

Three caskets they bore on their saddle-bows,
    Three caskets of gold with golden keys;
Their robes were of crimson silk with rows
Of bells and pomegranates and furbelows,
    Their turbans like blossoming almond-trees.

And so the Three Kings rode into the West,
    Through the dusk of the night, over hill and dell,
And sometimes they nodded with beard on breast,
And sometimes talked, as they paused to rest,
    With the people they met at some wayside well.

"Of the child that is born," said Baltasar,
    "Good people, I pray you, tell us the news;
For we in the East have seen his star,
And have ridden fast, and have ridden far,
    To find and worship the King of the Jews."

And the people answered, "You ask in vain;
    We know of no King but Herod the Great!"
They thought the Wise Men were men insane,
As they spurred their horses across the plain,
    Like riders in haste, who cannot wait.

And when they came to Jerusalem,
    Herod the Great, who had heard this thing,
Sent for the Wise Men and questioned them;
And said, "Go down unto Bethlehem,
    And bring me tidings of this new king."

So they rode away; and the star stood still,
    The only one in the grey of morn;
Yes, it stopped—it stood still of its own free will,
Right over Bethlehem on the hill,
    The city of David, where Christ was born.

And the Three Kings rode through the gate and the guard,
    Through the silent street, till their horses turned
And neighed as they entered the great inn-yard;
But the windows were closed, and the doors were barred,
    And only a light in the stable burned.

And cradled there in the scented hay,
    In the air made sweet by the breath of kine,
The little child in the manger lay,
The child, that would be king one day
    Of a kingdom not human, but divine.

His mother Mary of Nazareth
    Sat watching beside his place of rest,
Watching the even flow of his breath,
For the joy of life and the terror of death
    Were mingled together in her breast.

They laid their offerings at his feet:
　　The gold was their tribute to a King,
The frankincense, with its odor sweet,
Was for the Priest, the Paraclete,
　　The myrrh for the body's burying.

And the mother wondered and bowed her head,
　　And sat as still as a statue of stone,
Her heart was troubled yet comforted,
Remembering what the Angel had said
　　Of an endless reign and of David's throne.

Then the Kings rode out of the city gate,
　　With a clatter of hoofs in proud array;
But they went not back to Herod the Great,
For they knew his malice and feared his hate,
　　And returned to their homes by another way.

The Story of the Other Wise Man

Henry van Dyke

Who seeks for heaven alone to save his soul,
May keep the path, but will not reach the goal;
While he who walks in love may wander far,
Yet God will bring him where the blessed are.

You know the story of the Three Wise Men of the East, and how they travelled from far away to offer their gifts at the manger-cradle in Bethlehem. But have you ever heard the story of the Other Wise Man, who also saw the star in its rising, and set out to follow it, yet did not arrive with his brethren in the presence of the young child Jesus? Of the great desire of this fourth pilgrim, and how it was denied, yet accomplished in the denial; of his many wanderings and the probations of his soul; of the long way of his seeking, and the strange way of his finding, the One whom he sought—I would tell the tale as I have heard fragments of it in the Hall of Dreams, in the palace of the Heart of Man.

THE SIGN IN THE SKY

In the days when Augustus Caesar was master of many kings and Herod reigned in Jerusalem, there lived in the city of Ecbatana, among the mountains of Persia, a certain man named Artaban, the Median. His house stood close to the outermost of the seven walls which encircled the royal treasury. From his roof he could look over the rising battlements of black and white and crimson and blue and red and silver and gold, to the hill where the summer palace of the Parthian emperors glittered like a jewel in a sevenfold crown.

Around the dwelling of Artaban spread a fair garden, a tangle of flowers and fruit-trees, watered by a score of streams descending from the slopes of Mount Orontes, and made musical by innumerable birds. But all colour was lost in the soft and odorous darkness of the late September night, and all sounds were hushed in the deep charm of its silence, save the plashing of the water, like a voice half sobbing and half laughing under the shadows. High above the trees a dim glow of light shone through the curtained arches of the upper chamber, where the master of the house was holding council with his friends.

He stood by the doorway to greet his guests—a tall, dark man of about forty years, with brilliant eyes set near together under his broad brow, and firm lines graven around his fine, thin lips; the brow of a dreamer and the mouth of a soldier, a man of sensitive feeling but inflexible will—one of those who, in whatever age they may live, are born for inward conflict and a life of quest.

His robe was of pure white wool, thrown over a tunic of silk; and a white, pointed cap, with long lapels at the sides, rested on his flowing black hair. It was the dress of the ancient priesthood of the Magi, called the fire-worshippers.

"Welcome!" he said, in his low, pleasant voice, as one after another entered the room—"welcome, Abdus; peace be with you, Rhodaspes and Tigranes, and with you my father, Abgarus. You are all welcome, and this house grows bright with the joy of your presence."

There were nine of the men, differing widely in age, but alike in the richness of their dress of many-coloured silks, and in the massive golden collars around their necks, marking them as Parthian nobles, and in the winged circles of gold resting upon their breasts, the sign of the followers of Zoroaster.

They took their places around a small black altar at the end of the room, where a tiny flame was burning. Artaban, standing beside it, and waving a barsom of thin tamarisk branches above the fire, fed it with dry sticks of pine and fragrant oils. Then he began the ancient chant of the Yasna, and the voices of his companions joined in the beautiful hymn to Ahura-Mazda:

> We worship the Spirit Divine,
>   all wisdom and goodness possessing,
> Surrounded by Holy Immortals,
>   the givers of bounty and blessing.
> We joy in the works of His hands,
>   His truth and His power confessing.
>
> We praise all the things that are pure,
>   for these are His only Creation;
> The thoughts that are true, and the words
>   and deeds that have won approbation;
> These are supported by Him,
>   and for these we make adoration.
>
> Hear us, O Mazda! Thou livest
>   in truth and in heavenly gladness;
> Cleanse us from falsehood, and keep us
>   from evil and bondage to badness;

Pour out the light and the joy of Thy life
  on our darkness and sadness.

Shine on our gardens and fields,
  Shine on our working and weaving;
Shine on the whole race of man,
  Believing and unbelieving;
  Shine on us now through the night,
  Shine on us now in Thy might,
The flame of our holy love
  and the song of our worship receiving.

The fire rose with the chant, throbbing as if it were made of musical flame, until it cast a bright illumination through the whole apartment, revealing its simplicity and splendour.

The floor was laid with tiles of dark blue veined with white; pilasters of twisted silver stood out against the blue walls; the clearstory of round-arched windows above them was hung with azure silk; the vaulted ceiling was a pavement of sapphires, like the body of heaven in its clearness, sown with silver stars. From the four corners of the roof hung four golden magic-wheels, called the tongues of the gods. At the eastern end, behind the altar, there were two dark-red pillars of porphyry; above them a lintel of the same stone, on which was carved the figure of a winged archer, with his arrow set to the string and his bow drawn.

The doorway between the pillars, which opened upon the terrace of the roof, was covered with a heavy curtain of the colour of a ripe pomegranate, embroidered with innumerable golden rays shooting upward from the floor. In effect the room was like a quiet, starry night, all azure and silver, flushed in the East with rosy promise of the dawn. It was, as the house of a man should be, an expression of the character and spirit of the master.

He turned to his friends when the song was ended, and invited them to be seated on the divan at the western end of the room.

"You have come to-night," said he, looking around the circle, "at my call, as the faithful scholars of Zoroaster, to renew your worship and rekindle your faith in the God of Purity, even as this fire has been rekindled on the altar. We worship not the fire, but Him of whom it is the chosen symbol, because it is the purest of all created things. It speaks to us of one who is Light and Truth. Is it not so, my father?"

"It is well said, my son," answered the venerable Abgarus. "The enlightened are never idolaters. They lift the veil of the form and go in to the shrine of the reality, and new light and truth are coming to them continually through the old symbols." "Hear me, then, my father and my friends," said Artaban, very quietly, "while I tell you of the new light and truth that have come to me through the most ancient of all signs. We have searched the secrets of nature together, and studied the healing virtues of water and fire and the plants. We have read also the books of prophecy in which the future is dimly foretold in words that are hard to understand. But the highest of all learning is the knowledge of the stars. To trace their courses is to untangle the threads of the mystery of life from the beginning to the end. If we could follow them perfectly, nothing would be hidden from us. But is not our knowledge of them still incomplete? Are there not many stars still beyond our horizon—lights that are known only to the dwellers in the far south-land, among the spice-trees of Punt and the gold mines of Ophir?"

There was a murmur of assent among the listeners.

"The stars," said Tigranes, "are the thoughts of the Eternal. They are numberless. But the thoughts of man can be counted, like the years of his life. The wisdom of the Magi is the greatest of all wisdoms on earth, because it knows its own ignorance. And that is the secret of power. We keep men always looking and waiting for a new sunrise. But we ourselves know that the darkness is equal to the light, and that the conflict between them will never be ended."

"That does not satisfy me," answered Artaban, "for, if the waiting must be endless, if there could be no fulfilment of it, then it would not be wisdom to look and wait. We should become like those new teachers of the Greeks, who say that there is no truth, and that the only wise men are those who spend their lives in discovering and exposing the lies that have been believed in the world. But the new sunrise will certainly dawn in the appointed time. Do not our own books tell us that this will come to pass, and that men will see the brightness of a great light?"

"That is true," said the voice of Abgarus; "every faithful disciple of Zoroaster knows the prophecy of the Avesta and carries the word in his heart. 'In that day Sosiosh the Victorious shall arise out of the number of the prophets in the east country. Around him shall shine a mighty brightness, and he shall make life everlasting, incorruptible, and immortal, and the dead shall rise again.'"

"This is a dark saying," said Tigranes, "and it may be that we shall never understand it. It is better to consider the things that are near at hand, and to increase the influence of the Magi in their own country, rather than to look for one who may be a stranger, and to whom we must resign our power."

The others seemed to approve these words. There was a silent feeling of agreement manifest among them; their looks responded with that indefinable expression which always follows when a speaker has uttered the thought that has been slumbering in the hearts of his listeners. But Artaban turned to Abgarus with a glow on his face, and said:

"My father, I have kept this prophecy in the secret place of my soul. Religion without a great hope would be like an altar without a living fire. And now the flame has burned more brightly, and by the light of it I have read other words which also have come from the fountain of Truth, and speak yet more clearly of the rising of the Victorious One in his brightness."

He drew from the breast of his tunic two small rolls of fine linen, with writing upon them, and unfolded them carefully upon his knee.

"In the years that are lost in the past, long before our fathers came into the land of Babylon, there were wise men in Chaldea, from whom the first of the Magi learned the secret of the heavens. And of these Balaam the son of Beor was one of the mightiest. Hear the words of his prophecy: 'There shall come a star out of Jacob, and a sceptre shall arise out of Israel.'"

The lips of Tigranes drew downward with contempt, as he said:

"Judah was a captive by the waters of Babylon, and the sons of Jacob were in bondage to our kings. The tribes of Israel are scattered through the mountains like lost sheep, and from the remnant that dwells in Judea under the yoke of Rome neither star nor sceptre shall arise."

"And yet," answered Artaban, "it was the Hebrew Daniel, the mighty searcher of dreams, the counsellor of kings, the wise Belteshazzar, who was most honored and beloved of our great King Cyrus. A prophet of sure things and a reader of the thoughts of God, Daniel proved himself to our people. And these are the words that he wrote." (Artaban read from the second roll:) "'Know, therefore, and understand that from the going forth of the commandment to restore Jerusalem, unto the Anointed One, the Prince, the time shall be seven and threescore and two weeks.'"

"But, my son," said Abgarus, doubtfully, "these are mystical numbers. Who can interpret them, or who can find the key that shall unlock their meaning?"

Artaban answered: "It has been shown to me and to my three companions among the Magi—Caspar, Melchior, and Balthazar. We have searched the ancient tablets of Chaldea and computed the time. It falls in this year. We have studied the sky, and in the spring of the year we saw two of the greatest stars draw near together in the sign of the Fish, which is the house of the Hebrews. We also saw a new star there, which shone for one night and then vanished. Now again the two great planets are meeting. This night is their conjunction. My three brothers are watching at the ancient temple of the Seven Spheres, at Borsippa, in Babylonia, and I am watching here. If the star shines again, they will wait ten days for me at the temple, and then we will set out together for Jerusalem, to see and worship the promised one who shall be born King of Israel. I believe the sign will come. I have made ready for the journey. I have sold my house and my possessions, and bought these three jewels—a sapphire, a ruby, and a pearl—to carry them as tribute to the King. And I ask you to go with me on the pilgrimage, that we may have joy together in finding the Prince who is worthy to be served."

While he was speaking he thrust his hand into the inmost fold of his girdle and drew out three great gems—one blue as a fragment of the night sky, one redder than a ray of sunrise, and one as pure as the peak of a snow mountain at twilight—and laid them on the outspread linen scrolls before him.

But his friends looked on with strange and alien eyes. A veil of doubt and mistrust came over their faces, like a fog creeping up from the marshes to hide the hills. They glanced at each other with looks of wonder and pity, as those who have listened to incredible sayings, the story of a wild vision, or the proposal of an impossible enterprise.

At last Tigranes said: "Artaban, this is a vain dream. It comes from too much looking upon the stars and the cherishing of lofty thoughts. It would be wiser to spend the time in gathering money for the new fire-temple at Chala. No king will ever rise from the broken race of Israel, and no end will ever come to the eternal strife of light and darkness. He who looks for it is a chaser of shadows. Farewell."

And another said: "Artaban, I have no knowledge of these things, and my office as guardian of the royal treasure binds me here. The quest is not for me. But if thou must follow it, fare thee well."

And another said: "In my house there sleeps a new bride, and I cannot leave her nor take her with me on this strange journey. This quest is not for me. But may thy steps be prospered wherever thou goest. So, farewell."

And another said: "I am ill and unfit for hardship, but there is a man among my servants whom I will send with thee when thou goest, to bring me word how thou farest."

But Abgarus, the oldest and the one who loved Artaban the best, lingered after the others had gone, and said, gravely: "My son, it may be that the light of truth is in this sign that has appeared in the skies, and then it will surely lead to the Prince and the mighty brightness. Or it may be that it is only a shadow of the light, as Tigranes has said, and then he who follows it will have only a long pilgrimage and an empty search. But it is better to follow even the shadow of the best than to remain content with the worst. And those who would see wonderful things must often be ready to travel alone. I am too old for this journey, but my heart shall be a companion of the pilgrimage day and night, and I shall know the end of thy quest. Go in peace."

So one by one they went out of the azure chamber with its silver stars, and Artaban was left in solitude.

He gathered up the jewels and replaced them in his girdle. For a long time he stood and watched the flame that flickered and sank upon the altar. Then he crossed the hall, lifted the heavy curtain, and passed out between the dull red pillars of porphyry to the terrace on the roof.

The shiver that thrills through the earth ere she rouses from her night sleep had already begun, and the cool wind that heralds the daybreak was drawing downward from the lofty snow-traced ravines of Mount Orontes. Birds, half awakened, crept and chirped among the rustling leaves, and the smell of ripened grapes came in brief wafts from the arbours.

Far over the eastern plain a white mist stretched like a lake. But where the distant peak of Zagros serrated the western horizon the sky was clear. Jupiter and Saturn rolled together like drops of lambent flame about to blend in one.

As Artaban watched them, behold, an azure spark was born out of the darkness beneath, rounding itself with purple splendours to a crimson sphere, and spiring upward through rays of saffron and orange into a point of white radiance. Tiny and infinitely remote, yet perfect in every part, it pulsated in the enormous vault as if the three jewels in the Magian's breast had mingled and been transformed into a living heart of light. He bowed his head. He covered his brow with his hands.

"It is the sign," he said. "The King is coming, and I will go to meet him."

BY THE WATERS OF BABYLON

All night long Vasda, the swiftest of Artaban's horses, had been waiting, saddled and bridled, in her stall, pawing the ground impatiently, and shaking her bit as if she shared the eagerness of her master's purpose, though she knew not its meaning.

Before the birds had fully roused to their strong, high, joyful chant of morning song, before the white mist had begun to lift lazily from the plain, the other wise man was in the saddle, riding swiftly along the high-road, which skirted the base of Mount Orontes, westward.

How close, how intimate is the comradeship between a man and his favourite horse on a long journey. It is a silent, comprehensive friendship, an intercourse beyond the need of words. They drink at the same way-side springs, and sleep under the same guardian stars. They are conscious together of the subduing spell of nightfall and the quickening joy of daybreak. The master shares his evening meal with his hungry companion, and feels the soft, moist lips caressing the palm of his hand as they close over the morsel of bread. In the gray dawn he is roused from his bivouac by the gentle stir of a warm, sweet breath over his sleeping face, and looks up into the eyes of his faithful fellow-traveller, ready and waiting for the toil of the day. Surely, unless he is a pagan and an unbeliever, by whatever name he calls upon his God, he will thank Him for this voiceless sympathy, this dumb affection, and his morning prayer will embrace a double blessing—God bless us both, and keep our feet from falling and our souls from death!

And then, through the keen morning air, the swift hoofs beat their spirited music along the road, keeping time to the pulsing of two hearts that are moved with the same eager desire—to conquer space, to devour the distance, to attain the goal of the journey.

Artaban must indeed ride wisely and well if he would keep the appointed hour with the other Magi; for the route was a hundred and fifty parasangs, and fifteen was the utmost that he could travel in a day. But he knew Vasda's strength, and pushed forward without anxiety, making the fixed distance every day, though he must travel late into the night, and in the morning long before sunrise.

He passed along the brown slopes of Mt. Orontes, furrowed by the rocky courses of a hundred torrents.

He crossed the level plains of the Nisaeans, where the famous herds of horses, feeding in the wide pastures, tossed their heads at Vasda's approach, and galloped away with a thunder of many hoofs, and flocks of wild birds rose suddenly from the swampy meadows, wheeling in great circles with a shining flutter of innumerable wings and shrill cries of surprise.

He traversed the fertile fields of Concabar, where the dust from the threshing-floors filled the air with a golden mist, half hiding the huge temple of Astarte with its four hundred pillars.

At Baghistan, among the rich gardens watered by fountains from the rock, he looked up at the mountain thrusting its immense rugged brow out over the road, and saw the figure of King Darius trampling upon his fallen foes, and the proud list of his wars and conquests graven high upon the face of the eternal cliff.

Over many a cold and desolate pass, crawling painfully across the wind-swept shoulders of the hills; down many a black mountain-gorge, where the river roared and raced before him like a savage guide; across many a smiling vale, with terraces of yellow limestone full of vines and fruit-trees; through the oak-groves of Carine and the dark Gates of Zagros, walled in by precipices; into the ancient city of Chala, where the people of Samaria had been kept in captivity long ago; and out again by the mighty portal, riven through the encircling hills, where he saw the image of the High Priest of the Magi sculptured on the wall of rock, with hand uplifted as if to bless the centuries of pilgrims; past the entrance of the narrow defile, filled from end to end with orchards of peaches and figs, through which the river Gyndes foamed down to meet him; over the broad rice-fields, where the autumnal vapours spread their deathly mists; following along the course of the river, under tremulous shadows of poplar and tamarind, among the lower hills; and out upon the flat plain, where the road ran straight as an arrow through the stubble-fields and parched meadows; past the city of Ctesiphon, where the Parthian emperors reigned, and the vast metropolis of Seleucia which Alexander built; across the swirling floods of Tigris and the many channels of Euphrates, flowing yellow through the corn-lands—Artaban pressed onward until he arrived, at nightfall of the tenth day, beneath the shattered walls of populous Babylon.

Vasda was almost spent, and he would gladly have turned into the city to find rest and refreshment for himself and for her. But he knew that it was three hours' journey yet to the Temple of the Seven Spheres, and he must reach the place by midnight if he would find his comrades waiting. So he did not halt, but rode steadily across the stubble-fields.

A grove of date-palms made an island of gloom in the pale yellow sea. As she passed into the shadow Vasda slackened her pace, and began to pick her way more carefully.

Near the farther end of the darkness an access of caution seemed to fall upon her. She scented some danger or difficulty; it was not in her heart to fly from it— only to be prepared for it, and to meet it wisely, as a good horse should do. The grove was close and silent as the tomb; not a leaf rustled, not a bird sang.

She felt her steps before her delicately, carrying her head low, and sighing now and then with apprehension. At last she gave a quick breath of anxiety and dismay, and stood stock-still, quivering in every muscle, before a dark object in the shadow of the last palm-tree.

Artaban dismounted. The dim starlight revealed the form of a man lying across the road. His humble dress and the outline of his haggard face showed that he was probably one of the poor Hebrew exiles who still dwelt in great numbers in the vicinity. His pallid skin, dry and yellow as parchment, bore the mark of the deadly fever which ravaged the marsh-lands in autumn. The chill of death was in his lean hand, and, as Artaban released it, the arm fell back inertly upon the motionless breast.

He turned away with a thought of pity, consigning the body to that strange burial which the Magians deem most fitting—the funeral of the desert, from which the kites and vultures rise on dark wings, and the beasts of prey slink furtively away, leaving only a heap of white bones in the sand.

But, as he turned, a long, faint, ghostly sigh came from the man's lips. The brown, bony fingers closed convulsively on the hem of the Magian's robe and held him fast.

Artaban's heart leaped to his throat, not with fear, but with a dumb resentment at the importunity of this blind delay. How could he stay here in the darkness to minister to a dying stranger? What claim had this unknown fragment of human life upon his compassion or his service? If he lingered but for an hour he could hardly reach Borsippa at the appointed time. His companions would think he had given up the journey. They would go without him. He would lose his quest.

But if he went on now, the man would surely die. If he stayed, life might be restored. His spirit throbbed and fluttered with the urgency of the crisis. Should he risk the great reward of his divine faith for the sake of a single deed of human love? Should he turn aside, if only for a moment, from the following of the star, to give a cup of cold water to a poor, perishing Hebrew?

"God of truth and purity," he prayed, "direct me in the holy path, the way of wisdom which Thou only knowest."

Then he turned back to the sick man. Loosening the grasp of his hand, he carried him to a little mound at the foot of the palm-tree. He unbound the thick folds of the turban and opened the garment above the sunken breast. He brought water from one of the small canals near by, and moistened the sufferer's brow and mouth. He mingled a draught of one of those simple but potent remedies which he carried always in his girdle—for the Magians were physicians as well as astrologers—and poured it slowly between the colourless lips. Hour after hour he labored as only a skilful healer of disease can do; and, at last, the man's strength returned; he sat up and looked about him.

"Who art thou?" he said, in the rude dialect of the country, "and why hast thou sought me here to bring back my life?"

"I am Artaban the Magian, of the city of Ecbatana, and I am going to Jerusalem in search of one who is to be born King of the Jews, a great Prince and Deliverer for all men. I dare not delay any longer upon my journey, for the caravan that has waited for me may depart without me. But see, here is all that I have left of bread and wine, and here is a potion of healing herbs. When thy strength is restored thou can'st find the dwellings of the Hebrews among the houses of Babylon."

The Jew raised his trembling hands solemnly to heaven.

"Now may the God of Abraham and Isaac and Jacob bless and prosper the journey of the merciful, and bring him in peace to his desired haven. But stay; I have nothing to give thee in return—only this: that I can tell thee where the Messiah must be sought. For our prophets have said that he should be born not in Jerusalem, but in Bethlehem of Judah. May the Lord bring thee in safety to that place, because thou hast had pity upon the sick."

It was already long past midnight. Artaban rode in haste, and Vasda, restored by the brief rest, ran eagerly through the silent plain and swam the channels of the river. She put forth the remnant of her strength, and fled over the ground like a gazelle.

But the first beam of the sun sent her shadow before her as she entered upon the final stadium of the journey, and the eyes of Artaban anxiously scanning the great mound of Nimrod and the Temple of the Seven Spheres, could discern no trace of his friends.

The many-coloured terraces of black and orange and red and yellow and green and blue and white, shattered by the convulsions of nature, and crumbling under the repeated blows of human violence, still glittered like a ruined rainbow in the morning light.

Artaban rode swiftly around the hill. He dismounted and climbed to the highest terrace, looking out towards the west.

The huge desolation of the marshes stretched away to the horizon and the border of the desert. Bitterns stood by the stagnant pools and jackals skulked through the low bushes; but there was no sign of the caravan of the wise men, far or near.

At the edge of the terrace he saw a little cairn of broken bricks, and under them a piece of parchment. He caught it up and read: "We have waited past the midnight, and can delay no longer. We go to find the King. Follow us across the desert." Artaban sat down upon the ground and covered his head in despair.

"How can I cross the desert," said he, "with no food and with a spent horse? I must return to Babylon, sell my sapphire, and buy a train of camels, and provision for the journey. I may never overtake my friends. Only God the merciful knows whether I shall not lose the sight of the King because I tarried to show mercy."

FOR THE SAKE OF A LITTLE CHILD

There was a silence in the Hall of Dreams, where I was listening to the story of the other wise man. And through this silence I saw, but very dimly, his figure passing over the dreary undulations of the desert, high upon the back of his camel, rocking steadily onward like a ship over the waves.

The land of death spread its cruel net around him. The stony wastes bore no fruit but briers and thorns. The dark ledges of rock thrust themselves above the surface here and there, like the bones of perished monsters. Arid and inhospitable mountain ranges rose before him, furrowed with dry channels of ancient torrents, white and ghastly as scars on the face of nature. Shifting hills of treacherous sand were heaped like tombs along the horizon. By day, the fierce heat pressed its intolerable burden on the quivering air; and no living creature moved, on the dumb, swooning earth, but tiny jerboas scuttling through the parched bushes, or lizards vanishing in the clefts of the rock. By night the jackals prowled and barked in the distance, and the lion made the black ravines echo with his hollow roaring, while a bitter, blighting chill followed the fever of the day. Through heat and cold, the Magian moved steadily onward.

Then I saw the gardens and orchards of Damascus, watered by the streams of Abana and Pharpar, with their sloping swards inlaid with bloom, and their thickets of myrrh and roses. I saw also the long, snowy ridge of Hermon, and the dark groves of cedars, and the valley of the Jordan, and the blue waters of the Lake of Galilee, and the fertile plain of Esdraelon, and the hills of Ephraim, and the highlands of Judah. Through all these I followed the figure of Artaban moving steadily onward, until he arrived at Bethlehem. And it was the third day after the three wise men had come to that place and had found Mary and Joseph, with the young child, Jesus, and had laid their gifts of gold and frankincense and myrrh at his feet.

Then the other wise man drew near, weary, but full of hope, bearing his ruby and his pearl to offer to the King. "For now at last," he said, "I shall surely find him, though it be alone, and later than my brethren. This is the place of which the Hebrew exile told me that the prophets had spoken, and here I shall behold the rising of the great light. But I must inquire about the visit of my brethren, and to what house the star directed them, and to whom they presented their tribute."

The streets of the village seemed to be deserted, and Artaban wondered whether the men had all gone up to the hill-pastures to bring down their sheep. From the open door of a low stone cottage he heard the sound of a woman's voice singing softly. He entered and found a young mother hushing her baby to rest. She told him of the strangers from the far East who had appeared in the village three days ago, and how they said that a star had guided them to the place where Joseph of Nazareth was lodging with his wife and her new-born child, and how they had paid reverence to the child and given him many rich gifts.

"But the travellers disappeared again," she continued, "as suddenly as they had come. We were afraid at the strangeness of their visit. We could not understand it. The man of Nazareth took the babe and his mother and fled away that same night secretly, and it was whispered that they were going far away to Egypt. Ever since, there has been a spell upon the village; something evil hangs over it. They say that the Roman soldiers are coming from Jerusalem to force a new tax from us, and the men have driven the flocks and herds far back among the hills, and hidden themselves to escape it."

Artaban listened to her gentle, timid speech, and the child in her arms looked up in his face and smiled, stretching out its rosy hands to grasp at the winged circle of gold on his breast. His heart warmed to the touch. It seemed like a greeting of love and trust to one who had journeyed long in loneliness and perplexity, fighting with his own doubts and fears, and following a light that was veiled in clouds.

"Might not this child have been the promised Prince?" he asked within himself, as he touched its soft cheek. "Kings have been born ere now in lowlier houses than this, and the favourite of the stars may rise even from a cottage. But it has not seemed good to the God of wisdom to reward my search so soon and so easily. The one whom I seek has gone before me; and now I must follow the King to Egypt."

The young mother laid the babe in its cradle, and rose to minister to the wants of the strange guest that fate had brought into her house. She set food before him, the plain fare of peasants, but willingly offered, and therefore full of refreshment for the soul as well as for the body. Artaban accepted it gratefully; and, as he ate, the child fell into a happy slumber, and murmured sweetly in its dreams, and a great peace filled the quiet room.

But suddenly there came the noise of a wild confusion and uproar in the streets of the village, a shrieking and wailing of women's voices, a clangor of brazen trumpets and a clashing of swords, and a desperate cry: "The soldiers! the soldiers of Herod! They are killing our children."

The young mother's face grew white with terror. She clasped her child to her bosom, and crouched motionless in the darkest corner of the room, covering him with the folds of her robe, lest he should wake and cry.

But Artaban went quickly and stood in the doorway of the house. His broad shoulders filled the portal from side to side, and the peak of his white cap all but touched the lintel.

The soldiers came hurrying down the street with bloody hands and dripping swords. At the sight of the stranger in his imposing dress they hesitated with surprise. The captain of the band approached the threshold to thrust him aside. But Artaban did not stir. His face was as calm as though he were watching the stars, and in his eyes there burned that steady radiance before which even the half-tamed hunting leopard shrinks, and the fierce bloodhound pauses in his leap. He held the soldier silently for an instant, and then said in a low voice:

"There is no one in this place but me, and I am waiting to give this jewel to the prudent captain who will leave me in peace."

He showed the ruby, glistening in the hollow of his hand like a great drop of blood.

The captain was amazed at the splendour of the gem. The pupils of his eyes expanded with desire, and the hard lines of greed wrinkled around his lips. He stretched out his hand and took the ruby.

"March on!" he cried to his men, "there is no child here. The house is still."

The clamour and the clang of arms passed down the street as the headlong fury of the chase sweeps by the secret covert where the trembling deer is hidden. Artaban re-entered the cottage. He turned his face to the east and prayed:

"God of truth, forgive my sin! I have said the thing that is not, to save the life of a child. And two of my gifts are gone. I have spent for man that which was meant for God. Shall I ever be worthy to see the face of the King?"

But the voice of the woman, weeping for joy in the shadow behind him, said very gently:

"Because thou hast saved the life of my little one, may the Lord bless thee and keep thee; the Lord make His face to shine upon thee and be gracious unto thee; the Lord lift up His countenance upon thee and give thee peace."

IN THE HIDDEN WAY OF SORROW

Then again there was a silence in the Hall of Dreams, deeper and more mysterious than the first interval, and I understood that the years of Artaban were flowing very swiftly under the stillness of that clinging fog, and I caught only a glimpse, here and there, of the river of his life shining through the shadows that concealed its course.

I saw him moving among the throngs of men in populous Egypt, seeking everywhere for traces of the household that had come down from Bethlehem, and finding them under the spreading sycamore-trees of Heliopolis, and beneath the walls of the Roman fortress of New Babylon beside the Nile—traces so faint and dim that they vanished before him continually, as footprints on the hard river-sand glisten for a moment with moisture and then disappear.

I saw him again at the foot of the pyramids, which lifted their sharp points into the intense saffron glow of the sunset sky, changeless monuments of the perishable glory and the imperishable hope of man. He looked up into the vast countenance of the crouching Sphinx and vainly tried to read the meaning of her calm eyes and smiling mouth. Was it, indeed, the mockery of all effort and all aspiration, as Tigranes had said—the cruel jest of a riddle that has no answer, a search that never can succeed? Or was there a touch of pity and encouragement in that inscrutable smile—a promise that even the defeated should attain a victory, and the disappointed should discover a prize, and the ignorant should be made wise, and the blind should see, and the wandering should come into the haven at last?

I saw him again in an obscure house of Alexandria, taking counsel with a Hebrew rabbi. The venerable man, bending over the rolls of parchment on which the prophecies of Israel were written, read aloud the pathetic words which foretold the sufferings of the promised Messiah—the despised and rejected of men, the man of sorrows and the acquaintance of grief.

"And remember, my son," said he, fixing his deep-set eyes upon the face of

Artaban, "the King whom you are seeking is not to be found in a palace, nor among the rich and powerful. If the light of the world and the glory of Israel had been appointed to come with the greatness of earthly splendour, it must have appeared long ago. For no son of Abraham will ever again rival the power which Joseph had in the palaces of Egypt, or the magnificence of Solomon throned between the lions in Jerusalem. But the light for which the world is waiting is a new light, the glory that shall rise out of patient and triumphant suffering. And the kingdom which is to be established forever is a new kingdom, the royalty of perfect and unconquerable love. I do not know how this shall come to pass, nor how the turbulent kings and peoples of earth shall be brought to acknowledge the Messiah and pay homage to him. But this I know. Those who seek Him will do well to look among the poor and the lowly, the sorrowful and the oppressed."

So I saw the other wise man again and again, travelling from place to place, and searching among the people of the dispersion, with whom the little family from Bethlehem might, perhaps, have found a refuge. He passed through countries where famine lay heavy upon the land, and the poor were crying for bread. He made his dwelling in plague-stricken cities where the sick were languishing in the bitter companionship of helpless misery. He visited the oppressed and the afflicted in the gloom of subterranean prisons, and the crowded wretchedness of slave-markets, and the weary toil of galley-ships. In all this populous and intricate world of anguish, though he found none to worship, he found many to help. He fed the hungry, and clothed the naked, and healed the sick, and comforted the captive; and his years went by more swiftly than the weaver's shuttle that flashes back and forth through the loom while the web grows and the invisible pattern is completed.

It seemed almost as if he had forgotten his quest. But once I saw him for a moment as he stood alone at sunrise, waiting at the gate of a Roman prison. He had taken from a secret resting-place in his bosom the pearl, the last of his jewels. As he looked at it, a mellower lustre, a soft and iridescent light, full of shifting gleams of azure and rose, trembled upon its surface. It seemed to have absorbed some reflection of the colours of the lost sapphire and ruby. So the profound, secret purpose of a noble life draws into itself the memories of past joy and past sorrow. All that has helped it, all that has hindered it, is transfused by a subtle magic into its very essence. It becomes more luminous and precious the longer it is carried close to the warmth of the beating heart. Then, at last, while I was thinking of this pearl, and of its meaning, I heard the end of the story of the other wise man.

A PEARL OF GREAT PRICE

Three-and-thirty years of the life of Artaban had passed away, and he was still a pilgrim and a seeker after light. His hair, once darker than the cliffs of Zagros, was now white as the wintry snow that covered them. His eyes, that once flashed like flames of fire, were dull as embers smouldering among the ashes.

Worn and weary and ready to die, but still looking for the King, he had come for the last time to Jerusalem. He had often visited the holy city before, and had searched through all its lanes and crowded hovels and black prisons without finding any trace of the family of Nazarenes who had fled from Bethlehem long ago. But now it seemed as if he must make one more effort, and something whispered in his heart that, at last, he might succeed. It was the season of the Passover. The city was thronged with strangers. The children of Israel, scattered in far lands all over the world, had returned to the Temple for the great feast, and there had been a confusion of tongues in the narrow streets for many days.

But on this day there was a singular agitation visible in the multitude. The sky was veiled with a portentous gloom, and currents of excitement seemed to flash through the crowd like the thrill which shakes the forest on the eve of a storm. A secret tide was sweeping them all one way. The clatter of sandals, and the soft, thick sound of thousands of bare feet shuffling over the stones, flowed unceasingly along the street that leads to the Damascus gate.

Artaban joined company with a group of people from his own country, Parthian Jews who had come up to keep the Passover, and inquired of them the cause of the tumult, and where they were going.

"We are going," they answered, "to the place called Golgotha, outside the city walls, where there is to be an execution. Have you not heard what has happened? Two famous robbers are to be crucified, and with them another, called Jesus of Nazareth, a man who has done many wonderful works among the people, so that they love him greatly. But the priests and elders have said that he must die, because he gave himself out to be the Son of God. And Pilate has sent him to the cross because he said that he was the 'King of the Jews.'"

How strangely these familiar words fell upon the tired heart of Artaban! They had led him for a lifetime over land and sea. And now they came to him darkly and mysteriously like a message of despair. The King had arisen, but he had been denied and cast out. He was about to perish. Perhaps he was already dying. Could it be the same who had been born in Bethlehem, thirty-three years ago, at whose birth the star had appeared in heaven, and of whose coming the prophets had spoken?

Artaban's heart beat unsteadily with that troubled, doubtful apprehension which is the excitement of old age. But he said within himself, "The ways of God are stranger than the thoughts of men, and it may be that I shall find the King, at last, in the hands of His enemies, and shall come in time to offer my pearl for His ransom before He dies."

So the old man followed the multitude with slow and painful steps towards the Damascus gate of the city. Just beyond the entrance of the guard-house a troop of Macedonian soldiers came down the street, dragging a young girl with torn dress and dishevelled hair. As the Magian paused to look at her with compassion, she broke suddenly from the hands of her tormentors, and threw herself at his feet, clasping him around the knees. She had seen his white cap and the winged circle on his breast.

"Have pity on me," she cried, "and save me, for the sake of the God of Purity! I also am a daughter of the true religion which is taught by the Magi. My father was a merchant of Parthia, but he is dead, and I am seized for his debts to be sold as a slave. Save me from worse than death!"

Artaban trembled.

It was the old conflict in his soul, which had come to him in the palm-grove of Babylon and in the cottage at Bethlehem—the conflict between the expectation of faith and the impulse of love. Twice the gift which he had consecrated to the worship of religion had been drawn from his hand to the service of humanity. This was the third trial, the ultimate probation, the final and irrevocable choice.

Was it his great opportunity, or his last temptation? He could not tell. One thing only was clear in the darkness of his mind—it was inevitable. And does not the inevitable come from God?

One thing only was sure to his divided heart—to rescue this helpless girl would be a true deed of love. And is not love the light of the soul?

He took the pearl from his bosom. Never had it seemed so luminous, so radiant, so full of tender, living lustre. He laid it in the hand of the slave.

"This is thy ransom, daughter! It is the last of my treasures which I kept for the King."

While he spoke the darkness of the sky thickened, and shuddering tremors ran through the earth, heaving convulsively like the breast of one who struggles with mighty grief.

The walls of the houses rocked to and fro. Stones were loosened and crashed into the street. Dust clouds filled the air. The soldiers fled in terror, reeling like drunken men. But Artaban and the girl whom he had ransomed crouched helpless beneath the wall of the Praetorium.

What had he to fear? What had he to live for? He had given away the last remnant of his tribute for the King. He had parted with the last hope of finding

Him. The quest was over, and it had failed. But, even in that thought, accepted and embraced, there was peace. It was not resignation. It was not submission. It was something more profound and searching. He knew that all was well, because he had done the best that he could, from day to day. He had been true to the light that had been given to him. He had looked for more. And if he had not found it, if a failure was all that came out of his life, doubtless that was the best that was possible. He had not seen the revelation of "life everlasting, incorruptible and immortal." But he knew that even if he could live his earthly life over again, it could not be otherwise than it had been.

One more lingering pulsation of the earthquake quivered through the ground. A heavy tile, shaken from the roof, fell and struck the old man on the temple. He lay breathless and pale, with his gray head resting on the young girl's shoulder, and the blood trickling from the wound. As she bent over him, fearing that he was dead, there came a voice through the twilight, very small and still, like music sounding from a distance, in which the notes are clear but the words are lost. The girl turned to see if some one had spoken from the window above them, but she saw no one.

Then the old man's lips began to move, as if in answer, and she heard him say in the Parthian tongue:

"Not so, my Lord! For when saw I thee an hungered, and fed thee? Or thirsty, and gave thee drink? When saw I thee a stranger, and took thee in? Or naked, and clothed thee? When saw I thee sick or in prison, and came unto thee? Three-and-thirty years have I looked for thee; but I have never seen thy face, nor ministered to thee, my King."

He ceased, and the sweet voice came again. And again the maid heard it, very faintly and far away. But now it seemed as though she understood the words:

"*Verily I say unto thee, inasmuch as thou hast done it unto one of the least of these my brethren, thou hast done it unto me.*"

A calm radiance of wonder and joy lighted the pale face of Artaban like the first ray of dawn on a snowy mountain-peak. One long, last breath of relief exhaled gently from his lips.

His journey was ended. His treasures were accepted. The other Wise Man had found the King.

Tilly's Christmas

Louisa May Alcott

I'm so glad tomorrow is Christmas, because I'm going to have lots of presents."

"So am I glad, though I don't expect any presents but a pair of mittens."

"And so am I; but I shan't have any presents at all."

As the three little girls trudged home from school they said these things, and as Tilly spoke, both the others looked at her with pity and some surprise, for she spoke cheerfully, and they wondered how she could be happy when she was so poor she could have no presents on Christmas.

"Don't you wish you could find a purse full of money right here in the path?" said Kate, the child who was going to have "lots of presents."

"Oh, don't I, if I could keep it honestly!" and Tilly's eyes shone at the very thought.

"What would you buy?" asked Bessy, rubbing her cold hands, and longing for her mittens.

"I'd buy a pair of large, warm blankets, a load of wood, a shawl for mother, and a pair of shoes for me; and if there was enough left, I'd give Bessy a new hat, and then she needn't wear Ben's old felt one," answered Tilly.

The girls laughed at that; but Bessy pulled the funny hat over her ears, and said she was much obliged but she'd rather have candy.

"Let's look, and maybe we *can* find a purse. People are always going about with money at Christmas time, and someone may lose it here," said Kate.

So, as they went along the snowy road, they looked about them, half in earnest, half in fun. Suddenly Tilly sprang forward, exclaiming—

"I see it! I've found it!"

The others followed, but all stopped disappointed; for it wasn't a purse, it was only a little bird. It lay upon the snow with its wings spread and feebly fluttering, as if too weak to fly. Its little feet were benumbed with cold; its once bright eyes were dull with pain, and instead of a blithe song, it could only utter a faint chirp, now and then, as if crying for help.

"Nothing but a stupid old robin; how provoking!" cried Kate, sitting down to rest.

"I shan't touch it. I found one once, and took care of it, and the ungrateful thing flew away the minute it was well," said Bessy, creeping under Kate's shawl, and putting her hands under her chin to warm them.

"Poor little birdie! How pitiful he looks, and how glad he must be to see someone coming to help him! I'll take him up gently, and carry him home to mother. Don't be frightened, dear, I'm your friend"; and Tilly knelt down in the snow, stretching her hand to the bird, with the tenderest pity in her face.

Kate and Bessy laughed.

"Don't stop for that thing; it's getting late and cold: let's go on and look for the purse," they said moving away.

"You wouldn't leave it to die!" cried Tilly. "I'd rather have the bird than the money, so I shan't look any more. The purse wouldn't be mine, and I should only be tempted to keep it; but this poor thing will thank and love me, and I'm *so* glad I came in time."

Gently lifting the bird, Tilly felt its tiny cold claws cling to her hand, and saw its dim eyes brighten as it nestled down with a grateful chirp.

"Now I've got a Christmas present after all," she said, smiling, as they walked on. "I always wanted a bird, and this one will be such a pretty pet for me."

"He'll fly away the first chance he gets, and die anyhow; so you'd better not waste your time over him," said Bessy.

"He can't pay you for taking care of him, and my mother says it isn't worth while to help folks that can't help us," added Kate.

"My mother says, 'Do as you'd be done by'; and I'm sure I'd like anyone to help me if I was dying of cold and hunger. 'Love your neighbour as yourself,' is another of her sayings. This bird is my little neighbour, and I'll love him and care for him, as I often wish our rich neighbour would love and care for us," answered Tilly, breathing her warm breath over the benumbed bird, who looked up at her with confiding eyes, quick to feel and know a friend.

"What a funny girl you are," said Kate; "caring for that silly bird, and talking about loving your neighbour in that sober way. Mr. King don't care a bit for you, and never will, though he knows how poor you are; so I don't think your plan amounts to much."

"I believe it, though; and shall do my part, any way. Good-night. I hope you'll have a merry Christmas, and lots of pretty things," answered Tilly, as they parted.

Her eyes were full, and she felt so poor as she went on alone toward the little old house where she lived. It would have been so pleasant to know that she was going to have some of the pretty things all children love to find in their full stockings on Christmas morning. And pleasanter still to have been able to give her mother something nice. So many comforts were needed, and there was no hope of getting them; for they could barely get food and fire.

"Never mind, birdie, we'll make the best of what we have, and be merry in spite of every thing. *You* shall have a happy Christmas, any way; and I know God won't forget us if everyone else does."

She stopped a minute to wipe her eyes, and lean her cheek against the bird's soft breast, finding great comfort in the little creature, though it could only love her, nothing more.

"See, mother, what a nice present I've found," she cried, going in with a cheery face that was like sunshine in the dark room.

"I'm glad of that, dearie; for I haven't been able to get my little girl anything but a rosy apple. Poor bird! Give it some of your warm bread and milk."

"Why, mother, what a big bowlful! I'm afraid you gave me all the milk," said Tilly, smiling over the nice, steaming supper that stood ready for her.

"I've had plenty, dear. Sit down and dry your wet feet, and put the bird in my basket on this warm flannel."

Tilly peeped into the closet and saw nothing there but dry bread.

"Mother's given me all the milk, and is going without her tea, 'cause she knows I'm hungry. Now I'll surprise her, and she shall have a good supper too. She is going to split wood, and I'll fix it while she's gone."

So Tilly put down the old tea-pot, carefully poured out a part of the milk, and from her pocket produced a great, plummy bun, that one of the school-children had given her, and she had saved for her mother. A slice of the dry bread was nicely toasted, and the bit of butter set by for her put on it. When her mother came in there was the table drawn up in a warm place, a hot cup of tea ready, and Tilly and birdie waiting for her.

Such a poor little supper, and yet such a happy one; for love, charity, and contentment were guests there, and that Christmas eve was a blither one than that up at the great house, where lights shone, fires blazed, a great tree glittered, and music sounded, as the children danced and played.

"We must go to bed early, for we've only wood enough to last over tomorrow. I shall be paid for my work the day after, and then we can get some," said Tilly's mother, as they sat by the fire.

"If my bird was only a fairy bird, and would give us three wishes, how nice it would be! Poor dear, he can't give me any thing; but it's no matter," answered Tilly, looking at the robin, who lay in the basket with his head under his wing, a mere little feathery bunch.

"He can give you one thing, Tilly—the pleasure of doing good. That is one of the sweetest things in life; and the poor can enjoy it as well as the rich."

As her mother spoke, with her tired hand softly stroking her little daughter's hair, Tilly suddenly started and pointed to the window, saying, in a frightened whisper—

"I saw a face—a man's face, looking in! It's gone now; but I truly saw it."

"Some traveller attracted by the light perhaps. I'll go and see." And Tilly's mother went to the door.

No one was there. The wind blew cold, the stars shone, the snow lay white on field and wood, and the Christmas moon was glittering in the sky.

"What sort of a face was it?" asked Tilly's mother, coming back.

"A pleasant sort of face, I think; but I was so startled I don't quite know what it was like. I wish we had a curtain there," said Tilly.

"I like to have our light shine out in the evening, for the road is dark and lonely just here, and the twinkle of our lamp is pleasant to people's eyes as they go by. We can do so little for our neighbours, I am glad to cheer the way for them. Now put these poor old shoes to dry, and go to bed, dearie; I'll come soon."

Tilly went, taking her bird with her to sleep in his basket near by, lest he should be lonely in the night.

Soon the little house was dark and still, and no one saw the Christmas spirits at their work that night.

When Tilly opened the door next morning, she gave a loud cry, clapped her hands, and then stood still; quite speechless with wonder and delight. There, before the door, lay a great pile of wood, all ready to burn, a big bundle and a basket, with a lovely nosegay of winter roses, holly, and evergreen tied to the handle.

"Oh, mother! did the fairies do it?" cried Tilly, pale with her happiness, as she seized the basket, while her mother took in the bundle.

"Yes, dear, the best and dearest fairy in the world, called 'Charity.' She walks abroad at Christmas time, does beautiful deeds like this, and does not stay to be thanked," answered her mother with full eyes, as she undid the parcel.

There they were—the warm, thick blankets, the comfortable shawls, the new shoes, and, best of all, a pretty winter hat for Bessy. The basket was full of good things to eat, and on the flowers lay a paper, saying—

"For the little girl who loves her neighbour as herself."

"Mother, I really think my bird is a fairy bird, and all these splendid things come from him," said Tilly, laughing and crying with joy.

It really did seem so, for as she spoke, the robin flew to the table, hopped to the nosegay, and perching among the roses, began to chirp with all his little might. The sun streamed in on flowers, bird, and happy child, and no one saw a shadow glide away from the window; no one ever knew that Mr. King had seen and heard the little girls the night before, or dreamed that the rich neighbour had learned a lesson from the poor neighbour.

And Tilly's bird *was* a fairy bird; for by her love and tenderness to the helpless thing, she brought good gifts to herself, happiness to the unknown giver of them, and a faithful little friend who did not fly away, but stayed with her till the snow was gone, making summer for her in the winter-time.

Tessa's Surprises

Louisa May Alcott

I

Little Tessa sat alone by the fire, waiting for her father to come home from work. The children were fast asleep, all four in the big bed behind the curtain; the wind blew hard outside, and the snow beat on the window-panes; the room was large, and the fire so small and feeble that it didn't half warm the little bare toes peeping out of the old shoes on the hearth.

Tessa's father was an Italian plaster-worker, very poor, but kind and honest. The mother had died not long ago, and left twelve-year-old Tessa to take care of the little children. She tried to be very wise and motherly, and worked for them like any little woman; but it was so hard to keep the small bodies warm and fed, and the small souls good and happy, that poor Tessa was often at her wits' end. She always waited for her father, no matter how tired she was, so that he might find his supper warm, a bit of fire, and a loving little face to welcome him. Tessa thought over her troubles at these quiet times, and made her plans; for her father left things to her a good deal, and she had no friends but Tommo, the harp-boy upstairs, and the lively cricket who lived in the chimney. Tonight her face was very sober, and her pretty brown eyes very thoughtful as she stared at the fire and knit her brows, as if perplexed. She was not thinking of her old shoes, nor the empty closet, nor the boys' ragged clothes just then. No; she had a fine plan in her good little head, and was trying to discover how she could carry it out.

You see, Christmas was coming in a week; and she had set her heart on putting something in the children's stockings, as the mother used to do, for while she lived things were comfortable. Now Tessa had not a penny in the world, and didn't know how to get one, for all the father's earnings had to go for food, fire, and rent.

"If there were only fairies, ah! how heavenly that would be; for then I should tell them all I wish, and, pop! behold the fine things in my lap!" said Tessa to herself. "I must earn the money; there is no one to give it to me, and I cannot beg. But what can I do, so small and stupid and shy as I am? I *must* find some way to give the little ones a nice Christmas. I *must*! I *must*!" and Tessa pulled her long hair, as if that would help her think.

But it didn't, and her heart got heavier and heavier; for it did seem hard that in a great city full of fine things, there should be none for poor Nono, Sep, and little Speranza. Just as Tessa's tears began to tumble off her eyelashes on to her brown cheeks, the cricket began to chirp. Of course, he didn't say a word; but it really did seem as if he had answered her question almost as well as a fairy; for, before he had piped a dozen shrill notes, an idea popped into Tessa's head—such a truly splendid idea that she clapped her hands and burst out laughing. "I'll do it! I'll do it! if father will let me," she said to herself, smiling and nodding at the fire. "Tommo will like to have me go with him and sing, while he plays his harp in the streets. I know many songs, and may get money if I am not frightened; for people throw pennies to other little girls who only play the tambourine. Yes, I will try; and then, if I do well, the little ones shall have a Merry Christmas."

So full of her plan was Tessa that she ran upstairs at once, and asked Tommo if he would take her with him on the morrow. Her friend was delighted, for he thought Tessa's songs very sweet, and was sure she would get money if she tried.

"But see, then, it is cold in the streets; the wind bites, and the snow freezes one's fingers. The day is very long, people are cross, and at night one is ready to die with weariness. Thou art so small, Tessa, I am afraid it will go badly with thee," said Tommo, who was a merry, black-eyed boy of fourteen, with the kindest heart in the world under his old jacket.

"I do not mind cold and wet, and cross people, if I can get the pennies," answered Tessa, feeling very brave with such a friend to help her. She thanked Tommo, and ran away to get ready, for she felt sure her father would not refuse her anything. She sewed up the holes in her shoes as well as she could, for she had much of that sort of cobbling to do; she mended her only gown, and laid ready the old hood and shawl which had been her mother's. Then she washed out little Ranza's frock and put it to dry, because she would not be able to do it the next day. She set the table and got things ready for breakfast, for Tommo went out early, and must not be kept waiting for her. She longed to make the beds and dress the children over night, she was in such a hurry to have all in order; but, as that could not be, she sat down again, and tried over all the songs she knew. Six pretty ones were chosen; and she sang away with all her heart in a fresh little voice so sweetly that the children smiled in their sleep, and her father's tired face brightened as he entered, for Tessa was his cheery cricket on the hearth. When she had told her plan, Peter Benari shook his head, and thought it would never do; but Tessa begged so hard, he consented at last that she should try it for one week, and sent her to bed the happiest little girl in New York.

Next morning the sun shone, but the cold wind blew, and the snow lay thick in the streets. As soon as her father was gone, Tessa flew about and put everything in nice order, telling the children she was going out for the day, and they were to mind Tommo's mother, who would see about the fire and the dinner; for the good woman loved Tessa, and entered into her little plans with all her heart. Nono and Giuseppe, or Sep, as they called him, wondered what she was going away for, and little Ranza cried at being left; but Tessa told them they would know all about it in a week, and have a fine time if they were good; so they kissed her all round and let her go.

Poor Tessa's heart beat fast as she trudged away with Tommo, who slung his harp over his shoulder, and gave her his hand. It was rather a dirty hand, but so kind that Tessa clung to it, and kept looking up at the friendly brown face for encouragement.

"We go first to the *café*, where many French and Italians eat the breakfast. They like my music, and often give me sips of hot coffee, which I like much. You too shall have the sips, and perhaps the pennies, for these people are greatly kind," said Tommo, leading her into a large smoky place where many people sat at little tables, eating and drinking. "See, now, have no fear; give them 'Bella Monica'; that is merry and will make the laugh," whispered Tommo, tuning his harp.

For a moment Tessa felt so frightened that she wanted to run away; but she remembered the empty stockings at home, and the fine plan, and she resolved *not* to give it up. One fat old Frenchman nodded to her, and it seemed to help her very much; for she began to sing before she thought, and that was the hardest part of it. Her voice trembled, and her cheeks grew redder and redder as she went on; but she kept her eyes fixed on her old shoes, and so got through without breaking down, which was very nice. The people laughed, for the song *was* merry; and the fat man smiled and nodded again. This gave her courage to try another, and she sung better and better each time; for Tommo played his best, and kept whispering to her, "Yes; we go well; this is fine. They will give the money and the blessed coffee."

So they did; for, when the little concert was over, several men put pennies in the cap Tessa offered, and the fat man took her on his knee, and ordered a mug of coffee, and some bread and butter for them both. This quite won her heart; and when they left the *café*, she kissed her hand to the old Frenchman, and said to her friend, "How kind they are! I like this very much; and now it is not hard."

But Tommo shook his curly head, and answered, soberly, "Yes, I took you there first, for they love music, and are of our country; but up among the great houses we shall not always do well. The people there are busy or hard or idle, and care nothing for harps and songs. Do not skip and laugh too soon; for the day is long, and we have but twelve pennies yet."

Tessa walked more quietly, and rubbed her cold hands, feeling that the world was a very big place, and wondering how the children got on at home without the little mother. Till noon they did not earn much, for everyone seemed in a hurry, and the noise of many sleigh-bells drowned the music. Slowly they made their way up to the great squares where the big houses were, with fine ladies and pretty children at the windows. Here Tessa sung all her best songs, and Tommo played as fast as his fingers could fly; but it was too cold to have the windows open, so the pretty children could not listen long, and the ladies tossed out a little money, and soon went back to their own affairs.

All the afternoon the two friends wandered about, singing and playing, and gathering up their small harvest. At dusk they went home, Tessa so hoarse she could hardly speak, and so tired she fell asleep over her supper. But she had made half a dollar, for Tommo divided the money fairly, and she felt rich with her share. The other days were very much like this; sometimes they made more, sometimes less, but Tommo always "went halves"; and Tessa kept on, in spite of cold and weariness, for her plans grew as her earnings increased, and now she hoped to get useful things, instead of candy and toys alone.

On the day before Christmas she made herself as tidy as she could, for she hoped to earn a good deal. She tied a bright scarlet handkerchief over the old hood, and the brilliant color set off her brown cheeks and bright eyes, as well as the pretty black braids of her hair. Tommo's mother lent her a pair of boots so big that they turned up at the toes, but there were no holes in them, and Tessa felt quite elegant in whole boots. Her hands were covered with chilblains, for she had no mittens; but she put them under her shawl, and scuffled merrily away in her big boots, feeling so glad that the week was over, and nearly three dollars safe in her pocket. How gay the streets were that day! how brisk everyone was, and how bright the faces looked, as people trotted about with big baskets, holly-wreaths, and young evergreens going to blossom into splendid Christmas trees!

"If I could have a tree for the children, I'd never want anything again. But I can't; so I'll fill the socks all full, and be happy," said Tessa, as she looked wistfully into the gay stores, and saw the heavy baskets go by.

"Who knows what may happen if we do well?" returned Tommo, nodding wisely, for he had a plan as well as Tessa, and kept chuckling over it as he trudged through the mud. They did *not* do well somehow, for everyone seemed so full of their own affairs they could not stop to listen, even to "Bella Monica," but bustled away to spend their money in turkeys, toys, and trees. In the afternoon it began to rain, and poor Tessa's heart to fail her; for the big boots tired her feet, the cold wind made her hands ache, and the rain spoilt the fine red handkerchief. Even Tommo looked sober, and didn't whistle as he walked, for he also was disappointed, and his plan looked rather doubtful, the pennies came in so slowly.

"We'll try one more street, and then go home, thou art so tired, little one.

Come; let me wipe thy face, and give me thy hand here in my jacket pocket; there it will be as warm as any kitten"; and kind Tommo brushed away the drops which were not *all* rain from Tessa's cheeks, tucked the poor hand into his ragged pocket, and led her carefully along the slippery streets, for the boots nearly tripped her up.

II

At the first house, a cross old gentleman flapped his newspaper at them; at the second, a young gentleman and lady were so busy talking that they never turned their heads, and at the third, a servant came out and told them to go away, because someone was sick. At the fourth, some people let them sing all their songs and gave nothing. The next three houses were empty; and the last of all showed not a single face as they looked up anxiously. It was so cold, so dark and discouraging, that Tessa couldn't help one sob; and, as he glanced down at the little red nose and wet figure beside him, Tommo gave his harp an angry thump, and said something very fierce in Italian. They were just going to turn away; but they didn't, for that angry thump happened to be the best thing they could have done. All of a sudden a little head appeared at the window, as if the sound had brought it; then another and another, till there were five, of all heights and colors, and five eager faces peeped out, smiling and nodding to the two below.

"Sing, Tessa; sing! Quick! quick!" cried Tommo, twanging away with all his might, and showing his white teeth, as he smiled back at the little gentle-folk.

Bless us! How Tessa did tune up at that! She chirped away like a real bird, forgetting all about the tears on her cheeks, the ache in her hands, and the heaviness at her heart. The children laughed, and clapped their hands, and cried "More! more! Sing another, little girl! Please do!" And away they went again, piping and playing, till Tessa's breath was gone, and Tommo's stout fingers tingled well.

"Mamma says, come to the door; it's too muddy to throw the money into the street!" cried out a kindly child's voice as Tessa held up the old cap, with beseeching eyes.

Up the wide stone steps went the street musicians, and the whole flock came running down to give a handful of silver, and ask all sorts of questions. Tessa felt so grateful that, without waiting for Tommo, she sang her sweetest little song all alone. It was about a lost lamb, and her heart was in the song; therefore she sang it well, so well that a pretty young lady came down to listen, and stood watching the bright-eyed girl, who looked about her as she sang, evidently enjoying the light and warmth of the fine hall, and the sight of the lovely children with their gay dresses, shining hair, and dainty little shoes.

"You have a charming voice, child. Who taught you to sing?" asked the young lady kindly.

"My mother. She is dead now; but I do not forget," answered Tessa, in her pretty broken English.

"I wish she could sing at our tree, since Bella is ill," cried one of the children peeping through the banisters.

"She is not fair enough for the angel, and too large to go up in the tree. But she sings sweetly, and looks as if she would like to see a tree," said the young lady.

"Oh, so much!" exclaimed Tessa; adding eagerly, "my sister Ranza is small and pretty as a baby-angel. She could sit up in the fine tree, and I could sing for her from under the table."

"Sit down and warm yourself, and tell me about Ranza," said the kind elder sister, who liked the confiding little girl, in spite of her shabby clothes.

So Tessa sat down and dried the big boots over the furnace, and told her story, while Tommo stood modestly in the background, and the children listened with faces full of interest.

"O Rose! let us see the little girl; and if she will do, let us have her, and Tessa can learn our song, and it will be splendid!" cried the biggest boy, who sat astride of a chair, and stared at the harp with round eyes.

"I'll ask mamma," said Rose; and away she went into the dining-room close by. As the door opened, Tessa saw what looked to her like a fairy feast—all silver mugs and flowery plates and oranges and nuts and rosy wine in tall glass pitchers, and smoking dishes that smelt so deliciously she could not restrain a little sniff of satisfaction.

"Are you hungry?" asked the boy, in a grand tone.

"Yes, sir," meekly answered Tessa.

"I say, mamma; she wants something to eat. Can I give her an orange?" called the boy, prancing away into the splendid room, quite like a fairy prince, Tessa thought.

A plump motherly lady came out and looked at Tessa, asked a few questions, and then told her to come tomorrow with Ranza, and they would see what could be done. Tessa clapped her hands for joy—she didn't mind the chilblains now—and Tommo played a lively march, he was so pleased.

"Will you come, too, and bring your harp? You shall be paid, and shall have something from the tree, likewise," said the motherly lady, who liked what Tessa gratefully told about his kindness to her.

"Ah, yes; I shall come with much gladness, and play as never in my life before," cried Tommo, with a flourish of the old cap that made the children laugh.

"Give these to your brothers," said the fairy prince, stuffing nuts and oranges into Tessa's hands.

"And these to the little girl," added one of the young princesses, flying out of the dining-room with cakes and rosy apples for Ranza.

Tessa didn't know what to say; but her eyes were full, and she just took the mother's white hand in both her little grimy ones, and kissed it many times in her pretty Italian fashion. The lady understood her, and stroked her cheek softly, saying to her elder daughter, "We must take care of this good little creature. Freddy, bring me your mittens; these poor hands must be covered. Alice, get your play-hood; this handkerchief is all wet; and, Maud, bring the old chinchilla tippet."

The children ran, and in a minute there were lovely blue mittens on the red hands, a warm hood over the black braids, and a soft "pussy" round the sore throat.

"Ah! so kind, so very kind! I have no way to say 'thank you'; but Ranza shall be for you a heavenly angel, and I will sing my heart out for your tree!" cried Tessa, folding the mittens as if she would say a prayer of thankfulness if she knew how.

Then they went away, and the pretty children called after them, "Come again, Tessa! come again, Tommo!" Now the rain didn't seem dismal, the wind cold, nor the way long, as they bought their gifts and hurried home, for kind words and the sweet magic of charity had changed all the world to them.

I think the good spirits who fly about on Christmas Eve, to help the loving fillers of little stockings, smiled very kindly on Tessa as she brooded joyfully over the small store of presents that seemed so magnificent to her. All the goodies were divided evenly into three parts and stowed away in father's three big socks, which hung against the curtain. With her three dollars, she had got a pair of shoes for Nono, a knit cap for Sep, and a pair of white stockings for Ranza; to her she also gave the new hood; to Nono the mittens; and to Sep the tippet.

"Now the dear boys can go out, and my Ranza will be ready for the lady to see, in her nice new things," said Tessa, quite sighing with pleasure to see how well the gifts looked pinned up beside the bulging socks, which wouldn't hold them all. The little mother kept nothing for herself but the pleasure of giving everything away; yet, I think, she was both richer and happier than if she had kept them all. Her father laughed as he had not done since the mother died, when he saw how comically the old curtain had broken out into boots and hoods, stockings and tippets.

"I wish I had a gold gown and a silver hat for thee, my Tessa, thou art so good. May the saints bless and keep thee always!" said Peter Benari tenderly, as he held his little daughter close, and gave her the good-night kiss.

Tessa felt very rich as she crept under the faded counterpane, feeling as if she had received a lovely gift, and fell happily asleep with chubby Ranza in her arms, and the two rough black heads peeping out at the foot of the bed. She dreamed wonderful dreams that night, and woke in the morning to find real wonders before her eyes. She got up early, to see if the socks were all right, and there she found the most astonishing sight. Four socks, instead of three; and by the fourth, pinned out quite elegantly was a little dress, evidently meant for her—a warm, woollen dress, all made, and actually with bright buttons on it. It nearly took her breath away; so did the new boots on the floor, and the funny long stocking like a grey sausage, with a wooden doll staring out at the top, as if she said, politely, "A Merry Christmas, ma'am!" Tessa screamed and danced in her delight, and up tumbled all the children to scream and dance with her, making a regular carnival on a small scale. Everybody hugged and kissed everybody else, offered sucks of orange, bites of cake, and exchanges of candy; everyone tried on the new things, and pranced about in them like a flock of peacocks. Ranza skipped to and fro airily, dressed in her white socks and the red hood; the boys promenaded in their little shirts, one with his creaking new shoes and mittens, the other in his gay cap and fine tippet; and Tessa put her dress straight on, feeling that her father's "gold gown" was not all a joke. In her long stocking she found all sorts of treasures; for Tommo had stuffed it full of queer things, and his mother had made gingerbread into every imaginable shape, from fat pigs to full omnibuses.

Dear me! What happy little souls they were that morning; and when they were quiet again, how like a fairy tale did Tessa's story sound to them. Ranza was quite ready to be an angel; and the boys promised to be marvellously good, if they were only allowed to see the tree at the "palace," as they called the great house.

Little Ranza was accepted with delight by the kind lady and her children, and Tessa learned the song quite easily. The boys *were* asked; and, after a happy day, the young Italians all returned, to play their parts at the fine Christmas party. Mamma and Miss Rose drilled them all; and when the folding-doors flew open, one rapturous "Oh!" arose from the crowd of children gathered to the festival. I assure you, it was splendid; the great tree glittering with lights and gifts; and, on her invisible perch, up among the green boughs, sat the little golden-haired angel, all in white, with downy wings, a shining crown on her head, and the most serene satisfaction in her blue eyes, as she stretched her chubby arms to those below, and smiled her baby smile at them. Before anyone could speak, a voice, as fresh and sweet as a lark's, sang the Christmas Carol so blithely that everyone stood still to hear, and then clapped till the little angel shook on her perch, and cried out, "Be 'till, or me'll fall!" How they laughed at that; and what fun they had talking to Ranza, while Miss Rose stripped the tree, for the angel could not resist temptation, and amused herself by eating all the bonbons she could reach, till she was taken down, to dance about like a fairy in a white frock and red shoes. Tessa and her friends had many presents; the boys were perfect lambs, Tommo played for the little folks to dance, and everyone said something friendly to the strangers, so that they did not feel shy, in spite of shabby clothes. It was a happy night: and all their lives they remembered it as something too beautiful and bright to be quite true. Before they went home, the kind mamma told Tessa she should be her friend, and gave her a motherly kiss, which warmed the child's heart and seemed to set a seal upon that promise. It was faithfully kept, for the rich lady had been touched by Tessa's patient struggles and sacrifices; and for many years, thanks to her benevolence, there was no end to Tessa's Surprises.

A Christmas Dream, and How It Came True

Louisa May Alcott

I'm so tired of Christmas, I wish there never would be another one!" exclaimed a discontented-looking little girl, as she sat idly watching her mother arrange a pile of gifts two days before they were to be given.

"Why, Effie, what a dreadful thing to say! You are as bad as old Scrooge; and I'm afraid something will happen to you, as it did to him, if you don't care for dear Christmas," answered Mamma, almost dropping the silver horn she was filling with delicious candies.

"Who was Scrooge? What happened to him?" asked Effie, with a glimmer of interest in her listless face, as she picked out the sourest lemon-drop she could find; for nothing sweet suited her just then.

"He was one of Dickens's best people, and you can read the charming story some day. He hated Christmas until a strange dream showed him how dear and beautiful it was, and made a better man of him."

"I shall read it; for I like dreams, and have a great many curious ones myself. But they don't keep me from being tired of Christmas," said Effie, poking discontentedly among the sweeties for something worth eating.

"Why are you tired of what should be the happiest time of all the year?" asked mamma, anxiously.

"Perhaps I shouldn't be if I had something new. But it is always the same, and there isn't any more surprise about it. I always find heaps of goodies in my stocking. Don't like some of them, and soon get tired of those I do like. We always have a great dinner, and I eat too much, and feel ill next day. Then there is a Christmas tree somewhere, with a doll on top, or a stupid old Santa Claus, and children dancing and screaming over bonbons and toys that break, and shiny things that are of no use. Really, Mamma, I've had so many Christmases all alike that I don't think I *can* bear another one." And Effie laid herself flat on the sofa, as if the mere idea was too much for her.

Her mother laughed at her despair, but was sorry to see her little girl so discontented, when she had everything to make her happy, and had known but ten Christmas days.

"Suppose we don't give you *any* presents at all—how would that suit you?" asked Mamma, anxious to please her spoiled child.

"I should like one large and splendid one, and one dear little one, to remember some very nice person by," said Effie, who was a fanciful little body, full of odd whims and notions, which her friends loved to gratify, regardless of time, trouble, or money; for she was the last of three little girls, and very dear to all the family.

"Well, my darling, I will see what I can do to please you, and not say a word until all is ready. If I could only get a new idea to start with!" And Mamma went on tying up her pretty bundles with a thoughtful face, while Effie strolled to the window to watch the rain that kept her in-doors and made her dismal.

"Seems to me poor children have better times than rich ones. I can't go out, and there is a girl about my age splashing along, without any maid to fuss about rubbers and cloaks and umbrellas and colds. I wish I was a beggar-girl."

"Would you like to be hungry, cold, and ragged, to beg all day, and sleep on an ash-heap at night?" asked Mamma, wondering what would come next.

"Cinderella did, and had a nice time in the end. This girl out here has a basket of scraps on her arm, and a big old shawl all round her, and doesn't seem to care a bit, though the water runs out of the toes of her boots. She goes paddling along, laughing at the rain, and eating a cold potato as if it tasted nicer than the chicken and ice-cream I had for dinner. Yes, I do think poor children are happier than rich ones."

"So do I, sometimes. At the Orphan Asylum today I saw two dozen merry little souls who have no parents, no home, and no hope of Christmas beyond a stick of candy or a cake. I wish you had been there to see how happy they were, playing with the old toys some richer children had sent them."

"You may give them all mine; I'm so tired of them I never want to see them again," said Effie, turning from the window to the pretty baby-house full of everything a child's heart could desire.

"I will, and let you begin again with something you will not tire of, if I can only find it." And Mamma knit her brows trying to discover some grand surprise for this child who didn't care for Christmas.

Nothing more was said then; and wandering off to the library, Effie found "A Christmas Carol," and curling herself up in the sofa corner, read it all before tea. Some of it she did not understand; but she laughed and cried over many parts of the charming story, and felt better without knowing why.

All the evening she thought of poor Tiny Tim, Mrs. Cratchit with the pudding, and the stout old gentleman who danced so gayly that "his legs twinkled in the air." Presently bedtime arrived.

"Come, now, and toast your feet," said Effie's nurse, "while I do your pretty hair and tell stories."

"I'll have a fairy tale tonight, a very interesting one," commanded Effie, as she put on her blue silk wrapper and little fur-lined slippers to sit before the fire and have her long curls brushed.

So Nursey told her best tales; and when at last the child lay down under her lace curtains, her head was full of a curious jumble of Christmas elves, poor children, snow-storms, sugarplums, and surprises. So it is no wonder that she dreamed all night; and this was the dream, which she never quite forgot.

She found herself sitting on a stone, in the middle of a great field, all alone. The snow was falling fast, a bitter wind whistled by, and night was coming on. She felt hungry, cold, and tired, and did not know where to go nor what to do.

"I wanted to be a beggar-girl, and now I am one; but I don't like it, and wish somebody would come and take care of me. I don't know who I am, and I think I must be lost," thought Effie, with the curious interest one takes in one's self in dreams.

But the more she thought about it, the more bewildered she felt. Faster fell the snow, colder blew the wind, darker grew the night; and poor Effie made up her mind that she was quite forgotten and left to freeze alone. The tears were chilled on her cheeks, her feet felt like icicles, and her heart died within her, so hungry, frightened, and forlorn was she. Laying her head on her knees, she gave herself up for lost, and sat there with the great flakes fast turning her to a little white mound, when suddenly the sound of music reached her, and starting up, she looked and listened with all her eyes and ears.

Far away a dim light shone, and a voice was heard singing. She tried to run toward the welcome glimmer, but could not stir, and stood like a small statue of expectation while the light drew nearer, and the sweet words of the song grew clearer.

> *From our happy home*
> *Through the world we roam*
> *One week in all the year,*
> *Making winter spring*
> *With the joy we bring,*
> *For Christmas-tide is here.*
>
> *Now the eastern star*
> *Shines from afar*
> *To light the poorest home;*
> *Hearts warmer grow,*
> *Gifts freely flow,*
> *For Christmas-tide has come.*

Now gay trees rise
Before young eyes,
Abloom with tempting cheer;
Blithe voices sing,
And blithe bells ring,
For Christmas-tide is here.

Oh, happy chime,
Oh, blessed time,
That draws us all so near!
"Welcome, dear day,"
All creatures say,
For Christmas-tide is here.

A child's voice sang, a child's hand carried the little candle; and in the circle of soft light it shed, Effie saw a pretty child coming to her through the night and snow. A rosy, smiling creature, wrapped in white fur, with a wreath of green and scarlet holly on its shining hair, the magic candle in one hand, and the other outstretched as if to shower gifts and warmly press all other hands.

Effie forgot to speak as this bright vision came nearer, leaving no trace of footsteps in the snow, only lighting the way with its little candle, and filling the air with the music of its song.

"Dear child, you are lost, and I have come to find you," said the stranger, taking Effie's cold hands in his, with a smile like sunshine, while every holly berry glowed like a little fire.

"Do you know me?" asked Effie, feeling no fear, but a great gladness, at his coming.

"I know all children, and go to find them; for this is my holiday, and I gather them from all parts of the world to be merry with me once a year."

"Are you an angel?" asked Effie, looking for the wings.

"No; I am a Christmas spirit, and live with my mates in a pleasant place, getting ready for our holiday, when we are let out to roam about the world, helping make this a happy time for all who will let us in. Will you come and see how we work?"

"I will go anywhere with you. Don't leave me again," cried Effie, gladly.

"First I will make you comfortable. That is what we love to do. You are cold, and you shall be warm; hungry, and I will feed you; sorrowful, and I will make you gay."

With a wave of his candle all three miracles were wrought—for the snow-flakes turned to a white fur cloak and hood on Effie's head and shoulders, a bowl of hot soup came sailing to her lips, and vanished when she had eagerly drunk the last drop; and suddenly the dismal field changed to a new world so full of wonders that all her troubles were forgotten in a minute.

Bells were ringing so merrily that it was hard to keep from dancing. Green garlands hung on the walls, and every tree was a Christmas tree full of toys, and blazing with candles that never went out.

In one place many little spirits sewed like mad on warm clothes, turning off work faster than any sewing-machine ever invented, and great piles were made ready to be sent to poor people. Other busy creatures packed money into purses, and wrote checks which they sent flying away on the wind—a lovely kind of snow-storm to fall into a world below full of poverty.

Older and graver spirits were looking over piles of little books, in which the records of the past year were kept, telling how different people had spent it, and what sort of gifts they deserved. Some got peace, some disappointment, some remorse and sorrow, some great joy and hope. The rich had generous thoughts sent them; the poor, gratitude and contentment. Children had more love and duty to parents; and parents renewed patience, wisdom, and satisfaction for and in their children. No one was forgotten.

"Please tell me what splendid place this is?" asked Effie, as soon as she could collect her wits after the first look at all these astonishing things.

"This is the Christmas world; and here we work all the year round, never tired of getting ready for the happy day. See, these are the saints just setting off; for some have far to go, and the children must not be disappointed."

As he spoke the spirit pointed to four gates, out of which four great sleighs were just driving, laden with toys, while a jolly old Santa Claus sat in the middle of each, drawing on his mittens and tucking up his wraps for a long cold drive.

"Why, I thought there was only one Santa Claus, and even he was a humbug," cried Effie, astonished at the sight.

"Never give up your faith in the sweet old stones, even after you come to see that they are only the pleasant shadow of a lovely truth."

Just then the sleighs went off with a great jingling of bells and pattering of reindeer hoofs, while all the spirits gave a cheer that was heard in the lower world, where people said, "Hear the stars sing."

"I never will say there isn't any Santa Claus again. Now, show me more."

"You will like to see this place, I think, and may learn something here perhaps."

The spirit smiled as he led the way to a little door, through which Effie peeped into a world of dolls. Baby-houses were in full blast, with dolls of all sorts going on like live people. Waxen ladies sat in their parlors elegantly dressed; black dolls cooked in the kitchens; nurses walked out with the bits of dollies; and the streets were full of tin soldiers marching, wooden horses prancing, express wagons rumbling, and little men hurrying to and fro. Shops were there, and tiny people buying legs of mutton, pounds of tea, mites of clothes, and everything dolls use or wear or want.

But presently she saw that in some ways the dolls improved upon the manners and customs of human beings, and she watched eagerly to learn why they did these things. A fine Paris doll driving in her carriage took up a black worsted Dinah who was hobbling along with a basket of clean clothes, and carried her to her journey's end, as if it were the proper thing to do. Another interesting china lady took off her comfortable red cloak and put it round a poor wooden creature done up in a paper shift, and so badly painted that its face would have sent some babies into fits.

"Seems to me I once knew a rich girl who didn't give her things to poor girls. I wish I could remember who she was, and tell her to be as kind as that china doll," said Effie, much touched at the sweet way the pretty creature wrapped up the poor fright, and then ran off in her little gray gown to buy a shiny fowl stuck on a wooden platter for her invalid mother's dinner.

"We recall these things to people's minds by dreams. I think the girl you speak of won't forget this one." And the spirit smiled, as if he enjoyed some joke which she did not see.

A little bell rang as she looked, and away scampered the children into the red-and-green school-house with the roof that lifted up, so one could see how nicely they sat at their desks with mites of books, or drew on the inch-square blackboards with crumbs of chalk.

"They know their lessons very well, and are as still as mice. We make a great racket at our school, and get bad marks every day. I shall tell the girls they had better mind what they do, or their dolls will be better scholars than they are," said Effie, much impressed, as she peeped in and saw no rod in the hand of the little mistress, who looked up and shook her head at the intruder, as if begging her to go away before the order of the school was disturbed.

Effie retired at once, but could not resist one look in at the window of a fine mansion, where the family were at dinner, the children behaved so well at table, and never grumbled a bit when their mamma said they could not have any more fruit.

"Now, show me something else," she said, as they came again to the low door that led out of Doll-land.

"You have seen how we prepare for Christmas; let me show you where we love best to send our good and happy gifts," answered the spirit, giving her his hand again.

"I know. I've seen ever so many," began Effie, thinking of her own Christmases.

"No, you have never seen what I will show you. Come away, and remember what you see tonight."

Like a flash that bright world vanished, and Effie found herself in a part of the city she had never seen before. It was far away from the gayer places, where every store was brilliant with lights and full of pretty things, and every house wore a festival air, while people hurried to and fro with merry greetings. It was down among the dingy streets where the poor lived, and where there was no making ready for Christmas.

Hungry women looked in at the shabby shops, longing to buy meat and bread, but empty pockets forbade. Tipsy men drank up their wages in the bar-rooms; and in many cold dark chambers little children huddled under the thin blankets, trying to forget their misery in sleep.

No nice dinners filled the air with savory smells, no gay trees dropped toys and bonbons into eager hands, no little stockings hung in rows beside the chimney-piece ready to be filled, no happy sounds of music, gay voices, and dancing feet were heard; and there were no signs of Christmas anywhere.

"Don't they have any in this place?" asked Effie, shivering, as she held fast the spirit's hand, following where he led her.

"We come to bring it. Let me show you our best workers." And the spirit pointed to some sweet-faced men and women who came stealing into the poor houses, working such beautiful miracles that Effie could only stand and watch.

Some slipped money into the empty pockets, and sent the happy mothers to buy all the comforts they needed; others led the drunken men out of temptation, and took them home to find safer pleasures there. Fires were kindled on cold hearths, tables spread as if by magic, and warm clothes wrapped round shivering limbs. Flowers suddenly bloomed in the chambers of the sick; old people found themselves remembered; sad hearts were consoled by a tender word, and wicked ones softened by the story of Him who forgave all sin.

But the sweetest work was for the children; and Effie held her breath to watch these human fairies hang up and fill the little stockings without which a child's Christmas is not perfect, putting in things that once she would have thought very humble presents, but which now seemed beautiful and precious because these poor babies had nothing.

"That is so beautiful! I wish I could make merry Christmases as these good people do, and be loved and thanked as they are," said Effie, softly, as she watched the busy men and women do their work and steal away without thinking of any reward but their own satisfaction.

"You can if you will. I have shown you the way. Try it, and see how happy your own holiday will be hereafter."

As he spoke, the spirit seemed to put his arms about her, and vanished with a kiss.

"Oh, stay and show me more!" cried Effie, trying to hold him fast.

"Darling, wake up, and tell me why you are smiling in your sleep," said a voice in her ear; and opening her eyes, there was Mamma bending over her, and morning sunshine streaming into the room.

"Are they all gone? Did you hear the bells? Wasn't it splendid?" she asked, rubbing her eyes, and looking about her for the pretty child who was so real and sweet.

"You have been dreaming at a great rate—talking in your sleep, laughing, and clapping your hands as if you were cheering someone. Tell me what was so splendid," said mamma, smoothing the tumbled hair and lifting up the sleepy head.

Then, while she was being dressed, Effie told her dream, and Nursey thought it very wonderful; but Mamma smiled to see how curiously things the child had thought, read, heard, and seen through the day were mixed up in her sleep.

"The spirit said I could work lovely miracles if I tried; but I don't know how to begin, for I have no magic candle to make feasts appear, and light up groves of Christmas trees, as he did," said Effie, sorrowfully.

"Yes, you have. We will do it! we will do it!" And clapping her hands, Mamma suddenly began to dance all over the room as if she had lost her wits.

"How? how? You must tell me, Mamma," cried Effie, dancing after her, and ready to believe anything possible when she remembered the adventures of the past night.

"I've got it! I've got it!—the new idea. A splendid one, if I can only carry it out!" And Mamma waltzed the little girl round till her curls flew wildly in the air, while Nursey laughed as if she would die.

"Tell me! tell me!" shrieked Effie. "No, no; it is a surprise—a grand surprise for Christmas day!" sung Mamma, evidently charmed with her happy thought. "Now, come to breakfast; for we must work like bees if we want to play spirits tomorrow. You and Nursey will go out shopping, and get heaps of things, while I arrange matters behind the scenes."

They were running downstairs as Mamma spoke, and Effie called out breathlessly—

"It won't be a surprise; for I know you are going to ask some poor children here, and have a tree or something. It won't be like my dream; for they had ever so many trees, and more children than we can find anywhere."

"There will be no tree, no party, no dinner, in this house at all, and no presents for you. Won't that be a surprise?" And Mamma laughed at Effie's bewildered face.

"Do it. I shall like it, I think; and I won't ask any questions, so it will all burst upon me when the time comes," she said; and she ate her breakfast thoughtfully, for this really would be a new sort of Christmas.

All that morning Effie trotted after Nursey in and out of shops, buying dozens of barking dogs, woolly lambs, and squeaking birds; tiny tea-sets, gay picture-books, mittens and hoods, dolls and candy. Parcel after parcel was sent home; but when Effie returned she saw no trace of them, though she peeped everywhere. Nursey chuckled, but wouldn't give a hint, and went out again in the afternoon with a long list of more things to buy; while Effie wandered forlornly about the house, missing the usual merry stir that went before the Christmas dinner and the evening fun.

As for Mamma, she was quite invisible all day, and came in at night so tired that she could only lie on the sofa to rest, smiling as if some very pleasant thought made her happy in spite of weariness.

"Is the surprise going on all right?" asked Effie, anxiously; for it seemed an immense time to wait till another evening came.

"Beautifully! better than I expected; for several of my good friends are helping, or I couldn't have done it as I wish. I know you will like it, dear, and long remember this new way of making Christmas merry."

Mamma gave her a very tender kiss, and Effie went to bed.

The next day was a very strange one; for when she woke there was no stocking to examine, no pile of gifts under her napkin, no one said "Merry Christmas!" to her, and the dinner was just as usual to her. Mamma vanished again, and Nursey kept wiping her eyes and saying: "The dear things! It's the prettiest idea I ever heard of. No one but your blessed Ma could have done it."

"Do stop, Nursey, or I shall go crazy because I don't know the secret!" cried Effie, more than once; and she kept her eye on the clock, for at seven in the evening the surprise was to come off.

The longed-for hour arrived at last, and the child was too excited to ask questions when Nurse put on her cloak and hood, led her to the carriage, and they drove away, leaving their house the one dark and silent one in the row.

"I feel like the girls in the fairy tales who are led off to strange places and see fine things," said Effie, in a whisper, as they jingled through the gay streets.

"Ah, my deary, it *is* like a fairy tale, I do assure you, and you *will* see finer things than most children will tonight. Steady, now, and do just as I tell you, and don't say one word whatever you see," answered Nursey, quite quivering with excitement as she patted a large box in her lap, and nodded and laughed with twinkling eyes.

They drove into a dark yard, and Effie was led through a back door to a little room, where Nurse coolly proceeded to take off not only her cloak and hood, but her dress and shoes also. Effie stared and bit her lips, but kept still until out of the box came a little white fur coat and boots, a wreath of holly leaves and berries, and a candle with a frill of gold paper round it. A long "Oh!" escaped her then; and when she was dressed and saw herself in the glass, she started back, exclaiming, "Why, Nursey, I look like the spirit in my dream!"

"So you do; and that's the part you are to play, my pretty! Now wait while I blind your eyes and put you in your place."

"Shall I be afraid?" whispered Effie, full of wonder; for as they went out she heard the sound of many voices, the tramp of many feet, and, in spite of the bandage, was sure a great light shone upon her when she stopped.

"You needn't be; I shall stand close by, and your ma will be there."

After the handkerchief was tied about her eyes, Nurse led Effie up some steps, and placed her on a high platform, where something like leaves touched her head, and the soft snap of lamps seemed to fill the air.

Music began as soon as Nurse clapped her hands, the voices outside sounded nearer, and the tramp was evidently coming up the stairs.

"Now, my precious, look and see how you and your dear ma have made a merry Christmas for them that needed it!"

Off went the bandage; and for a minute Effie really did think she was asleep again, for she actually stood in "a grove of Christmas trees," all gay and shining as in her vision. Twelve on a side, in two rows down the room, stood the little pines, each on its low table; and behind Effie a taller one rose to the roof, hung with wreaths of popcorn, apples, oranges, horns of candy, and cakes of all sorts, from sugary hearts to gingerbread Jumbos. On the smaller trees she saw many of her own discarded toys and those Nursey bought, as well as heaps that seemed to have rained down straight from that delightful Christmas country where she felt as if she was again.

"How splendid! Who is it for? What is that noise? Where is Mamma?" cried Effie, pale with pleasure and surprise, as she stood looking down the brilliant little street from her high place.

Before Nurse could answer, the doors at the lower end flew open, and in marched twenty-four little blue-gowned orphan girls, singing sweetly, until amazement changed the song to cries of joy and wonder as the shining spectacle appeared. While they stood staring with round eyes at the wilderness of pretty things about them, Mamma stepped up beside Effie, and holding her hand fast to give her courage, told the story of the dream in a few simple words, ending in this way:

"So my little girl wanted to be a Christmas spirit too, and make this a happy day for those who had not as many pleasures and comforts as she has. She likes surprises, and we planned this for you all. She shall play the good fairy, and give each of you something from this tree, after which everyone will find her own name on a small tree, and can go to enjoy it in her own way. March by, my dears, and let us fill your hands."

Nobody told them to do it, but all the hands were clapped heartily before a single child stirred; then one by one they came to look up wonderingly at the pretty giver of the feast as she leaned down to offer them great yellow oranges, red apples, bunches of grapes, bonbons, and cakes, till all were gone, and a double row of smiling faces turned toward her as the children filed back to their places in the orderly way they had been taught.

Then each was led to her own tree by the good ladies who had helped mamma with all their hearts; and the happy hubbub that arose would have satisfied even Santa Claus himself—shrieks of joy, dances of delight, laughter and tears (for some tender little things could not bear so much pleasure at once, and sobbed with mouths full of candy and hands full of toys). How they ran to show one another the new treasures! how they peeped and tasted, pulled and pinched, until the air was full of queer noises, the floor covered with papers, and the little trees left bare of all but candles!

"I don't think heaven can be any gooder than this," sighed one small girl, as she looked about her in a blissful maze, holding her full apron with one hand, while she luxuriously carried sugar-plums to her mouth with the other.

"Is that a truly angel up there?" asked another, fascinated by the little white figure with the wreath on its shining hair, who in some mysterious way had been the cause of all this merry-making.

"I wish I dared to go and kiss her for this splendid party," said a lame child, leaning on her crutch, as she stood near the steps, wondering how it seemed to sit in a mother's lap, as Effie was doing, while she watched the happy scene before her.

Effie heard her, and remembering Tiny Tim, ran down and put her arms about the pale child, kissing the wistful face, as she said sweetly, "You may; but Mamma deserves the thanks. She did it all; I only dreamed about it."

Lame Katy felt as if "a truly angel" was embracing her, and could only stammer out her thanks, while the other children ran to see the pretty spirit, and touch her soft dress, until she stood in a crowd of blue gowns laughing as they held up their gifts for her to see and admire.

Mamma leaned down and whispered one word to the older girls; and suddenly they all took hands to dance round Effie, singing as they skipped.

It was a pretty sight, and the ladies found it hard to break up the happy revel; but it was late for small people, and too much fun is a mistake. So the girls fell into line, and marched before Effie and Mamma again, to say goodnight with such grateful little faces that the eyes of those who looked grew dim with tears. Mamma kissed everyone; and many a hungry childish heart felt as if the touch of those tender lips was their best gift. Effie shook so many small hands that her own tingled; and when Katy came she pressed a small doll into Effie's hand, whispering, "You didn't have a single present, and we had lots. Do keep that; it's the prettiest thing I got."

"I will," answered Effie, and held it fast until the last smiling face was gone, the surprise all over, and she safe in her own bed, too tired and happy for anything but sleep.

"Mamma, it was a beautiful surprise, and I thank you so much! I don't see how you did it; but I like it best of all the Christmases I ever had, and mean to make one every year. I had my splendid big present, and here is the dear little one to keep for love of poor Katy; so even that part of my wish came true."

And Effie fell asleep with a happy smile on her lips, her one humble gift still in her hand, and a new love for Christmas in her heart that never changed through a long life spent in doing good.

The Life and Adventures of Santa Claus

L. Frank Baum

PART ONE: YOUTH

CHAPTER I. BURZEE

Have you heard of the great Forest of Burzee? Nurse used to sing of it when I was a child. She sang of the big tree-trunks, standing close together, with their roots intertwining below the earth and their branches intertwining above it; of their rough coating of bark and queer, gnarled limbs; of the bushy foliage that roofed the entire forest, save where the sunbeams found a path through which to touch the ground in little spots and to cast weird and curious shadows over the mosses, the lichens and the drifts of dried leaves.

The Forest of Burzee is mighty and grand and awesome to those who steal beneath its shade. Coming from the sunlit meadows into its mazes it seems at first gloomy, then pleasant, and afterward filled with never-ending delights.

For hundreds of years it has flourished in all its magnificence, the silence of its inclosure unbroken save by the chirp of busy chipmunks, the growl of wild beasts and the songs of birds.

Yet Burzee has its inhabitants—for all this. Nature peopled it in the beginning with Fairies, Knooks, Ryls and Nymphs. As long as the Forest stands it will be a home, a refuge and a playground to these sweet immortals, who revel undisturbed in its depths.

Civilization has never yet reached Burzee. Will it ever, I wonder?

CHAPTER II. THE CHILD OF THE FOREST

Once, so long ago our great-grandfathers could scarcely have heard it mentioned, there lived within the great Forest of Burzee a wood-nymph named Necile. She was closely related to the mighty Queen Zurline, and her home was beneath the shade of a widespreading oak. Once every year, on Budding Day, when the trees put forth their new buds, Necile held the Golden Chalice of Ak to the lips of the Queen, who drank therefrom to the prosperity of the Forest.

So you see she was a nymph of some importance, and, moreover, it is said she was highly regarded because of her beauty and grace.

When she was created she could not have told; Queen Zurline could not have told; the great Ak himself could not have told. It was long ago when the world was new and nymphs were needed to guard the forests and to minister to the wants of the young trees. Then, on some day not remembered, Necile sprang into being; radiant, lovely, straight and slim as the sapling she was created to guard.

Her hair was the color that lines a chestnut-bur; her eyes were blue in the sunlight and purple in the shade; her cheeks bloomed with the faint pink that edges the clouds at sunset; her lips were full red, pouting and sweet. For costume she adopted oak-leaf green; all the wood-nymphs dress in that color and know no other so desirable. Her dainty feet were sandal-clad, while her head remained bare of covering other than her silken tresses.

Necile's duties were few and simple. She kept hurtful weeds from growing beneath her trees and sapping the earth-food required by her charges. She frightened away the Gadgols, who took evil delight in flying against the tree-trunks and wounding them so that they drooped and died from the poisonous contact. In dry seasons she carried water from the brooks and pools and moistened the roots of her thirsty dependents.

That was in the beginning. The weeds had now learned to avoid the forests where wood-nymphs dwelt; the loathsome Gadgols no longer dared come nigh; the trees had become old and sturdy and could bear the drought better than when fresh-sprouted. So Necile's duties were lessened, and time grew laggard, while succeeding years became more tiresome and uneventful than the nymph's joyous spirit loved.

Truly the forest-dwellers did not lack amusement. Each full moon they danced in the Royal Circle of the Queen. There were also the Feast of Nuts, the Jubilee of Autumn Tintings, the solemn ceremony of Leaf Shedding and the revelry of Budding Day. But these periods of enjoyment were far apart, and left many weary hours between.

That a wood-nymph should grow discontented was not thought of by Necile's sisters. It came upon her only after many years of brooding. But when once she had settled in her mind that life was irksome she had no patience with her condition, and longed to do something of real interest and to pass her days in ways hitherto undreamed of by forest nymphs. The Law of the Forest alone restrained her from going forth in search of adventure.

While this mood lay heavy upon pretty Necile it chanced that the great Ak visited the Forest of Burzee and allowed the wood-nymphs as was their wont—to lie at his feet and listen to the words of wisdom that fell from his lips. Ak is the

Master Woodsman of the world; he sees everything, and knows more than the sons of men.

That night he held the Queen's hand, for he loved the nymphs as a father loves his children; and Necile lay at his feet with many of her sisters and earnestly harkened as he spoke.

"We live so happily, my fair ones, in our forest glades," said Ak, stroking his grizzled beard thoughtfully, "that we know nothing of the sorrow and misery that fall to the lot of those poor mortals who inhabit the open spaces of the earth. They are not of our race, it is true, yet compassion well befits beings so fairly favored as ourselves. Often as I pass by the dwelling of some suffering mortal I am tempted to stop and banish the poor thing's misery. Yet suffering, in moderation, is the natural lot of mortals, and it is not our place to interfere with the laws of Nature."

"Nevertheless," said the fair Queen, nodding her golden head at the Master Woodsman, "it would not be a vain guess that Ak has often assisted these hapless mortals."

Ak smiled.

"Sometimes," he replied, "when they are very young—'children,' the mortals call them—I have stopped to rescue them from misery. The men and women I dare not interfere with; they must bear the burdens Nature has imposed upon them. But the helpless infants, the innocent children of men, have a right to be happy until they become full-grown and able to bear the trials of humanity. So I feel I am justified in assisting them. Not long ago—a year, maybe—I found four poor children huddled in a wooden hut, slowly freezing to death. Their parents had gone to a neighboring village for food, and had left a fire to warm their little ones while they were absent. But a storm arose and drifted the snow in their path, so they were long on the road. Meantime the fire went out and the frost crept into the bones of the waiting children."

"Poor things!" murmured the Queen softly. "What did you do?"

"I called Nelko, bidding him fetch wood from my forests and breathe upon it until the fire blazed again and warmed the little room where the children lay. Then they ceased shivering and fell asleep until their parents came."

"I am glad you did thus," said the good Queen, beaming upon the Master; and Necile, who had eagerly listened to every word, echoed in a whisper: "I, too, am glad!"

"And this very night," continued Ak, "as I came to the edge of Burzee I heard a feeble cry, which I judged came from a human infant. I looked about me and found, close to the forest, a helpless babe, lying quite naked upon the grasses and wailing piteously. Not far away, screened by the forest, crouched Shiegra, the lioness, intent upon devouring the infant for her evening meal."

"And what did you do, Ak?" asked the Queen, breathlessly.

"Not much, being in a hurry to greet my nymphs. But I commanded Shiegra to lie close to the babe, and to give it her milk to quiet its hunger. And I told her to send word throughout the forest, to all beasts and reptiles, that the child should not be harmed."

"I am glad you did thus," said the good Queen again, in a tone of relief; but this time Necile did not echo her words, for the nymph, filled with a strange resolve, had suddenly stolen away from the group.

Swiftly her lithe form darted through the forest paths until she reached the edge of mighty Burzee, when she paused to gaze curiously about her. Never until now had she ventured so far, for the Law of the Forest had placed the nymphs in its inmost depths.

Necile knew she was breaking the Law, but the thought did not give pause to her dainty feet. She had decided to see with her own eyes this infant Ak had told of, for she had never yet beheld a child of man. All the immortals are full-grown; there are no children among them. Peering through the trees Necile saw the child lying on the grass. But now it was sweetly sleeping, having been comforted by the milk drawn from Shiegra. It was not old enough to know what peril means; if it did not feel hunger it was content.

Softly the nymph stole to the side of the babe and knelt upon the sward, her long robe of rose leaf color spreading about her like a gossamer cloud. Her lovely countenance expressed curiosity and surprise, but, most of all, a tender, womanly pity. The babe was newborn, chubby and pink. It was entirely helpless. While the nymph gazed the infant opened its eyes, smiled upon her, and stretched out two dimpled arms. In another instant Necile had caught it to her breast and was hurrying with it through the forest paths.

CHAPTER III. THE ADOPTION

The Master Woodsman suddenly rose, with knitted brows. "There is a strange presence in the Forest," he declared. Then the Queen and her nymphs turned and saw standing before them Necile, with the sleeping infant clasped tightly in her arms and a defiant look in her deep blue eyes.

And thus for a moment they remained, the nymphs filled with surprise and consternation, but the brow of the Master Woodsman gradually clearing as he gazed intently upon the beautiful immortal who had wilfully broken the Law. Then the great Ak, to the wonder of all, laid his hand softly on Necile's flowing locks and kissed her on her fair forehead.

"For the first time within my knowledge," said he, gently, "a nymph has defied me and my laws; yet in my heart can I find no word of chiding. What is your desire, Necile?"

"Let me keep the child!" she answered, beginning to tremble and falling on her knees in supplication.

"Here, in the Forest of Burzee, where the human race has never yet penetrated?" questioned Ak.

"Here, in the Forest of Burzee," replied the nymph, boldly. "It is my home, and I am weary for lack of occupation. Let me care for the babe! See how weak and helpless it is. Surely it can not harm Burzee nor the Master Woodsman of the World!"

"But the Law, child, the Law!" cried Ak, sternly.

"The Law is made by the Master Woodsman," returned Necile; "if he bids me care for the babe he himself has saved from death, who in all the world dare oppose me?" Queen Zurline, who had listened intently to this conversation, clapped her pretty hands gleefully at the nymph's answer.

"You are fairly trapped, O Ak!" she exclaimed, laughing. "Now, I pray you, give heed to Necile's petition."

The Woodsman, as was his habit when in thought, stroked his grizzled beard slowly. Then he said:

"She shall keep the babe, and I will give it my protection. But I warn you all that as this is the first time I have relaxed the Law, so shall it be the last time. Never more, to the end of the World, shall a mortal be adopted by an immortal. Otherwise would we abandon our happy existence for one of trouble and anxiety. Good night, my nymphs!"

Then Ak was gone from their midst, and Necile hurried away to her bower to rejoice over her new-found treasure.

CHAPTER IV. CLAUS

Another day found Necile's bower the most popular place in the Forest. The nymphs clustered around her and the child that lay asleep in her lap, with expressions of curiosity and delight. Nor were they wanting in praises for the great Ak's kindness in allowing Necile to keep the babe and to care for it. Even the Queen came to peer into the innocent childish face and to hold a helpless, chubby fist in her own fair hand.

"What shall we call him, Necile?" she asked, smiling. "He must have a name, you know."

"Let him be called Claus," answered Necile, "for that means 'a little one.'"

"Rather let him be called Neclaus,"* returned the Queen, "for that will mean 'Necile's little one.'"

The nymphs clapped their hands in delight, and Neclaus became the infant's name, although Necile loved best to call him Claus, and in afterdays many of her sisters followed her example.

Necile gathered the softest moss in all the forest for Claus to lie upon, and she made his bed in her own bower. Of food the infant had no lack. The nymphs searched the forest for bell-udders, which grow upon the goa-tree and when opened are found to be filled with sweet milk. And the soft-eyed does willingly gave a share of their milk to support the little stranger, while Shiegra, the lioness, often crept stealthily into Necile's bower and purred softly as she lay beside the babe and fed it.

So the little one flourished and grew big and sturdy day by day, while Necile taught him to speak and to walk and to play.

His thoughts and words were sweet and gentle, for the nymphs knew no evil and their hearts were pure and loving. He became the pet of the forest, for Ak's decree had forbidden beast or reptile to molest him, and he walked fearlessly wherever his will guided him.

Presently the news reached the other immortals that the nymphs of Burzee had adopted a human infant, and that the act had been sanctioned by the great Ak. Therefore many of them came to visit the little stranger, looking upon him with much interest. First the Ryls, who are first cousins to the wood-nymphs, although so differently formed. For the Ryls are required to watch over the flowers and plants, as the nymphs watch over the forest trees. They search the wide world for the food required by the roots of the flowering plants, while the brilliant colors possessed by the full-blown flowers are due to the dyes placed in the soil by the Ryls, which are drawn through the little veins in the roots and the body of the plants, as they reach maturity. The Ryls are a busy people, for their flowers bloom and fade continually, but they are merry and light-hearted and are very popular with the other immortals.

Next came the Knooks, whose duty it is to watch over the beasts of the world, both gentle and wild. The Knooks have a hard time of it, since many of the beasts are ungovernable and rebel against restraint. But they know how to manage them, after all, and you will find that certain laws of the Knooks are obeyed by even the most ferocious animals. Their anxieties make the Knooks look old and worn and crooked, and their natures are a bit rough from associating with wild creatures continually; yet they are most useful to humanity and to the world in general, as

---

* Some people have spelled this name Nicklaus and others Nicolas, which is the reason that Santa Claus is still known in some lands as St. Nicolas. But, of course, Neclaus is his right name, and Claus the nickname given him by his adopted mother, the fair nymph Necile.

their laws are the only laws the forest beasts recognize except those of the Master Woodsman.

Then there were the Fairies, the guardians of mankind, who were much interested in the adoption of Claus because their own laws forbade them to become familiar with their human charges. There are instances on record where the Fairies have shown themselves to human beings, and have even conversed with them; but they are supposed to guard the lives of mankind unseen and unknown, and if they favor some people more than others it is because these have won such distinction fairly, as the Fairies are very just and impartial. But the idea of adopting a child of men had never occurred to them because it was in every way opposed to their laws; so their curiosity was intense to behold the little stranger adopted by Necile and her sister nymphs.

Claus looked upon the immortals who thronged around him with fearless eyes and smiling lips. He rode laughingly upon the shoulders of the merry Ryls; he mischievously pulled the gray beards of the low-browed Knooks; he rested his curly head confidently upon the dainty bosom of the Fairy Queen herself. And the Ryls loved the sound of his laughter; the Knooks loved his courage; the Fairies loved his innocence.

The boy made friends of them all, and learned to know their laws intimately. No forest flower was trampled beneath his feet, lest the friendly Ryls should be grieved. He never interfered with the beasts of the forest, lest his friends the Knooks should become angry. The Fairies he loved dearly, but, knowing nothing of mankind, he could not understand that he was the only one of his race admitted to friendly intercourse with them.

Indeed, Claus came to consider that he alone, of all the forest people, had no like nor fellow. To him the forest was the world. He had no idea that millions of toiling, striving human creatures existed.

And he was happy and content.

CHAPTER V. THE MASTER WOODSMAN

Years pass swiftly in Burzee, for the nymphs have no need to regard time in any way. Even centuries make no change in the dainty creatures; ever and ever they remain the same, immortal and unchanging.

Claus, however, being mortal, grew to manhood day by day. Necile was disturbed, presently, to find him too big to lie in her lap, and he had a desire for other food than milk. His stout legs carried him far into Burzee's heart, where he gathered supplies of nuts and berries, as well as several sweet and wholesome roots, which suited his stomach better than the belludders. He sought Necile's bower less frequently, till finally it became his custom to return thither only to sleep.

The nymph, who had come to love him dearly, was puzzled to comprehend the changed nature of her charge, and unconsciously altered her own mode of life to conform to his whims. She followed him readily through the forest paths, as did many of her sister nymphs, explaining as they walked all the mysteries of the gigantic wood and the habits and nature of the living things which dwelt beneath its shade.

The language of the beasts became clear to little Claus; but he never could understand their sulky and morose tempers. Only the squirrels, the mice and the rabbits seemed to possess cheerful and merry natures; yet would the boy laugh when the panther growled, and stroke the bear's glossy coat while the creature snarled and bared its teeth menacingly. The growls and snarls were not for Claus, he well knew, so what did they matter?

He could sing the songs of the bees, recite the poetry of the wood-flowers and relate the history of every blinking owl in Burzee. He helped the Ryls to feed their plants and the Knooks to keep order among the animals. The little immortals regarded him as a privileged person, being especially protected by Queen Zurline and her nymphs and favored by the great Ak himself.

One day the Master Woodsman came back to the forest of Burzee. He had visited, in turn, all his forests throughout the world, and they were many and broad.

Not until he entered the glade where the Queen and her nymphs were assembled to greet him did Ak remember the child he had permitted Necile to adopt. Then he found, sitting familiarly in the circle of lovely immortals, a broad-shouldered, stalwart youth, who, when erect, stood fully as high as the shoulder of the Master himself.

Ak paused, silent and frowning, to bend his piercing gaze upon Claus. The clear eyes met his own steadfastly, and the Woodsman gave a sigh of relief as he marked their placid depths and read the youth's brave and innocent heart. Nevertheless, as Ak sat beside the fair Queen, and the golden chalice, filled with rare nectar, passed from lip to lip, the Master Woodsman was strangely silent and reserved, and stroked his beard many times with a thoughtful motion.

With morning he called Claus aside, in kindly fashion, saying:

"Bid good by, for a time, to Necile and her sisters; for you shall accompany me on my journey through the world."

The venture pleased Claus, who knew well the honor of being companion of the Master Woodsman of the world. But Necile wept for the first time in her life, and clung to the boy's neck as if she could not bear to let him go. The nymph who had mothered this sturdy youth was still as dainty, as charming and beautiful as when she had dared to face Ak with the babe clasped to her breast; nor was her love less great. Ak beheld the two clinging together, seemingly as brother and sister to one another, and again he wore his thoughtful look.

CHAPTER VI. CLAUS DISCOVERS HUMANITY

Taking Claus to a small clearing in the forest, the Master said: "Place your hand upon my girdle and hold fast while we journey through the air; for now shall we encircle the world and look upon many of the haunts of those men from whom you are descended."

These words caused Claus to marvel, for until now he had thought himself the only one of his kind upon the earth; yet in silence he grasped firmly the girdle of the great Ak, his astonishment forbidding speech.

Then the vast forest of Burzee seemed to fall away from their feet, and the youth found himself passing swiftly through the air at a great height.

Ere long there were spires beneath them, while buildings of many shapes and colors met their downward view. It was a city of men, and Ak, pausing to descend, led Claus to its inclosure. Said the Master:

"So long as you hold fast to my girdle you will remain unseen by all mankind, though seeing clearly yourself. To release your grasp will be to separate yourself forever from me and your home in Burzee."

One of the first laws of the Forest is obedience, and Claus had no thought of disobeying the Master's wish. He clung fast to the girdle and remained invisible.

Thereafter with each moment passed in the city the youth's wonder grew. He, who had supposed himself created differently from all others, now found the earth swarming with creatures of his own kind.

"Indeed," said Ak, "the immortals are few; but the mortals are many."

Claus looked earnestly upon his fellows. There were sad faces, gay and reckless faces, pleasant faces, anxious faces and kindly faces, all mingled in puzzling disorder. Some worked at tedious tasks; some strutted in impudent conceit; some were thoughtful and grave while others seemed happy and content. Men of many natures were there, as everywhere, and Claus found much to please him and much to make him sad.

But especially he noted the children—first curiously, then eagerly, then lovingly. Ragged little ones rolled in the dust of the streets, playing with scraps and pebbles. Other children, gaily dressed, were propped upon cushions and fed with sugar-plums. Yet the children of the rich were not happier than those playing with the dust and pebbles, it seemed to Claus.

"Childhood is the time of man's greatest content," said Ak, following the youth's thoughts. "'Tis during these years of innocent pleasure that the little ones are most free from care."

"Tell me," said Claus, "why do not all these babies fare alike?"

"Because they are born in both cottage and palace," returned the Master. "The difference in the wealth of the parents determines the lot of the child. Some are carefully tended and clothed in silks and dainty linen; others are neglected and covered with rags."

"Yet all seem equally fair and sweet," said Claus, thoughtfully.

"While they are babes—yes," agreed Ak. "Their joy is in being alive, and they do not stop to think. In after years the doom of mankind overtakes them, and they find they must struggle and worry, work and fret, to gain the wealth that is so dear to the hearts of men. Such things are unknown in the Forest where you were reared." Claus was silent a moment. Then he asked:

"Why was I reared in the forest, among those who are not of my race?"

Then Ak, in gentle voice, told him the story of his babyhood: how he had been abandoned at the forest's edge and left a prey to wild beasts, and how the loving nymph Necile had rescued him and brought him to manhood under the protection of the immortals.

"Yet I am not of them," said Claus, musingly.

"You are not of them," returned the Woodsman. "The nymph who cared for you as a mother seems now like a sister to you; by and by, when you grow old and gray, she will seem like a daughter. Yet another brief span and you will be but a memory, while she remains Necile."

"Then why, if man must perish, is he born?" demanded the boy.

"Everything perishes except the world itself and its keepers," answered Ak. "But while life lasts everything on earth has its use. The wise seek ways to be helpful to the world, for the helpful ones are sure to live again."

Much of this Claus failed to understand fully, but a longing seized him to become helpful to his fellows, and he remained grave and thoughtful while they resumed their journey.

They visited many dwellings of men in many parts of the world, watching farmers toil in the fields, warriors dash into cruel fray, and merchants exchange their goods for bits of white and yellow metal. And everywhere the eyes of Claus sought out the children in love and pity, for the thought of his own helpless babyhood was strong within him and he yearned to give help to the innocent little ones of his race even as he had been succored by the kindly nymph.

Day by day the Master Woodsman and his pupil traversed the earth, Ak speaking but seldom to the youth who clung steadfastly to his girdle, but guiding him into all places where he might become familiar with the lives of human beings.

And at last they returned to the grand old Forest of Burzee, where the Master set Claus down within the circle of nymphs, among whom the pretty Necile anxiously awaited him.

The brow of the great Ak was now calm and peaceful; but the brow of Claus had become lined with deep thought. Necile sighed at the change in her foster-son, who until now had been ever joyous and smiling, and the thought came to her that never again would the life of the boy be the same as before this eventful journey with the Master.

CHAPTER VII. CLAUS LEAVES THE FOREST

When good Queen Zurline had touched the golden chalice with her fair lips and it had passed around the circle in honor of the travelers' return, the Master Woodsman of the World, who had not yet spoken, turned his gaze frankly upon Claus and said:

"Well?"

The boy understood, and rose slowly to his feet beside Necile. Once only his eyes passed around the familiar circle of nymphs, every one of whom he remembered as a loving comrade; but tears came unbidden to dim his sight, so he gazed thereafter steadfastly at the Master.

"I have been ignorant," said he, simply, "until the great Ak in his kindness taught me who and what I am. You, who live so sweetly in your forest bowers, ever fair and youthful and innocent, are no fit comrades for a son of humanity. For I have looked upon man, finding him doomed to live for a brief space upon earth, to toil for the things he needs, to fade into old age, and then to pass away as the leaves in autumn. Yet every man has his mission, which is to leave the world better, in some way, than he found it. I am of the race of men, and man's lot is my lot. For your tender care of the poor, forsaken babe you adopted, as well as for your loving comradeship during my boyhood, my heart will ever overflow with gratitude. My foster-mother," here he stopped and kissed Necile's white forehead, "I shall love and cherish while life lasts. But I must leave you, to take my part in the endless struggle to which humanity is doomed, and to live my life in my own way."

"What will you do?" asked the Queen, gravely.

"I must devote myself to the care of the children of mankind, and try to make them happy," he answered. "Since your own tender care of a babe brought to me happiness and strength, it is just and right that I devote my life to the pleasure of other babes. Thus will the memory of the loving nymph Necile be planted within the hearts of thousands of my race for many years to come, and her kindly act be recounted in song and in story while the world shall last. Have I spoken well, O Master?"

"You have spoken well," returned Ak, and rising to his feet he continued: "Yet one thing must not be forgotten. Having been adopted as the child of the Forest, and the playfellow of the nymphs, you have gained a distinction which forever separates you from your kind. Therefore, when you go forth into the world of men you shall retain the protection of the Forest, and the powers you now enjoy will remain with you to assist you in your labors. In any need you may call upon the Nymphs, the Ryls, the Knooks and the Fairies, and they will serve you gladly. I, the Master Woodsman of the World, have said it, and my Word is the Law!"

Claus looked upon Ak with grateful eyes.

"This will make me mighty among men," he replied. "Protected by these kind friends I may be able to make thousands of little children happy. I will try very hard to do my duty, and I know the Forest people will give me their sympathy and help."

"We will!" said the Fairy Queen, earnestly.

"We will!" cried the merry Ryls, laughing.

"We will!" shouted the crooked Knooks, scowling.

"We will!" exclaimed the sweet nymphs, proudly. But Necile said nothing. She only folded Claus in her arms and kissed him tenderly.

"The world is big," continued the boy, turning again to his loyal friends, "but men are everywhere. I shall begin my work near my friends, so that if I meet with misfortune I can come to the Forest for counsel or help."

With that he gave them all a loving look and turned away. There was no need to say good by, by for him the sweet, wild life of the Forest was over. He went forth bravely to meet his doom—the doom of the race of man—the necessity to worry and work.

But Ak, who knew the boy's heart, was merciful and guided his steps.

Coming through Burzee to its eastern edge Claus reached the Laughing Valley of Hohaho. On each side were rolling green hills, and a brook wandered midway between them to wind afar off beyond the valley. At his back was the grim Forest; at the far end of the valley a broad plain. The eyes of the young man, which had until now reflected his grave thoughts, became brighter as he stood silent, looking out upon the Laughing Valley. Then on a sudden his eyes twinkled, as stars do on a still night, and grew merry and wide.

For at his feet the cowslips and daisies smiled on him in friendly regard; the breeze whistled gaily as it passed by and fluttered the locks on his forehead; the brook laughed joyously as it leaped over the pebbles and swept around the green curves of its banks; the bees sang sweet songs as they flew from dandelion to daffodil; the beetles chirruped happily in the long grass, and the sunbeams glinted pleasantly over all the scene.

"Here," cried Claus, stretching out his arms as if to embrace the Valley, "will I make my home!"

That was many, many years ago. It has been his home ever since. It is his home now.

PART TWO: MANHOOD

CHAPTER I. THE LAUGHING VALLEY

When Claus came the Valley was empty save for the grass, the brook, the wildflowers, the bees and the butterflies. If he would make his home here and live after the fashion of men he must have a house. This puzzled him at first, but while he stood smiling in the sunshine he suddenly found beside him old Nelko, the servant of the Master Woodsman. Nelko bore an ax, strong and broad, with blade that gleamed like burnished silver. This he placed in the young man's hand, then disappeared without a word.

Claus understood, and turning to the Forest's edge he selected a number of fallen tree-trunks, which he began to clear of their dead branches. He would not cut into a living tree. His life among the nymphs who guarded the Forest had taught him that a live tree is sacred, being a created thing endowed with feeling. But with the dead and fallen trees it was different. They had fulfilled their destiny, as active members of the Forest community, and now it was fitting that their remains should minister to the needs of man.

The ax bit deep into the logs at every stroke. It seemed to have a force of its own, and Claus had but to swing and guide it.

When shadows began creeping over the green hills to lie in the Valley overnight, the young man had chopped many logs into equal lengths and proper shapes for building a house such as he had seen the poorer classes of men inhabit. Then, resolving to await another day before he tried to fit the logs together, Claus ate some of the sweet roots he well knew how to find, drank deeply from the laughing brook, and lay down to sleep on the grass, first seeking a spot where no flowers grew, lest the weight of his body should crush them.

And while he slumbered and breathed in the perfume of the wondrous Valley the Spirit of Happiness crept into his heart and drove out all terror and care and misgivings. Never more would the face of Claus be clouded with anxieties; never more would the trials of life weigh him down as with a burden. The Laughing Valley had claimed him for its own.

Would that we all might live in that delightful place!—but then, maybe, it would become overcrowded. For ages it had awaited a tenant. Was it chance that led young Claus to make his home in this happy vale? Or may we guess that his thoughtful friends, the immortals, had directed his steps when he wandered away from Burzee to seek a home in the great world?

Certain it is that while the moon peered over the hilltop and flooded with its soft beams the body of the sleeping stranger, the Laughing Valley was filled with the queer, crooked shapes of the friendly Knooks. These people spoke no words, but worked with skill and swiftness. The logs Claus had trimmed with his bright ax were carried to a spot beside the brook and fitted one upon another, and during the night a strong and roomy dwelling was built.

The birds came sweeping into the Valley at daybreak, and their songs, so seldom heard in the deep wood, aroused the stranger. He rubbed the web of sleep from his eyelids and looked around. The house met his gaze.

"I must thank the Knooks for this," said he, gratefully. Then he walked to his dwelling and entered at the doorway. A large room faced him, having a fireplace at the end and a table and bench in the middle. Beside the fireplace was a cupboard. Another doorway was beyond. Claus entered here, also, and saw a smaller room with a bed against the wall and a stool set near a small stand. On the bed were many layers of dried moss brought from the Forest.

"Indeed, it is a palace!" exclaimed the smiling Claus. "I must thank the good Knooks again, for their knowledge of man's needs as well as for their labors in my behalf."

He left his new home with a glad feeling that he was not quite alone in the world, although he had chosen to abandon his Forest life. Friendships are not easily broken, and the immortals are everywhere.

Upon reaching the brook he drank of the pure water, and then sat down on the bank to laugh at the mischievous gambols of the ripples as they pushed one another against rocks or crowded desperately to see which should first reach the turn beyond. And as they raced away he listened to the song they sang:

Rushing, pushing, on we go!
Not a wave may gently flow—
All are too excited.
Ev'ry drop, delighted,
Turns to spray in merry play
As we tumble on our way!

Next Claus searched for roots to eat, while the daffodils turned their little eyes up to him laughingly and lisped their dainty song:

> *Blooming fairly, growing rarely,*
> *Never flowerets were so gay!*
> *Perfume breathing, joy bequeathing,*
> *As our colors we display.*

It made Claus laugh to hear the little things voice their happiness as they nodded gracefully on their stems. But another strain caught his ear as the sunbeams fell gently across his face and whispered:

> *Here is gladness, that our rays*
> *Warm the valley through the days;*
> *Here is happiness, to give*
> *Comfort unto all who live!*

"Yes!" cried Claus in answer, "there is happiness and joy in all things here. The Laughing Valley is a valley of peace and good-will."

He passed the day talking with the ants and beetles and exchanging jokes with the light-hearted butterflies. And at night he lay on his bed of soft moss and slept soundly.

Then came the Fairies, merry but noiseless, bringing skillets and pots and dishes and pans and all the tools necessary to prepare food and to comfort a mortal. With these they filled cupboard and fireplace, finally placing a stout suit of wool clothing on the stool by the bedside.

When Claus awoke he rubbed his eyes again, and laughed, and spoke aloud his thanks to the Fairies and the Master Woodsman who had sent them. With eager joy he examined all his new possessions, wondering what some might be used for. But, in the days when he had clung to the girdle of the great Ak and visited the cities of men, his eyes had been quick to note all the manners and customs of the race to which he belonged; so he guessed from the gifts brought by the Fairies that the Master expected him hereafter to live in the fashion of his fellow-creatures.

"Which means that I must plow the earth and plant corn," he reflected; "so that when winter comes I shall have garnered food in plenty."

But, as he stood in the grassy Valley, he saw that to turn up the earth in furrows would be to destroy hundreds of pretty, helpless flowers, as well as thousands of the tender blades of grass. And this he could not bear to do.

Therefore he stretched out his arms and uttered a peculiar whistle he had learned in the Forest, afterward crying:

"Ryls of the Field Flowers—come to me!"

Instantly a dozen of the queer little Ryls were squatting upon the ground before him, and they nodded to him in cheerful greeting.

Claus gazed upon them earnestly.

"Your brothers of the Forest," he said, "I have known and loved many years. I shall love you, also, when we have become friends. To me the laws of the Ryls, whether those of the Forest or of the field, are sacred. I have never wilfully destroyed one of the flowers you tend so carefully; but I must plant grain to use for food during the cold winter, and how am I to do this without killing the little creatures that sing to me so prettily of their fragrant blossoms?"

The Yellow Ryl, he who tends the buttercups, made answer:

"Fret not, friend Claus. The great Ak has spoken to us of you. There is better work for you in life than to labor for food, and though, not being of the Forest, Ak has no command over us, nevertheless are we glad to favor one he loves. Live, therefore, to do the good work you are resolved to undertake. We, the Field Ryls, will attend to your food supplies."

After this speech the Ryls were no longer to be seen, and Claus drove from his mind the thought of tilling the earth.

When next he wandered back to his dwelling a bowl of fresh milk stood upon the table; bread was in the cupboard and sweet honey filled a dish beside it. A pretty basket of rosy apples and new-plucked grapes was also awaiting him. He called out "Thanks, my friends!" to the invisible Ryls, and straightway began to eat of the food.

Thereafter, when hungry, he had but to look into the cupboard to find goodly supplies brought by the kindly Ryls. And the Knooks cut and stacked much wood for his fireplace. And the Fairies brought him warm blankets and clothing.

So began his life in the Laughing Valley, with the favor and friendship of the immortals to minister to his every want.

CHAPTER II. HOW CLAUS MADE THE FIRST TOY

Truly our Claus had wisdom, for his good fortune but strengthened his resolve to befriend the little ones of his own race. He knew his plan was approved by the immortals, else they would not have favored him so greatly.

So he began at once to make acquaintance with mankind. He walked through the Valley to the plain beyond, and crossed the plain in many directions to reach the abodes of men. These stood singly or in groups of dwellings called villages, and in nearly all the houses, whether big or little, Claus found children.

The youngsters soon came to know his merry, laughing face and the kind glance of his bright eyes; and the parents, while they regarded the young man with some scorn for loving children more than their elders, were content that the girls and boys had found a playfellow who seemed willing to amuse them.

So the children romped and played games with Claus, and the boys rode upon his shoulders, and the girls nestled in his strong arms, and the babies clung fondly to his knees. Wherever the young man chanced to be, the sound of childish laughter followed him; and to understand this better you must know that children were much neglected in those days and received little attention from their parents, so that it became to them a marvel that so goodly a man as Claus devoted his time to making them happy. And those who knew him were, you may be sure, very happy indeed. The sad faces of the poor and abused grew bright for once; the cripple smiled despite his misfortune; the ailing ones hushed their moans and the grieved ones their cries when their merry friend came nigh to comfort them.

Only at the beautiful palace of the Lord of Lerd and at the frowning castle of the Baron Braun was Claus refused admittance. There were children at both places; but the servants at the palace shut the door in the young stranger's face, and the fierce Baron threatened to hang him from an iron hook on the castle walls. Whereupon Claus sighed and went back to the poorer dwellings where he was welcome.

After a time the winter drew near.

The flowers lived out their lives and faded and disappeared; the beetles burrowed far into the warm earth; the butterflies deserted the meadows; and the voice of the brook grew hoarse, as if it had taken cold.

One day snowflakes filled all the air in the Laughing Valley, dancing boisterously toward the earth and clothing in pure white raiment the roof of Claus's dwelling.

At night Jack Frost rapped at the door.

"Come in!" cried Claus.

"Come out!" answered Jack, "for you have a fire inside."

So Claus came out. He had known Jack Frost in the Forest, and liked the jolly rogue, even while he mistrusted him.

"There will be rare sport for me to-night, Claus!" shouted the sprite. "Isn't this glorious weather? I shall nip scores of noses and ears and toes before daybreak."

"If you love me, Jack, spare the children," begged Claus.

"And why?" asked the other, in surprise.

"They are tender and helpless," answered Claus.

"But I love to nip the tender ones!" declared Jack. "The older ones are tough, and tire my fingers."

"The young ones are weak, and can not fight you," said Claus.

"True," agreed Jack, thoughtfully. "Well, I will not pinch a child this night—if I can resist the temptation," he promised. "Good night, Claus!"

"Good night."

The young man went in and closed the door, and Jack Frost ran on to the nearest village.

Claus threw a log on the fire, which burned up brightly. Beside the hearth sat Blinkie, a big cat give him by Peter the Knook. Her fur was soft and glossy, and she purred never-ending songs of contentment.

"I shall not see the children again soon," said Claus to the cat, who kindly paused in her song to listen. "The winter is upon us, the snow will be deep for many days, and I shall be unable to play with my little friends."

The cat raised a paw and stroked her nose thoughtfully, but made no reply. So long as the fire burned and Claus sat in his easy chair by the hearth she did not mind the weather.

So passed many days and many long evenings. The cupboard was always full, but Claus became weary with having nothing to do more than to feed the fire from the big wood-pile the Knooks had brought him.

One evening he picked up a stick of wood and began to cut it with his sharp knife. He had no thought, at first, except to occupy his time, and he whistled and sang to the cat as he carved away portions of the stick. Puss sat up on her haunches and watched him, listening at the same time to her master's merry whistle, which she loved to hear even more than her own purring songs.

Claus glanced at puss and then at the stick he was whittling, until presently the wood began to have a shape, and the shape was like the head of a cat, with two ears sticking upward.

Claus stopped whistling to laugh, and then both he and the cat looked at the wooden image in some surprise. Then he carved out the eyes and the nose, and rounded the lower part of the head so that it rested upon a neck.

Puss hardly knew what to make of it now, and sat up stiffly, as if watching with some suspicion what would come next.

Claus knew. The head gave him an idea. He plied his knife carefully and with skill, forming slowly the body of the cat, which he made to sit upon its haunches as the real cat did, with her tail wound around her two front legs.

The work cost him much time, but the evening was long and he had nothing better to do. Finally he gave a loud and delighted laugh at the result of his labors and placed the wooden cat, now completed, upon the hearth opposite the real one.

Puss thereupon glared at her image, raised her hair in anger, and uttered a defiant mew. The wooden cat paid no attention, and Claus, much amused, laughed again.

Then Blinkie advanced toward the wooden image to eye it closely and smell of it intelligently: Eyes and nose told her the creature was wood, in spite of its natural appearance; so puss resumed her seat and her purring, but as she neatly washed her face with her padded paw she cast more than one admiring glance at her clever master. Perhaps she felt the same satisfaction we feel when we look upon good photographs of ourselves.

The cat's master was himself pleased with his handiwork, without knowing exactly why. Indeed, he had great cause to congratulate himself that night, and all the children throughout the world should have joined him rejoicing. For Claus had made his first toy.

CHAPTER III. HOW THE RYLS COLORED THE TOYS

A hush lay on the Laughing Valley now. Snow covered it like a white spread and pillows of downy flakes drifted before the dwelling where Claus sat feeding the blaze of the fire. The brook gurgled on beneath a heavy sheet of ice and all living plants and insects nestled close to Mother Earth to keep warm. The face of the moon was hid by dark clouds, and the wind, delighting in the wintry sport, pushed and whirled the snowflakes in so many directions that they could get no chance to fall to the ground.

Claus heard the wind whistling and shrieking in its play and thanked the good Knooks again for his comfortable shelter. Blinkie washed her face lazily and stared at the coals with a look of perfect content. The toy cat sat opposite the real one and gazed straight ahead, as toy cats should.

Suddenly Claus heard a noise that sounded different from the voice of the wind. It was more like a wail of suffering and despair.

He stood up and listened, but the wind, growing boisterous, shook the door and rattled the windows to distract his attention. He waited until the wind was tired and then, still listening, he heard once more the shrill cry of distress.

Quickly he drew on his coat, pulled his cap over his eyes and opened the door. The wind dashed in and scattered the embers over the hearth, at the same time blowing Blinkie's fur so furiously that she crept under the table to escape. Then the door was closed and Claus was outside, peering anxiously into the darkness.

The wind laughed and scolded and tried to push him over, but he stood firm. The helpless flakes stumbled against his eyes and dimmed his sight, but he rubbed them away and looked again. Snow was everywhere, white and glittering. It covered the earth and filled the air.

The cry was not repeated.

Claus turned to go back into the house, but the wind caught him unawares and he stumbled and fell across a snowdrift. His hand plunged into the drift and touched something that was not snow. This he seized and, pulling it gently toward him, found it to be a child. The next moment he had lifted it in his arms and carried it into the house.

The wind followed him through the door, but Claus shut it out quickly. He laid the rescued child on the hearth, and brushing away the snow he discovered it to be Weekum, a little boy who lived in a house beyond the Valley.

Claus wrapped a warm blanket around the little one and rubbed the frost from its limbs. Before long the child opened his eyes and, seeing where he was, smiled happily. Then Claus warmed milk and fed it to the boy slowly, while the cat looked on with sober curiosity. Finally the little one curled up in his friend's arms and sighed and fell asleep, and Claus, filled with gladness that he had found the wanderer, held him closely while he slumbered.

The wind, finding no more mischief to do, climbed the hill and swept on toward the north. This gave the weary snowflakes time to settle down to earth, and the Valley became still again.

The boy, having slept well in the arms of his friend, opened his eyes and sat up. Then, as a child will, he looked around the room and saw all that it contained.

"Your cat is a nice cat, Claus," he said, at last. "Let me hold it."

But puss objected and ran away.

"The other cat won't run, Claus," continued the boy. "Let me hold that one." Claus placed the toy in his arms, and the boy held it lovingly and kissed the tip of its wooden ear.

"How did you get lost in the storm, Weekum?" asked Claus.

"I started to walk to my auntie's house and lost my way," answered Weekum.

"Were you frightened?"

"It was cold," said Weekum, "and the snow got in my eyes, so I could not see. Then I kept on till I fell in the snow, without knowing where I was, and the wind blew the flakes over me and covered me up."

Claus gently stroked his head, and the boy looked up at him and smiled.

"I'm all right now," said Weekum.

"Yes," replied Claus, happily. "Now I will put you in my warm bed, and you must sleep until morning, when I will carry you back to your mother."

"May the cat sleep with me?" asked the boy.

"Yes, if you wish it to," answered Claus.

"It's a nice cat!" Weekum said, smiling, as Claus tucked the blankets around him; and presently the little one fell asleep with the wooden toy in his arms.

When morning came the sun claimed the Laughing Valley and flooded it with his rays; so Claus prepared to take the lost child back to its mother.

"May I keep the cat, Claus?" asked Weekum. "It's nicer than real cats. It doesn't run away, or scratch or bite. May I keep it?"

"Yes, indeed," answered Claus, pleased that the toy he had made could give pleasure to the child. So he wrapped the boy and the wooden cat in a warm cloak, perching the bundle upon his own broad shoulders, and then he tramped through the snow and the drifts of the Valley and across the plain beyond to the poor cottage where Weekum's mother lived.

"See, mama!" cried the boy, as soon as they entered, "I've got a cat!"

The good woman wept tears of joy over the rescue of her darling and thanked Claus many times for his kind act. So he carried a warm and happy heart back to his home in the Valley.

That night he said to puss: "I believe the children will love the wooden cats almost as well as the real ones, and they can't hurt them by pulling their tails and ears. I'll make another."

So this was the beginning of his great work.

The next cat was better made than the first. While Claus sat whittling it out the Yellow Ryl came in to make him a visit, and so pleased was he with the man's skill that he ran away and brought several of his fellows.

There sat the Red Ryl, the Black Ryl, the Green Ryl, the Blue Ryl and the Yellow Ryl in a circle on the floor, while Claus whittled and whistled and the wooden cat grew into shape.

"If it could be made the same color as the real cat, no one would know the difference," said the Yellow Ryl, thoughtfully.

"The little ones, maybe, would not know the difference," replied Claus, pleased with the idea.

"I will bring you some of the red that I color my roses and tulips with," cried the Red Ryl; "and then you can make the cat's lips and tongue red."

"I will bring some of the green that I color my grasses and leaves with," said the Green Ryl; "and then you can color the cat's eyes green."

"They will need a bit of yellow, also," remarked the Yellow Ryl; "I must fetch some of the yellow that I use to color my buttercups and goldenrods with."

"The real cat is black," said the Black Ryl; "I will bring some of the black that I use to color the eyes of my pansies with, and then you can paint your wooden cat black."

"I see you have a blue ribbon around Blinkie's neck," added the Blue Ryl. "I will get some of the color that I use to paint the bluebells and forget-me-nots with, and then you can carve a wooden ribbon on the toy cat's neck and paint it blue."

So the Ryls disappeared, and by the time Claus had finished carving out the form of the cat they were all back with the paints and brushes.

They made Blinkie sit upon the table, that Claus might paint the toy cat just the right color, and when the work was done the Ryls declared it was exactly as good as a live cat.

"That is, to all appearances," added the Red Ryl.

Blinkie seemed a little offended by the attention bestowed upon the toy, and that she might not seem to approve the imitation cat she walked to the corner of the hearth and sat down with a dignified air.

But Claus was delighted, and as soon as morning came he started out and tramped through the snow, across the Valley and the plain, until he came to a village. There, in a poor hut near the walls of the beautiful palace of the Lord of Lerd, a little girl lay upon a wretched cot, moaning with pain.

Claus approached the child and kissed her and comforted her, and then he drew the toy cat from beneath his coat, where he had hidden it, and placed it in her arms.

Ah, how well he felt himself repaid for his labor and his long walk when he saw the little one's eyes grow bright with pleasure! She hugged the kitty tight to her breast, as if it had been a precious gem, and would not let it go for a single moment. The fever was quieted, the pain grew less, and she fell into a sweet and refreshing sleep.

Claus laughed and whistled and sang all the way home. Never had he been so happy as on that day.

When he entered his house he found Shiegra, the lioness, awaiting him. Since his babyhood Shiegra had loved Claus, and while he dwelt in the Forest she had often come to visit him at Necile's bower. After Claus had gone to live in the Laughing Valley Shiegra became lonely and ill at ease, and now she had braved the snow-drifts, which all lions abhor, to see him once more. Shiegra was getting old and her teeth were beginning to fall out, while the hairs that tipped her ears and tail had changed from tawny-yellow to white.

Claus found her lying on his hearth, and he put his arms around the neck of the lioness and hugged her lovingly. The cat had retired into a far corner. She did not care to associate with Shiegra.

Claus told his old friend about the cats he had made, and how much pleasure they had given Weekum and the sick girl. Shiegra did not know much about children; indeed, if she met a child she could scarcely be trusted not to devour it. But she was interested in Claus' new labors, and said:

"These images seem to me very attractive. Yet I can not see why you should make cats, which are very unimportant animals. Suppose, now that I am here, you make the image of a lioness, the Queen of all beasts. Then, indeed, your children will be happy—and safe at the same time!"

Claus thought this was a good suggestion. So he got a piece of wood and sharpened his knife, while Shiegra crouched upon the hearth at his feet. With much care he carved the head in the likeness of the lioness, even to the two fierce teeth that curved over her lower lip and the deep, frowning lines above her wide-open eyes.

When it was finished he said:

"You have a terrible look, Shiegra."

"Then the image is like me," she answered; "for I am indeed terrible to all who are not my friends."

Claus now carved out the body, with Shiegra's long tail trailing behind it. The image of the crouching lioness was very life-like.

"It pleases me," said Shiegra, yawning and stretching her body gracefully. "Now I will watch while you paint."

He brought the paints the Ryls had given him from the cupboard and colored the image to resemble the real Shiegra.

The lioness placed her big, padded paws upon the edge of the table and raised herself while she carefully examined the toy that was her likeness.

"You are indeed skillful!" she said, proudly. "The children will like that better than cats, I'm sure."

Then snarling at Blinkie, who arched her back in terror and whined fearfully, she walked away toward her forest home with stately strides.

CHAPTER IV. HOW LITTLE MAYRIE BECAME FRIGHTENED

The winter was over now, and all the Laughing Valley was filled with joyous excitement. The brook was so happy at being free once again that it gurgled more boisterously than ever and dashed so recklessly against the rocks that it sent showers of spray high in the air. The grass thrust its sharp little blades upward through the mat of dead stalks where it had hidden from the snow, but the flowers were yet too timid to show themselves, although the Ryls were busy feeding their roots. The sun was in remarkably good humor, and sent his rays dancing merrily throughout the Valley.

Claus was eating his dinner one day when he heard a timid knock on his door.

"Come in!" he called.

No one entered, but after a pause came another rapping.

Claus jumped up and threw open the door. Before him stood a small girl holding a smaller brother fast by the hand.

"Is you Tlaus?" she asked, shyly.

"Indeed I am, my dear!" he answered, with a laugh, as he caught both children in his arms and kissed them. "You are very welcome, and you have come just in time to share my dinner."

He took them to the table and fed them with fresh milk and nut-cakes. When they had eaten enough he asked:

"Why have you made this long journey to see me?"

"I wants a tat!" replied little Mayrie; and her brother, who had not yet learned to speak many words, nodded his head and exclaimed like an echo: "Tat!"

"Oh, you want my toy cats, do you?" returned Claus, greatly pleased to discover that his creations were so popular with children.

The little visitors nodded eagerly.

"Unfortunately," he continued, "I have but one cat now ready, for I carried two to children in the town yesterday. And the one I have shall be given to your brother, Mayrie, because he is the smaller; and the next one I make shall be for you."

The boy's face was bright with smiles as he took the precious toy Claus held out to him; but little Mayrie covered her face with her arm and began to sob grievously.

"I—I—I wants a t—t—tat now!" she wailed.

Her disappointment made Claus feel miserable for a moment. Then he suddenly remembered Shiegra.

"Don't cry, darling!" he said, soothingly; "I have a toy much nicer than a cat, and you shall have that."

He went to the cupboard and drew out the image of the lioness, which he placed on the table before Mayrie.

The girl raised her arm and gave one glance at the fierce teeth and glaring eyes of the beast, and then, uttering a terrified scream, she rushed from the house. The boy followed her, also screaming lustily, and even dropping his precious cat in his fear.

For a moment Claus stood motionless, being puzzled and astonished. Then he threw Shiegra's image into the cupboard and ran after the children, calling to them not to be frightened.

Little Mayrie stopped in her flight and her brother clung to her skirt; but they both cast fearful glances at the house until Claus had assured them many times that the beast had been locked in the cupboard.

"Yet why were you frightened at seeing it?" he asked. "It is only a toy to play with!"

"It's bad!" said Mayrie, decidedly, "an'—an'—just horrid, an' not a bit nice, like tats!"

"Perhaps you are right," returned Claus, thoughtfully. "But if you will return with me to the house I will soon make you a pretty cat."

So they timidly entered the house again, having faith in their friend's words; and afterward they had the joy of watching Claus carve out a cat from a bit of wood and paint it in natural colors. It did not take him long to do this, for he had become skillful with his knife by this time, and Mayrie loved her toy the more dearly because she had seen it made.

After his little visitors had trotted away on their journey homeward Claus sat long in deep thought. And he then decided that such fierce creatures as his friend the lioness would never do as models from which to fashion his toys.

"There must be nothing to frighten the dear babies," he reflected; "and while I know Shiegra well, and am not afraid of her, it is but natural that children should look upon her image with terror. Hereafter I will choose such mild-mannered animals as squirrels and rabbits and deer and lambkins from which to carve my toys, for then the little ones will love rather than fear them."

He began his work that very day, and before bedtime had made a wooden rabbit and a lamb. They were not quite so lifelike as the cats had been, because they were formed from memory, while Blinkie had sat very still for Claus to look at while he worked.

But the new toys pleased the children nevertheless, and the fame of Claus' playthings quickly spread to every cottage on plain and in village. He always carried his gifts to the sick or crippled children, but those who were strong enough walked to the house in the Valley to ask for them, so a little path was soon worn from the plain to the door of the toy-maker's cottage.

First came the children who had been playmates of Claus, before he began to make toys. These, you may be sure, were well supplied. Then children who lived farther away heard of the wonderful images and made journeys to the Valley to secure them. All little ones were welcome, and never a one went away empty-handed.

This demand for his handiwork kept Claus busily occupied, but he was quite happy in knowing the pleasure he gave to so many of the dear children. His friends the immortals were pleased with his success and supported him bravely.

The Knooks selected for him clear pieces of soft wood, that his knife might not be blunted in cutting them; the Ryls kept him supplied with paints of all colors and brushes fashioned from the tips of timothy grasses; the Fairies discovered that the workman needed saws and chisels and hammers and nails, as well as knives, and brought him a goodly array of such tools.

Claus soon turned his living room into a most wonderful workshop. He built a bench before the window, and arranged his tools and paints so that he could reach everything as he sat on his stool. And as he finished toy after toy to delight the hearts of little children he found himself growing so gay and happy that he could not refrain from singing and laughing and whistling all the day long.

"It's because I live in the Laughing Valley, where everything else laughs!" said Claus.

But that was not the reason.

CHAPTER V. HOW BESSIE BLITHESOME CAME TO THE LAUGHING VALLEY

One day, as Claus sat before his door to enjoy the sunshine while he busily carved the head and horns of a toy deer, he looked up and discovered a glittering cavalcade of horsemen approaching through the Valley.

When they drew nearer he saw that the band consisted of a score of men-at-arms, clad in bright armor and bearing in their hands spears and battle-axes. In front of these rode little Bessie Blithesome, the pretty daughter of that proud Lord of Lerd who had once driven Claus from his palace. Her palfrey was pure white, its bridle was covered with glittering gems, and its saddle draped with cloth of gold, richly broidered. The soldiers were sent to protect her from harm while she journeyed.

Claus was surprised, but he continued to whittle and to sing until the cavalcade drew up before him. Then the little girl leaned over the neck of her palfrey and said:

"Please, Mr. Claus, I want a toy!"

Her voice was so pleading that Claus jumped up at once and stood beside her. But he was puzzled how to answer her request.

"You are a rich lord's daughter," said he, "and have all that you desire."

"Except toys," added Bessie. "There are no toys in all the world but yours."

"And I make them for the poor children, who have nothing else to amuse them," continued Claus.

"Do poor children love to play with toys more than rich ones?" asked Bessie.

"I suppose not," said Claus, thoughtfully.

"Am I to blame because my father is a lord? Must I be denied the pretty toys I long for because other children are poorer than I?" she inquired earnestly.

"I'm afraid you must, dear," he answered; "for the poor have nothing else with which to amuse themselves. You have your pony to ride, your servants to wait on you, and every comfort that money can procure."

"But I want toys!" cried Bessie, wiping away the tears that forced themselves into her eyes. "If I can not have them, I shall be very unhappy."

Claus was troubled, for her grief recalled to him the thought that his desire was to make all children happy, without regard to their condition in life. Yet, while so many poor children were clamoring for his toys he could not bear to give one to them to Bessie Blithesome, who had so much already to make her happy.

"Listen, my child," said he, gently; "all the toys I am now making are promised to others. But the next shall be yours, since your heart so longs for it. Come to me again in two days and it shall be ready for you."

Bessie gave a cry of delight, and leaning over her pony's neck she kissed Claus prettily upon his forehead. Then, calling to her men-at-arms, she rode gaily away, leaving Claus to resume his work.

"If I am to supply the rich children as well as the poor ones," he thought, "I shall not have a spare moment in the whole year! But is it right I should give to the rich? Surely I must go to Necile and talk with her about this matter."

So when he had finished the toy deer, which was very like a deer he had known in the Forest glades, he walked into Burzee and made his way to the bower of the beautiful Nymph Necile, who had been his foster mother.

She greeted him tenderly and lovingly, listening with interest to his story of the visit of Bessie Blithesome.

"And now tell me," said he, "shall I give toys to rich children?"

"We of the Forest know nothing of riches," she replied. "It seems to me that one child is like another child, since they are all made of the same clay, and that riches are like a gown, which may be put on or taken away, leaving the child unchanged. But the Fairies are guardians of mankind, and know mortal children better than I. Let us call the Fairy Queen."

This was done, and the Queen of the Fairies sat beside them and heard Claus relate his reasons for thinking the rich children could get along without his toys, and also what the Nymph had said.

"Necile is right," declared the Queen; "for, whether it be rich or poor, a child's longings for pretty playthings are but natural. Rich Bessie's heart may suffer as much grief as poor Mayrie's; she can be just as lonely and discontented, and just as gay and happy. I think, friend Claus, it is your duty to make all little ones glad, whether they chance to live in palaces or in cottages."

"Your words are wise, fair Queen," replied Claus, "and my heart tells me they are as just as they are wise. Hereafter all children may claim my services."

Then he bowed before the gracious Fairy and, kissing Necile's red lips, went back into his Valley.

At the brook he stopped to drink, and afterward he sat on the bank and took a piece of moist clay in his hands while he thought what sort of toy he should make for Bessie Blithesome. He did not notice that his fingers were working the clay into shape until, glancing downward, he found he had unconsciously formed a head that bore a slight resemblance to the Nymph Necile!

At once he became interested. Gathering more of the clay from the bank he carried it to his house. Then, with the aid of his knife and a bit of wood he succeeded in working the clay into the image of a toy nymph. With skillful strokes he formed long, waving hair on the head and covered the body with a gown of oakleaves, while the two feet sticking out at the bottom of the gown were clad in sandals.

But the clay was soft, and Claus found he must handle it gently to avoid ruining his pretty work.

"Perhaps the rays of the sun will draw out the moisture and cause the clay to become hard," he thought. So he laid the image on a flat board and placed it in the glare of the sun.

This done, he went to his bench and began painting the toy deer, and soon he became so interested in the work that he forgot all about the clay nymph. But next morning, happening to notice it as it lay on the board, he found the sun had baked it to the hardness of stone, and it was strong enough to be safely handled.

Claus now painted the nymph with great care in the likeness of Necile, giving it deep-blue eyes, white teeth, rosy lips and ruddy-brown hair. The gown he colored oak-leaf green, and when the paint was dry Claus himself was charmed with the new toy. Of course it was not nearly so lovely as the real Necile; but, considering the material of which it was made, Claus thought it was very beautiful.

When Bessie, riding upon her white palfrey, came to his dwelling next day, Claus presented her with the new toy. The little girl's eyes were brighter than ever as she examined the pretty image, and she loved it at once, and held it close to her breast, as a mother does to her child.

"What is it called, Claus?" she asked.

Now Claus knew that Nymphs do not like to be spoken of by mortals, so he could not tell Bessie it was an image of Necile he had given her. But as it was a new toy he searched his mind for a new name to call it by, and the first word he thought of he decided would do very well.

"It is called a dolly, my dear," he said to Bessie.

"I shall call the dolly my baby," returned Bessie, kissing it fondly; "and I shall tend it and care for it just as Nurse cares for me. Thank you very much, Claus; your gift has made me happier than I have ever been before!"

Then she rode away, hugging the toy in her arms, and Claus, seeing her delight, thought he would make another dolly, better and more natural than the first.

He brought more clay from the brook, and remembering that Bessie had called the dolly her baby he resolved to form this one into a baby's image. That was no difficult task to the clever workman, and soon the baby dolly was lying on the board and placed in the sun to dry. Then, with the clay that was left, he began to make an image of Bessie Blithesome herself.

This was not so easy, for he found he could not make the silken robe of the lord's daughter out of the common clay. So he called the Fairies to his aid, and asked them to bring him colored silks with which to make a real dress for the clay image. The Fairies set off at once on their errand, and before nightfall they returned with a generous supply of silks and laces and golden threads.

Claus now became impatient to complete his new dolly, and instead of waiting for the next day's sun he placed the clay image upon his hearth and covered it over with glowing coals. By morning, when he drew the dolly from the ashes, it had baked as hard as if it had lain a full day in the hot sun.

Now our Claus became a dressmaker as well as a toymaker. He cut the lavender silk, and neaty sewed it into a beautiful gown that just fitted the new dolly. And he put a lace collar around its neck and pink silk shoes on its feet. The natural color of baked clay is a light gray, but Claus painted the face to resemble the color of flesh, and he gave the dolly Bessie's brown eyes and golden hair and rosy cheeks.

It was really a beautiful thing to look upon, and sure to bring joy to some childish heart. While Claus was admiring it he heard a knock at his door, and little Mayrie entered. Her face was sad and her eyes red with continued weeping.

"Why, what has grieved you, my dear?" asked Claus, taking the child in his arms.

"I've—I've—bwoke my tat!" sobbed Mayrie.

"How?" he inquired, his eyes twinkling.

"I—I dwopped him, an' bwoke off him's tail; an'—an'—then I dwopped him an' bwoke off him's ear! An'—an' now him's all spoilt!"

Claus laughed.

"Never mind, Mayrie dear," he said. "How would you like this new dolly, instead of a cat?"

Mayrie looked at the silk-robed dolly and her eyes grew big with astonishment.

"Oh, Tlaus!" she cried, clapping her small hands together with rapture; "tan I have 'at boo'ful lady?"

"Do you like it?" he asked.

"I love it!" said she. "It's better 'an tats!"

"Then take it, dear, and be careful not to break it."

Mayrie took the dolly with a joy that was almost reverent, and her face dimpled with smiles as she started along the path toward home.

CHAPTER VI. THE WICKEDNESS OF
THE AWGWAS

I must now tell you something about the Awgwas, that terrible race of creatures which caused our good Claus so much trouble and nearly succeeded in robbing the children of the world of their earliest and best friend.

I do not like to mention the Awgwas, but they are a part of this history, and can not be ignored. They were neither mortals nor immortals, but stood midway between those classes of beings. The Awgwas were invisible to ordinary people, but not to immortals. They could pass swiftly through the air from one part of the world to another, and had the power of influencing the minds of human beings to do their wicked will.

They were of gigantic stature and had coarse, scowling countenances which showed plainly their hatred of all mankind. They possessed no consciences whatever and delighted only in evil deeds.

Their homes were in rocky, mountainous places, from whence they sallied forth to accomplish their wicked purposes.

The one of their number that could think of the most horrible deed for them to do was always elected the King Awgwa, and all the race obeyed his orders. Sometimes these creatures lived to become a hundred years old, but usually they fought so fiercely among themselves that many were destroyed in combat, and when they died that was the end of them. Mortals were powerless to harm them and the immortals shuddered when the Awgwas were mentioned, and always avoided them. So they flourished for many years unopposed and accomplished much evil.

I am glad to assure you that these vile creatures have long since perished and passed from earth; but in the days when Claus was making his first toys they were a numerous and powerful tribe.

One of the principal sports of the Awgwas was to inspire angry passions in the hearts of little children, so that they quarreled and fought with one another. They would tempt boys to eat of unripe fruit, and then delight in the pain they suffered; they urged little girls to disobey their parents, and then would laugh when the children were punished. I do not know what causes a child to be naughty in these days, but when the Awgwas were on earth naughty children were usually under their influence.

Now, when Claus began to make children happy he kept them out of the power of the Awgwas; for children possessing such lovely playthings as he gave them had no wish to obey the evil thoughts the Awgwas tried to thrust into their minds.

Therefore, one year when the wicked tribe was to elect a new King, they chose an Awgwa who proposed to destroy Claus and take him away from the children.

"There are, as you know, fewer naughty children in the world since Claus came to the Laughing Valley and began to make his toys," said the new King, as he squatted upon a rock and looked around at the scowling faces of his people. "Why, Bessie Blithesome has not stamped her foot once this month, nor has Mayrie's brother slapped his sister's face or thrown the puppy into the rain-barrel. Little Weekum took his bath last night without screaming or struggling, because his mother had promised he should take his toy cat to bed with him! Such a condition of affairs is awful for any Awgwa to think of, and the only way we can direct the naughty actions of children is to take this person Claus away from them."

"Good! good!" cried the big Awgwas, in a chorus, and they clapped their hands to applaud the speech of the King.

"But what shall we do with him?" asked one of the creatures.

"I have a plan," replied the wicked King; and what his plan was you will soon discover.

That night Claus went to bed feeling very happy, for he had completed no less than four pretty toys during the day, and they were sure, he thought, to make four little children happy. But while he slept the band of invisible Awgwas surrounded his bed, bound him with stout cords, and then flew away with him to the middle of a dark forest in far off Ethop, where they laid him down and left him.

When morning came Claus found himself thousands of miles from any human being, a prisoner in the wild jungle of an unknown land.

From the limb of a tree above his head swayed a huge python, one of those reptiles that are able to crush a man's bones in their coils. A few yards away crouched a savage panther, its glaring red eyes fixed full on the helpless Claus. One of those monstrous spotted spiders whose sting is death crept stealthily toward him over the matted leaves, which shriveled and turned black at its very touch.

But Claus had been reared in Burzee, and was not afraid.

"Come to me, ye Knooks of the Forest!" he cried, and gave the low, peculiar whistle that the Knooks know.

The panther, which was about to spring upon its victim, turned and slunk away. The python swung itself into the tree and disappeared among the leaves. The spider stopped short in its advance and hid beneath a rotting log.

Claus had no time to notice them, for he was surrounded by a band of harsh-featured Knooks, more crooked and deformed in appearance than any he had ever seen.

"Who are you that call on us?" demanded one, in a gruff voice.

"The friend of your brothers in Burzee," answered Claus. "I have been brought here by my enemies, the Awgwas, and left to perish miserably. Yet now I implore your help to release me and to send me home again."

"Have you the sign?" asked another.

"Yes," said Claus.

They cut his bonds, and with his free arms he made the secret sign of the Knooks.

Instantly they assisted him to stand upon his feet, and they brought him food and drink to strengthen him.

"Our brothers of Burzee make queer friends," grumbled an ancient Knook whose flowing beard was pure white. "But he who knows our secret sign and signal is entitled to our help, whoever he may be. Close your eyes, stranger, and we will conduct you to your home. Where shall we seek it?"

" 'Tis in the Laughing Valley," answered Claus, shutting his eyes.

"There is but one Laughing Valley in the known world, so we can not go astray," remarked the Knook.

As he spoke the sound of his voice seemed to die away, so Claus opened his eyes to see what caused the change. To his astonishment he found himself seated on the bench by his own door, with the Laughing Valley spread out before him. That day he visited the Wood-Nymphs and related his adventure to Queen Zurline and Necile.

"The Awgwas have become your enemies," said the lovely Queen, thoughtfully; "so we must do all we can to protect you from their power."

"It was cowardly to bind him while he slept," remarked Necile, with indignation.

"The evil ones are ever cowardly," answered Zurline, "but our friend's slumber shall not be disturbed again."

The Queen herself came to the dwelling of Claus that evening and placed her Seal on every door and window, to keep out the Awgwas. And under the Seal of Queen Zurline was placed the Seal of the Fairies and the Seal of the Ryls and the Seals of the Knooks, that the charm might become more powerful.

And Claus carried his toys to the children again, and made many more of the little ones happy.

You may guess how angry the King Awgwa and his fierce band were when it was known to them that Claus had escaped from the Forest of Ethop.

They raged madly for a whole week, and then held another meeting among the rocks.

"It is useless to carry him where the Knooks reign," said the King, "for he has their protection. So let us cast him into a cave of our own mountains, where he will surely perish."

This was promptly agreed to, and the wicked band set out that night to seize Claus. But they found his dwelling guarded by the Seals of the Immortals and were obliged to go away baffled and disappointed.

"Never mind," said the King; "he does not sleep always!"

Next day, as Claus traveled to the village across the plain, where he intended to present a toy squirrel to a lame boy, he was suddenly set upon by the Awgwas, who seized him and carried him away to the mountains.

There they thrust him within a deep cavern and rolled many huge rocks against the entrance to prevent his escape.

Deprived thus of light and food, and with little air to breathe, our Claus was, indeed, in a pitiful plight. But he spoke the mystic words of the Fairies, which always command their friendly aid, and they came to his rescue and transported him to the Laughing Valley in the twinkling of an eye.

Thus the Awgwas discovered they might not destroy one who had earned the friendship of the immortals; so the evil band sought other means of keeping Claus from bringing happiness to children and so making them obedient.

Whenever Claus set out to carry his toys to the little ones an Awgwa, who had been set to watch his movements, sprang upon him and snatched the toys from his grasp. And the children were no more disappointed than was Claus when he was obliged to return home disconsolate. Still he persevered, and made many toys for his little friends and started with them for the villages. And always the Awgwas robbed him as soon as he had left the Valley.

They threw the stolen playthings into one of their lonely caverns, and quite a heap of toys accumulated before Claus became discouraged and gave up all attempts to leave the Valley. Then children began coming to him, since they found he did not go to them; but the wicked Awgwas flew around them and caused their steps to stray and the paths to become crooked, so never a little one could find a way into the Laughing Valley.

Lonely days now fell upon Claus, for he was denied the pleasure of bringing happiness to the children whom he had learned to love. Yet he bore up bravely, for he thought surely the time would come when the Awgwas would abandon their evil designs to injure him.

He devoted all his hours to toy-making, and when one plaything had been completed he stood it on a shelf he had built for that purpose. When the shelf became filled with rows of toys he made another one, and filled that also. So that in time he had many shelves filled with gay and beautiful toys representing horses, dogs, cats, elephants, lambs, rabbits and deer, as well as pretty dolls of all sizes and balls and marbles of baked clay painted in gay colors.

Often, as he glanced at this array of childish treasures, the heart of good old

Claus became sad, so greatly did he long to carry the toys to his children. And at last, because he could bear it no longer, he ventured to go to the great Ak, to whom he told the story of his persecution by the Awgwas, and begged the Master Woodsman to assist him.

CHAPTER VII. THE GREAT BATTLE BETWEEN GOOD AND EVIL

Ak listened gravely to the recital of Claus, stroking his beard the while with the slow, graceful motion that betokened deep thought. He nodded approvingly when Claus told how the Knooks and Fairies had saved him from death, and frowned when he heard how the Awgwas had stolen the children's toys. At last he said:

"From the beginning I have approved the work you are doing among the children of men, and it annoys me that your good deeds should be thwarted by the Awgwas. We immortals have no connection whatever with the evil creatures who have attacked you. Always have we avoided them, and they, in turn, have hitherto taken care not to cross our pathway. But in this matter I find they have interfered with one of our friends, and I will ask them to abandon their persecutions, as you are under our protection."

Claus thanked the Master Woodsman most gratefully and returned to his Valley, while Ak, who never delayed carrying out his promises, at once traveled to the mountains of the Awgwas.

There, standing on the bare rocks, he called on the King and his people to appear.

Instantly the place was filled with throngs of the scowling Awgwas, and their King, perching himself on a point of rock, demanded fiercely:

"Who dares call on us?"

"It is I, the Master Woodsman of the World," responded Ak.

"Here are no forests for you to claim," cried the King, angrily. "We owe no allegiance to you, nor to any immortal!"

"That is true," replied Ak, calmly. "Yet you have ventured to interfere with the actions of Claus, who dwells in the Laughing Valley, and is under our protection."

Many of the Awgwas began muttering at this speech, and their King turned threateningly on the Master Woodsman.

"You are set to rule the forests, but the plains and the valleys are ours!" he shouted. "Keep to your own dark woods! We will do as we please with Claus."

"You shall not harm our friend in any way!" replied Ak.

"Shall we not?" asked the King, impudently. "You will see! Our powers are vastly superior to those of mortals, and fully as great as those of immortals."

"It is your conceit that misleads you!" said Ak, sternly. "You are a transient race, passing from life into nothingness. We, who live forever, pity but despise you. On earth you are scorned by all, and in Heaven you have no place! Even the mortals, after their earth life, enter another existence for all time, and so are your superiors. How then dare you, who are neither mortal nor immortal, refuse to obey my wish?"

The Awgwas sprang to their feet with menacing gestures, but their King motioned them back.

"Never before," he cried to Ak, while his voice trembled with rage, "has an immortal declared himself the master of the Awgwas! Never shall an immortal venture to interfere with our actions again! For we will avenge your scornful words by killing your friend Claus within three days. Nor you, nor all the immortals can save him from our wrath. We defy your powers! Begone, Master Woodsman of the World! In the country of the Awgwas you have no place."

"It is war!" declared Ak, with flashing eyes.

"It is war!" returned the King, savagely. "In three days your friend will be dead."

The Master turned away and came to his Forest of Burzee, where he called a meeting of the immortals and told them of the defiance of the Awgwas and their purpose to kill Claus within three days.

The little folk listened to him quietly.

"What shall we do?" asked Ak.

"These creatures are of no benefit to the world," said the Prince of the Knooks; "we must destroy them."

"Their lives are devoted only to evil deeds," said the Prince of the Ryls. "We must destroy them."

"They have no conscience, and endeavor to make all mortals as bad as themselves," said the Queen of the Fairies. "We must destroy them."

"They have defied the great Ak, and threaten the life of our adopted son," said beautiful Queen Zurline. "We must destroy them."

The Master Woodsman smiled.

"You speak well," said he. "These Awgwas we know to be a powerful race, and they will fight desperately; yet the outcome is certain. For we who live can never die, even though conquered by our enemies, while every Awgwa who is struck down is one foe the less to oppose us. Prepare, then, for battle, and let us resolve to show no mercy to the wicked!"

Thus arose that terrible war between the immortals and the spirits of evil which is sung of in Fairyland to this very day.

The King Awgwa and his band determined to carry out the threat to destroy Claus. They now hated him for two reasons: he made children happy and was a friend of the Master Woodsman. But since Ak's visit they had reason to fear the opposition of the immortals, and they dreaded defeat. So the King sent swift messengers to all parts of the world to summon every evil creature to his aid.

And on the third day after the declaration of war a mighty army was at the command of the King Awgwa. There were three hundred Asiatic Dragons, breathing fire that consumed everything it touched. These hated mankind and all good spirits. And there were the three-eyed Giants of Tatary, a host in themselves, who liked nothing better than to fight. And next came the Black Demons from Patalonia, with great spreading wings like those of a bat, which swept terror and misery through the world as they beat upon the air. And joined to these were the Goozzle-Goblins, with long talons as sharp as swords, with which they clawed the flesh from their foes. Finally, every mountain Awgwa in the world had come to participate in the great battle with the immortals.

The King Awgwa looked around upon this vast army and his heart beat high with wicked pride, for he believed he would surely triumph over his gentle enemies, who had never before been known to fight. But the Master Woodsman had not been idle. None of his people was used to warfare, yet now that they were called upon to face the hosts of evil they willingly prepared for the fray.

Ak had commanded them to assemble in the Laughing Valley, where Claus, ignorant of the terrible battle that was to be waged on his account, was quietly making his toys.

Soon the entire Valley, from hill to hill, was filled with the little immortals. The Master Woodsman stood first, bearing a gleaming ax that shone like burnished silver. Next came the Ryls, armed with sharp thorns from bramblebushes. Then the Knooks, bearing the spears they used when they were forced to prod their savage beasts into submission. The Fairies, dressed in white gauze with rainbow-hued wings, bore golden wands, and the Wood-nymphs, in their uniforms of oak-leaf green, carried switches from ash trees as weapons.

Loud laughed the Awgwa King when he beheld the size and the arms of his foes. To be sure the mighty ax of the Woodsman was to be dreaded, but the sweet-faced Nymphs and pretty Fairies, the gentle Ryls and crooked Knooks were such harmless folk that he almost felt shame at having called such a terrible host to oppose them.

"Since these fools dare fight," he said to the leader of the Tatary Giants, "I will overwhelm them with our evil powers!"

To begin the battle he poised a great stone in his left hand and cast it full against the sturdy form of the Master Woodsman, who turned it aside with his ax. Then rushed the three-eyed Giants of Tatary upon the Knooks, and the Goozzle-Goblins upon the Ryls, and the firebreathing Dragons upon the sweet Fairies.

Because the Nymphs were Ak's own people the band of Awgwas sought them out, thinking to overcome them with ease.

But it is the Law that while Evil, unopposed, may accomplish terrible deeds, the powers of Good can never be overthrown when opposed to Evil. Well had it been for the King Awgwa had he known the Law!

His ignorance cost him his existence, for one flash of the ax borne by the Master Woodsman of the World cleft the wicked King in twain and rid the earth of the vilest creature it contained.

Greatly marveled the Tatary Giants when the spears of the little Knooks pierced their thick walls of flesh and sent them reeling to the ground with howls of agony.

Woe came upon the sharp-taloned Goblins when the thorns of the Ryls reached their savage hearts and let their life-blood sprinkle all the plain. And afterward from every drop a thistle grew.

The Dragons paused astonished before the Fairy wands, from whence rushed a power that caused their fiery breaths to flow back on themselves so that they shriveled away and died.

As for the Awgwas, they had scant time to realize how they were destroyed, for the ash switches of the Nymphs bore a charm unknown to any Awgwa, and turned their foes into clods of earth at the slightest touch!

When Ak leaned upon his gleaming ax and turned to look over the field of battle he saw the few Giants who were able to run disappearing over the distant hills on their return to Tatary. The Goblins had perished every one, as had the terrible Dragons, while all that remained of the wicked Awgwas was a great number of earthen hillocks dotting the plain.

And now the immortals melted from the Valley like dew at sunrise, to resume their duties in the Forest, while Ak walked slowly and thoughtfully to the house of Claus and entered.

"You have many toys ready for the children," said the Woodsman, "and now you may carry them across the plain to the dwellings and the villages without fear."

"Will not the Awgwas harm me?" asked Claus, eagerly.

"The Awgwas," said Ak, "have perished!"

Now I will gladly have done with wicked spirits and with fighting and bloodshed. It was not from choice that I told of the Awgwas and their allies, and of their great battle with the immortals. They were part of this history, and could not be avoided.

CHAPTER VIII. THE FIRST JOURNEY
WITH THE REINDEER

Those were happy days for Claus when he carried his accumulation of toys to the children who had awaited them so long. During his imprisonment in the Valley he had been so industrious that all his shelves were filled with playthings, and after quickly supplying the little ones living near by he saw he must now extend his travels to wider fields.

Remembering the time when he had journeyed with Ak through all the world, he knew children were everywhere, and he longed to make as many as possible happy with his gifts.

So he loaded a great sack with all kinds of toys, slung it upon his back that he might carry it more easily, and started off on a longer trip than he had yet undertaken.

Wherever he showed his merry face, in hamlet or in farmhouse, he received a cordial welcome, for his fame had spread into far lands. At each village the children swarmed about him, following his footsteps wherever he went; and the women thanked him gratefully for the joy he brought their little ones; and the men looked upon him curiously that he should devote his time to such a queer occupation as toy-making. But every one smiled on him and gave him kindly words, and Claus felt amply repaid for his long journey.

When the sack was empty he went back again to the Laughing Valley and once more filled it to the brim. This time he followed another road, into a different part of the country, and carried happiness to many children who never before had owned a toy or guessed that such a delightful plaything existed.

After a third journey, so far away that Claus was many days walking the distance, the store of toys became exhausted and without delay he set about making a fresh supply.

From seeing so many children and studying their tastes he had acquired several new ideas about toys.

The dollies were, he had found, the most delightful of all playthings for babies and little girls, and often those who could not say "dolly" would call for a "doll" in their sweet baby talk. So Claus resolved to make many dolls, of all sizes, and to dress them in bright-colored clothing. The older boys—and even some of the girls—loved the images of animals, so he still made cats and elephants and horses. And many of the little fellows had musical natures, and longed for drums and cymbals and whistles and horns. So he made a number of toy drums, with tiny sticks to beat them with; and he made whistles from the willow trees, and horns from the bog-reeds, and cymbals from bits of beaten metal.

All this kept him busily at work, and before he realized it the winter season came, with deeper snows than usual, and he knew he could not leave the Valley with his heavy pack. Moreover, the next trip would take him farther from home than every before, and Jack Frost was mischievous enough to nip his nose and ears if he undertook the long journey while the Frost King reigned. The Frost King was Jack's father and never reproved him for his pranks.

So Claus remained at his work-bench; but he whistled and sang as merrily as ever, for he would allow no disappointment to sour his temper or make him unhappy.

One bright morning he looked from his window and saw two of the deer he had known in the Forest walking toward his house.

Claus was surprised; not that the friendly deer should visit him, but that they walked on the surface of the snow as easily as if it were solid ground, notwithstanding the fact that throughout the Valley the snow lay many feet deep. He had walked out of his house a day or two before and had sunk to his armpits in a drift.

So when the deer came near he opened the door and called to them:

"Good morning, Flossie! Tell me how you are able to walk on the snow so easily."

"It is frozen hard," answered Flossie.

"The Frost King has breathed on it," said Glossie, coming up, "and the surface is now as solid as ice."

"Perhaps," remarked Claus, thoughtfully, "I might now carry my pack of toys to the children."

"Is it a long journey?" asked Flossie.

"Yes; it will take me many days, for the pack is heavy," answered Claus.

"Then the snow would melt before you could get back," said the deer. "You must wait until spring, Claus."

Claus sighed. "Had I your fleet feet," said he, "I could make the journey in a day."

"But you have not," returned Glossie, looking at his own slender legs with pride.

"Perhaps I could ride upon your back," Claus ventured to remark, after a pause.

"Oh no; our backs are not strong enough to bear your weight," said Flossie, decidedly. "But if you had a sledge, and could harness us to it, we might draw you easily, and your pack as well."

"I'll make a sledge!" exclaimed Claus. "Will you agree to draw me if I do?"

"Well," replied Flossie, "we must first go and ask the Knooks, who are our guardians, for permission; but if they consent, and you can make a sledge and harness, we will gladly assist you."

"Then go at once!" cried Claus, eagerly. "I am sure the friendly Knooks will give their consent, and by the time you are back I shall be ready to harness you to my sledge."

Flossie and Glossie, being deer of much intelligence, had long wished to see the great world, so they gladly ran over the frozen snow to ask the Knooks if they might carry Claus on his journey.

Meantime the toy-maker hurriedly began the construction of a sledge, using material from his wood-pile. He made two long runners that turned upward at the front ends, and across these nailed short boards, to make a platform. It was soon completed, but was as rude in appearance as it is possible for a sledge to be.

The harness was more difficult to prepare, but Claus twisted strong cords together and knotted them so they would fit around the necks of the deer, in the shape of a collar. From these ran other cords to fasten the deer to the front of the sledge.

Before the work was completed Glossie and Flossie were back from the Forest, having been granted permission by Will Knook to make the journey with Claus provided they would to Burzee by daybreak the next morning.

"That is not a very long time," said Flossie; "but we are swift and strong, and if we get started by this evening we can travel many miles during the night."

Claus decided to make the attempt, so he hurried on his preparations as fast as possible. After a time he fastened the collars around the necks of his steeds and harnessed them to his rude sledge. Then he placed a stool on the little platform, to serve as a seat, and filled a sack with his prettiest toys.

"How do you intend to guide us?" asked Glossie. "We have never been out of the Forest before, except to visit your house, so we shall not know the way."

Claus thought about that for a moment. Then he brought more cords and fastened two of them to the spreading antlers of each deer, one on the right and the other on the left.

"Those will be my reins," said Claus, "and when I pull them to the right or to the left you must go in that direction. If I do not pull the reins at all you may go straight ahead."

"Very well," answered Glossie and Flossie; and then they asked: "Are you ready?"

Claus seated himself upon the stool, placed the sack of toys at his feet, and then gathered up the reins.

"All ready!" he shouted; "away we go!"

The deer leaned forward, lifted their slender limbs, and the next moment away flew the sledge over the frozen snow. The swiftness of the motion surprised Claus, for in a few strides they were across the Valley and gliding over the broad plain beyond.

The day had melted into evening by the time they started; for, swiftly as Claus had worked, many hours had been consumed in making his preparations. But the moon shone brightly to light their way, and Claus soon decided it was just as pleasant to travel by night as by day.

The deer liked it better; for, although they wished to see something of the world, they were timid about meeting men, and now all the dwellers in the towns and farmhouses were sound asleep and could not see them.

Away and away they sped, on and on over the hills and through the valleys and across the plains until they reached a village where Claus had never been before.

Here he called on them to stop, and they immediately obeyed. But a new difficulty now presented itself, for the people had locked their doors when they went to bed, and Claus found he could not enter the houses to leave his toys.

"I am afraid, my friends, we have made our journey for nothing," said he, "for I shall be obliged to carry my playthings back home again without giving them to the children of this village."

"What's the matter?" asked Flossie.

"The doors are locked," answered Claus, "and I can not get in."

Glossie looked around at the houses. The snow was quite deep in that village, and just before them was a roof only a few feet above the sledge. A broad chimney, which seemed to Glossie big enough to admit Claus, was at the peak of the roof.

"Why don't you climb down that chimney?" asked Glossie.

Claus looked at it.

"That would be easy enough if I were on top of the roof," he answered.

"Then hold fast and we will take you there," said the deer, and they gave one bound to the roof and landed beside the big chimney.

"Good!" cried Claus, well pleased, and he slung the pack of toys over his shoulder and got into the chimney.

There was plenty of soot on the bricks, but he did not mind that, and by placing his hands and knees against the sides he crept downward until he had reached the fireplace. Leaping lightly over the smoldering coals he found himself in a large sitting-room, where a dim light was burning.

From this room two doorways led into smaller chambers. In one a woman lay asleep, with a baby beside her in a crib.

Claus laughed, but he did not laugh aloud for fear of waking the baby. Then he slipped a big doll from his pack and laid it in the crib. The little one smiled, as if it dreamed of the pretty plaything it was to find on the morrow, and Claus crept softly from the room and entered at the other doorway.

Here were two boys, fast asleep with their arms around each other's neck. Claus gazed at them lovingly a moment and then placed upon the bed a drum, two horns and a wooden elephant.

He did not linger, now that his work in this house was done, but climbed the chimney again and seated himself on his sledge.

"Can you find another chimney?" he asked the reindeer.

"Easily enough," replied Glossie and Flossie.

Down to the edge of the roof they raced, and then, without pausing, leaped through the air to the top of the next building, where a huge, old-fashioned chimney stood.

"Don't be so long, this time," called Flossie, "or we shall never get back to the Forest by daybreak."

Claus made a trip down this chimney also and found five children sleeping in the house, all of whom were quickly supplied with toys.

When he returned the deer sprang to the next roof, but on descending the chimney Claus found no children there at all. That was not often the case in this village, however, so he lost less time than you might suppose in visiting the dreary homes where there were no little ones.

When he had climbed down the chimneys of all the houses in that village, and had left a toy for every sleeping child, Claus found that his great sack was not yet half emptied.

"Onward, friends!" he called to the deer; "we must seek another village."

So away they dashed, although it was long past midnight, and in a surprisingly short time they came to a large city, the largest Claus had ever visited since he began to make toys. But, nothing daunted by the throng of houses, he set to work at once and his beautiful steeds carried him rapidly from one roof to another, only the highest being beyond the leaps of the agile deer.

At last the supply of toys was exhausted and Claus seated himself in the sledge, with the empty sack at his feet, and turned the heads of Glossie and Flossie toward home.

Presently Flossie asked:

"What is that gray streak in the sky?"

"It is the coming dawn of day," answered Claus, surprised to find that it was so late.

"Good gracious!" exclaimed Glossie; "then we shall not be home by daybreak, and the Knooks will punish us and never let us come again."

"We must race for the Laughing Valley and make our best speed," returned Flossie; "so hold fast, friend Claus!"

Claus held fast and the next moment was flying so swiftly over the snow that he could not see the trees as they whirled past. Up hill and down dale, swift as an arrow shot from a bow they dashed, and Claus shut his eyes to keep the wind out of them and left the deer to find their own way.

It seemed to him they were plunging through space, but he was not at all afraid. The Knooks were severe masters, and must be obeyed at all hazards, and the gray streak in the sky was growing brighter every moment.

Finally the sledge came to a sudden stop and Claus, who was taken unawares, tumbled from his seat into a snowdrift. As he picked himself up he heard the deer crying:

"Quick, friend, quick! Cut away our harness!"

He drew his knife and rapidly severed the cords, and then he wiped the moisture from his eyes and looked around him.

The sledge had come to a stop in the Laughing Valley, only a few feet, he found, from his own door. In the East the day was breaking, and turning to the edge of Burzee he saw Glossie and Flossie just disappearing in the Forest.

CHAPTER IX. "SANTA CLAUS!"

Claus thought that none of the children would ever know where the toys came from which they found by their bedsides when they wakened the following morning. But kindly deeds are sure to bring fame, and fame has many wings to carry its tidings into far lands; so for miles and miles in every direction people were talking of Claus and his wonderful gifts to children. The sweet generousness of his work caused a few selfish folk to sneer, but even these were forced to admit their respect for a man so gentle-natured that he loved to devote his life to pleasing the helpless little ones of his race.

Therefore the inhabitants of every city and village had been eagerly watching the coming of Claus, and remarkable stories of his beautiful playthings were told the children to keep them patient and contented.

When, on the morning following the first trip of Claus with his deer, the little ones came running to their parents with the pretty toys they had found, and asked from whence they came, they was but one reply to the question.

"The good Claus must have been here, my darlings; for his are the only toys in all the world!"

"But how did he get in?" asked the children.

At this the fathers shook their heads, being themselves unable to understand how Claus had gained admittance to their homes; but the mothers, watching the glad faces of their dear ones, whispered that the good Claus was no mortal man but assuredly a Saint, and they piously blessed his name for the happiness he had bestowed upon their children.

"A Saint," said one, with bowed head, "has no need to unlock doors if it pleases him to enter our homes."

And, afterward, when a child was naughty or disobedient, its mother would say: "You must pray to the good Santa Claus for forgiveness. He does not like naughty children, and, unless you repent, he will bring you no more pretty toys."

But Santa Claus himself would not have approved this speech. He brought toys to the children because they were little and helpless, and because he loved them. He knew that the best of children were sometimes naughty, and that the naughty ones were often good. It is the way with children, the world over, and he would not have changed their natures had he possessed the power to do so.

And that is how our Claus became Santa Claus. It is possible for any man, by good deeds, to enshrine himself as a Saint in the hearts of the people.

CHAPTER X. CHRISTMAS EVE

The day that broke as Claus returned from his night ride with Glossie and Flossie brought to him a new trouble. Will Knook, the chief guardian of the deer, came to him, surly and ill-tempered, to complain that he had kept Glossie and Flossie beyond daybreak, in opposition to his orders.

"Yet it could not have been very long after daybreak," said Claus.

"It was one minute after," answered Will Knook, "and that is as bad as one hour. I shall set the stinging gnats on Glossie and Flossie, and they will thus suffer terribly for their disobedience."

"Don't do that!" begged Claus. "It was my fault."

But Will Knook would listen to no excuses, and went away grumbling and growling in his ill-natured way.

For this reason Claus entered the Forest to consult Necile about rescuing the good deer from punishment. To his delight he found his old friend, the Master Woodsman, seated in the circle of Nymphs.

Ak listened to the story of the night journey to the children and of the great assistance the deer had been to Claus by drawing his sledge over the frozen snow.

"I do not wish my friends to be punished if I can save them," said the toy-maker, when he had finished the relation. "They were only one minute late, and they ran swifter than a bird flies to get home before daybreak."

Ak stroked his beard thoughtfully a moment, and then sent for the Prince of the Knooks, who rules all his people in Burzee, and also for the Queen of the Fairies and the Prince of the Ryls.

When all had assembled Claus told his story again, at Ak's command, and then the Master addressed the Prince of the Knooks, saying:

"The good work that Claus is doing among mankind deserves the support of every honest immortal. Already he is called a Saint in some of the towns, and before long the name of Santa Claus will be lovingly known in every home that is blessed with children. Moreover, he is a son of our Forest, so we owe him our encouragement. You, Ruler of the Knooks, have known him these many years; am I not right in saying he deserves our friendship?"

The Prince, crooked and sour of visage as all Knooks are, looked only upon the dead leaves at his feet and muttered: "You are the Master Woodsman of the World!"

Ak smiled, but continued, in soft tones: "It seems that the deer which are guarded by your people can be of great assistance to Claus, and as they seem willing to draw his sledge I beg that you will permit him to use their services whenever he pleases."

The Prince did not reply, but tapped the curled point of his sandal with the tip of his spear, as if in thought.

Then the Fairy Queen spoke to him in this way: "If you consent to Ak's request I will see that no harm comes to your deer while they are away from the Forest."

And the Prince of the Ryls added: "For my part I will allow to every deer that assists Claus the privilege of eating my casa plants, which give strength, and my grawle plants, which give fleetness of foot, and my marbon plants, which give long life."

And the Queen of the Nymphs said: "The deer which draw the sledge of Claus will be permitted to bathe in the Forest pool of Nares, which will give them sleek coats and wonderful beauty."

The Prince of the Knooks, hearing these promises, shifted uneasily on his seat, for in his heart he hated to refuse a request of his fellow immortals, although they were asking an unusual favor at his hands, and the Knooks are unaccustomed to granting favors of any kind. Finally he turned to his servants and said:

"Call Will Knook."

When surly Will came and heard the demands of the immortals he protested loudly against granting them.

"Deer are deer," said he, "and nothing but deer. Were they horses it would be right to harness them like horses. But no one harnesses deer because they are free, wild creatures, owing no service of any sort to mankind. It would degrade my deer to labor for Claus, who is only a man in spite of the friendship lavished on him by the immortals."

"You have heard," said the Prince to Ak. "There is truth in what Will says."

"Call Glossie and Flossie," returned the Master.

The deer were brought to the conference and Ak asked them if they objected to drawing the sledge for Claus.

"No, indeed!" replied Glossie; "we enjoyed the trip very much."

"And we tried to get home by daybreak," added Flossie, "but were unfortunately a minute too late."

"A minute lost at daybreak doesn't matter," said Ak. "You are forgiven for that delay."

"Provided it does not happen again," said the Prince of the Knooks, sternly.

"And will you permit them to make another journey with me?" asked Claus, eagerly.

The Prince reflected while he gazed at Will, who was scowling, and at the Master Woodsman, who was smiling.

Then he stood up and addressed the company as follows:

"Since you all urge me to grant the favor I will permit the deer to go with Claus once every year, on Christmas Eve, provided they always return to the Forest by daybreak. He may select any number he pleases, up to ten, to draw his sledge, and those shall be known among us as Reindeer, to distinguish them from the others. And they shall bathe in the Pool of Nares, and eat the casa and grawle and marbon plants and shall be under the especial protection of the Fairy Queen. And now cease scowling, Will Knook, for my words shall be obeyed!"

He hobbled quickly away through the trees, to avoid the thanks of Claus and the approval of the other immortals, and Will, looking as cross as ever, followed him.

But Ak was satisfied, knowing that he could rely on the promise of the Prince, however grudgingly given; and Glossie and Flossie ran home, kicking up their heels delightedly at every step.

"When is Christmas Eve?" Claus asked the Master.

"In about ten days," he replied.

"Then I can not use the deer this year," said Claus, thoughtfully, "for I shall not have time enough to make my sackful of toys."

"The shrewd Prince foresaw that," responded Ak, "and therefore named Christmas Eve as the day you might use the deer, knowing it would cause you to lose an entire year."

"If I only had the toys the Awgwas stole from me," said Claus, sadly, "I could easily fill my sack for the children."

"Where are they?" asked the Master.

"I do not know," replied Claus, "but the wicked Awgwas probably hid them in the mountains."

Ak turned to the Fairy Queen.

"Can you find them?" he asked.

"I will try," she replied, brightly.

Then Claus went back to the Laughing Valley, to work as hard as he could, and a band of Fairies immediately flew to the mountain that had been haunted by the Awgwas and began a search for the stolen toys.

The Fairies, as we well know, possess wonderful powers; but the cunning Awgwas had hidden the toys in a deep cave and covered the opening with rocks, so no one could look in. Therefore all search for the missing playthings proved in vain for several days, and Claus, who sat at home waiting for news from the Fairies, almost despaired of getting the toys before Christmas Eve.

He worked hard every moment, but it took considerable time to carve out and to shape each toy and to paint it properly, so that on the morning before Christmas Eve only half of one small shelf above the window was filled with playthings ready for the children.

But on this morning the Fairies who were searching in the mountains had a new thought. They joined hands and moved in a straight line through the rocks that formed the mountain, beginning at the topmost peak and working downward, so that no spot could be missed by their bright eyes. And at last they discovered the cave where the toys had been heaped up by the wicked Awgwas.

It did not take them long to burst open the mouth of the cave, and then each one seized as many toys as he could carry and they all flew to Claus and laid the treasure before him.

The good man was rejoiced to receive, just in the nick of time, such a store of playthings with which to load his sledge, and he sent word to Glossie and Flossie to be ready for the journey at nightfall.

With all his other labors he had managed to find time, since the last trip, to repair the harness and to strengthen his sledge, so that when the deer came to him at twilight he had no difficulty in harnessing them.

"We must go in another direction to-night," he told them, "where we shall find children I have never yet visited. And we must travel fast and work quickly, for my sack is full of toys and running over the brim!"

So, just as the moon arose, they dashed out of the Laughing Valley and across the plain and over the hills to the south. The air was sharp and frosty and the starlight touched the snowflakes and made them glitter like countless diamonds. The reindeer leaped onward with strong, steady bounds, and Claus' heart was so light and merry that he laughed and sang while the wind whistled past his ears:

> *With a ho, ho, ho!*
> *And a ha, ha, ha!*
> *And a ho, ho! ha, ha, hee!*
> *Now away we go*
> *O'er the frozen snow,*
> *As merry as we can be!*

Jack Frost heard him and came racing up with his nippers, but when he saw it was Claus he laughed and turned away again.

The mother owls heard him as he passed near a wood and stuck their heads out of the hollow places in the tree-trunks; but when they saw who it was they whispered to the owlets nestling near them that it was only Santa Claus carrying toys to the children. It is strange how much those mother owls know.

Claus stopped at some of the scattered farmhouses and climbed down the chimneys to leave presents for the babies. Soon after he reached a village and worked merrily for an hour distributing playthings among the sleeping little ones. Then away again he went, signing his joyous carol:

> *Now away we go*
> *O'er the gleaming snow,*
> *While the deer run swift and free!*
> *For to girls and boys*
> *We carry the toys*
> *That will fill their hearts with glee!*

The deer liked the sound of his deep bass voice and kept time to the song with their hoofbeats on the hard snow; but soon they stopped at another chimney and Santa Claus, with sparkling eyes and face brushed red by the wind, climbed down its smoky sides and left a present for every child the house contained.

It was a merry, happy night. Swiftly the deer ran, and busily their driver worked to scatter his gifts among the sleeping children.

But the sack was empty at last, and the sledge headed homeward; and now again the race with daybreak began. Glossie and Flossie had no mind to be rebuked a second time for tardiness, so they fled with a swiftness that enabled them to pass the gale on which the Frost King rode, and soon brought them to the Laughing Valley.

It is true when Claus released his steeds from their harness the eastern sky was streaked with gray, but Glossie and Flossie were deep in the Forest before day fairly broke.

Claus was so wearied with his night's work that he threw himself upon his bed and fell into a deep slumber, and while he slept the Christmas sun appeared in the sky and shone upon hundreds of happy homes where the sound of childish laughter proclaimed that Santa Claus had made them a visit.

God bless him! It was his first Christmas Eve, and for hundreds of years since then he has nobly fulfilled his mission to bring happiness to the hearts of little children.

CHAPTER XI. HOW THE FIRST STOCKINGS WERE HUNG BY THE CHIMNEYS

When you remember that no child, until Santa Claus began his travels, had ever known the pleasure of possessing a toy, you will understand how joy crept into the homes of those who had been favored with a visit from the good man, and how they talked of him day by day in loving tones and were honestly grateful for his kindly deeds. It is true that great warriors and mighty kings and clever scholars of that day were often spoken of by the people; but no one of them was so greatly beloved as Santa Claus, because none other was so unselfish as to devote himself to making others happy. For a generous deed lives longer than a great battle or a king's decree of a scholar's essay, because it spreads and leaves its mark on all nature and endures through many generations.

The bargain made with the Knook Prince changed the plans of Claus for all future time; for, being able to use the reindeer on but one night of each year, he decided to devote all the other days to the manufacture of playthings, and on Christmas Eve to carry them to the children of the world.

But a year's work would, he knew, result in a vast accumulation of toys, so he resolved to build a new sledge that would be larger and stronger and better-fitted for swift travel than the old and clumsy one.

His first act was to visit the Gnome King, with whom he made a bargain to exchange three drums, a trumpet and two dolls for a pair of fine steel runners, curled beautifully at the ends. For the Gnome King had children of his own, who, living in the hollows under the earth, in mines and caverns, needed something to amuse them.

In three days the steel runners were ready, and when Claus brought the playthings to the Gnome King, his Majesty was so greatly pleased with them that he presented Claus with a string of sweet-toned sleigh-bells, in addition to the runners.

"These will please Glossie and Flossie," said Claus, as he jingled the bells and listened to their merry sound. "But I should have two strings of bells, one for each deer."

"Bring me another trumpet and a toy cat," replied the King, "and you shall have a second string of bells like the first."

"It is a bargain!" cried Claus, and he went home again for the toys.

The new sledge was carefully built, the Knooks bringing plenty of strong but thin boards to use in its construction. Claus made a high, rounding dash-board to keep off the snow cast behind by the fleet hoofs of the deer; and he made high sides to the platform so that many toys could be carried, and finally he mounted the sledge upon the slender steel runners made by the Gnome King.

It was certainly a handsome sledge, and big and roomy. Claus painted it in bright colors, although no one was likely to see it during his midnight journeys, and when all was finished he sent for Glossie and Flossie to come and look at it.

The deer admired the sledge, but gravely declared it was too big and heavy for them to draw.

"We might pull it over the snow, to be sure," said Glossie; "but we would not pull it fast enough to enable us to visit the far-away cities and villages and return to the Forest by daybreak."

"Then I must add two more deer to my team," declared Claus, after a moment's thought.

"The Knook Prince allowed you as many as ten. Why not use them all?" asked Flossie. "Then we could speed like the lightning and leap to the highest roofs with ease."

"A team of ten reindeer!" cried Claus, delightedly. "That will be splendid. Please return to the Forest at once and select eight other deer as like yourselves as possible. And you must all eat of the casa plant, to become strong, and of the grawle plant, to become fleet of foot, and of the marbon plant, that you may live long to accompany me on my journeys. Likewise it will be well for you to bathe in the Pool of Nares, which the lovely Queen Zurline declares will render you rarely beautiful. Should you perform these duties faithfully there is no doubt that on next Christmas Eve my ten reindeer will be the most powerful and beautiful steeds the world has ever seen!"

So Glossie and Flossie went to the Forest to choose their mates, and Claus began to consider the question of a harness for them all.

In the end he called upon Peter Knook for assistance, for Peter's heart is as kind as his body is crooked, and he is remarkably shrewd, as well. And Peter agreed to furnish strips of tough leather for the harness.

This leather was cut from the skins of lions that had reached such an advanced age that they died naturally, and on one side was tawny hair while the other side was cured to the softness of velvet by the deft Knooks. When Claus received these strips of leather he sewed them neatly into a harness for the ten reindeer, and it proved strong and serviceable and lasted him for many years.

The harness and sledge were prepared at odd times, for Claus devoted most of his days to the making of toys. These were now much better than the first ones had been, for the immortals often came to his house to watch him work and to offer suggestions. It was Necile's idea to make some of the dolls say "papa" and "mama." It was a thought of the Knooks to put a squeak inside the lambs, so that when a child squeezed them they would say "baa-a-a-a!" And the Fairy Queen advised Claus to put whistles in the birds, so they could be made to sing, and wheels on the horses, so children could draw them around. Many animals perished in the Forest, from one cause or another, and their fur was brought to Claus that he might cover with it the small images of beasts he made for playthings. A merry Ryl suggested that Claus make a donkey with a nodding head, which he did, and afterward found that it amused the little ones immensely. And so the toys grew in beauty and attractiveness every day, until they were the wonder of even the immortals.

When another Christmas Eve drew near there was a monster load of beautiful gifts for the children ready to be loaded upon the big sledge. Claus filled three sacks to the brim, and tucked every corner of the sledge-box full of toys besides.

Then, at twilight, the ten reindeer appeared and Flossie introduced them all to Claus. They were Racer and Pacer, Reckless and Speckless, Fearless and Peerless, and Ready and Steady, who, with Glossie and Flossie, made up the ten who have traversed the world these hundreds of years with their generous master. They were all exceedingly beautiful, with slender limbs, spreading antlers, velvety dark eyes and smooth coats of fawn color spotted with white.

Claus loved them at once, and has loved them ever since, for they are loyal friends and have rendered him priceless service.

The new harness fitted them nicely and soon they were all fastened to the sledge by twos, with Glossie and Flossie in the lead. These wore the strings of sleigh-bells, and were so delighted with the music they made that they kept prancing up and down to make the bells ring.

Claus now seated himself in the sledge, drew a warm robe over his knees and his fur cap over his ears, and cracked his long whip as a signal to start.

Instantly the ten leaped forward and were away like the wind, while jolly Claus laughed gleefully to see them run and shouted a song in his big, hearty voice:

> *With a ho, ho, ho!*
> *And a ha, ha, ha!*
> *And a ho, ho, ha, ha, hee!*
> *Now away we go*
> *O'er the frozen snow,*
> *As merry as we can be!*
> *There are many joys*
> *In our load of toys,*
> *As many a child will know;*
> *We'll scatter them wide*

On our wild night ride
O'er the crisp and sparkling snow!

Now it was on this same Christmas Eve that little Margot and her brother Dick and her cousins Ned and Sara, who were visiting at Margot's house, came in from making a snow man, with their clothes damp, their mittens dripping and their shoes and stockings wet through and through. They were not scolded, for Margot's mother knew the snow was melting, but they were sent early to bed that their clothes might be hung over chairs to dry. The shoes were placed on the red tiles of the hearth, where the heat from the hot embers would strike them, and the stockings were carefully hung in a row by the chimney, directly over the fireplace. That was the reason Santa Claus noticed them when he came down the chimney that night and all the household were fast asleep. He was in a tremendous hurry and seeing the stockings all belonged to children he quickly stuffed his toys into them and dashed up the chimney again, appearing on the roof so suddenly that the reindeer were astonished at his agility.

"I wish they would all hang up their stockings," he thought, as he drove to the next chimney. "It would save me a lot of time and I could then visit more children before daybreak."

When Margot and Dick and Ned and Sara jumped out of bed next morning and ran downstairs to get their stockings from the fireplace they were filled with delight to find the toys from Santa Claus inside them. In face, I think they found more presents in their stockings than any other children of that city had received, for Santa Claus was in a hurry and did not stop to count the toys.

Of course they told all their little friends about it, and of course every one of them decided to hang his own stockings by the fireplace the next Christmas Eve. Even Bessie Blithesome, who made a visit to that city with her father, the great Lord of Lerd, heard the story from the children and hung her own pretty stockings by the chimney when she returned home at Christmas time.

On his next trip Santa Claus found so many stockings hung up in anticipation of his visit that he could fill them in a jiffy and be away again in half the time required to hunt the children up and place the toys by their bedsides.

The custom grew year after year, and has always been a great help to Santa Claus. And, with so many children to visit, he surely needs all the help we are able to give him.

CHAPTER XII. THE FIRST CHRISTMAS TREE

Claus had always kept his promise to the Knooks by returning to the Laughing Valley by daybreak, but only the swiftness of his reindeer has enabled him to do this, for he travels over all the world.

He loved his work and he loved the brisk night ride on his sledge and the gay tinkle of the sleigh-bells. On that first trip with the ten reindeer only Glossie and Flossie wore bells; but each year thereafter for eight years Claus carried presents to the children of the Gnome King, and that good-natured monarch gave him in return a string of bells at each visit, so that finally every one of the ten deer was supplied, and you may imagine what a merry tune the bells played as the sledge sped over the snow.

The children's stockings were so long that it required a great many toys to fill them, and soon Claus found there were other things besides toys that children love. So he sent some of the Fairies, who were always his good friends, into the Tropics, from whence they returned with great bags full of oranges and bananas which they had plucked from the trees. And other Fairies flew to the wonderful Valley of Phunnyland, where delicious candies and bonbons grow thickly on the bushes, and returned laden with many boxes of sweetmeats for the little ones. These things Santa Claus, on each Christmas Eve, placed in the long stockings, together with his toys, and the children were glad to get them, you may be sure.

There are also warm countries where there is no snow in winter, but Claus and his reindeer visited them as well as the colder climes, for there were little wheels inside the runners of his sledge which permitted it to run as smoothly over bare ground as on the snow. And the children who lived in the warm countries learned to know the name of Santa Claus as well as those who lived nearer to the Laughing Valley.

Once, just as the reindeer were ready to start on their yearly trip, a Fairy came to Claus and told him of three little children who lived beneath a rude tent of skins on a broad plain where there were no trees whatever. These poor babies were miserable and unhappy, for their parents were ignorant people who neglected them sadly. Claus resolved to visit these children before he returned home, and during his ride he picked up the bushy top of a pine tree which the wind had broken off and placed it in his sledge.

It was nearly morning when the deer stopped before the lonely tent of skins where the poor children lay asleep. Claus at once planted the bit of pine tree in the sand and stuck many candles on the branches. Then he hung some of his prettiest toys on the tree, as well as several bags of candies. It did not take long to do all this, for Santa Claus works quickly, and when all was ready he lighted the candles and, thrusting his head in at the opening of the tent, he shouted:

"Merry Christmas, little ones!"

With that he leaped into his sledge and was out of sight before the children, rubbing the sleep from their eyes, could come out to see who had called them.

You can imagine the wonder and joy of those little ones, who had never in their lives known a real pleasure before, when they saw the tree, sparkling with lights that shone brilliant in the gray dawn and hung with toys enough to make them happy for years to come! They joined hands and danced around the tree, shouting and laughing, until they were obliged to pause for breath. And their parents, also, came out to look and wonder, and thereafter had more respect and consideration for their children, since Santa Claus had honored them with such beautiful gifts.

The idea of the Christmas tree pleased Claus, and so the following year he carried many of them in his sledge and set them up in the homes of poor people who seldom saw trees, and placed candles and toys on the branches. Of course he could not carry enough trees in one load of all who wanted them, but in some homes the fathers were able to get trees and have them all ready for Santa Claus when he arrived; and these the good Claus always decorated as prettily as possible and hung with toys enough for all the children who came to see the tree lighted.

These novel ideas and the generous manner in which they were carried out made the children long for that one night in the year when their friend Santa Claus should visit them, and as such anticipation is very pleasant and comforting the little ones gleaned much happiness by wondering what would happen when Santa Claus next arrived.

Perhaps you remember that stern Baron Braun who once drove Claus from his castle and forbade him to visit his children? Well, many years afterward, when the old Baron was dead and his son ruled in his place, the new Baron Braun came to the house of Claus with his train of knights and pages and henchmen and, dismounting from his charger, bared his head humbly before the friend of children.

"My father did not know your goodness and worth," he said, "and therefore threatened to hang you from the castle walls. But I have children of my own, who long for a visit from Santa Claus, and I have come to beg that you will favor them hereafter as you do other children."

Claus was pleased with this speech, for Castle Braun was the only place he had never visited, and he gladly promised to bring presents to the Baron's children the next Christmas Eve.

The Baron went away contented, and Claus kept his promise faithfully.

Thus did this man, through very goodness, conquer the hearts of all; and it is no wonder he was ever merry and gay, for there was no home in the wide world where he was not welcomed more royally than any king.

PART THREE: OLD AGE

CHAPTER I. THE MANTLE OF IMMORTALITY

And now we come to a turning-point in the career of Santa Claus, and it is my duty to relate the most remarkable circumstance that has happened since the world began or mankind was created.

We have followed the life of Claus from the time he was found a helpless infant by the Wood-Nymph Necile and reared to manhood in the great Forest of Burzee. And we know how he began to make toys for children and how, with the assistance and goodwill of the immortals, he was able to distribute them to the little ones throughout the world.

For many years he carried on this noble work; for the simple, hard-working life he led gave him perfect health and strength. And doubtless a man can live longer in the beautiful Laughing Valley, where there are no cares and everything is peaceful and merry, than in any other part of the world.

But when many years had rolled away Santa Claus grew old. The long beard of golden brown that once covered his cheeks and chin gradually became gray, and finally turned to pure white. His hair was white, too, and there were wrinkles at the corners of his eyes, which showed plainly when he laughed. He had never been a very tall man, and now he became fat, and waddled very much like a duck when he walked. But in spite of these things he remained as lively as ever, and was just as jolly and gay, and his kind eyes sparkled as brightly as they did that first day when he came to the Laughing Valley.

Yet a time is sure to come when every mortal who has grown old and lived his life is required to leave this world for another; so it is no wonder that, after Santa Claus had driven his reindeer on many and many a Christmas Eve, those stanch friends finally whispered among themselves that they had probably drawn his sledge for the last time.

Then all the Forest of Burzee became sad and all the Laughing Valley was hushed; for every living thing that had known Claus had used to love him and to brighten at the sound of his footsteps or the notes of his merry whistle.

No doubt the old man's strength was at last exhausted, for he made no more toys, but lay on his bed as in a dream.

The Nymph Necile, she who had reared him and been his foster-mother, was still youthful and strong and beautiful, and it seemed to her but a short time since this aged, gray-bearded man had lain in her arms and smiled on her with his innocent, baby lips.

In this is shown the difference between mortals and immortals.

It was fortunate that the great Ak came to the Forest at this time. Necile sought him with troubled eyes and told him of the fate that threatened their friend Claus.

At once the Master became grave, and he leaned upon his ax and stroked his grizzled beard thoughtfully for many minutes. Then suddenly he stood up straight, and poised his powerful head with firm resolve, and stretched out his great right arm as if determined on doing some mighty deed. For a thought had come to him so grand in its conception that all the world might well bow before the Master Woodsman and honor his name forever!

It is well known that when the great Ak once undertakes to do a thing he never hesitates an instant. Now he summoned his fleetest messengers, and sent them in a flash to many parts of the earth. And when they were gone he turned to the anxious Necile and comforted her, saying:

"Be of good heart, my child; our friend still lives. And now run to your Queen and tell her that I have summoned a council of all the immortals of the world to meet with me here in Burzee this night. If they obey, and harken unto my words, Claus will drive his reindeer for countless ages yet to come."

At midnight there was a wondrous scene in the ancient Forest of Burzee, where for the first time in many centuries the rulers of the immortals who inhabit the earth were gathered together.

There was the Queen of the Water Sprites, whose beautiful form was as clear as crystal but continually dripped water on the bank of moss where she sat. And beside her was the King of the Sleep Fays, who carried a wand from the end of which a fine dust fell all around, so that no mortal could keep awake long enough to see him, as mortal eyes were sure to close in sleep as soon as the dust filled them. And next to him sat the Gnome King, whose people inhabit all that region under the earth's surface, where they guard the precious metals and the jewel stones that lie buried in rock and ore. At his right hand stood the King of the Sound Imps, who had wings on his feet, for his people are swift to carry all sounds that are made. When they are busy they carry the sounds but short distances, for there are many of them; but sometimes they speed with the sounds to places miles and miles away from where they are made. The King of the Sound Imps had an anxious and careworn face, for most people have no consideration for his Imps and, especially the boys and girls, make a great many unnecessary sounds which the Imps are obliged to carry when they might be better employed.

The next in the circle of immortals was the King of the Wind Demons, slender of frame, restless and uneasy at being confined to one place for even an hour. Once in a while he would leave his place and circle around the glade, and each time he did this the Fairy Queen was obliged to untangle the flowing locks of her golden hair and tuck them back of her pink ears. But she did not complain, for it was not often that the King of the Wind Demons came into the heart of the Forest. After the Fairy Queen, whose home you know was in old Burzee, came the King of the Light Elves, with his two Princes, Flash and Twilight, at his back. He never went anywhere without his Princes, for they were so mischievous that he dared not let them wander alone.

Prince Flash bore a lightning-bolt in his right hand and a horn of gunpowder in his left, and his bright eyes roved constantly around, as if he longed to use his blinding flashes. Prince Twilight held a great snuffer in one hand and a big black cloak in the other, and it is well known that unless Twilight is carefully watched the snuffers or the cloak will throw everything into darkness, and Darkness is the greatest enemy the King of the Light Elves has.

In addition to the immortals I have named were the King of the Knooks, who had come from his home in the jungles of India; and the King of the Ryls, who lived among the gay flowers and luscious fruits of Valencia. Sweet Queen Zurline of the Wood-Nymphs completed the circle of immortals.

But in the center of the circle sat three others who possessed powers so great that all the Kings and Queens showed them reverence.

These were Ak, the Master Woodsman of the World, who rules the forests and the orchards and the groves; and Kern, the Master Husbandman of the World, who rules the grain fields and the meadows and the gardens; and Bo, the Master Mariner of the World, who rules the seas and all the craft that float thereon. And all other immortals are more or less subject to these three.

When all had assembled the Master Woodsman of the World stood up to address them, since he himself had summoned them to the council.

Very clearly he told them the story of Claus, beginning at the time when as a babe he had been adopted a child of the Forest, and telling of his noble and generous nature and his life-long labors to make children happy.

"And now," said Ak, "when he had won the love of all the world, the Spirit of Death is hovering over him. Of all men who have inhabited the earth none other so well deserves immortality, for such a life can not be spared so long as there are children of mankind to miss him and to grieve over his loss. We immortals are the servants of the world, and to serve the world we were permitted in the Beginning to exist. But what one of us is more worthy of immortality than this man Claus, who so sweetly ministers to the little children?"

He paused and glanced around the circle, to find every immortal listening to him eagerly and nodding approval. Finally the King of the Wind Demons, who had been whistling softly to himself, cried out:

"What is your desire, O Ak?"

"To bestow upon Claus the Mantle of Immortality!" said Ak, boldly.

That this demand was wholly unexpected was proved by the immortals springing to their feet and looking into each other's face with dismay and then upon Ak with wonder. For it was a grave matter, this parting with the Mantle of Immortality.

The Queen of the Water Sprites spoke in her low, clear voice, and the words sounded like raindrops splashing upon a window-pane.

"In all the world there is but one Mantle of Immortality," she said.

The King of the Sound Fays added:

"It has existed since the Beginning, and no mortal has ever dared to claim it."

And the Master Mariner of the World arose and stretched his limbs, saying:

"Only by the vote of every immortal can it be bestowed upon a mortal."

"I know all this," answered Ak, quietly. "But the Mantle exists, and if it was created, as you say, in the Beginning, it was because the Supreme Master knew that some day it would be required. Until now no mortal has deserved it, but who among you dares deny that the good Claus deserves it? Will you not all vote to bestow it upon him?"

They were silent, still looking upon one another questioningly.

"Of what use is the Mantle of Immortality unless it is worn?" demanded Ak. "What will it profit any one of us to allow it to remain in its lonely shrine for all time to come?"

"Enough!" cried the Gnome King, abruptly. "We will vote on the matter, yes or no. For my part, I say yes!"

"And I!" said the Fairy Queen, promptly, and Ak rewarded her with a smile.

"My people in Burzee tell me they have learned to love him; therefore I vote to give Claus the Mantle," said the King of the Ryls.

"He is already a comrade of the Knooks," announced the ancient King of that band. "Let him have immortality!"

"Let him have it—let him have it!" sighed the King of the Wind Demons.

"Why not?" asked the King of the Sleep Fays. "He never disturbs the slumbers my people allow humanity. Let the good Claus be immortal!"

"I do not object," said the King of the Sound Imps.

"Nor I," murmured the Queen of the Water Sprites.

"If Claus does not receive the Mantle it is clear none other can ever claim it," remarked the King of the Light Elves, "so let us have done with the thing for all time."

"The Wood-Nymphs were first to adopt him," said Queen Zurline. "Of course I shall vote to make him immortal."

Ak now turned to the Master Husbandman of the World, who held up his right arm and said "Yes!"

And the Master Mariner of the World did likewise, after which Ak, with sparkling eyes and smiling face, cried out:

"I thank you, fellow immortals! For all have voted 'yes,' and so to our dear Claus shall fall the one Mantle of Immortality that it is in our power to bestow!"

"Let us fetch it at once," said the Fay King; "I'm in a hurry."

They bowed assent, and instantly the Forest glade was deserted. But in a place midway between the earth and the sky was suspended a gleaming crypt of gold and platinum, aglow with soft lights shed from the facets of countless gems. Within a high dome hung the precious Mantle of Immortality, and each immortal placed a hand on the hem of the splendid Robe and said, as with one voice:

"We bestow this Mantle upon Claus, who is called the Patron Saint of Children!"

At this the Mantle came away from its lofty crypt, and they carried it to the house in the Laughing Valley.

The Spirit of Death was crouching very near to the bedside of Claus, and as the immortals approached she sprang up and motioned them back with an angry gesture. But when her eyes fell upon the Mantle they bore she shrank away with a low moan of disappointment and quitted that house forever.

Softly and silently the immortal Band dropped upon Claus the precious Mantle, and it closed about him and sank into the outlines of his body and disappeared from view. It became a part of his being, and neither mortal nor immortal might ever take it from him.

Then the Kings and Queens who had wrought this great deed dispersed to their various homes, and all were well contented that they had added another immortal to their Band.

And Claus slept on, the red blood of everlasting life coursing swiftly through his veins; and on his brow was a tiny drop of water that had fallen from the ever-melting gown of the Queen of the Water Sprites, and over his lips hovered a tender kiss that had been left by the sweet Nymph Necile. For she had stolen in when the others were gone to gaze with rapture upon the immortal form of her foster son.

CHAPTER II. WHEN THE WORLD GREW OLD

The next morning, when Santa Claus opened his eyes and gazed around the familiar room, which he had feared he might never see again, he was astonished to find his old strength renewed and to feel the red blood of perfect health coursing through his veins. He sprang from his bed and stood where the bright sunshine came in through his window and flooded him with its merry, dancing rays. He did not then understand what had happened to restore to him the vigor of youth, but in spite of the fact that his beard remained the color of snow and that wrinkles still lingered in the corners of his bright eyes, old Santa Claus felt as brisk and merry as a boy of sixteen, and was soon whistling contentedly as he busied himself fashioning new toys.

Then Ak came to him and told of the Mantle of Immortality and how Claus had won it through his love for little children.

It made old Santa look grave for a moment to think he had been so favored; but it also made him glad to realize that now he need never fear being parted from his dear ones. At once he began preparations for making a remarkable assortment of pretty and amusing playthings, and in larger quantities than ever before; for now that he might always devote himself to this work he decided that no child in the world, poor or rich, should hereafter go without a Christmas gift if he could manage to supply it.

The world was new in the days when dear old Santa Claus first began toy-making and won, by his loving deeds, the Mantle of Immortality. And the task of supplying cheering words, sympathy and pretty playthings to all the young of his race did not seem a difficult undertaking at all. But every year more and more children were born into the world, and these, when they grew up, began spreading slowly over all the face of the earth, seeking new homes; so that Santa Claus found each year that his journeys must extend farther and farther from the Laughing Valley, and that the packs of toys must be made larger and ever larger.

So at length he took counsel with his fellow immortals how his work might keep pace with the increasing number of children that none might be neglected. And the immortals were so greatly interested in his labors that they gladly rendered him their assistance. Ak gave him his man Kilter, "the silent and swift." And the Knook Prince gave him Peter, who was more crooked and less surly than any of his brothers. And the Ryl Prince gave him Nuter, the sweetest tempered Ryl ever known. And the Fairy Queen gave him Wisk, that tiny, mischievous but lovable Fairy who knows today almost as many children as does Santa Claus himself.

With these people to help make the toys and to keep his house in order and to look after the sledge and the harness, Santa Claus found it much easier to prepare his yearly load of gifts, and his days began to follow one another smoothly and pleasantly.

Yet after a few generations his worries were renewed, for it was remarkable how the number of people continued to grow, and how many more children there were every year to be served. When the people filled all the cities and lands of one country they wandered into another part of the world; and the men cut down the trees in many of the great forests that had been ruled by Ak, and with the wood they built new cities, and where the forests had been were fields of grain and herds of browsing cattle.

You might think the Master Woodsman would rebel at the loss of his forests; but not so. The wisdom of Ak was mighty and farseeing.

"The world was made for men," said he to Santa Claus, "and I have but guarded the forests until men needed them for their use. I am glad my strong trees can furnish shelter for men's weak bodies, and warm them through the cold winters. But I hope they will not cut down all the trees, for mankind needs the shelter of the woods in summer as much as the warmth of blazing logs in winter. And, however crowded the world may grow, I do not think men will ever come to Burzee, nor to the Great Black Forest, nor to the wooded wilderness of Braz; unless they seek their shades for pleasure and not to destroy their giant trees."

By and by people made ships from the tree-trunks and crossed over oceans and built cities in far lands; but the oceans made little difference to the journeys of Santa Claus. His reindeer sped over the waters as swiftly as over land, and his sledge headed from east to west and followed in the wake of the sun. So that as the earth rolled slowly over Santa Claus had all of twenty-four hours to encircle it each Christmas Eve, and the speedy reindeer enjoyed these wonderful journeys more and more.

So year after year, and generation after generation, and century after century, the world grew older and the people became more numerous and the labors of Santa Claus steadily increased. The fame of his good deeds spread to every household where children dwelt. And all the little ones loved him dearly; and the fathers and mothers honored him for the happiness he had given them when they too were young; and the aged grandsires and granddames remembered him with tender gratitude and blessed his name.

CHAPTER III. THE DEPUTIES OF SANTA CLAUS

However, there was one evil following in the path of civilization that caused Santa Claus a vast amount of trouble before he discovered a way to overcome it. But, fortunately, it was the last trial he was forced to undergo.

One Christmas Eve, when his reindeer had leaped to the top of a new building, Santa Claus was surprised to find that the chimney had been built much smaller than usual. But he had no time to think about it just then, so he drew in his breath and made himself as small as possible and slid down the chimney.

"I ought to be at the bottom by this time," he thought, as he continued to slip downward; but no fireplace of any sort met his view, and by and by he reached the very end of the chimney, which was in the cellar.

"This is odd!" he reflected, much puzzled by this experience. "If there is no fireplace, what on earth is the chimney good for?"

Then he began to climb out again, and found it hard work—the space being so small. And on his way up he noticed a thin, round pipe sticking through the side of the chimney, but could not guess what it was for.

Finally he reached the roof and said to the reindeer:

"There was no need of my going down that chimney, for I could find no fireplace through which to enter the house. I fear the children who live there must go without playthings this Christmas."

Then he drove on, but soon came to another new house with a small chimney. This caused Santa Claus to shake his head doubtfully, but he tried the chimney, nevertheless, and found it exactly like the other. Moreover, he nearly stuck fast in the narrow flue and tore his jacket trying to get out again; so, although he came to several such chimneys that night, he did not venture to descend any more of them.

"What in the world are people thinking of, to build such useless chimneys?" he exclaimed. "In all the years I have traveled with my reindeer I have never seen the like before."

True enough; but Santa Claus had not then discovered that stoves had been invented and were fast coming into use. When he did find it out he wondered how the builders of those houses could have so little consideration for him, when they knew very well it was his custom to climb down chimneys and enter houses by way of the fireplaces. Perhaps the men who built those houses had outgrown their own love for toys, and were indifferent whether Santa Claus called on their children or not. Whatever the explanation might be, the poor children were forced to bear the burden of grief and disappointment.

The following year Santa Claus found more and more of the new-fashioned chimneys that had no fireplaces, and the next year still more. The third year, so numerous had the narrow chimneys become, he even had a few toys left in his sledge that he was unable to give away, because he could not get to the children.

The matter had now become so serious that it worried the good man greatly, and he decided to talk it over with Kilter and Peter and Nuter and Wisk.

Kilter already knew something about it, for it had been his duty to run around to all the houses, just before Christmas, and gather up the notes and letters to Santa Claus that the children had written, telling what they wished put in their stockings or hung on their Christmas trees. But Kilter was a silent fellow, and seldom spoke of what he saw in the cities and villages. The others were very indignant.

"Those people act as if they do not wish their children to be made happy!" said sensible Peter, in a vexed tone. "The idea of shutting out such a generous friend to their little ones!"

"But it is my intention to make children happy whether their parents wish it or not," returned Santa Claus. "Years ago, when I first began making toys, children were even more neglected by their parents than they are now; so I have learned to pay no attention to thoughtless or selfish parents, but to consider only the longings of childhood."

"You are right, my master," said Nuter, the Ryl; "many children would lack a friend if you did not consider them, and try to make them happy."

"Then," declared the laughing Wisk, "we must abandon any thought of using these new-fashioned chimneys, but become burglars, and break into the houses some other way."

"What way?" asked Santa Claus.

"Why, walls of brick and wood and plaster are nothing to Fairies. I can easily pass through them whenever I wish, and so can Peter and Nuter and Kilter. Is it not so, comrades?"

"I often pass through the walls when I gather up the letters," said Kilter, and that was a long speech for him, and so surprised Peter and Nuter that their big round eyes nearly popped out of their heads.

"Therefore," continued the Fairy, "you may as well take us with you on your next journey, and when we come to one of those houses with stoves instead of fireplaces we will distribute the toys to the children without the need of using a chimney."

"That seems to me a good plan," replied Santa Claus, well pleased at having solved the problem. "We will try it next year."

That was how the Fairy, the Pixie, the Knook and the Ryl all rode in the sledge with their master the following Christmas Eve; and they had no trouble at all in entering the new-fashioned houses and leaving toys for the children that lived in them.

And their deft services not only relieved Santa Claus of much labor, but enabled him to complete his own work more quickly than usual, so that the merry party found themselves at home with an empty sledge a full hour before daybreak.

The only drawback to the journey was that the mischievous Wisk persisted in tickling the reindeer with a long feather, to see them jump; and Santa Claus found it necessary to watch him every minute and to tweak his long ears once or twice to make him behave himself.

But, taken all together, the trip was a great success, and to this day the four little folk always accompany Santa Claus on his yearly ride and help him in the distribution of his gifts.

But the indifference of parents, which had so annoyed the good Saint, did not continue very long, and Santa Claus soon found they were really anxious he should visit their homes on Christmas Eve and leave presents for their children.

So, to lighten his task, which was fast becoming very difficult indeed, old Santa decided to ask the parents to assist him.

"Get your Christmas trees all ready for my coming," he said to them; "and then I shall be able to leave the presents without loss of time, and you can put them on the trees when I am gone."

And to others he said: "See that the children's stockings are hung up in readiness for my coming, and then I can fill them as quick as a wink."

And often, when parents were kind and good-natured, Santa Claus would simply fling down his package of gifts and leave the fathers and mothers to fill the stockings after he had darted away in his sledge.

"I will make all loving parents my deputies!" cried the jolly old fellow, "and they shall help me do my work. For in this way I shall save many precious minutes and few children need be neglected for lack of time to visit them."

Besides carrying around the big packs in his swift-flying sledge old Santa began to send great heaps of toys to the toy-shops, so that if parents wanted larger supplies for their children they could easily get them; and if any children were, by chance, missed by Santa Claus on his yearly rounds, they could go to the toy-shops and get enough to make them happy and contented. For the loving friend of the little ones decided that no child, if he could help it, should long for toys in vain. And the toy-shops also proved convenient whenever a child fell ill, and needed a new toy to amuse it; and sometimes, on birthdays, the fathers and mothers go to the toy-shops and get pretty gifts for their children in honor of the happy event.

Perhaps you will now understand how, in spite of the bigness of the world, Santa Claus is able to supply all the children with beautiful gifts. To be sure, the old gentleman is rarely seen in these days; but it is not because he tries to keep out of sight, I assure you. Santa Claus is the same loving friend of children that in the old days used to play and romp with them by the hour; and I know he would love to do the same now, if he had the time. But, you see, he is so busy all the year making toys, and so hurried on that one night when he visits our homes with his packs, that he comes and goes among us like a flash; and it is almost impossible to catch a glimpse of him.

And, although there are millions and millions more children in the world than there used to be, Santa Claus has never been known to complain of their increasing numbers.

"The more the merrier!" he cries, with his jolly laugh; and the only difference to him is the fact that his little workmen have to make their busy fingers fly faster every year to satisfy the demands of so many little ones.

"In all this world there is nothing so beautiful as a happy child," says good old Santa Claus; and if he had his way the children would all be beautiful, for all would be happy.

A Kidnapped Santa Claus

L. Frank Baum

Santa Claus lives in the Laughing Valley, where stands the big, rambling castle in which his toys are manufactured. His workmen, selected from the ryls, knooks, pixies and fairies, live with him, and every one is as busy as can be from one year's end to another.

It is called the Laughing Valley because everything there is happy and gay. The brook chuckles to itself as it leaps rollicking between its green banks; the wind whistles merrily in the trees; the sunbeams dance lightly over the soft grass, and the violets and wild flowers look smilingly up from their green nests. To laugh one needs to be happy; to be happy one needs to be content. And throughout the Laughing Valley of Santa Claus contentment reigns supreme.

On one side is the mighty Forest of Burzee. At the other side stands the huge mountain that contains the Caves of the Daemons. And between them the Valley lies smiling and peaceful.

One would think that our good old Santa Claus, who devotes his days to making children happy, would have no enemies on all the earth; and, as a matter of fact, for a long period of time he encountered nothing but love wherever he might go.

But the Daemons who live in the mountain caves grew to hate Santa Claus very much, and all for the simple reason that he made children happy.

The Caves of the Daemons are five in number. A broad pathway leads up to the first cave, which is a finely arched cavern at the foot of the mountain, the entrance being beautifully carved and decorated. In it resides the Daemon of Selfishness. Back of this is another cavern inhabited by the Daemon of Envy. The cave of the Daemon of Hatred is next in order, and through this one passes to the home of the Daemon of Malice—situated in a dark and fearful cave in the very heart of the mountain. I do not know what lies beyond this. Some say there are terrible pitfalls leading to death and destruction, and this may very well be true. However, from each one of the four caves mentioned there is a small, narrow tunnel leading to the fifth cave—a cozy little room occupied by the Daemon of Repentance. And as the rocky floors of these passages are well worn by the track of passing feet, I judge that many wanderers in the Caves of the Daemons have escaped through the tunnels to the abode of the Daemon of Repentance, who is said to be a pleasant sort of fellow who gladly opens for one a little door admitting you into fresh air and sunshine again.

Well, these Daemons of the Caves, thinking they had great cause to dislike old Santa Claus, held a meeting one day to discuss the matter.

"I'm really getting lonesome," said the Daemon of Selfishness. "For Santa Claus distributes so many pretty Christmas gifts to all the children that they become happy and generous, through his example, and keep away from my cave."

"I'm having the same trouble," rejoined the Daemon of Envy. "The little ones seem quite content with Santa Claus, and there are few, indeed, that I can coax to become envious."

"And that makes it bad for me!" declared the Daemon of Hatred. "For if no children pass through the Caves of Selfishness and Envy, none can get to *my* cavern."

"Or to mine," added the Daemon of Malice.

"For my part," said the Daemon of Repentance, "it is easily seen that if children do not visit your caves they have no need to visit mine; so that I am quite as neglected as you are."

"And all because of this person they call Santa Claus!" exclaimed the Daemon of Envy. "He is simply ruining our business, and something must be done at once."

To this they readily agreed; but what to do was another and more difficult matter to settle. They knew that Santa Claus worked all through the year at his castle in the Laughing Valley, preparing the gifts he was to distribute on Christmas Eve; and at first they resolved to try to tempt him into their caves, that they might lead him on to the terrible pitfalls that ended in destruction.

So the very next day, while Santa Claus was busily at work, surrounded by his little band of assistants, the Daemon of Selfishness came to him and said:

"These toys are wonderfully bright and pretty. Why do you not keep them for yourself? It's a pity to give them to those noisy boys and fretful girls, who break and destroy them so quickly."

"Nonsense!" cried the old graybeard, his bright eyes twinkling merrily as he turned toward the tempting Daemon. "The boys and girls are never so noisy and fretful after receiving my presents, and if I can make them happy for one day in the year I am quite content."

So the Daemon went back to the others, who awaited him in their caves, and said:

"I have failed, for Santa Claus is not at all selfish."

The following day the Daemon of Envy visited Santa Claus. Said he: "The toy shops are full of playthings quite as pretty as those you are making. What a shame it is that they should interfere with your business! They make toys by machinery much quicker than you can make them by hand; and they sell them for money, while you get nothing at all for your work."

But Santa Claus refused to be envious of the toy shops.

"I can supply the little ones but once a year—on Christmas Eve," he answered; "for the children are many, and I am but one. And as my work is one of love and kindness I would be ashamed to receive money for my little gifts. But throughout all the year the children must be amused in some way, and so the toy shops are able to bring much happiness to my little friends. I like the toy shops, and am glad to see them prosper."

In spite of the second rebuff, the Daemon of Hatred thought he would try to influence Santa Claus. So the next day he entered the busy workshop and said:

"Good morning, Santa! I have bad news for you."

"Then run away, like a good fellow," answered Santa Claus. "Bad news is something that should be kept secret and never told."

"You cannot escape this, however," declared the Daemon; "for in the world are a good many who do not believe in Santa Claus, and these you are bound to hate bitterly, since they have so wronged you."

"Stuff and rubbish!" cried Santa.

"And there are others who resent your making children happy and who sneer at you and call you a foolish old rattlepate! You are quite right to hate such base slanderers, and you ought to be revenged upon them for their evil words."

"But I don't hate 'em!" exclaimed Santa Claus positively. "Such people do me no real harm, but merely render themselves and their children unhappy. Poor things! I'd much rather help them any day than injure them."

Indeed, the Daemons could not tempt old Santa Claus in any way. On the contrary, he was shrewd enough to see that their object in visiting him was to make mischief and trouble, and his cheery laughter disconcerted the evil ones and showed to them the folly of such an undertaking. So they abandoned honeyed words and determined to use force.

It was well known that no harm can come to Santa Claus while he is in the Laughing Valley, for the fairies, and ryls, and knooks all protect him. But on Christmas Eve he drives his reindeer out into the big world, carrying a sleighload of toys and pretty gifts to the children; and this was the time and the occasion when his enemies had the best chance to injure him. So the Daemons laid their plans and awaited the arrival of Christmas Eve.

The moon shone big and white in the sky, and the snow lay crisp and sparkling on the ground as Santa Claus cracked his whip and sped away out of the Valley into the great world beyond. The roomy sleigh was packed full with huge sacks of toys, and as the reindeer dashed onward our jolly old Santa laughed and whistled and sang for very joy. For in all his merry life this was the one day in the year when he was happiest—the day he lovingly bestowed the treasures of his workshop upon the little children.

It would be a busy night for him, he well knew. As he whistled and shouted and cracked his whip again, he reviewed in mind all the towns and cities and farmhouses where he was expected, and figured that he had just enough presents to go around and make every child happy. The reindeer knew exactly what was expected of them, and dashed along so swiftly that their feet scarcely seemed to touch the snow-covered ground.

Suddenly a strange thing happened: a rope shot through the moonlight and a big noose that was in the end of it settled over the arms and body of Santa Claus and drew tight. Before he could resist or even cry out he was jerked from the seat of the sleigh and tumbled head foremost into a snowbank, while the reindeer rushed onward with the load of toys and carried it quickly out of sight and sound.

Such a surprising experience confused old Santa for a moment, and when he had collected his senses he found that the wicked Daemons had pulled him from the snowdrift and bound him tightly with many coils of the stout rope. And then they carried the kidnapped Santa Claus away to their mountain, where they thrust the prisoner into a secret cave and chained him to the rocky wall so that he could not escape.

"Ha, ha!" laughed the Daemons, rubbing their hands together with cruel glee. "What will the children do now? How they will cry and scold and storm when they find there are no toys in their stockings and no gifts on their Christmas trees! And what a lot of punishment they will receive from their parents, and how they will flock to our Caves of Selfishness, and Envy, and Hatred, and Malice! We have done a mighty clever thing, we Daemons of the Caves!"

Now it so chanced that on this Christmas Eve the good Santa Claus had taken with him in his sleigh Nuter the Ryl, Peter the Knook, Kilter the Pixie, and a small fairy named Wisk—his four favorite assistants. These little people he had often found very useful in helping him to distribute his gifts to the children, and when their master was so suddenly dragged from the sleigh they were all snugly tucked underneath the seat, where the sharp wind could not reach them.

The tiny immortals knew nothing of the capture of Santa Claus until some time after he had disappeared. But finally they missed his cheery voice, and as their master always sang or whistled on his journeys, the silence warned them that something was wrong.

Little Wisk stuck out his head from underneath the seat and found Santa Claus gone and no one to direct the flight of the reindeer.

"Whoa!" he called out, and the deer obediently slackened speed and came to a halt.

Peter and Nuter and Kilter all jumped upon the seat and looked back over the track made by the sleigh. But Santa Claus had been left miles and miles behind.

"What shall we do?" asked Wisk anxiously, all the mirth and mischief banished from his wee face by this great calamity.

"We must go back at once and find our master," said Nuter the Ryl, who thought and spoke with much deliberation.

"No, no!" exclaimed Peter the Knook, who, cross and crabbed though he was, might always be depended upon in an emergency. "If we delay, or go back, there will not be time to get the toys to the children before morning; and that would grieve Santa Claus more than anything else."

"It is certain that some wicked creatures have captured him," added Kilter thoughtfully, "and their object must be to make the children unhappy. So our first duty is to get the toys distributed as carefully as if Santa Claus were himself present. Afterward we can search for our master and easily secure his freedom."

This seemed such good and sensible advice that the others at once resolved to adopt it. So Peter the Knook called to the reindeer, and the faithful animals again sprang forward and dashed over hill and valley, through forest and plain, until they came to the houses wherein children lay sleeping and dreaming of the pretty gifts they would find on Christmas morning.

The little immortals had set themselves a difficult task; for although they had assisted Santa Claus on many of his journeys, their master had always directed and guided them and told them exactly what he wished them to do. But now they had to distribute the toys according to their own judgment, and they did not understand children as well as did old Santa. So it is no wonder they made some laughable errors.

Mamie Brown, who wanted a doll, got a drum instead; and a drum is of no use to a girl who loves dolls. And Charlie Smith, who delights to romp and play out of doors, and who wanted some new rubber boots to keep his feet dry, received a sewing box filled with colored worsteds and threads and needles, which made him so provoked that he thoughtlessly called our dear Santa Claus a fraud.

Had there been many such mistakes the Daemons would have accomplished their evil purpose and made the children unhappy. But the little friends of the absent Santa Claus labored faithfully and intelligently to carry out their master's ideas, and they made fewer errors than might be expected under such unusual circumstances.

And, although they worked as swiftly as possible, day had begun to break before the toys and other presents were all distributed; so for the first time in many years the reindeer trotted into the Laughing Valley, on their return, in broad daylight, with the brilliant sun peeping over the edge of the forest to prove they were far behind their accustomed hours.

Having put the deer in the stable, the little folk began to wonder how they might rescue their master; and they realized they must discover, first of all, what had happened to him and where he was.

So Wisk the Fairy transported himself to the bower of the Fairy Queen, which was located deep in the heart of the Forest of Burzee; and once there, it did not take him long to find out all about the naughty Daemons and how they had kidnapped the good Santa Claus to prevent his making children happy. The Fairy Queen also promised her assistance, and then, fortified by this powerful support, Wisk flew back to where Nuter and Peter and Kilter awaited him, and the four counseled together and laid plans to rescue their master from his enemies.

It is possible that Santa Claus was not as merry as usual during the night that succeeded his capture. For although he had faith in the judgment of his little friends he could not avoid a certain amount of worry, and an anxious look would creep at times into his kind old eyes as he thought of the disappointment that might await his dear little children. And the Daemons, who guarded him by turns, one after another, did not neglect to taunt him with contemptuous words in his helpless condition.

When Christmas Day dawned the Daemon of Malice was guarding the prisoner, and his tongue was sharper than that of any of the others.

"The children are waking up, Santa!" he cried. "They are waking up to find their stockings empty! Ho, ho! How they will quarrel, and wail, and stamp their feet in anger! Our caves will be full today, old Santa! Our caves are sure to be full!"

But to this, as to other like taunts, Santa Claus answered nothing. He was much grieved by his capture, it is true; but his courage did not forsake him. And, finding that the prisoner would not reply to his jeers, the Daemon of Malice presently went away, and sent the Daemon of Repentance to take his place.

This last personage was not so disagreeable as the others. He had gentle and refined features, and his voice was soft and pleasant in tone.

"My brother Daemons do not trust me overmuch," said he, as he entered the cavern; "but it is morning, now, and the mischief is done. You cannot visit the children again for another year."

"That is true," answered Santa Claus, almost cheerfully; "Christmas Eve is past, and for the first time in centuries I have not visited my children."

"The little ones will be greatly disappointed," murmured the Daemon of Repentance, almost regretfully; "but that cannot be helped now. Their grief is likely to make the children selfish and envious and hateful, and if they come to the Caves of the Daemons today I shall get a chance to lead some of them to my Cave of Repentance."

"Do you never repent, yourself?" asked Santa Claus, curiously.

"Oh, yes, indeed," answered the Daemon. "I am even now repenting that I assisted in your capture. Of course it is too late to remedy the evil that has been done; but repentance, you know, can come only after an evil thought or deed, for in the beginning there is nothing to repent of."

"So I understand," said Santa Claus. "Those who avoid evil need never visit your cave."

"As a rule, that is true," replied the Daemon; "yet you, who have done no evil, are about to visit my cave at once; for to prove that I sincerely regret my share in your capture I am going to permit you to escape."

This speech greatly surprised the prisoner, until he reflected that it was just what might be expected of the Daemon of Repentance. The fellow at once busied himself untying the knots that bound Santa Claus and unlocking the chains that fastened him to the wall. Then he led the way through a long tunnel until they both emerged in the Cave of Repentance.

"I hope you will forgive me," said the Daemon pleadingly. "I am not really a bad person, you know; and I believe I accomplish a great deal of good in the world."

With this he opened a back door that let in a flood of sunshine, and Santa Claus sniffed the fresh air gratefully.

"I bear no malice," said he to the Daemon, in a gentle voice; "and I am sure the world would be a dreary place without you. So, good morning, and a Merry Christmas to you!"

With these words he stepped out to greet the bright morning, and a moment later he was trudging along, whistling softly to himself, on his way to his home in the Laughing Valley.

Marching over the snow toward the mountain was a vast army, made up of the most curious creatures imaginable. There were numberless knooks from the forest, as rough and crooked in appearance as the gnarled branches of the trees they ministered to. And there were dainty ryls from the fields, each one bearing the emblem of the flower or plant it guarded. Behind these were many ranks of pixies, gnomes and nymphs, and in the rear a thousand beautiful fairies floated along in gorgeous array.

This wonderful army was led by Wisk, Peter, Nuter, and Kilter, who had assembled it to rescue Santa Claus from captivity and to punish the Daemons who had dared to take him away from his beloved children.

And, although they looked so bright and peaceful, the little immortals were armed with powers that would be very terrible to those who had incurred their anger. Woe to the Daemons of the Caves if this mighty army of vengeance ever met them!

But lo! coming to meet his loyal friends appeared the imposing form of Santa

Claus, his white beard floating in the breeze and his bright eyes sparkling with pleasure at this proof of the love and veneration he had inspired in the hearts of the most powerful creatures in existence.

And while they clustered around him and danced with glee at his safe return, he gave them earnest thanks for their support. But Wisk, and Nuter, and Peter, and Kilter, he embraced affectionately.

"It is useless to pursue the Daemons," said Santa Claus to the army. "They have their place in the world, and can never be destroyed. But that is a great pity, nevertheless," he continued musingly.

So the fairies, and knooks, and pixies, and ryls all escorted the good man to his castle, and there left him to talk over the events of the night with his little assistants.

Wisk had already rendered himself invisible and flown through the big world to see how the children were getting along on this bright Christmas morning; and by the time he returned, Peter had finished telling Santa Claus of how they had distributed the toys.

"We really did very well," cried the fairy, in a pleased voice; "for I found little unhappiness among the children this morning. Still, you must not get captured again, my dear master; for we might not be so fortunate another time in carrying out your ideas."

He then related the mistakes that had been made, and which he had not discovered until his tour of inspection. And Santa Claus at once sent him with rubber boots for Charlie Smith, and a doll for Mamie Brown; so that even those two disappointed ones became happy.

As for the wicked Daemons of the Caves, they were filled with anger and chagrin when they found that their clever capture of Santa Claus had come to naught. Indeed, no one on that Christmas Day appeared to be at all selfish, or envious, or hateful. And, realizing that while the children's saint had so many powerful friends it was folly to oppose him, the Daemons never again attempted to interfere with his journeys on Christmas Eve.

The Gift of the Magi

O. Henry

One dollar and eighty-seven cents. That was all. And sixty cents of it was in pennies. Pennies saved one and two at a time by bulldozing the grocer and the vegetable man and the butcher until one's cheeks burned with the silent imputation of parsimony that such close dealing implied. Three times Della counted it. One dollar and eighty-seven cents. And the next day would be Christmas.

There was clearly nothing to do but flop down on the shabby little couch and howl. So Della did it. Which instigates the moral reflection that life is made up of sobs, sniffles, and smiles, with sniffles predominating.

While the mistress of the home is gradually subsiding from the first stage to the second, take a look at the home. A furnished flat at $8 per week. It did not exactly beggar description, but it certainly had that word on the lookout for the mendicancy squad.

In the vestibule below was a letter-box into which no letter would go, and an electric button from which no mortal finger could coax a ring. Also appertaining thereunto was a card bearing the name "Mr. James Dillingham Young."

The "Dillingham" had been flung to the breeze during a former period of prosperity when its possessor was being paid $30 per week. Now, when the income was shrunk to $20, though, they were thinking seriously of contracting to a modest and unassuming D. But whenever Mr. James Dillingham Young came home and reached his flat above he was called "Jim" and greatly hugged by Mrs. James Dillingham Young, already introduced to you as Della. Which is all very good.

Della finished her cry and attended to her cheeks with the powder rag. She stood by the window and looked out dully at a gray cat walking a gray fence in a gray backyard. Tomorrow would be Christmas Day, and she had only $1.87 with which to buy Jim a present. She had been saving every penny she could for months, with this result. Twenty dollars a week doesn't go far. Expenses had been greater than she had calculated. They always are. Only $1.87 to buy a present for Jim. Her Jim. Many a happy hour she had spent planning for something nice for him. Something fine and rare and sterling—something just a little bit near to being worthy of the honor of being owned by Jim.

There was a pier-glass between the windows of the room. Perhaps you have seen a pier-glass in an $8 flat. A very thin and very agile person may, by observing his reflection in a rapid sequence of longitudinal strips, obtain a fairly accurate conception of his looks. Della, being slender, had mastered the art.

Suddenly she whirled from the window and stood before the glass. Her eyes were shining brilliantly, but her face had lost its color within twenty seconds. Rapidly she pulled down her hair and let it fall to its full length.

Now, there were two possessions of the James Dillingham Youngs in which they both took a mighty pride. One was Jim's gold watch that had been his father's and his grandfather's. The other was Della's hair. Had the queen of Sheba lived in the flat across the airshaft, Della would have let her hair hang out the window some day to dry just to depreciate Her Majesty's jewels and gifts. Had King Solomon been the janitor, with all his treasures piled up in the basement, Jim would have pulled out his watch every time he passed, just to see him pluck at his beard from envy.

So now Della's beautiful hair fell about her rippling and shining like a cascade of brown waters. It reached below her knee and made itself almost a garment for her. And then she did it up again nervously and quickly. Once she faltered for a minute and stood still while a tear or two splashed on the worn red carpet.

On went her old brown jacket; on went her old brown hat. With a whirl of skirts and with the brilliant sparkle still in her eyes, she fluttered out the door and down the stairs to the street.

Where she stopped the sign read: "Mne. Sofronie. Hair Goods of All Kinds." One flight up Della ran, and collected herself, panting. Madame, large, too white, chilly, hardly looked the "Sofronie."

"Will you buy my hair?" asked Della.

"I buy hair," said Madame. "Take yer hat off and let's have a sight at the looks of it."

Down rippled the brown cascade.

"Twenty dollars," said Madame, lifting the mass with a practised hand.

"Give it to me quick," said Della.

Oh, and the next two hours tripped by on rosy wings. Forget the hashed metaphor. She was ransacking the stores for Jim's present.

She found it at last. It surely had been made for Jim and no one else. There was no other like it in any of the stores, and she had turned all of them inside out. It was a platinum fob chain simple and chaste in design, properly proclaiming its value by substance alone and not by meretricious ornamentation—as all good things should do. It was even worthy of The Watch. As soon as she saw it she knew that it must be Jim's. It was like him. Quietness and value—the description applied to both. Twenty-one dollars they took from her for it, and she hurried home with the 87 cents. With that chain on his watch Jim might be properly anxious about the time in any company. Grand as the watch was, he sometimes looked at it on the sly on account of the old leather strap that he used in place of a chain.

When Della reached home her intoxication gave way a little to prudence and reason. She got out her curling irons and lighted the gas and went to work repairing the ravages made by generosity added to love. Which is always a tremendous task, dear friends—a mammoth task.

Within forty minutes her head was covered with tiny, close-lying curls that made her look wonderfully like a truant schoolboy. She looked at her reflection in the mirror long, carefully, and critically.

"If Jim doesn't kill me," she said to herself, "before he takes a second look at me, he'll say I look like a Coney Island chorus girl. But what could I do—oh! what could I do with a dollar and eighty-seven cents?"

At 7 o'clock the coffee was made and the frying-pan was on the back of the stove hot and ready to cook the chops.

Jim was never late. Della doubled the fob chain in her hand and sat on the corner of the table near the door that he always entered. Then she heard his step on the stair away down on the first flight, and she turned white for just a moment. She had a habit for saying little silent prayer about the simplest everyday things, and now she whispered: "Please God, make him think I am still pretty."

The door opened and Jim stepped in and closed it. He looked thin and very serious. Poor fellow, he was only twenty-two—and to be burdened with a family! He needed a new overcoat and he was without gloves.

Jim stopped inside the door, as immovable as a setter at the scent of quail. His eyes were fixed upon Della, and there was an expression in them that she could not read, and it terrified her. It was not anger, nor surprise, nor disapproval, nor horror, nor any of the sentiments that she had been prepared for. He simply stared at her fixedly with that peculiar expression on his face.

Della wriggled off the table and went for him.

"Jim, darling," she cried, "don't look at me that way. I had my hair cut off and sold because I couldn't have lived through Christmas without giving you a present. It'll grow out again—you won't mind, will you? I just had to do it. My hair grows awfully fast. Say 'Merry Christmas!' Jim, and let's be happy. You don't know what a nice—what a beautiful, nice gift I've got for you."

"You've cut off your hair?" asked Jim, laboriously, as if he had not arrived at that patent fact yet even after the hardest mental labor.

"Cut it off and sold it," said Della. "Don't you like me just as well, anyhow? I'm me without my hair, ain't I?"

Jim looked about the room curiously.

"You say your hair is gone?" he said, with an air almost of idiocy.

"You needn't look for it," said Della. "It's sold, I tell you—sold and gone, too. It's Christmas Eve, boy. Be good to me, for it went for you. Maybe the hairs of my head were numbered," she went on with sudden serious sweetness, "but nobody could ever count my love for you. Shall I put the chops on, Jim?"

Out of his trance Jim seemed quickly to wake. He enfolded his Della. For ten seconds let us regard with discreet scrutiny some inconsequential object in the other direction. Eight dollars a week or a million a year—what is the difference? A mathematician or a wit would give you the wrong answer. The magi brought valuable gifts, but that was not among them. This dark assertion will be illuminated later on.

Jim drew a package from his overcoat pocket and threw it upon the table.

"Don't make any mistake, Dell," he said, "about me. I don't think there's anything in the way of a haircut or a shave or a shampoo that could make me like my girl any less. But if you'll unwrap that package you may see why you had me going a while at first."

White fingers and nimble tore at the string and paper. And then an ecstatic scream of joy; and then, alas! a quick feminine change to hysterical tears and wails, necessitating the immediate employment of all the comforting powers of the lord of the flat.

For there lay The Combs—the set of combs, side and back, that Della had worshipped long in a Broadway window. Beautiful combs, pure tortoise shell, with jewelled rims—just the shade to wear in the beautiful vanished hair. They were expensive combs, she knew, and her heart had simply craved and yearned over them without the least hope of possession. And now, they were hers, but the tresses that should have adorned the coveted adornments were gone.

But she hugged them to her bosom, and at length she was able to look up with dim eyes and a smile and say: "My hair grows so fast, Jim!"

And then Della leaped up like a little singed cat and cried, "Oh, oh!"

Jim had not yet seen his beautiful present. She held it out to him eagerly upon her open palm. The dull precious metal seemed to flash with a reflection of her bright and ardent spirit.

"Isn't it a dandy, Jim? I hunted all over town to find it. You'll have to look at the time a hundred times a day now. Give me your watch. I want to see how it looks on it."

Instead of obeying, Jim tumbled down on the couch and put his hands under the back of his head and smiled.

"Dell," said he, "let's put our Christmas presents away and keep 'em a while.

They're too nice to use just at present. I sold the watch to get the money to buy your combs. And now suppose you put the chops on."

The magi, as you know, were wise men—wonderfully wise men—who brought gifts to the Babe in the manger. They invented the art of giving Christmas presents. Being wise, their gifts were no doubt wise ones, possibly bearing the privilege of exchange in case of duplication. And here I have lamely related to you the uneventful chronicle of two foolish children in a flat who most unwisely sacrificed for each other the greatest treasures of their house. But in a last word to the wise of these days let it be said that of all who give gifts these two were the wisest. O all who give and receive gifts, such as they are wisest. Everywhere they are wisest. They are the magi.

The Christmas Surprise at Enderly Road

Lucy Maud Montgomery

Phil, I'm getting fearfully hungry. When are we going to strike civilization?"

The speaker was my chum, Frank Ward. We were home from our academy for the Christmas holidays and had been amusing ourselves on this sunshiny December afternoon by a tramp through the "back lands," as the barrens that swept away south behind the village were called. They were grown over with scrub maple and spruce, and were quite pathless save for meandering sheep tracks that crossed and recrossed, but led apparently nowhere.

Frank and I did not know exactly where we were, but the back lands were not so extensive but that we would come out somewhere if we kept on. It was getting late and we wished to go home.

"I have an idea that we ought to strike civilization somewhere up the Enderly Road pretty soon," I answered.

"Do you call *that* civilization?" said Frank, with a laugh.

No Blackburn Hill boy was ever known to miss an opportunity of flinging a slur at Enderly Road, even if no Enderly Roader were by to feel the sting.

Enderly Road was a miserable little settlement straggling back from Blackburn Hill. It was a forsaken looking place, and the people, as a rule, were poor and shiftless. Between Blackburn Hill and Enderly Road very little social intercourse existed and, as the Road people resented what they called the pride of Blackburn Hill, there was a good deal of bad feeling between the two districts.

Presently Frank and I came out on the Enderly Road. We sat on the fence a few minutes to rest and discuss our route home. "If we go by the road it's three miles," said Frank. "Isn't there a short cut?"

"There ought to be one by the wood-lane that comes out by Jacob Hart's," I answered, "but I don't know where to strike it."

"Here is someone coming now; we'll inquire," said Frank, looking up the curve of the hard-frozen road. The "someone" was a little girl of about ten years old, who was trotting along with a basketful of school books on her arm. She was a pale, pinched little thing, and her jacket and red hood seemed very old and thin.

"Hello, missy," I said, as she came up, and then I stopped, for I saw she had been crying.

"What is the matter?" asked Frank, who was much more at ease with children than I was, and had always a warm spot in his heart for their small troubles. "Has your teacher kept you in for being naughty?"

The mite dashed her little red knuckles across her eyes and answered indignantly, "No, indeed. I stayed after school with Minnie Lawler to sweep the floor."

"And did you and Minnie quarrel, and is that why you are crying?" asked Frank solemnly.

"Minnie and I *never* quarrel. I am crying because we can't have the school decorated on Monday for the examination, after all. The Dickeys have gone back on us . . . after promising, too," and the tears began to swell up in the blue eyes again.

"Very bad behaviour on the part of the Dickeys," commented Frank. "But can't you decorate the school without them?"

"Why, of course not. They are the only big boys in the school. They said they would cut the boughs, and bring a ladder tomorrow and help us nail the wreaths up, and now they won't . . . and everything is spoiled . . . and Miss Davis will be so disappointed."

By dint of questioning Frank soon found out the whole story. The semi-annual public examination was to be held on Monday afternoon, the day before Christmas. Miss Davis had been drilling her little flock for the occasion; and a program of recitations, speeches, and dialogues had been prepared. Our small informant, whose name was Maggie Bates, together with Minnie Lawler and several other little girls, had conceived the idea that it would be a fine thing to decorate the schoolroom with greens. For this it was necessary to ask the help of the boys. Boys were scarce at Enderly school, but the Dickeys, three in number, had promised to see that the thing was done.

"And now they won't," sobbed Maggie. "Matt Dickey is mad at Miss Davis 'cause she stood him on the floor today for not learning his lesson, and he says he won't do a thing nor let any of the other boys help us. Matt just makes all the boys do as he says. I feel dreadful bad, and so does Minnie."

"Well, I wouldn't cry any more about it," said Frank consolingly. "Crying won't do any good, you know. Can you tell us where to find the wood-lane that cuts across to Blackburn Hill?" Maggie could, and gave us minute directions. So, having thanked her, we left her to pursue her disconsolate way and betook ourselves homeward.

"I would like to spoil Matt Dickey's little game," said Frank. "He is evidently trying to run things at Enderly Road school and revenge himself on the teacher. Let us put a spoke in his wheel and do Maggie a good turn as well."

"Agreed. But how?"

Frank had a plan ready to hand and, when we reached home, we took his sisters, Carrie and Mabel, into our confidence; and the four of us worked to such good purpose all the next day, which was Saturday, that by night everything was in readiness.

At dusk Frank and I set out for the Enderly Road, carrying a basket, a small step-ladder, an unlit lantern, a hammer, and a box of tacks. It was dark when we reached the Enderly Road schoolhouse. Fortunately, it was quite out of sight of any inhabited spot, being surrounded by woods. Hence, mysterious lights in it at strange hours would not be likely to attract attention.

The door was locked, but we easily got in by a window, lighted our lantern, and went to work. The schoolroom was small, and the old-fashioned furniture bore marks of hard usage; but everything was very snug, and the carefully swept floor and dusted desks bore testimony to the neatness of our small friend Maggie and her chum Minnie.

Our basket was full of mottoes made from letters cut out of cardboard and covered with lissome sprays of fir. They were, moreover, adorned with gorgeous pink and red tissue roses, which Carrie and Mabel had contributed. We had considerable trouble in getting them tacked up properly, but when we had succeeded, and had furthermore surmounted doors, windows, and blackboard with wreaths of green, the little Enderly Road schoolroom was quite transformed.

"It looks nice," said Frank in a tone of satisfaction. "Hope Maggie will like it."

We swept up the litter we had made, and then scrambled out of the window.

"I'd like to see Matt Dickey's face when he comes Monday morning," I laughed, as we struck into the back lands.

"I'd like to see that midget of a Maggie's," said Frank. "See here, Phil, let's attend the examination Monday afternoon. I'd like to see our decorations in daylight."

We decided to do so, and also thought of something else. Snow fell all day Sunday, so that, on Monday morning, sleighs had to be brought out. Frank and I drove down to the store and invested a considerable share of our spare cash in a varied assortment of knick-knacks. After dinner we drove through to the Enderly Road schoolhouse, tied our horse in a quiet spot, and went in. Our arrival created quite a sensation for, as a rule, Blackburn Hillites did not patronize Enderly Road functions. Miss Davis, the pale, tired-looking little teacher, was evidently pleased, and we were given seats of honour next to the minister on the platform.

Our decorations really looked very well, and were further enhanced by two large red geraniums in full bloom which, it appeared, Maggie had brought from home to adorn the teacher's desk. The side benches were lined with Enderly Road parents, and all the pupils were in their best attire. Our friend Maggie was there, of course, and she smiled and nodded towards the wreaths when she caught our eyes.

The examination was a decided success, and the program which followed was very creditable indeed. Maggie and Minnie, in particular, covered themselves with glory, both in class and on the platform. At its close, while the minister was making his speech, Frank slipped out; when the minister sat down the door opened and Santa Claus himself, with big fur coat, ruddy mask, and long white beard, strode into the room with a huge basket on his arm, amid a chorus of surprised "Ohs" from old and young.

Wonderful things came out of that basket. There was some little present for every child there—tops, knives, and whistles for the boys, dolls and ribbons for the girls, and a "prize" box of candy for everybody, all of which Santa Claus presented with appropriate remarks. It was an exciting time, and it would have been hard to decide which were the most pleased, parents, pupils, or teacher.

In the confusion Santa Claus discreetly disappeared, and school was dismissed. Frank, having tucked his toggery away in the sleigh, was waiting for us outside, and we were promptly pounced upon by Maggie and Minnie, whose long braids were already adorned with the pink silk ribbons which had been their gifts.

"*You* decorated the school," cried Maggie excitedly. "I know you did. I told Minnie it was you the minute I saw it."

"You're dreaming, child," said Frank.

"Oh, no, I'm not," retorted Maggie shrewdly, "and wasn't Matt Dickey mad this morning! Oh, it was such fun. I think you are two real nice boys and so does Minnie—don't you Minnie?"

Minnie nodded gravely. Evidently Maggie did the talking in their partnership.

"This has been a splendid examination," said Maggie, drawing a long breath. "Real Christmassy, you know. We never had such a good time before."

"Well, it has paid, don't you think?" asked Frank, as we drove home.

"Rather," I answered.

It did "pay" in other ways than the mere pleasure of it. There was always a better feeling between the Roaders and the Hillites thereafter. The big brothers of the little girls, to whom our Christmas surprise had been such a treat, thought it worthwhile to bury the hatchet, and quarrels between the two villages became things of the past.

Clorinda's Gifts

Lucy Maud Montgomery

"It is a dreadful thing to be poor a fortnight before Christmas," said Clorinda, with the mournful sigh of seventeen years.

Aunt Emmy smiled. Aunt Emmy was sixty, and spent the hours she didn't spend in a bed, on a sofa or in a wheel chair; but Aunt Emmy was never heard to sigh.

"I suppose it is worse then than at any other time," she admitted.

That was one of the nice things about Aunt Emmy. She always sympathized and understood.

"I'm worse than poor this Christmas . . . I'm stony broke," said Clorinda dolefully. "My spell of fever in the summer and the consequent doctor's bills have cleaned out my coffers completely. Not a single Christmas present can I give. And I did so want to give some little thing to each of my dearest people. But I simply can't afford it . . . that's the hateful, ugly truth."

Clorinda sighed again.

"The gifts which money can purchase are not the only ones we can give," said Aunt Emmy gently, "nor the best, either."

"Oh, I know it's nicer to give something of your own work," agreed Clorinda, "but materials for fancy work cost too. That kind of gift is just as much out of the question for me as any other."

"That was not what I meant," said Aunt Emmy.

"What did you mean, then?" asked Clorinda, looking puzzled.

Aunt Emmy smiled.

"Suppose you think out my meaning for yourself," she said. "That would be better than if I explained it. Besides, I don't think I could explain it. Take the beautiful line of a beautiful poem to help you in your thinking out: 'The gift without the giver is bare.'"

"I'd put it the other way and say, 'The giver without the gift is bare,'" said Clorinda, with a grimace. "That is my predicament exactly. Well, I hope by next Christmas I'll not be quite bankrupt. I'm going into Mr. Callender's store down at Murraybridge in February. He has offered me the place, you know."

"Won't your aunt miss you terribly?" said Aunt Emmy gravely.

Clorinda flushed. There was a note in Aunt Emmy's voice that disturbed her.

"Oh, yes, I suppose she will," she answered hurriedly. "But she'll get used to it very soon. And I will be home every Saturday night, you know. I'm dreadfully tired of being poor, Aunt Emmy, and now that I have a chance to earn something for myself I mean to take it. I can help Aunt Mary, too. I'm to get four dollars a week."

"I think she would rather have your companionship than a part of your salary, Clorinda," said Aunt Emmy. "But of course you must decide for yourself, dear. It is hard to be poor. I know it. I am poor."

"You poor!" said Clorinda, kissing her. "Why, you are the richest woman I know, Aunt Emmy—rich in love and goodness and contentment."

"And so are you, dearie . . . rich in youth and health and happiness and ambition. Aren't they all worth while?"

"Of course they are," laughed Clorinda. "Only, unfortunately, Christmas gifts can't be coined out of them."

"Did you ever try?" asked Aunt Emmy. "Think out that question, too, in your thinking out, Clorinda."

"Well, I must say bye-bye and run home. I feel cheered up—you always cheer people up, Aunt Emmy. How grey it is outdoors. I do hope we'll have snow soon. Wouldn't it be jolly to have a white Christmas? We always have such faded brown Decembers."

Clorinda lived just across the road from Aunt Emmy in a tiny white house behind some huge willows. But Aunt Mary lived there too—the only relative Clorinda had, for Aunt Emmy wasn't really her aunt at all. Clorinda had always lived with Aunt Mary ever since she could remember.

Clorinda went home and upstairs to her little room under the eaves, where the great bare willow boughs were branching athwart her windows. She was thinking over what Aunt Emmy had said about Christmas gifts and giving.

"I'm sure I don't know what she could have meant," pondered Clorinda. "I do wish I could find out if it would help me any. I'd love to remember a few of my friends at least. There's Miss Mitchell . . . she's been so good to me all this year and helped me so much with my studies. And there's Mrs. Martin out in Manitoba. If I could only send her something! She must be so lonely out there. And Aunt Emmy herself, of course; and poor old Aunt Kitty down the lane; and Aunt Mary and, yes—Florence too, although she did treat me so meanly. I shall never feel the same to her again. But she gave me a present last Christmas, and so out of mere politeness I ought to give her something."

Clorinda stopped short suddenly. She had just remembered that she would not have liked to say that last sentence to Aunt Emmy. Therefore, there was something wrong about it. Clorinda had long ago learned that there was sure to be something wrong in anything that could not be said to Aunt Emmy. So she stopped to think it over.

Clorinda puzzled over Aunt Emmy's meaning for four days and part of three nights. Then all at once it came to her. Or if it wasn't Aunt Emmy's meaning it was a very good meaning in itself, and it grew clearer and expanded in meaning during the days that followed, although at first Clorinda shrank a little from some of the conclusions to which it led her.

"I've solved the problem of my Christmas giving for this year," she told Aunt Emmy. "I have some things to give after all. Some of them quite costly, too; that is, they will cost me something, but I know I'll be better off and richer after I've paid the price. That is what Mr. Grierson would call a paradox, isn't it? I'll explain all about it to you on Christmas Day."

On Christmas Day, Clorinda went over to Aunt Emmy's. It was a faded brown Christmas after all, for the snow had not come. But Clorinda did not mind; there was such joy in her heart that she thought it the most delightful Christmas Day that ever dawned.

She put the queer cornery armful she carried down on the kitchen floor before she went into the sitting room. Aunt Emmy was lying on the sofa before the fire, and Clorinda sat down beside her.

"I've come to tell you all about it," she said.

Aunt Emmy patted the hand that was in her own.

"From your face, dear girl, it will be pleasant hearing and telling," she said.

Clorinda nodded.

"Aunt Emmy, I thought for days over your meaning . . . thought until I was dizzy. And then one evening it just came to me, without any thinking at all, and I knew that I *could* give some gifts after all. I thought of something new every day for a week. At first I didn't think I could give some of them, and then I thought how selfish I was. I would have been willing to pay any amount of money for gifts if I had had it, but I wasn't willing to pay what I had. I got over that, though, Aunt Emmy. Now I'm going to tell you what I did give.

"First, there was my teacher, Miss Mitchell. I gave her one of father's books. I have so many of his, you know, so that I wouldn't miss one; but still it was one I loved very much, and so I felt that that love made it worth while. That is, I felt that on second thought. At first, Aunt Emmy, I thought I would be ashamed to offer Miss Mitchell a shabby old book, worn with much reading and all marked over with father's notes and pencillings. I was afraid she would think it queer of me to give her such a present. And yet somehow it seemed to me that it was better than something brand new and unmellowed—that old book which father had loved and which I loved. So I gave it to her, and she understood. I think it pleased her so much, the real meaning in it. She said it was like being given something out of another's heart and life.

"Then you know Mrs. Martin . . . last year she was Miss Hope, my dear Sunday School teacher. She married a home missionary, and they are in a lonely part of the west. Well, I wrote her a letter. Not just an ordinary letter; dear me, no. I took a whole day to write it, and you should have seen the postmistress's eyes stick out when I mailed it. I just told her everything that had happened in Greenvale since she went away. I made it as newsy and cheerful and loving as I possibly could. Everything bright and funny I could think of went into it.

"The next was old Aunt Kitty. You know she was my nurse when I was a baby, and she's very fond of me. But, well, you know, Aunt Emmy, I'm ashamed to confess it, but really I've never found Aunt Kitty very entertaining, to put it mildly. She is always glad when I go to see her, but I've never gone except when I couldn't help it. She is very deaf, and rather dull and stupid, you know. Well, I gave her a whole day. I took my knitting yesterday, and sat with her the whole time and just talked and talked. I told her all the Greenvale news and gossip and everything else I thought she'd like to hear. She was so pleased and proud; she told me when I came away that she hadn't had such a nice time for years.

"Then there was . . . Florence. You know, Aunt Emmy, we were always intimate friends until last year. Then Florence once told Rose Watson something I had told her in confidence. I found it out and I was so hurt. I couldn't forgive Florence, and I told her plainly I could never be a real friend to her again. Florence felt badly, because she really did love me, and she asked me to forgive her, but it seemed as if I couldn't. Well, Aunt Emmy, that was my Christmas gift to her . . . my forgiveness. I went down last night and just put my arms around her and told her that I loved her as much as ever and wanted to be real close friends again.

"I gave Aunt Mary her gift this morning. I told her I wasn't going to Murraybridge, that I just meant to stay home with her. She was so glad—and I'm glad, too, now that I've decided so."

"Your gifts have been real gifts, Clorinda," said Aunt Emmy. "Something of you—the best of you—went into each of them."

Clorinda went out and brought her cornery armful in.

"I didn't forget you, Aunt Emmy," she said, as she unpinned the paper.

There was a rosebush—Clorinda's own pet rosebush—all snowed over with fragrant blossoms.

Aunt Emmy loved flowers. She put her finger under one of the roses and kissed it.

"It's as sweet as yourself, dear child," she said tenderly. "And it will be a joy to me all through the lonely winter days. You've found out the best meaning of Christmas giving, haven't you, dear?"

"Yes, thanks to you, Aunt Emmy," said Clorinda softly.